CREEPY STORIES

CREEPY STORIES

—A Classic Collection—

INTRODUCTION BY
FRED URQUHART

BRACKEN BOOKS
LONDON

Creepy Stories

This edition published in 1994 by Bracken Books, an imprint of Studio Editions Ltd, Princess House, 50 Eastcastle Street, London W1N 7AP, England

ISBN 1 85891 136 2

Printed at Thomson Press (I) Ltd.

INTRODUCTION

It is remarkable that one creepy story read at the same time as another by the same author lingers far longer in the mind than its fellow. For instance, when I was twelve I read Edgar Allan Poe's *The Fall of the House of Usher* and *The Black Cat*. One of Poe's most famous stories, *The Fall of the House of Usher* must not have impressed me, for I remember nothing about it. And every time I've read it since, I keep forgetting what it's about. Yet *The Black Cat* has haunted me at intervals during the past seventy years. At times this horrifying tale of the two cats, whose affection was spurned by their evil and murderous master, who cut out their eyes and hanged one, has given me nightmares, and I've never forgotten the second cat's terrible revenge.

I suppose that this forgetting one story and remembering the other arises from the temperament of the reader, but it is an extremely strange thing. Another example of this is that I never forget M.R. James' *Rats*, whereas I seem always to re-read some of his others as if they are new. But I keep being haunted by the rats beneath the sheets covering the corpse with a chain around his neck. Indeed, in nightmares I always see the rats, although in the story they never come from beneath the bedclothes.

In my teens I worked in an Edinburgh book shop. I was the only assistant, the boss was often out, there were not many customers, so I was often left to my own devices. I wrote sometimes and I read a lot. My reading varied from Gibbon's *Decline and Fall* to Proust; from Henry James to Edgar Wallace, I swallowed *The Four Just Men* and *Sanders of the River* and many others by this popular author. So I was delighted to find in this creepy volume a story *Circumstantial Evidence* by Wallace which I'd never read. I read with excitement and great horror that the fate of many people tried for murder often hangs on very faint circumstantial evidence.

The same circumstantial evidence appears in E.F. Benson's *The Hanging of Alfred Wadham*. This tragic story, told by a priest, is about the hanging of an innocent young man, whose confession he hears on the scaffold. The priest knows Alfred is innocent, but he can do nothing to save him, and he is haunted on the scaffold and thereafter by Alfred's purple face, protruding eyes and the noose around his neck.

Creepy Stories is a superb collection. Besides those already mentioned, there are stories by Ambrose Bierce, Washington Irving, Daniel Defoe, Hugh Walpole, Oliver Onions, Clemence Dane, D.H. Lawrence and Mary Webb.

I read Oliver Onion's novel *In Accordance With the Evidence* when I was sixteen and I've admired his work ever since, particularly his historical novel *The Story of Ragged Robyn*. I have read very few of his short stories, so it was a delight to find three in this collection.

I was captivated too by Denis Mackail's *The Lost Tragedy*, a story set in a bookshop. As an ex-bookseller I found it of the greatest interest, not only for its background, the odd habits of both bookseller and his customers, but also for its strange tale about the ghosts of Shakespeare and Ben Johnson. Denis Mackail, a grandson of Burne-Jones, was a very popular novelist in the middle years of this century. He was also the author of *The Story of J.M.B.*, the life of Sir James Barrie, the famous Scottish playwright who wrote *Peter Pan*, *Mary Rose* and *Quality Street* and many other plays and books, including *A Window in Thrums* and *Tommy and Grizel*.

I had never read the stories by some of the authors in this collection and I found most of them very much to my taste for creepiness. Although I read many Hugh Walpole novels when I was young, this is the first time I've read any of his short stories. The four here are wonderful, and I won't forget his portrait of the ghost of that malicious, malevolent old *Mrs Lunt*. C.B.H. Kitchin is also new to me as a short story writer, but I have read and greatly admire his novel *Death of My Aunt*. I was very struck by Flavia Richardson's *The Red Turret*, a diabolical tale of Roy Erringham's great-grandfather, 'the wizard, the devotee of the Black One,' whose ghost haunts Roy and his Canadian wife when they arrive in England to take possession of the Erringham property that has been in the family for generations. I shall look for more of Flavia Richardson's stories. I'll look too for more of Oscar Cook's weird tales of Borneo. Also for more by Hilda Hughes, whose two stories here are among the finest in the book, particularly *The Birthright*, a terrifying story about the undying hatred between father and son.

I'm sure you will agree that they make a grand bunch of stories, and I hope that, like me, you will read them again and again.

Fred Urquart

CONTENTS

CONTENTS

CONTENTS

CONTENTS

HUGH WALPOLE

THE SNOW

THE second Mrs. Ryder was a young woman not easily frightened, but now she stood in the dusk of the passage leaning back against the wall, her hand on her heart, looking at the grey-faced window beyond which the snow was steadily falling against the lamplight.

The passage where she was led from the study to the dining-room and the window looked out on to the little paved path that ran at the edge of the Cathedral green. As she stared down the passage she couldn't be sure whether the woman were there or no. How absurd of her! She knew the woman was not there. But if the woman was not, how was it that she could discern so clearly the old-fashioned grey cloak, the untidy grey hair and the sharp outline of the pale cheek and pointed chin? Yes, and more than that, the long sweep of the grey dress, falling in folds to the ground, the flash of a gold ring on the white hand. No. No. NO. This was madness. There was no one and nothing there. Hallucination. . . .

Very faintly a voice seemed to come to her: "I warned you. This is for the last time. . . ."

The nonsense! How far now was her imagination to carry her? Tiny sounds about the house, the running of a tap somewhere, a faint voice from the kitchen, these and something more had translated themselves into an imagined voice. "The last time . . ."

But her terror was real. She was not normally frightened by anything. She was young and healthy and bold, fond of sport, hunting, shooting, taking any risk. Now she was truly *stiffened* with terror—she could not move, could not advance down the passage as she wanted to and find light, warmth, safety in the dining-room. All the time the snow fell steadily, stealthily, with its own secret purpose, maliciously, beyond the window in the pale glow of the lamplight.

Then unexpectedly there was noise from the hall, opening of doors, a rush of feet, a pause and then in clear beautiful voices the well-known strains of "Good King Wenceslas". It was the Cathedral choirboys on their regular Christmas round. This was Christmas Eve. They always came just at this hour on Christmas Eve.

With an intense, almost incredible relief she turned back into the hall. At the same moment her husband came out of the study. They stood together smiling at the little group of mufflered, becoated boys who were singing, heart and soul in the job, so that the old house simply rang with their melody.

Reassured by the warmth and human company, she lost her terror. It had been her imagination. Of late she had been none too well. That was why she had been so irritable. Old Doctor Bernard was no good : he didn't understand her case at all. After Christmas she would go to London and have the very best advice. . . ..

Had she been well she could not, half an hour ago, have shown such miserable temper over nothing. She knew that it was over nothing, and yet that knowledge did not make it any easier for her to restrain herself. After every bout of temper she told herself that there should never be another— and then Herbert said something irritating, one of his silly muddle-headed stupidities, and she was off again !

She could see now, as she stood beside him at the bottom of the staircase, that he was still feeling it. She had certainly half an hour ago said some abominably rude personal things —things that she had not at all meant—and he had taken them in his meek, quiet way. Were he not so meek and quiet, did he only pay her back in her own coin, she would never lose her temper. Of that she was sure. But who wouldn't be irritated by that meekness and by the only reproachful thing that he ever said to her : "Elinor understood me better, my dear" ? To throw the first wife up against the second ! Wasn't that the most tactless thing that a man could possibly do ? And Elinor, that old, worn, elderly woman, the very opposite of her own gay, bright, amusing self ! That was why Herbert had loved her, because she was gay and bright and young. It was true that Elinor had been devoted, that she had been so utterly wrapped up in Herbert that she lived only for him. People were always recalling her devotion, which was sufficiently rude and tactless of them.

Well, she could not give anyone that kind of old-fashioned sugary devotion; it wasn't in her, and Herbert knew it by this time.

Nevertheless, she loved Herbert in her own way, as he must know, know it so well that he ought to pay no attention to the bursts of temper. She wasn't well. She would see a doctor in London. . . .

The little boys finished their carols, were properly rewarded and tumbled like feathery birds out into the snow again. They went into the study, the two of them, and stood beside the big open log-fire. She put her hand up and stroked his thin, beautiful cheek.

"I'm so sorry to have been cross just now, Bertie. I didn't mean half I said, you know."

But he didn't, as he usually did, kiss her and tell her that it didn't matter. Looking straight in front of him he answered:

"Well, Alice, I do wish you wouldn't. It hurts horribly. It upsets me more than you think. And it's growing on you. You make me miserable. I don't know what to do about it. And it's all about nothing."

Irritated at not receiving the usual commendation for her sweetness in making it up again, she withdrew a little and answered:

"Oh, all right. I've said I'm sorry. I can't do any more."

"But tell me," he insisted, "I want to know. What makes you so angry, so suddenly—and about nothing at all?"

She was about to let her anger rise, her anger at his obtuseness, obstinacy, when some fear checked her, a strange unanalysed fear, as though someone had whispered to her, "Look out! This is the last time!"

"It's not altogether my own fault," she answered and left the room.

She stood in the cold hall, wondering where to go. She could feel the snow falling outside the house and shivered. She hated the snow, she hated the winter, this beastly, cold, dark English winter that went on and on only at last to change into a damp, soggy English spring.

It had been snowing all day. In Polchester it was unusual to have so heavy a snowfall. This was the hardest winter that they had known for many years.

When she urged Herbert to winter abroad—which he

could quite easily do—he answered her impatiently ; he had the
strongest affection for this poky dead-and-alive Cathedral town.
The Cathedral seemed to be precious to him ; he wasn't happy
if he didn't go and see it every day ! She wouldn't wonder
if he didn't think more of the Cathedral than he did of herself.
Elinor had been the same ; she had even written a little book
about the Cathedral, about the Black Bishop's tomb and the
stained glass and the rest. . . .

What was the Cathedral after all ? Only a building !

She was standing in the drawing-room looking out over
the dusky, ghostly snow to the great hulk of the Cathedral, that
Herbert said was like a flying ship, but to herself was more like
a crouching beast licking its lips over the miserable sinners
that it was for ever devouring.

As she looked and shivered, feeling that in spite of herself
her temper and misery were rising so that they threatened to
choke her, it seemed to her that her bright and cheerful firelit
drawing-room was suddenly open to the snow. It was exactly
as though cracks had appeared everywhere, in the ceiling, the
walls, the windows, and that through these cracks the snow
was filtering, dribbling in little tracks of wet down the walls,
already perhaps making pools of water on the carpet.

This was of course imagination, but it was a fact that the
room was most dreadfully cold, although a great fire was burning and it was the cosiest room in the house.

Then, turning, she saw the figure standing by the door.
This time there could be no mistake. It was a grey shadow,
and yet a shadow with form and outline—the untidy grey
hair, the pale face like a moon-lit leaf, the long grey clothes
and something obstinate, vindictive, terribly menacing in its
pose.

She moved and the figure was gone ; there was nothing
there and the room was warm again, quite hot in fact. But
young Mrs. Ryder, who had never feared anything in all her
life save the vanishing of her youth, was trembling so that she
had to sit down, and even then her trembling did not cease.
Her hand shook on the arm of her chair.

She had created this thing out of her imagination of
Elinor's hatred of her and her own hatred of Elinor. It was
true that they had never met, but who knew not that the spiritualists were right, and Elinor's spirit, jealous of Herbert's
love for her, had been there driving them apart, forcing her

to lose her temper and then hating her for losing it. Such things might be! But she had not much time for speculation. She was preoccupied with her fear. It was a definite, positive fear, the kind of fear that one has just before one goes into an operation. Someone or something was threatening her. She clung to her chair as though to leave it was to plunge into disaster. She looked around her everywhere; all the familiar things, the pictures, the books, the little tables, the piano, were different now, isolated, strange, hostile, as though they had been won over by some enemy power.

She longed for Herbert to come and protect her; she felt most kindly to him. She would never lose her temper with him again—and at that same moment some cold voice seemed to whisper in her ear: "You had better not. It will be for the last time."

At length she found courage to rise, cross the room and go up to dress for dinner. In her bedroom courage came to her once more. It was certainly very cold, and the snow, as she could see when she looked between her curtains, was falling more heavily than ever, but she had a warm bath, sat in front of her fire and was sensible again.

For many months this odd sense that she was watched and accompanied by someone hostile to her had been growing. It was the stronger perhaps because of the things that Herbert told her about Elinor; she was the kind of woman, he said, who, once she loved anyone, would never relinquish her grasp; she was utterly faithful. He implied that her tenacious fidelity had been at times a little difficult.

"She always said," he added once, "that she would watch over me until I rejoined her in the next world. Poor Elinor!" he sighed. "She had a fine religious faith, stronger than mine, I fear."

It was always after one of her tantrums that young Mrs. Ryder had been most conscious of this hallucination, this dreadful discomfort of feeling that someone was near you who hated you—but it was only during the last week that she began to fancy that she actually saw anyone, and with every day her sense of this figure had grown stronger.

It was of course only nerves, but it was one of those nervous afflictions that became tiresome indeed if you did not rid yourself of it. Mrs. Ryder, secure now in the warmth and intimacy of her bedroom, determined that henceforth

everything should be sweetness and light. No more tempers !
Those were the things that did her harm.

Even though Herbert were a little trying, was not that
the case with every husband in the world ? And was it not
Christmas-time ? Peace and Good Will to men ! Peace
and Good Will to Herbert !

They sat down opposite to one another in the pretty little
dining-room hung with Chinese woodcuts, the table gleaming
and the amber curtains richly dark in the firelight.

But Herbert was not himself. He was still brooding, she
supposed, over their quarrel of the afternoon. Weren't men
children ? Incredible the children that they were !

So when the maid was out of the room she went over to
him, bent down and kissed his forehead.

"Darling . . . you're still cross, I can see you are. You
mustn't be. Really you mustn't. It's Christmas-time, and,
if I forgive you, you must forgive me."

"You forgive me ?" he asked, looking at her in his most
aggravating way. "What have you to forgive me for ?"

Well, that was really too much—when she had taken
all the steps, humbled her pride.

She went back to her seat, but for a while could not
answer him because the maid was there. When they were
alone again she said, summoning all her patience :

"Bertie dear, do you really think that there's anything to
be gained by sulking like this ? It isn't worthy of you. It
isn't really."

He answered her quietly.

"Sulking ? No, that's not the right word. But I've got
to keep quiet. If I don't I shall say something I'm sorry for."
Then, after a pause, in a low voice, as though to himself :
"These constant rows are awful."

Her temper was rising again ; another self that had nothing
to do with her real self, a stranger to her and yet a very old,
familiar friend.

"Don't be so self-righteous," she answered, her voice
trembling a little. "These quarrels are entirely my own fault,
aren't they ?"

"Elinor and I never quarrelled," he said, so softly that she
scarcely heard him.

"No ! Because Elinor thought you perfect. She adored
you. You've often told me. I don't think you perfect. I'm

not perfect either. But we've both got faults. I'm not the only one to blame."

"We'd better separate," he said, suddenly looking up. "We don't get on now. We used to. I don't know what's changed everything. But, as things are, we'd better separate."

She looked at him and knew that she loved him more than ever, but because she loved him so much she wanted to hurt him, and because he had said that he thought he could get on without her she was so angry that she forgot all caution. Her love and her anger helped one another. The more angry she became the more she loved him.

"I know why you want to separate," she said. "It's because you're in love with someone else." ("How funny!" something inside her said. "You don't mean a word of this.") "You've treated me as you have, and then you leave me."

"I'm not in love with anyone else," he answered her steadily, "and you know it. But we are so unhappy together that it's silly to go on . . . silly. . . . The whole thing has failed."

There was so much unhappiness, so much bitterness, in his voice that she realized that at last she had truly gone too far. She had lost him. She had not meant this. She was frightened and her fear made her so angry that she went across to him.

"Very well, then . . . I'll tell everyone . . . what you've been, how you've treated me."

"Not another scene," he answered wearily. "I can't stand any more. Let's wait. To-morrow is Christmas Day. . . .'"

He was so unhappy that her anger with herself maddened her. She couldn't bear his sad, hopeless disappointment with herself, their life together, everything.

In a fury of blind temper she struck him; it was as though she were striking herself. He got up and without a word left the room. There was a pause and then she heard the hall door close. He had left the house.

She stood there, slowly coming to her control again. When she lost her temper it was as though she sank under water. When it was all over she came once more to the surface of life, wondering where she'd been and what she had been doing. Now she stood there, bewildered, and then at once she was aware of two things, one that the room was bitterly cold and the other that someone was in the room with her.

This time she did not need to look around her. She did not turn at all but only stared straight at the curtained windows, seeing them very carefully, as though she were summing them up for some future analysis, with their thick green folds, gold rod, white lines—and beyond them the snow was falling.

She did not need to turn, but, with a shiver of terror, she was aware that that grey figure who had, all these last weeks, been approaching ever more closely was almost at her very elbow. She heard quite clearly : "I warned you. That was the last time."

At the same moment Onslow the butler came in. Onslow was broad, fat and rubicund—a good, faithful butler with a passion for church music. He was a bachelor and, it was said, disappointed of women. He had an old mother in Liverpool to whom he was greatly attached.

In a flash of consciousness she thought of all these things when he came in. She expected him also to see the grey figure at her side. But he was undisturbed, his ceremonial complacency clothed him securely.

"Mr. Fairfax has gone out," she said firmly. Oh, surely he must see something, feel something ?

"Yes, madame !" Then, smiling rather grandly : "It's snowing hard. Never seen it harder here. Shall I build up the fire in the drawing-room, madame ?"

"No, thank you. But Mr. Fairfax's study . . ."

"Yes, madame. I only thought that as this room was so warm you might find it chilly in the drawing-room."

This room warm, when she was shivering from head to foot ; but holding herself lest he should see ! . . . She longed to keep him there, to implore him to remain ; but in a moment he was gone, softly closing the door behind him.

Then a mad longing for flight seized her, and she could not move. She was rooted there to the floor, and even as, wildly trying to cry, to scream, to shriek the house down, she found that only a little whisper would come, she felt the cold touch of a hand on hers.

She did not turn her head ; her whole personality, all her past life, her poor little courage, her miserable fortitude was summoned to meet this sense of approaching death which was as unmistakable as a certain smell or the familiar ringing of a gong. She had dreamt in nightmares of approaching death and it had always been like this, a fearful constriction of the heart, a paralysis of the limbs, a choking sense of disaster like an anaesthetic.

"You were warned," something said to her again.

She knew that if she turned she would see Elinor's face, set, white, remorseless. The woman had always hated her, been vilely jealous of her, protecting her wretched Herbert.

A certain vindictiveness seemed to release her. She found that she could move, her limbs were free.

She passed to the door, ran down the passage, into the hall. Where would she be safe? She thought of the Cathedral, where to-night there was a carol service. She opened the hall door and just as she was, meeting the thick, involving, muffling snow, she ran out.

She started across the green toward the Cathedral door. Her thin black slippers sank in the snow. Snow was every-where—in her hair, her eyes, her nostrils, her mouth, on her bare neck, between her breasts.

"Help! Help! Help!" she wanted to cry, but the snow choked her. Lights whirled about her. The Cathedral rose like a huge black eagle and flew towards her.

She fell forward, and even as she fell a hand, far colder than the snow, caught her neck. She lay struggling in the snow, and as she struggled there two hands of an icy fleshless chill closed about her throat.

Her last impression was of the hard outline of a ring pressing into her neck. Then she lay still, her face in the snow, and the flakes eagerly, savagely, covered her.

THE TARN

As Foster moved unconsciously across the room, bent towards
the bookcase, and stood leaning forward a little, choosing now
one book, now another, with his eyes, his host, seeing the
muscles of the back of his thin, scraggy neck stand out above
his low flannel collar, thought of the ease with which he could
squeeze that throat, and the pleasure, the triumphant, lustful
pleasure, that such an action would give him.

The low, white-walled, white-ceilinged room was flooded
with the mellow, kindly Lakeland sun. October is a wonderful month in the English Lakes, golden, rich, and perfumed,
slow suns moving through apricot-tinted skies to ruby evening
glories ; the shadows lie then thick about that beautiful
country, in dark purple patches, in long web-like patterns of
silver gauze, in thick splotches of amber and grey. The
clouds pass in galleons across the mountains, now veiling, now
revealing, now descending with ghost-like armies to the very
breast of the plains, suddenly rising to the softest of blue skies
and lying thin in lazy languorous colour.

Fenwick's cottage looked across to Low Fells ; on his
right, seen through side windows, sprawled the hills above
Ullswater.

Fenwick looked at Foster's back and felt suddenly sick,
so that he sat down, veiling his eyes for a moment with his
hand. Foster had come up there, come all the way from
London, to explain. It was so like Foster to want to explain,
to want to put things right. For how many years had he
known Foster ? Why, for twenty at least, and during all
those years Foster had been for ever determined to put things
right with everybody. He could never bear to be disliked ;
he hated that anyone should think ill of him ; he wanted everyone to be his friends. That was one reason, perhaps, why

Foster had got on so well, had prospered so in his career ;
one reason, too, why Fenwick had not.

For Fenwick was the opposite of Foster in this. He
did not want friends, he certainly did not care that people should
like him—that is people for whom, for one reason or another,
he had contempt—and he had contempt for quite a number
of people.

Fenwick looked at that long, thin, bending back and felt
his knees tremble. Soon Foster would turn round and that
high, reedy voice would pipe out something about the books.
"What jolly books you have, Fenwick !" How many, many
times in the long watches of the night, when Fenwick could
not sleep, had he heard that pipe sounding close there—yes,
in the very shadows of his bed ! And how many times had
Fenwick replied to it : "I hate you ! You are the cause of
my failure in life ! You have been in my way always. Always,
always, always ! Patronizing and pretending, and in truth
showing others what a poor thing you thought me, how great
a failure, how conceited a fool ! I know. You can hide
nothing from me ! I can hear you !"

For twenty years now Foster had been persistently in
Fenwick's way. There had been that affair, so long ago now,
when Robins had wanted a sub-editor for his wonderful
review, the *Parthenon*, and Fenwick had gone to see him and
they had had a splendid talk. How magnificently Fenwick
had talked that day ; with what enthusiasm he had shown
Robins (who was blinded by his own conceit, anyway) the
kind of paper the *Parthenon* might be ; how Robins had caught
his own enthusiasm, how he had pushed his fat body about
the room, crying : "Yes, yes, Fenwick—that's fine ! That's
fine indeed !"—and then how, after all, Foster had got
that job.

The paper had only lived for a year or so, it is true, but the
connection with it had brought Foster into prominence just
as it might have brought Fenwick !

Then, five years later, there was Fenwick's novel, *The
Bitter Aloe*—the novel upon which he had spent three years
of blood-and-tears endeavour—and then, in the very same
week of publication, Foster brings out *The Circus*, the novel
that made his name ; although, Heaven knows, the thing was
poor enough sentimental trash. You may say that one novel
cannot kill another—but can it not ? Had not *The Circus*

appeared would not that group of London know-alls—that
conceited, limited, ignorant, self-satisfied crowd, who nevertheless can do, by their talk, so much to affect a book's good
or evil fortunes—have talked about *The Bitter Aloe* and so
forced it into prominence ?   As it was, the book was still-
born and *The Circus* went on its prancing, triumphant way.

After that there had been many occasions—some small,
some big—and always in one way or another that thin,
scraggy body of Foster's was interfering with Fenwick's
happiness.

The thing had become, of course, an obsession with
Fenwick.   Hiding up there in the heart of the Lakes, with
no friends, almost no company, and very little money, he
was given too much to brooding over his failure.   He *was*
a failure and it was not his own fault.   How could it be his
own fault with his talents and his brilliance ?   It was the
fault of modern life and its lack of culture, the fault of the stupid
material mess that made up the intelligence of human beings—
and the fault of Foster.

Always Fenwick hoped that Foster would keep away
from him.   He did not know what he would not do did he
see the man.   And then one day, to his amazement, he
received a telegram :

*Passing through this way.   May I stop with you Monday and
Tuesday ?—Giles Foster.*

Fenwick could scarcely believe his eyes, and then—from
curiosity, from cynical contempt, from some deeper, more
mysterious motive that he dared not analyse—he had telegraphed—*Come.*

And here the man was.   And he had come—would you
believe it ?—to "put things right".   He had heard from
Hamlin Eddis that Fenwick was hurt with him, had some
kind of grievance.

"I didn't like to feel that, old man, and so I thought I'd
just stop by and have it out with you, see what the matter
was, and put it right."

Last night after supper Foster had tried to put it right.
Eagerly, his eyes like a good dog's who is asking for a bone
that he knows he thoroughly deserves, he had held out his
hand and asked Fenwick to "say what was up".

Fenwick simply had said that nothing was up ; Hamlin Eddis was a damned fool.

"Oh, I'm glad to hear that !" Foster had cried, springing up out of his chair and putting his hand on Fenwick's shoulder. "I'm glad of that, old man. I couldn't bear for us not to be friends. We've been friends so long."

Lord ! How Fenwick hated him at that moment

II

"What a jolly lot of books you have !" Foster turned round and looked at Fenwick with eager, gratified eyes. "Every book here is interesting ! I like your arrangement of them, too, and those open bookshelves—it always seems to me a shame to shut up books behind glass !"

Foster came forward and sat down quite close to his host. He even reached forward and laid his hand on his host's knee. "Look here ! I'm mentioning it for the last time—positively ! But I do want to make quite certain. There *is* nothing wrong between us, is there, old man ? I know you assured me last night, but I just want . . ."

Fenwick looked at him and, surveying him, felt suddenly an exquisite pleasure of hatred. He liked the touch of the man's hand on his knee ; he himself bent forward a little and, thinking how agreeable it would be to push Foster's eyes in, deep, deep into his head, crunching them, smashing them to purple, leaving the empty, staring, bloody sockets, said :

"Why, no. Of course not. I told you last night. What could there be ?"

The hand gripped the knee a little more tightly.

"I *am* so glad ! That's splendid ! Splendid ! I hope you won't think me ridiculous, but I've always had an affection for you ever since I can remember. I've always wanted to known you better. I've admired your talent so greatly. That novel of yours—the—the—the one about the aloe——"

"*The Bitter Aloe ?*"

"Ah yes, that was it. That was a splendid book. Pessimistic, of course, but still fine. It ought to have done better. I remember thinking so at the time."

"Yes, it ought to have done better."

"Your time will come, though.   What I say is that good
work always tells in the end."

"Yes, my time will come."

The thin, piping voice went on :

"Now, I've had more success than I deserved.   Oh yes,
I have.   You can't deny it.   I'm not falsely modest.   I mean
it.   I've got some talent, of course, but not so much as people
say.   And you !   Why, you've got so *much* more than they
acknowledge.   You have, old man.   You have indeed.
Only—I do hope you'll forgive my saying this—perhaps
you haven't advanced quite as you might have done.   Living
up here, shut away here, closed in by all these mountains, in
this wet climate—always raining—why, you're out of things !
You don't see people, don't talk and discover what's really
going on.   Why, look at me !"

Fenwick turned round and looked at him.

"Now, I have half the year in London, where one gets the
best of everything, best talk, best music, best plays ;   and then
I'm three months abroad, Italy or Greece or somewhere, and
then three months in the country.   Now, that's an ideal
arrangement.   You have everything that way."

Italy or Greece or somewhere !

Something turned in Fenwick's breast, grinding, grinding,
grinding.   How he had longed, oh, how passionately, for just
one week in Greece, two days in Sicily !   Sometimes he had
thought that he might run to it, but when it had come to the
actual counting of the pennies . . .   And how this fool, this
fat-head, this self-satisfied, conceited, patronizing . . .

He got up, looking out at the golden sun.

"What do you say to a walk ?" he suggested.   "The sun
will last for a good hour yet."

III

As soon as the words were out of his lips he felt as though
someone else had said them for him.   He even turned half
round to see whether anyone else were there.   Ever since
Foster's arrival on the evening before he had been conscious
of this sensation.   A walk ?   Why should he take Foster for
a walk, show him his beloved country, point out those curves
and lines and hollows, the broad silver shield of Ullswater, the

cloudy purple hills hunched like blankets about the knees of some recumbent giant? Why? It was as though he had turned round to someone behind him and had said: "You have some further design in this."

They started out. The road sank abruptly to the lake, then the path ran between trees at the water's edge. Across the lake tones of bright yellow light, crocus-hued, rode upon the blue. The hills were dark.

The very way that Foster walked bespoke the man. He was always a little ahead of you, pushing his long, thin body along with little eager jerks, as though, did he not hurry, he would miss something that would be immensely to his advantage. He talked, throwing words over his shoulder to Fenwick as you throw crumbs of bread to a robin.

"Of course I was pleased. Who would not be? After all, it's a new prize. They've only been awarding it for a year or two, but it's gratifying—really gratifying—to secure it. When I opened the envelope and found the cheque there —well, you could have knocked me down with a feather. You could, indeed. Of course, a hundred pounds isn't much. But it's the honour. . . ."

Whither were they going? Their destiny was as certain as though they had no free will. Free will? There is no free will. All is Fate. Fenwick suddenly laughed aloud.

Foster stopped.

"Why, what is it?"

"What's what?"

"You laughed."

"Something amused me."

Foster slipped his arm through Fenwick's.

"It *is* jolly to be walking along together like this, arm in arm, friends. I'm a sentimental man. I won't deny it. What I say is that life is short and one must love one's fellow-beings, or where is one? You live too much alone, old man." He squeezed Fenwick's arm. "That's the truth of it."

It was torture, exquisite, heavenly torture. It was wonderful to feel that thin, bony arm pressing against his. Almost you could hear the beating of that other heart. Wonderful to feel that arm and the temptation to take it in your hands and to bend it and twist it and then to hear the bones crack . . . crack . . . crack. . . . Wonderful to feel that temptation rise through one's body like boiling water and yet

not to yield to it.   For a moment Fenwick's hand touched
Foster's.   Then he drew himself apart.

"We're at the village.   This is the hotel where they all
come in the summer.   We turn off at the right here.   I'll
show you my tarn."

IV

"Your tarn ?" asked Foster.   "Forgive my ignorance,
but what *is* a tarn exactly ?"

"A tarn is a miniature lake, a pool of water lying in the lap
of the hill.   Very quiet, lovely, silent.   Some of them are
immensely deep."

"I should like to see that."

"It is some little distance—up a rough road.   Do you
mind ?"

"Not a bit.   I have long legs."

"Some of them are immensely deep—unfathomable—
nobody touched the bottom—but quiet, like glass, with
shadows only——"

"Do you know, Fenwick, I have always been afraid of
water—I've never learnt to swim.   I'm afraid to go out of
my depth.   Isn't that ridiculous ?   But it is all because at my
private school, years ago, when I was a small boy, some big
fellows took me and held me with my head under the water
and nearly drowned me.   They did indeed.   They went
farther than they meant to.   I can see their faces."

Fenwick considered this.   The picture leapt to his mind.
He could see the boys—large, strong fellows, probably—and
this skinny thing like a frog, their thick hands about his throat,
his legs like grey sticks kicking out of the water, their laughter,
their sudden sense that something was wrong, the skinny
body all flaccid and still. . . .

He drew a deep breath.

Foster was walking beside him now, not ahead of him,
as though he were a little afraid and needed reassurance.
Indeed, the scene had changed.   Before and behind them
stretched the uphill path, loose with shale and stones.   On
their right, on a ridge at the foot of the hill, were some quarries,
almost deserted, but the more melancholy in the fading afternoon because a little work still continued there ; faint sounds

came from the gaunt listening chimneys, a stream of water ran
and tumbled angrily into a pool below, once and again a black
silhouette, like a question-mark, appeared against the darken-
ing hill.

It was a little steep here, and Foster puffed and blew.

Fenwick hated him the more for that.   So thin and spare
and still he could not keep in condition!   They stumbled,
keeping below the quarry, on the edge of the running water,
now green, now a dirty white-grey, pushing their way along
the side of the hill.

Their faces were set now towards Helvellyn.   It rounded
the cup of hills, closing in the base and then sprawling to the
right.

"There's the tarn!" Fenwick exclaimed; and then added,
"The sun's not lasting as long as I had expected.   It's growing
dark already."

Foster stumbled and caught Fenwick's arm.

"This twilight makes the hills look strange—like living
men.   I can scarcely see my way."

"We're alone here," Fenwick answered.   "Don't you
feel the stillness?   The men will have left the quarry now
and gone home.   There is no one in all this place but ourselves.   If you watch you will see a strange green light steal
down over the hills.   It lasts for but a moment and then it is
dark.

"Ah, here is my tarn.   Do you know how I love this place,
Foster?   It seems to belong especially to me, just as much
as all your work and your glory and fame and success seem
to belong to you.   I have this and you have that.   Perhaps
in the end we are even, after all.   Yes. . . .

"But I feel as though that piece of water belonged to me
and I to it, and as though we should never be separated—yes.
. . . Isn't it black?

"It is one of the deep ones.   No one has ever sounded it.
Only Helvellyn knows, and one day I fancy that it will take
me, too, into its confidence, will whisper its secrets——"

Foster sneezed.

"Very nice.   Very beautiful, Fenwick.   I like your tarn.
Charming.   And now let's turn back.   That is a difficult
walk beneath the quarry.   It's chilly, too."

"Do you see that little jetty there?" Fenwick led Foster
by the arm.   "Someone built that out into the water.   He

had a boat there, I suppose. Come and look down. From
the end of the little jetty it looks so deep and the mountains
seem to close round."

Fenwick took Foster's arm and led him to the end of the
jetty. Indeed, the water looked deep here. Deep and very
black. Foster peered down, then he looked up at the hills
that did indeed seem to have gathered close around him.
He sneezed again.

"I've caught a cold, I am afraid. Let's turn homewards,
Fenwick, or we shall never find our way."

"Home, then," said Fenwick, and his hands closed about
the thin, scraggy neck. For the instant the head half turned,
and two startled, strangely childish eyes stared ; then, with
a push that was ludicrously simple, the body was impelled forward, there was a sharp cry, a splash, a stir of something white
against the swiftly gathering dusk, again and then again, then
far-spreading ripples, then silence.

V

The silence extended. Having enwrapped the tarn, it
spread as though with finger on lip to the already quiescent
hills. Fenwick shared in the silence. He luxuriated in it.
He did not move at all. He stood there looking upon the inky
water of the tarn, his arms folded, a man lost in intensest
thought. But he was not thinking. He was only conscious
of a warm, luxurious relief, a sensuous feeling that was not
thought at all.

Foster was gone—that tiresome, prating, conceited, self-
satisfied fool ! Gone, never to return. The tarn assured him
of that. It stared back into Fenwick's face approvingly as
though it said : "You have done well—a clean and necessary
job. We have done it together, you and I. I am proud of
you."

He was proud of himself. At last he had done something definite with his life. Thought, eager, active thought,
was beginning now to flood his brain. For all these years
he had hung around in this place doing nothing but cherish
grievances, weak, backboneless—now at last there was
action. He drew himself up and looked at the hills. He was
proud—and he was cold. He was shivering. He turned up

the collar of his coat. Yes, there was that faint green light that always lingered in the shadows of the hills for a brief moment before darkness came. It was growing late. He had better return.

Shivering now so that his teeth chattered, he started off down the path, and then was aware that he did not wish to leave the tarn. The tarn was friendly—the only friend he had in all the world. As he stumbled along in the dark this sense of loneliness grew. He was going home to an empty house. There had been a guest in it last night. Who was it ? Why, Foster, of course—Foster with his silly laugh and amiable, mediocre eyes. Well, Foster would not be there now. No, he never would be there again.

And Suddenly Fenwick started to run. He did not know why, except that, now that he had left the tarn, he was lonely. He wished that he could have stayed there all night, but because it was cold he could not, and so now he was running so that he might be at home with the lights and the familiar furniture—and all the things that he knew to reassure him.

As he ran the shale and stones scattered beneath his feet. They made a tit-tattering noise under him, and someone else seemed to be running too. He stopped, and the other runner also stopped. He breathed in the silence. He was hot now. The perspiration was trickling down his cheeks. He could feel a dribble of it down his back inside his shirt. His knees were pounding. His heart was thumping. And all around him the hills were so amazingly silent, now like india-rubber clouds that you could push in or pull out as you do those india-rubber faces, grey against the night sky of a crystal purple, upon whose surface, like the twinkling eyes of boats at sea, stars were now appearing.

His knees steadied, his heart beat less fiercely, and he began to run again. Suddenly he had turned the corner and was out at the hotel. Its lamps were kindly and re-assuring. He walked then quietly along the lake-side path, and had it not been for the certainty that someone was treading behind him he would have been comfortable and at his ease. He stopped once or twice and looked back, and once he stopped and called out, "Who's there ?" Only the rustling trees answered.

He had the strangest fancy, but his brain was throbbing

so fiercely that he could not think, that it was the tarn that was following him, the tarn slipping, sliding along the road, being with him so that he should not be lonely.   He could almost hear the tarn whisper in his ear : "We did that together, and so I do not wish you to bear all the responsibility yourself.   I will stay with you, so that you are not lonely."

He climbed down the road towards home, and there were the lights of his house.   He heard the gate click behind him as though it were shutting him in.   He went into the sitting-room, lighted and ready.   There were the books that Foster had admired.

The old woman who looked after him appeared.

"Will you be having some tea, sir ?"

"No, thank you, Annie."

"Will the other gentleman be wanting any ?"

"No ; the other gentleman is away for the night."

"Then there will be only one for supper ?"

"Yes, only one for supper."

He sat in the corner of the sofa and fell instantly into a deep slumber.

VI

He woke when the old woman tapped him on the shoulder and told him that supper was served.   The room was dark save for the jumping light of two uncertain candles.   Those two red candlesticks—how he hated them up there on the mantelpiece !   He had always hated them, and now they seemed to him to have something of the quality of Foster's voice—that thin, reedy, piping tone.

He was expecting at every moment that Foster would enter, and yet he knew that he would not.   He continued to turn his head towards the door, but it was so dark there that you could not see.   The whole room was dark except just there by the fireplace, where the two candlesticks went whining with their miserable twinkling plaint.

He went into the dining-room and sat down to his meal. But he could not eat anything.   It was odd—that place by the table where Foster's chair should be.   Odd, naked, and made a man feel lonely.

He got up once from the table and went to the window,

opened it and looked out. He listened for something.
A trickle as of running water, a stir, through the silence, as
though some deep pool were filling to the brim. A rustle
in the trees, perhaps. An owl hooted. Sharply, as though
someone had spoken to him unexpectedly behind his shoulder,
he closed the window and looked back, peering under his dark
eyebrows into the room.

Later on he went up to bed.

VII

Had he been sleeping, or had he been lying lazily, as one
does, half dozing, half luxuriously not thinking? He was
wide awake now, utterly awake, and his heart was beating
with apprehension. It was as though someone had called him
by name. He slept always with his window a little open and
the blind up. To-night the moonlight shadowed in sickly
fashion the objects in his room. It was not a flood of light nor
yet a sharp splash, silvering a square, a circle, throwing the rest
into ebony darkness. The light was dim, a little green, perhaps, like the shadow that comes over the hills just before dark.

He stared at the window, and it seemed to him that something moved there. Within, or rather against the green-grey
light, something silver-tinted glistened. Fenwick stared.
It had the look, exactly, of slipping water.

Slipping water! He listened, his head up, and it seemed
to him that from beyond the window he caught the stir of
water, not running, but rather welling up and up, gurgling
with satisfaction as it filled and filled.

He sat up higher in bed, and then saw that down the wallpaper beneath the window water was undoubtedly trickling.
He could see it lurch to the projecting wood of the sill, pause,
and then slip, slither down the incline. The odd thing was
that it fell so silently.

Beyond the window there was that odd gurgle, but in the
room itself absolute silence. Whence could it come? He
saw the line of silver rise and fall as the stream on the window-
ledge ebbed and flowed.

He must get up and close the window. He drew his legs
above the sheets and blankets and looked down.

He shrieked. The floor was covered with a shining

film of water. It was rising. As he looked it had covered
half the short stumpy legs of the bed. It rose without a wink,
a bubble, a break! Over the sill it poured now in a steady
flow, but soundless. Fenwick sat up in the bed, the clothes
gathered up to his chin, his eyes blinking, the Adam's apple
throbbing like a throttle in his throat.

But he must do something, he must stop this. The water
was now level with the seats of the chairs, but still was soundless. Could he but reach the door!

He put down his naked foot, then cried again. The
water was icy cold. Suddenly, leaning, staring at its dark,
unbroken sheen, something seemed to push him forward.
He fell. His head, his face was under the icy liquid; it seemed
adhesive and, in the heart of its ice, hot like melting wax. He
struggled to his feet. The water was breast-high. He
screamed again and again. He could see the looking-glass,
the row of books, the picture of Dürer's "Horse", aloof, im-
pervious. He beat at the water, and flakes of it seemed to
cling to him like scales of fish, clammy to his touch. He
struggled, ploughing his way towards the door.

The water now was at his neck. Then something had
caught him by the ankle. Something held him. He struggled,
crying: "Let me go! Let me go! I tell you to let me go!
I hate you! I hate you! I will not come down to you!
I will not——"

The water covered his mouth. He felt that someone
pushed in his eyeballs with bare knuckles. A cold hand
reached up and caught his naked thigh.

VIII

In the morning the little maid knocked and, receiving no
answer, came in, as was her wont, with his shaving-water.
What she saw made her scream. She ran for the gardener.

They took the body with its staring, protruding eyes, its
tongue sticking out between the clenched teeth, and laid it on
the bed.

The only sign of disorder was an overturned water-jug.
A small pool of water stained the carpet.

It was a lovely morning. A twig of ivy idly, in the little
breeze, tapped the pane.

A LITTLE GHOST

GHOSTS ?   I looked across the table at Truscott and had a sudden desire to impress him.   Truscott has, before now, invited confidences in just that same way, with his flat impassivity, his air of not caring whether you say anything to him or no, his determined indifference to your drama and your pathos.   On this particular evening he had been less impassive. He had himself turned the conversation towards Spiritualism, séances, and all that world of humbug, as he believed it to be, and suddenly I saw, or fancied that I saw, a real invitation in his eyes, something that made me say to myself : "Well, hang it all, I've known Truscott for nearly twenty years ; I've never shown him the least little bit of my real self ; he thinks me a writing money-machine, with no thought in the world beside my brazen serial stories and the yacht that I purchased out of them."

So I told him this story, and I will do him the justice to say that he listened to every word of it most attentively, although it was far into the evening before I had finished. He didn't seem impatient with all the little details that I gave. Of course, in a ghost story, details are more important than anything else.   But was it a ghost story ?   Was it a story at all ?   Was it true even in its material background ?   Now, as I try to tell it again, I can't be sure.   Truscott is the only other person who has ever heard it, and at the end of it he made no comment whatever.

It happened long ago, long before the War, when I had been married for about five years, and was an exceedingly prosperous journalist, with a nice little house and two children in Wimbledon.

I lost suddenly my greatest friend.   That may mean little or much as friendship is commonly held, but I believe that most

Britishers, most Americans, most Scandinavians, know before they die one friendship at least that changes their whole life experience by its depth and colour. Very few Frenchmen, Italians or Spaniards, very few Southern people at all, understand these things.

The curious part of it in my particular case was that I had known this friend only four or five years before his death, that I had made many friendships both before and since that have endured over much longer periods, and yet this particular friendship had a quality of intensity and happiness that I have never found elsewhere.

Another curious thing was that I met Bond only a few months before my marriage, when I was deeply in love with my wife, and so intensely preoccupied with my engagement that I could think of nothing else. I met Bond quite casually at someone's house. He was a large-boned, broad-shouldered, slow-smiling man with close-cropped hair turning slightly grey, and our meeting was casual; the ripening of our friendship was casual; indeed, the whole affair may be said to have been casual to the very last. It was, in fact, my wife who said to me one day, when we had been married about a year or so: "Why, I believe you care more for Charlie Bond than for anyone else in the world." She said it in that sudden, disconcerting, perceptive way that some women have. I was entirely astonished. Of course I laughed at the idea. I saw Bond frequently. He came often to the house. My wife, wiser than many wives, encouraged all my friendships, and she herself liked Charlie immensely. I don't suppose that anyone disliked him. Some men were jealous of him; some men, the merest acquaintances, called him conceited; women were sometimes irritated by him because so clearly he could get on very easily without them; but he had, I think, no real enemy.

How could he have had? His good nature, his freedom from all jealousy, his naturalness, his sense of fun, the absence of all pettiness, his common sense, his manliness, and at the same time his broad-minded intelligence, all these things made him a most charming personality. I don't know that he shone very much in ordinary society. He was very quiet and his wit and humour came out best with his intimates.

I was the showy one, and he always played up to me, and I think I patronized him a little and thought deep down in my subconscious self that it was lucky for him to have such a brilliant friend, but he never gave a sign of resentment. I believe now that he knew me, with all my faults and vanities and absurdities, far better than anyone else, even my wife, did, and that is one of the reasons, to the day of my death, why I shall always miss him so desperately.

However, it was not until his death that I realized how close we had been. One November day he came back to his flat, wet and chilled, didn't change his clothes, caught a cold, which developed into pneumonia, and after three days was dead. It happened that that week I was in Paris, and I returned to be told on my doorstep by my wife of what had occurred. At first I refused to believe it. When I had seen him a week before he had been in splendid health ; with his tanned, rather rough and clumsy face, his clear eyes, no fat about him anywhere, he had looked as though he would live to a thousand, and then, when I realized that it was indeed true, I did not during the first week or two grasp my loss.

I missed him, of course ; was vaguely unhappy and dis-contented ; railed against life, wondering why it was always the best people who were taken and the others left ; but I was not actually aware that for the rest of my days things would be different, and that that day of my return from Paris was a crisis in my human experience. Suddenly one morning, walking down Fleet Street, I had a flashing, almost blinding need of Bond that was like a revelation. From that moment I knew no peace. Everyone seemed to me dull, profitless and empty. Even my wife was a long way away from me, and my children, whom I dearly loved, counted nothing to me at all. I didn't, after that, know what was the matter with me. I lost my appetite, I couldn't sleep, I was grumpy and nervous. I didn't myself connect it with Bond at all. I thought that I was overworked, and when my wife suggested a holiday, I agreed, got a fortnight's leave from my newspaper, and went down to Glebeshire.

Early December is not a bad time for Glebeshire, it is just then the best spot in the British Isles. I knew a little village beyond St. Mary's Moor, that I had not seen for ten years, but always remembered with romantic gratitude, and I felt that that was the place for me now.

I changed trains at Polchester and found myself at last in a little jingle driving out to sea. The air, the wide open moor,

B*

the smell of the sea delighted me, and when I reached my little
village, with its sandy cove and the boats drawn up in two rows
in front of a high rocky cave, and when I ate my eggs and bacon
in the little parlour of the inn overlooking the sea, I felt happier
than I had done for weeks past ; but my happiness did not last
long.   Night after night I could not sleep.   I began to feel
acute loneliness and knew at last in full truth that it was my
friend whom I was missing, and that it was not solitude I
needed, but his company.   Easy enough to talk about having
his company, but I only truly knew, down here in this little
village, sitting on the edge of the green cliff, looking over into
limitless sea, that I was indeed never to have his company again.
There followed after that a wild, impatient regret that I had
not made more of my time with him.   I saw myself, in a sudden vision, as I had really been with him, patronizing, indulgent,
a little contemptuous of his good-natured ideas.   Had I only
a week with him now, how eagerly I would show him that I
was the fool and not he, that I was the lucky one every time !

One connects with one's own grief the place where one feels
it, and before many days had passed I had grown to loathe the
little village, to dread, beyond words, the long, soughing groan
of the sea as it drew back down the slanting beach, the melancholy wail of the seagull, the chattering women under my little
window.   I couldn't stand it.   I ought to go back to London,
and yet from that, too, I shrank.   Memories of Bond lingered
there as they did in no other place, and it was hardly fair to
my wife and family to give them the company of the dreary,
discontented man that I just then was.

And then, just in the way that such things always happen,
I found on my breakfast-table one fine morning a forwarded
letter.   It was from a certain Mrs. Baldwin, and, to my surprise, I saw that it came from Glebeshire, but from the top of
the county and not its southern end.

John Baldwin was a Stock Exchange friend of my brother's,
a rough diamond, but kindly and generous, and not, I believed,
very well off.   Mrs. Baldwin I had always liked, and I think
she always liked me.   We had not met for some little time and
I had no idea what had happened to them.   Now in her letter
she told me that they had taken an old eighteenth-century

house on the north coast of Glebeshire, not very far from Dry-
mouth, that they were enjoying it very much indeed, that Jack
was fitter than he had been for years, and that they would be
delighted, were I ever in that part of the country, to have me
as their guest.   This suddenly seemed to me the very thing.
The Baldwins had never known Charlie Bond, and they would
have, therefore, for me no association with his memory.
They were jolly, noisy people, with a jolly, noisy family, and
Jack Baldwin's personality was so robust that it would surely
shake me out of my gloomy mood.   I sent a telegram at once
to Mrs. Baldwin, asking her whether she could have me for a
week, and before the day was over I received the warmest of
invitations.

Next day I left my little fishing village and experienced
one of those strange, crooked, in-and-out little journeys that
you must undergo if you are to find your way from one
obscure Glebeshire village to another.

About midday, a lovely, cold, blue December midday, I
discovered myself in Polchester with an hour to wait for my
next train.   I went down into the town, climbed the High
Street to the magnificent cathedral, stood beneath the famous
Arden Gate, looked at the still more famous tomb of the
Black Bishop, and it was there, as the sunlight, slanting through
the great east window, danced and sparkled about the wonderful blue stone of which that tomb is made, that I had a sudden
sense of having been through all this before, of having stood
just there in some earlier time, weighed down by some earlier
grief, and that nothing that I was experiencing was unexpected.   I had a curious sense, too, of comfort and condo-
lence, that horrible grey loneliness that I had felt in the fishing
village suddenly fell from me, and for the first time since
Bond's death I was happy.   I walked away from the cathedral,
down the busy street, and through the dear old market-place,
expecting I know not what.   All that I knew was that I was
intending to go to the Baldwins' and that I would be happy
there.

The December afternoon fell quickly, and during the last
part of my journey I was travelling in a ridiculous little train,
through dusk, and the little train went so slowly and so casually that one was always hearing the murmurs of streams
beyond one's window, and lakes of grey water suddenly

stretched like plates of glass to thick woods, black as ink, against a faint sky.   I got out at my little wayside station, shaped like a rabbit-hutch, and found a motor waiting for me.   The drive was not long, and suddenly I was outside the old eighteenth-century house, and Baldwin's stout butler was conveying me into the hall with that careful, kindly patronage, rather as though I were a box of eggs that might very easily be broken.

It was a spacious hall, with a large open fireplace, in front of which they were all having tea.   I say "all" advisedly, because the place seemed to be full of people, grown-ups and children, but mostly children.   There were so many of these last that I was not, to the end of my stay, to be able to name most of them individually.

Mrs. Baldwin came forward to greet me, introduced me to one or two people, sat me down and gave me my tea, told me that I wasn't looking at all well, and needed feeding up, and explained that Jack was out shooting something, but would soon be back.

My entrance had made a brief lull, but immediately everyone recovered and the noise was terrific.   There is a lot to be said for the freedom of the modern child.   There is a lot to be said against it, too.   I soon found that in this party, at any rate, the elders were completely disregarded and of no account. Children rushed about the hall, knocked one another down, shouted and screamed, fell over grown-ups as though they were pieces of furniture, and paid no attention at all to the mild "Now, children" of a plain, elderly lady who was, I supposed, a governess.   I fancy that I was tired with my criss-cross journey, and I soon found a chance to ask Mrs. Baldwin if I could go up to my room.   She said : "I expect you find these children noisy.   Poor little things.   They must have their fun.   Jack always says that one can only be young once, and I do so agree with him."

I wasn't myself feeling very young that evening (I was really about nine hundred years old), so that I agreed with her and eagerly left youth to its own appropriate pleasures. Mrs. Baldwin took me up the fine broad staircase.   She was a stout, short woman, dressed in bright colours, with what is known, I believe, as an infectious laugh.   To-night, although I was fond of her, and knew very well her good, generous heart, she irritated me, and for some reason that I could not quite define.   Perhaps I felt at once that she was out of place there and that the house resented her, but in all this account, I am puzzled by the question as to whether I imagine now, on looking back, all sorts of feelings that were not really there at all, but come to me now because I know of what happened afterwards. But I am so anxious to tell the truth, the whole truth, and nothing but the truth, and there is nothing in the world so difficult to do as that.

We went through a number of dark passages, up and down little pieces of staircase that seemed to have no beginning, no end, and no reason for their existence, and she left me at last in my bedroom, said that she hoped I would be comfortable, and that Jack would come and see me when he came in, and then paused for a moment, looking at me. "You really don't look well," she said. "You've been overdoing it. You're too conscientious. I always said so. You shall have a real rest here. And the children will see that you're not dull."

Her last two sentences seemed scarcely to go together. I could not tell her about my loss. I realized suddenly, as I had never realized in our older acquaintance, that I should never be able to speak to her about anything that really mattered.

She smiled, laughed and left me. I looked at my room and loved it at once. Broad and low-ceilinged, it contained very little furniture, an old four-poster, charming hangings, some old rose-coloured damask, an old gold mirror, an oak cabinet, some high-backed chairs, and then, for comfort, a large armchair with high elbows, a little quaintly shaped sofa dressed in the same rose colour as the bed, a bright crackling fire, and a grandfather clock. The walls, faded primrose, had no pictures, but on one of them, opposite my bed, was a gay sampler worked in bright colours of crimson and yellow and framed in oak.

I liked it, I loved it, and drew the armchair in front of the fire, nestled down into it, and before I knew, I was fast asleep.

How long I slept I don't know, but I suddenly woke with a sense of comfort and well-being which was nothing less than exquisite. I belonged to it, that room, as though I had been in it all my days. I had a curious sense of companionship that was exactly what I had been needing during these last weeks. The house was very still, no voices of children came to me, no sound anywhere, save the sharp crackle of the fire and the friendly ticking of the old clock. Suddenly I thought that there was someone in the room with me, a rustle of something that might have been the fire and yet was not.

I got up and looked about me, half smiling, as though I expected to see a familiar face. There was no one there, of course, and yet I had just that consciousness of companionship that one has when someone whom one loves very dearly and knows very intimately is sitting with one in the same room. I even went to the other side of the four-poster and looked around me, pulled for a moment at the silver-coloured curtains, and of course saw no one. Then the door suddenly opened, and Jack Baldwin came in, and I remember having a curious feeling of irritation as though I had been interrupted. His large, breezy, knickerbockered figure filled the room. "Hullo!" he said. "Delighted to see you. Bit of luck your being down this way. Have you got everything you want?"

II

That was a wonderful old house. I am not going to attempt to describe it, although I have stayed there quite recently. Yes, I stayed there on many occasions since that first of which I am now speaking. It has never been quite the same to me since that first time. You may say, if you like, that the Baldwins fought a battle with it and defeated it. It is certainly now more Baldwin than—well, whatever it was before they rented it. They are not the kind of people to be defeated by atmosphere. Their chief duty in this world, I gather, is to make things Baldwin, and very good for the world too ; but when I first went down to them the house was still challenging them. "A wee bit creepy," Mrs. Baldwin confided to me on the second day of my visit.

"What exactly do you mean by that ?" I asked her. "Ghosts ?"

"Oh, there are those, of course," she answered. "There's an underground passage, you know, that runs from here to the sea, and one of the wickedest of the smugglers was killed in it, and his ghost still haunts the cellar. At least, that's what we were told by our first butler here ; and then, of course, we found that it was the butler, not the smuggler, who was haunting the cellar, and since his departure the smuggler hasn't been visible." She laughed. "All the same, it isn't a comfortable place. I'm going to wake up some of those old rooms. We're going to put in some more windows. And then there are the children," she added.

Yes, there were the children. Surely the noisiest in all the world. They had reverence for nothing. They were the wildest savages, and especially those from nine to thirteen, the cruellest and most uncivilized age for children. There were two little boys, twins I should think, who were nothing less than devils, and regarded their elders with cold, watching eyes, said nothing in protest when scolded, but evolved plots afterwards that fitted precisely the chastiser. To do my host and hostess justice, all the children were not Baldwins, and I fancy that the Baldwin contingent was the quietest.

Nevertheless, from early morning until ten at night, the noise was terrific and you were never sure how early in the morning it would recommence. I don't know that I personally minded the noise very greatly. It took me out of myself and gave me something better to think of, but, in some obscure and unanalysed way, I felt that the house minded it. One knows how the poets have written about old walls and rafters rejoicing in the happy, careless laughter of children. I do not think this house rejoiced at all, and it was queer how consistently I, who am not supposed to be an imaginative person, thought about the house.

But it was not until my third evening that something really happened. I say "happened", but did anything really happen? You shall judge for yourself.

I was sitting in my comfortable armchair in my bedroom, enjoying that delightful half-hour before one dresses for dinner. There was a terrible racket up and down the passages, the children being persuaded, I gathered, to go into the schoolroom and have their supper, when the noise died down and there was nothing but the feathery whisper of the snow— snow had been falling all day—against my window-pane. My thoughts suddenly turned to Bond, directed to him as actually and precipitately as though he had suddenly sprung before me. I did not want to talk of him. I had been fighting his memory these last days, because I had thought that the wisest thing to do, but now he was too much for me.

I luxuriated in my memories of him, turning over and over all sorts of times that we had had together, seeing his smile, watching his mouth that turned up at the corners when he was amused, and wondering finally why he should obsess me the way that he did, when I had lost so many other friends for whom I had thought I cared much more, who, nevertheless, never bothered my memory at all.   I sighed, and it seemed to me that my sigh was very gently repeated behind me.   I turned sharply round.   The curtains had not been drawn. You know the strange, milky pallor that reflected snow throws over objects, and although three lighted candles shone in the room, moon-white shadows seemed to hang over the bed and across the floor.   Of course there was no one there, and yet I stared and stared about me as though I were convinced that I was not alone.   And then I looked especially at one part of the room, a distant corner beyond the four-poster, and it seemed to me that someone was there.   And yet no one was there. But whether it was that my mind had been distracted, or that the beauty of the old snow-lit room enchanted me, I don't know, but my thoughts of my friend were happy and reassured. I had not lost him, I seemed to say to myself.   Indeed, at that special moment, he seemed to be closer to me than he had been while he was alive.

From that evening a curious thing occurred.   I only seemed to be close to my friend when I was in my own room— and I felt more than that.   When my door was closed and I was sitting in my armchair, I fancied that our new companionship was not only Bond's, but was something more as well. I would wake in the middle of the night or in the early morning and feel quite sure that I was not alone ; so sure that I did not even want to investigate it further, but just took the companionship for granted and was happy.

Outside that room, however, I felt increasing discomfort. I hated the way in which the house was treated.   A quite unreasonable anger rose within me as I heard the Baldwins discussing the improvements that they were going to make, and yet they were so kind to me, and so patently unaware of doing anything that would not generally be commended, that it was quite impossible for me to show my anger.   Nevertheless, Mrs. Baldwin noticed something.   "I am afraid the children are worrying you," she said one morning, half interrogatively. "In a way it will be a rest when they go back to school, but the Christmas holidays is their time, isn't it ?   I do like to see them happy, poor little dears."

The poor little dears were at that moment being Red Indians all over the hall.

"No, of course, I like children," I answered her. "The only thing is that they don't—I hope you won't think me foolish—somehow quite fit in with the house."

"Oh, I think it's so good for old places like this," said Mrs. Baldwin briskly, "to be woken up a little. I'm sure if the old people who used to live here came back they'd love to hear all the noise and laughter."

I wasn't so sure myself, but I wouldn't disturb Mrs. Baldwin's contentment for anything.

That evening in my room I was so convinced of companionship that I spoke.

"If there's anyone here," I said aloud, "I'd like them to know that I'm aware of it and am glad of it."

Then, when I caught myself speaking aloud, I was suddenly terrified. Was I really going crazy? Wasn't that the first step towards insanity when you talked to yourself? Nevertheless, a moment later I was reassured. There *was* someone there.

That night I woke, looked at my luminous watch and saw that it was a quarter past three. The room was so dark that I could not even distinguish the posters of my bed, but—there was a very faint glow from the fire, now nearly dead. Opposite my bed there seemed to me to be something white. Not white in the accepted senses of a tall, ghostly figure ; but, sitting up and staring, it seemed to me that the shadow was very small, hardly reaching above the edge of the bed.

"Is there anyone there ?" I asked. "Because, if there is, do speak to me. I'm not frightened. I know that someone has been here all this last week, and I am glad of it."

Very faintly then, and so faintly that I cannot to this day be sure that I saw anything at all, the figure of a child seemed to me to be visible.

We all know how we have at one time and another fancied that we have seen visions and figures, and then have discovered that it was something in the room, the chance hanging of a coat, the reflection of a glass, a trick of moonlight that has fired our imagination. I was quite prepared for that in this case, but it seemed to me then that as I watched the shadow moved directly in front of the dying fire, and delicate as the leaf of a silver birch, like the trailing rim of some evening cloud, the figure of a child hovered in front of me.

Curiously enough the dress, which seemed to be of some silver tissue, was clearer than anything else. I did not, in fact, see the face at all, and yet I could swear in the morning that I had seen it, that I knew large, black, wide-open eyes, a little mouth very faintly parted in a timid smile, and that beyond anything else I had realized in the expression of that face fear and bewilderment and a longing for some comfort.

III

After that night the affair moved very quickly to its little climax.

I am not a very imaginative man, nor have I any sympathy with the modern craze for spooks and spectres. I have never seen, nor fancied that I had seen, anything of a supernatural kind since that visit, but then I have never known since that time such a desperate need of companionship and comfort, and is it not perhaps because we do not want things badly enough in this life that we do not get more of them ? However that may be, I was sure on this occasion that I had some companion-ship that was born of a need greater than mine. I suddenly took the most frantic and unreasonable dislike of the children in that house. It was exactly as though I had discovered some-where in a deserted part of the building some child who had been left behind by mistake by the last occupants and was terri-fied by the noisy exuberance and ruthless selfishness of the new family.

For a week I had no more definite manifestations of my little friend, but I was as sure of her presence there in my room as I was of my own clothes and the armchair in which I used to sit.

It was time for me to go back to London, but I could not go. I asked everyone I met as to legends and stories con-nected with the old house, but I never found anything to do with a little child. I looked forward all day to my hour in my room before dinner, the time when I felt the companionship closest. I sometimes woke in the night and was conscious of its presence, but, as I have said, I never saw anything.

One evening the older children obtained leave to stay up

later. It was somebody's birthday. The house seemed to be full of people, and the presence of the children led after dinner to a perfect riot of noise and confusion. We were to play hide-and-seek all over the house. Everybody was to dress up. There was, for that night at least, to be no privacy anywhere. We were all, as Mrs. Baldwin said, to be ten years old again. I hadn't the least desire to be ten years old, but I found myself caught into the game, and had, in sheer self-defence, to run up and down the passages and hide behind doors. The noise was terrific. It grew and grew in volume. People got hysterical. The smaller children jumped out of bed and ran about the passages. Somebody kept blowing a motor-horn. Somebody else turned on the gramophone.

Suddenly I was sick of the whole thing, retreated into my room, lit one candle and locked the door. I had scarcely sat down in my chair when I was aware that my little friend had come. She was standing near to the bed, staring at me, terror in her eyes. I have never seen anyone so frightened. Her little breasts panting beneath her silver gown, her very fair hair falling about her shoulders, her little hands clenched. Just as I saw her there were loud knocks on the door, many voices shouting to be admitted, a perfect babel of noise and laughter. The little figure moved, and then—how can I give any idea of it?—I was conscious of having something to protect and comfort. I saw nothing, physically I felt nothing, and yet I was murmuring. "There, there, don't mind. They shan't come in. I'll see that no one touches you. I understand. I understand." For how long I sat like that I don't know. The noises died away, voices murmured at intervals, and then were silent. The house slept. All night I think I stayed there comforting and being comforted.

I fancy now—but how much of it may not be fancy?—that I knew that the child loved the house, had stayed so long as was possible, at last was driven away, and that that was her farewell, not only to me, but all that she most loved in this world and the next.

I do not know—I could swear to nothing. Of what I am sure is that my sense of loss in my friend was removed from that night and never returned. Did I argue with myself that that child companionship included also my friend? Again, I do not know. But of one thing I am now sure, that if love is strong enough, physical death cannot destroy it, and however platitudinous that may sound to others, it is platitudinous no longer when you have discovered it by actual experience for yourself.

That moment in that fire-lit room, when I felt that spiritual heart beating with mine, is and always will be enough for me.

One thing more.   Next day I left for London, and my wife was delighted to find me so completely recovered—happier, she said, than I had ever been before.

Two days afterwards, I received a parcel from Mrs. Baldwin.   In the note that accompanied it, she said :

I think that you must have left this by mistake behind you.   It was found in the small drawer in your dressing-table.

I opened the parcel and discovered an old blue silk handkerchief, wrapped round a long, thin wooden box.   The cover of the box lifted very easily, and I saw inside it an old painted wooden doll, dressed in the period, I should think, of Queen Anne.   The dress was very complete, even down to the little shoes, and the little grey mittens on the hands.   Inside the silk skirt there was sewn a little tape, and on the tape, in very faded letters, "Ann Trelawney, 1710."

MRS. LUNT

I

"Do you believe in ghosts?" I asked Runciman. I had to
ask him this very platitudinous question more because he was
so difficult a man to spend an hour with rather than for any
other reason. You know his books, perhaps, or more probably you don't know them—*The Running Man*, *The Elm
Tree*, and *Crystal and Candlelight*. He is one of those little
men who are constant enough in this age of immense over-
production of books, men who publish every autumn their
novel, who arouse by that publication in certain critics eager
appreciation and praise, who have a small and faithful public,
whose circulation is very small indeed, who, when you meet
them, have little to say, are often shy and nervous, pessimistic
and remote from daily life. Such men do fine work, are made
but little of in their own day, and perhaps fifty years after
their death are rediscovered by some digging critic and become
a sort of cult with a new generation.

I asked Runciman that question because, for some
unknown reason, I had invited him to dinner at my flat,
and was now faced with a long evening filled with that most
tiresome of all conversations, talk that dies every two minutes
and has to be revived with terrific exertions. Being myself a
critic, and having on many occasions praised Runciman's
work, he was the more nervous and shy with me ; had I
abused it, he would perhaps have had plenty to say—he was
that kind of man. But my question was a lucky. one : it
roused him instantly, his long, bony body became full of a
new energy, his eyes stared into a rich and exciting reminiscence, he spoke without pause, and I took care not to interrupt him. He certainly told me one of the most astounding
stories I have ever heard. Whether it was true or not I
cannot, of course, say. These ghost stories are nearly always

at second or third hand. I had, at any rate, the good fortune
to secure mine from the source. Moreover, Runciman was
not a liar ; he was too serious for that. He himself admitted
that he was not sure, at this distance of time, as to whether
the thing had gained as the years passed. However, here
it is as he told it.

'It was some fifteen years ago," he said. "I went down
to Cornwall to stay with Robert Lunt. Do you remember
his name ? No, I suppose you do not. He wrote several
novels ; some of those half-and-half things that are not quite
novels, not quite poems, rather mystical and picturesque,
and are the very devil to do well. De la Mare's *Return* is a
good example of the kind of thing. I had reviewed somewhere his last book, and reviewed it favourably, and received
from him a really touching letter showing that the man was
thirsting for praise, and also, I fancied, for company. He
lived in Cornwall somewhere on the sea-coast, and his wife
had died some two years before ; he said he was quite alone
there, and would I come and spend Christmas with him ;
he hoped I would not think this impertinent ; he expected
that I would be engaged already, but he could not resist the
chance. Well, I wasn't engaged ; far from it. If Lunt was
lonely, so was I ; if Lunt was a failure, so was I ; I was touched,
as I have said, by his letter, and I accepted his invitation.
As I went down in the train to Penzance I wondered what
kind of a man he would be. I had never seen any photographs
of him ; he was not the sort of author whose picture the newspapers publish. He must be, I fancied, about my own age—
perhaps rather older. I know when we're lonely how some of
us are for ever imagining that a friend will somewhere turn
up, that ideal friend who will understand all one's feelings,
who will give one affection without being sentimental, who
will take an interest in one's affairs without being impertinent
—yes, the sort of friend one never finds.

"I fancy that I became quite romantic about Lunt before
I reached Penzance. We would talk, he and I, about all
those literary questions that seemed to me at that time so
absorbing ; we would perhaps often stay together and even
travel abroad on those little journeys that are so swiftly
melancholy when one is alone, so delightful when one has a
perfect companion. I imagined h m as sparse and delicate
and refined, with a sort of wistfulness and rather childish

play of fancy. We had both, so far, failed in our careers, but perhaps toge her we would do great things.

"When I arrived at Penzance it was almost dark, and the snow, threatened all day by an overhanging sky, had begun gently and timorously to fall. He had told me in his letter that a fly would be at the station to take me to his house ; and there I found it—a funny old weather-beaten carriage with a funny old weather-beaten driver. At this distance of time my imagination may have created many things, but I fancy that from the moment I was shut into that carriage some dim suggestion of fear and apprehension attacked me. I fancy that I had some absurd impulse to get out of the thing and take the night train back to London again—an action that would have been very unlike me, as I had always a sort of obstinate determination to carry through anything that I had begun. In any case, I was uncomfortable in that carriage ; it had, I remember, a nasty, musty smell of damp straw and stale eggs, and it seemed to confine me so closely as though it were determined that, once I was in, I should never get out again. Then, it was bitterly cold ; I was colder during that drive than I have ever been before or since. It was that penetrating cold that seems to pierce your very brain, so that I could not think with any clearness, but only wish again and again that I hadn't come. Of course, I could see nothing—only feel the jolt over the uneven road— and once and again we seemed to fight our way through dark paths, because I could feel the overhanging branches of the trees knock against the cab with mysterious taps, as though they were trying to give me some urgent message.

"Well, I mustn't make more of it than the facts allow, and I mustn't see into it all the significance of the events that followed. I only know that as the drive proceeded I became more and more miserable : miserable with the cold of my body, the misgivings of my imagination, the general loneliness of my case.

"At last we stopped. The old scarecrow got slowly off his box, with many heavings and sighings, came to the cab door and, with great difficulty and irritating slowness, opened it. I got out of it, and found that the snow was now falling very heavily indeed, and that the path was lightened with its soft, mysterious glow. Before me was a humped and ungainly shadow : the house that was to receive me. I could

make nothing of it in that darkness, but only stood there
shivering while the old man pulled at the door-bell with a
sort of frantic energy as though he were anxious to be rid of
the whole job as quickly as possible and return to his own
place.   At last, after what seemed an endless time, the door
opened, and an old man, who might have been own brother
to the driver, poked out his head.   The two old men talked
together, and at last my bag was shouldered and I was permitted to come in out of the piercing cold.

"Now this, I know, is not imagination.   I have never
at any period of my life hated at first sight so vigorously
any dwelling-place into which I have ever entered as I did
that house.   There was nothing especially disagreeable about
my first vision of the hall.   It was a large, dark place, lit by
two dim lamps, cold and cheerless ;   but I got no particular
impression of it because at once I was conducted out of it,
led along a passage, and then introduced into a room which
was, I saw at once, as warm and comfortable as the hall had
been dark and dismal.   I was, in fact, so eagerly pleased at the
large and leaping fire that I moved towards it at once, not
noting, at the first moment, the presence of my host ;   and
when I did see him I could not believe that it was he.   I have
told you the kind of man that I had expected ;   but, instead
of the sparse, sensitive artist, I found facing me a large, burly
man, over six foot, I should fancy, as broad-shouldered as he
was tall, giving evidence of great muscular strength, the lower
part of his face hidden by a black, pointed beard.

"But if I was astonished at the sight of him, I was doubly
amazed when he spoke.   His voice was thin and piping,
like that of some old woman, and the little nervous gestures
that he made with his hands were even more feminine than
his voice.   But I had to allow, perhaps, for excitement, for
excited he was ;   he came up to me, took my hand in both of
his, and held it as though he would never let it go.   In the
evening, when we sat over our port, he apologized for this.
'I was so glad to see you,' he said ;   'I couldn't believe that
really you would come ;   you are the first visitor of my own
kind that I have had here for ever so long.   I was ashamed,
indeed, of asking you, but I had to snatch at the chance—it
means so much to me.'

"His eagerness, in fact, had something disturbing about
it ;   something pathetic, too.   He simply couldn't do too

much for me : he led me through funny crumbling old passages, the boards creaking under us at every step, up some
dark stairs, the walls hung, so far as I could see in the dim
light, with faded yellow photographs of places, and showed
me into my room with a deprecating agitated gesture as
though he expected me at the first sight of it to turn and run.
I didn't like it any more than I liked the rest of the house ;
but that was not my host's fault. He had done everything he
possibly could for me : there was a large fire flaming in the
open fireplace, there was a hot bottle, as he explained to me,
in the big four-poster bed, and the old man who had opened
the door to me was already taking my clothes out of my bag
and putting them away. Lunt's nervousness was almost
sentimental. He put both his hands on my shoulders and
said, looking at me pleadingly : 'If you only knew what it is
for me to have you here, the talks we'll have. Well, well, I
must leave you. You'll come down and join me, won't you,
as soon as you can ?'

"It was then, when I was left alone in my room, that
I had my second impulse to flee. Four candles in tall old
silver candlesticks were burning brightly, and these, with the
blazing fire, gave plenty of light ; and yet the room was in
some way dim, as though a faint smoke pervaded it, and I
remember that I went to one of the old lattice windows and
threw it open for a moment as though I felt stifled. Two
things quickly made me close it. One was the intense cold
which, with a fluttering scamper of snow, blew into the room ;
the other was the quite deafening roar of the sea, which
seemed to fling itself at my very face as though it wanted to
knock me down. I quickly shut the window, turned round,
and saw an old woman standing just inside the door. Now
every story of this kind depends for its interest on its verisi-
militude. Of course, to make my tale convincing I should
be able to prove to you that I saw that old woman ; but I
can't. I can only urge upon you my rather dreary reputation
of probity. You know that I'm a teetotaller, and always
have been, and, most important evidence of all, I was not
expecting to see an old woman ; and yet I hadn't the least
doubt in the world but that it was an old woman I saw. You
may talk about shadows, clothes hanging on the back of the
door, and the rest of it. I don't know. I've no theories
about this story, I'm not a spiritualist, I don't know that I

believe in anything especially, except the beauty of beautiful things.

"We'll put it, if you like, that I fancied that I saw an old woman, and my fancy was so strong that I can give you to this day a pretty detailed account of her appearance. She wore a black silk dress and on her breast was a large, ugly gold brooch ; she had black hair, brushed back from her forehead and parted down the middle ; she wore a collar of some white stuff round her throat ; her face was one of the wickedest, most malignant, and furtive that I have ever seen —very white in colour. She was shrivelled enough now, but might once have been rather beautiful. She stood there quietly, her hands at her side. I thought that she was some kind of housekeeper. 'I have everything I want, thank you,' I said. 'What a splendid fire !' I turned for a moment towards it, and when I looked back she was gone. I thought nothing of this, of course, but drew up an old chair covered with green faded tapestry, and thought that I would read a little from some book that I had brought down with me before I went to join my host. The fact was that I was not very intent upon joining him before I must. I didn't like him. I had already made up my mind that I would find some excuse to return to London as soon as possible. I can't tell you why I didn't like him, except that I was myself very reserved and had, like many Englishmen, a great distrust of demonstrations, especially from another man. I hadn't cared for the way in which he had put his hands on my shoulders, and I felt perhaps that I wouldn't be able to live up to all his eager excitement about me.

"I sat in my chair and took up my book, but I had not been reading for more than two minutes before I was conscious of a most unpleasant smell. Now, there are all sorts of smells —healthy and otherwise—but I think the nastiest is that chilly kind of odour that comes from bad sanitation and stuffy rooms combined ; you meet it sometimes at little country inns and decrepit town lodgings. This smell was so definite that I could almost locate it ; it came from near the door. I got up, approached the door, and at once it was as though I were drawing near to somebody who, if you'll forgive the impoliteness, was not accustomed to taking too many baths. I drew back just as I might had an actual person been there. Then quite suddenly the smell was gone, the room

was fresh, and I saw, to my surprise, that one of the windows
had opened and that snow was again blowing in. I closed it
and went downstairs.

"The evening that followed was odd enough. My
host was not in himself an unlikeable man ; he did his very
utmost to please me. He had a fine culture and a wide
knowledge of books and things. He became quite cheerful
as the evening went on ; gave me a good dinner in a funny
little old dining-room hung with some admirable mezzotints.
The old serving man looked after us—a funny old man, with
a long white beard like a goat—and, oddly enough, it was from
him that I first recaught my earlier apprehension. He had
just put the dessert on the table, had arranged my plate in front
of me, when I saw him give a start and look towards the door.
My attention was attracted to this because his hand, as it
touched the plate, suddenly trembled. My eyes followed,
but I could see nothing. That he was frightened of something was perfectly clear, and then (it may, of course, very
easily have been fancy) I thought that I detected once more
that strange unwholesome smell.

"I forgot this again when we were both seated in front
of a splendid fire in the library. Lunt had a very fine collection of books, and it was delightful to him, as it is to every
book-collector, to have somebody with him who could really
appreciate them. We stood looking at one book after another
and talking eagerly about some of the minor early English
novelists who were my especial hobby—Bage, Godwin,
Henry Mackenzie, Mrs. Shelley, Mat Lewis, and others—
when once again he affected me most unpleasantly by putting
his arm round my shoulders. I have all my life disliked
intensely to be touched by certain people. I suppose we all
feel like this. It is one of those inexplicable things ; and I
disliked this so much that I abruptly drew away.

"Instantly he was changed into a man of furious and
ungovernable rage ; I thought that he was going to strike me.
He stood there quivering all over, the words pouring out
of his mouth incoherently, as though he were mad and did not
know what he was saying. He accused me of insulting him,
of abusing his hospitality, of throwing his kindness back
into his face, and of a thousand other ridiculous things ; and
I can't tell you how strange it was to hear all this coming out
in that shrill piping voice as though it were from an agitated

woman, and yet to see with one's eyes that big, muscular frame, those immense shoulders, and that dark bearded face.

"I said nothing. I am, physically, a coward. I dislike, above anything else in the world, any sort of quarrel. At last I brought out, 'I am very sorry. I didn't mean anything. Please forgive me,' and then hurriedly turned to leave the room. At once he changed again ; now he was almost in tears. He implored me not to go ; said it was his wretched temper, but that he was so miserable and unhappy, and had for so long now been alone and desolate that he hardly knew what he was doing. He begged me to give him another chance, and if I would only listen to his story I would perhaps be more patient with him.

"At once, so oddly is man constituted, I changed in my feelings towards him. I was very sorry for him. I saw that he was a man on the edge of his nerves, and that he really did need some help and sympathy, and would be quite distracted if he could not get it. I put my hand on his shoulder to quieten him and to show him that I bore no malice, and I felt that his great body was quivering from head to foot. We sat down again, and in an odd, rambling manner he told me his story. It amounted to very little, and the gist of it was that, rather to have some sort of companionship than from any impulse of passion, he had married, some fifteen years before, the daughter of a neighbouring clergyman. They had had no very happy life together, and at the last, he told me quite frankly, he had hated her. She had been mean, overbearing, and narrow-minded ; it had been, he confessed, nothing but a relief to him when, just a year ago, she had suddenly died from heart failure. He had thought then that things would go better with him, but they had not ; nothing had gone right with him since. He hadn't been able to work, many of his friends had ceased to come to see him, he had found it even difficult to get servants to stay with him, he was desperately lonely, he slept badly——that was why his temper was so terribly on edge.

"He had no one in the house with him save the old man, who was, fortunately, an excellent cook, and a boy——the old man's grandson. 'Oh, I thought,' I said, 'that that excellent meal to-night was cooked by your housekeeper.' 'My housekeeper ?' he answered. 'There's no woman in the house.' 'Oh, but one came to my room,' I replied,

'this evening—an old lady-like looking person in a black
silk dress.' 'You were mistaken,' he answered in the
oddest voice, as though he were exerting all the strength that
he possessed to keep himself quiet and controlled. 'I am sure
that I saw her.' I answered. 'There couldn't be any mistake.'
And I described her to him. 'You were mistaken,' he repeated
again. 'Don't you see that you must have been when I tell
you there is no woman in the house?' I reassured him
quickly lest there should be another outbreak of rage. Then
there followed the oddest kind of appeal. Urgently, as though
his very life depended upon it, he begged me to stay with
him for a few days. He implied, although he said nothing
definitely, that he was in great trouble, that if only I would
stay for a few days all would be well, that if ever in all my
life I had had a chance of doing a kind action I had one now,
that he couldn't expect me to stop in so dreary a place, but
that he would never forget it if I did. He spoke in a voice
of such urgent distress that I reassured him as I might a child,
promising that I would stay, and shaking hands with him on
it as though it were a kind of solemn oath between us.

II

. "I am sure that you would wish me to give you this
incident as it occurred, and if the final catastrophe seems
to come, as it were, accidentally, I can only say to you that
that was how it happened. It is since the event that I have
tried to put two and two together, and that they don't
altogether make four is the fault that mine shares, I suppose,
with every true ghost story.

"But the truth is that after that very strange episode
between us I had a very good night. I slept the sleep of all
justice, cosy and warm, in my four-poster, with the murmur
of the sea beyond the windows to rock my slumbers. Next
morning, too, was bright and cheerful, the sun sparkling
down on the snow, and the snow sparkling back to the sun
as though they were glad to see one another. I had a very
pleasant morning looking at Lunt's books, talking to him,
and writing one or two letters. I must say that, after all, I
liked the man. His appeal to me on the night before had
touched me. So few people, you see, had ever appealed

to me about anything. His nervousness was there and the
constant sense of apprehension, yet he seemed to be putting
the best face on it, doing his utmost to set me at my ease in
order to induce me to stay, I suppose, and to give him a little
of that company that he so terribly needed. I dare say if I
had not been so busy about the books I would not have been
so happy. There was a strange eerie silence about that house
if one ever stopped to listen ; and once, I remember, sitting
at the old bureau writing a letter, I raised my head and looked
up, and caught Lunt watching as though he wondered whether
I had heard or noticed anything. And so I listened too, and
it seemed to me as though someone were on the other side
of the library door with their hand raised to knock ; a quaint
notion, with nothing to support it, but I could have sworn
that if I had gone to the door and opened it suddenly someone
would have been there.

"However, I was cheerful enough, and after lunch quite
happy. Lunt asked me if I would like a walk, and I said I
would ; and we started out in the sunshine over the crunching
snow towards the sea. I don't remember of what we talked ;
we seemed to be now quite at our ease with one another.
We crossed the fields to a certain point, looked down at the
sea—smooth now, like silk—and turned back. I remember
that I was so cheerful that I seemed suddenly to take a happy
view of all my prospects. I began to confide in Lunt, telling
him of my little plans, of my hopes for the book that I was
then writing, and even began rather timidly to suggest to him
that perhaps we should do something together ; that what
we both needed was a friend of common taste with ourselves.
I know that I was talking on, that we had crossed a little village
street, and were turning up the path towards the dark avenue
of trees that led to his house, when suddenly the change came.

"What I first noticed was that he was not listening to
me ; his gaze was fixed beyond me, into the very heart of the
black clump of trees that fringed the silver landscape. I
looked too, and my heart bounded. There, standing just
in front of the trees, as though she were waiting for us, was
the old woman whom I had seen in my room the night before.
I stopped. 'Why, there she is !' I said. 'That's the old
woman of whom I was speaking—the old woman who came
to my room.' He caught my shoulder with his hand.
'There's nothing there,' he said. 'Don't you see that that's

shadow? What's the matter with you? Can't you see that there's nothing?' I stepped forward, and there was nothing, and I wouldn't, to this day, be able to tell you whether it was hallucination or not. I can only say that, from that moment, the afternoon appeared to become dark.

"As we entered into the avenue of trees, silently and hurrying as though someone were behind us, the dusk seemed to have fallen so that I could scarcely see my way. We reached the house breathless. He hastened into his study as though I were not with him, but I followed and, closing the door behind me, said, with all the force that I had at command : 'Now, what is this? What is it that's troubling you? You must tell me! How can I help you if you don't?' And he replied, in so strange a voice that it was as though he had gone out of his mind : 'I tell you there's nothing! Can't you believe me when I tell you there's nothing at all? I'm quite all right. . . . Oh, my God!—my God! . . . don't leave me! . . . This is the very day—the very night she said . . . But I did nothing, I tell you—I did nothing—it's only her beastly malice. . . .' He broke off. He still held my arm with his hand. He made strange movements, wiping his forehead as though it were damp with sweat, almost pleading with me ; then suddenly angry again, then beseeching once more, as though I had refused him the one thing he wanted.

"I saw that he was truly not far from madness, and I began myself to have a sudden terror of this damp, dark house, this great, trembling man, and something more that was worse than they. But I pitied him. How could you or any man have helped it? I made him sit down in the arm-chair be ide the fire, which had now dwindled to a few glimmering red coals. I let him hold me close to him with his arm and clutch my hand with his, and I repeated, as quiet as I might : 'But tell me ; don't be afraid, whatever it is you have done. Tell me what danger it is you fear, and then we can face it together.' 'Fear! fear!' he repeated ; and then, with a mighty effort which I could not but admire, he summoned all his control. 'I'm off my head,' he said, 'with loneliness and depression. My wife died a year ago on this very night. We hated one another. I couldn't be sorry when she died, and she knew it. When that last heart attack came on, between her gasps she told me that she would return, and I've always dreaded this night. That's partly why I asked you to come, to have anyone here, anybody, and you've been very kind—more kind than I had any right to expect. You must think me insane going on like this, but see me through to-night and we'll have splendid times together. Don't desert me now—now, of all times !' I promised that I would not. I soothed him as best I could. We sat there, for I know not how long, through the gathering dark ; we neither of us moved, the fire died out, and the room was lit with a strange dim glow that came from the snowy landscape beyond the uncurtained windows. Ridiculous, perhaps, as I look back at it. We sat there, I in a chair close to his, hand in hand, like a couple of lovers ; but, in real truth, two men terrified, fearful of what was coming, and unable to do anything to meet it.

"I think that that was perhaps the strangest part of it ; a sort of paralysis that crept over me. What would you or anyone else have done—summoned the old man, gone down to the village inn, fetched the local doctor ? I could do nothing but see the snow-shine move like trembling water about the furniture and hear, through the urgent silence, the faint hoot of an owl from the trees in the wood.

III

"Oddly enough, I can remember nothing, try as I may, between that strange vigil and the moment when I myself, wakened out of a brief sleep, sat up in bed to see Lunt standing inside my room holding a candle. He was wearing a night-shirt, and looked huge in the candlelight, his black beard falling intensely dark on the white stuff of his shirt. He came very quietly towards my bed, the candle throwing flickering shadows about the room. When he spoke it was in a voice low and subdued, almost a whisper. 'Would you come,' he asked, 'only for half an hour—just for half an hour ?' he repeated, staring at me as though he didn't know me. 'I'm unhappy without somebody—very unhappy.' Then he looked over his shoulder, held the candle high above his head, and stared piercingly at every part of the room. I could see that something had happened to him, that he had taken another step into the country of Fear—a step that had withdrawn him from me and from every other human being.

He whispered : 'When you come, tread softly ; I don't want anyone to hear us.' I did what I could. I got out of bed, put on my dressing-gown and slippers, and tried to persuade him to stay with me. The fire was almost dead, but I told him that we would build it up again, and that we would sit there and wait for the morning ; but no, he repeated again and again : 'It's better in my own room ; we're safer there.' 'Safe from what ?' I asked him, making him look at me. 'Lunt, wake up ! You're as though you were asleep. There's nothing to fear. We've nobody but ourselves. Stay here and let us talk, and have done with this nonsense.' But he wouldn't answer ; only drew me forward down the dark passage, and then turned into his room, beckoning me to follow. He got into bed and sat hunched up there, his hands holding his knees, staring at the door, and every once and again shivering with a little tremor. The only light in the room was that from the candle, now burning low, and the only sound was the purring whisper of the sea.

"It seemed to make little difference to him that I was there. He did not look at me, but only at the door, and when I spoke to him he did not answer me nor seem to hear what I had said. I sat down beside the bed and, in order to break the silence, talked on about anything, about nothing, and was dropping off, I think, into a confused doze, when I heard his voice breaking across mine. Very clearly and distinctly he said : 'If I killed her, she deserved it ; she was never a good wife to me, not from the first ; she shouldn't have irritated me as she did—she knew what my temper was. She had a worse one than mine, though. She can't touch me ; I'm as strong as she is.' And it was then, as clearly as I can now remember, that his voice suddenly sank into a sort of gentle whisper, as though he were almost glad that his fears had been confirmed. He whispered : 'She's there !' I cannot possibly describe to you how that whisper seemed to let Fear loose like water through my body. I could see nothing—the candle was flaming high in the last moment of its life—I could see nothing ; but Lunt suddenly screamed, with a shrill cry like a tortured animal in agony : 'Keep her off me, keep her away from me, keep her off— keep her off !' He caught me, his hands digging into my shoulders ; then, with an awful effect of constricted muscles, as though rigor had caught and held him, his arms slowly

C

fell away, he slipped back on to the bed as though someone
were pushing him, his hands fell against the sheet, his whole
body jerked with a convulsive effort, and then he rolled over.
I saw nothing ; only quite distinctly in my nostrils was that
same fetid odour that I had known on the preceding evening.
I rushed to the door, opened it, shouted down the long passage
again and again, and soon the old man came running.   I sent
him for the doctor, and then could not return to the room,
but stood there listening, hearing nothing save the whisper
of the sea, the loud ticking of the hall clock.   I flung open
the window at the end of the passage ;   the sea rushed in with
its precipitant roar ;   some bells chimed the hour.   Then
at last, beating into myself more courage, I turned back
towards the room. . . ."

"Well ?" I asked as Runciman paused.   "He was dead,
of course ?"

"Dead, the doctor afterwards said, of heart failure."

"Well ?" I asked again.

"That's all."   Runciman paused.   "I don't know whether
you can even call it a ghost story.   My idea of the old woman
may have been all hallucination.   I don't even know whether
his wife was like that when she was alive.   She may have
been large and fat.   Lunt died of an evil conscience."

"Yes," I said.

"The only thing," Runciman added at last, after a long
pause, "is that on Lunt's body there were marks—on his
neck especially, some on his chest—as of fingers pressing in,
scratches and dull blue marks.   He may, in his terror, have
caught at his own throat. . . ."

"Yes," I said again.

"Anyway"—Runciman shivered—"I don't like Cornwall
—beastly county.   Queer things happen there—something
in the air. . . ."

"So I've heard," I answered.   "And now have a drink.
We both will."

ARTHUR MACHEN

THE ISLINGTON MYSTERY

I

THE public taste in murders is often erratic, and sometimes, I think, fallible enough. Take, for example, that Crippen business. It happened seventeen years ago, and it is still freshly remembered and discussed with interest. Yet it was by no means a murder of the first rank. What was there in it? The outline is crude enough; simple, easy, and disgusting, as Dr. Johnson observed of another work of art. Crippen was cursed with a nagging wife of unpleasant habits; and he cherished a passion for his typist. Whereupon he poisoned Mrs. Crippen, cut her up and buried the pieces in the coal-cellar. This was well enough, though elementary; and if the foolish little man had been content to lie quiet and do nothing, he might have lived and died peaceably. But he must needs disappear from his house—the action of a fool—and cross the Atlantic with his typist absurdly and obviously disguised as a boy: sheer, bungling imbecility. Here, surely, there is no single trace of the master's hand; and yet, as I say, the Crippen Murder is reckoned amongst the masterpieces. It is the same tale in all the arts: the low comedian was always sure of a laugh if he cared to tumble over a pin; and the weakest murderer is sure of a certain amount of respectful attention if he will take the trouble to dismember his subject. And then, with respect to Crippen: he was caught by means of the wireless device, then in its early stages. This, of course, was utterly irrelevant to the true issue; but the public wallows in irrelevance. A great art critic may praise a great picture, and make his criticism a masterpiece in itself. He will be unread; but let some asinine paragraphist say that the painter always sings "Tom Bowling" as he sets his palette, and dines on boiled fowl and apricot sauce three times a week —then the world will proclaim the artist great.

II

The success of the second-rate is deplorable in itself ; but it is more deplorable in that it very often obscures the genuine masterpiece.   If the crowd runs after the false, it must neglect the true.   The intolerable *Romola* is praised ; the admirable *Cloister and the Hearth* is waived aside.   So, while the very indifferent and clumsy performance of Crippen filled the papers, the extraordinary Battersea Murder was served with a scanty paragraph or two in obscure corners of the Press.   Indeed, we were so shamefully starved of detail that I only retain a bare outline of this superb crime in my memory ; but, roughly, the affair was shaped as follows : In the first floor of one of the smaller sets of flats in Battersea a young fellow (? 18—20) was talking to an actress, a "touring" actress of no particular fame, whose age, if I recollect, was drawing on from thirty to forty.   A shot, a near shot, broke in suddenly on their talk. The young man dashed out of the flat, down the stairs, and there, in the entry of the flats, found his own father, shot dead. The father, it should be remarked, was a touring actor, and an old friend of the lady upstairs.   But here comes the magistral element in this murder.   Beside the dead man, or in the hand of the dead man, or in a pocket of the dead man's coat—I am not sure how it was—there was found a weapon made of heavy wire—a vile and most deadly contraption, fashioned with curious and malignant ingenuity.   It was night-time, but the bright light of a moon ten days old was shining, and the young man said he saw someone running and leaping over walls.

But mark the point : the dead actor was hiding beneath his friend's flat, hiding and lying in wait, with his villainous weapon to his hand.   He was expecting an encounter with some enemy, on whom he was resolved to work at least deadly mischief, if not murder.

Who was that enemy ?   Whose bullet was it that was swifter than the dead man's savage and premeditated desire ?

We shall probably never know.   A murder that might have stood in the very first rank, that might have vied with the affair of Madeleine Smith—there were certain indications that made this seem possible—was suffered to fade into obscurity, while the foolish crowd surged about elementary

Crippen and his bungling imbecilities. So there were once people who considered *Robert Elsmere* as a literary work of palmary significance.

III

Naturally, and with some excuse, the war was responsible for a good deal of this sort of neglect. In those appalling years there was but one thing in men's heads ; all else was blotted out. So, little attention was paid to the affair of the woman's body, carefully wrapped in sacking, which was found in Regent's Square, by the Gray's Inn Road. A man was hanged without phrases, but there were one or two curious points in the case.

Then, again, there was the Wimbledon Murder, a singular business. A well-to-do family had just moved into a big house facing the Common, so recently that many of its goods and chattels were still in the packing-cases. The master of the house was murdered one night by a man who made off with his booty. It was a curious haul, consisting of a mackintosh worth, perhaps, a couple of pounds, and a watch which would have been dear at ten shillings. This murderer, too, was hanged without comment ; and yet, on the face of it, his conduct seems in need of explanation. But the most singular case of all those that suffered from the pre-occupations of the war was, there is no doubt, the Islington Mystery, as the Press called it. It was a striking headline, but the world was too busy to attend. The affair got abroad, so far as it did get abroad, about the time of the first employment of the tanks ; and people were trying not to see through the war correspondents, not to perceive that the inky fandangoes and corroborees of these gentlemen hid a sense of failure and disappointment.

IV

But as to the Islington Mystery—this is how it fell out. There is an odd street, not far from the region which was once called Spa Fields, not far from the Pentonville or Islington Fields. where Grimaldi the clown was once accused of inciting the mob to chase an overdriven ox. It goes up a steep hill, and the rare adventurer who pierces now and then into this unknown quarter of London is amazed and bewildered at the very outset, since there are no steep hills in the London of his knowledge, and the contours of the scene remind him of the cheap lodging-house area at the back of hilly seaside resorts. But if the site is strange, the buildings on it are far stranger. They were no doubt set up at the high tide of Sir Walter Scott Gothic, which has left such queer memorials behind it. The houses of Lloyd Street are in couples, and the architect, combining the two into one design, desired to create an illusion of a succession of churches, in the Perpendicular or Third Pointed manner, climbing up the hill. The detail is rich, there are finials to rejoice the heart, and gargoyles of fine fantasy, all carried out in the purest stucco. At the lowest house on the right-hand side lived Mr. Harol l Boale and his wife, and a brass plate on the Gothic door said, "Taxidermist : Skeletons Articulated". As it chanced, this lowest house of Lloyd Street has a longer garden than its fellows, giving on a contractor's yard, and at the end of the garden Mr. Boale had set up the apparatus of his craft in an outhouse, away from the noses of his fellow-men.

So far as can be gathered, the stuffer and articulator was a harmless and inoffensive little fellow. His neighbours liked him, and he and the Boule cabinet-maker from next door, the Shell box-maker over the way, the seal-engraver and the armourer from Baker Square at the top of the hill, and the old mercantile marine skipper who lived round the corner in Marchmont Street, at the house with the ivory junk in the window, used to spend many a genial evening together in the parlour of the Quill in the days before everything was spoilt by the war.

They did not drink very much or talk very much, any of them ; but they enjoyed their moderate cups and the snug comfort of the place, and stared solemnly at the old coaching prints that were upon the walls, and at the large glass painting depicting the landing of England's Injured Queen, which hung over the mantelpiece, between two Pink Dogs with gold collars. Mr. Boale passed as a very nice sort of man in this circle and everybody was sorry for him. Mrs. Boale was a tartar and a scold. The men of the quarter kept out of her way ; the women were afraid of her. She led poor Boale the devil's own life. Her voice, often enough, would be heard at the Quill door, vomiting venom at her husband's address ; and he, poor man, would tremble and go forth, lest some worse thing might happen. Mrs. Boale was a short dark woman. Her hair was coal-black, her face wore an expression of acid malignity, and she walked quickly but with a decided limp. She was full of energy and the pest of the neighbourhood, and more than a pest to her husband.

The war, with its scarcity and its severe closing-hours, made the meetings at the Quill rarer than before, and deprived them of a good deal of their old comfort. Still, the circle was not wholly broken up, and one evening Boale announced that his wife had gone to visit relations in Lancashire, and would most likely be away for a considerable time.

"Well, there's nothing like a change of air, so they say," said the skipper, "though I've had more than enough of it myself."

The others said nothing, but congratulated Boale in their hearts. One of them remarked afterwards that the only change that would do Mrs. Boale good was a change to King-dom Come, and they all agreed. They were not aware that Mrs. Boale was enjoying the advantages of the recommended treatment.

V

As I recollect, Mr. Boale's worries began with the appear-ance of Mrs. Boale's sister, Mary Aspinall, a woman almost as ill-tempered and malignant as Mrs. Boale herself. She had been for some years nurse with a family in Capetown, and had come home with her mistress. In the first place, the woman had written two or three letters to her sister, and there had been no reply. This struck her as odd, for Mrs. Boale had been a very good correspondent, filling her letters with "nasty things" about her husband. So, on her first afternoon off after her return, Mary Aspinall called at the house in Lloyd Street to get the truth of the matter from her sister's own lips. She strongly suspected Boale of having suppressed her letters. "The dirty little tyke ; I'll serve him," she said to herself. So came Miss Aspinall to Lloyd Street and brought out Boale from his workshop. And when he saw her his heart

C*

sank. He read her letters. But the decision to return to England had been taken suddenly ; Miss Aspinall had, therefore, said not a word about it. Boale had thought of his wife's sister as established at the other end of the world for the next ten, twenty years, perhaps ; and he meant to go away and lose himself under a new name in a year or two. And so, when he saw the woman, his heart sank.

Mary Aspinall went straight to the point.

"Where's Elizabeth ?" she asked. "Upstairs ? I wonder she didn't come down when she heard the bell."

"No," said Boale. He comforted himself with the thought of the curious labyrinth he had drawn about his secret ; he felt secure in the centre of it.

"No, she's not upstairs. She's not in the house."

"Oh, indeed. Not in the house. Gone to see some friends, I suppose. When do you expect her back ?"

"The truth is, Mary, that I don't expect her back. She's left me—three months ago, it is."

"You mean to tell me that ! Left you ! Showed her sense, I think. Where has she gone ?"

"Upon my word, Mary, I don't know. We had a bit of a to-do one evening, though I don't think I said much. But she said she'd had enough, and she packed a few things in a bag, and off she went. I ran after her and called to her to come back, but she wouldn't so much as turn her head, and went off King's Cross way. And from that day to this I've never seen her, nor had a word from her. I've had to send all her letters back to the post office."

Mary Aspinall stared hard at her brother-in-law and pondered. Beyond telling him that he had brought it on himself, there seemed nothing to say. So she dealt with Boale on those lines very thoroughly, and made an indignant exit from the parlour. He went back to stuff peacocks, for all I know. He was feeling comfortable again. There had been a very unpleasant sensation in the stomach for a few seconds—a very horrible fear at the moment that one of the outer walls of that labyrinth of his had been breached ; but now all was well again.

And all might have been permanently well if Miss Aspinall had not happened to meet Mrs. Horridge in the main road, close to the bottom of Lloyd Street. Mrs. Horridge was the wife of the Shell box-maker, and the two had met once or twice long ago at Mrs. Boale's tea-table. They recognized each other, and, after a few unmeaning remarks, Mrs. Horridge asked Miss Aspinall if she had seen her sister since her return to England.

"How could I see her when I don't know where she is ?" asked Miss Aspinall with some ferocity.

"Dear me, you haven't seen Mr. Boale, then ?"

"I've just come from him this minute."

"But he can't have lost the Lancashire address, surely ?"

And so one thing led to another, and Mary Aspinall gathered quite clearly that Boale had told his friends that his wife was paying a long visit to relations in Lancashire. In the first place the Aspinalls had no relations in Lancashire— they came from Suffolk—and secondly Boale had informed her that Elizabeth had gone away in a rage, he knew not where. She did not pay him another visit then and there, as she had at first intended. It was growing late, and she took her considerations back with her to Wimbledon, determined on thinking the matter out.

Next week she called again at Lloyd Street. She charged Boale with deliberate lying, placing frankly before him the two tales he had told. Again that horrid sinking sensation lay heavy upon Boale. But he had reserves.

"Indeed," he said, "I've told you no lies, Mary. It all happened just as I said before. But I did make up that tale about Lancashire for the people about here. I didn't like them to have my troubles to talk over, especially as Elizabeth is bound to come back some time, and I hope it will be soon."

Miss Aspinall stared at the little man in a doubtful, threatening fashion for a moment, and then hurried upstairs. She came down soon afterwards.

"I've gone through Elizabeth's drawers," she said with defiance. "There's a good many things missing. I don't see those bits of lace she had from Granny, and the set of jet is gone, and so is the garnet necklace, and the coral brooch. I couldn't find the ivory fan, either."

"I found all the drawers wide open after she'd gone," sighed Mr. Boale. "I supposed she'd taken the things away with her."

It must be confessed that Mr. Boale, taught, perhaps, by the nicety of his craft, had paid every attention to detail. He had tealized that it would be vain to tell a tale of his wife going away and leaving her treasures behind her. And so the treasures had disappeared.

Really, the Aspinall vixen did not know what to say. She had to confess that Boale had explained the difficulty of his two stories quite plausibly. So she informed him that he was more like a worm than a man, and banged the hall door. Again Boale went back to his workshop with a warmth about his heart. His labyrinth was still secure, its secret safe. At first, when confronted again by the accusing Aspinall, he had thought of bolting the moment he got the woman out of the house; but that was unreasoning panic. He was in no danger. And he remembered, like the rest of us, the Crippen case. It was running away that had brought Crippen to ruin; if he had sat tight he would have sat secure, and the secret of the cellar would never have been known. Though, as Mr. Boale reflected, anybody was welcome to search his cellar, to search here and there and anywhere on his premises, from the hall door in front to the workshop at the back. And he proceeded to give his calm, whole-souled attention to a fine raven that had been sent round in the morning.

Miss Aspinall took the extraordinary disappearance of her sister back with her to Wimbledon and thought it over. She thought it over again and again, and she could make nothing of it. She did not know that people are constantly disappearing for all sorts of reasons; that nobody hears anything about such cases unless some enterprising paper sees matter for a "stunt", and rouses all England to hunt for John Jones or Mrs. Carraway. To Miss Aspinall, the vanishing of Elizabeth Boale seemed a portent and a wonder, a unique and terrible event; and she puzzled her head over it, and still could find no exit from her labyrinth—a different structure from the labyrinth maintained by the serene Boale. The Aspinall had no suspicions of her brother-in-law; both his manner and his matter were straightforward, clear, and square. He was a worm, as she had informed him, but he was certainly telling the truth. But the woman was fond of her sister, and wanted to know where she had gone and what had happened to her; and so she put the matter into the hands of the police.

VI

She furnished the best description that she could of the missing woman, but the officer in charge of the case pointed out that she had not seen her sister for many years, and that Mr. Boale was obviously the person to be consulted in the matter. So the taxidermist was again drawn from his scientific labours. He was shown the information laid by Miss Aspinall and the description furnished by her. He told his simple story once more, mentioning the incident of his lying to his neighbours to avoid unpleasant gossip, and added several details to Miss Aspinall's picture of his wife. He then furnished the constable with two photographs, pointed out the better likeness of the two, and saw his visitor off the premises with cheerful calm.

In due course, the "Missing" bill, garnished with a reproduction of the photograph selected by Mr. Boale, with minute descriptive details, including the "marked limp", was posted up at the police-stations all over the country, and glanced at casually by a few passers-by here and there. There was nothing sensational about the placard ; and the statement "Last seen going in the direction of King's Cross" was not a very promising clue for the amateur detective. No hint of the matter got into the Press ; as I have pointed out, hardly one per cent of these cases of "missing" does get into the Press. And just then we were all occupied in reading the pæans of the war correspondents, who were proving that an advance of a mile and a half on a nine-mile front constituted a victory which threw Waterloo into the shade. There was no room for discussing the whereabouts of an obscure woman whom Islington knew no more.

It was sheer accident that brought about the catastrophe. James Curry, a medical student who had rooms in Percy Street, Tottenham Court Road, was prowling about his quarter one afternoon in an indefinite and idle manner, gazing at shop windows and mooning at street corners. He knew that he would never want a cash register, but he inspected the stock with the closest attention, and chose a fine specimen listed at £75. Again, he invested heavily in costly Oriental rugs, and furnished a town mansion in the Sheraton manner at very considerable expense. And so his tour of inspection brought him to the police-station; and there he proceeded to read the bills posted outside, including the bill relating to Elizabeth Boale.

"Walks with a marked limp."

James Curry felt his breath go out of his body in a swift gasp. He put out a hand towards the railing to steady himself as he read that amazing sentence over again. And then he walked straight into the police-station.

The fact was that he had bought from Harold Boale, three weeks after the date on which Elizabeth Boale was last seen, a female skeleton. He had got it comparatively cheaply because of the malformation of one of the thigh-bones. And now it struck him that the late owner of that thigh-bone must have walked with a very marked limp.

VII

M'Aulay made his reputation at the trial. He defended Harold Boale with magnificent audacity. I was in court—it was a considerable part of my business in those days to frequent the Old Bailey—and I shall never forget the opening phrases of his speech for the prisoner. He rose slowly, and let his glance go slowly round the court. His eyes rested at last with grave solemnity on the jury. At length he spoke, in a low, clear, deliberate voice, weighing, as it seemed, every word he uttered.

"Gentlemen," he began, "a very great man, and a very wise man, and a very good man once said that probability is the guide of life. I think you will agree with me that this is a weighty utterance. When we once leave the domain of pure mathematics, there is very little that is certain. Supposing we have money to invest : we weigh the pros and cons of this scheme and that, and decide at last on probable grounds. Or it may be our lot to have to make an appointment ; we have to choose a man to fill a responsible position in which both honesty and sagacity are of the first consequence. Again probability must guide us to a decision. No one man can form a certain and infallible judgment of another. And so through all the affairs of life : we must be content with probability, and again and again with probability. Bishop Butler was right.

"But every rule has its exception. The rule which we have just laid down has its exception. That exception confronts you terribly, tremendously, at this very moment. You may think—I do not say that you do think—but you may think that Harold Boale, the prisoner at the bar, in all probability murdered his wife, Elizabeth Boale."

There was a long pause at this point. Then :

"*If* you think that, then it is your imperative duty to acquit the prisoner at the bar. The only verdict which you dare give is a verdict of "Not Guilty'."

Up to this moment, Counsel had maintained the low, deliberate utterance with which he had begun his speech, pausing now and again and seeming to consider within himself the precise value of every word that came to his lips. Suddenly his voice rang out, resonant, piercing. One word followed swiftly on another :

"This, remember, is not a court of probability. Bishop Butler's maxim does not apply here. Here there is no place for probability. This is a court of certainty. And unless you are certain that my client is guilty, unless you are as certain of his guilt as you are certain that two and two make four, then you must acquit him.

"Again, and yet again—this is a court of certainty. In the ordinary affairs of life, sa we have seen, we are guided by probability. We sometimes make mistakes ; in most cases these mistakes may be rectified. A disastrous investment may be counterbalanced by a prosperous investment ; a bad servant may be replaced by a good one. But in this place, where life and death hang in the balances which are in your hands, there is no room for mistakes, since here mistakes are irreparable. Tou cannot bring a dead man back to life. You must not say, 'this man is probably a murderer, and therefore he is guilty'. Before you bring in such a verdict, you must be able to say, 'This man is certainly a murderer'. And *that* you cannot say, and I will tell you w*æ*y."

M'Aulay then took the evidence piece by piece. Scientific witnesses had declared that the malformation of the thighbone in the skeleton exhibited would produce exactly the sort of limp which had characterized Elizabeth Boale. Counsel for the defence had worried the doctors, had made them admit that such a malformation was by no means unique. It was uncommon. Yes, but not very uncommon ? Perhaps not.

Finally, one doctor admitted that in the course of thirty years of hospital and private practice he had known of five such cases of malformation of the thigh-bone. M'Aulay gave an inaudible sigh of relief ; he felt that he had got his verdict.

He made all this quite clear to the jury. He dwelt on the principle that no one can be condemned unless the *corpus delicti*, the body, or some identifiable portion of the body of the murdered person can be produced. He told them the story of the Campden Wonder ; how the "murdered" man walked into his village two years after three people had been hanged for murdering him. "Gentlemen," he said, "for all I know, and for all you know, Elizabeth Boale may walk into this court at any moment. I say boldly that we have no earthly right to assume that she is dead."

Of course Boale's defence was a very simple one. The skeleton which he sold to Mr. Curry had been gradually assembled by him in the course of the last three years. He pointed out that the two hands were not a very good match ; and, indeed, this was a little detail that he had not overlooked.

The jury took half an hour to consider their verdict. Harold Boale was found "Not Guilty".

He was seen by an old friend a couple of years ago. He had emigrated to America, and was doing prosperously in his old craft in a big town of the Middle West. He had married a pleasant girl of Swedish extraction.

"You see," he explained, "the lawyers told me I should be safe in presuming poor Elizabeth's death."

He smiled amiably.

And finally, I beg to state that this account of mine is a grossly partial narrative. For all I know, assuming for a moment the severe standards of M'Aulay, Boale was an innocent man. It is possible that his story was a true one. Elizabeth Boale may, after all, be living ; she may return after the fashion of the "murdered" man in the Campden Wonder. All the thoughts, devices, meditations that I have put into the heart and mind of Boale may be my own malignant inventions without the shadow of true substance behind them.

In theory, then, the Islington Mystery is an open question. Certainly ; but in fact ?

THE COSY ROOM

I

AND he found to his astonishment that he came to the appointed place with a sense of profound relief. It was true that the window was somewhat high up in the wall, and that, in case of fire, it might be difficult, for many reasons, to get out that way ; it was barred like the basement windows that one sees now and then in London houses, but as for the rest it was an extremely snug room. There was a gay flowering paper on the walls, a hanging bookshelf—his stomach sickened for an instant—a little table under the window with a board and draughtsmen on it, two or three good pictures, religious and ordinary, and the man who looked after him was arranging the tea-things on the table in the middle of the room. And there was a nice wicker chair by a bright fire. It was a thoroughly pleasant room ; snug you would call it. And, thank God, it was all over, anyhow.

II

It had been a horrible time for the last three months, up to an hour ago. First of all there was the trouble ; all over in a minute, that was, and couldn't be helped, though it was a pity, and the girl wasn't worth it. But then there was the getting out of the town. He thought at first of just going about his ordinary business and knowing nothing about it ; he didn't think that anybody had seen him following Joe down to the river. Why not loaf about as usual, and say nothing, and go into the Ringland Arms for a pint ? It might be days before they found the body under the alders ; and there would be an inquest, and all that. Would it be the best plan just to stick it out, and hold his tongue if the police came

63

asking him questions. But then, how could he account for himself and his doings that evening ? He might say he went for a stroll in Bleadon Woods and home again without meeting anybody. There was nobody who could contradict him that he could think of.

And now, sitting in the snug room with the bright wallpaper, sitting in the cosy chair by the fire—all so different from the tales they told of such places—he wished he had stuck it out and faced it out, and let them come on and find out what they could. But, then, he had got frightened. Lots of men had heard him swearing it would be outing dos for Joe if he didn't leave the girl alone. And he had shown his revolver to Dick Haddon, and "Lobster" Carey, and Finniman, and others, and then they would be fitting the bullet into the revolver, and it would be all up. He got into a panic and shook with terror, and knew he could never stay in Ledham, not another hour.

III

Mrs. Evans, his landlady, was spending the evening with her married daughter at the other side of the town, and would not be back till eleven. He shaved off his stubbly black beard and moustache, and slunk out of the town in the dark and walked all through the night by a lonely by-road, and got to Darnley, twenty miles away, in the morning in time to catch the London excursion. There was a great crowd of people, and, so far as he could see, nobody that he knew, and the carriages packed full of Darnleyites and Lockwood weavers all in high spirits and taking no notice of him. They all got out at King's Cross, and he strolled about with the rest, and looked round here and there as they did and had a glass of beer at a crowded bar. He didn't see how anybody was to find out where he had gone.

IV

He got a back room in a quiet street off the Caledonian Road, and waited. There was something in the evening paper that night, something that you couldn't very well make

out. By the next day Joe's body was found, and they got to
Murder—the doctor said it couldn't be suicide. Then his
own name came in, and he was missing and was asked to come
forward. And then he read that he was supposed to have
gone to London, and he went sick with fear. He went hot and
he went cold. Something rose in his throat and choked him.
His hands shook as he held the paper, his head whirled with
terror He was afraid to go home to his room, because he
knew he could not stay still in it ; he would be tramping up and
down, like a wild beast, and the landlady would wonder. And
he was afraid to be in the streets, for fear a policeman would
come behind him and put a hand on his shoulder. There was
a kind of small square round the corner and he sat down on
one of the benches there and held up the paper before his face,
with the children yelling and howling and playing all about
him on the asphalt paths. They took no notice of him,
and yet they were company of a sort ; it was not like being
all alone in that little, quiet room. But it soon got dark and
the man came to shut the gates.

V

And after that night ; nights and days of horror and sick
terrors that he never had known a man could suffer and
live. He had brought enough money to keep him for a while,
but every time he changed a note he shook with fear, wondering whether it would be traced. What could he do ; where
could he go ? Could he get out of the country ? But there
were passports and papers of all sorts ; that would never do.
He read that the police held a clue to the Ledham Murder
Mystery ; and he trembled to his lodgings and locked himself
in and moaned in his agony, and then found himself chattering
words and phrases at random, without meaning or relevance ;
strings of gibbering words : "all right, all right, all right . . .
yes, yes, yes, yes . . . there, there, there . . . well, well,
well, well . . ." just because he must utter something,
because he could not bear to sit still and silent, with that
anguish tearing his heart, with that sick horror choking him,
with that weight of terror pressing on his breast. And then,
nothing happened ; and a little, faint, trembling hope fluttered

in his breast for a while, and for a day or two he felt he might have a chance after all.

One night he was in such a happy state that he ventured round to the little public-house at the corner, and drank a bottle of Old Brown Ale with some enjoyment, and began to think of what life might be again, if by a miracle —he recognized, even then, that it would be a miracle —all this horror passed away, and he was once more just like other men, with nothing to be afraid of. He was relishing the Brown Ale, and quite plucking up a spirit, when a chance phrase from the bar caught him : "looking for him not far from here, so they say". He left the glass of beer half full, and went out wondering whether he had the courage to kill himself that night. As a matter of fact the men at the bar were talking about a recent and sensational cat burglar ; but every such word was doom to this wretch. And ever and again, he would check himself in his horrors, in his mutterings and gibberings, and wonder with amazement that the heart of a man could suffer such bitter agony, such rending torment. It was as if he had found out and discovered, he alone of all men living, a new world of which no man before had ever dreamed, in which no man could believe, if he were told the story of it. He had woken up in his past life from such night-mares, now and again, as most men suffer. They were terrible, so terrible that he remembered two or three of them that had oppressed him years before ; but they were pure delight to what he now endured. Not endured, but writhed under as a worm twisting amidst red, burning coals.

He went out into the streets, some noisy, some dull and empty, and considered in his panic-stricken confusion which he should choose. They were looking for him in that part of London ; there was deadly peril in every step. The streets where people went to and fro and laughed and chattered might be the safer ; he could walk with the others and seem to be of them, and so be less likely to be noticed by those who were hunting on his track. But then, on the other hand, the great electric lamps made these streets almost as bright as day, and every feature of the passers-by was clearly seen. True, he was clean-shaven now, and the pictures of him in the papers showed a bearded man, and his own face in the glass still looked strange to him. Still, there were sharp eyes that could penetrate such disguises ; and they might have brought down

some man from Ledham who knew him well, and knew
the way he walked ; and so he might be haled and held at
any moment.   He dared not walk under the clear blaze of the
electric lamps.   He would be safe in the dark, quiet by-ways.

He was turning aside, making for a very quiet street close
by, when he hesitated.   This street, indeed, was still enough
after dark, and not over well lighted.   It was a street of low,
two-storied houses of grey brick that had grimed, with three
or four families in each house.   Tired men came home here
after working hard all day, and people drew their blinds early
and stirred very little abroad, and went early to bed ; footsteps were rare in this street and in other streets into which it
led, and the lamps were few and dim compared with those in
the big thoroughfares.   And yet, the very fact that few people
were about made such as were all the more noticeable and
conspicuous.   And the police went slowly on their beats in
the dark streets as in the bright, and with few people to look
at no doubt they looked all the more keenly at such as passed
on the pavement.   In his world, that dreadful world that he
had discovered and dwelt in alone, the darkness was brighter
than the daylight, and solitude more dangerous than a multitude of men.   He dared not go into the light, he feared the
shadows, and went trembling to his room and shuddered there
as the hours of the night went by ; shuddered and gabbled
to himself his infernal rosary : "all right, all right, all right
. . . splendid, splendid . . . that's the way, that's the way,
that's the way, that's the way . . . yes, yes, yes . . . first
rate, first rate . . . all right . . . one, one, one, one"—
gabbled in a low mutter to keep himself from howling like a
wild beast.

VI

It was somewhat in the manner of a wild beast that he
beat and tore against the cage of his fate.   Now and again
it struck him as incredible.   He would not believe that it
was so.   It was something that he would wake from, as he
had waked from those nightmares that he remembered, for
things did not really happen so.   He could not believe it,
he would not believe it.   Or, if it were so indeed, then all
these horrors must be happening to some other man into whose

torments he had mysteriously entered. Or he had got into a book, into a tale which one read and shuddered at, but did not for one moment credit ; all make-believe, it must be, and presumably everything would be all right again. And then the truth came down on him like a heavy hammer, and beat him down, and held him down—on the burning coals of his anguish.

Now and then he tried to reason with himself. He forced himself to be sensible, as he put it ; not to give way, to think of his chances. After all, it was three weeks since he had got into the excursion train at Darnley, and he was still a free man, and every day of freedom made his chances better. These things often die down There were lots of cases in which the police never got the man they were after. He lit his pipe and began to think things over quietly. It might be a good plan to give his landlady notice, and leave at the end of the week, and make for somewhere in South London, and try to get a job of some sort : that would help to put them off his track. He got up and looked thoughtfully out of the window ; and caught his breath. There, outside the little newspaper shop opposite, was the bill of the evening paper : New Clue in Ledham Murder Mystery.

VII

The moment came at last. He never knew the exact means by which he was hunted down. As a matter of fact, a woman who knew him well happened to be standing outside Darnley station on the Excursion Day morning, and she had recognized him, in spite of his beardless chin. And then, at the other end, his landlady, on her way upstairs, had heard his mutterings and gabblings, though the voice was low. She was interested, and curious, and a little frightened, and wondered whether her lodger might be dangerous, and naturally she talked to her friends. So the story trickled down to the ears of the police, and the police asked about the date of the lodger's arrival. And there you were. And there was our nameless friend, drinking a good, hot cup of tea, and polishing off the bacon and eggs with rare appetite ; in the cosy room with the cheerful paper ; otherwise the Condemned Cell.

OPENING THE DOOR

THE newspaper reporter, from the nature of the case, has generally to deal with the commonplaces of life. He does his best to find something singular and arresting in the spectacle of the day's doings ; but, in spite of himself, he is generally forced to confess that whatever there may be beneath the surface, the surface itself is dull enough.

I must allow, however, that during my ten years or so in Fleet Street, I came across some tracks that were not devoid of oddity. There was that business of Campo Tosto, for example. That never got into the papers. Campo Tosto, I must explain, was a Belgian, settled for many years in England, who had left all his property to the man who looked after him.

My news editor was struck by something odd in the brief story that appeared in the morning paper, and sent me down to make enquiries. I left the train at Reigate ; and there I found that Mr. Campo Tosto had lived at a place called Burnt Green—which is a translation of his name into English— and that he shot at trespassers with a bow and arrows. I was driven to his house, and saw through a glass door some of the property which he had bequeathed to his servant : fifteenth-century triptychs, dim and rich and golden ; carved statues of the saints ; great spiked altar candlesticks : storied censers in tarnished silver ; and much more of old church treasure. The legatee, whose name was Turk, would not let me enter ; but, as a treat, he took my newspaper from my pocket and read it upside down with great accuracy and facility. I wrote this very queer story, but Fleet Street would not suffer it. I believe it struck them as too strange a thing for their sober columns.

And then there was the affair of the J.H.V.S. Syndicate, which dealt with a Cabalistic cipher, and the phenomenon, called in the Old Testament, "the Glory of the Lord", and the discovery of certain objects buried under the site of the Temple

at Jerusalem : that story was left half told, and I never heard
the ending of it.   And I never understood the affair of the
hoard of coins that a storm disclosed on the Suffolk coast near
Aldeburgh.   From the talk of the longshoremen, who were
on the look-out amongst the dunes, it appeared that a great
wave came in and washed away a slice of the sand cliff just
beneath them.   They saw glittering objects as the sea washed
back, and retrieved what they could.   I viewed the treasure—
it was a collection of coins ; the earliest of the twelfth century,
the latest, pennies, three or four of them, of Edward VII, and
a bronze medal of Charles Spurgeon.   There are, of course,
explanations of the puzzle ; but there are difficulties in the way
of accepting any one of them.   It is very clear, for example,
that the hoard was not gathered by a collector of coins ; neither
the twentieth-century pennies nor the medal of the great
Baptist preacher would appeal to a numismatologist.

But perhaps the queerest story to which my newspaper
connections introduced me was the affair of the Reverend
Secretan Jones, the "Canonbury Clergyman", as the headlines
called him.

To begin with, it was a matter of sudden disappearance.
I believe people of all sorts disappear by dozens in the course of
every year, and nobody hears of them or their vanishings.
Perhaps they turn up again, or perhaps they don't ; anyhow,
they never get so much as a line in the papers, and there is an
end of it.   Take, for example, that unknown man in the burning car, who cost the amorous commercial traveller his life.
In a certain sense, we all heard of him ; but he must have
disappeared from somewhere in space, and nobody knew that
he had gone from his world.   So it is often ; but now and
then there is some circumstance that draws attention to the
fact that A. or B. was in his place on Monday and missing
from it on Tuesday and Wednesday ; and then enquiries are
made and usually the lost man is found, alive or dead, and the
explanation is often simple enough.

But as to the case of Secretan Jones.   This gentleman, a
cleric as I have said, but seldom, it appeared, exercising his
sacred office, lived retired in a misty, 1830-40 square in the
recesses of Canonbury.   He was understood to be engaged in
some kind of scholarly research, was a well-known figure in
the Reading Room of the British Museum, and looked anything between fifty and sixty.   It seems probable that if he

had been content with that achievement, he might have disappeared as often as he pleased, and nobody would have troubled ; but one night as he sat late over his books in the stillness of that retired quarter, a motor-lorry passed along a road not far from Tollit Square, breaking the silence with a heavy rumble and causing a tremor of the ground that penetrated into Secretan Jones's study. A teacup and saucer on a side-table trembled slightly, and Secretan Jones's attention was taken from his authorities and notebooks.

This was in February or March of 1907, and the motor industry was still in its early stages. If you preferred a horse-bus, there were plenty left in the streets. Motor coaches were non-existent, hansom cabs still jogged and jingled on their cheerful way ; and there were very few heavy motor-vans in use. But to Secretan Jones, disturbed by the rattle of his cup and saucer, a vision of the future, highly coloured, was vouchsafed, and he began to write to the papers. He saw the London streets almost as we know them to-day ; streets where a horsed vehicle would be almost a matter to show one's children for them to remember in their old age ; streets in which a great procession of huge omnibuses carrying fifty, seventy, a hundred people was continually passing ; streets in which vans and trailers loaded far beyond the capacity of any manageable team of horses would make the ground tremble without ceasing.

The retired scholar, with the happy activity which does sometimes, oddly enough, distinguish the fish out of water, went on and spared nothing. Newton saw the apple fall, and built up a mathematical universe ; Jones heard the teacup rattle, and laid the universe of London in ruins. He pointed out that neither the roadways nor the houses beside them were constructed to withstand the weight and vibration of the coming traffic. He crumbled all the shops in Oxford Street and Piccadilly into dust ; he cracked the dome of St. Pauls', brought down Westminster Abbey, reduced the Law Courts to a fine powder. What was left was dealt with by fire, flood, and pestilence. The prophetic Jones demonstrated that the roads must collapse, involving the various services beneath them. Here, the water-mains and the main drainage would flood the streets ; there, huge volumes of gas would escape, and electric wires fuse ; the earth would be rent with explosions, and the myriad streets of London would go up in a great flame of fire. Nobody really believed that it would happen, but it made good reading, and Secretan Jones gave interviews, started discussions, and enjoyed himself thoroughly Thus he became the "Canonbury Clergyman". "Canonbury Clergyman says that Catastrophe is Inevitable" ; "Doom of London pronounced by Canonbury Clergyman" ; "Canonbury Clergyman's Forecast : London a Carnival of Flood, Fire and Earthquake"—that sort of thing.

And thus Secretan Jones, though his main interests were liturgical, was able to secure a few newspaper paragraphs when he disappeared—rather more than a year after his great campaign in the Press, which was not quite forgotten, but not very clearly remembered.

A few paragraphs, I said, and stowed away, most of them, in out-of-the-way corners of the papers. It seemed that Mrs. Sedger, the woman who shared with her husband the business of looking after Secretan Jones, brought in tea on a tray to his study at four o'clock as usual, and came, again as usual, to take it away at five. And, a good deal to her astonishment, the study was empty. She concluded that her master had gone out for a stroll, though he never went out for strolls between tea and dinner. He didn't come back for dinner ; and Sedger, inspecting the hall, pointed out that the master's hats and coats and sticks and umbrellas were all on their pegs and in their places. The Sedgers conjectured this, that, and the other, waited a week, and then went to the police, and the story came out and perturbed a few learned friends and correspondents : Prebendary Lincoln, author of *The Roman Canon in the Third Century* ; Dr. Brightwell, the authority on the Rite of Malabar ; and Stokes, the Mozarabic man. The rest of the populace did not take very much interest in the affair, and when, at the end of six weeks, there was a line or two stating that "the Rev. Secretan Jones, whose disappearance at the beginning of last month from his house in Tollit Square, Canonbury, caused some anxiety to his friends, returned yesterday", there was neither enthusiasm nor curiosity. The last line of the paragraph said that the incident was supposed to be the result of a misunderstanding ; and nobody even asked what that statement meant.   •

And there would have been the end of it—if Sedger had not gossiped to the circle in the private bar of "The King of Prussia" ... Some mysterious and unofficial person, in touch with this circle, insinuated himself into the presence of my news editor and told him Sedger's tale. Mrs. Sedger, a careful woman, had kept all the rooms tidy and well dusted. On the Tuesday afternoon she had opened the study door and saw, to her amazement and delight, her master sitting at his table with a great book open beside him and a pencil in his hand. She exclaimed :

"Oh, sir, I *am* glad to see you back again !"

"Back again ?" said the clergyman. "What do you mean ? I think I should like some more tea."

"I don't know in the least what it's all about," said the news editor, "but you might go and see Secretan Jones and have a chat with him. There may be a story in it." There was a story in it, but not for my paper, or any other paper.

I got into the house in Tollit Square on some unhandsome pretext connected with Secretan Jones's traffic scare of the year before. He looked at me in a dim, abstracted way at first— the "great book" of his servant's story, and other books, and many black quarto notebooks were about him—but my introduction of the proposed design for a "mammoth carrier" clarified him, and he began to talk eagerly, and as it seemed to me lucidly, of the grave menace of the new mechanical transport.

"But what's the use of talking ?" he ended. "I tried to wake people up to the certain dangers ahead. I seemed to succeed for a few weeks ; and then they forgot all about it. You would really say that the great majority are like dreamers, like sleepwalkers. Yes ; like men walking in a dream ; shutting out all the actualities, all the facts of life. They know that they are, in fact, walking on the edge of a precipice ; and yet they are able to believe, it seems, that the precipice is a garden path ; and they behave as if it were a garden path, as safe as that path you see down there, going to the door at the bottom of my garden."

The study was at the back of the house, and looked on the long garden, heavily overgrown with shrubs run wild, mingling with one another, some of them flowering richly, and altogether and happily obscuring and confounding the rigid grey walls that doubtless separated each garden from its neighbours. Above the tall shrubs, taller elms and planes and ash trees grew unlopped and handsomely neglected ; and under this deep concealment of green boughs the path went down to a green door, just visible under a cloud of white roses.

"As safe as that path you see there," Secretan Jones

repeated, and, looking at him, I thought his expression changed
a little ; very slightly, indeed, but to a certain questioning, one
might say to a meditative doubt.   He suggested to me a man
engaged in an argument, who puts his case strongly, decisively;
and then hesitates for the fraction of a second as a point occurs
to him of which he had never thought before ; a point as yet
unweighed, unestimated ; dimly present, but more as a shadow
than a shape.

The newspaper reporter needs the gestures of the serpent
as well as its wisdom.   I forget how I glided from the safe
topic of the traffic peril to the dubious territory which I had
been sent to explore.   At all events, my contortions were the
most graceful that I could devise ;   but they were altogether
vain.   Secretan Jones's kind, lean, clean-shaven face took on
an expression of distress.   He looked at me as one in perplexity ; he seemed to search his mind not for the answer
that he should give me, but rather for some answer due to
himself.

"I am extremely sorry that I cannot give you the information you want," he said, after a considerable pause.   "But I
really can't go any farther into the matter.   In fact, it is quite
out of the question to do so.   You must tell your editor—
or sub-editor ; which is it ?—that the whole business is due
to a misunderstanding, a misconception, which I am not at
liberty to explain.   But I am really sorry that you have come
all this way for nothing."

There was real apology and regret, not only in his words,
but in his tones and in his aspect.   I could not clutch my hat
and get on my way with a short word in the character of a
disappointed and somewhat disgusted emissary ; so we fell
on general talk, and it came out that we both came from the
Welsh borderland, and had long ago walked over the same hills
and drank of the same wells.   Indeed, I believe we proved
cousinship, in the seventh degree or so, and tea came in, and
before long Secretan Jones was deep in liturgical problems, of
which I knew just enough to play the listener's part.   Indeed,
when I had told him that the *hwyl*, or chanted eloquence, of the
Welsh Methodists was, in fact, the Preface Tone of the Roman
Missal, he overflowed with grateful interest, and made a note
in one of his books, and said the point was most curious and
important.   It was a pleasant evening, and we strolled through
the french windows into the green-shadowed, blossoming

garden, and went on with our talk, till it was time—and high time—for me to go. I had taken up my hat as we left the study, and as we stood by the green door in the wall at the end of the garden, I suggested that I might use it.

"I'm so sorry," said Secretan Jones, looking, I thought, a little worried, "but I am afraid it's jammed, or something of that kind. It has always been an awkward door, and I hardly ever use it."

So we went through the house, and on the doorstep he pressed me to come again, and was so cordial that I agreed to his suggestion of the Saturday sennight. And so at last I got an answer to the question with which my newspaper had originally entrusted me ; but an answer by no means for newspaper use. The tale, or the experience, or the impression, or whatever it may be called, was delivered to me by very slow degrees, with hesitations, and in a manner of tentative suggestion that often reminded me of our first talk together. It was as if Jones were, again and again, questioning himself as to the matter of his utterances, as if he doubted whether they should not rather be treated as dreams, and dismissed as trifles without consequence.

He said once to me : "People do tell their dreams, I know ; but isn't it usually felt that they are telling nothing ? That's what I am afraid of."

I told him that I thought we might throw a great deal of light on very dark places if more dreams were told.

"But there," I said, "is the difficulty. I doubt whether the dreams that I am thinking of *can* be told. There are dreams that are perfectly lucid from beginning to end, and also perfectly insignificant. There are others which are blurred by a failure of memory, perhaps only on one point : you dream of a dead man as if he were alive. Then there are dreams which are prophetic : there seems, on the whole, no doubt of that. Then you may have sheer clotted nonsense ; I once chased Julius Cæsar all over London to get his recipe for curried eggs. But, besides these, there is a certain dream of another order : utter lucidity up to the moment of waking, and then perceived to be beyond the power of words to express. It is neither sense nor nonsense ; it has, perhaps, a notation of its own, but . . . well, you can't play Euclid on the violin."

Secretan Jones shook his head. "I am afraid my experiences are rather like that," he said. It was clear, indeed, that he found great difficulty in finding a verbal formula which should convey some hint of his adventures.

But that was later. To start with, things were fairly easy; but, characteristically enough, he began his story before I realized that the story was begun. I had been talking of the queer tricks a man's memory sometimes plays him. I was saying that a few days before, I was suddenly interrupted in some work I was doing. It was necessary that I should clear my desk in a hurry. I shuffled a lot of loose papers together and put them away, and awaited my caller with a fresh writing-pad before me. The man came. I attended to the business with which he was concerned, and went back to my former affair when he had gone. But I could not find the sheaf of papers. I thought I had put them in a drawer. They were not in the drawer; they were not in any drawer, or in the blotting-book, or in any place where one might reasonably expect to find them. They were found next morning by the servant who dusted the room, stuffed hard down into the crevice between the seat and the back of an armchair, and carefully hidden under a cushion.

"And," I finished, "I hadn't the faintest recollection of doing it. My mind was blank on the matter."

"Yes," said Secretan Jones, "I suppose we all suffer from that sort of thing at times. About a year ago I had a very odd experience of the same kind. It troubled me a good deal at the time. It was soon after I had taken up that question of the new traffic and its probable—its certain—results. As you may have gathered, I have been absorbed for most of my life in my own special studies, which are remote enough from the activities and interests of the day. It hasn't been at all my way to write to the papers to say there are too many dogs in London, or to denounce street musicians. But I must say that the extraordinary dangers of using our present road system for a traffic for which it was not designed did impress themselves very deeply upon me; and I dare say I allowed myself to be over-interested and over-excited.

"There is a great deal to be said for the Apostolic maxim: 'Study to be quiet and to mind your own business'. I am afraid I got the whole thing on the brain, and neglected my own business, which at that particular time, if I remember, was the investigation of a very curious question—the validity or non-validity of the Consecration Formula of the *Grand*

Saint Graal : *Car chou est li sanc di ma nouviele loy, li miens meismes*. Instead of attending to my proper work I allowed myself to be drawn into the discussion I had started, and for a week or two I thought of very little else : even when I was looking up authorities at the British Museum, I couldn't get the rumble of the motor-van out of my head. So, you see, I allowed myself to get harried and worried and distracted, and I put down what followed to all the bother and excitement I was going through. The other day, when you had to leave your work in the middle and start on something else, I dare say you felt annoyed and put out, and shoved those papers of yours away without really thinking of what you were doing, and I suppose something of the same kind happened to me. Though it was still queerer, I think."

He paused, and seemed to meditate doubtfully, and then broke out with an apologetic laugh, and : "It really sounds quite crazy !" And then : "I forgot where I lived."

"Loss of memory, in fact, through overwork and nervous excitement ?"

"Yes, but not quite in the usual way. I was quite clear about my name and my identity. And I knew my address perfectly well : Thirty-nine, Tollit Square, Canonbury."

"But you said you forgot where you lived."

"I know ; but there's the difficulty of expression we were talking about the other day. I am looking for the notation, as you called it. But it was like this : I had been working all the morning in the Reading Room with the motor danger at the back of my mind, and as I left the Museum, feeling a sort of heaviness and confusion, I made up my mind to walk home. I thought the air might freshen me a little. I set out at a good pace. I knew every foot of the way, as I had often done the walk before, and I went ahead mechanically, with my mind wrapt up in a very important matter relating to my proper studies. As a matter of fact, I had found in a most unexpected quarter a statement that threw an entirely new light on the Rite of the Celtic Church, and I felt that I might be on the verge of an important discovery. I was lost in a maze of conjectures, and when I looked up I found myself standing on the pavement by the 'Angel', Islington, totally unaware of where I was to go next.

"Yes, quite so : I knew the 'Angel' when I saw it, and I

knew I lived in Tollit Square ; but the relation between the
two had entirely vanished from my consciousness. For
me, there were no longer any points of the compass ; there
was no such thing as direction, neither north nor south, nor
left nor right, an extraordinary sensation, which I don't feel
I have made plain to you at all. I was a good deal disturbed,
and felt that I must move somewhere, so I set off—and found
myself at King's Cross railway station. Then I did the only
thing there was to be done : took a hansom and got home,
feeling shaky enough.''

I gathered that this was the first incident of significance
in a series of odd experiences that befell this learned and
amiable clergyman. His memory became thoroughly un-
reliable, or so he thought at first.

He began to miss important papers from his table in the
study. A series of notes, on three sheets lettered A, B, and
C, were placed by him on the table under a paperweight one
night, just before he went up to bed. They were missing
when he went into his study the next morning. He was
certain that he had put them in that particular place, under the
bulbous glass weight with the pink roses embedded in its
depths : but they were not there. Then Mrs. Sedger knocked
at the door and entered with the papers in her hand. She
said she had found them between the bed and the mattress
in the master's bedroom, and thought they might be
wanted.

Secretan Jones could not make it out at all. He supposed
he must have put the papers where they were found and then
forgotten all about it, and he was uneasy, feeling afraid that
he was on the brink of a nervous breakdown. Then there
were difficulties about his books, as to which he was very
precise, every book having its own place. One morning
he wanted to consult the *Missale de Arbuthnot*, a big red quarto,
which lived at the end of a bottom shelf near the window.
It was not there. The unfortunate man went up to his bedroom, and felt the bed all over and looked under his shirts
in the chest of drawers, and searched all the room in vain.
However, determined to get what he wanted, he went to the
Reading Room, verified his reference, and returned to Canonbury : and there was the red quarto in its place. Now here,
it seemed certain, there was no room for loss of memory ;
and Secretan Jones began to suspect his servants of playing

tricks with his possessions, and tried to find a reason for their imbecility or villainy—he did not know what to call it. But it would not do at all. Papers and books disappeared and reappeared, or now and then vanished without return. One afternoon, struggling, as he told me, against a growing sense of confusion and bewilderment, he had with considerable difficulty filled two quarto sheets of ruled paper with a number of extracts necessary to the subject he had in hand. When this was done, he felt his bewilderment thickening like a cloud about him : "It was, physically and mentally, as if the objects in the room became indistinct, were presented in a shimmering mist or darkness." He felt afraid, and rose, and went out into the garden. The two sheets of paper he had left on his table were lying on the path by the garden door.

I remember he stopped dead at this point. To tell the truth, I was thinking that all these instances were rather matter for the ear of a mental specialist than for my hearing. There was evidence enough of a bad nervous breakdown, and, it seemed to me, of delusions. I wondered whether it was my duty to advise the man to go to the best doctor he knew, and without delay. Then Secretan Jones began again :

"I won't tell you any more of these absurdities. I know they are drivel, pantomime tricks and traps, children's conjuring; contemptible, all of it.

"But it made me afraid. I felt like a man walking in the dark, beset with uncertain sounds and faint echoes of his footsteps that seem to come from a vast depth, till he begins to fear that he is treading by the edge of some awful precipice. There was something unknown about me ; and I was holding on hard to what I knew, and wondering whether I should be kept up.

"One afternoon I was in a very miserable and distracted state. I could not attend to my work. I went out into the garden, and walked up and down trying to calm myself. I opened the garden door and looked into the narrow passage which runs at the end of all the gardens on this side of the square. There was nobody there—except three children playing some game or other. They were horrible, stunted little creatures, and I turned back into the garden and walked into the study. I had just sat down, and had turned to my work hoping to find relief in it, when Mrs. Sedger, my servant,

D

came into the room and cried out, in an excited sort of way, that she was glad to see me back again.

"I made up some story. I don't know whether she believes it. . I suppose she thinks I have been mixed up in something disreputable."

"And what had happened ?"

"I haven't the remotest notion."

We sat looking at each other for some time.

"I suppose what happened was just this," I said at last. "Your nervous system had been in a very bad way for some time. It broke down utterly : you lost your memory, your sense of identity—everything. You may have spent the six weeks in addressing envelopes in the City Road."

He turned to one of the books on the table and opened it. Between the leaves there were the dimmed red and white petals of some flower that looked like an anemone.

"I picked this flower," he said, "as I was walking down the path that afternoon. It was the first of its kind to be in bloom—very early. It was still in my hand when I walked back into this room, six weeks later, as everybody declares. But it was quite fresh."

There was nothing to be said. I kept silent for five minutes, I suppose, before I asked him whether his mind was an utter blank as to the six weeks during which no known person had set eyes on him ; whether he had no sort of recollection, however vague.

"At first, nothing at all. I could not believe that more than a few seconds came between my opening the garden door and shutting it. Then in a day or two there was a vague impression that I had been somewhere where everything was absolutely right. I can't say more than that. No fairy-land joys, or bowers of bliss, or anything of that kind ; no sense of anything strange or unaccustomed. But there was no care there at all. *Est enim magnum chaos.*"

But that means "For there is a great void", or "A great gulf".

We never spoke of the matter again. Two months later he told me that his nerves had been troubling him, and that he was going to spend a month or six weeks at a farm near Llanthony, in the Black Mountains, a few miles from his old home. In three weeks I got a letter, addressed in Secretan Jones's hand. Inside was a slip of paper on which he had written the words :

Est enim magnum chaos.

The day on which the letter was posted he had gone out in wild autumn weather, late one afternoon, and had never come back. No trace of him has ever been found.

MUNITIONS OF WAR

THERE was a thick fog, acrid and abominable, all over London when I set out for the West.   And at the heart of the fog, as it were, was the shudder of the hard frost that made one think of those winters in Dickens that had seemed to have become fabulous.   It was a day on which to hear in dreams the iron ring of the horses' hoofs on the Great North Road, to meditate the old inns with blazing fires, the coach going onward into the darkness, into a frozen world.   A few miles out of London the fog lifted.   The horizon was still vague in a purple mist of cold, but the sun shone brilliantly from a pale clear sky of blue, and all the earth was a magic of whiteness.   White fields stretched to that dim violet mist far away, white hedges divided them, and the trees were all snowy white with the winter blossom of the frost.   The train had been delayed a little by the thick fog about London ; now it was rushing at a tremendous speed through this strange white world.

My business with the famous town in the West was to attempt to make some picture of it as it faced the stress of war, to find out whether it prospered or not.   From what I had seen in other large towns, I expected to find it all of a bustle on the Saturday, its shops busy, its streets thronged and massed with people.   Therefore, it was with no small astonishment that I found the atmosphere of Westpool wholly different from anything I had observed at Sheffield or Birmingham. Hardly anybody seemed to leave the train at the big station, and the broad road into the town wore a shy, barred-up air ; it reminded one somewhat of the streets by which the traveller passes into forgotten places, little villages that once were great cities.   I remember how in the town of my birth, Caerleon-on-Usk, the doctor's wife would leave the fire and run to the window if a step sounded in the main street outside ; and strangely I was reminded of this as I walked from

82

the Westpool station. Save for one thing : at intervals there were silent parties huddled together as if for help and comfort, and all making for the outskirts of the city.

There is a fair quarter of an hour's walk between West-pool station and the centre of the town. And here I would say that though Westpool is one of the biggest and busiest cities in England, it is also, in my judgment, one of the most beautiful. Not only on account of the ancient timbered houses that still overhang many of its narrower streets, not only because of its glorious churches and noble old traditions of splendour—I am known to be weak and partial where such things are concerned—but rather because of its site. For through the very heart of the great town a narrow, deep river runs, full of tall ships, bordered by bustling quays ; and so you can often look over your garden wall and see a cluster of masts, and the shaking out of sails for a fair wind. And this bringing of deep-sea business into the middle of the dusty streets has always seemed to me an enchantment ; there is something of Sindbad and Basra and Bagdad and the Nights in it. But this is not all the delight of Westpool ; from the very quays of the river the town rushes up to great heights, with streets so steep that often they are flights of steps as in St. Peter Port, and ladder-like ascents. And as I came to Middle Quay in Westpool that winter day, the sun hovered over the violet mists, and the windows of the houses on the heights flamed and flashed red, vehement fires.

But the slight astonishment with which I had noted the shuttered and dismal aspect of the station road now became bewilderment. Middle Quay is the heart of Westpool, and all its business. I had always seen it swarm like an anthill. There were scarcely half a dozen people there on Saturday afternoon ; and they seemed to be hurrying away. The Vintry and the Little Vintry, those famous streets, were deserted. I saw in a moment that I had come on a fool's errand : in Westpool assuredly there was no hurry or rush of war-business, no swarm of eager shoppers for me to describe. I had an introduction to a well-known Westpool man. "Oh no," he said, "we are very slack in Westpool. We are doing hardly anything. There's an aeroplane factory out at Oldham, and they're making high explosives by Portdown, but that doesn't affect us. Things are quiet, very quiet." I suggested that they might brighten up a little at night. "No," he said, "it really wouldn't be worth your while to stay on ; you wouldn't find anything to write about, I assure you."

I was not satisfied. I went out and about the desolate streets of the great city ; I made inquiries at random, and always heard the same story—"Things were very slack". And I began to receive an extraordinary impression : that the few I met were frightened, and were making the best of their way, either out of the town, or to the safety of their own bolted doors and barred shutters. It was only the very special mention of a friendly commercial traveller of my acquaintance that got me a room for the night at the "Pineapple" on Middle Quay, overlooking the river. The landlord assented with difficulty, after praising the express to town. "It's a noisy place, this," he said, "if you're not used to it." I looked at him. It was as quiet as if we were in the heart of the forest or the desert. "You see," he said, "we don't do much in munitions, but there's a lot of night transport for the docks at Portdown. You know those climbing motors that they use in the Army, caterpillars or whatever they call them. We get a lot of them through Westpool ; we get all sorts of heavy stuff, and I expect they'll wake you at night. I wouldn't go to the window, if I were you, if you do wake up. They don't like anybody peering about."

And I woke up in the dead of night. There was a thundering and a rumbling and a trembling of the earth such as I had never heard. And shouting too ; and rolling oaths that sounded like judgment. I got up and drew the blind a little aside, in spite of the landlord's warning, and there was that desolate Middle Quay swarming with men, and the river full of great ships, faint and huge in the frosty mist, and sailing-ships too. Men were rolling casks by the hundred down to the ships. "Hurry up, you lazy lubbers, you damned sons of guns, damn ye !" said a great voice. "Shall the King's Majesty lack powder ?" "No, by God, he shall not !" roared the answer. "I rolled it aboard for old King George, and young King George shall be none the worse for me."

"And who the devil are you to speak so bold ?"

"Blast ye, bos'n ; I fell at Trafalgar."

FLAVIA RICHARDSON

THE RED TURRET

AFTER a lapse of nearly half a century an Erringham came once more to the home of his fathers. Roy Erringham had spent the first thirty years of his life abroad : born and bred in Canada, he never saw his old home till he walked into it by right of succession one October evening.

Jerome Erringham, his father, was dead : going abroad, a poverty-stricken younger son, he had carved his way to fame and wealth, if not fortune, by his own efforts and those of his wife. Roy, the only child, had inherited the bulk of his wealth. Ten years before, his father had come into the Erringham property, but business necessities had kept him from coming to take possession ; moreover, he counted himself an outcast and a working-man—one who had but little desire to live in the lordly home of his fathers.

Now there was only one Erringham left in the world— the last of a once proud and spreading family—and that one was Roy. True, there was hope for the future, for Helen, Roy's wife, of a year was a healthy woman and there was no reason why she should not bear sons.

Together, Roy and Helen walked into the old house on the day after they landed in England.

Roy loved it. Helen hated and feared it.

"But it's beautiful," he said, as he led her from one room to another. "Beautiful. Can't you see it ?"

She shook her head. "I can't bear it. Roy, I don't think I can live here. It's too—too gloomy. There is something uncanny about it. The house seems to be watching us. Don't you feel it ?"

He shook his head and patted her on the shoulder.

"Of course it's watching us, silly. Why not ? It's the old home of the Erringhams. We've been here for centuries. It's glad we've come back. It wants to make sure that we're the right sort."

"The right sort," Helen repeated, with a shiver. "Yes, Roy, but what sort does this house want ?" Her voice shrilled a little.

"You're tired." He spoke with masterful decision. "Come and rest for a bit. We'll go over the rest of the house to-morrow."

Away in the newer wing which the housekeeper, engaged by the lawyers, had rendered habitable, Helen felt less disturbed. She determined that, come what might, she would have her own rooms in this new and more comfortable quarter. Not for her the stone-walled grandeur of the great dining-room or the panels of the long saloon : she admitted that though she could appreciate grandeur in the abstract, she wanted modernity and comfort in real life. Tucked up on the luxurious chesterfield, a shaded electric standard at her elbow, a new magazine on the occasional-table, she felt at peace. This was home : she began to get a touch of warmth into her feeling for the old house. After all, it was only natural that so old a place should have an atmosphere.

"Perhaps it's me," she murmured, half asleep. "I'm the thing that's wrong. I don't belong here. I belong to Canada. I'm not really an Erringham—it thinks I'm an interloper."

In the morning various business claimed both her and Roy. In the afternoon, neighbours, forgetful of the bother of settling into a house that had been shut up for years, insisted on coming to call.

Not till dinner was over did Roy have time to finish his tour.

"You'll come with me, darling ?" he said, a little anxiously.

Helen assented. After all, it was her home ; she must make it like her, must herself grow accustomed to the atmosphere.

They went through the long succession of rooms that they had seen the day before till at last they reached the picture gallery.

It ran the whole width of the house on the first floor. Above it was nothing but the roof. The high ceiling had been built to give an impression of space. The bedrooms on the floor above were all in the other wing.

Helen went to one of the long mullioned windows and looked out.

"We look down on the terrace here," she observed, over her shoulder. Then she added : "Roy, the door to the turret ought to be somewhere here. It's at this end of the house."

"Of course." He joined her at the window and took his bearings.

"That's funny," he said, looking back into the room. "There's no sign of a door here. Wonder where it is."

He strolled over to the end of the room, and Helen followed him, scanning the Erringham ancestors idly as she passed. Suddenly she gave a little cry and covered her face with her hands.

"What's the matter?" Roy was beside her in an instant.

"That picture!" she cried, pointing to the corner in deepest shadow. "It moved! I'm sure it did! . . ." Her voice rose a trifle.

"Steady on, darling!" Roy spoke reprovingly. "You never used to have nerves like these. Of course it didn't move. Let's go over and look at it. I can't see who it is from here, it's so dark."

He stepped to the wall to turn on the electric light, but the switch was dead, and with an exclamation of annoyance he turned back.

"I've got my flashlight with me," he said. "Come on, Helen. We'll kill this bogy of yours before we go downstairs."

He pressed the button of the torch and directed the glare on to the picture in the corner.

"Great-grandfather," he said, his eye catching the date on the frame. "He—he—not a very pleasant-looking old bird, eh?"

Helen laughed nervously. She saw the distinctive Erringham features; saw, too, how they were reproduced in Roy. Standing there with the faint radiance on his face, he might almost have been his great-grandfather come back to life.

"I believe there was some sort of scandal about the old man," said Roy, as he looked at the portrait again. "I don't know what it was: Dad never mentioned it. But when I went through his papers after he was dead, I found some funny passages in some old letters that his mother sent him. She was daughter-in-law to this old man and lived here with my grandfather before he came into the property. I gather he was a bit of a queer fish, but I don't know why."

"I don't like him," Helen whispered. "He looks so evil."

"Not too prepossessing," agreed Roy. "Got the worst type of Erringham face, hasn't he." He lifted the torch and looked at the picture from another angle. "Hello," he said, "what's that ? Do you see, a handle or something on the side of the frame. I believe it's the entrance to the door of the turret. Let's go and see."

"Oh, don't, Roy," Helen pleaded, urged by some instinct for which she could not account. "Please don't. Do wait for daylight."

"Not I," he returned. "The moon's coming up. The view from the turret over to the hills will be perfectly marvellous. Come along, Helen. Don't be a 'fraid cat," he taunted.

She set her lips and waited while he pulled at the handle.

As they had expected, the whole portrait swung round and a narrow flight of steps was disclosed to view.

"I wonder why they hid it," said Roy, as he swung the light up.

"Not much hidden, was it ? We should have seen the lever at once in daylight." Helen was determined to make the whole matter as uninteresting and commonplace as she could. Somehow she sensed that in the turret lay danger— danger not so much to herself as to Roy, and she was determined to give it no aid by preparing to be afraid.

"Perhaps," Roy assented a little unwillingly.

He gave one glance at the portrait of his great-grandfather and then began to climb up the staircase. It wound round in a narrow spiral, evidently built in the thickness of the outer wall, while the turret itself rested on the roof of the picture gallery.

Helen followed, partly because she did not dare to trust Roy alone with what might happen, and partly because she herself did not dare to stop alone in the picture gallery with the Erringhams around. To her sensitive mind an air of repellent contempt came from the pictured faces. She knew they were not so much resentful of her as pitying, but pitying with a sneer.

Setting her teeth, she tossed her head at the lot of them and put her foot on the first stair.

The staircase was only the height of the gallery, and three or four turns took them to the door at the top which barred the way.

Roy turned the great iron handle and pushed the door ajar. It was a heavy oaken affair, clamped with metal bands and screws. No one could have passed it without immense effort had it been barred.

"Here's the turret," said Roy, throwing the beam forward. Helen pressed to his side, and together they looked in amazement.

The turret was much larger than it looked from the ground, whence it gave the impression of being merely a pepper-box. It was deceptively built, its size running inwards along the width of the roof so that the chimney-stacks broke the line and hid much of it.

On three sides were windows, deep-set, filled with thick glass, on which strange designs had been painted, evidently by amateur hands. Helen walked over to them and looked at them closely. The moon was shining full into the little room, and its strange furnishings were clearly picked out. Roy snapped off the torch, for it was not needed, and he knew that the battery was wearing low. He would want what light he had to help them down the spiral stairs and through the picture gallery.

The moon passed behind a cloud, and for a moment the room was plunged into darkness. Before Helen could implore Roy to put on the torch, there came a strange unearthly radiance, filling the whole place and yet appearing from a source unknown.

Helen shrank back into the embrasure of the window, frightened.

Roy stood still in the middle of the room, taken unawares, yet amazed rather than scared. He knew all at once that he had dimly expected this. That as an Erringham he must be present at some strange, mysterious rite and make a choice. He waited.

Helen waited also. She grew less afraid. Her eyes roamed round the room. In the dim yet clear red of the light, it was easy to pick out the objects on the floor. In the wall that had no window was set a table. On it stood a golden plate and cup. Before it was a narrow mat, ivory white, worked in black. The light was so clear that she could distinguish the pattern of fir-cones that formed the chief feature of the scrolled design.

In the distance a clock struck ten times. The normal

sound would ordinarily have reassured her, suggesting as it did a house inhabited by servants, a sane and pleasant life to which she could return at any moment if she so chose. But at the moment of the first stroke of the clock some new power seemed to fill the room.

It was so subtle, so strong, and so unexpected, that for the moment Helen was nearly overwhelmed by it. It gave her no time to prepare : it caught her, as it were, in a web of fine tissue and held her, unable to speak or move, yet conscious of all that went on.

She tried to cry out to Roy, but her voice was strangled in her throat. She tried to go to him, but her limbs seemed paralysed.

Her eyes fixed themselves on him and saw the change that came over his features. He had lost some of the wonder that had marked them when the phenomenal light began to appear. He was looking absorbed, interested, almost, Helen shuddered mentally, as if he were about to enjoy himself. He seemed to be expecting something, as if he knew what was about to happen and why.

Out of the radiance of the red light a figure seemed to materialize—the figure of an old man wearing the robes of a priest. He turned, and Helen caught sight of his mocking, sardonic face. Her head reeled, she found she could not faint. Roy's great-grandfather stood in the middle of the room, beckoning to Roy—and Roy went to him, gladly, as if it were natural thing !

"Erringham of the Erringhams, you have come !" The words could have issued from no living mouth, yet Helen would have sworn that she heard them clearly spoken.

Roy took another step towards that strange figure clad in gold and black, with touches of white that gleamed red in the light.

"I have come," he said, with assurance, as one who saw no cause for fear. "What do you want ?"

"To-night you have your choice," the strange, unearthly voice went on. "Your father refused to choose : he died a stranger in a strange land rather than face the choice of the Erringhams. Your grandfather died : your uncle died. You have come back."

"I am here," Roy reiterated. "What do I choose ?"

"Whether you will eat of the Tree of Knowledge of Good

and Evil, whether you will learn the control of the Life Force, whether you will be as God, even as I am, and conquer even the last great enemy, Death, that rides upon the Pale Horse and passes no one by."

"And the price?"

"There is none. Knowledge is Power. What more do you desire? Death shall pass you by, so shall you escape the final reckoning, since only the dead can be judged by God."

"I choose. I will follow you."

The old man's eyes seemed to gleam more brightly, and the face he turned towards Helen was distorted with devilish glee. She tried again to scream, to warn Roy, but she could not make a sound.

"And the ritual?" Roy asked. He had not moved, but it was plain that he was beginning to suffer from suppressed excitement. His face was very pale and the sweat began to show on his forehead.

"The Service of Sacrifice shall be held to-night."

The strange apparition went to the table built against the wall, which Helen, her heart sinking again, now recognized as an altar. He busied himself for a moment with the golden vessels. Then he bent down and touched a spring in the front of the table. It swung open, and, controlled by the same spring, a stone slab slid quietly forward, resting some six inches above the ground. On it lay a strangely shaped knife, the handle glittering with jewels.

"All is prepared," said the man, as he drew himself up again.

In obedience to a sign, Roy came forward to the altar and flung himself on his knees.

Old Erringham stood before the stone slab and raised his arms. He began to chant, softly at first, then more loudly in that terrible room. At first Helen could not pick out the words, was only aware that they were in a strange tongue. Then gradually something familiar yet mysterious about them struck her and she realized with a further pang of horror that she was listening to that foulest of all rites, the Black Mass.

"But there should be a sacrifice. There must be blood," she heard herself saying, able to speak for the first time, but seemingly unable to control her words.

"There shall be blood. There shall be blood and a burnt-offering. There shall be a willing sacrifice," came back to her, chanted by the priest.

Moving in spite of herself, with no power over her limbs, walking as if hypnotized, Helen found herself crossing the floor to that terrible altar. Roy still knelt, his face buried in his hands. She tried to speak to him but could not. She could not even touch him as she went by. She must move as if in a dream.

Still without conscious volition, yet terribly aware of all that was going on, Helen found herself lying on the slab. Staring up into the face of the Erringham apostate, she was nearly rendered unconscious by the malevolence of his look. Suddenly an inner power came to her; she knew that she could only save herself by a supreme effort—still more, that only so could she save Roy.

Summoning every ounce of will power, she broke the bonds that controlled her. She found her voice. Brokenly, only half consciou of what she said, she began to recite the Pater Noster. . . . At the first words, a fury seized the demon bending above her. He seized the jewelled-handled knife and thrust it into Roy's hands.

"It is the moment of the Sacrifice," he chanted, his voice drowning Helen's feeble tones. "It is the moment for the spilling of the blood. See, my son, I place the golden cup beneath the Stone that it may catch the precious drops as they run, that you and I may drink from them and live."

As one in a dream, Roy rose from his knees and took the knife that was held out to him. He tested the blade against his nail, swung it in the air, and——

"Roy !" Helen screamed.

The sound startled him. He dropped the knife. It fell across his leg, gashing the shin through his sock. A little blood trickled out and across the altar-stone.

With a cry of baffled fury, mingled with desire, old Erringham bent down and tried to catch the flow in the golden chalice.

Helen, on her feet by now, caught the cup, making the Sacred Sign as she did so. There was a blinding flash of light, that seemed to come from the altar. The room was lighted up and at the same moment a crashing peal of thunder broke over the house. As it died away, came another ominous crash, and the roof of the turret started to crumble and fall in.

Helen seized Roy and dragged him to the head of the stairs. Behind them was the rumbling of falling stones and plaster, with a crash at intervals, as one of the big roof-beams came down.

Somehow they staggered down the stairs and through the picture gallery, till they roused the frightened servants to action.

The storm had been sharp and sudden : only that one flash and one crack of thunder had been heard.

In the morning they went upstairs to see the damage done. The picture gallery seemed unharmed in spite of the masonry that had fallen on its roof. But when they went to the door of the staircase Roy and Helen started back in amazement.

The picture of old Erringham, the wizard, the devotee of the Black One, had been torn from its frame and lay, a great cut in the canvas over the heart, face downwards on the floor.

They dragged it to one side and forced their way up to the turret. One wall still stood, the one against which had been built the altar-stone. For the rest, Roy and Helen stood under the sweet blue sky and the clean sunlight.

Beneath the altar was a heap of rubbish. Roy went over to examine it. He came back, his face graver than before.

"Don't go to look," he said. "I—I must get someone to help. They are—bones. There must have been a body buried there."

Helen turned white. "Your great-grandfather," she said.

"I expect so. You remember they always said his grave was empty in the churchyard. Last night the Devil came for his own."

Helen shivered. "I am glad the turret has gone," she said, and led Roy to the head of the stairs.

OSCAR COOK

WHEN GLISTER WALKED

DENNIS, district officer of the Labuk district in British North
Borneo, had been spending a few days' "local leave" on
Tingling Estate, for Walkely, the manager, and he were great
friends. The night before his departure the two men had
sat together in the latter's mosquito-room, fitted up like a
"den", and with pipes well lit had roamed in desultory
manner over many fields of conversation.

For the last ten minutes or so there had been silence
between them—the silence of friends in complete accord.
Dennis broke it.

"Throw me a match, Walley," he said.

Walkely moved as though to comply, then stopped as
his "boy" entered, carrying a tray containing whisky and
soda, which he placed on a table near his master. He was
about to depart when Walkely spoke.

"The *Tuan* is leaving to-morrow before breakfast, Amat.
Tell Cookie to make some sandwiches and see the Thermos
flask is filled with hot tea."

"*Tuan*."

"And hand these to the *Tuan*." Walkely pointed to the
matches.

Amat obeyed and went out.

Walkely rose from his long chair, mixed the drinks and
held out a glass to Dennis.

"To our next meeting," he said, and raised his glass.

Dennis followed suit.

Then, yawning, Dennis rose, and stretching his arms
well above his head, looked sleepily in the direction of his
bedroom.

Walkely nodded assent and held open the mosquito-door.

A few minutes later the house was in darkness, save for
the lights that shone through the open windows of the two
bedrooms.

The rooms were on either side of a large dining-room, which in turn opened out from the main verandah, off one side of which was built the mosquito-room. At the far end of the dining-room were two folding doors that led to a passage and pantry, and thence down some steps to the kitchen and "boys' " quarters at the rear of the house.

As Dennis undressed he sleepily hummed the latest fox-trot record received from England. Then, dimming the light, he got into bed.

From where he lay he could hear Walkely moving about his room, and could see the reflection his light cast on the exposed *attap* * roof of the house. As he idly watched, speculating dreamily on Walley's success as a manager, Walkely's lamp in turn was lowered. Followed the creaking noise of a body turning on a spring mattress—then silence.

Dennis rolled from his left to right side preparatory to sleep.

"Nighty-night, Old Thing," he grunted.

"Night," came back the sleepy reply.

Then all was quiet save for the gentle rustling of the rubber trees and the occasional hoot of an owl.

Presently Dennis awoke to full alertness. He was not strung up; no sound nor fear nor nightmare had aroused him. He was simply and quietly awake. Turning on his side he looked at his watch. The hands pointed to 2 a.m. He closed his eyes, but sleep would not be wooed.

For a long time Dennis lay in the nearly darkened room, watching the waving branch of a rubber tree outside the window, that moved gently to the sighing of the breeze.

Suddenly he heard the sound of feet ascending the steps that led from garden to verandah doors.

But half awake, he listened.

Slowly the footsteps mounted the stairs; then came the lifting of the latch that fastened the low wooden gates, and the creaking of moving hinges. The footsteps entered, continued the full length of the verandah, to pass into the dining-room beyond. Here for a moment they halted. Then they moved again, shuffling uncertainly—forward, backward, sideways—as those of a person trying to locate something in the dark.

---

* Dried sago leaves.

Again they moved with steady tread and reached the intervening doors that shut off the passage.

Dennis listened and waited. What the devil was old Walley doing, he sleepily wondered.

A sudden rush of cool air struck on him over the top of the bedroom wall, billowing out his mosquito net.

Creak—creak—creak—the doors were opening. The footsteps went along the passage and came to a standstill at the end.

"Boy!"

The call was clear and decisive, but Dennis failed to quite recognize the voice, though he realized it was a European's.

There came no answer.

"Boy!"

This time the call was sharper, and impatience was in its tone. Still no reply.

In the silence Dennis, wondering greatly, waited, for he was still uncertain whether the voice was Walkely's or another's.

The footsteps sounded again as they descended the stairs that led to the servants' quarters. On the bottom step they halted.

"Boy!"

The call was long, loud, and angry. Yet still no answer came.

Up the stairs the footsteps returned. They strode along the passage, paused as the doors were closed and the latch clicked, then swiftly moved through the dining-room out on to the wide verandah. Here for a moment they rested.

Sounded the fumbling for a latch, the squeak of a faulty hinge, and from the sharp banging of a door Dennis knew the footsteps had entered the mosquito-room.

He sprang out of bed, and sitting on its edge, hurriedly pushed his feet into slippers. Then, as he was about to move, the lamp in the room went out.

"Damn!" he muttered, and fumbled for his matches, but before he found them he was listening to the opening and shutting of drawers.

He struck a match, and by its light crossed to the lamp, the wick of which, however, refused to burn, though he wasted many matches upon it.

In the gathering darkness, for the moon was setting, he moved toward the door, but with his hand upon the knob, stood still, for the footsteps were shuffling again and the sharp banging to of the mosquito-door made him jump.

Through the verandah the footsteps went, gaining sureness with every stride. The gates creaked and the latch fell to. Down the stairs the footsteps clumped, the sound growing fainter till it became lost in the night.

Three deep-toned notes from the office gong boomed on the air. Dennis shivered, kicked off his slippers and returned to bed. The air was cold, so he drew his blanket well around him.

"Old Walley's walking in his sleep or else indulging in a midnight prowl," he muttered. Half a minute later he was sound asleep.

.   .   .   .

As Dennis's eyes opened to the beauties of a tropic dawn, the clink of silver spoons against china reached his ears and the scent of a cigarette crept into the room. He plunged his head into a basin of cold water, brushed his hair, and still in his *sarong* and *kabaiah*,* went out on to the verandah, where Walkely paused in the act of conveying a cup to his mouth.

"Morning, Dennis," he grunted, and continued drinking his tea.

He was never very talkative the first thing in the morning.

Dennis answered and busied himself with the teapot. Then, under cover of meticulously choosing a piece of toast, he studied Walkely, who showed no signs of having spent a sleepless night.

Suddenly Walkely looked up and caught Dennis's eye upon him.

"Well ?" he asked ; "what is it ?"

"Nothing," Dennis curtly replied.

"Then why look at me like that ?"

"Sorry, Old Thing," Dennis stammered. "I was only wondering——"

"Yes ?"

"What the devil were you up to last night ?—walking all over the house and shouting for your boy."

---

* Sleeping-garments.

"Then you heard it too?"   Walkely asked the question with relief.

"It ?   What's *it* ?" Dennis retorted.   "Didn't I hear *you* come up the verandah steps, open the gates and walk to the back ?   You called 'Boy' three times, but got no answer. Then you walked back through the house and down the steps.   What was wrong, Walley ?"

Walkely looked Dennis full in the eyes as he slowly answered:

"Nothing ! Nothing was wrong, and I never moved from my room till this morning."

"But—then who the—— ?"

"I never moved," Walkely repeated.   "What you heard was Glister."

"Glister ! What on earth do you mean ? Who's Glister ?"

"You know. The chap who was manager here before Bellamy. He shot himself. Died in your room—on your bed. He's buried in the garden at the foot of the hill below your window. Great pity, but—drink and a native woman— nice chap too."

Walkely ceased as the light of recollection shone on Dennis's face.

"Yes, I remember," he spoke almost to himself.   "I met him once at a Jesselton Race Meeting. A tall, good-looking fellow ?"

Walkely nodded, and Dennis continued :

"He was awfully keen on a beautiful native woman—a Dusun named Jebee."

"Yes. She was lured away from Glister by another man. It was a dirty thing to do."

"The swine ! I only hope——"

"You needn't worry," Walkely interrupted. "He rues the day all right, I'll bet, for she's got him body and soul— doped to the eyes—and her temper is that of a fiend incarnate. She is priestess, too, of the *Gusi*, and he daren't call his soul his own."

"So poor old Glister's loss was really his gain, if only he'd known !" Dennis's words were gently spoken.

"Yes. But he felt her absence, and in the loneliness that followed, the drink got him again."

For nearly a minute there was silence between the two.

It was as if their memories had recalled Glister's spirit to his old home, almost as if he were sitting at the table with them, while the tinkling of Jebee's anklets sounded from an adjoining room. . . .

Dennis broke the silence.

"And you mean that—that was he, last night ?" he asked.

"Yes." The word seemed drawn reluctantly from Walkely's lips.

"But, good lord, man ! — you don't mean ?—you can't—it's preposterous."

"I know." Walkely spoke slowly. "It sounds absurd, doesn't it ? But Old Bellamy went through it, saw him and spoke to him, and once even shot at him."

"Bellamy ! Bellamy shot him ?"

"Yes. And there isn't much mysticism about him—he's as much imagination as a turnip."

"But——"

"All the 'buts' in the world won't alter matters. Bellamy's seen him. I've seen him, and you've heard him. He's there—and it happens, and it's always the same—only——"

"What ?" The word was wrung from Dennis.

"He's never entered the mosquito-room before."

"You think——"

"I don't know ! How can I ? I'm only wondering why he went there—what he was searching for."

"Drink, perhaps ?"

Walkely shook his head.

"No," he said. "The room wasn't built in his days. No ; there's something worrying him, something that's caused this variation of his usual walk."

His eyes met Dennis's and he gave a short, half-ashamed laugh. Then :

"Get on with your tea. When you've finished we'll go and look at his grave. I always inspect it twice a month and put a coolie on cleaning it up and looking after the flowers. We'll have a look to-day."

. . . . . .

As Dennis dressed with unusual slowness his mind was full of the tragedy so strangely recalled. "Poor old Glister !" he muttered. "What an end !"

An impatient call roused Dennis from his reverie and he

hastened to the verandah, to find Walkely already on the garden steps conversing with Gaga, the head *mandor* * of many years' standing.

The three at once set off. Down well-laid cement steps, along a broad path that wound among a profusion of bright coloured flowers they went. Overhead a flaming sun rode in an azure sky, and a faint breeze fanned their faces with its cooling breath, perfumed with the scent of dew and the fragrant, elusive blossoms of the rubber trees.

At the foot of the hill they turned and went in single file along a narrow path that followed the winding contour of the hill.

The three walked in silence, for speech was difficult along that narrow track. Suddenly the path, dipping down, turned sharply, and Walkely, who was leading, became for an instant lost to view. Dennis, humming a Dusun love song, followed close behind, but as he reached the turn the tune died abruptly on his lips and he stood stone-still.

"Good lord ! What can it mean ?"

The words were gasped by Walkely, who stood transfixed, staring with horror-struck eyes straight before him.

Instinctively Walkely turned to Dennis, who, like himself, stood with gaze fixed and staring eyes.

"What can it mean ?" he gasped a second time.

For they had reached the grave, and *it was open*. Heaped under the railings surrounding it, which were intact, were piles of fresh-dug earth, and all round lay the scattered flowers, withered and trampled into twisted shapes.

The eyes of Dennis and Walkely met. In each there lurked a question that neither dared to ask. Each heard again the shuffling footsteps of the previous night, and the opening and shutting of the drawers in the mosquito-room.

A shadow fell across them as they stood. There came a startled cry, the quick pattering of bare feet, and Gaga flung himself upon his knees, burying his hands in the earth.

"Gaga !"

The word was a sharp command of outraged wrath. But the man did not heed, and his hands continued fumbling, fingering, searching.

Walkely stooped down to seize the kneeling *mandor* by

---

* Overseer.

the shoulder, then straightened up as the latter rose and, turning, showed a face pallid under the yellow of his skin, from which stark horror shone.

"The *pandang**, *Tuan*," he gasped. "The *pandang*! It has gone!"

Walkely looked at him in stupefaction.

"Gaga——" he began, but got no further, for the man, heedless of Walkely's upraised hand, broke in :

"The *pandang*, *Tuan*, the silver *pandang* that Jebee used to wear as token of her priesthood, of the *Gusi*, has gone. The silver *pandang* is no more!"

He ceased, and for a moment there was silence among the three.

On Walkely's face there showed a blank amazement, but Dennis's brows had gathered in a frown and his lips had closed in a deep straight line. He was the first to speak.

"Walkely," he said, "may I ask Gaga questions ?"

Walkely nodded his assent, and Dennis turned to Gaga.

"Gaga, tell me, what makes you say the silver *pandang* is no more ?"

"Because," Gaga stammered in his emotion, "because— when Tuan Glister was buried, the *pandang* was buried too— and—now——"

His gaze sought for the coffin for a moment, and he fingered a charm of monkey's teeth that hung around his neck.

"Tell me, Gaga," Dennis's voice was very gentle, "all you know. Begin at the beginning."

.   .   .   .

Gaga looked relieved, for a native resents questioning and loves to tell a story in his own way.

"The *Tuans* know," he began, "that Tuan Glister had a *nyai†* named Jebee. She came to him when she was very young, but vowed by the oaths of her parents to the priesthood of the *Gusi*, the sacred jars we Dusuns worship, which only our womenkind may tend. But she was young and beautiful and full of life. Her beauty was unmatched in all this land of Sabah‡ ; her form was lithe, her footsteps light ; her

---

* Buckle.   † Native housekeeper.   ‡ Borneo.

waist was small ; yet she was vowed in wifehood to a jar, the sacred *Gusi* ! Her lips and eyes, though warring with her blood, were innocent of love till Tuan Glister visited the village in search of coolies for the estate.

"Then"—Gaga paused, seeming for a moment at a loss to find his words—"then—the *Tuan* was tall and handsome, and possessed golden hair. He had a laughing, winning way and eyes that darted here and there and made the warm blood race within your veins when once his glance had rested on you. His eyes discovered Jebee, and——"

Gaga looked nervously from Dennis and Walkely as he shuffled his feet, frightened of saying too much concerning a white man before others of his race.

Dennis read the meaning of his glance.

"Yes, Gaga. You may speak," he said, "for the *Tuan Besar** and I are friends and we would give Tuan Glister's wandering spirit peace. Say all that is in your heart. We understand."

"*Tuan !*" Gaga's tone conveyed a depth of grateful meaning. "That night there was dancing and feasting in the village, and pitcher after pitcher of *tapai*† was consumed. The *Tuan* drank too, but none could stand against him and one by one they sank into a heavy sleep. Only the *Tuan* remained. He left the headman's house, and going through the village reached Jebee's home.

"It was that darkest hour before dawn when the chill wind blows, yet she was seated on the topmost step. The light of the dying moon seemed focused on the silver buckle that she wore, hung from a rotan girdle round her waist.

"Their eyes met. No word was said. The *Tuan* stretched out his arms and Jebee went to him, and the *Tuan's* arms enfolded her."

Gaga ceased. The silence lengthened till the office gong, booming eight deep notes, shattered the spell.

"How do you know all this, Gaga ?" Walkely asked, at length. "You never mentioned it before !"

A look of surprise flitted over the *mandor's* face, then he quietly replied :

"The *Tuan* never asked me my story before, nor is it customary for the white man to discuss others of his race

---

with natives. How do I know? Why, *Tuan Besar*, was I not present on that night, and is not Jebee my sister, though of a different mother?

"The *Tuan* had saved my life, and Jebee was young. The warm blood danced in her veins, and her heart cried out for a mate. And so . . . The river, *Tuan*, flowed far from the village. The *Tuan's* boat was there. All in the village slept. The *Tuan* led her to the boat, while I stole up the steps, entered the house and made a bundle of her clothes. Then to the waiting boat I followed. The *Tuan* had covered Jebee with his coat and she was sleeping, but the silver buckle hung round his neck. And from that day it never left him. We three were alone in the boat. The *Tuan* and I picked up the paddles, and as their blades in silence touched the water the moon slipped beneath the earth and the *Burong hantu** hooted thrice. An evil omen, which the *Tuan* heeded not and Jebee did not hear.

"Till the sun was high we paddled and by noon were far beyond pursuit, for the river flowed very swiftly and one does not wake early from such a sleep as those in the village were sleeping."

Gaga paused, then he added:

"The rest of the story the *Tuans* know. For a little while the *Tuan* and Jebee were happy. But the omen of the *Burong hantu* and the dying moon would not be denied.

"And the shadow of the *Gusi* lay between them. So though the *Tuan* loved her he drank too deeply, and she found favour in another's sight and went away. But the *Tuans* know the rest. I buried him—there was no white man on the estate—and, as he died, he made me promise to bury the buckle with him, hanging round his neck. It was the only thing of Jebee's that he kept."

"And now?"

Dennis put the question sharply, and his eyes held Gaga's gaze.

"I am afraid, *Tuan*—sore afraid."

"Of what?"

"I do not know; and the silver *pandang* has been stolen, though its hiding-place was unknown. To none has it value, save to my people, and for years now they have let it

---

* Owl.

rest. But, *Tuan*, they never forget, and the *Gusi* is most sacred. In the great blue jar that Jebee used to tend, and should have wedded, Maboga, the bad Spirit, dwells. Of late evil has befallen my people : the buffaloes bring forth no young, and the crops refuse to ripen ; so, *Tuan*, I am afraid."

Gaga ceased, and once again a silence fell upon the three.

Suddenly it was broken by the hurrying footsteps and laboured breathing of a man who ran, and round the bend appeared an *opas*.

All three looked up at his approach and saw stark fear upon his face.

"*Tuan !   Tuan !*" he gasped. "Tuan Glister cannot be found. His house is empty, and his bedroom disarranged, and on the floor is a pool of blood——"

His eyes caught sight of the open grave. The words faltered on his tongue, then ceased, and he stood silent, trembling like a leaf.

At the mention of that name Dennis started, but before he could speak Walkely answered the question hovering on his lips.

"Young Glister's imy new assistant, Dennis," he spoke in a queer, strained vo ce ; "he came only last month ; you haven't met him yet."

"But——"

"He's a younger brother of . . ." Walkely looked toward the grave. "It's horrible !" he muttered.

In a flash the meaning of the rifled grave and Glister's disappearance grew plain, and the frown on Dennis's face grew deeper and his lips grew more compressed. Heedless of Walkely's questionings of the jibbering *opas* he turned to Gaga.

"Gaga," he said, "I see the hand of Mabago stretching out, seeking revenge for the insult of years ago. His arm is long. It stretches from the *Tuan's* grave to a village in the hills. Is it not so ?"

"*Tuan ?*" Gaga answered.

"It stretches," Dennis continued, "from the village to the new *Tuan's* house as well, for what the white man took must be repaid with interest. What think you, Gaga ?"

"That the *Tuan* is wise and reads the Dusun as a book."

"Dennis !" Walkely had dismissed the *opas*, and putting out his hand, grasped Dennis's arm. "Dennis," he cried, "what do you mean ? Glister has disappeared, there's blood upon his floor and we stand here while heaven knows what devil's work is being done ! What do you mean—with interest ?"

"Listen, Walley." Dennis weighed his words and spoke with slow conviction. "I'm in the dark almost as much as you—but I know the Dusuns and the fetish of their *Gusi* worship. When Glister took Jebee from her people, she broke their vows and outraged the sacred jars ; but while the years were plentiful and their calves were strong they did not worry ; when, as now, the inevitable lean year comes they seek a reason for their troubles."

"You mean . . . ?" asked Walkely, still perplexed.

"That reason is Maboga. They think he will not be appeased unless . . ."

Dennis did not finish, but his glance wandered to the open grave and back to Walkely's strained white face, on which the dawning light of comprehension showed.

"Good heavens !" he muttered ; "you really think . . . ?"

Dennis nodded ; then turned to Gaga.

"Gaga," he said, "tell me exactly what happens at the Feast."

"The silver buckles of the priestesses, *Tuan*, are hung upon the *Gusis'* lips. Then when the dying moon is half-way set, the mateless wives say prayers and wash the sacred jars, and call upon the spirits to come forth and give their judgment on the village for the year. This year I think Maboga's jar will once again be decked. But who will cleanse the sacred lips I cannot think, for while Jebee lives the *pandang* may be worn by no one else. Tuan Glister dared, and paid the price."

"And Maboga ?" Dennis's voice was low, almost a whisper.

For a moment Gaga hesitated, then he replied : "The *Tuan* himself has said : 'What the white man took must be repaid—with interest."

He paused ; then he added : "A white man's head has never yet hung in a Dusun house, but three days hence Maboga will decide."

The eyes of Dennis and Walkely met. Both seemed to hear again the shufflings in the night, the opening and the shutting of the drawers. Both understood the object of that search.

"I'll borrow Glister's revolver, Walley, for we'll go alone with only Gaga as our guide, and attend this Feast," said Dennis.

    .   .   .   .   .

For hours the booming of gongs had been borne upon the breeze, yet though the three had been steadily ascending, the deep-toned notes still sounded far away.

On the crest of a hill Dennis and his companion halted for a brief rest, and then onward and upward the trio climbed, while the track grew narrower and stonier and the jungle pressed closer on every side, and long trailing thorn-edged creepers, hanging from the trees, whipped their faces and tore their clothes.

The leading beast stopped and Gaga raised his hand. Without a word the two white men drew level, for the path had widened out and they stood upon the border of a glade, dissected by a muddy stream, whose banks were scored with a myriad hoof-marks.

Gaga slipped from his animal and softly spoke.

"We are nearly there, *Tuan*. This is their grazing ground, but all the animals are at the village, for all have ridden to the Feast."

Dennis nodded and proceeded, like the others, to tether his beast.

Then on foot the three moved forward but with a quicker pace, for the gongs were loudly booming with a beat that would not be denied. Even as they crossed the muddy stream, the swaying rhythmic time, rising and falling with the cadence of a dance, gave place to an insistent note that rose and rose, till only one intense vibration, one single throbbing note, beat on the heavy air with a malignant strength sapping all kindly thoughts and fanning to flame the primal lusts of hate and vengeance.

A little farther and the path rose with a sudden precipitousness that forced them to mount the well-worn stones as though they climbed a stair. They reached the top, to stand upon a tiny plain, on which the shadows of the encircling trees were slowly lengthening.

Even as they rested to regain their breath that one insistent note ceased, and for an instant silence reigned.

Then from the glade's farther end arose a cry, faint at

first, then slowly louder, harsher, stronger, swelling to a
mighty pæan, to a tumultuous cry, "Maboga ; Maboga !
Aki* Mabogo !" And stillness once again, save for the
hurried padding of running feet as the three raced across the
shadow-flecked glade.

Panting, they reached a wall of jungle, pierced by a sunken
path that twined its short length through the heart of a moss-
clad hill, whose riven sides were lit with weird, fantastic
lights, thrown from countless torches that burned upon a
plateau at its end.

In the shadow of a belt of trees they paused to take stock
of their surroundings.

The plateau formed a horseshoe, and at its apex stood a
native house built eight feet off the ground, whose length
stretched three hundred feet. At either end, leading to the
only doors, were rough-hewn steps, carved from solid logs of
timber, and from these steps arose two poles, six feet in
height, between which was stretched a length of knotted
rotan. From this, like a gruesome necklace, hung two rows
of ghastly human heads—blackened and dried from the
smoke of years—save at each end. And there hung two heads
with staring, sightless eyes, and bared lips exposing whitened
teeth ; and from them the red blood dripped.

Upon the ground, placed in a semicircle, stood the jars—
the sacred *Gusi*—ranged in accordance with their height and
rank. From either end they tapered up towards the central
spot, where, side by side, rose two of flaming blue that reached
the height of a man's shoulder.

The rim, or lip, of each was of a different hue—one
black, one white—while from the neck of those whose lip
was black grew four large ears, and in the lobes of each was
placed a human skull.

Behind each jar, save one, a woman stood ; her thick
black hair piled high upon her head, framing her lime-washed
face from which her dark eyes shone ; her figure swathed
from chin to toe in shrouded black, girt at the waist with a
girdle of mice and monkeys' teeth.

A silver *pandang* hung under the lip of every jar but one,
and resting on its swelling shoulder shimmered and winked
in the torches' fantastic light.

---

* Father.

Facing the jars, the Dusuns sat in rows, immobile and intent. There shone upon the face of every one a strained expectancy, showing in the taut muscles of the back and the restless, twining fingers of the hands. Thus they waited— in that strange, uncanny silence—for the answer to their cry, "Maboga, Maboga, *Aki* Maboga !"

Almost forgetful of the purpose of their errand, Dennis and Walkely watched, fascinated by the scene before them, lit by the waning moon and the lurid flickering torches. Something of its primeval instincts and the tension of the squatting natives crept into their veins and held them spell-bound as they gazed upon the coloured jars, with their glittering shining buckles, each with its dumb, attendant white-faced woman, backed by the long, unbroken shadow of the palm-roofed house.

While the moon sank slowly in the west, until its lower rim began to kiss the topmost ridge of the roof, the silence lengthened, till it seemed as if Nature slept and those rows of squatting natives were graven images devoid of breath.

But all at once there came a creaking sound, and the tension snapped. A long, rippling murmur, half-sigh, half-gasp, filled the air, and Gaga's hand gripped Dennis's arm.

"Look, *Tuan*, look !" he whispered, and pointed to a hut which stood alone and almost hidden in the shade of a mighty billian tree.

The two men obeyed, following the line of Gaga's pointing finger.

The hut door opened slowly as the noise increased. But though no light burned within, a shadowy form was faintly visible moving toward the glade. Slowly, silently, though still half hidden by the shade, the form drew near. Then as all eyes were turned upon it a glinting speck of light winked in the gloom. And as the figure moved the winking light moved too.

Slowly, steadily from the shade into the flickering fringe of torches ; from the fringe into the full lurid glare moved the figure and the light.

A quick intake of many breaths ; a long, loud gasp of terrified surprise. Then silence—and a woman, with a silver buckle hanging from a girdle round her waist, stood before-the great blue sacred jar, from under whose deep black lip no silver buckle hung.

Over the silence, that like a living spirit lay upon the glade, Gaga's excited whisper just reached Dennis's and Walkely's ears.

"*Tuan*, it is Jebee, and she wears the silver *pandang* that I buried in Tuan Glister's grave! *Tuan, Tuan*, I am afraid!"

Even as he spoke the woman raised her rounded arms, on which no gleaming bangles shone, and with a single gesture unloosed the coils of her high-wound hair. The long, thick tresses fell around her like a black cloak.

Again she raised her arms, this time in supplication, and her low, clear voice went chanting through the glade.

"*Aki* Maboga of the Sacred *Gusi*, Spirit of Evil who dwelleth in the great blue jar, hear now thy erring daughter, thy forsworn priestess, and forgive. Here in my shame I stand before thee and the assembled people, bearing the silver *pandang*, symbol of thy might and power, which in my youth and wilful love I disgraced.

"Thou, who for long hast been neglected, till thy just wrath burst into flame, so that the crops no longer ripen and the herds cease to bring forth young, lift, I beseech thee, *Aki* Maboga, the shadow of thy anger from off my race.

"Through me and for my sin my people have been punished; through me, O *Aki*, pronounce the penance thou dost claim."

She ceased, and as a wailing cry rose from the assembled natives, slipped slowly to her knees, and flinging her arms round the great jar's neck, rested her lips upon its blackened rim.

Walkely stirred, but Dennis's warning hand bade him keep still. Gaga, speechless and with bulging eyes, stared at the kneeling figure.

A wind was stirring in the trees. The moon had sunk completely out of sight, and here and there a flickering torch gutted and burnt out.

Thus in the creeping darkness they waited, while the moments grew to minutes burdened with suspense—waited for Maboga's answer that his deep black lips would whisper in Jebee's listening ear.

At length, with infinite grace she rose, and stood clothed

in her long black hair behind the great blue jar; for on its swelling shoulders, glinting against its deep black lip, the silver *pandang* lay.

The wind was sighing in the trees. The rustling leaves made soft accompaniment to her voice, which trembled with emotion.

"My lips have kissed the sacred *Gusi*—my tears have washed its deep black lip. The silver *pandang* has returned to deck the shrine of the Great Spirit, who has spoken, for my ears have caught his whispering breath."

A murmur rose, then faded, and she continued:

"Rejoice, O people, for I see the crops on all the hillsides ripening and herds with their young. But for his clemency Maboga asks a price."

She paused; then stretching out her arms cried in a ringing voice: "What will you give, my people, to allay your desperate plight?"

Quick as the summer lightning, swift as an adder's tongue came the answer from those rows of waiting natives.

"What the white man took, let him repay with interest. The head of the white man's brother we will give, as a make-peace to Maboga, and as thy wedding gift."

She raised her hand, and there was silence.

"Thy words are good; thy offering acceptable unto——"

Her words were drowned in a great shout of fear, as a lighted torch fell from its bamboo socket on to the palm-roofed house.

Like running water, fanned by the rising breeze, the flames spread rapidly, till in the twinkling of an eye the wooden house was nothing but three hundred feet of sheeted flame.

Then pandemonium reigned and terror stalked the glade.

But to the watching three the fire was providential, for the burning house lit up the hut, till now hidden in the gloom, and at its single window they beheld young Glister's blood-stained face.

Under the shadow of the trees, skirting the edge of the tiny plain, they raced. A few more yards and they would reach the door; another second—out of the shadows by the hut a naked figure sprang, her long black hair streaming in the breeze, a glittering sharp-edged sword in her hand.

With an oath, Walkely forged ahead, but, missing his footing on a twisted root, stumbled and fell.

The sudden, instinctive tightening of his fingers, a flare and a sharp report ; a cry of pain, a sagging, drooping form— and Jebee lay a crumpled figure across the threshold of the hut.

SI URAG OF THE TAIL

DENNIS sat on the verandah of his bungalow and gazed meditatively around him. He could not look at the view, because there was none to speak of since the house was built on an island in the middle of the Luago River. On all sides of the island grew the tall rank elephant-grass and nipa-palm. Here and there a stunted, beetle-ridden coconut tree just topped the dense vegetation, a relic of some clearing and plantation commenced by a native, then left to desolation and the ever-encroaching jungle.

Dennis was bored. He was two years overdue for leave ; also the day was unusually hot. The hour was about four, but though the sun was beginning to slant there was no abatement in the fierceness of its rays. After lunch he had followed the immemorial custom and undressed for a short siesta, but sleep was denied him. The mechanical action of undressing had quickened his brain. The room seemed stifling ; the bed felt warm. He bathed, dressed and betook himself to the verandah. Here he smoked and thought.

And his thoughts were none too pleasant, for there was much that was troubling him. Throughout the morning he had been listening to the endless intricacies of a native land case—a dispute over boundaries and ownership. He had reserved his judgment till the morrow, for the evidence had been involved and contradictory. He had meant to go over the salient points during the afternoon, and instead, here he was seated on his verandah smoking and thinking of an entirely different matter. Try as he would, his mind would not keep on the subject of the land, but roamed ever and ever over the mystery that was fast setting its seal of terror and fear on the district.

From a village in the *ulu** of the river, strange rumours

---

* Source.

E*

had come floating downstream. At first they were as light and airy as thistledown—just a passing whisper— a fairy story over which to smile ; then they passed, but came again, more substantial and insistent, stronger and sterner and not to be denied. Their very number compelled a hearing ; their very sameness breathed a truth. Inhabitants from the village had gone forth and never returned ; never a trace of them had been found. First a young girl, then her father. She had been absent six days, and he had gone to look for her. But he looked in vain and in his turn disappeared. Then a young boy, and next an aged woman. Then, after a longer period a tame ape, and finally the headman's favourite wife.

Fear settled on the village ; its inhabitants scarce dared leave their houses, save in batches to collect water and food. But fear travels fast, and the rumours reached Klagan and came to Dennis's ears. In the end the mystery caught him in its toils, weaved itself into his every waking moment and excited his interest beyond control.

An idle native story : the tale of a neighbouring village with an axe of its own to grind. He was a fool to worry over it. Such mare's nests were of almost daily occurrence, thus Dennis argued ; and then from two other villages came similar tales. Two little girls had gone to bathe in the height of the noonday sun. At moonrise they had not returned. Nor in the days that passed were they ever seen again. Two lovers met one moonlight night and waded to a boulder in midstream of the river. Here they sat oblivious of the world around them. They were seen by a couple of natives passing downstream in their boat and then—never again.

Down the river crept the cold, insidious Fear like a plague, taking toll of every village in its path. In their houses huddled the natives, while crops were unsown and pigs uprooted the plantations ; while crocodiles devoured untended buffaloes, and squirrels and monkeys rifled the fruit trees. From source to mouth the Fear crept down and in the end forced Dennis's hand, compelling him to action.

Thus as he sat on his verandah and cursed the heat of the sun and the humidity of the tropics, unbidden and unsought the mystery filled his thoughts ; and he began to wonder as to if and when his native sergeant and three police would return. For he had sent them to the *ulu* to probe and solve the meaning of the rumours. They had been gone three weeks, and throughout this time no word had been heard of or come from them.

In the office a clock struck five. Its notes came booming across to Dennis. Then silence—not complete and utter stillness ; such is never possible in the tropics, but the silence of that hour when the toilers—man and animal—by day realize that night is approaching ; when the toilers by night have not yet awakened.

Lower and lower sank the sun. In the sky a moon was faintly visible. Dennis rose, about to call for tea, then checked the desire. From afar upstream came the chug, chug, chug of a motor-boat. Its beat just reached his ears. He looked at his wrist-watch. In ten minutes he would go down to the floating wharf. That would give him plenty of time to watch the boat round the last bend of the river. In the meanwhile . . .

But he went at once to the wharf after all, for mystery gripped him, causing him feverishly to pace up and down the tiny floating square. Chug, chug, chug, louder and louder came the noise ; then fainter and fainter, and then was lost altogether as the dense jungle cut off the sound as the boat traversed another bend of the river. Chug, chug, chug, faintly, then louder and stronger. A long-drawn note from the horn of a buffalo smote the air, and the boat swung round the final bend. Only a quarter of a mile separated it now from Dennis.

As the boat drew nearer he saw that she was empty save for the *serang** and boatmen. Then the Fear gripped him too, and he quickly returned to the house. With shaking hand he poured out a whisky-and-soda, flung himself into a chair and shouted for his "boy".

"*Tuan* !" The word, though quietly spoken, made him flinch, for the "boy" had approached him silently, as all well-trained servants do. Quickly, too, he had obeyed the summons, but in that brief space of time Dennis's mind had escaped his body and immediate wants to roam the vast untrodden fields of speculation and fear.

With an effort he pulled himself together.

---

* Helmsman.

"The motor-boat is returning. Tell the *serang* to come to me as soon as he has tied her up. See that no one is within earshot."

"*Tuan.*" And the boy departed.

Scarcely had the boy left than the *serang* stood in front of Dennis. His story was brief, though harrowing, but it threw no light upon the mystery. For two days, till they reached the rapids, they had used the motor-boat. Then they transhipped into a native dug-out, leaving the motor in charge of a village headman. For three days they had paddled and poled upstream till they came to the mouth of the Buis River. Here the sergeant and police left them, telling them to wait for their return, and struck inland along a native track. For sixteen days they waited, though their food had given out and they had taken turns to search the jungle for edible roots. Then on the sixteenth day it happened—the horrible coming of Nuin.

The boatmen had gone to look for roots. The *serang* was dozing in a dug-out. Suddenly it shook and rocked. Something clutched the *serang's* arm. It was Nuin's hand. Startled into wakefulness, the *serang* sat up ; then he screamed and covered his eyes with his hands. When he dared look again Nuin was lying on the river bank. His clothes were in rags. Round his chest and back ran a livid weal four inches wide. His left leg hung broken and twisted. His right arm was entirely missing. His face was caked in congealed blood.

As the *serang* looked, Nuin opened his lips to speak, but his voice was only a whisper. Tremblingly, haltingly, the *serang* went to him and put his ear to his mouth. "Sergeant—others—dead—three days—west—man—with—big—big—others." The whisper faded away ; Nuin gave a shudder and was dead.

They buried him near the river and then left, paddling night and day till they reached the rapids. A night they spent in the village, for they were racked with sleeplessness, and they left the next morning, reaching Klagan the same day.

Such was the *serang's* report.

The Fear spread farther down the river till it reached the sea and spread along the coast.

In the barracks that night were two women who would

never see their men again ; was born a baby, who would never know his father ; wept a maiden for the lover whose lips she would never kiss again.

As the earliest streaks of dawn came stealing across the sky, the chugging of a motor-boat broke the stillness of the night. Dennis himself was at the wheel, for the *serang* was suffering with fever. With him were nine police and a corporal. They carried stores for twenty days.

The journey was a replica of the *serang's*, save that at the village by the rapids no friendly headman or villagers took charge of the motor-boat. The village had fled before the Fear. On the fifth day Buis was reached as the setting sun shot the sky with blood-red streamers.

On the banks of the river the earth was uprooted ; among the loosened earth were human bones and the marks of pigs' feet. Among the bones was a broken tusk, sure sign of some fierce conflict that had raged over Nuin's remains.

Dennis shuddered as he saw the scene ; his Murut police, pagans from the interior of North Borneo, fingered their charms of monkeys' teeth and dried snake-skins that hung around their necks or were attached to the rotan belts around their waists, that carried their heavy *parangs*.*

Occasionally throughout the night the droning noise of myriad insects was broken by the shrill bark of deer or kijang. Sometimes the sentry, gazing into the vast blackness of the jungle, saw the beady eyes of a pig, lit up for a moment by the flames of the campfire. Sometimes a snake, attracted by the glare, glided through the undergrowth, then passed on. Once or twice a nightjar cried and an owl hooted—eerie sounds in the pitch-black night. Otherwise a heavy brooding stillness, like an autumn mist, crept over the jungle and enveloped the camp. Hardly a policeman slept ; but dozed and waked and dozed again, only to wake once more and feel the Fear grow ever stronger. Dennis, on his camp-bed under a *kajang* awning, tossed and tossed the long night through.

Dawn broke to a clap of thunder. Rain heralded in the new day.

"Three days—west." This was all Dennis knew ; all he had to guide him. For this and the next two days the party followed a track that led steadily in a westerly direction.

---

* Swords.

On the evening of the third day it came out into a glade. Here Dennis pitched his camp. The tiny space of open sky and glittering stars breathed a cooler air and purer fragrance than the camps roofed in by the canopy of mighty trees. Thus the tired and haunted police slept, and Dennis ceased his tossing. Only the sentry was awake—or should have been. Perhaps he too dozed or fell fast asleep, for a few unconscious moments. If so he paid a heavy penalty.

Dennis awoke the next morning at a quarter to six to see only the smouldering remains of the campfire.

"Sentry!" he called. But no answer was vouchsafed. "Sentry!" he cried again, but no one came. Aroused by his voice, the sleeping camp stirred to wide and startled awakeness.

The corporal came across to Dennis, saluted, then stood at attention, waiting.

"The fire's nearly out; where's the sentry?" Dennis queried.

The corporal looked around him, gazed at the smouldering fire, counted his men, then looked at Dennis with fear-stricken eyes.

"*Tuan !*" he gasped; "he is not—there are only eight men !"

"Is not? What d'you mean? Where's he gone?" As Dennis snapped his question cold fear gripped his heart. He knew; some inner sense told him that the man had disappeared in the same mysterious fashion as those early victims. Here, in the midst of his camp, the terrible, unseen thing had power !

"Where's he gone?" Dennis repeated his question fiercely to quench his rising fear. "What d'you mean?"

For answer the corporal only stood and trembled. His open, twitching mouth produced no sound.

With an oath Dennis flung himself from his bed. "Search the glade, you fool," he cried, "and find his tracks ! He can't be far away. No, stay," he added as the corporal was departing. "Who is it?"

"Bensaian, *Tuan*," gasped the terrified man.

Dennis's eyes narrowed and a frown spread over his face. "Bensaian !" he repeated. "He was Number Three. His watch was from twelve till two."

"*Tuan !*"

"Then he's never been relieved. From two o'clock at least, he's been missing !"

"*Tuan !* I must have slept. I saw Auraner relieve Si Tuah, but I was tired and——"

"Search for his tracks," Dennis cried, breaking in on his protestations, "but see no man enters the jungle."

In that tiny glade the search was no prolonged affair, but no traces of the missing man were found—save one. A brass button, torn from his tunic, lay at the foot of a mighty billian tree. But where and how he had gone remained a mystery. Only the regular footprints as he had walked to and fro on his beat were just discernible, and these crossed and recrossed each other in hopeless confusion.

Over the tops of the trees the sun came stealing, bathing the glade in its warming light, but Dennis heeded it not.

"Three days—west." The words kept hammering in his brain as he sat on the edge of his bed and smoked cigarette after cigarette. Up and down the glade a sentry walked. Round the fire the police were crouched cooking their rice ; over another Dennis's boy prepared his *tuan's* breakfast.

At length, when ready, he brought it over to him, poured out his coffee and departed to join the whispering police. But though the coffee grew cold and flies settled on the food, Dennis sat on, unmoved, deep in his distraction.

This was the fourth day ! For three days they had journeyed west, following Nuin's almost last conscious words. The glade was hemmed in by the impenetrable jungle ; no path led out of it save that along which they had come. It formed a *cul-de-sac* indeed ! And Bensaian was missing !

As Dennis sat and pondered, this one great fact became predominant. Bensaian was missing. Then what did it mean ? Only that here the thing had happened, lived or breathed or moved about. Here, then, would be found the answer to the riddle ! In this little glade of sunlight must they watch and wait. Into the trackless jungle he dared not enter, even if his men could hack a path. To return the way they had come would make his errand worse than fruitless. Watching and waiting only remained.

So they waited. Day turned to evening and evening into night ; the dawn of another day displaced the night ; the sun again rode over the tops of the jungle. But nothing happened. Only the policemen grew more frightened ; only Dennis's nerves grew more frayed. Then once again the night descended, but no one in the camp dared really sleep.

Up and down walked the sentry, resting every now and then, as he turned against the billian tree. A gentle breeze stirred the branches of the encircling trees, bearing on the air a faint aromatic smell, that soothed the nervous senses of the resting camp, as a narcotic dispels pain. One by one the police ceased whispering and gently dozed, calmed by the sweet fragrance. Dennis ceased his endless smoking; stretched himself at ease upon his bed. The sense of mystery seemed forgotten by all ; a sense of peace seemed brooding over them.

Midnight came and the wakeful sentry was relieved. His relief, but half awake, railed at his fate—the half-unconscious dozing was so pleasant, and this marching up and down the glade, while others rested, so utterly to his distaste.

As for the fortieth time he turned about at the base of the great billian tree, he lowered his rifle, rested for a few seconds with his hands upon its barrel, then leaned against the dark ridged stem ; just for a moment he would rest, his rifle in his hands—just for a moment only, then once again take up his beat.

The wind in the trees was gradually increasing; the fragrance on the air became more pronounced. The camp was almost wrapt in slumber. On his bed Dennis sleepily wondered whence came the pleasing, soothing odour, that seemed to breathe so wondrous a peace. Against the billian tree the sentry still was leaning ; his rifle slipped from the faint grasp of his hands, but he heeded not the rattle as it struck the ground.

Peace in the glade from whence came so much mystery ! Peace while the dread, though unknown, agent drew near apace !

Down from the top of the billian tree it slowly descended, branch by branch ; slowly, carefully, silently, till it rested on the lowest branch still thirty feet above the sentry.

The bark of a deer broke the stillness of the night. From afar came an answering note. Somehow the sound awakened the sentry. He looked around him, saw the fire was burning bright, picked up his fallen rifle and commenced to walk about.

Down the far side of the tree a bark rope descended till

its weighted end just rested on the ground. Down the rope a man, naked save for a bark-made loin-cloth, descended till he too reached the earth. Then, pressed flatly to the great tree's trunk, he waited.

Across the glade the sentry turned about. With listless, heavy steps he was returning. Nearer and nearer he approached. At the foot of the billian tree he halted, turned and leaned against its trunk. The tension of his limbs relaxed. The rifle slipped from his grasp, but hung suspended by the strap that had become entangled over his arm. A light unconsciousness, hardly to be designated sleep, stole over him. From the camp there was no sign of wakefulness.

Slowly a figure crept noiselessly round the tree and stood gazing at the policeman. Naked indeed he was save for the *chawat** of bark; his thick black hair hung over his neck and reached beyond his shoulders, framing a face out of which gleamed two fanatical shining eyes. His body to the waist was covered with tattoo. From each of his breasts the designs started, spreading to waist-line and round to the back. The nipple of each breast gleamed a fiery burnished gold, while from their fringe spread outward, like a full-blown flower, five oval petals of wondrous purple hue. From the golden centre of each flower ten long pistils spread, curving downward and round his body. At their source they too were of a purple hue, but as they reached the petals their colour turned to gleaming gold which slowly changed to glistening silver as their ridged ends were reached. These ridged ends were circular, and their silver rims framed brilliant scarlet mouths, shaped like the sucking orifice with which the huge and slimy horse-leech gluts its loathsome thirst for blood.

The man's arms were unusually long; his finger-nails had never been clipped; the splay of his toes, especially between the big and the next one, uncommonly wide.

One hand still clutched the bark rope; the other hung loosely at his side. Though he was tall, standing five feet ten inches, and heavily built, he moved as lightly as a cat.

Lightly he let go the rope and extended his two long arms toward his unconscious prey. The cry of a nightjar sounded close at hand. The somnolent sentry stirred as the sound

---

* Loin-cloth.

just reached his brain. With a spring the man was upon him. One hand upon his mouth ; one arm around his chest pinioning his arms to his side. With a swiftness incredible he reached the far side of the tree, let go his grasp upon the sentry's mouth, and using the rope as a rail, commenced to climb step over step with an amazing agility.

"*Tolong !*"* The cry, laden with overwhelming fear, rent the stillness of the night. "*Tol——*"

All further sound ended in a gurgle as the relentless pressure round the sentry's chest squeezed out all breath from his body. The camp at that sudden cry of human agony and fear awoke to life. Instinctively the police seized their rifles ; the corporal blew fiercely on his whistle ; Dennis hurriedly pulled on his mosquito boots and picked up his revolver from under his pillow.

"Corporal !"

"*Tuan !*"

"*Siapa itu ?*"†

The cries rent the air simultaneously. Then came silence for the fraction of a second, as everyone stared hopelessly at one another as they realized the glade was empty of the sentry.

"Si Tuah ! Tuah !" Dennis's voice rose in a long cry, breaking the sudden silence that followed the camp's awakening. "Tu-ah," he called again.

Somewhere from among the trees came a sound—a kind of muffled sob—a choking, gurgling cry of fear. To the edge of the jungle close to the billian tree Dennis and the corporal darted.

"Look, *Tuan*, a rope !" the latter gasped.

"My God !" Dennis whispered. "What does it mean ?"

"It's made of bark and——" began the corporal, but the rest of his words were drowned by a loud report.

"*Jaga ! Tuan, Jaga !*"‡ he cried, as a jumbled shape came hurtling down from the branches of the tree and the frayed ends of the rope came writhing about them. The snapping of a twig overhead, and a smoking rifle fell at their feet.

As the shape reached the ground with a sickening bump, two figures fell apart and then lay still.

---

* Help !   † Who's that ?   ‡ Look out!

"Seize that man and bind him!" Dennis cried, pointing to the naked form, as he bent over the prostrate figure of Si Tuah. "Gently, men, gently," he added, as four police picked him up and carried him over to their *kajang* shelter.

His left arm hung loosely by his side, two ribs were also broken, but his heart still faintly beat. Dennis poured a little brandy down his throat. Slowly Si Tuah came to. He tried to rise to sitting posture, but fell back with a groan of pain.

"He came upon me from behind the tree—I must have dozed," he muttered. "He picked me up—the pressure of his grasp was awful—and then commenced to climb the tree, holding the rope as a rail and walking up step by step. I struggled—just as we neared the branches his grip slackened— I could not cry—I had no breath—I only groaned, I struggled once again—my foot kicked the butt of my rifle—my toe found the trigger and I pressed and pressed—there came a report—we fell—and——"

Si Tuah had fainted again. Dennis's eyes met those of the corporal. "The shot must have severed the rope," he whispered.

"*Tuan*, his *nasib** was good," the corporal answered, and they crossed to where the human vulture lay, one leg twisted under him, his *chawat* all awry. As the policemen rolled him over on his face to knot the ropes—they showed but little pity for his unconscious state—the *chawat* came undone and slipped from his waist.

"Look, *Tuan*, look!" the corporal gasped, and pointed with shaking finger. "Look, he has a tail—it's not a man—it has a tail!" And feverishly he fingered the charms that hung around his neck.

Dennis looked, following the pointing finger, then bending down, looked long and closely. It was as the corporal said. The man possessed a tail—a long, hard protuberance that projected from his spine for about four inches.

"Bring him to the camp," he ordered. "Place two sentries; one over him, one on the camp. He is only stunned; there are no bones broken. In the morning when Tuah's better we'll learn some more."

---

* Fate.

Dennis walked across to his bed. The Fear was gone, but the mystery was still unexplained. The camp-fire burnt brightly, giving out a smell of pungent wood smoke. The soothing aromatic scent of an hour ago was no more. From the police came intermittent whisperings ; from the man with the tail naught but heavy breathing. On his bed Dennis tossed and wondered.

As the early dawn first faintly flooded the sky, shriek upon shriek rent the air. Si Tuah had become delirious. The man with the tail awoke and listened. From a group of police squatting over a fire their voices reached him. His eyes blinked in perplexity. Quietly as he lay, he dug with his nails a small round hole in the earth about five inches deep. Then gingerly he moved, and in spite of his bonds sat up. From his bed Dennis watched him. Into the hole he fitted his tail, then looked at his bonds and the group of police. He opened his mouth, but no sound came forth. His tied hands he stretched out to them. His face expressed a yearning. It was as if their voices brought a comfort or recalled a past. Then tear after tear rolled down his cheeks.

Calling the corporal, Dennis crossed to the weeping man. At Dennis's approach he looked up, then with a cry buried his face in his bound hands and rocked his body to and fro. He was afraid—afraid of a white man, the like of which he had never seen before.

"Peace, fool," the corporal said roughly, speaking unconsciously in Murut ; "stop your wailing, the *tuan* is no ghost but a man, albeit all-powerful."

Slowly the tailed being ceased his weeping and looked up. "A man !" he muttered. "A man and the colour of the gods !" He spoke a bastard Murut and Malay that caused Dennis to start and the corporal to frown in perplexity, for his meaning was clear, though many of the words, akin to either language, were yet unlike either. But they understood him.

"And your name ?" Dennis asked in Malay, but the being only shook his head in fear, extending his hands in supplication.

"Loosen his bonds," Dennis commanded. "Ask him his name and tribe and village."

The corporal obeyed, and then translated.

The man's name was Si Urag. He came of a Murut

race that years ago had captured some Malay traders. All had been killed except the women. These had been made to marry the head-men. Then came a plague and nearly all died. The remnants, according to custom, moved their village. For days and days they walked in the trackless jungle. Then from the trees they were attacked by a race of dwarfs who lived in houses in the branches. All save him were killed. He lay stunned ; when he recovered consciousness he saw that the dwarfs had tails and that they were disembowelling the dead and dying and hanging their entrails round their necks. Fear seized him. He tried to rise and run away. He staggered to his feet, tottered a yard or two and then collapsed. Terrified, face downward, he waited for his foes. With a rush of feet they came. He waited for the blow. It never fell. Suddenly he felt a gentle pull upon his tail—the tail over which all his life he had been ridiculed ; then came a muttering of voices. From the face of the moon a cloud passed by. He was in a glade and lying near a pool. Over the air a heavy scent was hanging. Suddenly the waters stirred. Out of their depths a flaming gold and purple flower arose. Ten tentacles spread out with gaping, wide-open, blood-red mouths. Shriek upon shriek of utter agony rent the air. Into the flaming golden centre each tentacle, curving inward, dropped a dwarf. Into the depths of the pool the flower sank down. All was still. Si Urag was alone.

That night he slept in a house among the branches of a tree. The surviving dwarfs had fled.

In the morning he collected the corpses of his friends and placed them near the lake. That night from his tree-house he watched. The moon was one day off the full. When at its highest point in the sky, the waters of the pool became disturbed. Again the golden-purple flower arose from its depths and the soothing scent spread over the jungle. Again the red-mouthed tentacles spread over the shore and sucked up the corpses, curved themselves in toward the golden centre, dropped in its bell-shaped mouth the stiffened bodies. Once again the human-feeding flower sank beneath the waters. Once again all was still. Gradually the narcotic smell grew less ; slowly the moon sank in the west. All was dark and silent.

On the next and two following nights the flower appeared.

Each night the hungry tentacles sought for food—human or animal. Then with the waning of the moon the flower rose up no more. Still in his tree-house Si Urag watched and lived. Where else was he to go? His tribe was killed; the dwarfs had fled, and of them he was afraid. On account of his tail he was shy to intermingle with other humans, even if he knew where to find them. Here was his house, safe from wild beasts that roamed at night; in the pool were many fish, in the jungle many roots and fruit. Here was the wondrous flower that fed on men, that spread its wondrous scent, to whom he felt he owed his life. Here, then, he would live and consecrate his life in a kind of priesthood to the flaming gold-and-purple orchid.

The corporal ceased and his eyes met those of Dennis. There was no need to answer the unspoken question in them. The mystery of those disappearances was explained.

"And that?" Dennis pointed to the tattooing on the prisoner's body.

Si Urag understood the gesture, if not the words.

"Is the picture of the flower I serve," he answered, looking at the corporal. "Two nights ago I fed it with a man clothed like that"—and he pointed to the police. "A night ago I caught a pig and deer; last night I caught a man"— he pointed to where Si Tuah lay in his delirium—"but a magic spoke from out a tube that flashed fire and the rope was severed and . . ." He shrugged his shoulders with a world of meaning, then, "I am hungry; give me some rice," he begged.

For a while he ate his fill. Then when the sun rose high over the little glade Dennis questioned him further, and from his answers formed a great resolve.

The glade of the golden-purple flower was but a few miles away. A little cutting of the jungle, and a hidden path— Si Urag's path—would be found. That night the moon would be but two days past its zenith, the wondrous flower would rise for the last time for a month—or rise never to rise again, hoped Dennis.

Si Urag was complacent. Was it fear or cunning? Who could tell? His face was like a mask as he agreed to lead the little party to the pool where dwelt the sacred flower.

The hour was after midnight. In the camp three police watched the delirious Si Tuah. Along a narrow track that led from the jungle to a pool, silently stole eight men. In the west a clipped moon was slowly sinking. Out of the jungle crept the men, into a glade silvered by the light of the moon.

"To the right ten paces ex——" Dennis's whispered orders faded away, giving place to a breathless gasp of surprise. There in the middle of the pool was the great golden-purple flower, its centre flaming gold, its petals deepest purple, its ten pistils curling and waving about—curling and waving toward the little group of men as they emerged from the track ; the blood-red, silver-rimmed mouths opening and shutting in hungry expectation. Over the glade lay the heavy aromatic scent.

Speechless, spellbound, the little party looked at the wondrous, beautiful sight. The deadening spell of that narcotic scent was spreading through their veins. Lower and lower slowly sank the moon.

Si Urag fell upon his knees, covered his face with his hands and commenced to mumble a prayer. His action jerked the rope with which he was attached to Dennis and the corporal. With a start the former awoke as from a trance. All the waving pistils were pointing and stretching toward the huddled group. The moon was nearly touching the farther edge of the sky. Soon—soon . . .

"To the right ten paces extend !" Like pistol shots Dennis's words broke in upon the night. Unconsciously, automatically, the police obeyed. Si Urag remained in prayer. "Load !" The one word cut the stillness like a knife. The waving pistils changed their curves—followed the extending men, stretched and strained their blood-red mouths.

"At point-blank—fire !" Six tongues of flame ; one loud and slightly jagged report. Four pistils writhed and twisted in an agony of death. In the flaming golden centre, a jagged hole. The heavy aromatic scent came stealing stronger and stronger from the maimed and riddled centre. The moon just touched the far horizon. Slowly the wondrous flower began to sink, the waters became disturbed, the pistils seemed to shrink.

Si Urag rose from his knees and prayers ; uncovered his ears, over which he had placed his hand at the sound of the report. From Dennis to the corporal he looked

Aird's eyes opened and he sat up with a je...
awake, the chance of a siesta a thing of th...
from his chair, picked up his terai, whist...
descended the zigzag path that led to the off...

A few minutes later he stood by his ...
the perspiration from his forehead. Ther...
trend of thought he had had in the long ...
to a pile of dusty papers that rose three fee...
and picking up a bundle tied with red tape...
desk.

"I wonder," he muttered, as he turned ...
page. "I wonder if that old tale is true. ...
married—if a daughter *were* born whom a...
ever seen ! Surely there'll be some record...
former D.O. !"

The sun set. Dusk gave place to the ...
night. A sentry brought a lamp which he ...
desk. The puny light cast weird shadow...
Still Aird searched on. The pile on the ...
scarcely six inches high. The air was ho...
fingered the corner of a sheet, his brow pud...
The stillness of night lay over the static...
revelry would be at its height. Just for the ...
—peace.

Suddenly there came the most vivid flas...
had ever seen and the most terrific clap of thu...
heard. The paper slipped from Aird's hand...
with others it fell, and they were scattered a...

Aird grumbled annoyance and stooped ...
As he did so he slipped. To save a fall he ...
the unexamined papers gave way under the ...
they slithered, and in their turn scattered ove...
rustling noise which yet just failed to drow...
tiny thud. Aird heard it, and his eyes s...
sought and were held by something bright...
little way apart from the papers, winked up...
dark well-worn boards.

For a long minute he gazed at the winkin...
slowly stooped down again and picked it up...

It lay on his desk beside the lamp, a thin...
liance and delicate beauty, the exquisitely carv...
buckle. Beside it lay a sheet of formal-lo...

in mute and utter supplication. From head to foot he trembled.

Slowly the moon and flower were sinking. One pistil, bigger, stronger, fuller-mouthed than the rest, seemed reluctant to retreat, but pointed and waved at the silent three.

Into his *chawat* Si Urag dived his hand. Quick as lightning he withdrew it. A slash to the right, another to the left, and he was free. A mighty spring, a piercing cry and he hurled himself, as a devotee, into the great ravenous, blood-red mouth. Slowly the pistil curved inward. Over the golden bell-shaped centre it poised. Then it bent its head ; its silver rim distended and then closed. Si Urag was no more.

The moon sank down out of sight ; the wondrous flower with its maddened, fanatical victim slipped beneath the waters of the pool. The stillness of the jungle remained ; the scent of dew-laden earth arose. Darkness—and a memory—surrounded the group of seven.

The tropic sleepiness of 3 p.m. hung over Klagan. Suddenly the chugging of a motor-boat was heard coming from afar upstream. Down to the tiny floating wharf the populace descended, headed by the *serang*. Round the last bend swung the motor-boat, drew alongside the wharf and came to rest. Out of it silently stepped Dennis and the weary police. One of them carried two rifles, which told the wondering people of a death. Two of them supported Si Tuah, which told them a struggle had taken place. Over his features spread a smile as his hands met those of his wife. " 'Twas a near thing, Miang," he murmured, "and it happened at the dead of night. A man with a tail and a golden-purple orchid which he worshipped."

From the people rose a gasp of wonder and cries of disbelief. Then Dennis raised his hand.

"Si Tuah speaks the truth," he said, "but Si Urag of the Tail no longer lives, and the flower no more can blossom. The Fear is dead."

Then unsteadily he walked to his house.

THE GREAT WH

MERVYN AIRD was essentially e
capable district officer and a qui
long chair on the veranda of h
cursed the enforced idleness of thr
proclaimed by Government in h
festival. In view of the holiday, it
district ; no one would wish to se
(district officer) at such a time.
office bare of papers.   His clerks
to infringe their right of three day
insistent enough to find work for
the long chair on his veranda, smo
the future.

The plans forming in his head
thought. He moved restlessly in
sought a roof just visible through
fringed the lower slopes of the hill
was built. The roof made a dark
divided the green of the palms from
sea that formed the waters of Bru
left by a long, low, rocky promonto
The line of the roof and the line of

Aird's gaze followed from the
brow puckered. What if there w
after all ? If the sacred rocks wer
Spirit of the Great White Death ?
at all, but a living woman, as som
the rocks rested the answer to the
and Cranfield's daughter ?

Mervyn Aird's lids drooped
minute and his plans would have turn

From the district office sounded
gong, struck slowly four times by th

ancient district register of marriage, the top right-hand corner
of which was torn.

Aird's eyes travelled as if by instinct from the half-buckle
to the register. No word or movement escaped him as he
read :

Cranfield, John Edward, bachelor.   And underneath, *Martin,*
Mary Enid, spinster.

In silence he read on, tracing with his forefinger the
various columns that were ruled across the page, till at the
extreme right he came to one headed "Nationality". Then
at last a sigh escaped him as his finger came to an abrupt
stop, pointing to the word "British" written twice.

Through the open window the moonlight warred with
the yellow flame of the hurricane lantern. From the smooth
waters of the bay a cooling breeze had sprung up. Suddenly
Aird realized that the hour was late, that he was tired, that
with the settling of the old gnawing doubt reaction had come,
that he had neither bathed nor dined. With an abrupt gesture
he looked at his watch ; the hands pointed to nearly seven
o'clock.

Picking up the half-buckle and torn register, he passed
out of the office, subconsciously answering the sentry's smart
salute, and climbed the hill leading to his house. When near
the top the heavy notes of the office gong flung him once
again into the present with a duty which he must perform.
As district officer he must be present, if only for a brief while,
at the forthcoming native dance.

The riddle, nearly solved, intrigued him ; his eyes
brightened, for he realized to the full what the possibilities
of his discovery might be.

.   .   .   .   .

Aird looked round at the sea of faces that circled the
small patch of earth doing duty as a stage—men's faces
that glistened bright with sweat, out of which shone dark,
fanatical eyes ; women's faces, painted white with lime,
now smudged unevenly into unsightly blotches, yet which
made startling contrasts to eyes alluring, sensuous, slum-
brous, made bright as stars by a secret native juice ; children's
faces, panting with excitement, yet heavy with sleep.

tribe and village would give thanks to its particular deity—
to Allah, to Kinaringan, to the ruling spirits of the rivers and
the sea. Then would follow a solemn presentation to him,
the Tuan ; then sports, and in the evening and far into the
night, a mighty dance.

From the contemplation of the scene he turned to an
aged, wrinkled woman by his side—Pangiran Haji Alimah—
grandmother of the dead Pangiran Piut.

"Well, Mother ?" he said. Between them, when alone,
ceremonious address was always banished. They understood
each other, and to Pangiran Alimah, Aird was as a son.

She took his right hand in both her winkled ones and
carried it to her breast, to her forehead. Then, gently releasing
it, folded both her own upon her breast.

"It is well, Tuan," she answered. "Yet I am afraid.
I love the Tuan, and of my love see deeper than many, and
so I am afraid because . . ." She paused.

"Because ?" Aird questioned.

A smile of inexpressible sadness passed over Pangiran
Alimah's face as she turned away from Aird and gazed towards
the distant corner of the bay, where the sharp lines of Scrip's
Cave broke the merging blues of sky and sea.

"Because, Mother ?" Aird gently repeated.

She turned, and lifting a small leather satchel that hung
by a string of camel's hair round her neck to her lips, answered :

"Because the Tuan of the wisdom and knowledge of the
white man is not content, but ever seeks and digs and probes.
To the Tuan there is no such thing as the Great White Fear ;
but I who am old and have made the pilgrimage know. My
eyes are dim, their beauty is no more, their sparkle dead ;
yet, Tuan, they see deep into the future, whose pages are not
those of a sealed book. For all things are written ; it is ever
so. The cholera is fled, but it will come again. In the bowels
of the earth, in the depth of the sea, on the breath of the wind
it lurks and hides. At the appointed time it will come forth
again and the White Spirit with the four attendant dwarfs
once more appear, and she who the Tuan seeks and loves
shall be his ruin. And so I am afraid."

Aird's hands were gripping the sides of his chair ; his
eyes were riveted on Pangiran Alimah's face.

"You mean ?" he whispered.

"Only that I can see into the Tuan's heart. Throughout

the cholera he has sung, and a light—the light of love—has been in his eyes. The White Spirit, which is no spirit at all, but a woman of flesh and blood, has him in her toils, and we for whom he toiled and whom he loved will count no more."

"Pangiran !" The cry was wrung from Aird, but Pangiran Haji Alimah went on :

"She lives, Tuan, over there among the caves of Serip's rocks"—her wrinkled forefinger pointing to the distant cape ; "and she is evil. She desecrates the holy spot, knowing that none dare turn her out, for the rocks mark the spot where the boat bearing the Serip's remains came to anchor at the setting of the sun, where next morning no boat rocked longer on the tide's ebb and flow, but in its place rose up out of the sea the holy rocks, symbol of man's puny efforts to climb to heaven."

"You say, Pangiran, that she—she lives." Aird could not speak for the emotion that was tearing at his heart.

Again Pangiran Alimah smiled, and again the smile was sad.

"Tuan," she said, "is it not even as I have said ? Is not the Tuan's heart beating but for her ?"

"But—but——" he gasped.

"And she is as beautiful as she is bad." The aged voice was low but strong. "As wise as she is evil, trading on ignorance and beliefs. To all except to me she is a spirit— the Spirit of the Great White Death, that stalks the land instilling in the people the Great White Fear. But I who am old, and have made the pilgrimage, know. She steals and lives upon the offerings and alms of the Tuan's people to the Serip. Tuan, I know, I, Pangiran Haji Alimah binti Pangiran Haji Mahomed, know, yet I will not, cannot, speak—because in the days gone by I nursed her, the daughter of Tuan Cranfield and the unknown memsahib whom he took to his side. A daughter of sin, she is cursed and pays."

Aird, risen from his chair, stood towering over the aged, wrinkled woman. His upraised hand was clenched, his face a frozen mask of anger, yet Pangiran Haji Alimah did not flinch.

On the garden path outside sounded the heavy tread of boots. The native sergeant swung into view. Aird sat down slowly. A cold sweat broke out on his forehead as,

waiting the sergeant's approach, he realized how near he had
been to striking a woman.

· · ·

Breathlessly, silently, Aird waited, his rifle resting lightly
in his hands, his body tense with expectation, his eyes alight
with the zest of a hunter. He was alone—he always hunted
alone, leaving his boys in camp. For two days he had followed
the spoor—tracks of unusual size and deepness—and now by
a curious chance the deer had doubled on its tracks. Nearer
and nearer it came, a magnificent stag, the spread of whose
antlers caused Aird to gasp. At that short range—a hundred
yards—he could not miss the broad chest or forehead.

He raised his rifle ; the butt settled surely in his shoulder ;
his finger curved round the trigger, curved and pressed,
pressed slowly, inexorably. A flash, a report, a puff of smoke.
Aird ran to the spot where the deer had stood when it dropped;
yet when he got there it was gone. He looked around ; the
spoor was faint, for the ground was hard and stony. His ear
caught the slight sound of snapping twigs. He followed.
A little way and the bushes were here and there splashed
with blood. A little farther and blood stained the ground ;
the hoof-marks grew uneven.

Aird quickened his pace as excitement rose. The blood-
stains grew in size and number ; here and there a rock or a
bush was smeared. Aird followed hot-foot, exalted. Those
antlers on his wall—the biggest he had ever seen, the whole
majestic head, a trophy worthy of recall, the end of a glorious,
laborious hunt !

Suddenly the jungle lessened, the light grew and a strange
sound reached his ears—a restless, never-ending sound—the
sound of sea swelling and rolling round rocks. Involuntarily
Aird paused, looked round and listened. As he did so the
sound of weeping broke the deep noise of the sea. Without
a thought Aird ran forward, blindly obeying the instinct of
his race. The stag must wait. Someone—a woman—was
weeping, was in trouble ; all else must wait. The sound of
the sea grew nearer and the jungle thinned. He turned a
corner of the tract, and then stood still.

Before a cave knelt a woman robed in white, whose
flaming hair hung around her like a golden cloak. The

massive antlers of a mighty stag arched over her head like
the candles of an altar arch above the Holy Cross. The
big brown head, with eyes now glazed in death, was held
to her breast. Two arms of purest white encircled the long,
graceful neck. The light of love and pity and horror was
in her eyes from which the tears were flowing on the sad
brown face.

Aird looked. He could not speak or move. He only
trembled. There before him knelt the Spirit of the Great
White Death. Death was in her arms—the arms of the
woman he loved with the madness of his race and faith—
the arms of the woman who had danced that night—the
daughter of Cranfield—daughter of sin, who therefore was
accursed and paid. . . .

Their eyes met.

Her arms released their hold upon the dead stag. Slowly
the great head slid to her knees, to the ground, to fall with a
tiny thud. Aird shivered. On her white robe splashes of
blood appeared; the mighty antlers had torn through the
fabric and pierced her slender form. Her blood! Aird
shivered again. She was the Spirit of the Great White Death
—and she had clasped death in her arms—death which he had
dealt—death which had led him to her at her home on Serip's
Cave.

She rose to her feet, her arms held rigidly to her sides
—a symbol of eternal stillness—death—her flaming golden
hair a mantle to her long white robe backed by the blue of
the endless sky and sea. Eternal Enigma : Woman—Eternal
Power : Death.

"You—thief !"

Aird started. The words, spoken in English though with
a faint Malay intonation, were biting and clear, yet withal
were of a timbre that set his heart beating fast, more from
love than surprise. There was a quality of richness, of conscious pride, which spoke of breeding and race, that found an
immediate echo in his own heart.

Without a thought he raised his soft felt hat and with
bowed head stood speechless before her.

"You—brute !"

Again she spoke ; again Aird kept silent. Then with a
flood of tears she fell across the dead stag's body, murmuring
words of endearment.

The setting sun, about to sink behind the ocean's rim, cast a blood-red shaft of light across her prostrate form. It lengthened till it reached the spot where Aird stood immovable, and bathed him too in its crimson light. Its dying flame held no warmth, yet seemed to scorch the two, awakening them to consciousness.

She raised her head, her body, to her knees. Aird moved towards her.

"Death," she murmured. "Death! Its blood-red flame reaches you too—you who have just dealt death. Why, why did you do it? Was there no other deer, no pig, within your reach, Tuan Aird—but you must slay my soul?"

Aird stumbled; a stone caught in his boot caused him to trip. She put out a hand. He grasped it in his own and raised it to his lips.

"Forgive!" he whispered. "Oh, my love, my love, forgive!"

He drew closer. Slowly she rose to her feet and swayed towards him. One arm, white as the purest alabaster, crept round his neck. He bowed his head. Over the stag's stiff body, cold in death, their warm lips met.

. . . . . .

The sweet music of the *kriedings* filled the cave—distant yet near, pervading yet not persistent. Aird, reclining on a sky-blue mattress, resting against a pile of cushions, looked meditatively at the smouldering end of his last cigarette. From this alone he knew how many days had passed since unconsciously he had found himself on Serip's Cave.

Five days! His strict ration, when hunting, of ten cigarettes a day now finished! Five days of . . . The rustling of a curtain of dried seaweed reached him. He raised his eyes, and Cranfield's daughter stood before him, and the music of the *kriedings* ceased.

"Beloved." The murmur of the sea was in her voice.

He struggled to his feet, but in a swirl of gold and white she reached his side, pressing him back upon the cushions, covering him with her flaming hair, stifling the murmured words with her kisses.

Through a deep embrasure in the rock wall the light of a full moon streamed. As the blood-red sun had scorched them, so now the cold silver light seemed pregnant with a chilly breath. The woman shivered and crept closer yet to Aird.

"Beloved, and all you say is true ?" she whispered.

"True—all true—as true as . . ." Aird was going to say "death", but checked himself in time.

"As ?" She looked him in the eyes.

"As that I love you, Saiang," he quietly answered, stroking her head of flame-gold hair.

"And you have seen the register—read the words ?" Aird nodded.

"There is no need for me longer to live accursed, despised by white and brown—a daughter of sin and shame—a harbinger of death—my hand against all men—my soul in chains —trading on superstition as the Spirit of the Great White Death—no need ?"

"None." Aird spoke the word with all the force at his command. Then he pointed to the silver buckle which she wore, which he had given her, the two halves of which he had found.

"Look, Saiang," he continued. "Look, the lost halves are one, locked in a strong embrace, the complement of each other, making a union perfect in design, unsullied, pure. There is no need, dear heart, for you to be ashamed, I swear."

"And you will take me to your house across the bay, let me sail you there in what I call my phantom boat, *Berballen* ? And show me all ? And you will keep me with you—me, an untamed child—a daughter of the wild—and—and our little children, born of the sun and moon and sea, shall one day clamber on your knees in a gabled house in England, far, far across the sea ? You swear, beloved ?"

Her eyes held his and at her gaze he trembled—trembled with a man's overwhelming primitive desire, for in her eyes was the glad, ever-willing surrender, woman's transcendent gift which, being omnipotent, is yet the ruin of the world.

"I swear."

In the hush of night, in the depth of the Serip's Cave, cradled in the waters of the sphinx-like China Sea, the words, though softly spoken, seemed like a clarion-call.

Aird closed his eyes. Some things there are men dare not see. He shivered. Cramp seized his calves. He stretched his legs, and the sudden pain wrung from him a cry. Two arms stole round his neck ; cool feet caressed his own, burning and on fire. Breath, fragrant as the perfume of the flowers, fanned his hot forehead. Close to his body a form, yielding, delicious, alluring, nestled. Two lips parted and breathed the word "Beloved", then found his in an age-long, momentary kiss.

The moon rode on in an almost starless sky. The dawn of another day broke to the murmur of the sea and the slow, languorous rhythm of the *kriedings*. And Death—the Great White Death itself—met and wrestled with a woman's love.

. . . . .

The phantom boat *Berballen*, flying Aird's flag, drew nearer and nearer to the shore. In its stern, propped up among pillows, his head resting on his love's lap, Mervyn lay weakly. Worn to a shadow, his body a skeleton clothed in skin, with eyes that seemed sunk into the middle of his head, he greedily yet faintly drank in the warmth of the glorious sun. He stirred. With the quickness of a streak of summer lightning Saiang's hand found his : her full red lips pressed closely, lightly, against his, ridged and purple-black and drawn.

"My love." Her voice was as a mermaid's breath, fragrant and faint, yet full of the murmur of the sea.

Aird smiled weakly and turned his head. Her eyes, aflame with shameless love, held his, and once again their lips met.

The boat drew nearer to the shore, whence came the sound of gongs and chanting. Out of the houses, down to the wharf, streamed a laughing crowd of happy people.

Only Pangiran Haji Alimah binti Pangiran Haji Mahomed remained on shore—alone in her house. She knew, and she was afraid. The wind was lessening, and its faint breath grew cold—cold as Death. The phantom boat was *bethantu** the woman of Serip's Cave accursed ; the Tuan Pegawei had forgotten his people.

The boat drew nearer, riding so lightly and mysteriously upon the water that it left no wake. The sail flapped in the lessening breeze, flapped and hung still ; yet *Berballen* glided on and nearer, till her gunwale almost scraped the timbers of the wharf.

---

* Haunted.

A mighty shout went ringing to the sky, cloudless and blue, yet somehow pitiless in its immeasurable immensity.

"The Tuan, the Tuan! The Tuan has come back at last. Allah is wonderful! Allah be praised!"

Pangiran Haji Alimah heard the cries, and a twisted smile crept over her aged face as she waited.

Then came the realization of her fears.

The cries of joy turned to cries of wonder, of surprise, of disappointment, then of fear. The sail filled faintly, as a breeze stirred, bearing an odour of decay and death. *Berballen* glided on, on past the wharf, on and out to sea, where on the horizon, faint yet definite and foreboding, dark clouds were scudding, gathering, growing larger, nearer.

Berballen glided on. Mervyn neither moved nor spoke. The woman looked at him. Then she understood, and a great cry of anguish rent the air. Love was dead. But in its death Love triumphed, for it killed the Great White Fear.

The woman took Mervyn in her arms, straining his cold, tortured body to her own, warm and glowing. But Death made no response.

The boat was gathering speed, the wind was freshening and the clouds coming up apace. The people on the wharf were silent, amazed. Then they fell upon their knees and covered their eyes as two figures balanced for one dizzy moment on the gunwale of the haunted boat. . . .

Then the storm broke and *Berballen* was no more.

BOOMERANG

WARWICK threw himself into a chair beside me, hitched up his trousers, and, leaning across, tapped me on the knee.

"You remember the story about Mendingham which you told me ?" he asked.

I nodded. I was not likely to forget that affair.

"Well," he went on, "I've got as good a one to tell you. Had it straight from the filly's mouth, so to speak—and it's red-hot."

I edged away in my chair, for there was something positively ghoulish in his delight, in the coarse way in which he referred to a woman, and one who, if my inference were correct, must have known tragedy. But there is no stopping Warwick: he knows or admits no finer feelings or shame when his thirst for "copy" is aroused. Like the little boy in the well-known picture, "he won't be happy till he's 'quenched' it".

I ordered drinks, and when they had been served and we were alone, bade him get on with his sordid story.

"It's a wild tale," he began, "of two planter fellows in the interior of Borneo—and, as usual, there's a woman."

"*The* woman ?" I could not refrain from asking, thinking of his earlier remark.

"The same," he replied. "A veritable golden-haired filly, only her mane is streaked with grey and there's a great livid scar or weal right round her neck. She's the wife of Leopold Thring. The other end of the triangle is Clifford Macy."

"And where do you come in ?" I inquired.

Warwick closed one eye and pursed his lips.

"As a spinner of yarns," he answered sententiously. Then, with a return to his usual cynicism, "The filly is down and out, but for some silly religious scruples feels she must

live. I bought the story, therefore, after verifying the facts.
Shall I go on ?"

I nodded, for I must admit I was genuinely interested.
The eternal triangle always intrigues : set in the wilds of
Borneo it promised a variation of incident unusually refresh-
ing in these sophisticated days. Besides, that scar was
eloquent.

Warwick chuckled.

"The two men were partners," he went on, "on a small
experimental estate far up in the interior. They had been at
it for six years and were just about to reap the fruits of their
labours very handsomely. Incidentally, Macy had been out
in the Colony the full six years—and the strain was beginning
to tell. Thring had been home eighteen months before, and
on coming back had brought his bride, Rhona.

"That was the beginning of the trouble. It split up the
partnership : brought in a new element : meant the building
of a new bungalow."

"For Macy ?" I asked.

"Yes. And he didn't take kindly to it. He had got
set. And then there was the loneliness of night after night
alone, while the others—you understand ?"

I nodded.

"Well," Warwick continued, "the expected happened.
Macy flirted, philandered, and then fell violently in love.
He was one of those fellows who never do things by halves.
If he drank, he'd get fighting drunk : if he loved, he went
all out on it : if he hated, well, hell was let loose."

"And—Mrs. Thring ?" I queried, for it seemed to me
that she might have a point of view.

"Fell between two stools—as so many women of a certain
type do. She began by being just friendly and kind—you
know the sort of thing—cheering the lonely man up, drifted
into woman's eternal game of flirting, and then began to
grow a little afraid of the fire she'd kindled. Too late she
realized that she couldn't put the fire out—either hers or
Macy's—and all the while she clung to some hereditary
religious scruples.

"Thring was in many ways easygoing, but at the same
time possessed of a curiously intense strain of jealous posses-
siveness. He was generous, too. If asked, he would share
or give away his last shirt or crust. But let him think or feel

that his rights or dues were being curtailed or taken and—
well, he was a tough customer of rather primitive ideas.

"Rhona—that's the easiest way to think of the filly—
soon found she was playing a game beyond her powers.
Hers was no poker face, and Thring began to sense that
something was wrong. She couldn't dissemble, and Macy
made no attempt to hide his feelings. He didn't make it
easy for her, and I guess from what the girl told me, life
about this time was for her a sort of glorified hell—a suspicious
husband on one hand, and an impetuous, devil-may-care
lover on the other. She was living on a volcano."

"Which might explode any minute," I quietly nodded.
Warwick nodded.

"Exactly; or whenever Thring chose to spring the mine.
He held the key to the situation, or, should I say, the time-
fuse? The old story, but set in a primitive land full of
possibilities. You've got me?"

For answer, I offered Warwick a cigarette, and, taking
one myself, lighted both.

"So far," I said, "with all your journalistic skill you've
not got off the beaten track. Can't you improve?"

He chuckled, blew a cloud of smoke, and once again
tapped my knee in his irritating manner.

"Your cynicism," he countered, "is but a poor cloak for
your curiosity. In reality you're jumping mad to know the
end, eh?"

I made no reply, and he went on.

"Well, matters went on from day to day till Rhona became
worn to the proverbial shadow. Thring wanted to send her
home, but she wouldn't go. She owed a duty to her husband :
she couldn't bear to be parted from her lover, and she didn't
dare leave the two men alone. She was terribly, horribly afraid.

"Macy grew more and more openly amorous and less
restrained. Thring watched whenever possible with the
cunning of an iguana. Then came a rainy, damp spell that
tried nerves to the uttermost and the inevitable stupid little
disagreements between Rhona and Thring—mere trifles, but
enough to let the lid off. He challenged her——."

"And she?" I could not help asking, for Warwick has,
I must admit, the knack of keeping one on edge.

"Like a blithering but sublime little idiot admitted that
it was all true."

For nearly a minute I was speechless. Somehow, although underneath I had expected Rhona to behave so, it seemed such a senseless, unbelievable thing to do. Then at last I found my voice.

"And Thring?" I said simply.

Warwick emptied his glass at a gulp.

"That's the most curious thing in the whole yarn," he answered slowly. "Thring took it as quietly as a lamb."

"Stunned?" I suggested.

"That's what Rhona thought: what Macy believed when Rhona told him what had happened. In reality he must have been burning mad, a mass of white-hot revenge controlled by a devilish, cunning brain : he waited. A scene or a fight—and Macy was a big man—would have done no good. He would get his own back in his own time and in his own way. Meanwhile, there was the lull before the storm.

"Then, as so often happens, Fate played a hand. Macy went sick with malaria—really ill—and even Thring had to admit the necessity for Rhona to nurse him practically night and day. Macy owed his eventual recovery to her care, but even so his convalescence was a long job. In the end Rhona too crocked up through overwork, and Thring had them both on his hands. This was an opportunity better than he could have planned—it separated the lovers and gave him complete control.

"Obviously the time was ripe, ripe for Thring to score his revenge.

"The rains were over, the jungle had ceased wintering, and spring was in the air. The young grass and vegetation were shooting into new life : concurrently all the creepy, crawly insect life of the jungle and estate was young and vigorous and hungry too. These facts gave Thring the germ of an idea which he was not slow to perfect—an idea as devilish as man could devise."

Warwick paused to press out the stub of his cigarette, and noticing that even he seemed affected by his recital, I prepared myself as best I could for a really gruesome horror. All I said, however, was, "Go on."

"It seems," he continued, "that in Borneo there is a kind of mammoth earwig—a thing almost as fine and gossamer as a spider's web, as long as a good-sized caterpillar, that lives on waxy secretions. These are integral parts of some flowers and trees, and lie buried deep in their recesses. It is one of the terrors of these particular tropics, for it moves and rests so lightly on a human being that one is practically unconscious of it, while, like its English relation, it has a decided liking for the human ear : on account of man's carnivorous diet the wax in this has a strong and very succulent taste."

As Warwick gave me those details, he sat upright on the edge of his easy chair. He spoke slowly, emphasizing each point by hitting the palm of his left hand with the clenched fist of his right. It was impossible not to see the drift and inference of his remarks.

"You mean——?" I began.

"Exactly," he broke in quickly, blowing a cloud of smoke from a fresh cigarette which he had nervously lighted. "Exactly. It was a devilish idea. To put the giant earwig on Macy's hair just above the ear."

"And then . . .?" I knew the fatuousness of the question, but speech relieved the growing sense of ticklish horror that was creeping over me.

"Do nothing. But rely on the filthy insect running true to type. Once in Macy's ear, it was a thousand-to-one chance against it ever coming out the same way : it would not be able to turn : to back out would be almost an impossibility, and so, feeding as it went, it would crawl right across inside his head, with the result that——"

The picture Warwick was drawing was more than I could bear : even my imagination, dulled by years of legal dryasdust affairs, saw and sickened at the possibilities. I put out a hand and gripped Warwick's arm.

"Stop, man !" I cried hoarsely. "For God's sake, don't say any more. I understand. My God, but the man Thring must be a fiend !"

Warwick looked at me, and I saw that even his face had paled.

"*Was*," he said meaningly. "Perhaps you're right, perhaps he *was* a fiend. Yet, remember, Macy stole his wife."

"But a torture like that ! The deliberate creation of a living torment that would grow into madness. Warwick, you can't condone that !"

He looked at me for a moment and then slowly spread out his hands.

"Perhaps you're right," he admitted. "It was a bit thick, I know. But there's more to come."

I closed my eyes and wondered if I could think of an excuse for leaving Warwick; but in spite of my real horror, my curiosity won the day.

"Get on with it," I muttered, and leant back, eyes still shut, hands clenched. With teeth gritted together as if I myself were actually suffering the pain of that earwig slowly, daily creeping farther into and eating my brain, I waited.

Warwick was not slow to obey.

"I have told you," he said, "that Rhona had to nurse Macy, and even when he was better, though still weak, Thring insisted on her looking after him, though now he himself came more often.

"One afternoon Rhona was in Macy's bungalow alone with him : the house-boy was out. Rhona was on the verandah : Macy was asleep in the bedroom. Dusk was just falling : bats were flying about : the flying foxes, heavy with fruit, were returning home : the inevitable house rats were scurrying about the floors : the lamps had not been lit. An eerie devastating hour. Rhona dropped some needlework and fought back tears. Then from the bedroom came a shriek. 'My head ! My ear ! Oh, God ! My ear ! Oh, God ! The pain !'

"That was the beginning. The earwig had got well inside. Rhona rushed in and did all she could. Of course, there was nothing to see. Then for a little while Macy would be quiet because the earwig was quiet, sleeping or gorged. Then the vile thing would move or feed again, and Macy once more would shriek with the pain.

"And so it went on, day by day. Alternate quiet and alternate pain, each day for Macy, for Rhona a hell of nerve-rending expectancy. Waiting, always waiting for the pain that crept and crawled and twisted and writhed and moved slowly, ever slowly, through and across Macy's brain."

Warwick paused so long that I was compelled to open my eyes. His face was ghastly. Fortunately I could not see my own.

"And Thring ?" I asked.

"Came often each day. Pretended sorrow and served out spurious dope—Rhona found the coloured water afterwards. He cleverly urged that Macy should be carried down to the coast for medical treatment, knowing full well that he was too ill and worn to bear the smallest strain. Then when Macy was an utter wreck, broken completely in mind and body, with hollow, hunted eyes, with ever-twitching fingers, with a body no part of which he could properly control or keep still, the earwig came out—at the other ear.

"As it happened, both Thring and Rhona were present. Macy must have suffered an excruciating pain, followed as usual by a period of quiescence : then, feeling a slight ticklish sensation on his cheek put up his hand to rub or scratch. His fingers came in contact with the earwig and its fine gossamer hairs. Instinct did the rest. You follow ?"

My tongue was still too dry to enable me to speak. Instead I nodded, and Warwick went on.

"He naturally was curious and looked to see what he was holding. In an instant he realized. Even Rhona could not be in doubt. The hairs were faintly but unmistakably covered here and there with blood, with wax and with grey matter.

"For a moment there was absolute silence between the three. At last Macy spoke.

" 'My God !' he just whispered. 'Oh, my God ! What an escape !'

"Rhona burst into tears. Only Thring kept silent, and that was his mistake. The silence worried Macy, weak though he was. He looked from Rhona to Thring, and at the critical moment Thring could not meet his gaze. The truth was out. With an oath Macy threw the insect, now dead from the pressure of his fingers, straight into Thring's face. Then he crumpled up in his chair and sobbed and sobbed till even the chair shook."

Again Warwick paused till I thought he would never go on. I had heard enough, I'll admit, and yet it seemed to me that at least there should be an epilogue.

"Is that all ?" I tentatively asked.

Warwick shook his head.

"Nearly, but not quite," he said. "Rhona had ceased weeping and kept her eyes fixed on Thring—she dared not go and comfort Macy now. She saw him examine the dead earwig, having picked it up from the floor to which it had fallen, turn it this way and that, then produce from a pocket a magnifying-glass which he used daily for the inspection and

detection of leaf disease on certain of the plants. As she
watched, she saw the fear and disappointment leave his face,
to be replaced by a look of cunning and evil satisfaction. Then
for the first time he spoke.

" 'Macy l' he called, in a sharp, loud voice.

"Macy looked up.

"Thring held up the earwig. 'This is dead, now,' he said,
—'dead. As dead a my friendship for you, you swine of a
thief, as dead as my love for that whore who was my wife.
It's dead, I tell you, dead, but it's a female. D'you get me ?
A female, and a female lays eggs, and before it died, it——'

"He never finished. His baiting at last roused Macy,
endowing him with the strength of madness and despair.
With one spring he was at Thring's throat, bearing him down
to the ground. Over and over they rolled on the floor,
struggling for possession of the great hunting-knife stuck in
Thring's belt. One moment Macy was on top, the next,
Thring. Their breath and oaths came in great trembling
gasps. They kicked and bit and scratched. And all the
while Rhona watched, fascinated and terrified. Then Thring
got definitely on top. He had one hand on Macy's throat,
both knees on his chest, and with his free hand he was feeling
for the knife. In that instant Rhona's religious scruples went
by the board. She realized she only loved Macy, that her
husband didn't count. She rushed to Macy's help. Thring
saw her coming and let drive a blow at her head which almost
stunned her. She fell on top of him just as he was whipping
out the knife. Its edge caught her neck. The sudden spurt
of blood shot into Thring's eyes, and blinded him. It was
Macy's last chance. He knew it, and he took it.

"When Rhona came back to consciousness, Thring was dead.
Macy was standing beside the body, which was gradually
swelling to huge proportions as he worked, weakly but
steadily, at the white ant exterminator pump, the nozzle of
which was pushed down the dead man's throat."

Warwick ceased. This last had been a long, unbroken
recital, and mechanically he picked up his empty glass as if
to drain it. The action brought me back to nearly normal.
I rang for the waiter—the knob of the electric bell luckily
being just over my head. While waiting, I had time to
speak.

"I've heard enough," I said hurriedly, "to last me a

lifetime. You've made me feel positively sick. But there's just one point. What happened to Macy? Did he live?"

Warwick nodded.

"That's another strange fact. He still lives. He was tried for the murder of Thring, but there was no real evidence. On the other hand, his story was too tall to be believed, with the result—well, you can guess."

"A lunatic asylum—for life?" I asked.

Warwick nodded again. Then I followed his glance. A waiter was standing by my chair.

"Two double whisky-and-sodas," I ordered tersely, and then, with shaking fingers, lighted a cigarette.

OLIVER ONIONS

TWO TRIFLES

THE ETHER-HOGS

I

WITH one foot thrust into an angle to brace himself against the motion of the ship, the twin telephone-receivers about his head, and one hand on the transmitting key, while the other hovered over screws and armatures, the young wireless operator was trying to get into tune. He had had the pitch, but had either lost it again, or else something had gone wrong on the ship from which that single urgent call had come. The pear-shaped incandescent light made cavernous shadows under his anxiously drawn brows; it shone harshly on dials and switchboards, on bells and coils, and milled screws and tubes; and the whole white-painted room now heeled slowly over this way, and then steeved as violently back the other, as the liner rolled to the storm.

The operator seemed to be able to get any ship except the one he wanted. As a keyed-up violin-string answers to tension after tension, or as if a shell held to the ear should sing, not one Song of the Sea, but a multitude, so he fluctuated through level after level of the diapason of messages that the installation successively picked up. They were comically various, had the young operator's face not been so ghastly anxious and set. "Merry Christmas . . . the *Doric* . . . buy Erie Railroads . . . Merry Christmas . . . overland from Marseilles . . . closing price copper . . . good night . . . Merry Christmas"—the night hummed with messages as a telephone exchange hums; and many decks overhead, and many scores of feet above that again, his own antennæ described vast loops and arcs in the wintry sky, and from time to time spoke with a roar that gashed the night.

But of all the confusion of intercourse about him, what

follows is a Conference that the young wireless operator did *not* hear.

The spirits of the Special Committee on Ethereal Traffic and Right of Way were holding an Extraordinary General Meeting. They were holding it because the nuisance had finally become intolerable. Mortal messages tore great rents through space with such a reckless disregard of the Ethereal Regulations that not a ghost among them was safe. A spectre would be going peacefully about his haunting ; there would come one of these radio-telegraphic blasts ; and lo, his essence would be shattered into fragments, which could only be reassembled after the hideous racket had passed away.

And by haunting they meant, not merely the old-fashioned terrorizing by means of white sheets and clanking fetters, nor yet only the more modern forms of intimidation that are independent of the stroke of midnight and the crowing of the first cock, but also benigner suggestions—their gentle promptings to the poets of the world, their whispered inspirations to its painters, their care for the integrity of letters, their impulses to kindliness, their spurs to bravery, and, in short, any other noble urging that earth-dwellers know, who give their strength and labour for the unprofitable things they believe without ever having seen them.

A venerable spirit with a faint aura of silver beard still clinging about him spoke.

"I think we are agreed something must be done," he said. "Even now, one of the most amiable junior ghosts of my acquaintance, on his way with a *motif* to a poor, tired musician, was radio'd into flinders, and though his own essence is not permanently harmed, his inspiration was shocked quite out of him, and may never be recovered again."

"That is so," another bore witness. "I happened to be projecting myself not far from the spot, and saw the whole occurrence—poor fellow, he had no chance whatever to escape. It was one of these 'directive' messages, as they call them, and no ghost of his grade could have stood up for a moment against it."

"But it is the universal messages, sent out equally in all directions, that are the most serious menace to our state," another urged.

"Quite so. We have a chance of getting out of the way of the directive ones, but the others leave us no escape."

"Look—there goes one now," said another, suddenly pointing; "luckily it's far enough away."

There was an indignant clamour.

"Vandals !" "Huns !" "Hooligans !" "Shame !"

Then a female spirit spoke. It was known that she owed her condition to a motor accident on earth.

"I remember a name the grosser ones used to have for those who exceeded the speed limit in their motor-cars. They were called road-hogs. In the same way the creators of these disturbances ought to be called ether-hogs."

There was applause at this, which the young wireless operator, still seeking his pitch, mistook for the general radio-commotion about him.

"Yes," the female spirit went on (she had always been a little garrulous under encouragement), "I was afflicted with deafness, and in that horrible instrument they call an Insurance Policy I had to pay an extra premium on that account ; dear, dear, the number of times my heart jumped into my mouth as their cars whizzed by !"

But at this point two attendant spirits, whose office it was, gently but firmly "damped" her, that is, merged into her and rarefied her astral coherence ; they had heard her story many, many times before. The deliberations continued.

Punitive measures were resolved on. With that the question arose, of whom were they to make an example ?

"Take a survey," said the spirit with the aura of silver beard ; and a messenger was gone, and immediately back again, with the tidings that at that very moment a young operator, in an admirably susceptible condition of nerves, was seeking to compass a further outrage.

"Good !" said the venerable one, dismissing his minion again. "We have now to decide who shall haunt him. The Chair invites suggestions."

Now the selection of a haunter is always a matter for careful thought. Not every ghost can haunt everybody. Indeed, the superior attenuations have often difficulty in manifesting themselves at all, so that in practice a duller spirit becomes their deputy. Thus it is only the less ghostly ghosts we of earth know, those barely yet weaned from the breast of the world, and that is the weakness of haunting from the ghostly point of view. The perfect message must go through the imperfect channel. The great ghosts may plan, but the coarser ones execute.

But as this is not unknown on earth also, we need hardly dwell on it.

Now the Committee had no more redoubtable haunter in certain respects than it had in the spirit of an old Scottish engineer, who had suffered translation in the middle days of steam. True, they had to watch him rather carefully, for he had more than once been suspected of having earthly hankerings and regrets ; but that, a demerit in one sense, meant added haunting-efficacy in another, and no less a spirit than Vanderdecken himself had recommended him for a certain class of seafaring commission. He was bidden to appear, and his errand was explained to him.

"You understand," they said a little severely when all had been made clear. "Your instructions are definite, remember, and you are not to exceed them."

"Ay, ay, sir," said that blunt ghost. "I kenned sail, and I kenned steam, and I ha' sairved on a cable-ship. Ye canna. dae better than leave a' tae me."

There was the ring, at any rate, of sincere intention in his tone, and they were satisfied.

"Very well," said the presiding spirit. "You know where to find him. Be off."

"Ay, ay, sir—dinna fash yersel'—I'll gi'e the laddie a twisting !"

But at that moment a terrific blast from the Cape Cod Station scattered the meeting as if it had been blown from the muzzle of a gun.

And you are to understand that the foregoing took no time at all, as earthly time is reckoned.

II

"Oh, get out of my way, you fool ! I want the ship that called me five minutes ago—the *Bainbridge*. Has she called you ? . . . O Lord, here's another lunatic—wants to know who's won the prizefight ! Are you the *Bainbridge* ? Then buzz off ! . . . You there—have you had a call from the *Bainbridge* ? Yes, five minutes ago ; I think she said she was on fire, but I'm not sure, and I can't get her note again !

You try—shove that Merry Christmas fool out—— B-a-i-n
. . . No, but I think—I say I think—she said so—perhaps
she can't transmit any more. . . ."

Dot, dash—dot, dash—dot, dash——

Again he was running up and down the gamut, seeking
the ship that had given him that flickering, uncertain message,
and then—silence.

A ship on fire—somewhere——

He was almost certain she had said she was on fire——

And perhaps she could no longer transmit——

Anyway, half a dozen ships were trying for her now.

It was at this moment, when the whole stormy night
throbbed with calls for the *Bainbridge*, that the ghost came
to make an example of the young wireless operator for the
warning of Ethereal Trespassers at large.

Indeed, the ships were making an abominable racket.
The Morse tore from the antennæ through the void, and if a
homeless spectre missed one annihilating wavelength he
encountered another. They raged. What was the good of
their being the Great Majority if they were to be bullied by
a mortal minority with these devastating devices at its
command ?

Even as that ghostly avenger, in a state of imminent
precipitation, hung about the rocking operating-room, he
felt himself racked by disintegrating thrills. The young
operator's fingers were on the transmitting key again.

"Can't you get the *Bainbridge* ? Oh, try, for God's sake !
. . . Are you there ? Nothing come through yet ? . . .
Doric. Can't you couple ? . . ."

Lurch, heave ; crest, trough ; a cant to port, an angle of
forty-five degrees to starboard ; on the vessel drove, with the
antennæ high overhead describing those dizzy loops and
circles and rending the night with the sputtering Morse.

Dot, dash—dot, dash—dot, dash . . .

But already that old ghost, who in his day had known sail
and steam and had served on a cable-ship, had hesitated even
on the brink of manifestation. He knew that he was only a
low-grade ghost, charged rather than trusted with an errand,
and their own evident mistrust of him was not a thing greatly
to strengthen his allegiance to them. He began to remember
his bones and blood, and his past earthly passion for his job.
He had been a fine engineer, abreast of all the knowledge of his

day, and what he now saw puzzled him exceedingly. By
virtue of his instantaneousness and ubiquity, he had already
taken a complete conspectus of the ship. Much that he had
seen was new, more not. The engines were more powerful,
yet essentially the same. In the stokeholds, down the inter-
minable escalades, all was much as it had formerly been. Of
electric lighting he had seen more than the beginnings, so
that the staring incandescents were no wonder to him, and on
the liner's fripperies of painted and gilded saloons and
gymnasium and staterooms and swimming-baths he had
wasted little attention. And yet even in gathering himself
for visibility he had hesitated. He tried to tell himself why
he did so. He told himself that, formidable haunter as he
was, it is no easy matter to haunt a deeply preoccupied man.
He told himself that he would be able to haunt him all the
more soundly did he hold off for awhile and find the hauntee's
weak spot. He told himself that his superiors (a little con-
descending and sniffy always) had after all left a good deal to
his discretion. He told himself that, did he return with his
errand unaccomplished, they would at all events be no worse
off than they had been before.

In a word, he told himself all the things that we mere
mortals tell ourselves when we want to persuade ourselves
that our inclinations and our consciences are one and the
same thing.

And in the meantime he was peering and prying about a
little moving band of wires that passed round two wooden
pulleys geared to a sort of clock, with certain coils of wire
and a couple of horseshoe magnets, the whole attached to the
telephone clasped about the young ether-hog's head. He
was tingling to know what the thing was for.

It was, of course, the Detector, the instrument's vital ear.

Then the young man's finger began to tap on the transmitter key again.

"*Doric* . . . Anything yet? . . . You're the *Imperator*?
. . . Are you calling the *Bainbridge*?"

Now the ghost, who could not make head or tail of the
Detector, nevertheless knew Morse; and though it had not
yet occurred to him to squeeze himself in between the operator's
ears and the telephone receiver, he read the transmitted message.
Also he saw the young man's strained and sweating face.
He wanted some ship—the *Bainbridge*; from the corrugations

of his brows, a grid in the glare of the incandescent, and the glassy set of his eyes, he wanted her badly ; and so apparently did those other ships whose mysterious apparatus harrowed the fields of ether with long and short . . .

Moreover, on board a ship again that wistful old ghost felt himself at home—or would do so could he but grasp the operations of that tapping key, of that air-wire that barked, and oscillated overhead, and of that slowly moving endless band that passed over the magnets and was attached to the receivers about the young ether-hog's ears.

Whatever they thought of him who had sent him, he *had* been a person of no small account on earth, and a highly skilled mechanic into the bargain.

Suddenly he found himself in temptation's grip. He didn't want to haunt this young man. If he did, something might go wrong with that unknown instrument, and then they might not get this ship they were hunting through the night.

And if he could only ascertain *why* they wanted her so badly, it would be the simplest thing in space for a ghost to find her.

Then, as he nosed about the Detector, it occurred to him to insinuate a portion of his imponderable fabric between the receiver and the young man's ear.

The next moment he had started resiliently back again, as like pole repels like pole of the swinging needle. He was trembling as no radio-message had ever set him trembling yet.

Fire ! A ship on fire ! . . .

That was why these friendly young engineers and operators were blowing a lot of silly ghosts to smithereens ! . . .

The *Bainbridge*—on fire ! . . .

What did all the ghosts of the universe matter if a ship was on fire ?

That faithless emissary did not hesitate for an instant. The ghostly Council might cast him out if they liked ; he didn't care ; they should be hogged till Doomsday if, on all the seas of the world, a single ship were on fire ! A ship on fire ? He had once seen a ship on fire, and didn't want, even as a ghost, to see another.

Even while you have been reading this he was off to find the *Bainbridge*.

Of course he hadn't really to go anywhere to find her at all. Low-class and ill-conditioned ghost as he was, he still had that property of ubiquity. An instantaneous double change in his own tension and he was there and back again, with the *Bainbridge's* bearings, her course, and the knowledge that it was still not too late. The operator was listening in an agony into the twin receivers; a thrill of thankfulness passed through the ghost that he had not forgotten the Morse he had learned on the cable-ship. Swiftly he precipitated himself into a point of action on the transmitter key.

Long, short—long, short—long, short . . .

The operator heard. He started up as if he had been hogged himself. His eyes were staring, his mouth horridly open. What was the matter with his instrument?

Long, short—long, short—long, short . . .

It was not in the telephone. The young man's eyes fell on his own transmitter key. It was clicking up and down. He read out *"Bainbridge"*, and a bearing, and of course his instrument was spelling it out to the others.

Feverishly he grabbed the telephone.

Already the *Doric* was acknowledging. So was the *Imperator*.

He had sent no message. . . .

Yet, though it made him a little sick to think of it, he would let it stand. If one ship were fooled, all would be fooled. At any rate, he did not think he had dreamed that *first* call, that first horrifying call of *"Bainbridge—fire!"*

He sprang to the tube and called up the bridge.

They picked them up from the *Bainbridge's* boats towards the middle of Christmas morning; but that unrepentant, old seafaring spectre, returning whence he had come, gave little satisfaction to his superiors. Against all their bullying he was proof; he merely repeated doggedly over and over again, "The laddie's nairves o' steel! Ower and ower again I manifested mysel' tae him, but it made na mair impression on him than if I'd tried to ha'nt Saturn oot o' his Rings! It's my opeenion that being a ghaistie isna what it was. They hae ower mony new-fangled improvements in these days."

But his spectral heart was secretly sad because he had not been able to make head or tail of the Detector.

THE MORTAL

I

"Oh, Egbert," the White Lady implored, "let me beg of you to abandon this mad, wicked idea!"

Sir Egbert the Dauntless was in the act of passing himself through the wainscot of the North Gallery; he turned, half on this side of the panel, half already in the Priest's Hole in the thickness of the wall.

"No, Rowena," he replied firmly. "You saw fit to cast doubts upon my courage before all the Family Ancestors, and now I intend to do it. If anything happens to me my essence will be upon your head."

The Lady Rowena wailed. In her agitation she clasped her hands awry, so that they interpenetrated.

"Nay, Egbert, I did but jest! On earth you were known as the Dauntless; our descendants are proud of you; cannot you forget my foolish words?"

"No," replied Sir Egbert sternly. "Though it cost me my Non-existence I will spend the night in a Human Chamber!"

"Egbert—Egbert—stay—not *that* one—*not* the Parson's! Think—should he exorcise you——!"

"Too late; I have spoken!" said Sir Egbert, with an abrupt wave of his hand. He vanished into the Fifth Dimension. No sooner had he done so than the general lamentation broke out.

"Oh, he'll Be, he'll Be, I *know* he'll Be!" the White Lady sobbed.

To be re-confined in Matter, so that there is no speech save with a tongue and no motion save with limbs—to be once more subject to the Three Dimensions of the grosser life— is the final menace to the spectral Condition.

"Poor chap—I fancied I detected a trace of Visibility about him already," grim Sir Hugo muttered.

"Oh, it's playing with Flesh!" another cried, with a shiver.

"Almost Human folly!"

"Already his glide isn't what it was," said the melancholy Lady Annice, who on Earth had been a famous attender at funerals.

"I shall never behold his dear Aura again," moaned the White Lady, already half opaque herself. "It will be the Existence of me!"

"If only it had not been a Parson's Chamber," said the Lady Annice, with mournful relish.

"Here—catch her quick—she's solidifying!" half a dozen of them cried at once.

It was with difficulty that they brought the White Lady even to a state of semi-evaporation again.

II

It was midnight, and the Parson snored. He turned uneasily in his sleep. Perhaps already he was conscious of Sir Egbert's presence.

Sir Egbert himself dared approach no nearer to the Mortal Bed than the lattice. Fear had given him the pink gossamer look that is the perilous symptom of veins and blood, and he knew that he received faintly the criss-crossed shadow of the lattice. To save his Nonentity he could not have glided up the shaft of moonlight that streamed in at the window.

Suddenly a violent Hertzian Wave passed through Sir Egbert's ether. He jumped almost clear out of his Dimension. The Parson had opened his eyes. To Be or not to Be? Had he seen him?

He had. His horrible embodied eyes were on the poor harmless Spectre. The two looked at one another, the one quailing in the moonlight, the other sitting in all the horror of Solidity bolt upright in bed.

Then the Mortal began to practise his fearsome devices.

First he gave the hoarse cry that all ghosts dread, and Sir Egbert felt himself suddenly heavier by a pound. But he remembered his name—the Dauntless. He would not yield.

Then the Parson's teeth began to chatter. He gibbered, and Sir Egbert wondered whether this was the beginning of the Exorcism. If it was, he would never see the happy old Ancestral Gallery again, never hold his dear Rowena in perfect interpermeation again—never pass himself through a Solid again—never know again the jolly old lark of being nowhere and everywhere at once.

"Mercy, mercy !" he tried to cry ; and indeed his voice all but stirred the palpable air.

But there was no mercy in that grisly Parson. His only reply was to shoot the hair up on his head, straight on end.

Then he protruded his eyes.

Then he grinned.

And then he began to talk, as it were, the deaf and dumb alphabet on his fingers.

Sir Egbert's semi-Substance was like reddish ground glass ; it was the beginning of the agony. How near to the Mortal Precipitation he was he knew when suddenly he found himself thinking, almost with fright, of his own dear White Lady. *She was a Ghost.*

Then the Mortal began to gabble words. It was the Exorcism.

Oh, why, why, why had Sir Egbert not chosen a Layman ?

The gabbling continued. Colour—warmth—weight— these settled down on Sir Egbert the Dauntless. He half Was. And as he continued steadily to Become, the words increased in speed. Sir Egbert's feet felt the floor ; he cried ; a faint windy moan came. The Parson bounded a foot up on the bed and tossed his pillow into the air.

Could nothing save Sir Egbert ?

Ah yes. They that lead a meek and blameless Non-existence shall not be cast down ; they shall not be given over at last to the terrors of the Solid and Known. From somewhere outside in the moonlight there came a shrill sound.

It was the crowing of a Cock.

The Parson had had the pillow over his face. It fell, and he looked again.

Nothing was there.

Sir Egbert, back in his comfortable Fourth Dimension, was of the loved indivisible texture of his dear White Lady again

THE SMILE OF KAREN

(To June)

I

ALTHOUGH the sleigh had come to a standstill, I do not think that half the people in it had any idea of what was happening. All that they seemed to hear, besides their own cheerful voices, was the dull rush of the torrent below and a little clamour of bells whenever a horse moved his head. But another sound, a leisurely "Cric-crac, cric-cric", had seemed to me to grow more formidable every moment, and I had climbed out of the sleigh and was watching the man who was the cause of it.

We could hardly have come upon the timber-cart at a more perilous spot. The road at that point, besides being deep in snow, was not more than ten feet wide, and the timber-cart had the right to the inside berth, the one with the sheer face of precipitous rock that seemed to rise to the skies. Only a low parapet separated the sleigh from the abyss of tree-tops below. The problem was how to pass.

The largest tree was sixty feet if it were an inch, and if that could be cleared all would be well. It was against the tree that the young man in the velvet jacket and voluminous corduroys had set the jack. Without haste, a pound or so at a time, he was slowly pumping power into it, with the wall of rock to take the resistance. I learned soon enough that he could neither read nor write. This that he was doing was his revelation of himself, his signature upon the world. A slip of the jack, a fragment of ice, a faltering of the man's nerve, and there was no second chance. He knew it, and he, his task, and the way he set himself to it, made on me an impression of fatalistic beauty that has never left me.

Imperceptibly, relentlessly, the tree became bowed like a

163

catapult. At every grind it gave on the rock's face my heart
leaped into my mouth. But he only stepped back once or
twice to see how much more there was to do, and then bent
to the ratchet again. The handsome black brows under the
black wideawake were hardly knitted.

"Cric-cric, cric-cric, cric-cric. . . ." Still he went on,
though the tree could have whisked us into the abyss as easily
as a finger flicks a pea.

"Cric-cric, cric-cric, cric-cric. . . ."

And even did he bend the tree sufficiently to allow the
sleigh to pass he still had the task of rendering the dreadful
engine harmless again.

We did pass, or I should not be writing about Walther
Blum. The passengers did not resume their chatter, because
they had barely interrupted it. An hour later we had arrived
at our destination, but I confess that my dreams that night
were of elemental things—of masses and weights and forces
and how man tames the devils that abide in them. I was
haunted by thoughts of the precarious margins of safety by
which we live, and by the still more precarious assumption
that a man will never fail of having himself in control. And,
above all, there seemed to hang between me and the night a
slightish figure in a black velvet jacket and baggy corduroys,
with handsome dark brows over dark fatalistic eyes, who
himself seemed to possess something of that very inimicality
of the Nature against which he wrought. As long as things
went well he held, as a dam holds ; but if they went ill he was
himself a tree to break, with a dreadful sound, a rock to come
thundering down.

II

It has more than once happened to me that a powerfully
received impression has been followed almost immediately
by another one, as if in some way I myself were specially
attuned and open to it. I am of a restless disposition, and
did not propose to make any long stay in Haarheim ; and if
Walther Blum (as I presently learned his name to be) had made
such an impression on me, and was indeed a timber-carrier,
well, these fellows spend three-quarters of their lives on the
road, and the chances were that I should never see him again.

But I did see him again, and, as it happened, within a couple of nights of that perilous exploit of his with the jack.

I am permitted a moderate amount of walking, though not "winter sports"; and as hotel life has long since lost its attraction for me, I like to turn my back on the ringing *eisbahn* and to seek the higher slopes, where the clearings and the sawmills are, and the hydraulic mains lean on the mountains like rods against a wall, and, higher still, where the kites circle, and a thousand trees can be cut and the face of the landscape is hardly changed. With the close of the season the hotels shut down; direction and staff and clientele move elsewhere; but the timbermen and the men of the power-stations and the cattlemen and sawyers remain. In the meantime their wives sweep the floors and carry the pails and make the beds at the hotels.

It was in these high regions that I saw Walther Blum again. And I say that I saw him at night, though in that electricity-flooded country of snowy tops and wooded scarps, "artificial day" would serve as well, since they hold midnight carnivals on the *eisbahn* under the great sputtering arcs, while frequently lights burn unheeded at noon. There was, in fact, a carnival that night, and I relied on its illumination to guide me home again, for to tell the truth, I had no very clear idea where I was. It was in order to ascertain this that I was making towards another light, along a rough, snowy track that skirted a clearing.

The light was a sort of blurred square, as if the window were draped with some curtain-stuff, and as I drew nearer I saw that it came from the window of a house or hut of logs, apparently of two rooms that communicated. The communicating door must have been open, for a remnant of light was visible in the second window also. And then I saw what it was that veiled the first window. They were icicles. They made another bloated pane outside the inner one, some of them three fingers thick, others mere films, as if it had thawed and blown a gale and frozen again simultaneously, and one liquefying finger had passed its drops on to the next. This shutter of ice gave the place an uncared-for look, for it could have been cleared away in a couple of minutes, and even the light within was no certain indication that there was anybody there. I therefore approached the window before knocking at the door.

I dimly saw that a hatted man sat inside at a table, alone. The naked incandescent was immediately above his head, and he appeared to be moving something smoothly and regularly a few inches along the table, to and fro. The rest was a mere distorted blur, through which it was impossible that he should have seen me, and I turned away quietly enough; but suddenly I heard the moving of his chair and his voice that called:

"Is that you, Karen ?"

The next moment the door was flung open and I stood full in the light.

In the German I make shift with, I told him that I had missed my way and would be grateful if he would direct me to the Haarheim Palast. He stood aside to allow me to enter.

"Come in," he said, and he closed the door behind me.

It was a rough and neglected interior, and it gave the impression of having been shut up for some time. The walls were of yellow pine, and there was probably an airspace between them and the outer logs. The furniture consisted of the table I had seen, a couple of chairs, a sort of home-made settee with blankets and a great-coat on it, a rack of crockery, a stopped fretwork clock, and the stove. There was not so much as a print on the walls, but ranged along a narrow shelf were the usual trifles in carved wood—paper-knives, boxes, blotters, toy cattle, a bear, and the rest of the things people buy in the picture-postcard shops and bring home as mementoes. To make these things was evidently his way of passing the evenings, as indeed the litter on the table showed, for the light shone down on a handful of chisels and a small saw; and, mingled with chips and sawdust, on a newspaper he couldn't read, stood a loaf of black bread and half a sausage. The oilstone was there too, for the smooth, regular movement I had seen through the icicled window had been the sharpening of his penknife.

He showed no sign of recognizing me as the passenger who had got out of the sleigh to watch him at work with the jack. He had taken off his wide hat, and its removal showed a broad brow beneath thick rumpled hair, the low growth of which made more emphatic still the handsomeness of his brows. His youthful face—he could not have been more than five or six and twenty—was weathered to a clear even brown, and possibly he shaved twice a week or so, for his small moustache was continued downwards in a soft smudge, which seemed to give a richness to the fine line of his jaw. His eyes were very bright, and even his wide corduroys did not conceal his powerful grace of movement as he crossed to get the other chair for me.

"You are from the Haarheim Palast, Herr Doktor?" he said.

I told him yes, but that there was a carnival that had not greatly amused me, and I had taken a walk instead. I also told him that I was neither Doktor nor Professor, but he continued to call me "Herr Doktor" till the end.

"There are many people there?" he asked.

"In the hotel? It is full. They are even sleeping in the bathrooms."

"So. So. I was told so. It all makes work."

"And brings money to Haarheim?" I suggested.

"People lived here before the Palast was built," he answered moodily.

Then, as I looked again round the poor and brilliantly lighted interior, my eyes were attracted by something that apparently he had made a hasty effort to conceal. Although the table was strewn with fresh chippings, no trinket-box or paper-knife was to be seen; but half hidden behind the newspaper on which the bread and sausage stood was the object on which he had been at work. I saw the head and shoulders of a small wooden statuette.

There was that about the glimpse that made me wish to see more, and in matters of that kind I permit myself a little curiosity. He did not appear to have seen my glance.

"I interrupted you at work?" I said.

"No, Herr Doktor, my time is my own."

"You carve these animals and things?"

"Everybody here carves them. They are made in every house."

"I am a kind of artist too. May I see that?" And I nodded towards the figure.

His bright eyes were mistrustfully on mine. Thinking it might help matters if I gave him my name, which is known here and there, I did so; but he only shook his head. He had never heard it. Nevertheless, the fact that apparently I had a name worth giving seemed to impress him, and his eyes

dropped. He muttered something I didn't catch. He took
up the penknife, as if he would have resumed his sharpening.
And then suddenly he yielded. He rose, pushed the newspaper aside, and placed the statuette in my hands.

I suppose I am about the last man in the world to lose my
head over a work of art. It has always seemed to me that the
more claims a thing makes the higher must be the standard by
which it is judged, and this is to reduce the number of the
world's masterpieces considerably. Masterpieces? Why do
I mention the word? A masterpiece has detachment, and
this statuette had none. Its merit was vehemently the other
way. It banished the very word "classic". It was as much
his own as his own reluctant speech. If his fatalistic handling
of the jack had impressed me, all that I could now do was to
stare at the piece of wood in my hands. And as I like to be
right about my facts, let me first give its dimensions.

It was a woman's figure, about ten inches high, in the
attitude of dancing. Allowing a minimum for wastage,
the block in which it had slept before it came to life was
about 11 by 4 by 5 inches. Call it 12 by 6 by 6 inches, or
a quarter of a cubic foot. Those, I say, were the dimensions
of the original block. But the figure itself contained nothing
like that. Perhaps 6 cubic inches for the trunk and head, 4
for the thighs and legs, and 2 for the arms—total, 12 : out of
432 cubic inches all but 12 had had to be laboriously cut away
before the figure emerged, and that at the risk of an oversawing
or a fracture at any moment. "What on earth made you
choose wood?" one wanted to cry to him. "Why, you could
have set up a wire armature in an hour! Is there no clay in
Haarheim? Couldn't you have bought a pound or two of
wax on one of your timber-journeys to the towns? Why
this immense toil? Are you truly of a nature so tormented
by itself that if no difficulties exist you must create them?"

For that was precisely what it looked like. He had gone
wilfully out of his way to postpone the consummation of his
work as long as possible. But now that the thing was
finished, or almost so, I had to admit that it was neither wood
nor wax, but flesh. The tendon of that supporting ankle
would be hard between the fingers, a thumb run up that spine
would feel the vertebræ. Feet, ankles, neck were exquisitely
finished. But the face, the face only, was left. The cheeks
remained rough and pitted by the tool. And in some obscure

way this was a relief. For the figure was not merely a statuette of a woman. It was of one *given* woman, in all the idiom of her beauty, and to have given her a face would have been to shout her name as well.

"Where," I asked slowly, "did you learn all this ?"

He did not seem to understand. "To carve wood ? Everybody here carves wood. Our fathers carved wood, and their fathers."

"Yes, paper-knives and Noah's Ark cows. But *this* ? You have then studied ?"

He shook his head. At the schools ? No.

"But, man ! I know what I am saying. One can get a resemblance, even of anatomy. Nine people out of ten are deceived. But not the tenth. It is *not* Nature, where you can trace the effect back to the cause. It is Art, where, if you do not understand the cause, the effect cannot possibly be right."

For the anatomy of that piece of wood left not a single anatomical question unanswered. The heads of the gastrocnemius *would* swell so, the soleus behave so, the thin, taut flank stretch precisely so.

"I can set bones," he said, as if in apology. "Often there are accidents in the woods. Then they send for me."

"But are you not often away ?"

"Not now. That is finished. Josef Speck broke his leg. I set it and took his team till he was well. Now I am back. I help the second forester."

"I saw you on the road, when the sleigh could not pass."

"I did not see you, Herr Doktor."

"I saw you bend the pole with the jack."

"So ?" he said indifferently. "Something had to be done."

"Tell me," I said after a pause, "why you carved the figure in wood when there were easier ways. Why make it so difficult for yourself ?"

He hesitated, at a loss for words. He muttered :

"I don't know. How should I know ? I am not as the Herr Doktor. It was as it was. It is still as it is. It has always been so. And it is more difficult than you know. More difficult—more difficult . . ." His voice sank, and then his manner changed. He had questions to put to me, too, quick little questions, so far as I could see without import."

"It is pleasant at the Palast?"

I shrugged my shoulders. "Hotels are very much alike."

"You are staying there long?"

"Most likely not. No. Not long."

"They are"—the bright eyes were earnestly on mine as he used the German equivalent—"they are run off their feet there? I mean the service?"

"I really don't know. The hotel is full. I don't suppose they employ more people than they have work for."

"No. I believe they work late," he said, frowning, his fingers drumming on the table again.

Light began to dawn on me. His first words on hearing my foot on the snow outside had been, "Is that you, Karen?" His questions about the hotel, the service, the degree of its busyness, could only mean that he had a wife at the hotel and was expecting her home. I was looking intently at the tool-marked space where the statuette's face should have been.

"Why don't you finish it?" I asked him.

He fixed me with his stare, as if I had committed an impertinence, which quite possibly I had.

"What?" he demanded.

"The hands, the feet, are wonderfully done. You have even put life into the braiding of the hair. Why leave the face like that?"

I have seldom seen a man's expression change so swiftly. A fire seemed to blaze up in him. Something looked for a moment out of his eyes that made me afraid, not, understand, for myself, but for the latent things so imperfectly safeguarded in himself. I have stood on a spot where they say the crust of the earth is only twelve feet thick, and the ground rings hollow to your tread. Sulphurous vapours trickle up from the crevices, and to run a torch along them is to wake the whole region into activity. I felt that I was experimenting with some such torch now. His voice, which had been a pleasant soft guttural, became strained and harsh.

"Why?" he said, with sudden loudness. "The Herr Dokter asks me why? Why, indeed! I will tell you. It is because she smiles! Always she smiles! Once she did not smile, not, at least, like that, and I was happy. Now she smiles, and it drives me mad. . . ."

And with an abrupt movement he was on his feet and struggling into the great-coat that lay on the settee.

I protested that it was not necessary that he should accompany me. It would suffice if he indicated the way. But his voice fell to a mutter again.

"No. I will come. There is a branch of the paths—I will come. I will come to the hotel. It is nothing. Often I have been later than this. We will leave the light. There is a branch of two paths—she knows it too ; if the Herr Doktor will please . . ."

Together we passed out of the hut, leaving the light burning behind us.

Yes, it seemed clear enough—all but one thing. He had been sitting up for this wife who worked at the hotel, and was now going to fetch her, as a husband should. But the other thing remained. Most husbands are happy in the smiles of their wives, but he was not. Once she had not smiled, or not after that fashion, and he said he had been happy. Now she smiled, smiled always, and he left that portion of his carving blank and expressionless. What sort of a smile was that ? I wondered deeply as we trudged together along the cart-track at the wood's edge and began to descend by rounded, monotonous hummocks of snow.

But he said not another word. At the junction of the tracks of which he had spoken he paused for a moment, looking along both portions. Then he took the right-hand one, which was obviously the more direct. A quarter of an hour later I fancied I had picked up my bearings again, and told him so, but still he tramped on at my side without replying. A little later still we came upon ski-tracks, and in one quarter the night seemed to have paled perceptibly. We rounded a shoulder of the mountain and gained its crest. Over the pines below was a mist of light, from which faint sounds reached us. They were still keeping up the carnival. We dropped down the track to the Palast Hotel.

A plantation straggles upwards from the rear of the hotel premises, and as we approached this Walther Blum began to tread more carefully. His care increased as the lights of the servants' quarters at the back began to appear through the trees. Most of the lower windows were in darkness, for the kitchens were hardly likely to be troubled again at that hour of the night, but the floors above shone out

K

brightly enough, and through corridor windows a shadow could even be seen to pass from time to time. My own room was in the front of the hotel, where the long balconies are, and one can look down on the *eisbahn*. From this now came a confused babble of sound—music, a faint rattle of applause, the thin hum of skates. A swept path ran round the hotel in that direction. I was about to thank Walther Blum and to take this path when from the darkness there came the sound of a door being softly closed. Two low voices were heard, the one a woman's, the other a man's.

"No, go in now," the woman's voice was saying. "If he says he came to meet me I shall say I went the other way round."

"*Dis bonsoir.*"

"No, not now—be careful—return to the bar——"

"The colleague Otto is there; just ten minutes, in the wood——"

"No, I say——"

We had drawn into the shadow of the trees. For all her protests, there was the sound of a kiss. A door closed, and in the semi-darkness a shadow was seen to steal away. The shadow went, not in the direction by which Blum and I had come, but by the other path. I looked round for Blum.

He was not there. He was a dozen yards away. And he was hurrying, not after the woman, but by the shorter way we had taken, as if he wished to reach home first.

III

Unless one has need of something and rings for it, one usually sees little of one's chambermaid, and I had no idea who performed this office for me at the Haarheim Palast. Indeed, it was at my own risk if I concluded that Walther Blum's wife was a chambermaid at all, and not employed in some other branch of the service. My data for her identification were, on the one hand, uniquely ample, and on the other, scanty to a degree. For all practical purposes they resolved themselves into one distinguishing feature—hair braided in a thick coronal round the head, as if two heavy plaits had been brought forward and woven together.

I have already remarked how, before what later seems a

hidden plan is unfolded and revealed, trifling events add themselves to one another with increasing swiftness, until the last trifling accident or two have almost the force of a foregone conclusion. I was not thinking of Walther Blum when I rang my bell some two mornings later. Nor could I possibly know that, just as he had been doing an injured timber-driver's job in an emergency, so she now was temporarily taking over somebody else's duties. She knocked and entered in answer to my ring ; and she was so indubitably the woman of the statuette that I could have called her by her name : Karen.

To my astonishment she seemed to be hardly more than seventeen. Young to be married, I thought, and to a husband in whom was something—I do not know if "timeless" is the right word ; I mean something that the years can neither add to nor take away from. She was blue-eyed, fair as Ceres, and had a mouth like a sealed rose. If, hastily summoning and dismissing a recollection, I found her on the small side, these things, after all, are more a matter of proportion than of actual size. Her ample blue print skirt filled the doorway like a bell, and her expression was one of petulant gravity, as if, young as she was, she must struggle with things beyond her years, while resenting and hating them. It was right too that she should be a chambermaid. She fitted in better with linen-closets and brush-cupboards than if she had worn a smart apron or sat behind a cash-desk. And I confess that it came over me with a shock that not only could she apparently hold her vows loosely, but was also capable of telling her husband that she had gone one way home when, in fact, she had taken another.

I had no excuse for detaining her, and I told her what I wanted ; but I missed not a single one of her movements as she stooped to the pile of linen on the floor and began to sort it. Then she looked up.

"The *gnädiger* Herr has made a list ?" she asked in good German.

"No."

"Then I will count it."

So at least she could read and write. I continued to watch her as she made her list. Once she turned her head, and it was the identical turn of the statuette ; and the wreath of the honey-fair hair was the same ; but her face was hidden. She gathered the linen together, placed it on a towel, and knotted the corners crosswise. She rose with the bundle.

"The *gnädiger* Herr would wish them quickly?" she said, the grave, resentful eyes on mine.

"As quickly as possible."

"It is done in the hotel. It will be ready at half past eight o'clock on Thursday evening. I shall do it myself."

The door closed on her and her bundle.

So this was Karen of the smile! Certainly I had seen little smile enough, but possibly she was not yet restored to a smiling humour, for had I been a woman I should not have cared to return to that hut with the icicled window and tell such a husband as Walther Blum a pack of lies in his teeth. I would as soon not have gone home at all. I wondered what her life with him was up there. He had been away on the road. She too, so far as I could gather, was temporarily undertaking other duties. But these were interruptions to the routine. Soon the hotel would close. She would return home, and all day long he would not be far away—merely in some neighbouring portion of the forest, helping the second forester. A couple of strokes with a brush-handle and that raffle of icicles would come splintering down. The interior would be set to rights. Normal cohabitation would go on as before.

But I checked my thoughts, suddenly still. Everything as before! How then had that been? Since she was certainly not yet eighteen, there could not have been a great deal of "before". And why should his statuette, so betrayingly evidential in everything else, keep that blank, mocking, unfeatured face? What was this reason he gave of a smile? A smile is a peaceful, happy thing. So much can it do that, let a man but have it, and a load falls from him, as the mass of late snow, slipping away, suddenly shows the green all new and tender beneath. Yet he had said it himself. She smiled, and the chisel was arrested in his hand. She smiled, and every other perfection that those few cubic inches of wood contained became anonymous. She smiled, and at the mere recollection of it he broke out in fury before a stranger. "Why? I will tell you why! *Because* she smiles! Once she did not smile, and I was happy. Now she smiles—always, always smiles— and it is driving me mad!"

Sufficiently occupied with these thoughts, I turned my attention to the other man.

For I already knew who *he* was. Even the few words I had overheard at the back of the hotel had had that caressing yet acrid Neapolitan timbre. He was Nicolo, the white-jacketed waiter in the American bar, and his type is repugnant to me. He could not hide the fulsome meanings in his strongly staring black eyes, nor keep the vain and conquering smile from his shaven lips. Shaven? He was shaven *au bleu*. He must have shaved twice a day to keep the indigo so smoothly down. I learned that he did, in fact, shave for the second time before coming on to serve the evening cock-tails, for, seeking a way up to the roof early one evening to see what the view was like up there, I came by chance upon the little room where daily the barber attended, and there was Nicolo, with the napkin tucked about the cauliflower of soap, his head back, and that ineffable smile on his face at something imaginary between him and the ceiling. His teeth, too, were as white as his barman's jacket, and as he polished his glasses behind the counter he might have been under glass himself, so sleek and unspotted a picture did he make.

In the circumstances I saw no reason why, over my modest *apéritif*, I should not find out as much about Nicolo as I could.

I soon had him marked down as a diligent fellow, with ambitions. A German-Swiss hotel is no bad stepping-stone from Naples to London, and Nicolo was making the most of his time. He was continually checking his stock, marking bottles, and copying the remaining quantities into a little book; and he had another book, too, with coloured edges, in French, German, Italian and English. It was a book of cookery recipes, and his short straight nose was never out of it. One of these days he was going to have his own hotel. Every *pfennig* of change that was pushed back to him as *trinkgeld* was set aside, and presently he would be leaving Haarheim, not to return. He would take his cookery-book with him in his trunk, and his hard-boiled shirts, and his black bows and starched white jackets. But he would not take his mistress, if she were that. Why pay excess on superfluous luggage? There were mistresses enough in London for a handsome, far-seeing, ambitious fellow such as our Nicolo.

So there was dapper Nicolo, with his English lessons in

his spare hours, and his serenely insolent way of looking at women, and his smooth, plump hands that would let them go like so many water-drops when he reached for a towel.   And there was Walther Blum, muttering, morose, half-savage as regarded one part of his nature, the other half mingled flame and passion and nameless desire.   And apparently Nicolo got the kisses and Walther got the smiles.   It doesn't matter by what processes I pieced all this together.   I hardly think I did piece it together.   It fell together of itself.   It was simply the final assembly of elements that had long been preparing, and I doubt if anything could have changed the complete pattern into which they finally fell.   On my walks, at my solitary table in the corner, leaning over the balcony at night and watching the waltzings and acrobatics on the *eisbahn*, I pondered much about it all, and one of the resolutions to which I came was that when Karen brought my linen back at half past eight o'clock on the Thursday evening I would be there to have, if possible, a word with her.

IV

For I am no stranger to hotels, and I know what their promises about laundry usually amount to.   It comes when it comes.   But here was a promise much more precisely made. It was made even to the half-hour.   She was doing it herself, and it was to be in my room at half past eight.   Of course it might not come, but I was inclined to dismiss that.   There were too many things against it.   Say, for one thing, she was in love with this fellow.   At half past eight the hotel, including myself, would be dining.   The bedrooms would long since have been made ready for the night, except for the final touches that would only take a few minutes.   And at half past eight Otto, as I knew, relieved Nicolo at the American bar.   It was the one interval of the day that they might reasonably expect to have to themselves.   That, briefly, was my guess at the position.

Yet I was dissatisfied with my guess.   It seemed to condemn her too summarily.   There must be some reason for the hate and resentfulness that dwelt so contradictorily side by side with the gravity in her clear eyes, and I began to play with hypotheses.   Suppose, I argued to myself, that she had been married a year. If she had had even a little happiness during that year it was as much as could have been expected from a man so palpably at odds with the world and human life as he found it as Walther Blum. The chances were that he avoided his kind, or classed them, too, as phenomena with the trees and the rocks and the snows. He must have been a very difficult man to live with.

Yet it was a woman he had married, not a rock or a tree ; and there had been something very steadfast in the eyes she had turned up to me as she had packed my linen on the floor. Apparently this man, who took life hardly himself, had passed a hard portion on to her too, and she had flown to one who took it more easily, cajoled her, flattered her, and would turn her off the moment he got what he wanted. In that case I was sorry for her, but except to tell her to make the best of her Walther and leave the other alone, I should not have known how to advise her.

I had intended to be in my room when Karen came at half past eight on Thursday ; as it turned out I had no choice in the matter. A slight indisposition necessitated my seeing the doctor that afternoon ; I was told that a couple of days in bed would set me right ; and to bed I was sent. I had been in bed some hours when I heard Karen's tap at the door.

One minor difficulty at least was out of the way. I could not very well have detained her had she wished to finish the errand and be gone, but she, if she chose, might in the circumstances linger as long as she wished. She came in with my parcel. She wore the same little jacket and wide blue print skirt as before. In anybody else I should have called her salutation a curtsey, but in her it was somehow both given and withheld. Then, in the act of setting down the parcel, she paused.

"The *gnädiger* Herr is not well ?" she asked, as if she had only just noticed that I was in bed.

I told her that it was nothing, and that I should be all right in a couple of days.

"Is it the *gnädiger* Herr's pleasure that I should count the linen and put it away ?"

"If you would be so kind, Karen."

She unfastened the parcel, checked its contents, and began to open drawers. She did not ask where anything was to

be put, but went about her light task smoothly and efficiently.
Only towards the end of her shirt-and-collar sorting did she
delay a little. Then she turned, with the last of the washing
still in her hand.

"The *gnädiger* Herr then knows my name ?"

"Yes. You are Karen, the wife of Walther Blum. I have
spoken with your husband."

"You know him ?"   The limpid blue eyes were on mine,
and she seemed to have forgotten the third-personal address.

"Very slightly," I answered, though I felt this to be, in
some odd way, untrue.   "Among others, I am not at all sure
that he didn't save my life."

Most people would have asked how that had come about,
but she only knitted the brows above the blue eyes. She
put away the last of the linen and closed the drawer. I
thought she was about to leave. But she stood there with
her hands on her hips (she seemed incapable of an attitude
that was not alive with grace, and her hands and wrists in
particular were full of the most moving beauty), the small foot
under the bell-shape of blue print tapping, her teeth catching
at that half-rose of a lower lip. No wonder Blum had given
forth her shape so passionately in his wood. I could hardly
take my eyes from her. And then her own eyes, which had
been on the polished floor, met mine again.

"I am also grateful to your husband for directing me when
I had missed my way," I went on.

And that she did take up. "When ?" she demanded,
almost imperiously.

"Let me see. Four nights ago."

She betrayed herself completely in her next question,
for I might have met him anywhere ; but she didn't seem to
care. "And you went in ?" she challenged me.

"Yes," I answered. There was no need to say where.
She herself went straight to the point.

"And he walked back to the hotel with you ?"

"Yes. . . . Though I didn't say so."

Still she didn't seem to care, though she bit her lip again.
I would have given a fortune to have known all that was
passing behind those rounds of palest blue under the wreath of
fairest hair, but a very little I thought I did know. I had
been in her husband's house four nights before. He had
walked back to the hotel with me, and she herself had slipped

away like a shadow by another path. There must have been—
let us call it a situation—when she had climbed the mountain
and pushed at the door of that solitary hut again. And above
all, if I had been inside I had seen the statuette.

"The *gnädiger* Herr speaks the truth," she said; "since I
knew all that," she added, with a lift of her head.

Then suddenly it came out, as if somebody else spoke for
me. Up to that moment it had not entered my head to ask
such a question.

"Why do you smile, Karen? I want to know why you
smile."

Ah! (the eyes seemed to say). So I knew that too!
Well, if I already knew it it saved the time and trouble of
explanation. All could be understood without further ado.
Nevertheless, she repeated my question.

"Why do I smile?"

"Why do you smile?"

"You have been in the house?"

"I said so."

"And you saw—it?"

I spoke slowly: "By 'it' you mean the thing that doesn't
smile?"

"I knew you had seen it. It never will smile. It will
never be finished. But I—I shall smile the more. . . . So
he told you that too?"

"He told me that you smiled, and that it drove him mad."

"It is no worse to be mad than to be killed, as I have been
killed," she answered, with compressed lips. "One can be
killed, and yet go on living."

Killed! She in the bloom and freshness of her seventeen
short years! . . . But girls have these fancies. In another
year or two she would be laughing at them herself. I leaned
up on my pillow and looked at her attentively.

"What do you mean, Karen?"

She returned my look disdainfully, as if I and all like me
were things of so little importance that the truth could be
flung to us as one tosses a bone to a dog. But her hands had
left her hips, and were clenched at her sides.

"Why should I not tell you? Why should I not tell
everybody? It is only *he* who doesn't understand!" broke
from her. "Listen! Do you know how old I am? I am
seventeen and a half years old. And I have been married to

K*

Walther Blum one year—one whole year! I didn't want to marry him. He made me marry him. We didn't even belong to the same valley. He lived in one valley and I in another, with the Huldhorn between. Among us we marry in the same valley—because of the mountain, because of the Huldhorn. Hardly a man can pass the cornice in the winter. Even in the summer it is a toil. So our young men marry the girls at home. But he came over, down into our village from the skies. He came over whatever the weather was, with runners on his feet that he had made himself. He could have settled among us, for he lived alone, but he would not. He told me that he would not come every night, but I soon learned what *that* meant. It meant that he might not arrive every night. But he set out every night. I asked him once, when he was very late, whether he had got lost, but he said he had a compass in his breast. I used to open the shutters and look up at the crest of the hill for his lantern."

So he had made even his love difficult to the verge of impossibility! Her words pictured it all the more vividly because of their very abruptness—him in his hut making ready his lantern; his setting-out; the diamonded night sky overhead or else the blinding scurries of snow; the soft sliding thunder of a distant avalanche, the creep round the cornice of the Huldhorn; the pause to look down on the handful of houses that made the hamlet—and all guided by that in his breast that he called a compass. I saw the child of sixteen peering past the shutter for the winking light of his lantern. And I was quite prepared to hear that she had been afraid of him even then.

"My parents were against it, *gnädiger* Herr," she went on more quietly. "They said it was not natural that he should not be able to get a girl without coming over the mountain. But he said: Get a girl! He had seen them—girls. They were nothing. If *those* were girls, then *I* was something else, and he wanted me, whatever I was, if those others were girls! He said that my smile made him warm even on the cornice of the Huldhorn. My father said that was high-falutin talk, and not good. Let him come and make his home among us and then it would be time to talk, my father said. And the Herr Pastor, who was also my schoolmaster, said the same. But I began not to listen to them. At first, all the same, I didn't want to marry Walther. I told him not to come.

But he made me marry him, *gnädiger* Herr. He gave me no peace. There is no peace where he is. If there is a moment's peace an avalanche follows. And when I learned that he set out every night, then the nights when he didn't arrive were terrible. I felt that I had killed him by not marrying him sooner. I was very young, *gnädiger* Herr. I am older now. And so I married him."

That, too, I could believe—that he had made her marry him. He had compelled her a little at a time, as he had loaded up that sixty-foot tree, forcing it to bend. And suddenly she stamped her small foot so that the blue print bell shook with the passionate gesture.

"And what was it? *Lieber Gott!* Do the other men do so to the other girls? Why, then, do they not die? But I have seen them laughing, these young married girls; how can they do it? I tell you, you who lie there, that it was endless! Always it was so, always, always. . . . And there, with the Huldhorn between, where was there to run to? And what was the good of crying? No, I do not wish! He broke me, he broke me. It arrived that he might do as he wished; what did I care? Then he reproached me, but it no longer mattered to me. Nothing mattered. And so I was contented, thinking I knew the worst.

"But I did *not* know the worst, you who lie there!" she cried, in a voice that mounted. "Having broken my body he began to break my mind too! I had had lessons from the Herr Pastor. I could read and write; I could speak a little French; and he could neither read nor write nor speak French. And because I could not answer his questions he called me a fool! His questions, *lieber Gott!* He did not understand them himself. They were not questions! I have heard him say that he did not know what it was he wanted to know! How, then, should *I* know? He called us all fools. Even the Herr Pastor he called a fool. He said that we knew no more than he, and that if he learned to read and write he would be the greatest fool of all. And when one is called a fool sufficiently one ceases to open one's mouth. Days passed when I never spoke to him. Even at night I never spoke to him. All was without words or speech, since he wished it so. Why should one speak when one is a fool?"

Poor, hapless pair! What was there to say? I said what I could.

"Much is laid on him, Karen."

"What is laid on him ? How, laid on him ?" she flashed.

"It hasn't got a name. He is right in saying that the Herr Pastor knows no more of the reason of everything than he. Nevertheless, it is fastened on him as they fasten the trees to the carts—with a chain and a winch."

"It is on *me* that it is fastened !" she cried. "Listen to me ! Listen heedfully ! What had I left ? My beauty remained. I do not mean my beauty as at first, though he might please himself about that. My beauty to his eyes remained. That was all—all ! And his eyes never left me. They followed me about like the piercings in a dark shutter. And then the other—all else—stopped. I existed in his eyes only. I was his *Gliederpuppe*, his thing that he copied from. Even in mid-winter I must go about—yes, even when I was sweeping up his chippings or cooking the supper . . . but the *gnädiger* Herr has seen. Soon I ceased to blush. That was not his first statuette. Many he cast into the stove, saying it was all they were fit for—more true to say it was all *I* was fit for ! I was a fool. That other was finished. But this remained. I had married a man who growled over pieces of wood. I was something to turn into a piece of wood. If I could tell you, you who lie there listening—if I could tell you——"

I put up my hand to calm her. It was not necessary to tell me ; the statuette had done that. I thought of that lonely hut far up the Huldhorn. Terrible houses of men, of which we see the outside only ! A mansion in a London square, a crowded Paris tenement, a cabin on a vineyard's slope, a log-hut high and lonely in a world of snows—just once in a while a chink opens, a curtain is left a little aside. One learns the reasons why a will was made, why a divorce-action was entered, why a crime was committed. Then the chink closes again and the curtain slips back into its place. But one has seen. I saw in Walther Blum a man scourged by life and his station in it, dwelling in solitude of soul up there, saturating his eyes with anguishing and untranslatable beauty, and with curses casting his wretched images into the stove. I saw a young girl, shy with the shyness of young girls, modest with a peasant's flinching modesty, shrivelling Semele-like under the fierce heat of a passion elemental and beyond her comprehension, forced to yield up her very superficies as her

sole remaining value. Comprehend it? Because she did
not comprehend it, it was the last violation. The little he had
left her of her own, to do as she pleased with, he used up in
order that the eyes of strangers might know as much of her
as he. I had seen. Anybody might see. And she no
longer cared.

"But all this, Karen—it might explain why you weep.
It does not explain why you smile," I said, after a long silence.

"Does it not?" she taunted me. "To you, no, perhaps;
but *he* knows! Listen! It is not all. I now give way to
him in everything. From here to here"—she put out one
foot and, with a gesture terrible in its very slightness, lightly
touched her chin—"*that* is his. He may look at it, embrace it,
burn it, cut it with knives. I now run to let him do as he
wishes with it. 'Yes, Walther; assuredly, Walther,' I say—
for we speak now. But he pays. There is still something in
me he cannot touch." And the smile, with all its hideous
meanings for him, stole over the young rose of a mouth.
"Is it not so, *gnädiger* Herr? And when he groans and weeps
and prays for that something—for the *gnädiger* Herr is right
when he says it has no name, but it is *that* he wants—is not
that alone enough to make the smile come? For I cannot
give that something now if I would. It is me, but it is not
mine. He has all the rest instead. And so it is even wifely
to smile."

"If it drives him mad, Karen?" I asked gravely. For I
had remembered Nicolo's absence from the American bar.
"If it drives him—or you—to something desperate?"

She now spoke quite lightly with a little stretch of herself.
"At least it would be an end. . . . Please would the *gnädiger*
Herr like me to send the valet as I go down?"

"No, Karen."

"Or any service. . .?"

"There is nothing, thank you. But I should like to see
you again."

With the smile still about her mouth, the steady scornful
look in her clear eyes, and her hands upon her hips again,
she said a mocking and a bitter thing: "The *gnädiger* Herr
has only to ring."

"Karen! . . . Why do you not go to your home over
the Huldhorn for a short time?"

"I come here instead," she answered; and the next moment

she was gone, leaving me gazing at the "Flight into Egypt" carved in high relief in brown wood on the wall opposite my bed.

V

How much better for Walther Blum, I thought, could he have contented himself with work of that kind, carving what every peasant in the district carved, the edelweiss paper-knives, the clock faces, and the other objects of the stationers' shops! But what was the good of thoughts like that? He was what he was, and who shall justify the ways of man to woman, of woman to man? It was much more to the point that apparently his wife was carrying on this intrigue with the Neapolitan. Or was it not an intrigue at all? Was it, so to speak, part of the smile? Was it designed to show him that all that he had destroyed in her might still revive at the beck of somebody else?

Our conversation, which I have abbreviated, had taken some time. If she had had an assignation with Nicolo at half past eight she had certainly not kept it. She might or might not be with him now. It was truly no affair of mine. And yet I felt restless and anxious.

My indisposition was a short one. After two days I was up and about again. I received the congratulations of such of the guests as had any interest in me, and was told that I had missed little during my lying-up. The weather had broken. A strong thaw had set in. The *eisbahn* was a deserted waste, and there were trunks at the door of the hotel—for those who were not departing immediately were preparing to do so, and within a few days the clientele would probably be diminished by half. The signs of the winter's end were not confined to the guests. There was a stir in the natural life of the district, too. Down the lower slopes one saw more cattle, and multitudinous sounds of deliquescence and break-up were everywhere. Upstairs in the hotel they were already closing unneeded rooms, and downstairs Nicolo, checking his stock and poring over his book in four languages, had the American bar to himself.

The incident to which I am coming happened at five o'clock one afternoon upstairs in the already half-empty hotel. They were stripping beds and rolling up the bolsters and mattresses, and as a portion of the staff had already been discharged the rest of the remaining personnel was bearing a hand. Among them was Nicolo, in his shirt-sleeves, a plump cock among the print-skirted hens, smiling, showing his white teeth, and within an hour of his second daily shave. His jests, as he dragged out the mattresses and carried the stacks of sheets, caused an incessant tittering among the maids, and I suppose it is because I have no such success with women as he that I liked him less than ever.

Something had taken me to my room, which was, of course, untouched, and I had seen all this in passing. I did whatever it was that had brought me up, and came out again. A few yards along the corridor stood an addition to the group. Walther Blum had joined it.

He was standing by the half-open door of a linen-room, watching his wife and Nicolo as they folded a blanket between them. For two reasons I did not pass on : I was interested in the situation, and I had a fancy to pass the time of day with Blum. Thus, as I lingered, I heard what passed between Nicolo and Karen Blum, in French.

"When one folds blankets you know what happens ?" the Neapolitan was saying.

Karen shook the plaited head.

"It cannot happen this time, for a reason. The reason stands there watching us. But one folds, so—and so"—the blanket was halved and quartered as the two holders of it approached—"and the one who takes the blanket takes something else also."

"What ?"

"Ah, so little when one thinks of the rest ! (*Comme il fait les yeux féroces !*)"

"*Il fait toujours les yeux féroces.*"

"*Mais les tiens* . . ." His own black bull's-eyes rolled to her clear rounds, and the look itself was the kiss of which he spoke. She made way for me to pass, and I sought Blum.

The man from Naples was certainly taking risks. I myself should hesitate before I provoked on a man's face the sort of look that was on Blum's. When I greeted him he did not at first speak. When he did speak it was not in answer to my greeting.

"The Herr Doktor speaks languages. What was that he was saying ?" he said under his breath.

"I heard nothing. What brings you here, Blum ?"

"Those things that the Herr Doktor does not hear bring me here," he replied grimly. "There is no longer any reason why she should remain. Half of them have left already. It is time she left."

"It is only a matter of a few days."

"I have come to fetch her to-day," he answered curtly.

At that moment there was a further interesting passage between the pair who folded the blankets. She had loaded him with a pile of them for carrying away, and the pile bulged and tottered. He looked back over his shoulder.

"Give a hand or they will be down and all to fold again," he panted, for he was of a sedentary habit, and the blankets had lodged stiffly against some small projection of the wall. She tripped after him.

But she did not reach him. Blum's voice was raised.

"Karen !"

She turned. One would have thought she had not known of his presence.

"Yes, Walther ?"

"You are to come home. You are to come now. Go and make yourself ready."

It was peremptory, perhaps a little unreasonable ; but she ignored that. The look she turned on him was not mere yielding ; it was the deliberate strangling of a will of any kind to set against his. Already she was close on him, hastening to whatever room she occupied. At me she did not glance. The look was all for him—as also was the smile that accompanied it.

"Yes, Walther."

"Go and pack your box. I will carry it up the mountain."

"Yes, Walther."

"At once. Get your wages and wait for me."

"Yes, Walther." The next moment she was gone.

I thought for a moment that Walther Blum was going to seek out Nicolo there and then, for he stood irresolute, watching him with wrathful, smouldering eyes. But all at once he turned away. I thought he was going to take some domestics' staircase or other, but he didn't. In his black jacket and spacious corduroys, though carrying his broad hat in his hand, he marched down the main staircase, as if he had

been staying in the hotel. I followed him, and on the broad
outer verandah called his name. He turned.

"Herr Doktor?"

"Could I have a word with you?"

He bowed, for he had the peasant's courtesy.

"Properly speaking, what I want to say is none of my
business, unless I can be of use. But you yourself spoke of it
one night, and since then an accident has brought about a talk
with your wife also."

"She shall come away to-day," he muttered.

"But you speak as if she had left your roof. She has
returned late perhaps, but she has worked late. There has
been much to do. You will remember that you asked me the
question."

He made no reply, and again I wondered what had passed
between them on the night when he had overheard her words
to Nicolo and been a witness to their kiss. The next moment
he had told me.

"I have warned her!" he cried. "That man, anybody
can see what he is! Would I had the shaving of him; I
would make the blade keen for *that*! . . . What was he
saying in that language?" he demanded once more.

"I scarcely heard. It was harmless."

"It was *not* harmless! Those eyes do not go with harmless
things!"

I was much of the same opinion, but, "He is going away
in a week," I said. "Do not think of him."

But the empty verandah boomed with Walther Blum's
outbreak.

"In a week! And what does *that* mean? He has not
possessed her. I made her tell me that night, and it would
have given her pleasure to say 'Yes', but she does not lie.
He has not possessed her. But there is still time! All these
months he has planned it, and he has one week left! I do
not wish to kill. It is better to take her away. But if, within
a week, I find him one yard above that plantation's edge . . ."
He stopped.

This was a dangerous turn for things to take. Not only
was he capable of doing it; he was capable of finding, out of
that chaotic tormented mind of his, overwhelming reason why
it should be done. If the lore of the Herr Pastor over the
mountain was ignorance and confusion to him, he would

make as little of a Commandment.   Neither was it safe that he should boom out menaces of this kind under the verandah of the Haarheim Palast Hotel.

"Your wife will not come out this way," I said.   "Will you take a little walk ?"   And to make sure of his doing so I took his arm.   We turned by the path that led round the hotel, under the plantation beyond which if Nicolo went a single yard it would be at his own risk.   A little way up the plantation was an old wooden cattle-trough, with the bent and rusty remains of the pipe that had fed it.   It was half full of snow, but we should see from there when Karen came out, and its thick worn edge made a seat.   We sat down side by side.

We might have been waiting for Karen and nothing else, for we were as silent as if our minds had been unoccupied. It would have been like him not to speak at all.   It was therefore I who took the word.

"Walther," I said, using the name for the first time, "to what kind of a life do you take Karen when she goes up there ?"

"To mine," he said.   "To the only one I have.   But she gets the whole of it.   *I* want no light-o'-love !" he added contemptuously.

"But is it necessary to give her the whole of it ?   May not the whole be too much ?   She is very young."

His eyes were past the hotel, over the valley furrowed with white, thinned and mottled into dark unsightly patches. Soon the gentian and anemone would smile there and the sweet cold freshets thread themselves downward under the grass, and the tonk of the bells be borne on the wind.   And he seemed to be thinking of gentler things than murder, too, for he began to speak in a voice from which the anger had died away.

"It may be so, Herr Doktor," he said.   "It should not be so, for what is to love if it is not to give ?   But sometimes I ask myself whether only I am right, and I cannot answer.   It is *here*"—he placed a clenched hand on his breast—"and if I feel it there, how can I lie to myself and say I do not feel it ? We cannot all be right, I and they.   Then come times when I tell myself that it is easy for *them* to say 'I give all', when *their* all perhaps is so little.   And yet again there are times when I rage, and say they are wrong, were they as countless as the pines, and only *I* understand.   Is that too much, Herr Doktor ?"

"Much too much."

"When I love her ?"

"Love her a little less, Walther."

The brown hand gripped the remains of the rusty trough-pipe, and I could see its fierce tension. Then his head sank suddenly to his breast. He spoke in a shaky voice.

"Herr Doktor, I have no words of my own. The words I have are carved and filed smooth by others. They are a great number, the others, and I am only one, and ignorant at that. Therefore I do not say I loved her, Herr Doktor. She happened to me. I say she happened to me. She happened to me as rain happens, or sun, or the fall of the tree, or the avalanche. She happened as sickness happens, or healing, or thirst, or hunger. Sometimes, when she looked beautiful, I could even love myself a little, that I should be the cause of her looking beautiful. She lived in the valley over the Huldhorn. What was the Huldhorn? I have crossed it in all weathers. They do not love, these young men who will not take the trouble if the one they love lives a couple of pastures away ! Herr Doktor, if I have no words to speak of these things, was it not word enough to cross the Huldhorn for her ? I could have carried her, too, as I shall carry her box to-day. So she happened to me in that valley.

"And I said to myself, 'Have a care, Walther Blum ! You are rude and unlettered. *They* have been to school with the Herr Pastor ! Therefore contradict nobody. If they seem to you to talk foolish and vain things, things that will not bear examination, say nothing. Look at Karen instead. Look at her as she takes down the platters, as she serves the cheese, as she kisses her father before going to bed. Look at her as if she were the mountain air you breathed, the mountain pool in which you swam.' All the way back over the Huldhorn it remained with me. Beauty is agony to me, Herr Doktor. She cannot move a hand but I feel that no woman's hand has ever moved so before. And even these are words, that other people use. Let them pass. They are nothing . . . ah !"

What else he would have said I cannot tell, for at that moment there was a little bustle at the back of the hotel. Nicolo appeared, bearing in front of him a small trunk of metal, corded. Karen followed, in a queer stiff little round hat. Nicolo set the trunk on the ground, with a gesture that seemed to say, *Ach*, but that was heavy ! Blum had risen.

I continued to sit where I was. He dropped down through
the plantation and joined the pair at the door. As far as I
could see he did not look at Nicolo. He threw the box up
to his shoulder and made a gesture of his head to his wife. A
few minutes later they had passed me, she a few paces in
front, he with the corded box on his shoulder, on their way to
their home among the melting snows.

VI

It chanced that I had an acquaintance at the hotel who was
among the last to leave, and I might well have left with him ;
but for reasons I need not go into it was not to be so, and I
went to see him off instead.   The station is twelve miles away,
and whereas we had come in sleighs, we went back in Swiss
carts.   I said good bye to my friend, and the heads of the
horses were turned homeward again.   Halfway back I saw
Walther Blum.   He was sitting on a timber-cart.   The
vehicles passed without incident.   I think he saw me, but was
not sure.   He gave no sign of recognition.

"Has Josef Speck fallen ill again ?" I asked of the driver.
Josef Speck was the man whose leg Blum had set, driving
his cart for him until his recovery.

"No, *gnädiger* Herr.   Josef Speck is well and on his
journey."

"Then what does Walther Blum going to the town ?"

The man laughed.   "Oh, Walther Blum is unaccountable,
gnädiger Herr.   Nobody asks himself why Walther Blum
does anything."

We drove on.

As I look back on this incident I find it difficult to justify
the apprehension I felt.   Walther Blum was on a timber-cart,
going to the town ; why should he not be on a timber-cart,
going to the town ?   He was not even driving, but sitting by
the driver's side ; why, if he had business that way, should
he not take the chance of a lift ?   For all I knew he was going
to dispose of his paper-knives and blotters and fretwork
clock-faces.   If he were away for a couple of days it would be
lonely for his wife, but they do not mind loneliness up there,
and possibly he had sent her to her people.   It was as natural

that Walther Blum should be taking a journey on a cart as that I myself should be saying good-bye to my friend.

None the less, I could not get rid of it like that. "Nobody asks why Walther Blum does anything," my driver had just said ; but I asked. Say he was not going away at all. Say he merely wished it to be supposed he had gone away. Say, in short, that he was setting a trap for Nicolo. Had it been possible, I would have bidden my driver turn and follow Walther Blum wherever he went. That was not possible. But something else was. I couldn't follow Walther Blum, but I could keep an eye on Nicolo. He would not know he was being watched, and watched, moreover, for his own health and safety.

It was the first thing I did on my return to the hotel to walk into the American bar. He happened to be there. Disliking him as I did, I nevertheless made myself talk to him.

"So another has left, Nicolo," I said, with an assumption of cheerfulness. "It is drawing near the end."

"Monsieur will be the last," he said, busily polishing.

"When do you go to London ?"

"In four days, Monsieur."

"Well, this country is beautiful in the winter, and beautiful in the summer, but it is not much in between."

He showed his close white teeth in a smile. "It is Monsieur who sees the country," he said. "We of the staff work too long hours to see much of it."

"But you go up the mountain sometimes for a walk and to breathe the air ?"

"Not I, Monsieur. I do not like the cold. I like Capri and Sorrento and the sun on Naples Bay."

And, having ascertained that he was in the hotel, I left him, but did not go too far away.

I well believed that he was not fond of mountain climbing. He might even have to run the gauntlet of jests if he, the smooth lazy one, were seen toiling up past the plantation during the day. For many reasons he would prefer the night. And I had no evidence that he intended to go at all. But I was persuaded by something more subtly strong than evidence. There were vast gaps in my information. I only knew in outline what had passed between Blum and his wife on that first night of all. That she and Nicolo exchanged kisses I did know, but not every kiss is an adultery, and it

would be an unfeeling heart that found no forgiveness for
her. But while I did not know the details, I did know the
sum and result of them. Blum himself was satisfied that no
guilty act had been committed. At the same time, he was
equally satisfied that the attempt would be made, and had
cunningly and deliberately provided the opportunity. If
Nicolo did not climb the mountain it was even possible that
he might prevail on her to make a pretext to come to the
hotel. Or nothing at all might happen.

But as the day wore on and I wandered aimlessly about
the precincts of the hotel, I thought so less and less.

I come now to the moment when Nicolo did leave the
hotel, setting his face up the mountain. With the passing
of time I can survey the events of that evening almost calmly ;
but time has had to pass. I have ceased to call myself a young
man. I apprehend, too constantly, the meaning of such
words as causation and fatality and absence of design. I
have learned how events themselves take charge and fall into
inhuman and unpremeditated patterns. I think it was so with
Walther and Karen Blum. As she had "happened" to him,
so the world had happened to him and he to the world, and
there was no escape from the dreadful logic of the upshot.
It had to be so, and it was so, and I had to be a witness of it.

Nicolo did not steal out of the hotel like a man on a
guilty errand. He strolled out, apparently with no other
purpose than to take the air. He wore his waiter's black
trousers, but had changed his white jacket for one of purplish
cloth, and on his head was a green velours hat with feathers
in it. To English eyes his appearance was incongruous yet
somehow dandified, and he himself was evidently well content
with it. All this I saw from where I stood at the verandah's
end. He sauntered round to the back of the hotel, and I
ascended quickly to my room. Not that there was any hurry.
I had to let him get ahead. I do not carry firearms, but if I
had had a pistol I should certainly have slipped it into my
pocket. For moral effect, naturally.

He was not quite out of sight when I descended ; he was
well up the plantation, giving a backward glance, as if he
wondered how much longer it was necessary to keep up
appearances. I stepped out of his line of vision. There was
one chance and one only that I should lose him, and even
that did not matter—for if he took the longer and less steep

of the two paths that met again farther on, I could take the
other one and be there before him. That might be the best.
At least I should escape the hateful appearance of watching
another man unobserved. As he was of a corpulent build he
probably would take the easier path. In fact he did so, and
I the other.

I made haste. If Blum should appear he would hardly
resent it that one such as I should be found alone with his
wife, and if he did not appear Nicolo would be likely to
find an empty house at the end of his journey. It may seem
odd, but it seemed somehow part of what I have called the
pattern that I made no attempt to divert Nicolo himself.
He was a contemptible fellow, and must take his chance.
He was away to the right, somewhere over the shoulder of the
hill, and as I passed the point that he, too, would presently
have to pass, I quickened my pace to something like a run,
that he might not see me ahead.

More snow than in the valleys still lay on the ground,
and as I reached the beginning of the dark clearing the ghostly
mass of the Huldhorn rose miles ahead, just discernible. Not
a quarter of a mile away Blum's light showed, almost as
watery as on my first visit—for I discovered that the icicles
had not been broken away, but still formed a screen, though
a perforated and attentuated one only. This time I did not
look in. I walked up to the door and knocked. Only when
I had done so did it occur to me that my knock might be
taken for the knock of somebody else.

There was no reply, and I knocked more loudly. Still
I had no answer, though I heard a muffled sound within.
There was nothing for it but the window. I advanced and
looked through a ribbed and ragged hole.

Karen sat there alone. She sat where her husband had
sat, under the powerful incandescent, and her round eyes
appeared to be staring straight into mine. But I don't think
they saw. She was rigid, as if the sound of my knock had
frozen both the sight and speech of her. The table at which
she sat was empty. On the little shelf stood the row of wooden
cattle and carved knives, but I did not see the statuette. I
called; I gave my name; and as if my name had been a magic
word, she broke into life. She sprang up and disappeared
for an instant from my view. I heard the shooting of a bolt.
By this time I was at the door. She flung it open, dragged

me in, and shot the bolt again almost in one movement. Then she clasped both her hands on one of my shoulders, and I had to save her from falling.

"Oh, the dear God has sent you!" she moaned on my breast. "Do not go. Keep me so. Keep me so till morning, for God knows what is going to happen this night!"

"I know what is going to happen this night if you will, Karen. You cannot stay here alone. Put your things on and come with me back to the hotel."

She shook convulsively. "I cannot! I dare not! I was told I must stay here! Stay here with me!"

"Certainly I will stay with you; but who told you you must stay here?"

"He told me—Walther——"

"But he has gone to the town?"

"He has not gone to the town. I do not know where he is. But he is not far away. He was here an hour ago. He has kept me here all day, that I might neither go nor send word to the hotel."

"Why should you wish to send word to the hotel, Karen? Word to whom, and about what?"

But she only said, "Oh! Oh! Oh!" and crushed herself harder against me.

"When I knocked, Karen, did you think it might be somebody else, that you did not answer?" I asked.

I felt her nod.

"Walther?" (The door had been bolted, and the visitor might have been he.)

"No."

"The somebody else—has he ever been here?"

"Never—never—never!" she said, with a passion that utterly convinced me.

"You know what I mean?" I whispered.

"Yes."

"Then shall I go and turn him back?"

She bounded from my arms in fright. "What! Then he *is* coming?"

"There may be time to warn him."

She sank to the floor. "If he is on the mountain—Walther can run like a hare and leap like the chamois——"

And I remembered Blum's words: "If he steps a yard beyond the plantation——"

It had been plain enough before; it was bright as a sunburst now. My first unworthy idea, that Blum had turned his house into a mousetrap and baited it with a piece of cheese, was utterly wrong. Nobody was luring Nicolo. He was free to stay away. But he was free *only* as long as he stayed away. Once he set foot on those mountain wastes he entered a cage of which the door closed behind him. What chance had he, the keeper of an American bar, against a man who could run like a hare and leap like a chamois? . . . And yet a panic took me too. I must have caught it from her, sunk to a huddle on the floor. I could not see a human being walk into an open trap like that. I must warn him. I sprang to the bolt of the door.

But I was too late. I heard the faint sound of a distant scream. I flung open the door with such force that the wall shook.

"*Eee-eee-eee !*" It was the tight-drawn, inarticulate scream of pure terror, and it came from somewhere in the wood. He had sought safety in the wood—and from a pursuing woodsman !

"*Eee-eee-eee !*" Again came the squeal. My shadow streamed from the doorway, and the beginning of the wood beyond was illuminated as if by the headlights of a car. Karen had stopped her ears.

"*Eee-eee-eee !*"

And then, a little way within the wood, I saw him, if that shadow was he. The sounds of the last scream had died away, as if he had merely continued to scream as a child screams, having once begun. He seemed to be listening. Blum I did not see. This made matters no better. Better to see Blum than to know all the time that he was near, stealing noiselessly from tree to tree, ushering, shepherding, getting his man where he wanted him.

"*Eeee-eeee-eeee ! . . . Eeee-eeee-eeee !*"

Such an added extreme of terror would have seemed inexpressible, but he did it. The next moment he was flying straight for the hut, as a moth makes for a lamp. His arms were above his head, and Blum was after him.

Do not tell me how feeble was my effort to bang the door between the two. I cannot leap like a chamois nor cover the mountains like a hare. Loudly the door swung to and back again. As it did so something fell to the floor with a little snap. I do not know on what ledge or shelf it had been standing, but it was Blum's statuette, and the violent jar of the door had brought it down. Breathing easily, Blum slowly bolted the door.

"Walther," I cried sharply, "open that door! No harm is done! Let the fellow go!"

He did not appear to hear me. His bright eyes were on the other's white and sweating face.

"Then I will open it——" and I took a step forward.

But I seemed merely to precipitate the thing I wished to forestall. Even in a light-built man I should not have thought so swift a movement possible. I fell back with a ringing head and one useless elbow, and Blum was not calm now. He was trembling and his face was advanced towards the Neapolitan's.

"So you thought you would come? The coast was clear? Just one little peep past the plantation before you left?"

Nicolo was licking his lips. His purple jacket was fouled and burred, and his green velours hat had gone.

"You said to yourself, 'Walther Blum is away, and his wife must be lonely, and it would be neighbourly to sit with her an hour'?"

I saw Nicolo's fleeting look at the window. I read his thoughts: a sudden leap to the table and a header, through icicles and all—Blum could have done it—it was all there was to do. It was, as a matter of fact, Nicolo who struck first, a desperate and futile blow. He did not even succeed in getting on to the table. He was caught and tripped, and in a moment both men were on the floor.

Karen had fallen back behind the stove, with eyes that peeped dreadfully between her fingers. And there was no more screaming now. Blum had his left forearm under the Neapolitan's nape, and his right palm was pressed on his forehead. He was looking at him earnestly, attentively. And he had ceased to speak. Why should he speak? Words were things used up and outworn by others. To creep in midwinter round the cornice of the Huldhorn had been one of his words. And this was its companion word, that he was doing now.

Then my heart stood still as I saw the slow grope of his powerful hand along the floor. In a flash I knew beforehand

what he intended to do. I tried to kick at the hand, but
once more I was too late. I looked wildly round. Karen
had sunk to the floor by the stove, but I saw her raise her
head. . . .

And that at least—her seeing what I foresaw—I *could*
stop. Those blue, already overburdened eyes were not
made for *that*. I do not know whether or not I was in time.
I sprang to the middle of the room and with my unhurt hand
dashed out the incandescent.

I dash out the light from this page, too. As the player
rises from the board without making the final move, as the
pattern is all there without the addition of the last piece
of all, so let it be with the tale. Say—I do not know—
that the whole thing took ten minutes, half an hour, an hour,
before the silence came. It was in the dead silence that I
heard Blum get up from the floor. I heard his feet pass me,
heard his groping in some cupboard behind me. There were
sounds as he did something in the middle of the room.

Then suddenly the hut was flooded with the light of the
new bulb he had fitted.

My eyes rested on Karen first. She lay on her back, wide-
eyed and still. I had heard no sound from her—believe me,
if you had been there you would have had ears for one set of
sounds only—but deep in her breast was Walther's slenderest
carving-chisel. He was standing there, but he had not yet
seen her; he was looking down at his other piece of work.
I think, when I remember the cleared table at which Karen
had sat, that he had intended to make a man-to-man business
of it. He had cleared away all other weapons, intending to
finish him with his hands, and Karen had probably hidden
the thin chisel somewhere about her. But what I saw I seemed
already to have known. Only the arm of the statuette was
to be seen, the one that had broken off when it had fallen
from behind the door. All else of that thing of loveliness
was indistinguishable from the rest of the red on the floor.
Blum had broken it to splinters in cramming it where he
conceived it to belong—where he conceived the smile itself
to belong—in between Nicolo's white teeth and down his
throat.

"JOHN GLADWIN SAYS . . ."

IF we are to believe John Gladwin, the oncoming car made no attempt to avoid him, but held straight on. It held on at top speed, he says, for the first he saw of it was the sudden blinding gold of the afternoon sun on its screen, almost on top of him. He was not wool-gathering or thinking of anything else at the time, and he has been for years a teetotaller. As for there not being any other car there at all, he naturally scouts the idea, for if there had been no other car why should he have made that violent and instinctive swerve? He did swerve; something hurtled past him; into the hedge and through it he and his car plunged; and where a moment before the white secondary road had run straight as a ruler for miles, he found himself on soft green, startled out of his wits, still at the wheel, his screen unbroken, his engine still running.

He says that his first thought was this—people ought not to drive like that. All was quiet on the road behind him, but the fellow could hardly be out of sight yet. John Gladwin came to life. He climbed as quickly as he was able out of the car and pushed through the hole he had made in the hedge.

Properly speaking, he had not come through the hedge at all. He had broken through a thin part of it, a gap, thinly tangled over, and his car had come to rest on an old grass-grown track beyond. He looked first down the long white road. There was no sign of any other car, and no other roads ran into it. Then he looked at his own wheelmarks in the dust, and they rather scared him. Heavens! What a mercy he had been crawling along! It would be just as well to report a lunatic who drove like that.

But what was there to report, except that golden flash, gone in a moment, the empty road, and his own tracks in the dust?

He scrambled back through the broken hedge and climbed into the car again. At any rate, he was alive.

Something had happened to the car, none the less. The lever would not go into reverse. Again and again he tried; it went with ease into the other speeds, but not into the one that would take him out backwards again into the road he had left. He got out and set his shoulder to the car, but that was a younger man's job, and the car remained immovable. Then he looked ahead and thought he saw the best thing to do.

Old Harkness Bottom, he knew the region to be called, and from the pocket of the car he fetched out the map. It was an old map, mounted on linen, in tatters with much use, but it told him what he wanted to know. Harkness itself—New Harkness the older people still called it—lay away over the hill and out of sight, and New Harkness was almost a bustling sort of place. A tarred main road ran through it, with traffic at all hours, and it has red and yellow petrol-pumps, and a church already old, as new churches go, with its shrine and flowers at the lychgate, and its tablet with the names of seven Harkness lads inside. But nobody ever went near Old Harkness. Something had happened about the price of corn, and its very stones had been carted away to make the new village.

But here was probably a way through, and out again beyond, and John Gladwin, unable to go back, decided to go forward.

On the left of the green lane along which he bumped rose a rough slope covered with ragwort and thistles, and on his right he brushed another hedge so closely that clusters of berries, vivid and rank, scarlet and bright green and glossy black all on the same bunch, broke off and fell into the car, with strippings of deadly-nightshade and fat-fruited bryony. Swish, snap, rip; it was far from being a new car, and a loose mudguard rattled, and the headlamps vibrated with the jolting. For half a mile or so he drove, winding now to the left, now to the right. And then suddenly he came upon a whole world of palest pinkish-silver.

It rose steeply round three sides of a deep dell—the seeding willow-herb, deadly-soft, wreathed, billowing, with here and there a maple of a gold so vibrant that the eye was almost sensible of a twang. A week or two before it must have been a dyer's vat of the flagrant purple; now the very air was thickened with the fleece of its procreation.

And down in the Bottom, in the only patch the weeds had not invaded, stood a church.

John Gladwin would hardly have known it was a church, he says, if it had not been for the tombstones. There were perhaps a score of these, lying and leaning at all angles, and some of them were not stones at all, but nameboards of ancient wood, with finials sticking up at the ends like prick-ears, John Gladwin says. As for the church—well, there it was, what remained of it, that wrecked and ivied hummock in the middle of the field. The gap into the field had no gate. John Gladwin imagines he must have stopped his engine, for this pink-and-silver bowl in the hills was filled with an immense quiet. He got out of the car. Picking his way among the tombstones, he pushed through coarse grass to the ruin.

The stone-movers had been there, too, John Gladwin says, for half of the broken buttress over which he clambered had gone ; but that ragged "V" against the sky where the belfry had been had probably fallen down of itself. He could only just force his way in for brambles and tangled rose, and a mountain-ash filled the chancel, its berries already turning red. The whole church was not more than fifteen strides long. A greenish, semi-darkness filled it, says John Gladwin.

And over all brooded that stillness, not of peace (he says), but of the desolation of things lost to the world. He started when, with a harsh beating of wings, a thrush flew out of the chancel where the mountain-ash was.

But he jumped nearly a foot into the air when, loud and immediately above his head, there clanged out the single stroke of a bell.

Of course, he knew there was no bell. The nearest bell was the thin-noted bell of New Harkness Church, away over the hill, and, anyway, its sound would have passed unheard overhead. Nevertheless, John Gladwin looked up. And naturally he saw only the ragged "V" where once a bell had been.

And then the note came again, urgent and earnest, as if it summoned somebody to make haste. John Gladwin, suddenly remembering that he was in a church, took off his hat.

The bell that wasn't there rang a third time, and he bent

his knee and crossed himself.   As he did so he heard his name
spoken behind him.

Now the most astounding statement of a number that
John Gladwin makes is that of a sudden all this seemed
reasonable and natural and right.   Indubitably there had
been a bell in that crumbling "V" above his head.   It had had
its own voice, earnest and urgent and compelling.   But in
another moment he had forgotten all about the bell, he says.
What was a bell by the side of the voice that had called him
by name ?   It was a young voice, of a lingering sweetness,
that finished each syllable exquisitely and had always moved
John Gladwin past telling.   It took him back more than
thirty years—and already John Gladwin was fifty-eight years
old when he says all this happened.   And then the voice spoke
his name again.

"John !"

This time he did not turn round, as a minute or two
before he had looked up at that startling ringing of the bell.
What, he asks, is the use of turning round to see something
that is as much you as your heart itself ?   Instead, he replied
to the voice, and his own tones shook with a still passion of
tenderness.

"Emily !"

"So you were able to come ?"

"I was not able to stay away."

"You rode over on Grey Boy ?"

"Yes, most loved."

"I have his piece of sugar.   It is in my muff."

"How beautiful you are !"

"Am I ?"

"Have you no kiss for me ?"

And the voice said :

"Hush—we are in a church."

She had always been like that, John says, sweet and cir-
cumspect, decorous and right, so that those other moments,
when there had been no need for circumspection, had been
by contrast unutterably full.   And when a love like that
has been, it still is, and dies only with the heart it has visited.
So in that sense I should say that every word John Gladwin
says is to be believed.   He was in a church with her once
more, with Grey Boy contentedly cropping in the adjoining
pasture.   Not the leprous silver of the willow-herb disgraced

the hill outside, but the corn whispering in the sun, and the
horseless reaper left where it was until Monday morning.
He was less aware of the hymn-book they shared than of her
hand so near to his own ; and he wore a cravat, and she an
adorable little bonnet with ribands, and a flounced skirt
with a waterfall behind. And John Gladwin says that it did
not seem to be any particular Sunday. The Sundays seemed
to run together, he says, as snowy Christmases run together
in our memories, and sunny summers, and indistinguishable
daisy-fields, that somehow seem the same daisies year after
year. But there came suddenly into his head a Sunday that
did stand out from the rest. As plainly as he had heard the
bell he heard the parson's voice again, pronouncing his name
with hers who sat there in the square pew so consciously
glowing by his side.

"I publish the Banns of Marriage . . ."

There was a rustle in the mountain-ash that filled the
chancel ; the thrush had returned. Through a fissure where
the ivy had forced the stones apart two butterflies could be
seen at play. Morsels of fleece settled on John Gladwin's
new black arm-band, and something stirred among the thigh-
deep nettles. But to John Gladwin it was her voice again.
Thrice the Banns had been proclaimed, and none had known
of any let or impediment.

"So now you can hardly run away !" the voice laughed.

"Away ! Where, away from you, when you are everywhere ?"

"So that's what you mean when you say I am the world
to you !"

"You are both worlds, the bread I eat and the prayers
I say."

"Listen to him, Grey Boy ! Did ever you hear such a
man ?"

"We are not in church now, love. Have you no kiss
for me ?"

And the remembered kiss was as fresh to John Gladwin
as on the day it had been given.

At this point John Gladwin admits to a certain confusion as to what was really happening. His actual surroundings, he says, stood out clearly enough before his
eyes. Looking up, he saw the gap where the bell had been ;
looking out of the breach by which he had entered he saw

L

the spilth of silver seed, the raw gold of the maples, his car not a hundred yards away. But in some way he cannot explain the things he saw were doubled with other things, just as, by mechanical ingenuity, pictures are imposed on pictures and made to come and go. It was, he says, as if one looked at a half-obliterated sketch and saw brightly through it, drawing nearer and nearer, a golden-hued irradiation behind.

Unfortunately, to question him too closely is to confuse him and make him give different answers. He acknowledges, for example, that he is not a Harkness man, and that his Banns were never called in Old Harkness Church. It was in a church two hundred miles away that they were published. But Holy Church, he says, is one, no matter where the location of its fabric, and wedding-bells are the same, whether they be a merry peal or a single blithe note. For it was his marriage, he says, that that vanished bell next gave tongue to.

Not nettles and brambles, but guests filled the church, the friends of the bride on the one side, those of the groom on the other. The gilded pipes of the little organ reared themselves among the berries of the mountain-ash. The fissure where the butterflies played healed itself, and there floated into its place the white marble tablet of Henry Gladwin, Justice of the Peace, benefactor of the church, and owner of acres, long before things happened about the price of corn. The altar was raised again, a roof of oak shut out the September sky, John Gladwin says. And she came in on her father's arm and was brought to where he waited. She wore her great-grandmother's lace, that lace that had outlasted herself, and never, the village declared, had bride looked lovelier.

And John Gladwin thinks that as he stood there, as one might say in two churches at once, he saw something no man has seen before—two faces also at once, not as one sees them in some old album, with the gradations of the years coming calmly and imperceptibly in between, but vividly and violently contrasted, the unwrinkled face side by side with the wrinkled one, the veined hand by the flower-smooth one, and nothing to account for the fading and change. And one face was shrouded in lavendered lace, and the other had lain now a week in another shroud. The two faces looked together at him, different yet the same as his love had

been different yet the same. She had neither utterly died
nor utterly grown old. Something as inalienable as her name
had persisted throughout—Emily.

So she said, "I will," that day, and there was a hush,
because they were in a church.

John Gladwin says that he saw himself, too. He saw
himself in a pouting grey cravat and beautiful tubular trousers,
and he was straight-backed then and strong-limbed, and
could, if need be, walk his thirty miles in a day instead of being
glad of a coughing old two-seater to trundle him about. But
he did not see himself twice over, side by side, as he had seen
her, for what was there to look at in the John Gladwin who
stood that afternoon among the brambles that choked Old
Harkness Church, friendless, alone, and very tired? Life
was a thing to look back on, not forward to, and now, in his
unique experience, he had nothing but thanks for that mad
driver who, dashing past him with a flash of gold, had pushed
him through the hedge and into the old lane. He heard the
organ in the mountain-ash again, and the words joined in of
themselves—"The voice that breathed o'er Eden that earliest
wedding day". He saw the throng at the sunny church door,
saw the waiting carriage and the coloured favours of the horses,
the showers of rice, an old shoe. He says he turned himself
about in Old Harkness Church and actually saw these things,
and not merely his old two-seater waiting for him beyond the
overturned tombstones. If they were not there, he says, he
saw them none the less.

But some richness of light had passed away from the
golden maples, a tarnish had come over the silver of the
shedding weed. One could hardly have imagined a greater
stillness than before, and yet the pause and hush seemed
intensified, John said, as he suddenly remembered a pause
and hush in his life before. Here again he admits to a certain
amount of confusion. He was no longer in a church, but
in his own office or study, where he kept his guns and account
books, and received his rent from his tenants, regaling them
in the cleared barn afterwards with beef and beer. He had
taken off his boots, quite unnecessarily, since his walking
about could not possibly have been heard ; and sometimes
his brown hands were clasped together before him, and sometimes they touched grain samples or farm plans, or his magnify-
ing glass, or a strap, or some other of the objects that littered

the room. He was waiting with tense nerves for news from upstairs—news of Emily.

It was brought to him, less by the doctor's words than by his shining face. The child was a boy, and all was well. John Gladwin pulled his boots on again, and put his hand to the little porcelain bell-knob by the side of the mantel-piece. Wine and glasses were brought—and then, without warning, he says, he was back in the church again. He was standing by the font, and when the priest said, "Name this child," John Gladwin answered, "George," and by that name he was baptized in the Name of the Father, and of the Son, and of the Holy Ghost.

And a year and a half later it happened again, and the name this time was William.

John Gladwin says quite frankly that he is by no means certain as to what came next. As the light had died out of the maples, so the pictures became a little less distinct, a little more run together. Perhaps that was because on the whole his life had been a peaceful and eventless one. He had brought up his two sons in the fear of the Lord. On Sundays, in the square pew, and while they were yet quite small, he had had to tell them to hush, because they were in a church ; and as they grew older, and those things began to happen about the price of corn, and the lads shot up to the height of their mother's waist, and then to her breast, churchgoing lads they remained, as was right in the successors of that Henry Gladwin whose tablet looked down on the pew from the fissure where the butterflies were no longer at play.

John had not noticed the departure of the butterflies ; butterflies go everywhere ; and neither had he noticed the further sombring of the maples, nor the change of light that turned the pink of the willow-herb to a whity-brown. He was still, he supposed, half in a church two hundred miles away, and the Sabbaths ran together as the snowy Christmases had run together, and the hot summers and the daisied fields, and the birthdays of the boys. He was troubled about the boys, he says. The price of corn was becoming less and less what it should have been. The marble Henry Gladwin, gazing steadfastly from the wall into the square pew, might presently find one of the boys missing. Probably it would be George, the elder one. He spoke of Canada and South Africa. And it might be a good thing, for it was not right that John Glad-win's labourers only should bear the brunt of a period of agricultural depression. John talked with Emily about it.

"But you have had an offer for the shooting, John," she said again, now in Old Harkness Church.

"Which I shall take, but it is only delaying matters for another year. It is no remedy."

"George only wants to go because he thinks it may ease matters."

"George is not the only one who is going."

"And then I suppose William will want to go after him."

John Gladwin vows that he heard all this again, in the broken church in Old Harkness Bottom.

"We must do what we can. And if you are going to read let me get you your glasses."

But as things chanced it was neither Canada nor South Africa that took George and William. If John Gladwin is to be believed, that vanished bell against the now un-naturally hued sky spoke loudly once again. And, knowing now what was happening, he did not jump a foot into the air this time. Quietly he sank to his knees among the nettles.

"Let them go," he said with bowed head. "I will go too. We shall all be needed."

"John!" her voice rang sharply out. "They cannot take them! They did not bear them! They are mine!"

"They will go laughing. You will not be able to keep them."

"But I shall be alone!"

"There is nursing. There is cooking. I will find you something to do."

And again, says John Gladwin, the bell rang warningly out, as if to summon the women as well as the men.

But in the end neither did he find anything for her to do, nor yet anything for himself. They wanted captains of twenty-five, not forty-five, they said, and he must wait his turn. Youngest and best first; and go George and William did. Shortly after, John Gladwin, seizing an occasion, sold his land two hundred miles away, brought his wife south, and settled her in a small house not far from Harkness, and himself became a special constable, since that was all they seemed able to find him to do.

And now, though he was on his knees, he was not in a

place that at all resembled a church, but in some dim twilight of mud and flashes, and roaring and death, that naturally he could not see clearly because he had never been there. An occasional "Pretty hectic" was all he could get out of the letters of his sons, varied once in a while with a jest about its healthiness. The light through the brambles and the mountain-ash became of a more sullen green. The wall-tablet of Henry Gladwin, John says, dissolved away, and another slid relentlessly into its place. This one was of oak, with names upon it in gold, and there was one exactly like it in the New Harkness Church, as well as where John Gladwin knelt. Even the names were the same :

GEORGE GLADWIN
WILLIAM GLADWIN

—they were the first two of the seven on the tablet. The names only survived. What had become of the rest of them neither John Gladwin nor anybody else knew.

A low muttering filled the air. It was the first rumble of a storm. There was a pale flash, like the flash of a shell in daylight, and if John Gladwin wanted to get home before it came he had best put his hood up and be gone. But he remained where he was, so still that the very field-mice might have approached him. Then the muttering was no longer muttering. Suddenly the heavens cracked and pealed harshly above his head. A chill gust filled the air with fleece, and a bright flash showed every leaf and berry of the ash. But between it and the crash that followed John Gladwin says he heard another voice, the voice of the white-haired New Harkness vicar, who had put the names of John Gladwin's sons in gold on the wall.

"We bring nothing into this world, and it is certain that we can carry nothing out . . . the Lord gave, and the Lord hath taken away : blessed be the name of the Lord. . . . We, therefore, commit her body to the ground. . . . Not to be sorry, as men without hope . . ."

Three days before, the words had been spoken, and John Gladwin says he heard their very vibrations still.

"Amen," he said, with bowed head, and rose as the first great drop struck his bare crown like a falling pebble.

He was hardly out of the church when the rain crashed

down. Every broken tombstone was hidden in a mist and spray of it. The maples were not to be seen, the craven silver of the weed seemed to cower under its thrashing. Rivers coursed between the old graves, and, at the gap where the wedding carriage had stood with favours on the horses and flowers in the lamps, it was John Gladwin's car that stood there, twanging like a drum and spouting out valances of water. Soaked to his spine, John Gladwin bent over the starting-handle. The engine broke into a rattle. He climbed into the sodden seat, and sat for a moment wondering whether he should turn round or go forward. He decided to go forward. A gate might close the old track at its other end, but he would risk it. The other would be miles round to where he wanted to be—standing before a gold-lettered nameboard, standing at a mound of earth three days old.

And John Gladwin says, and stands to it, that it was to the tolling of the bell of Old Harkness Church heard above the shout of the rain that he swayed and splashed in the car round the churchyard and skirted the beaten-down silver of the weeds.

First, he says, he found roofless buildings, then a solitary inhabited farm, and then a straggle of cottages along a cart-track, but ever getting nearer to the known world. Then, almost suddenly because of the rain, he saw the tree-line of the tarred main road. As suddenly, at the crest, the shower ceased as if an invisible hand had turned it off at the main. Swiftly the clouds packed themselves away behind him, and ahead there flashed on his eyes a dazzle of gold. It glittered on the still-showering branches ; it made prisms in the air ; and as John Gladwin swung out of the lane into the tarred main road he saw nothing but a glow of molten light. He says it was like looking into the middle of the Sun Himself.

And the manner of his going out of Old Harkness Bottom was as the manner of his entering it. I think myself that Death did not ride on a Pale Horse that afternoon, but took a trip in a Golden Car. John Gladwin was driving slowly ; at his time of life he never did anything else. He never even saw what rushed towards him (he says), but only the effulgent road. And this time it was too late to swerve. It was just where the red and yellow petrol-pumps stood, backed by the coloured sheet-iron advertisements. New Harkness Church, with its shrine and lych-gate, was a bare hundred yards away.

John Gladwin thinks, and says, that it was the same car as before.

The noise of the smash was heard by a Bentley, more than a mile away.

The Bentley came up and drew to a standstill. It had come from that direction, but it had met no other car. And it was the Bentley that took John Gladwin to the cottage hospital with a broken back.

I myself have never been to Old Harkness Bottom, and have only John Gladwin's word for it that there is a church there at all. We go to see him where he lies. He lies on a white bedstead, with a white-uniformed nurse to make things easy for the remaining time, which we, like himself, hope won't be too long. And he tells us these things with the dreadful candour of a man about to die.

But sometimes, with the screen at his feet and the chart over his head, without regard to where he is, in a red-roofed cottage hospital with white woodwork and a privet hedge round it, he breaks off with a gesture. His fingers go to his lips and his eyes steal round. He is in Old Harkness Bottom again, and for all I know his boys are being naughty once more.

"Hush!" he says reproachfully. "We are in church!"

E. F. BENSON

THE HANGING OF ALFRED WADHAM

I HAD been telling Father Denys Hanbury about a very extraordinary séance which I had attended a few days before. The medium in trance had said a whole series of things which were unknown to anybody but myself and a friend of mine who had lately died, and who, so she said, was present and was speaking to me through her. Naturally, from the strictly scientific point of view in which alone we ought to approach such phenomena, such information was not really evidence that the spirit of my friend was in touch with her, for all this was already known to me, and might by some process of telepathy have been communicated to the medium from my brain and not through the agency of the dead. She spoke, too, not in her own ordinary voice, but in a voice which certainly was very like his. Then again, however, his voice was known to me; it was in my memory even as were the things she had been saying. All this, therefore, as I was remarking to Father Denys, must be ruled out as positive evidence that communications had been coming from the other side of death.

"A telepathic explanation was possible," I said, "and we have to accept any known explanation which covers the facts before we conclude that the dead have come back into touch with the material world."

The room was quite warm, but I saw that he shivered slightly, and, hitching his chair a little nearer the fire, he spread out his hands to the blaze. Such hands they were; beautiful and expressive of him, and so like the praying hands of Albert Dürer; the blaze shone through them as through rose-red alabaster. He shook his head.

"It's a terribly dangerous thing to attempt to get into communication with the dead," he said. "If you seem to get into touch with them, you run the risk of establishing connection not with them but with awful and perilous intelligences.   Study telepathy by all means, for that is one of the marvels of the mind which we are meant to investigate like any other of the wonderful secrets of Nature.   But I interrupt you ; you said something else occurred.   Tell me about it.''

Now I knew Father Denys's creed about such things and deplored it.   He holds, as his Church commands him, that intercourse with the spirits of the dead is impossible, and that when it appears to occur, as it undoubtedly does, the inquirer is really in touch with some species of dramatic demon, who is impersonating the spirit of the dead.   Such a thing has always seemed to me as monstrous as it is without foundation, and there is nothing I can discover in the recognized sources of Christian doctrine which justifies such a view.

"Yes ! Now comes the queer part," I said.   "For, still speaking in the voice of my friend, the medium told me something which instantly I believed to be untrue.   It could not therefore have been drawn telepathically from me.   After that the séance came to an end, and in order to convince myself that this could not have come from him, I looked up the diary of my friend which had been left me at his death, and which had just been sent me by his executors, and was still unpacked.   There I found an entry which proved that what the medium had said was absolutely correct.   A certain thing—I needn't go into it—had occurred precisely as she had stated, though I should have been willing to swear to the contrary.   That cannot have come into her mind from mine, and there is no source that I can see from which she could have obtained it except from my friend.   What do you say to that ?"

He shook his head.   "I don't alter my position at all," he said.   "That information, given it did not come from your mind, which certainly seems to be impossible, came from some discarnate agency.   But it didn't come from the spirit of your friend : it came from some evil and awful intelligence."

"But isn't that pure assumption ?" I asked.   "It is surely much simpler to say that the dead can, under certain conditions, communicate with us.   Why drag in the devil ?"

He glanced at the clock.

"It's not very late," he said.   "Unless you want to go to bed, give me your attention for half an hour, and I will try to show you."

The rest of my story is what Father Denys told me, and what happened immediately afterwards.

"Though you are not a Catholic," he said. "I think you would agree with me about an institution which plays a very large part in our ministry, namely Confession, as regards the sacredness and the inviolability of it. A soul laden with sin comes to his Confessor knowing that he is speaking to one who has the power to pronounce or withhold forgiveness, but who will never, for any conceivable reason, repeat or hint at what has been told him. If there were the slightest chance of the penitent's confession being made known to anyone, unless he himself, for purposes of expiation or of righting some wrong, chooses to repeat it, no one would ever come to Confession at all. The Church would lose the greatest hold it possesses over the souls of men, and the souls of men would lose that inestimable comfort of knowing (not hoping merely, but knowing) that their sins are forgiven them. Of course the priest may withhold Absolution, if he is not convinced that he is dealing with a true penitent, and before he gives it, he will insist that the penitent makes such reparation as is in his power for the wrong he has done. If he has profited by his dishonesty he must make good ; whatever crime he has committed he must give warrant that his penitence is sincere. But I think you would agree that in any case the priest cannot, whatever the result of his silence may be, repeat what has been told him. By doing so he might right or avert some hideous wrong, but it is impossible for him to do so. What he has heard, he has heard under the seal of Confession, concerning the sacredness of which no argument is conceivable."

"It is possible to imagine awful consequences resulting from it," I said. "But I agree."

"Before now awful consequences have come of it," he said, "but they don't touch the principle. And now I am going to tell you of a certain confession that was once made to me."

"How can you ?" I said. "That's impossible surely ?"

"For a certain reason, which we shall come to later," he said, "you will see that secrecy is no longer incumbent on me. But the point of my story is not that : it is to warn you about attempting to establish communication with the dead. Signs and tokens, voices and apparitions appear to come through to us from them, but who sends them? You will see what I mean."

I settled myself down to listen.

"You will probably not remember with any distinctness, if at all, a murder committed a year ago, when a man called Gerald Selfe met his death. There was no enticing mystery about it, no romantic accessories, and it aroused no public interest. Selfe was a man of loose life, but he held a respectable position, and it would have been disastrous for him if his private irregularities had come to light. For some time before his death he had been receiving blackmailing letters regarding his relations with a certain married woman, and, very properly, he had put the matter into the hands of the police. They had been pursuing certain clues, and on the afternoon before Selfe's death one of the officers of the Criminal Investigation Department had written to him that everything pointed to his manservant, who certainly knew of his intrigue, being the culprit.

"This was a young man named Alfred Wadham: he had only lately entered Selfe's service, and his past history was of the most unsavoury sort. They had baited a trap for him, of which details were given, and suggested that Selfe should display it, which, within an hour or two, he successfully did. This information and these instructions were conveyed in a letter which, after Selfe's death, was found in a drawer of his writing-table, of which the lock had been tampered with. Only Wadham and his master slept in his flat; and a woman came in every morning to cook breakfast and do the housework, and Selfe lunched and dined at his club, or in the restaurant on the ground floor of this house of flats, and here he dined that night. When the woman came in next morning she found the outer door of the flat open, and Selfe lying dead on the floor of his sitting-room with his throat cut. Wadham had disappeared, but in the slop-pail of his bedroom was water which was stained with human blood. He was caught two days afterwards and at his trial elected to give evidence. His story was that he suspected he had fallen into a trap, and that while Mr. Selfe was at dinner he searched his drawers and found the letter sent by the police, which proved that this was the case. He therefore decided to bolt, and he left the flat that evening

before his master came back to it after dinner. Being in the
witness-box, he was of course subjected to a searching cross-
examination, and contradicted himself in several particulars.
Then there was that incriminating evidence in his room,
and the motive for the crime was clear enough. After a
very long deliberation the jury found him guilty, and he was
sentenced to death. His appeal, which followed, was dismissed.

"Wadham was a Catholic, and since it is my office to
minister to Catholic prisoners at the gaol where he was
lying under sentence of death, I had many talks with him,
and entreated him for the sake of his immortal soul to confess
his guilt. But though he was even eager to confess other
misdeeds of his, some of which it was ugly work to speak of,
he maintained his innocence on this charge of murder. Nothing shook him, and though so far as I could judge he was
sincerely penitent for other misdeeds, he swore to me that the
story he told in court was, in spite of the contradictions in
which he had involved himself, essentially true, and that if
he were hanged, he died unjustly. Up till the last afternoon
of his life, when I sat with him for two hours, praying and
pleading with him, he stuck to that. Why he should do that,
unless indeed he was innocent, when he was eager to search
his heart for the confession of other gross wickednesses, was
curious ; the more I pondered it, the more inexplicable I
found it, and during that afternoon, doubt as to his guilt
began to grow in me. A terrible thought it was, for he had
lived in sin and error, and to-morrow his life was to be broken
like a snapped stick. I was to be at the prison again before
six in the morning, and I still had to determine whether I
should give him the Sacrament. If he went to his death guilty
of murder, but refusing to confess, I had no right to give it
him, but if he were innocent, my withholding of it was as terrible
as any miscarriage of justice. Then on my way out I had a
word with one of the warders, which brought my doubt
closer to me.

" 'What do you make of Wadham ?' I asked.
"He drew aside to let a man pass, who nodded to him :
somehow I knew that he was the hangman.

" 'I don't like to think of it, sir,' he said. 'I know he
was found guilty, and that his appeal failed. But if you ask
me whether I believe him to be a murderer, why no, I don't.'

"I spent the evening alone : about ten o'clock, as I was on the point of going to bed, I was told that a man called Horace Kennion was below, and wanted to see me. He was a Catholic, and though I had been friends with him at one time, certain things had come to my knowledge which made it impossible for me to have anything more to do with him, and I had told him so. He was wicked—oh, don't mis-understand me ; we all do wicked things constantly : the life of us all is a tissue of misdeeds, but he alone of all men I had ever met seemed to me to love wickedness for its own sake. I said I could not see him, but the message came back that his need was urgent, and up he came. He wanted, he told me, to make his Confession, not to-morrow, but now, and his Confessor was away. I could not as a priest resist that appeal. And his confession was that he had killed Gerald Selfe.

"For a moment I thought this was some impious joke, but he swore he was speaking the truth, and still under the seal of Confession gave me a detailed account. He had dined with Selfe that night, and had gone up afterwards to his flat for a game of piquet. · Selfe told him with a grin that he was going to lay his servant by the heels to-morrow for blackmail. 'A smart spry young man to-day,' he said. 'Perhaps a bit off colour to-morrow at this time.' He rang the bell for him to put out the card-table ; then saw it was ready, and he forgot that his summons remained unanswered. They played high points and both had drunk a good deal. Selfe lost partie after partie and eventually accused Kennion of cheating. Words ran high, and boiled over into blows, and Kennion in some rough and tumble of wrestling and hitting, picked up a knife from the table and stabbed Selfe in the throat, through jugular vein and carotid artery. In a few minutes he had bled to death. . . . Then Kennion remembered that unanswered bell, and went tiptoe to Wad-ham's room. He found it empty ; empty, too, were the other rooms in the flat. Had there been anyone there, his idea was to say he had come up at Selfe's invitation and found him dead. But this was better yet : there was no more than a few spots of blood on him, and he washed them in Wadham's room, emptying the water into his slop-pail. Then, leaving the door of the flat open, he went downstairs and out.

"He told me this in quite a few sentences, even as I have told it you, and looked up at me with a smiling face.

" 'So what's to be done next, Venerable Father ?' he said gaily.

" 'Ah, thank God you've confessed !' I said. "We're in time yet to save an innocent man. You must give yourself up to the police at once.' But even as I spoke my heart misgave me.

"He rose, dusting the knees of his trousers.

" 'What a quaint notion,' he said. 'But there's nothing further from my thoughts.'

"I jumped up.

" 'I shall go myself then,' I said.

"He laughed outright at that.

" 'Oh, no, indeed you won't,' he said. 'What about the seal of Confession ? Indeed, I rather fancy it's a deadly sin for a priest ever to think of violating it. Really, I'm ashamed of you, my dear Denys. Naughty fellow ! But perhaps it was only a joke ; you didn't mean it.'

" 'I do mean it,' I said. 'You shall see if I mean it.' But even as I spoke, I knew I did not. 'Anything is allowable to save an innocent man from death.'

"He laughed again.

" 'Pardon me : you know perfectly well that it isn't," he said. 'There's one thing in our creed far worse than death, and that is the damnation of the soul. You've got no intention of damning yours. I took no risk at all when I confessed to you.'

" 'But it will be murder if you don't save this man,' I said.

" 'Oh, certainly, but I've got murder on my conscience already,' he said. 'One gets used to it very quickly. And having got used to it, another murder doesn't seem to matter an atom. Poor young Wadham : to-morrow, isn't it ? I'm not sure it won't be a sort of rough justice. Blackmail is a disgusting offence.'

"I went to the telephone, and took off the receiver.

" 'Really this is most interesting,' he said. 'Walton Street is the nearest police station. You don't need the number : just say "Walton Street police". But you can't. You can't say, "I have a man with me now, Horace Kennion, who has confessed to me that he murdered Selfe." So why bluff ! Besides, if you could do any such thing, I should merely say that I had done nothing of the kind. Your word, the word of a priest who has broken the most sacred vow, against mine. Childish !'

" 'Kennion,' I said, 'for the love of God, and for the fear of hell, give yourself up ! What does it matter whether you or I live a few years less, if at the end we pass into the vast infinite with our sins confessed and forgiven ? Day and night I will pray for you.'

" 'Charming of you,' said he. 'But I've no doubt that now you will give Wadham full absolution. So what does it matter if he goes into—into the vast infinite at eight o'clock to-morrow morning ?'

" 'Why did you confess to me then,' I asked, 'if you had no intention of saving him, and making atonement ?'

" 'Well, not long ago you were very nasty to me,' he said. 'You told me no decent man would consort with me. So it struck me quite suddenly only to-day that it would be pleasant to see you in the most awful hole. I dare say I've got Sadic tastes, too, and they are being wonderfully indulged. You're in torment, you know : you would choose any physical agony other than to be in such a torture-chamber of the soul. It's entrancing : I adore it. Thank you very much, Denys.'

"He got up.

" 'I kept my taxi waiting,' he said. 'No doubt you'll be busy to-night. Can I give you a lift anywhere ? Penton-ville ?'

"There are no words to describe certain darknesses and ecstasies that come to the soul, and I can only tell you that I can imagine no hell of remorse that could equal the hell that I was in. For in the bitterness of remorse we can see that our suffering is a needful and salutary experience : only through it can our sin be burned away. But here was a torture blank and meaningless. . . . And then my brain stirred a little, and I began to wonder whether without breaking the seal of Confession I might not be able to effect some-thing. I saw from my window that the light was burning in the clock-tower at Westminster : the House therefore was sitting, and it seemed possible that without violation I might tell the Home Secretary that a confession had been made me, whereby I knew that Wadham was innocent. He would ask me for any details I could give him, and I could tell him—and then I saw that I could tell him nothing : I could not say that the murderer had gone up with Selfe to his room, for through that information it might be found that Kennion had dined with him.   But before I did anything, I must have guidance, and I went to the Cardinal's house by our Cathedral.   He had gone to bed, for it was now after midnight, but in answer to the urgency of my request he came down to see me.   I told him, without giving any clue, what had happened, and his verdict was what in my heart I knew it would be.   Certainly I might see the Home Secretary and tell him that such a confession had been made me, but no word or hint must escape me which could lead to identification.   Personally, he did not see how the execution could be postponed on such information as I could give.

" 'And whatever you suffer, my son,' he said, 'be sure that you are suffering not from having done wrong, but from having done right.   Placed as you are, your temptation to save an innocent man comes from the devil, and whatever you may be called upon to endure for not yielding to it, is of that origin also."

"I saw the Home Secretary in his room at the House within the hour.   But unless I told him more, and he realized that I could not, he was powerless to move.

" 'He was found guilty at his trial,' he said, 'and his appeal was dismissed.   Without further evidence I can do nothing.'

He sat thinking a moment : then jumped up.

" 'Good God, it's ghastly !' he said.   'I entirely believe, I needn't tell you, that you've heard this confession, but that doesn't prove it's true.   Can't you see the man again ?   Can't you put the fear of God into him ?   If you can do anything at all, which gives me any justification for acting, up till the moment the drop falls, I will give a reprieve at once.   There's my telephone number :   ring me up here or at my house at any hour.'

"I was back at the prison before six in the morning.   I told Wadham that I believed in his innocence, and I gave him Absolution for all else.   He received the Holy and Blessed Sacrament with me, and went without flinching to his death."

Father Denys paused.

"I have been a long time coming to that point in my story," he said, "which concerns that séance you spoke of, but it was necessary for your understanding of what I am going to tell you now that you should know all this.   I said that these messages and communications from the dead come not from them but from some evil and awful power impersonating them. You answered, I remember, 'Why drag in the Devil?' I will tell you.

"When it was over, when the drop on which he stood yawned open, and the rope creaked and jumped, I went home. It was a dark winter's morning, still barely light, and in spite of the tragic scene I had just witnessed I felt serene and peaceful. I did not think of Kennion at all, only of the boy—he was little more—who had suffered unjustly, and that seemed a pitiful mistake, but no more. I did not touch him, his essential living soul, it was as if he had suffered the sacred expiation of martyrdom. And I was humbly thankful that I had been enabled to act rightly, and had Kennion now, through my agency, been in the hands of the police and Wadham alive, I should have been branded with the most terrible crime a priest can commit.

"I had been up all night, and after I had said my office, I lay down on my sofa to get a little sleep. And I dreamed that I was in the cell with Wadham and that he knew I had proof of his innocence. It was within a few minutes of the hour of his death, and I heard along the stone-flagged corridor outside the steps of those who were coming. He heard them too, and stood up, pointing at me.

"'You're letting an innocent man die, when you could save him,' he said. 'You can't do it, Father Denys. Father Denys!' he shrieked, and the shriek broke off in a gulp and a gasp as the door opened.

"I woke, knowing that which had roused me was my own name, screamed out from somewhere close at hand, and I knew whose voice it was. But there I was alone in my quiet empty room, with the dim day peering in. I had been asleep, I saw, for only a few minutes, but now all thought or power of sleep had fled, for somewhere by me, invisible but awfully present, was the spirit of the man whom I had allowed to perish. And he called me.

"But presently I convinced myself that this voice coming to me in sleep was no more than a dream, natural enough in the circumstances, and some days passed tranquilly enough. And then one day when I was walking down a sunny crowded street, I felt some definite and dreadful change in what I may call the psychic atmosphere which surrounds us all, and my soul grew black with fear and with evil imaginings. And there was Wadham coming towards me along the pavement, gay and debonair. He looked at me, and his face became a mask of hate. 'We shall meet often, I hope, Father Denys,' he said as he passed. Another day I returned home in the twilight, and suddenly, as I entered my room, I heard the creak and strain of a rope, and his body with head covered by the death-cap swung in the window against the sunset. And sometimes when I was at my books the door opened quietly and closed again, and I knew he was there. The apparition or the token of it did not come often or perhaps my resistance would have been quickened, for I knew it was devilish in origin. But it came when I was off my guard at long intervals, so that I thought I had vanquished it, and then sometimes I felt my faith to reel. But always it was preceded by this sense of evil power bearing down on me, and I have made haste to seek the shelter of the House of Defence which is set very high. And this last Sunday only——"

He broke off, covering his eyes with his hand, as if shutting out some appalling spectacle.

"I had been preaching," he resumed, "for one of our missions. The church was full, and I do not think there was another thought or desire in my soul but to further the holy cause for which I was speaking. It was a morning service, and the sun poured in through the stained windows in a glow of coloured light. But in the middle of my sermon some bank of cloud drove up, and with it this horrible forewarning of the approach of a tempest of evil. So dark it got that, as I was drawing near the end of my sermon, the lights in the church were switched on, and it leaped into brightness. There was a lamp on the desk in the pulpit, where I had placed my notes, and now when it was kindled it shone full on the pew just below. And there, with his head turned upwards towards me, with his face purple and eyes protruding and with the strangling noose round his neck, sat Wadham.

"My voice faltered a second, and I clutched at the pulpit-rail as he stared at me and I at him. A horror of the spirit, black as the eternal night of the lost, closed round me, for I had let him go innocent to his death, and my punishment was just. . . . And then, like a star shining out through some merciful rent in this soul-storm, came again that ray of conviction that as a priest I could not have done otherwise, and with it the sure knowledge that this apparition could not be of God, but of the devil, to be resisted and defied even as we defy with contempt some sweet and insidious temptation. It could not therefore be the spirit of the man at which I gazed, but some diabolical counterfeit. And I looked back from him to my notes, and went on with my sermon, for that alone was my business. That pause had seemed to me eternal : it had the quality of timelessness, but I learned afterwards that it had been barely perceptible. And from my own heart I learned that it was no punishment that I was undergoing, but the strengthening of a faith that had faltered."

Suddenly he broke off. There came into his eyes as he fixed them on the door a look, not of fear at all, but of savage relentless antagonism.

"It's coming," he said to me, "and now if you hear or see anything, despise it, for it is evil."

The door swung open and closed again, and though nothing visible entered, I knew that there was now in the room a living intelligence other than Father Denys's and mine, and it affected my being, my self, just as some horrible odour of putrefaction affects one physically : my soul sickened in it. Then, still seeing nothing, I perceived that the room, warm and comfortable just now, with a fire of coal prospering in the grate, was growing cold, and that some strange eclipse was veiling the light. Close to me on the table stood an electric lamp : the shade of it fluttered in the icy draught that stirred in the air, and the luminous wire was no longer incandescent, but red and dull like the embers in the grate. I scrutinized the dimness, but as yet no material form manifested itself.

Father Denys was sitting very upright in his chair, his eyes fixed and focused on something invisible to me. His lips were moving and muttering, his hands grasped the crucifix he was wearing. And then I saw what I knew he was seeing too : a face was outlining itself on the air in front of him, a face swollen and purple, with tongue lolling from the mouth, and as it hung there it oscillated to and fro. Clear and clearer it grew, suspended there by the rope that now became visible to me, and though the apparition was of a man hanged by the neck, it was not dead but active and alive, and the spirit that awfully animated it was no human one, but something diabolical.

Suddenly Father Denys rose to his feet, and his face was within an inch or two of that suspended horror. He raised his hands which held the sacred emblem.

"Begone to your torment," he cried, "until the days of it are over, and the mercy of God grants you eternal death."

There rose a wailing in the air : some blast shook the room so that the corners of it quaked, and then the light and the warmth were restored to it, and there was no one there but our two selves. Father Denys's face was haggard and dripping with the struggle he had been through, but there shone on it such radiance as I have never seen on human countenance.

"It's over," he said. "I saw it shrivel and wither before the power of His presence. . . . And your eyes tell me you saw it too and you know now that what wore the semblance of humanity was pure evil."

We talked a little longer, and he rose to go.

"Ah, I forgot," he said ; "you wanted to know how I could reveal to you what was told me in confession. Horace Kennion died this morning by his own hand. He left with his lawyer a packet to be opened on his death, with instructions that it should be published in the daily Press. I saw it in an evening paper, and it was a detailed account of how he killed Gerald Selfe. He wished it to have all possible publicity."

"But why ?" I asked.

Father Denys paused.

"He gloried in his wickedness, I think," he said. "He loved it, as I told you, for its own sake, and he wanted every-one to know of it as soon as he was safely away."

SHANE LESLIE

AS IN A GLASS DIMLY

As a rule nobody enjoys better health than the race of Egyptian archæologists. Yet they are supposed to live under a curse and to be liable to weird accidents and sudden deaths. How can they walk the street as other men and sleep quiet of nights when it is known that they have roused the vengeful passions of many disturbed mummies?

Have they not broken into the sacred resting-places of the dead and breathed the baleful air which rushes out of the tombs laden with the dust and something more than the dust of a thousand years? Regardless of the warnings and entreaties of occultists (many of advanced adeptship) who write to men of science and curators of museums from boarding-houses in Brighton and Brixton, they live their official lives and continue sorting the mummies as though they were birdskins or corked insects. They receive threats and curses by post from folk who believe they are reborn out of the land of Egypt into modern life. From others they receive propitiatory offerings, talismans, or money to buy flowers to lay before the desecrated dead behind glass cases. Spirits, which like tumours can be malignant, are supposed to cling to embalmed bodies which have been dispossessed of life since before Greece or Rome were, and even to possess those dry, painted coffins which adorn our museums. Our ancestors had less fear, though perhaps not more sense, for they pounded mummies into medicines.

In more nervous days the strangest stories have been told of the fate which indirectly reaches the vandalizer of mummies. Gossip and journalism have spread strong rumours of the succession of disasters and sudden mis-adventures which invariably follow the excavator or collector. Burnt houses and sunken liners are sometimes connected with the shipment of a mummy. Still, there is no record of the unexpected salvage of a mummy from the scene of a naval disaster. And the percentage of burnt mansions in which there were Egyptian curiosities is so small that it has not attracted the attention of the insurance companies.

Nevertheless, the great Egyptian myth has proceeded gaily. Who does not know a friend whose friend slipped and broke an ankle on the steps of the British Museum after peering too inquisitively into a mummy? Who has not heard of the explorer and hunter who, after shipping a mummy home, proceeded into the African bush never to be seen alive again? Years afterwards his companions relate that he was killed by a buffalo or lion and his remains hastily buried in a river bank. They returned later to find that it had been carried away by the floods. A strange corroboration follows in England. Some expert, who is quite unaware of the circumstances of the mummy, has deciphered the inscription on the coffin wood and found stated in hieroglyphics as plain as many pikestaffs that the violator of this particular mummy will perish by a sudden and violent death.

"Out of the forest shall the destroyer come upon him, and the voice of the waters shall be lifted against him, and the place of his burial shall not be known."

And the legend assumes a very sturdy size. It is believed and vouched for. And wherever the mummy is placed, troubles begin. One legend spreads the seed of others, and there is no sifting of the different tales. Egyptologists find themselves tripping up on staircases and on ballroom floors. Their houses are mysteriously ignited, and they do not live out the period which is set for the life of man. A series of inexplicable accidents are reserved for those who photograph mummies. Nothing seems to cause such annoyance to the dead as photography. The troubles which befall curators and vanmen are nothing in comparison. Nothing is more resented by the mummy than reduplication upon sensitized plates. Curses take effect upon honest photographers which are collected and retailed by honest journalists, and these, in turn, are investigated and pronounced upon by honest spiritualists.

The general reader accumulates a hazy memory of these yarns, but decides to wait the day until an Egyptian expert crosses his path before taking a final opinion. Such an occasion once came to us. An old Egyptian explorer had joined the same house party in the south of England, and it was easy to draw him on the only subject about which he would speak at all.

We told him some of these fantastic tales and asked him about his health. Had he ever had any accidents during his work ? He smiled and then laughed. We laughed and then smiled as he made fun of the whole type of story. His burly health and sound common sense seemed an assurance in favour of the life he led. He looked like a retired football-player with a sense of humour, not in the least like a man who devoted his soul to unwrapping the dead and, when possible, to deciphering their hidden secrets. He told us some interesting things, but quite scientific, about Egyptians and their writings.

After dinner we tried him again, especially about the famous mummy in the British Museum which had wrought such devastation. This particular case had never crossed his path. He had read about it in the papers. In fact he looked to the daily Press for all the exciting sidelights of his profession, but those kind of things didn't happen as a rule. He was disinclined to believe this wonderful tale, and he smiled and laughed in turn. But the simpler theories of the spiritualists which we propounded to him he was willing to accept, because, he said, there were no facts to prove or controvert them.

As far as facts stood, he insisted that he must remain a materialist. He had never investigated the spirits of those whom he unravelled, but he was interested when we suggested that the Egyptians were thinking of their spirits rather than their bodies when they went to such elaborate lengths of bodily preservation ; our theory being that the astral body or ghost is entirely distributed by fire or cremation, but in the case of earth-burial is liable to linger perhaps as long as the process of decay itself. This was more so the case when the body was laid away secretly or ill-buried behind panelling or under flooring.

Suicides were often earth-bound, and this seemed to be the reason why in the Middle Ages their bodies were staked at the cross-roads. Somebody suggested that people who had been burnt never left a ghost. By the burning of the astral body they escaped instantly to the next plane. But no cut-and-dried rule could be laid down. Some occultists were deeply opposed to the destruction of the astral body involved in cremation.   Others welcomed the great release.

The Egyptians seem to have gone to the opposite extreme, as their complicated burial system was an effort to retain the body and its astral shape together in the indefinite silence of the tombs.   As long as the body was undecayed, the astral body remained.   There must be some powerful reason behind the amazing immobility which they decreed to their dead.   No other race had made the tomb its national monument.   What a people !   Their art was devoted to the dead, and their Hierarchy was one of Undertakers !

Naturally, our view, being based a little on rumoured happenings, was that the ghost was unable to escape from the undecaying mummy, but that when the coffins were opened and the spices and preservatives were interfered with anything might happen.   Astral forms, though reduced to feeble transparency by time, were bound to pass out.   In some cases it was possible that they should assume a malevolent medium, but it was difficult to say how long they survived the opening of the coffins in which they had been immobile so long.

This was pure theory, and our wise old friend took it very well.   He was even considerate.   Yes, it might be so. He was bound to take a scientific attitude himself towards mummies.   He had dug them up as stolidly as other men dig up potatoes or nuggets, according to their respective callings.   He had examined, dissected, labelled and exported them.   He had packed them for the post and arranged them on shelves.   He had lectured about them, holding specimens in his hand, and here he was !   He had often arranged for them to be photographed.   We listened very humbly.

But when he mentioned photography, he ceased in his talk.   We thought he became rather more solemn, and, as though unwilling to carry us over relentlessly to his own arguments, he was giving us a chance of recovery.

"Talking of photography, I do remember something happening which to my mind remains quite unexplained."

We begged him to tell us.   He seemed unwilling, but with great fairness he told us what seemed to be a singular exception against his theories and belief that mummies could be dealt with like merchandise from the grocer or the apothecary.

"Yes, there was one event in my life which remains

inexplicable. I was collecting Egyptian curios for an amateur who had commissioned me to buy whatever genuine stuff came into the market. One day a traveller called and asked me if I were interested in mummy-cases. I replied I certainly was, provided they had not been manufactured in Paris with French paupers' bodies wrapped up in modern preservatives. He said he had no mummy, but an Egyptian coffin-board to dispose of, and that immediately. He asked me if I could feel interested in a single board, which was painted with hieroglyphics from the Book of the Dead. This was rare and interesting, and I asked him the price.

" 'Oh, it's valuable, is it?' he asked. 'May I inquire what it would fetch in the auction rooms?' I was prepared to do an honest deal with him, and I said that such a rarity was worth two hundred pounds to me.

" 'Well,' he snapped, 'suppose I were to let you have it for nothing!'

" 'As a gift? Well, I should be very grateful.'

"Before I could speak further, he said, 'Done! You can have it, but on one condition—that you fetch it from my address to-day.'

"It was already late in the afternoon, and I doubted if I could get my furnisher's van round to him before it was put away for the night. I suggested coming next day. No, it must be that afternoon; before midnight or never. I did not wish to lose such a chance, and called my workmen back from supper to perform a special job. That evening the painted plank stood in my study, and my benefactor with a sigh of relief shook my hands and I never saw him again.

"That night the plank remained in my rooms and I was complimenting myself on my luck in picking up such a good item. Suddenly the bell rang, and some excitable gentlemen arrived who said they were spiritualists as hot in the search of their science as I was in my line. They were very interested in this famous mummy-plank, which had already given some rather wonderful results to their medium. Unfortunately the owner had become nervous or frightened, thought he was incurring bad luck, and had sold it. I did not inform them that he had been very glad to give it away.

"The upshot of their visit was that they were anxious to carry out a séance with this object, and, if I would permit them, to make a photograph of it. After a little questioning

I learnt from them that it had been photographed once and that the plate had revealed an unpleasant face in the wood. They were unwilling to show it to me, as there had been some question of a fraud. I made up my mind. I said I had no intention of allowing a séance, especially as they proposed to sit up all night in my rooms. But I was willing to allow the plank to be photographed under my own conditions, which were that I should choose the photographer and use the firm who usually developed my plates for me, and that six negatives should be taken and kept locked in a box for future reference.

"To these conditions they agreed, and for a week I was left alone.

"When they returned to the charge I was ready for them. I had communicated with my photographer and my trustworthy firm, who agreed to take every precaution against the slightest fake. Mr. Bashford, the photographer, arrived, and the head of the firm I had mentioned the matter to. The latter had been so interested that he had the box for the negatives prepared under his own supervision and a special lock fitted. The plank was photographed six times in the presence of witnesses and the negatives taken away to be developed.

"On the morning following I was surprised, though not alarmed, to receive a telegram from Bashford asking me to telegraph him money to return to London with. As he lived at Enfield I was surprised to notice that he telegraphed from Edinburgh. The resemblance between the two names was slight. However, I forwarded him the money and he returned that night. He came to see me, a little worried and not quite coherent. He had fallen down my steps when leaving my house and struck his head. He must have asked for the wrong train, for he knew nothing about it until he found himself at Edinburgh. That was all he had to say.

"The next day I was sorry to receive word that the gentleman who was developing my negatives had had an accident in his family. A daughter of his had fallen through a glass window and severely cut her face. I remember pulling myself together and resolutely assuring myself that these were both accidental happenings and that neither could have had anything to do with the coffin-plank they had shared in photographing.

"I waited till my spiritualist friends applied to see the results, and I went round to the shop where they were to have been developed. The head of the firm talked with me for half an hour before we touched on the photographs. I was glad to hear that his daughter was well on the way to recovery. It was now only a question of scars. As for the negatives, he had developed them successfully and placed them in the box, which he had locked and left in his safe. His safe was never interfered with and, indeed, he had unlocked it that morning and found the box exactly as he had stored it. He had unlocked it only an hour back. He was sorry he had not studied the negatives when they were first developed. They were now impossible to make out!

" 'What,' I insisted, 'they haven't changed colour since you put them away?' He was silent for a minute. Then he said very quietly : 'They have not only changed colour, but they have changed substance. There are six thin trails of dust where the glass plates stood last night. I am very sorry, and that is all that is to be said about it. Such a thing has never happened to me before.'

"He showed the box to me, and I touched the thin grey dust on my fingertip.

"As I say, there has been one occurrence in my life which remains absolutely inexplicable to this day. I leave it there."

Some time had passed after recording the Egyptian experience and that at second-hand. I had recorded it in a cell of memory, for one does incline to save up little fragments of the supernatural during life in the hope that one may meet a clue or a piece of the missing jigsaw later.

I was asked by a friend to visit a church in the Diocese of London which was giving the Rector a considerable amount of trouble. Not a mile from Kensington, it was a peaceful little church in its way, but it had become disagreeable spiritually. Moderate in ritual, and old-fashioned in doctrine, it lay in an ecclesiastical backwater. My friend called me on the telephone and asked me to come round and have a talk with the Rector. I agreed at a few hours' notice, and we found ourselves passing rapidly out of the maelstrom of a bus-route through narrow and short streets until we caught sight of a Georgian chapel with Victorian additions.

M

It was a dull and drab edifice, and if it was a haunted building this was its only distinction.

There are, of course, many haunted churches in London. There is a Catholic Church where the interior confessional bell is frequently rung at night and Masses are said as though in response to the call of unknown souls. There is an Anglican Church where the stamp of the lame clergyman, long dead, is heard pacing round his aisles as though for ever counting his absent congregation. But this was a different case, we were told, and impossible to explain.

We called on the Rector, who said he would show us over his church before he gave us any indication of what was worrying him. We passed solemnly up and down the quiet, dusty pews. There had not been many improvements and there was little beauty to restore from the beginning. Except for some stained-glass windows of recent origin there was nothing of colour to relieve the dull walls. These the Rector pointed out to us, and begged us to take stock of them. Besides the conventional English saints, whose dullness in the case of Bishops, and plainness in the case of Holy Virgins, seems to ensure against any temptation to invoke their aid, there was a Last Supper, in which the only lifelike figure was that of Judas as he hurried from the upper room. There was also a scene from the Miracles, which was concealed by a board partition. We glimpsed behind it at the conventional picture—quite unnoteworthy. Then we searched the whole church very thoroughly, and, finding less than nothing to remark, we withdrew to the Rectory. Over a strong brew of tea the Rector explained his difficulties. Morning Prayer was all right and Evening Prayer likewise. His trouble always came at the Communion Service.

"I might tell you that in the eighteen months I have been quartered here I have not yet been able to bring the most sacred of services to a decorous finish. The service is held in the early morning to very small congregations. The majority prefer the choral midday with a very short sermon."

I asked him whether the assistants were troubled as well as he. He answered that there were different communicants at the services. Some had perceived these incidents once or twice and had mistaken them for accidents. But he had celebrated on each occasion and felt that the strange

hand of coincidence could not have been exerted Sunday after
Sunday. In the end he had abandoned the early service for
some months, but he felt uneasy about having done so, and
was anxious to resume them. It was some time before he
would give us any inkling into his past experiences. But
they had not been pleasant. On one occasion the window-
covered by the boarding had blown in and an icy air had
penetrated as far as the Communion Table, where he had felt
too chilly to proceed and had dismissed the communicants.
On another occasion the Cup had been snatched from his
hands and the unconsecrated wine poured over the cloth.
He had never commenced the service without a feeling of
dread creeping upon him. He never felt nervous at the
services later in the day. The climax had come when he
had turned towards the congregation and, as he believed,
noticed one of the figures in the boarded window standing
reflected against the opposite wall with its tongue hanging
out. It gave him so considerable a shock that he had
abandoned the service straight away, and had the window
boarded under the pretext that it was in need of repairs.

We returned to the church and examined the window
carefully. He showed us the figure which had, in his imagination, apparently become separated from its glazing. But
there were two remarkable things about it. First of all, it
was impossible that the sun could ever have thrown the shape
like a magic-lantern, because the window looked out on a
blank wall. Secondly, the leaded mouth in the figure was
tightly closed. It was apparently meant to represent the
young man with the loaves and fishes.

It was puzzling to know why such an innocent figure
should have taken upon itself so gruesome an aspect. Again
the Rector assured us that on two occasions he had seen the
window reflected almost in facsimile upon the opposite wall,
but with the awful change in the tongue which he was certain
was hanging out of the lips. Under careful examination
we elicited the fact that the two appearances had occurred
at the same service and that the glass had been made by a
reputable firm in Birmingham, though the designs had been
suggested by the Rector's predecessor. About him we knew
nothing, but fortunately the old pew-opener, who had accompanied us, was at this juncture able to offer a valuable comment—to wit, that the last Rector of the church, in her

opinion, went mad, and that was why he resigned the living.
It turned out that he was dead, or he would have afforded a
valuable witness.   The pew-opener, on being further
examined, remembered that the late Rector had been interested
in prison work and that his brother had been a Deputy-
Governor in some gaol.   That was all that could be remembered.

Never did a psychic hunting-ground provide less clues.
The structure of the church proved drab, modern and feature-
less.   The boards were taken down from the suspected
window.   We arranged mirrors in a number of positions
to catch the stained glass, but the effect was always the same.
The young man with the loaves and the fishes always preserved
his well-mannered look.   When the light threw the colours
against the opposite wall they seemed blurred but not in the
least ghastly or unpleasant.   Suddenly I heard a groan from
the Rector, who was holding a mirror in a far corner of the
church.   We both hurried to his side, where he stood petrified
with terror.   It seemed obvious, at the moment, that the
solution of everything lay in his own nervous disorders.   He
stood there holding out the mirror and clasping it with both
hands.   We glanced over his shoulder.   The stained-glass
window was reflected small and clearly against the quicksilver.
Every detail was discernible, including one which was not in
the original—a wagging tongue.   It was so uncalled-for and
so inexplicable that we both uttered a cry of bewilderment,
passing into a groan.   This was too much for the Rector,
who dropped the mirror with a crash to the floor and sank
upon his knees into the nearest pew.

We hurried back to the original and scrutinized with
eye and finger.   It was exactly as when it left the Birmingham
makers.   But we made no further experiments with mirrors.

There was nothing more to be done, and the next morning
the boards were restored to the window and church services
were resumed.   We put ourselves into communication
with the manufacturers.   Our correspondence conveyed, of
course, not the least hint that their fine work of art had been
behaving in such disorderly fashion.   But we represented
that we were interested in the work and would be anxious
to know if the firm could reproduce a similar window from the
old designs.   In any case we wished to know the name of the
designer.   The firm replied that they would be happy to supply

us with a similar, or, rather, better example of their art.
Unfortunately the designs for the particular window we
mentioned could not be found. They were able to put their
hands on any others of their work during the past fifty years.
It was very curious (to us a little more than curious) that it
should be so, but they were not to be found. So scent failed
there at an important point.

A few weeks passed, and we received a letter from the
firm to say that the reason why they had not been able to
find the designs of the window in which we were interested
was that, unlike all others produced by the firm, this one
had been drawn by a brother of the former Rector, the
Deputy-Governor of —— Gaol. This was the first unusual
fact we had discovered, and the next step was to visit the gaol
in question. Though the Deputy-Governor was dead, there
were several warders who remembered him. I fell into
conversation with one of these and asked him if the late
Deputy was very fond of drawing. The warder thought
for a moment and said : "Well, now I think about him, he was,
and he sometimes drew sketches of the prisoners here."

I tried a long shot. "Do you remember if he ever made
any designs for the Prison Chapel ?"

"Why, yes," replied the warder, "he most certainly did.
The whole of the altar was painted by him, and he drew
pictures for the walls from faces in the prison."

We visited the chapel, and the warder was amused, pointing out the pictures of various characters, such as the previous
Governor, warders he had known, and several prisoners
who had been used as models. Suddenly my eye fell on a
visage which I remembered in a flash. In one of the frescoes
was a young, perfectly expressionless face, identical with the
young man who had given us so much trouble in the window
of the London church. I asked very quietly if he remembered the model who had been used.

"It's curious you should ask that," answered the warder,
"for, though you would never think it, that was a young and
desperate criminal. I was in the prison when he was executed,
and very unpleasant it was. The Deputy-Governor was
taken by his looks from an artistic point of view and tried to
draw him when he was in his cell, but the prisoner objected
so much that the Governor came one day with an old camera
and photographed him while he was asleep, and I believe he

used the photograph to make a drawing for the picture on the chapel wall. It certainly looks uncommonly like that prisoner. . . ."

There was no need to tell the warder that the photograph must have been later enlarged and used to make a light in a London church. When we returned we told the Rector the curious clue we had discovered. He could judge for himself whether the glass was haunted and whether the spirit of the hanged man had been able to possess itself of the texture of the glass. I do not know whether hanging has any effect on a man's tongue or whether it could cause it to protrude. We decided that would be an unnecessary inquiry. We also forwent any research into the career of the prisoner. It was sufficient once to have heard his name. But, at our advice, the Rector removed the whole window, which we buried subsequently in a country churchyard and left to its fate.

I always connected the evil possession of this glass with the curious story I had heard about the negative plates of the Egyptian coffin-board. In each case some malefic power had installed itself invisibly in the glass. There was no conclusion to come to except that they were parallels. Neither really made a story, but the two episodes remained not utterly unrelated in my memory. I could at least say that two and two make four, but further I could not carry any calculation into the world of ghostly relativity.

THE HOSPITAL NURSE

A STUDY IN MURDER

Miss Turberah Doole was the middle-aged, hard-worked, uninteresting and unenterprising nurse and slavey employed by Hosanna Smith to tend Mrs. Smith's father, old Sir Athelstone Penguin, the master-plumber, who, by an ingenious series of inventions, had collected half the Royal Blasonry of Christendom on his Appointments. In his senility he had added Arms of his own to the venerable collection of Burke. His fortune was large and his family was small. There was a disinherited son in Australia, Edward, who had speculated so considerably on his father's death that his father had cut him off in his own lifetime. His dull but inexpensive daughter and the good-or-bad-for-nothing husband she had bought for herself on an excursion to Switzerland lived like a pair of caretakers or sentries in his gaunt Palladian house a couple of miles outside Reading. As far as the baronet's health was concerned they were caretakers, but of his fortune they were sentries. They watched against the return of the prodigal son. They had watched for ten years, day and night, post after post. One of them had always been within reach of the telephone, and telegrams were humanely opened before they could give the old man any kind of shock.

It was very unlikely that the son would return after a career which had been continued in the Antipodes long after his enforced trip from the Old Country and the old folks at home. His mother had since died of her son's and husband's behaviour in equal parts, and her death had extinguished the last flicker of daughterly love on the part of Mrs. Smith for her father. Edward had never acknowledged the notification of his mother's death, but continued to sully the old name in the Australian dust. No longer able to pledge and pawn Sir Athelstone's credit, he had danced, drunk, devilled and disappeared. Hosanna's husband, Jordan, developed an unsuspected interest in keeping the family annals, and all that could be recorded to Edward's discredit by letter or by news-cutting was kept in a black copy-book to refresh the baronet's memory if need arose.

Nurse Doole was seldom disturbed of a morning by the family, who left her about her duties. She was surprised when Mr. Smith interrupted her once before noon and asked for *The Times* which she generally read to her patient in the course of the day. He brought it back with a paragraph cut out by scissors. Three days later *The Times* was brought to her with an excision previously committed.

She was a harmless old soul with one ambition and one vice. Her ambition was the cottage she intended buying with her savings at the end of this case, and her vice was curiosity. It was her curiosity to know what had been cut from *The Times* which was to change her whole life. As she went only to Reading on Sundays, she saw no way of securing that cutting except by letting Sir Athelstone notice the gap. She read several paragraphs to him through the missing square. When he noticed, he was very angry and stopped her reading. He examined the sheet and ordered the butler to be sent into Reading for a clean copy. Her curiosity was gratified an hour later by reading aloud a few sentences reporting the sudden rise into political fame of the young Australian, who had been selected to join the Imperial Tramway Visiting Committee and had left the Antipodes with the other members the previous day. They would reach England in six weeks. An interesting rather than a pleasant programme appeared to have been arranged for them. The name of the young politician was Edward Penguin.

All this caused the greatest panic and distress among the Smiths, but as neither they nor the old man mentioned the news, the old life proceeded. Only the nurse's position changed perceptibly. The Smiths no longer treated her as a hireling. They began consulting her. They were particularly anxious to know how the news had affected Sir Athelstone. The nurse reported that he had not turned a hair. The next six weeks became a nightmare for the Smiths, who slept considerably worse than the invalid. The nurse alone slept with a careless content. In a few months she would be able to purchase her cottage. For thirty years she had slaved in ward and hospital and on private cases. Freedom and Respectability, a Cottage and the Crematorium beyond lay comfortably before her. Money she had never had and never would. She could enjoy the sleep denied to the Smiths, whose agonies increased as the possible spoiler of their long-awaited treasure approached.

The return of Edward carried nightmarish possibilities. They knew they were the inheritors in Sir Athelstone's will, but they knew his pride in his name. They had once offered to assume it after his death by Royal Licence, and he had scorned the idea. The old name must be carried on by son of his but by nobody else. The Smiths knew well his attitude to the idea of sonship and inheritance, apart from the filial curse with which Heaven had visited him. They knew that he was immensely rich. They knew they would be so at his death. They knew they had waited for twenty years. They were ready to wait ten more, but in six weeks this wretched son would have risen from the dead. They could not forbear asking the nurse once if she thought the old man would live through the summer. They hoped so, they said, because he was so fond of roses. Nurse answered that he would see the last rose of several summers yet. He was not ill, only old.

It was an injudicious question, for it enabled the nurse to read what was in their minds and it gave her a sense of power. She was enjoying the nervous alarm which the Australian Special Correspondent of *The Times* was causing in the household. She had nothing to win or lose herself. She was not in the will. Whoever inherited the money would pay her her wage and she would buy her cottage. When she thought of the years she had slaved and slaved and served for others, she felt a slight anger against the wealthy people who could hire her services for so little. The nervous anxiety of the Smiths, amounting to despair, offered her a form of slight revenge. Four weeks passed, and there was a long paragraph in *The Times* about the coming Committee from Australia. This time the Smiths threw away all reserve and Hosanna Smith asked nurse as a favour not to read it to the old man. She could easily skip it. Nurse said nothing, biding her counsel, but an envelope was brought to her at lunch. It contained a five-pound note. For the first time for many months Turberah Doole smiled. The winning game seemed to have been placed in her lap. She would have a

M*

garden as well as a cottage in the country by the time this case was over.

She skipped reading the passage about Edward Penguin to his father and reassured the Smiths. A week later she noticed a tiny news item containing the dreaded name, and pointed it out to the Smiths with the malicious query whether she ought to read it aloud or not. That evening her bank account received another five-pound note. The condition of the Smiths was pitiable. They seemed unable to act or think for themselves. They looked to the nurse for initiative. What was the patient thinking or wanting? Did he ever mention his son or his lawyers, and what could be his feelings? Perhaps he had forgotten. Nurse was never very reassuring, but she went on reading and skipping paragraphs until the very day when the Australian visitors were expected to arrive. An unfortunate scene occurred that day. The aged baronet questioned her. He had been apparently counting the days, and when she hesitated he demanded the paper, which he read for himself. He found all he had looked for. The names of the Australian Committee filled a corner. His son was due to reach Southampton that day. His wrath was considerable and expressed itself in wriggling convulsions. But his wrath was not directed against his son or his nurse, although both had failed him, but against the Smiths.

He sat up and ordered Miss Doole to telephone for his lawyers.

Nurse rushed below. It was half an hour before she could find the Smiths, and to both she broke the news.

Hosanna burst into hysterical tears and Mr. Smith "blinked his blee" or, in other words, changed colour. There was a general collapse. Nurse alone stood rocklike. What was she to do? The Smiths weakly bade her get busy on the telephone. Nearly an hour had passed, and before she called for a trunk call she ran upstairs to look at her patient. When she entered Sir Athelstone's bedroom she received her second shock. The baronet lay stretched upon his bed. He lay dead of sheer wrath. The arteries or plumbing of his heart had given way under the stress. Miss Doole did everything that professional humanity or science could suggest. Then she telephoned to the doctor.

As she hung up the telephone, the Smiths came to her in the passage. "Is the lawyer coming?" they asked. Their

faces were disconsolate to the lowest state of anguish.   She
drew them into her own bedroom and her brain worked with
fierce rapidity.

"No, I have sent for a doctor instead."

"Why, is he really ill ?"

"Dead ! Dead ! Dead !"

"Thank God," muttered the injudicious Mr. Smith.   Mrs.
Smith almost struck him.   "Oh, my dear, dear father ! Nurse,
you must have killed him !"   And she burst into sobs.

Miss Doole staggered with fear and fury.   Her emotions
gave her the only brain-wave of her life, and she answered :
"Well, you both told me to."   It was possible that the Smiths
attibuted the miracle to foul play.   Miss Doole suddenly saw
her Cottage become a Boarding-House, and a Conservatory
added to her Garden.   Where there is fear, money becomes
fluidic.   If the Smiths really thought she was a murderess, she
could make them pay for their mistake.   "It will be all right,
but you must give me a thousand pounds before the funeral.
I will go, and trouble you no more," was her ultimatum.
The Smiths turned haggardly to face the first peck that was
made at the fortune before their own hands could close
upon it.   They consented and were taken to view the corpse.
When the doctor arrived, Sir Athelstone's daughter was
kneeling at the foot of the bed in prolonged prayer.

The excitement of waiting for the will precluded any
anxiety the Smiths might have felt over the doctor's investigation.   He rapidly pronounced death due to heart failure,
and departed after signing his certificate.   By the time the
will had been brought by the lawyers from London, a third
most interested party had arrived in time to hear the reading
of the clauses and codicils.   Edward Athelstone arrived in
England that morning, and the evening papers were full of
the tragic coincidence.   Headlines described the race across
the ocean of the long-lost son to receive forgiveness at his
dying father's bedside.

The deceased baronet had placed a short will in legal
hands.   His entire fortune was left to the Smiths, and there
was no mention of his son or of his nurse.   A large legacy
was set aside to endow the hospital in the Midlands in which
he had always been interested.   His creed had been strictly
utilitarian, and, to mark the practice of his lifetime, he bequeathed his body to the same Institution for purposes of

dissection, after which all remains were to be interred on the premises—if any remains there were from the laboratory. The codicil affecting his body was a surprise, and Mrs. Smith burst into tears, insisting that her dear father must receive Christian burial. All present were much edified, with the exception of Edward the disinherited. He had preserved a grim silence during the reading of the will, which he realized was final. It was only when the proviso for dissecting his father was opposed by the Smiths that he raised his voice to insist that this wish of his father's should be carried out to the letter. Had some fearful suspicion crossed his mind? Was he hopeful that some damning grains of poison would be found in the body? It was the only chance of invalidating the will, and he watched filially over his father's body until it was despatched under medical conduct.

That evening Edward's lawyer arrived and advised him to interview the nurse very carefully and friendly-like pending a possible doctor's report from the Middle Midlands Hospital. The lawyer himself left to give a hint to the dissecting doctors. In view of the baronet's bounty they could not be too careful or minute in investigating his atoms. Nearly a quarter of a million had been left to their Institution.

Edward could not have interviewed the nurse at a more fruitful moment than that evening, for she had just been refused the immediate payment of her thousand pounds' bonus by the Smiths, who had plucked courage after the doctor's harmless pronouncement. If the nurse had surreptitiously done the baronet out of his few remaining weeks of life, she had employed agencies which left no trace. The Smiths continued to whine for a Christian funeral, ordering the nurse to leave the following day. A cheque for eighty pounds was handed to her. The amount placed a bare cottage in sight, and she decided to stay until she was pushed out. When Edward interviewed her, she promptly let him know that the old man had been aware of his coming and had sent for his lawyers on the very day that his arrival was scheduled in *The Times*. Edward's foulest suspicions were instantly confirmed. The alarmed and sullen behaviour of the Smiths the next day almost tempted him to send for the police. He waited feverishly for the hospital report, telegraphing to his lawyer to bring back the remains. He had a theory that the sight of the dissected corpse would terrify the Smiths into confession. He had no doubt, no possible doubt now, and, when the nurse allowed the Smiths to know how much she had confessed to Edward, their behaviour passed from distress to distraction. They became as psychologically convinced as Edward himself that the old man had met with an unnatural end. And that damnable nurse refused to go. She was waiting for her thousand pounds of hush money. They realized that, even if they inherited the fortune, she would blackmail them all their lives. Gradually she would bleed their pockets until the whole fortune was transferred into her lap. They would be lucky if they escaped with their necks ! They writhed with mental gangrene.

There was the ghastly atmosphere of a morgue about that noble old Palladian house crowning the heights above Reading. It was three days before the remains of Sir Athelstone were brought back. The dissector had left no flesh upon the bones, and the lawyers were discussing whether the will would be invalidated unless they were buried as well as the flesh under the walls of the great hospital, which would always bear the baronet's name. The doctors had not found one suspicious atom, though their researches had been conducted under the eyes of Edward's lawyer. There was nothing to be done but to accept the medical opinion concerning his death and to return or bury the fragments, which were recognizable neither to eye nor nostril, so exhaustively had scalpel and spirit done their work. Mrs. Smith's prayers and tears prevailed, and the undertakers were ordered to bring a rich satinwood coffin that night. Before they arrived, Edward left in pursuit of his Australian Committee, which was being entertained at the Mansion House that night. How he became the worse for drink later in the evening and how he met his host, the Lord Mayor, on the Bench the following morning, forms another story, often told in Australian political circles.

The Smiths, Hosanna and Jordan watched the bones of Sir Athelstone being slowly nailed into the coffin. It was very simple, and the undertakers left the coffin under a pall in the front hall, promising an early return. As the last nail sounded, a heavy gloom seemed to lift from the Smiths, and Hosanna wore a beatific expression worthier to deck a Queen of the May than a mourning daughter. It remained now to deal with Turberah Doole, and in their temporary exultation they decided to pay her her thousand pounds and be done with her on condition that she left before the funeral and signed a paper that she would present no further claims.

Miss Doole was awaiting their offer and quietly doubled it. Two thousand pounds down and the first train to-morrow ! The Smiths blanched, but not with fear. Avarice and anger overwhelmed them. They refused point-blank. . . . Miss Doole must have insisted and threatened and bluffed, and Smith must have threatened in reply. Miss Doole must have been determined that if she could not live in comfort for the rest of her life they should swing, all three. She might have been prepared to confess that she had choked the old man at their suggestion soon after he had threatened to send for his lawyers, and presumably to alter his will. They would become accessories before the fact. Nobody will ever know. . . . It was late before the lights were extinguished that night, and only a faint whiff of deodorized disinfectants bespoke the morrow's funeral.

The funeral took place with a certain amount of grim grandeur, but there was an absence of friends and neighbours. Some ugly rumours had already circulated. Comment was roused by the absence of Edward, the only son of deceased. The absence of the nurse was not noticed. She had been under notice to leave by the first train. The Smiths, looking very sheepish and sulky, officiated as principal mourners. A large crowd had gathered outside the local churchyard and waited. The Governors of the Middle Midlands Hospital attended in their robes. As the Smiths emerged, a slow, perceptible hiss broke through the huddled spectators, followed by silence. Edward's hot tongue had loosed the local gossip.

In the few years which followed they were never able to rid themselves of the scent of foul play. The late Sir Athelstone was often alluded to in the neighbourhood as the "murdered baronet". Two matters of proof were often adduced. One was the disappearance of the nurse with, presumably, enough hush money to keep her in some distant part of the world, and secondly, the fact that the Smiths would never erect a monument or even visit the grave of the man whose vast fortune they enjoyed.

As the Smiths distinctly treated themselves as in the

light of a guilty couple, the public feeling was not blameable for their resentment. They lived wealthily and unhappily ever afterwards within the gloomy walls of the Palladian super-villa which they had inherited. In due time they died, childless and intestate. They had been forgotten long before their deaths and would have been totally forgotten afterwards, had it not been for the celebrated legislation which arose over Sir Athelstone's fortune. By his will it reverted to the Middle Midlands Hospital, provided that all his wishes were fulfilled. When it was recalled that one of his requests had been that his dissected body should be interred on the premises of the Institution he had endowed, the representatives of Edward Penguin brought an action on the grounds that the remains, or some of them, had been buried in the churchyard near his house.

The Governors of the Hospital were seriously alarmed, and after taking legal advice applied to the Home Office for permission to disinter and recover the remains of their founder, according to his last Will and Testament. In this way they felt that they could make themselves legally secure. Permission was granted, and a shrine was prepared in the very walls of the hospital as an adequate resting-place. Arrangements for a form of ceremony of deposition had been made, when the Governors of the hospital and their legal advisers were considerably disconcerted by one of those utterly unexpected surprises which thrill and mystify the English public. The coffin of Sir Athelstone Penguin was brought to the surface in the presence of legal, medical, and police authorities. It contained the mummified and scarcely decayed body of a middle-aged woman. After so short a lapse of time there could be no doubt that it was the right grave. Although no monument had been erected, the vault had preserved a number of immortelles in their glass cases. On one the printed card of inscription was still legible. It read :

SIR ATHELSTONE PENGUIN, BART.
FROM HIS DEVOTED NURSE.

THE LORD-IN-WAITING

I SPENT my last and happiest fortnight as an undergraduate at Cambridge indulging myself in the leisure which rowing and reading had previously not permitted. A friend, whom I will call Peter Enright, was with me most of the time. We had both secured our release from final examinations and we spent day after day in voyages of discovery on the Cam. They began in a desire to find the native swallow-tailed butterfly. They ended in our paddling down as far as the sea. The more important result was that from henceforth we became very resolute friends. We decided to sign on for lifelong friendship. Life· was simple then, and the children of Victorians could not conceive any change affecting the structure of society. The Victorian age seemed bound to reproduce itself over and over again with variations. Oxford and Cambridge seemed to symbolize eternal truths. Germany appeared inefficient in professordom, futile in diplomacy and fantastic in armour. Definitely the German was unsporting, and the Great War, which swept Peter Enright out of past, present and future, was as incredible to the imagination as the story of the Deluge to the people of the Sahara.

Peter's life was destined to be remarkably short, had he known it. All his hardly earned knowledge of mathematics (for he was a seventeenth Wrangler) as well as his fine physical development were destined to be quenched in a moment of time. Fortunately, of that moment he had no prevision, and his few years subsequent to Cambridge were very cheerful. He was destined however to add more than one singular experience to the normal collection of reactions with which Cambridge had endowed him. ∩ Peter told me, while we were paddling among the Fens, that he had decided to take a curacy in the country under very old-fashioned conditions. That he was willing to take Orders in the Church of England showed what a very normal and unmetaphysical person he was. He was no doubt a muscular Christian, though not in any offensive sense. We had both belonged to one of the minor and neglected Colleges, which for that reason imposed a certain freemasonry among their Fellows and followers. We were sworn to help each other in the after-passages of life, and though I immediately rehearsed the names of people I knew in possession of livings suitable to my friend's talents, I had a feeling that it would be long before he needed my help or influence. At the same time I always believed that Peter was one of those protected beings who had unseen powers working for them. At a lecture on Spiritualism given in the College he had once been selected, to his huge amusement, by the lecturer as possessing the makings of a first-class medium. As he looked more like a medium-weight boxer the amusement became general, and he was called "Mrs. Piper", after a well-known sorceress, for some time to come.

Though Peter never strayed into the paths of psychical science so called, a singular thing had happened to him in his first year which caused him no little scruple of conscience. He had entered for a minor prize or scholarship, which he was anxious to obtain rather for the ready pocket-money than for its distinction. He had crammed himself steadily for several weeks and worked abnormal hours at night until his brain was no doubt in a worried condition, but in those days there was no other acceptable manner of preparing for examinations, and Peter underwent the process with a wet towel round his head, stewing over gallons of hot tea. The night previous to the examination he fell asleep over his books and dreamed that he was already in the examination room. He found himself confronted there by a paper which he was unable to answer very well. When he woke in the early hours he carried it in his head, and referring to his books he learnt the answers by heart.

In the morning he found himself a surprised but easy examinee sitting in front of the same identical questions. It was not the figures which surprised him so much as the colour of the examination paper on which he was expected to write. In his dream during the night he remembered that the paper was tinted a greenish colour. To his genuine amazement this was the case in daylight. The paper was tinted green. There was nothing for him to do but to write a very successful paper and inquire quietly afterwards why the paper was of such unusual colour. The explanation was simple. The examiner was suffering from a disease of the eyes which made it necessary for him to use tinted paper. Peter was awarded the prize and was filled with distress. Finally he explained to his tutor that he did not believe he had come by the reward fairly, that he must have wandered and found the paper somewhere in his sleep. How else could he have known beforehand that green was the colour of the paper to be given him in the examination room ? His tutor, having kept the papers locked in his drawer the night previous to the examination, dismissed the idea as the fancy of an overwrought brain, and insisted on giving Peter his *exeat* for a few days' holiday. Any further discussion was thus pleasantly quashed and Peter was not allowed to dream of refusing the prize. As his tutor had expected, a few days' holiday restored his normality and for two years he worked and rowed steadily until academical freedom and honour had been attained. Nothing of the kind ever remotely occurred to him again during his Cambridge time, and his desire to receive Orders from some ghostly Father and Lord of the Established Church seemed to arise from a healthy optimism in life rather than from any wish to wrestle with the terrors of the spiritual world.

To the outer world in those days we fancied ourselves impregnable. Why three years of unflagging rowing should have bred so hearty a contempt for the world, that doth not row nor give instruction in rowing, I could never guess. Even in a Cambridge degree each imagined he had secured a combined shield and spear to present to the outside hosts of folly, disorder and unsportingness. Incidentally we had each escaped damage to our hearts on the river or elsewhere. We felt so successful in advance that it seemed a little difficult to know what the world would do with us.

Before we left the college portals for good, Peter decided he must make some deal with the world, into which he was entering with less than the price of a clerical outfit, so he took a tutorship in the County of Huntingdon, hoping to clear a few pounds by the end of the Long Vacation. Let us say that he engaged himself to coach the son of Lord Mountstable at Mountstable Towers. It covers all identities. It was falsely called the Towers, if Towers it was called, for it bore no resemblance to any castle. It was Georgian and highly modernized at the time when the Victorians were putting their houses in order for the Millennium so abundantly foreshown at the Great Exhibition of 1851.

We parted, promising to meet regularly in life; at the Boat Race, at the annual tea-crawl given to the senile or the College on Founders' Day, at the Oxford-and-Cambridge cricket match at Lord's, and to help and succour each other whenever overwhelmed by debts, taxes or Christmas collections. We went our ways, and in a few hours our College life had passed out of the realm of working reality into the pleasant background of a dream. Our whole year scattered, never to meet again. Peter undertook his tutorship and I spent the Long in the Touraine, where the weeks of perfect health and weather passed by as quickly as the sunlit fields seen from a passing railway-carriage. Though Peter never left my general remembrance, it was a surprise to receive a telegram from him at the little French post office a week before I intended to return. It was simple :

Remember old promises can you join me immediately wire Mountstable Rectory Mountstable.

Peter.

There was no refusing so direct a call, and that evening I was following my own reply as fast as the train could take me to Paris. The next day I was met by Peter at a Huntingdonshire station and driven in a horse-gig to Mountstable Towers. "I thought you had better have a preliminary look at it," he said, when we drew within sight of a singularly modern and ugly building. It seemed deprived of all romance or history, exhibiting only the squat and gilded squalor by which the Victorian middle class announced their arrival among the County families. "It's not much to look at," added Peter. "It looks like the College kitchens worked up into a Ritz hotel. It's modern and new, and everything is as comfortable as you could wish, but I am not going to sleep there again till I have finished my tutorship. I'm staying in the Rectory over there and I hope you'll stay with me as my friend." Otherwise he had absolutely no communication to make. I was curious and acquiescent.

Beyond the elm avenue was a much more ancient structure, an old broken-down Rectory apparently only held together by festoons of wistaria and passion-flowers. Behind the tithe-barn in the background was a neat medieval church. Peter introduced me to the Rector, who gave us supper and left us to ourselves. The Rector, nervous, tactful, silent, and an ardent Baconian, as I quickly learnt, was also the happy possessor of a cook who could make good coffee. Peter and I sat up till midnight, our quickened wits wrestling with each other, for Peter would not broach what had induced him to send me such a pressing telegram. I learnt a good deal else of his circumstances. It seemed a comfortable billet. The present Lord Mountstable was a recluse. He was delicate and almost deformed. His poor, twisted limbs had never allowed him to share the life of public school or university. But he was anxious that his son, who was a healthy youngster in his teens, should enjoy those advantages to the full. He had made Peter comfortable in every way. There was a squash tennis court at his disposal. Every suggestion he made was met regardless of cost. The boy was intelligent and showed no particular contempt for the Binomial Theorem. As to his change of quarters, Peter would only say that he preferred not to sleep in the Towers. He had given his host and employer no reason, but, as he was an admirable tutor, he had been given rooms in the Rectory, whence he telegraphed to me and whither I had come. Peter said that he liked his pupil immensely. He had found traces of real mathematical power. "Such a curious brain. He has had no grounding, but he often knows the answers of difficult problems before he understands the nature of the problems at all. He is really a queer boy. I am told by the Rector that he takes after his grandfather, the first in the present line. He was an amazing man. Made his great fortune in business and then educated himself into a very learned personage. His hobby was science, and he had a wonderful collection of medieval scientific books. Instead of a racehorse stable he used to keep a laboratory with trained assistants. There was an awful explosion once or twice and the assistants were killed. When the second happened, the Government gave him a hint to close his laboratory. He still carried on experiments in the house, but nobody saw him except his servants, and often days passed during which they prepared and left his food in a locked room without catching a glimpse of their employer. I learnt all this from the Rector." And, as it was midnight, Peter suggested we should go to bed.

Night in the quiet old house was peaceful, and the awakening was lovely and benign.   In the morning the Rector took
us round the church.   There was little of the picturesque to
note as the result of three thorough restorations, but in the
vestry there was a small chained library, of which he showed
us the catalogue.   Most of the books were still on their chains,
but bibliophiles during the years had wrested a number away
from their places.   Some of the most tantalizing in the catalogue, especially as they were in manuscript, had disappeared.
For instance I looked in vain for a tome that had been in-
scribed *De Succubis et Incubis Animadversaria* . . .   The rest of
the title had been erased.   The Rector informed us that they
had disappeared with some others in his predecessor's time,
under the first Lord Mountstable.   Until then they had been
known to medieval scholars.   Unfortunately they had never
been printed, though the editing had often been mooted.
Something had always happened to prevent it.   One scholar
had died while actually transcribing them.   Another, in
Germany, curiously enough, had never brought out his edition,
although he lived past his century of years.   Eventually the
books had disappeared and no inquiries had ever replaced
them.   In that way a definite scrap of medieval superstition
had perished for ever.

Peter returned to his charge, and, after the morning's work
and lunch at the Towers, returned to the Rectory.   That
afternoon we went a long walk together and he began to
expound.   "I'm dreadfully ashamed to haul you back from
France and all because of a bad dream."   I assured him that
I knew that he must have felt abundant reasons or he would
never have sent me the telegram.   "Well, there was a reason.
It was more than a dream and I will show you something that
I didn't dream, for it remained over.   They gave me the room
at the top of the house where the old grandfather had lived the
last years of his life.   I can't say it's haunted, for I shouldn't
mind that much.   A ghost is a ghost and nothing more.   The
room felt unpleasant and I shouldn't have minded, however much it continued to feel unpleasant.   I never heard a
step or a sound.   Nobody ever has from those rooms, but
then nobody ever slept in them since the last man died.   That's
all I know about the place and I slept five nights there and each
was worse than the other.   I intend to sleep a sixth night when
my tutorship is over if you will stay in the room with me.

That's why I telegraphed to you.   I wanted you here for a few days to prepare you.   I should feel a coward if I quitted that house without going upstairs again."

I agreed to stand by him, but out of more than personal curiosity I inquired what manner of visitation had befallen him.   "It is difficult to say what it is, but I dreamed horribly every night.   The dream was the same with more or less intensity each time.   I could not remember what it was except that it was terrible.   The moment I awoke, it seemed to go, only leaving me with a feeling that there was something in the bed beside me, something not alive, but cold and prickly. When I woke, it was to dead silence.   I could hear and see nothing nor could I feel anything in the physical sense of feeling.   It is more truthful to say that I couldn't feel at all.   At last there came the night when I couldn't stand it any longer. I woke, but so quickly this time that I carried a clearer reminiscence of my dream with me.   In the anguish of a moment I found myself tied by cords to some being, some person or some spirit who was wriggling and writhing in my embrace as though we were both drowning together at the bottom of a well.   It was so appalling that I had to let my mind race through and through my state of awakenedness until I could assure myself that it was all a dream.   Even so I found myself lying on the floor with the bedclothes twisted in knots, and round and round the clothes these old electric wires.   I could not imagine where they came from, for all the wires lighting the room were intact.   I must have walked in my sleep and dragged them out of some old corner.   I still have them. Here they are."

Peter handed me a heavy entanglement of old wires wrapped in worn silk, rusty, bent and twisted.   They were thicker than modern wires, they were knotted and held in a design, but Peter had not tried to unravel them.   "Come, let us play cats'-cradle," I said, and gradually we pulled them into some shape.   Five sets of wiring could be pulled away from the main body.   It was not for an hour that we smoothed them out.   There was then no need to remark that as a whole it made a cage for a human body.   It struck us both rather horribly at the same time.   Then I suggested that it was the sort of thing that might be used to hang criminals who had been condemned to be gibbeted.   But that was not likely. What on earth would it be doing here ?   We preferred not to think and returned to spend a second night of peace and rest in the Rectory. It seemed decidedly cowardly to let that room keep its mystery to itself. That had been Peter's chief feeling in telegraphing to me, and the adventurous challenge of youth rose in our blood.

The next day was the last of the tutorship, and we both made up our minds to pass the last night in that room. We told the Rector of our purpose. He wished us well but he would not encourage or dissuade us. Towards evening he appeared a little nervous and asked us if we held to our determination. We replied that we did, as we felt there was something to be explained and that, if we did not find an explanation, nobody ever would.

"There are many things which have never been explained in that house," said the Rector. But he remained uncommunicative until tea-time. . . . He talked to us a good deal before we set out for Mountstable Towers after dinner. His tale was more or less this:

"You must do what you feel best. I cannot advise you. Lord Mountstable may be grateful to you if you penetrate the mystery, if there is a mystery. He is certainly pleased with the progress which his boy has made and was very distressed that you could not remain under his roof at night. Unfortunately that was the only wing on which he could offer accommodation. It has never had the repute of being haunted. Frankly, there is no ghost, but, if there is any trouble, it can only date from the first lord. All I know about him comes to me from my predecessor.

"Lord Mountstable was of ancient but poverty-stricken origin. He made money quickly and easily and retired from business. He rebuilt the old house that was standing here and he experimented in advance of his days. He certainly frightened the neighbourhood thoroughly. When they saw his electric flashes at night they thought he was in league with the devil. It used to be said with some terror that oil and tallow were never needed for lighting at the Towers. Whence I presume he had hit upon incandescent light in a glass bulb before the great American discoveries. He was supposed to have raised fiends from below, when voices were heard resounding from hollow boards attached to wires at a distance from the house. I presume again that he had stumbled on the telephone before his time. He was never able to make any commercial use of his weird pre-knowledge, and after a few years he passed on to another series of experiments which may have been premonitions of that future which still remains undisclosed. They necessitated a laboratory and assistants.

About this time he very unexpectedly inherited a peerage, which made him the first of a new line in his family. This, together with his self-made fortune and his very Radical opinions, called attention to him for the first time in his life, and there was a proposal that the Liberal Government should make him a Lord-in-Waiting. But this he declined very firmly and consequently was never heard of again, except for some unfortunate accidents which befell his laboratory.

He was looked upon as a remarkable amateur, and from time to time he communicated theories to the University of Oxford which brought him an honorary degree, though the scientists seldom carried his papers into the experimental stage. They took him seriously enough to supply him with laboratory assistants, whom he paid well. All would have proceeded well, had not one been found dead for no assignable cause. Lord Mountstable alleged the explosion of a new gas. There were no witnesses or traces of chemical disaster and nobody had heard an explosion. The young man was allowed by the coroner to be buried on Lord Mountstable's explanations, and nothing could be said. Four years later the same thing happened. Only the second time there remained nothing of the assistant at all. A coroner sat again and there was an inquiry, which was regarded rather grimly in the neighbourhood.

It was then that counsel published the fact that Lord Mountstable had once been offered a Lordship-in-Waiting at Court. No particular conclusions could be reached. Lord Mountstable evidenced a silent and internal explosion and showed some molten glass and twisted wires, which experts agreed had been subjected at some time to tremendous forces. There was a good deal of ill-natured comment, for the total disappearance of the assistant could scarcely be accounted for according to known rules of chemistry. An Oxford professor admitted that the papers which his Lordship had been submitting of late were considerably in advance of such laws as were accepted or dreamed of in the world of science, but he remained noncommittal. The best evidence in Lord Mountstable's favour was the fact that he had been very seriously burnt himself and appeared in court with bandages over his shoulders. He could remember little except that he had left his assistant at one end of the laboratory while he was making tests at the other, when an unexpected accident wrenched the whole building. The electrical fire which followed had reduced glass and metal to a solvent condition. His assistant had been caught in the wires and had perished in the glow. He himself had only been saved by being precipitated from the window. He could not explain his own wounds, but it looked as though the wires had entered his own flesh. When he was asked questions on the nature of his experiments, he distanced his questioners by a knowledge which the Professor of Chemistry in Oxford described as uncanny. In the end he was asked to close his laboratory and to pay a pension to the assistant's family, which he consented to do. He was asked whether he thought his experiments would lead to any result beneficial to the human race. He answered that he had already proposed means for the electrical transmission of the human voice. He also thought that electrical currents would be used to cure the most malignant diseases in time. Both these suggestions caused a great deal of amusement. Lord Mountstable was considered eccentric to the verge of insanity, but he was cloaked from general ridicule by the veneration which then happily hedged a peer."

The Rector had paused in his narrative and fumbled with the leaves of his Bacon. "There is a quotation from the *Novum Organum* which might well have been applied, that the race of chemists out of a few experiments of the furnace have built up a fantastic philosophy." Peter asked whether it was not possible to regard Lord Mountstable as a pioneer. There had been Darwinians before Darwin. It was possible that there had been a pre-Edisonian in England. The Rector replied again from Bacon in the philosopher's words, that the subtlety of Nature is greater many times than the subtlety of the understanding. Undoubtedly the understanding of early Victorian times was not equal to the subtlety which Lord Mountstable suspected in Nature. As to initiating any celebration of his name, the Rector spoke doubtfully : "I have every belief that his mind was as remarkable a mind for his own day as Bacon's was for his. I would be the first to encourage national recognition and I am sure a very good case could be made from his papers. But I should feel uneasy of booming what appears to me now in the light of a sinister character.

"As I think I told you, there have been occurrences at the Towers which have never been properly explained. Some fame could be attached to his earlier speculations, but I think his latter series of experiments had better remain out of notice. The inquests held at the time left matters veiled, and veiled they will probably always remain. The public suspicion at the time that all was not well was based on a truer instinct than juries or coroners could follow. Even at this distant time I think it is best for the sake of the family and especially of the boy, on whom the good wishes of the neighbourhood continue to rest, that mystery should be left even where it is most mysterious. For that reason I do not particularly encourage your expedition this evening. I can quite understand your wishes to settle the restlessness begotten of your unpleasant experiences, which we may call hallucinations until we know better. At the same time you may catch the clue to certain grave matters, of which I shall speak to you before you leave to-morrow. You would be only confused if I mentioned them to-night, and your imagination might be set upon the wrong track. It is possible that you may find no cause for feeling that the place is in the least haunted. In this case it would be better to let sleeping dogs lie, or, shall we say, to leave Lords-in-Waiting to continue waiting."

All this the old gentleman said in the wisest and kindest way. It was obvious that his long knowledge of the neighbourhood had made him aware of things of which he was unwilling to speak unless they proved to correspond with some new happening. Before we started for the Towers we could not help inviting him to divulge a little more. "I really cannot give you more facts," he answered. "I have only put together suspicions of what may have been the nature of those latter experiments of the first lord. The present lord has never spoken to me once on the subject of his father, whom he holds in incredible hatred. So much so that it is dangerous to allude to him, for the son appears to foam at the mouth at such mention. Although he was brought up entirely outside any religious belief, he has not been unfriendly to me, and it was on my advice that you were selected as the tutor of his son, who I regret to say has been brought up in the same negative opinions. When he goes to Cambridge I hope he will meet

redeeming influences. Meantime, I can only assume a
position of watchful benevolence."

We still begged him to advise what we might understand
by the influences which had troubled Peter during the nights
he had spent at the Towers. He hesitated and answered us
rather nervously. "You must not regard me as either superstitious or professional in what I say. The present Lord
Mountstable was never baptized. It was given out at the time
that he was too delicate, but this my predecessor never
admitted. His old nurse, who lived for years, almost half a
century, at the Towers, passed through my hands at the end.
Hers was a very troubled deathbed. I could not take all she
told me seriously, but certainly she took blame upon herself
that she had never brought the child to be baptized in spite of
his father's positive orders. One thing she insisted upon was
that when under her charge he had been a strong, well-built
boy. Whatever happened to him after he passed out of her
care she attributed to the vengeance of God. Of course I
could not encourage such a detestable view of the Divinity.
Lord Mountstable's deformity could only have been caused
by a natural accident or by some condition dating from birth.
He has always given me the appearance of a shrunken man and
one who has suffered from a sense of inferiority. The old
nurse used to speak of him as though he were not the same
being as the bonny bairn she had tended, and as though some
changeling had taken his place. I felt that there was always
something which she dared not tell me. But she was a
pensionary of the family and perhaps it was not until the close
of her life that a desire to cleanse her soul of horrible memories
affected her. Certainly I shall always remember her agony
and terror at the approach of death. It was only with the
greatest will-power that I composed her and caused her to
die in comparative peace."

As we all walked together on our way, we passed the
churchyard and he pointed out her grave. "Yes, there have
been inexplicable things over a considerable time, and they
do not necessarily dovetail. I shall give you my general
deduction to-morrow, but of facts I have no more. There
is one thing I shall show you to-morrow and that is one of the
chained books which was a long time missing from the vestry
library. It was returned after many years anonymously from
Oxford, but I understand it had remained in the possession

of the family of one of the assistants, who must have abstracted
it before he met with the fatal explosion.   I have never restored
it to the library.   I keep it in the parish safe, but you may
examine it before you leave to-morrow.''

That night, with Lord Mountstable's permission, we both
took up quarters in the unoccupied wing of the Towers.   We
did not undress, as we had already packed our suitcases, nor
did we occupy beds.   We each took blankets and prepared
opposite corners.   To begin with, we made a thorough search
through the whole wing, rooms and corridors.   It was all
strictly Victorian and in order.   There was not a worm-bite
nor a crack in the heavy carved panelling, surmounted with
crockets made of deal.   It was a solid example of carpenter's
Gothic. •The furniture and fittings were added in similar
taste.   Curtains, staircase rods and brass bedsteads all signified
an era of materialism tinged by pharisaism.   On the stairs
was a cupboard which showed signs of recent opening.   The
lock had been forced at some time.   It was a housekeeper's
receptacle, the height of a man, and it was crammed with dusty
old apparatus, apparently all the relics of the destroyed
laboratory.   There were large copper batteries greened by the
breath of time, and coils of heavy silk-coated wires.   "This
is the most prehistoric thing here," I observed.   "This is
where I must have picked up my little sample in my sleep,''
laughed Peter.   "Now we know where it came from.''

We pulled the cupboard inside out.   It was a melancholy
collection, as grim as a dead man's suit of clothes when it has
been given over to the moth.   This was the mechanical outfit
occupied once by a strenuous and possibly sinister mind, now
gone utterly from amongst mankind.   It is always difficult
to place such minds as Lord Mountstable's in the hereafter.
They seem equally unfitted for heaven or hell.   We replaced
the stuff and returned to our room.   It might have been
pictured as the model of a comfortable and unhaunted room.
We lay down in our respective corners and became somnolent.

But we were not heavily sunk in sleep.   If a board cracked
for dryness or a breath of air rustled the blinds, we both found
ourselves awake and staring at each other across the room.
Sometimes we dozed and sometimes we dreamed.   And all
the while the night hours were creeping along.   If our bodies
slept, our minds were subconsciously awake.   Certainly they
were not resting themselves, for our vigil charged them with

that mental heaviness which comes from a strain. And as the hours passed, the autumn dawn floated into the atmosphere. The window sashes became clearly discernible against the light like great squares of arid phosphorescence. Still there was no stir within or without. Not a moth moved out of a curtain, and for all the herbal treasures surrounding us in the park no bird sang. The sunrise itself, as though it were intimidated by the general lack of welcome, seemed to hang and hesitate. It was only a dull ray which filtered finally through the panes, and we had both fallen into the last lap of the night's slumber, when a distinct cry woke us from the corridor.

We both sat up instantly and Peter rushed to open the door. The cry came to us again. We could only see the grey clamminess streak down the empty passage. We moved towards the other wing when we heard a voice. "Good God, it is the boy!" shouted Peter, and we ran into the next wing, where we found his door was ajar. We entered, but the bed was empty and the linen lay in a heap. I felt it. It was warm and wet, as though the last drop of his sweat had been wrung out of him. We returned down the corridor in time to catch a groan from the direction of the cupboard we had fingered that evening. I thrust it open and Peter caught the boy as he fell out in a swoon. "Hold him!" called Peter, and we both closed our arms round him. He was swaying to and fro as though in the clutch of another. His face was pallid, his eyes were tightly closed and his tongue was hanging. We could feel and hold him, but our combined strength was insufficient to keep him still. He eluded our strength like one of the demoniacs of the Bible.

As he swayed in our arms without exerting any muscular effort on us, I became subject to a growing sensation of horror. There was nothing between my elbows except this bundled youth, but my limbs seemed to be tied to his. I felt as a very sensitive fly might feel when engaged in its first struggle against the flypaper before losing all hope. I could feel nothing external, but in my own skin I felt cold and prickly, but colder than I had ever felt before, and more prickly than any attack of pins and needles in bed had ever left me. Something that I could not define or disengage from was drawing the very marrow out of my bones. A faintness overcame me, which was not that which arises from physical pain, but rather from the senses when they are sinking under a subtle narcotic.

One latent sense remained only too vividly awake, that sense which human beings possess between dormant superstition and the stupor of the reason. I felt that I was giving up the ghost and began to sway limply with the unfortunate boy whom we held like a corpse between us—but a galvanized corpse. . . . Seconds seemed swollen into hours. A minute would have been as long as a day. . . . I felt my head becoming larger and larger until it seemed on the point of dissolving itself into a cloud of chill mist. . . . Peter, gradually exerting all his sturdiness of body and mind, was able to soothe the unconscious boy in his arms. He seemed to be passing from ridigity into languor. Peter picked him up and replaced him in his bed. I followed, and we spent some time rearranging the blankets around him. He was profoundly asleep, but his heart beat normally, and we thought it safer to leave him where he lay. The atmosphere cleared rapidly. The sun had extracted itself out of the cloud and a warmer light was penetrating the corridors. We fell into two or three hours of ordinary sleep. When we awoke, it was past breakfast-time and all seemed very like a dream.

We tidied ourselves and made our way down for breakfast, where Peter's pupil greeted us as though nothing had happened. He appeared paler than usual but showed no hectic sign. Apparently he had slept directly through his experiences and, whatever they had been to him, they had flown forgotten as as a dream. We, remembering more of the night, were far more upset and found it difficult to eat more than one of the many courses which make the rural British breakfast. Peter went along afterwards to say good-bye to his host, who hoped he had had one good night at least under his roof. Peter felt bound to say that he had not been personally disturbed. He would not promise to return the next vacation, as he expected to secure his curacy by then. He thought the boy would do very well under a regular coach and eventually be able to face the Mathematical Tripos.

We strolled back to the Rectory, where our venerable friend awaited us, and behind closed doors we repeated our experiences of the night. He listened with fascinated attention. "I am not surprised," he remarked. "It does not explain everything but it shows in what direction explanation may lie."

We begged him to suggest his ideas. "I think," he resumed, "the late Lord Mountstable carried out some very advanced experiments. I think that late in life he read some medieval ideas of the kind which used to appeal to the alchemists and which he endeavoured to subject to modern appliances. I think his assistants formed part of the experiment and that they perished under his wires. The body of the first assistant was reported to have been marked as though strangled with red-hot wire. The body of the second was probably disposed of for reasons best known to the experimenter. I imagine that last experiment was a failure. He never tried it again, at least during his own lifetime. The nickname of Lord-in-Waiting seemed to suit him thereafter rather grimly, for I feel he was always waiting to complete his experiment as far as a disembodied spirit is able to frequent the plane which he has left."

He then opened a drawer and showed us the missing chained book which had been returned by the assistant's family. "They were of course unable to read the characters and always mistook it for a chemical notebook. In time they heard of the collection here and made a gift." He pulled out the heavy vellum MS. It was written in black letters with cabalistic designs. It had been scored by modern pencil-marks.

"I have read it," said the Rector, "and it makes ill reading for Christian folks. It is in cipher at times, but I think I can read through the lines. Discoveries were always handed down in the form of secret anagram during the Middle Ages. This book describes demoniacal possession and the transference of personality, and includes speculations on the possibility of transference of natural forces from a young body into an older one. The requisite of the medieval sorcerer was always some magical medium. It was that which failed him all the centuries he spent questing for the Philosophers' Stone. Nor did he succeed in attaining the conservation of youthful energy by foul means or fair. This book must have come under the notice of Lord Mountstable soon after two attempts had been made to edit and translate it. Both editors died before they made any publication from the volume, unless you care to imagine that the one who became a centenarian had profited by his secret reading. Lord Mountstable had completed his magnetic discoveries without any idea how richly they would affect modern life. Then he took a wrong turning. To apply electricity while still an unknown force to a medieval theory appealed to him disastrously. Personally

I have no doubt of the use of his assistants and I only pray that their ends were not prolonged. . . .

"The experimenter's survival in time and space after death may be attributed to laws which even the Society for Psychical Research has not yet penetrated. The force of his mind has remained in solution in the atmosphere, which it would not be untrue to describe at times as electrical, and it has been posthumously turned against his own kin. The present lord no doubt received his disfigurement while that force was still virulent. Its recent manifestations seem to have shown a decreasing potency. I trust sincerely that it has exhausted itself in this final attempt at obsession. Bacon wrote that the study of Nature is engaged in by the mechanic, the mathematician, the physician, the alchemist and the magician. But the latter two are only the illegitimate forerunners of the others. In the fresh-eyed beginning of religious and scientific movements the pioneers sometimes received glimpses that were concealed from their successors. When the laws of Nature have been discovered in their entirety, it will be found that though all things are not permitted, all things are possible. . . ."

BARRY PAIN

A CONSIDERABLE MURDER

Mr. Albert Trusworth Mackinder, having made much
money in the City of London, retired to a house by the sea
at Helmstone. He was at this time a widower of fifty-eight
and he was accompanied by his only daughter, Elsa, a pretty
child of sixteen. Mr. Mackinder was satisfactory to the local
society and was not displeased with it himself. But he had
had many ideas in his life, and the idea which possessed him
most strongly at present was that he was interested in the
onward march of science. For this reason he interested himself
deeply in Dr. Bruce Perthwell. Dr. Perthwell attended Miss
Mackinder once and Mr. Mackinder twice—on all three
occasions for colds. When Dr. Perthwell recommended
that they should stay in bed, feed light, and take the medicine
which he would send up to the house, results had been satisfactory on each occasion. But this did not impress Mr.
Mackinder nearly so much as the way in which Dr. Perthwell
spoke of the mysteries and magic of science. Dr. Perthwell
was a clean-shaven man, grey-haired, with an authoritative
face and a very convincing manner.

Mr. Mackinder liked him and asked him to dinner frequently, for though Mr. Mackinder knew that it was too late
in life for him to take up any really serious study of science,
he was quite glad to have such scientific facts as Dr. Perthwell
might be disposed to let drop, duly prepared and seasoned to
suit the appetite of the elderly. In this way Mr. Mackinder
learnt what was, roughly speaking, the velocity of light, and,
if he happened to require Vitamin C, in what articles of diet
he would do best to search for it. This was all very good for
Mr. Mackinder and kept him up in his belief that the world
was an interesting place.

Now it happened that Elsa Mackinder invited to stay with
her a friend to whom she had been long attached, Miss Jessie
Palkinshaw, of the same age as herself and destined for the

nursing profession.   On the night of her arrival Mr. Mackinder, to square the table, invited Dr. Perthwell to join them
at dinner, which he did.   Dr. Perthwell got, perhaps, a little
tired of preaching extreme moderation and temperance all
day, and liked to relax a little in the evening.   Mr. Mackinder's
dinners were good.   His cellar was good.   There was no intolerable excess, but Mr. Mackinder and his guest generally,
as is sometimes said, did themselves fairly well.   It was
after the two ladies had retired to the drawing-room that Mr.
Mackinder refilled Dr. Perthwell's glass with '96 and addressed
himself to a subject which had been somewhat in his mind that
day.

"You know, Doctor, I was reading that murder case in
the papers this morning.   It puzzles me.   Why do those
poison people always bungle it ?   Why do they choose
poison such as arsenic which can so easily be traced ?"

Dr. Perthwell fixed his meditative eyes on the ceiling.

"I should say it is principally from ignorance.   No
doctor, of course, would make such a blunder.   But not even
every doctor, not by a long way, knows what is actually
possible.

"And what is actually possible ?" asked Mr. Mackinder
eagerly.

"Well," said Dr. Perthwell, "there are two drugs which
can be procured at any chemist's without any formalities, and
neither of them is in the least degree injurious.   But if you
mix, say, a quarter of a teaspoonful of one with a quarter of a
teaspoonful of the other and give that in a glass of water to any
person, in less than an hour that person will be dead.   And no
post-mortem, no examination of any kind will ever find the
slightest trace of poison in the body."

"Amazing," said Mr. Mackinder.   "Perfectly amazing.
That is really so ?"

"It is."

"I suppose I shouldn't ask it," said Mr. Mackinder, "but
could you tell me what the names of these two drugs are ?"

"Undoubtedly I could," said the doctor, "but——"

Mr. Mackinder refilled the doctor's glass.

"After all," said Dr. Perthwell, "you are a student of
science.   You are no ordinary layman.   I have no doubt that
your interest is quite legitimate.   Would you be willing to
swear to me on your word of honour that you have no intention

of murdering anybody, and that if I give you these names you will keep them strictly to yourself?"

"Certainly," said Mr. Mackinder. "I am at peace with the world, and have no desire to injure anybody whatever—let alone murder them."

Dr. Perthwell went to the door of the dining-room, opened it, closed it again, and returned to his seat.

"You will pardon me, Mr. Mackinder. I had to be quite certain that I could not be overheard."

He gave the names of the two drugs and Mr. Mackinder wrote them down in his note-book. He put each name down on a different page and the two pages were at some distance apart. Mr. Mackinder was cunning.

On the following day Mr. Mackinder purchased, without question or suspicion being roused, one ounce of each of these drugs, at two different chemists'. He was surprised at the vast amount he got for sixpence. He had enough to murder the entire neighbourhood if he had had any spite against it.

He was a methodical man. He took two large sheets of white paper and cut them into small squares. Into each square he put a quarter of a teaspoon of the first drug and folded it into a neat packet. He then took two sheets of blue paper and did the same thing with the other drug, being perhaps inspired with the classical example of the Seidlitz powder. There was still some of each drug remaining, and this he destroyed in the fire. He placed the packets neatly in a cardboard cigarette-box and put the box in a large desk which in theory he always kept locked, and quite frequently did.

He had now the means at hand to destroy forty-eight people. He positively tingled with power. If the worst came to the worst—and at present there was no worst and it was not coming to anything—he felt that he could deal with it.

And the years went on. It happened that once Elsa asked her father:

"What are all those funny little papers in the cigarette-box in your writing-desk? I noticed them to-day when I went there to get stamps. By the way, you don't keep as many stamps as you used to."

"Well," said Mr. Mackinder, "as regards the papers in the box, I think I may tell you about them because they are of extraordinary interest. But so far as I remember, I am to some extent restricted. You would have to promise me that you would tell nobody what I am going to tell you."

"Of course," said Elsa.

Mr. Mackinder then told his daughter precisely what Dr. Perthwell had told him.

And the years still went on and Miss Jessie Palkinshaw became a fully qualified nurse and went in for private work. And then came the letter from Robert Filminster.

Mr. Mackinder knew Mr. Filminster, whose age was at this time verging on the nineties, quite well. He knew that Mr. Filminster had been a friend of his father's and had, in fact, financed him over various crises before the business came to a position of steady security. He had been assured by Mr. Filminster that the greater part of his property would go to Mr. Mackinder for life and to his daughter after him.

Mr. Filminster's letter was simply pathetic. He said that he knew he was on the verge of death. The end of the lease of his house was up and he had been unable, even by a most extravagant offer, to obtain just two or three weeks' prolongation. He felt that he could not go into an hotel, for that would kill him painfully and at once. He knew that he asked much, but would Mr. Mackinder consent to put him up, together with his nurse, Jessie Palkinshaw, until the end came?

Mr. Mackinder felt that he could not do otherwise than accept. His daughter Elsa agreed with him. She was also glad of this coincidence which brought Jessie Palkinshaw back into her life. Questioned, Mr. Mackinder could say very little about Mr. Filminster. He remembered him as a very quiet and scholarly old gentleman. He reproached himself that they had not met more frequently in recent years.

So Mr. Filminster was accepted and arrived in his own expensive car with his nurse by his side. He seemed somewhat wearied with the journey and glad to get to bed. Not till he was safely asleep did Jessie Palkinshaw descend to talk things over with the eager Elsa Mackinder. They both rejoiced at the renewal of their rapturous friendship. Miss Palkinshaw looked like a saint of wonderful serenity in her nurse's uniform. Elsa, with her shingled hair, felt worldly and common in comparison.

"Tell me now, darling," said Elsa. "What kind of a man is this Mr. Filminster?"

"I think," said Nurse Palkinshaw, "that you are likely to have trouble with him. It cannot be for long, however, because his own doctor assured me that he could not last for more than a week, and there was even some question whether he would not die in the car coming down here. But Mr. Filminster does not like doctors and cannot be expected to do everything they say."

"But what kind of man is he?"

"He's more than one kind of man. The first week I was with him he was always very patient and nice and behaved himself. He can do it still if he wants to do it. He was all right when he arrived here to-day, for instance. Otherwise he has become so eccentric and wild—no doubt owing to his disease—that sometimes it is very, very difficult to put up with him. Of course, a nurse who is any good must be prepared to put up with absolutely anything. I was sent to him by a doctor who is well disposed towards me and has plenty of work to give. I don't want to lose my market. Whatever Mr. Filminster does or does not do I shall hang on until the lid's screwed down. When he is in one of his bad moods he uses the most terrific language you ever heard."

"Blasphemous?"

"That of course. Only yesterday in three words he implied that my soul was lost, that I had the haemorrhagic diathesis, and that I was of illegitimate birth. But that's not all, by a long way. He often uses language which is—well, physiological."

"But they have physiological language in books, don't they?"

"There are two kinds of physiological language. His is the other. I advise you to keep out of his way as much as possible."

"Oh, but I do want to help," said Elsa. "I don't want you to be worked to death. If you can put up with things, I must make up my mind to put up with them too."

"Well," said the nurse, "he's not perhaps been quite so bad lately. He's had a good deal of pain and that always keeps him quiet. I don't think he's actually broken a measuring-glass for three days."

"I suppose the poor old man can't hold them properly."

N*

"That's not it. He throws them, you know. He throws pretty well everything.   He says it's the only form of exercise that he's got now. We buy our measuring-glasses by the dozen, and they don't last long.   Every now and then he gets a fit of wonderful activity and would go out into the street if he were allowed to have any clothes in his room.   But he isn't. Of course, I have to use a good deal of tact.   As a matter of fact I could pick the old chap up and carry him.   But if he used any great effort that might bring on the end suddenly. No, I shouldn't describe it as a soft case—not easy, by any means."

At dinner that night Mr. Mackinder heard much of the story and was calmly philosophical.

"We must make up our minds to be patient," he said.   "It is a question of a few days only.   Surely we can put up with that.   To-morrow Dr. Perthwell will be in to see him.   No doubt he will be able to tell us something."

On the next morning at breakfast Nurse looked a little worn. Mr. Mackinder asked kindly how her patient was getting on.

"If anything he seems a little stronger. He had one of his fits of activity, but he's safely asleep again now. He's started porridge-sloshing again."

"Started which ?" asked Mr. Mackinder.

"Porridge-sloshing is what he calls it. He always will have porridge for breakfast, and the doctors say he is to have anything he likes. Some days he will eat it and some days he won't. It's when he won't that he starts this porridge-sloshing. He fills the spoon full with porridge, holds the end of the handle in one hand, and with a finger of the other draws back the tip of the spoon and suddenly lets go. He can send it quite a considerable distance that way. He generally aims at the different pictures in the room, but he's got me with it two or three times. It always seems to amuse him. Of course, it makes a good deal of work clearing up afterwards."

"Naturally," said Mr. Mackinder.   "I should hate to be unkind, but I think I must just ask Perthwell if he doesn't think the poor old chap had better be put into a—one of those institutions where those old chaps are put, you know."

But Dr. Perthwell gave no support to these hopes.

"My dear Mackinder," he said, "I could not possibly certify this Mr. Filminster. He is eccentric, no doubt, and his temperament is much altered by his illness, as any medical man would expect. But he has no delusions and he is not dangerous to anybody. Even if he were I should advise you to let him remain. So far as I can see, in three days he must be dead. You do not want to stuff him into an asylum just for those last three days of his life."

"Certainly not," said Mr. Mackinder. "I had not realized that the end was so near. Three days, I think you said."

"I may be wrong, but from my observations to-day I should think three days would be the limit."

But Mr. Filminster had no great belief in doctors. He lived on for another two months, and by that time the nerves of Mr. Mackinder, his daughter Elsa, and Nurse Palkinshaw were frazzled and pulped. Most of the work fell on them. The butler had already left on the grounds that he had been engaged for a private house and not for Bedlam. And Mr. Mackinder did not care to risk losing any other of the upper servants. He and his daughter and the nurse saw it through, relieving one another at intervals. All Dr. Perthwell could say was that he had never seen such a case before. He had never met with such extraordinary vitality. Any ordinary man must have been dead long before.

Mr. Mackinder, his daughter and the nurse used no hypocrisy. They longed for Mr. Filminster's death. As a concession to decency they said it would be a blessed release for all concerned.

After luncheon Nurse Palkinshaw and Elsa Mackinder were taking two hours off duty for the preservation of their health and sanity. The nurse had had a fit of hysterics of brief duration just before luncheon. Mr. Mackinder remained on duty. From his study he could easily hear Mr. Filminster's bell if he struck it. However, Mr. Filminster was now asleep and Mr. Mackinder hoped that, as usual, there would be nothing for him to do. Requiring a postcard, he opened his desk, and he left it open. And then he heard the whir of the bell on the table by Mr. Filminster's bedside. Almost immediately it was repeated. Mr. Mackinder hurried upstairs.

He had hardly got inside the door when a slipper, thrown with considerable force, struck him in the face, the heel of the slipper barking his nose.

"Why don't you pay attention?" said Mr. Filminster.

"I want a whisky-and-soda.   The doctors said I could have
anything I liked, didn't they ?   When you're on duty you're
jolly well on duty, and don't you forget it another time or I
might hop out of bed and twist your blessed nose."

(The more salient and picturesque adjectives have been
omitted or substitutes have been provided.)

"That is hardly the way to speak to me," said Mr. Mackinder.   "And you've caused the bridge of my nose to bleed.
However, I will bring you what you require."

Mr. Mackinder went downstairs with blue murder in his
heart.   He remembered the open desk and the cigarette-box
with the papers in it.   Without hesitation he took a glass and
emptied into it a white powder and a blue powder.   In this he
poured whisky and subsequently soda-water.   Mr. Filminster
took the contents of the glass in one draught, told Mr. Mackinder where he could go, and then flung the glass after him, but
fortunately missed.   In two minutes more Mr. Filminster
was asleep again.

Downstairs, Mr. Mackinder wrestled with his agonized
conscience.   But as he summed up the question he could not
see that he had done much harm.   There was not a day when
Mr. Filminster did not beg them to give him something to
put an end to it all.   There was the best medical opinion that
he could only live for a few hours now.   The man was simply
killing his daughter Elsa and Nurse Palkinshaw and they were
both absolute wrecks.   On the whole Mr. Mackinder decided
he had acted wisely.   He then put a small strip of pink plaster
across the bridge of his nose.

He waited impatiently for the return of his daughter and
the nurse about an hour later.   In reply to their inquiries he
said that he had taken up a whisky-and-soda to Mr. Filminster
and this was all there had been for him to do.

He waited for them to go upstairs and to come down
quickly announcing that Filminster was dead.

They did not come down quickly.   When they appeared
in the drawing-room Elsa rang for tea quite casually and
Nurse Palkinshaw said that Mr. Filminster seemed stronger
but was not in a good temper.

Mr. Mackinder reflected.   Those drugs had been in his
desk for some time.   Possibly they had now lost their efficacy.
He was in reality not sorry to think so.

On the following morning, as Mr. Mackinder sat at his

early breakfast at eight o'clock, Nurse Palkinshaw entered the room.

"Mr. Filminster is dead," she said. "He seems to have passed away in his sleep. I have telephoned to Dr. Perthwell. But that is not all. I was tried beyond human endurance. I have a confession to make to you."

She made it.

"What am I to do?" she cried despairingly.

"Nothing whatever at present," said Mr. Mackinder. "Leave things entirely in my hands. I will tell you more after the funeral."

And then, after the nurse had gone out, Elsa entered. She helped herself to a poached egg and a cup of China tea and then burst into tears and said she must confess all. Her father heard the confession and gave his instructions.

"At present," he said, "say nothing to anybody. After the funeral we must decide what is the right and moral thing to do."

Dr. Perthwell had not the least hesitation in giving a certificate that the death was due to natural causes, and in due course the funeral took place. Afterwards, by appointment, Dr. Perthwell attended Mr. Mackinder at his house.

"I think," said Mr. Mackinder, "by your certificate you attribute poor Filminster's death to his illness."

"Of course I did. It was the truth. Why not?"

"I have your promise of secrecy? I am speaking, so to say, under the seal of the professional?"

"Yes, yes."

"Well, I may tell you that Filminster was murdered."

"Murdered?"

"Yes. What is more, he was murdered three times."

"Three times?"

"Yes, and not only that. He also committed suicide."

"I think you'd better give me the details of this extraordinary story."

Mr. Mackinder then narrated how he himself had murdered Filminster. He showed that his motives were the best possible and said nothing about the abrasion on his nose.

"And then," Mr. Mackinder continued, "my daughter and the nurse came back. My daughter is absolutely devoted to Jessie Palkinshaw. She heard the language that Mr. Filminster was using to his nurse and felt absolutely unable to endure it.   Unluckily, my desk was still wide open on the study table.   She emptied one of each of the powders into the tea which was being taken up to him."

"Go on," said Dr. Perthwell.   "He was murdered three times, you say."

"And also committed suicide.   I think the nurse did what she did in a fit of temporary insanity caused by the awful overstrain.   In the evening she took up to his room the cigar-ette-box containing the poisons and put the powders into his last whisky-and-soda.   I cannot understand it, but she left that box on the table by his bedside.   There was also there a jug of water and a glass.   In the morning she found that the glass had been used and one of the white papers and one of the blue lay on the table.   He had taken his own life."

"I don't think so," said Dr. Perthwell cheerily.   "What's all this about white and blue papers ?"

"Surely you remember that you once told me that there were two drugs—you gave me the name of them—which were innocuous in themselves but would be fatal in one hour if mixed together ?"

"Well," said Dr. Perthwell, "you rather tempted me, you know.   You did like to have a sensational story, didn't you ?   As a matter of fact, those drugs are both of them, singly or in conjunction, absolutely harmless.   Had it been otherwise, you can't suppose that any conscientious medical man would have told you the facts ?"

"Why not ?"

"You promised me absolute secrecy, you know."

"Yes," said Mr. Mackinder.   "I think there was something said.   As a matter of fact, I told nobody but my own daughter, and the supposed poisons were very frequently kept locked up."

"Then how did the nurse know about it ?"

"Well, the nurse is one of my daughter's most intimate friends and she promised Elsa that it shouldn't go any further."

The doctor yawned.

"I see," he said.   "Well, I must be getting on.   I shouldn't let it worry me if I were you.   I don't suppose any one of the three was completely sane at the time."

That afternoon, I regret to say, Mr. Mackinder, his daughter and the nurse went to the Pictures.

LADY CYNTHIA ASQUITH

THE LOVELY VOICE

I WONDER why it is that in my old age I should feel prompted to set down this experience of a far-off girlhood. Partly, perhaps, because of our last night's conversation concerning murder.

We argued so long as to whether there was necessarily anything exceptional about the character of a murderer, my grandson maintaining that murder, like other actions, was in most cases merely the result of circumstances and no indication of the essential man.

"The act of murder," he asserted, "is far more of a fluke than many deeds not punishable by law. If you tell me that a man is habitually rude to his servant, you give me some insight into his personality and character, but by merely informing me of the fact that he has committed murder, you leave me in complete ignorance as to his nature."

I wonder.

Long, long ago, when I was thirteen years old, for the sake of acquiring French and health I passed a whole summer in an hotel in France. There is no object in giving the name of the town. Let it suffice that it was large and on the edge of a magnificent forest. My governess and I shared a double room, one in which we did lessons as well as slept. An admirable woman, Mademoiselle Plage, but by no means an entertaining companion. By sheer force of will she succeeded in holding my attention during lesson hours, but for the remainder of the day she did nothing whatever to occupy my mind. Her conversation offered neither instruction nor amusement. But I was very far from being bored. At that age the mere fact of staying in a large hotel was sufficient entertainment. The glamour of "pricky" water (plain was considered unsafe) never palled. The waiters were friendly, and it was lovely to be asked *which* sweet I would have. Above all, there was my unfailing interest in the varied visitors who perpetually came and went. Unlike us, these were mostly birds of swift passage, and nearly every time I entered the *table d'hôte* there would be some newcomer to stare at.

I wonder how often Mademoiselle told me that it was "rude to stare". She wasted her breath. She might just as well have asked me to stop breathing, so enthralled was I by this succession of human beings—by their faces, their voices, their clothes, and their manners.

Towards the end of July the stream of visitors thinned, and during that peculiarly sultry August the hotel was far too empty to please me. I mention this and the fact of Mademoiselle's dullness to show that my mind was unoccupied and therefore all the more liable to receive vivid impressions. If I was not consciously hungry for distraction, I was at least especially susceptible to it. One day towards the end of the month the heat was so intense that we were obliged to leave the door as well as the window of our room wide open. I always found lessons particularly difficult in hot weather, and just then was staring in sticky despair at the sum confronting me. Any distraction would have been most welcome, and at the sound of approaching footsteps and the chatter of voices I pricked up my ears. Through the open door I saw the concierge, bowing and smiling, followed by two vividly dressed, rustling ladies. It was only a fleeting glimpse that I caught, but it was enough to give an impression of almost startlingly brilliant smartness, and even now I can still smell the strong whiff of sweet, exotic perfume that came with the new arrivals. Most children have a dislike of artificial scent, and I remember wrinkling my nose with repugnance.

"*Par ici,*" said the concierge, and I heard the silken dresses of the ladies rustle into the room next to ours.

A peculiarly pleasant, fluting voice complained of the *grande chaleur*, and their door was left wide open. Thus, for the remaining half-hour of my lessons, I could plainly hear the two foreign voices. I understood French as easily as English and, to the destruction of my arithmetic, I listened to their ceaseless conversation. It was real chatter, a bright babble of words punctuated by gay laughter.

The voice I had first distinguished—an enchanting voice —appeared to do practically all the talking. Certainly it initiated every topic. In strong contrast to its rippling vivacity, the other voice was markedly toneless ; a sort of flat lifelessness conveying the impression of a rather dull personality. Yet her animated friend seemed sufficiently satisfied with her company.

They talked of their journey, their clothes, their plans for the morrow. Scattered through the converation I frequently heard "*Ma chérie*"—occasionally "*Mon ange*".

The chambermaid who brought in our hot water announced that two "*Parisiennes d'une grande élégance*" had arrived. Anxious to be in time to see the entry of the new arrivals, I hurried downstairs to the dining-room.

They were late, but when they did appear my expectations were far from disappointed. A lovely, slender young woman sailed—there is no other word for such motion—into the room, followed by her equally well-dressed but otherwise unprepossessing companion. To my delight they sat down at the nearest table to ours, and the lovely one began to speak in the voice that I had already thought so enchanting upstairs.

I was riveted by the beauty of this young Parisian. Not only was she utterly lovely with a peculiarly dewy loveliness, but there was about her a flowing grace such as I have never seen equalled. She seemed to bask in her own beauty, of which she was inevitably and simply aware.

"What fun it all is ! How lucky we are to be alive !" her glittering glance seemed to say even when it fell on the jaded, slatternly waiter from whom she might have been ordering so much nectar and ambrosia instead of gigôt and mineral water.

Even Mademoiselle, who was not addicted to personal remarks, actually sighed out the word "*Ravissante !*" as she blinked at the lovely being. The flower-like skin of the radiant young woman struck me as being of a fairness amazingly in contrast to her extremely dark hair, eyebrows, and lashes. I have never seen such startling whiteness crowned by black hair.

She shimmered.

Her companion was indeed an admirable foil, the one being as opaque as the other was translucent. Probably she was still nearly as young as she had ever seemed, but in her slow, unventilated face and her flat, springless voice there was something definitely dreary.

I wondered why two such utterly different women should be together, and concluded that they must be related. Not that there were any signs of strain. The lovely woman's talk never flagged. Her voice was like running water from which a delicious spray of laughter was frequently shaken. If her companion contributed but little, she was at least a rapt and most appreciative listener. Evidently she doted on her brilliant friend. So spoke the humble, adoring eyes and the delighted, unmusical chuckles with which she greeted her sallies. After all these obliterating years, I can still hear the quality of the voice to which she listened. Not only so lovely and liquid in tone, but of such flexibility that its intonations seemed, as it were, to thread the intricate mazes of a minuet and to curtsey with wincing appreciation of what it told. Her conversation was of people, of books, of plays, of clothes, and, to a child inured in schoolroom routine, redolent of varied interest and amusement.

After luncheon we moved into what would now be called the lounge, where my governess pounced on a dreary newspaper. To my delight, the two ladies soon came in. Catching sight of me, the lovely one's eyes lit up. "Hurrah! A child! Perhaps she'll be fun," they seemed to say.

Tall, undulating, smiling as she swayed across the room, in a moment she had joined me, and in charming broken English began to talk, not condescendingly as a grown-up person to a child, but rationally as to an equal.

I don't know how to convey to what extent I was fascinated. Suffice it to say that I became a complete convert to the use of scent. She drew me towards her friend, saying she must let me hear her repeating watch, which "loffly chimes played". The other woman obligingly showed me her pretty toy, and beneath her drab exterior and commonplace manners, child as I was, I could see the floor of her nature's steady kindliness shining like metal through muddy waters.

Reluctantly I was dragged away for my afternoon's walk, and, to my great disappointment, the ladies did not appear in the lounge for tea. I was never allowed to come down to the evening meal, and at seven I was sent to bed. I went upstairs the victim of a raging cult. I was obsessed by the lovely stranger.

The night was stifling—the hottest of all that grilling year—and it was considered necessary to leave our door wide open. Even so, there seemed no air to breathe. I lay and panted in my bed, and when Mademoiselle joined me at about ten o'clock I was still wide awake. Her complaints of the heat soon subsided into noisy slumber, but I had now determined to stay awake until the ladies in the next room came upstairs.

I pined to hear that enchanting voice again, for, lovely as was her face, it was her voice that had so completely captivated me.

It must have been long past eleven when at last the sultry silence was broken by the sound of fashionable high heels clicking along the parquet floor, and the notes of the voice for which I so eagerly listened. They passed by. I heard the lovely voice say that the door must be kept open on account of the heat. I was delighted. Hurrah! I should be able to hear their talk. This night there would be no slipping off to sleep from a dreary, lonely silence.

"It is so lovely to be here with you, *mon ange*," said the dull voice. She spoke, of course, in French, but I have forgotten her exact words. "With you one cannot have one dull moment," she went on, and I heard the sound of repeated kisses. I was struck by such demonstrative devotion. "You are looking so lovely," she continued, "but, oh, how I miss your glorious red-gold hair! How could you have spoilt it just for the sake of this one ball?"

"Oh, well," answered the voice, "Medea cannot possibly have anything but black hair, can she? And wigs always look so unnatural. You can't get them right! Besides, the man who dyed it swears it will be quite itself again in three months."

"I admire your zeal," said her friend, "but I deplore the sacrifice."

It did, indeed, seem extraordinary zeal to dye your hair for a fancy-dress ball. With the natural Puritanism of childhood, only the day before such an idea would have disgusted me, but in my present state of infatuation it seemed yet another symptom of her adorable zest for life. Excessive vitality mocks at a sense of proportion.

Besides, I rejoiced to hear that my lovely lady's hair was naturally auburn—my favourite colour. Against the dazzling fairness of her complexion, the intense darkness of her hair had seemed almost hard. Yes, a red-gold aureole would be far more becoming and immensely enhance her fairy-tale loveliness. I longed to see her as Nature had designed her.

For several minutes the conversation ran on about the fancy-dress ball—as to who was going, as which character, how much this and that lady had paid for their costumes, and so on.

"What an extraordinary whim of Madame de B——," said the dull voice, "that she must needs give a big charity ball now, when no one is naturally in Paris. But she never did do anything like anyone else."

"No; and can you wonder?" said *the* lovely voice, and here it dropped to inaudible whispering, which was followed by such loud laughter from both friends that, to my annoyance, Mademoiselle woke up.

"I cannot stand such chatter!" she exclaimed angrily. "Even heat is preferable. Let us cook in silence and peace."

She banged the door, and my evening's entertainment was at an end.

It had been such a treat listening to their conversation, and now, alas, I could no longer distinguish their words, though, as the wall was thin, I could still hear the sound of ceaseless talk and laughter. On and on it went. The first streaks of dawn were thinning the darkness before I fell asleep, but even then the ladies had not yet finished what my daughters—before they shingled—would have called their "hair-combing".

They did not come down to breakfast whilst I was in the dining-room, and you may be sure that I lingered as long as possible. Probably they had trays upstairs, but they must have gone out fairly early, for no sound came from their room during my dreary lesson hours.

The day was distinctly cooler, and at half past eleven we were able to start out for a walk.

During this long summer, my main hope of excitement lay in desperate attempts to get lost in the huge forest on whose borders our hotel stood. This craving for adventure was never gratified. Mademoiselle's bump of locality was incon-

veniently well developed. Unerringly she could find the
shortest way home. However, she was blessedly passive as
to the direction in which we took our walks. In fact, she was
completely indifferent as to where we went. Provided that
I followed her home directly she pronounced it time, I was
allowed to ramble at will through the more out-of-the-way
and unfrequented paths of that lovely forest.

That morning, after three-quarters of an hour's walk,
when we came to a sudden turning which disclosed a new
long vista, to my great delight I saw at some distance—
I suppose about fifty yards off—two figures that I immediately recognized as the two Parisian ladies, one of whom had
occupied most of my thoughts during the walk. Surrounded
by the paraphernalia of a picnic, they were both leaning
against the broad trunk of an oak tree whose spreading branches
overshadowed the little footpath leading past it. Their sun-
flecked dresses made gay splashes of colour against the heavy
green of late summer. My yesterday's interview with the
lady of the lovely voice made me feel quite confident
of a delightful welcome, and, with all the impetus of a
bored child in sight of diversion, I ran towards them. I was
disappointed; not in the lady's beauty—she was dressed in
dryad green and her complexion glowed in the strong
sunshine—but in the expression of her face. Though she
smiled quite civilly, her eyes showed no pleasure, and
yesterday they had literally shone with welcome.

I felt dashed. I had so looked forward to the tonic of
her gay responsiveness.

Oddly enough, it was her sallow friend who appeared
most pleased to see me. A placid good-humour irradiated
her plain face. She offered me chocolates, and her
accomplished watch was again put through its tricks. By
this time Mademoiselle had reached us. Characteristically
she announced that it was time to go back for *déjeuner*—
"*tout de suite*".

"It is to-day so luffly," said the plain lady, "that we are
going to—how you say?—peek-neek. I wish that you might
join vith us, but unhappily ve have not enough of provee-
sions."

The lovely lady, on whose face I had seen a fleeting frown,
now beamed, agreeing that it was a "big peety".

Reluctantly I followed Mademoiselle's remorseless back.

To eat in one's fingers under that glorious tree and in such enchanting company would indeed have been a romantic break in the monotonous routine of my *tête-à-tête* with Mademoiselle.

In spite of her disappointing greeting, which had greatly disconcerted me, the attraction of the lady with the lovely voice was still so strong that, when we set out for our afternoon walk, I felt irresistibly drawn back to the site of the picnic in the hope that the two friends might still be lingering in so pleasant a spot.

I had no difficulty in finding the way back. I hurried, outstripping Mademoiselle, and, when I turned the corner which brought the great oak into sight, to my delight I saw that the two ladies were still there. The tall figure in green had risen to her feet, and, with her back towards me, stood stooping down over the other, who still leant against the tree.

I was so delighted to see them that, waving my hand, I shouted a joyous "Hullo!" The tall green figure, dappled by sunshine, turned round suddenly and signalled to me to stop. At that distance I could, of course, not see the expression of her face, but there was no mistaking her almost violent gesture. She was waving me back, checking my approach, as might a nurse in charge of a sleeping child. Surprised, I stood still and stared.

The graceful green figure stooped low. Obviously she was kissing her friend. Again I was struck by such demonstrative affection. At least three kisses must have been given before she turned round and began to walk towards me. Half-way between me and the tree she looked back, and, waving her hand, called out, "*Au revoir, chérie!*" To my surprise there was no response from her friend, not even a nod of the head or a wave of the hand as she reclined, rather stiffly, propped up against the tree-trunk, her smart winged hat slightly tilted to one side, one hand holding up her somewhat garish parasol, the other lying in her lap beside a few wild flowers and one half of an orange. I remember noticing how almost exactly the orange matched the parasol, the top of which rested against the tree. Obviously she must have closed her eyes, else I could not imagine her failing to return her friend's wave of the hand. Asleep she could not be—the elbow of the arm holding up the parasol was bent in too acute an angle. In fact, in her whole attitude there was nothing to suggest sleep.

But I had scarcely had time to know that I had noticed any of these details before the lady with the lovely voice reached me and Mademoiselle, who had just joined me. She looked flushed and spoke quickly.

"My friend is feeling the heat," she said. "So she stays here to repose herself. I go back to the hotel to pay ze bill and fetch our baggage, and vill pick her up. Ze road comes not so very far off, I know, for we drove out zis morning, and only valked perhaps a quarter of an hour. I did not vant you to come close just now, because my poor friend is so nervous when she has the *migraine*. Absolute quiet is to her then necessary. It will no doubt be yesterday's sun that has her made ill."

I paid little heed to her account of her friend's indisposition. The mention of luggage and paying the bill had quenched my spirits. So they were going away to-day! Somehow I had assumed that they were to make a long stay, and I felt ridiculously dejected. Probably I should never see her again. Tears of disappointment came into my eyes, but they were not observed. Mademoiselle's corns were worrying her, and the lady seemed agitated about her friend's *migraine*.

"Now, little one," she said, still speaking very quickly, and in a voice not quite the one I loved, "please show me the quickest way back to the hotel. The sooner I get the tabloids my friend always takes the better."

Glad to be of any use, I took her at her word and started off at a rapid pace. Our short cut involved pursuing paths scarcely worthy of the name.

She was as fleet of foot as myself, and poor Mademoiselle followed in our wake as best she could.

About half-way home I received a shock which greatly troubled me. As I have said, I chose some very unorthodox paths, and, as I was threading my way along one across which the over-spreading boughs were scarcely cleared, forgetting how closely I was followed, I carelessly allowed a branch I had pushed away from my face to swing back. I heard a sharp cry of annoyance. The released branch had caught the lady's hat, almost knocking it off her head. In a flash she adroitly righted it, but not before I had seen the jet-black hair, beneath the displaced hat, surprisingly shift to one side, as it did so revealing some two inches of glowing *red* hair !

I'm not sure whether she saw that I had seen, but she looked flushed and disconcerted, and it was in complete silence that we finished our helter-skelter walk to the hotel.

I don't quite know why I was so disquieted by my chance discovery, but somehow I felt a sudden sagging of my natural trustfulness. Whether straightforward or not themselves, I think that most children attach great importance to truthfulness in those they love. It may seem absurd to use the word "love" in connection with a stranger, but no other word describes the emotion this lady had inspired in me.

Why, oh, why, in that conversation to which I had so eagerly listened last night, had she taken the trouble to tell her friend that she had had her hair *dyed*? "Wigs always look so unnatural. You can't get them right." I remembered her very words.

I expostulated with myself. How she achieved a desired disguise was surely a trivial matter, and no doubt there was some quite simple explanation. Perhaps she was going to surprise her friend by appearing in her natural colouring that very evening. A sort of practical joke. Nevertheless, I could not quite banish the distress from my mind. Her annoyance, too, over the mishap of the branch, seemed out of all proportion to the calamity of a displaced hat. One way and another I felt disillusioned. On our arrival I heard her ask for her luggage to be brought down and a carriage ordered. Dejectedly I went up to my room. Not very long afterwards, hearing the clatter of horses' hoofs, I leant out of the window. A carriage driven by a fat man with a black patch over one eye had drawn up. Some luggage was piled on to the back seat, and the lady, now dressed in a plain beige cloak and a small blue hat, stepped into the carriage. As the fat man with the black patch cracked his whip, she glanced upwards, and, seeing me, kissed her hand and smiled with all the radiance that had enslaved me the day before. My discouraged devotion flared up. Let her wear as many wigs as she chose and make any sort of a fool of her dull friend, what cared I ? I would remain her devoted slave. But, alas, should I ever see her again ?

The rattling carriage had now disappeared. She was gone. . . .

Lessons had never seemed so pointless, nor Mademoiselle so dreary.   At tea-time she discovered that a hole in her pocket had led to the loss of her purse.   In high agitation she announced that we must retrace our footsteps in the hope of finding the lost property.   Indifferent, I acquiesced.   All ways in that vast and senselessly beautiful forest were not equally uninteresting to me.   It was already quite four hours since the lady's departure.   No doubt she was already long since in Paris, the centre of the brilliance and gaiety her personality suggested.

I tried to concentrate on the diligent search for the lost purse.   Mademoiselle promised me a half-holiday as a reward if I should find it, but I had no particular use for a half-holiday. With bent heads, progressing at a snail's pace, the walk seemed endless, and it was not until we were within ten yards of the corner leading to the ladies' picnicking place that, with a cry of joy, Mademoiselle descried her purse lying, as it had fallen, right in the middle of the path.   Her anxiety thus relieved, she became excruciatingly conscious of the corns to which she was, as she constantly complained, an "absolute martyr".

"Ah!" she exclaimed.   "My feet burn!   I will take my boots off and give them a few moments' rest."

"All right," I answered.   "I'll stroll on and turn back in two minutes."   In my dejected state, movement was at least preferable to standing still.   A few listless strides brought me to the turning.   The familiar oak tree came in sight, and I stopped dead and stared in amazement.   I literally rubbed my eyes, for the scene was not the empty one I had expected. There, in full view, her back propped against the broad oak, her bent arm supporting the garish parasol, still reclined the figure of her whom I had come to think of as "the other lady".   The flowers and the half of an orange still lay in her lap, the disengaged hand beside them.   She was in exactly the same position as when I had last seen her.   How extraordinary!   I remembered the lovely lady's obvious anxiety to catch the next train.   Had she, then, failed to find her friend?   Was she perhaps still vainly searching through the forest?   She might be quite close.   Possibly I should see her again!   But fancy her friend having slept on through all these hours!   Slept she must have, else why was she still in the same position?   It *was* precisely the same position.   I remembered noticing the acute angle at which the elbow of the arm holding up the parasol was bent.

Surely it was a peculiarly stiff position for a sleeper. And what a long sleep! Why, it must be quite six hours since I last saw her. Mademoiselle and I had walked so slowly whilst searching for the purse.

I now noticed with surprise that she was bare-headed; and where was the small, smart, winged hat? Nowhere in sight.

As I stared at the still figure, I felt a strange drumming in my ears, and my breath came fast and rather painfully because of the queer way in which my heart was thumping.

My thoughts scarcely shaped the misgiving which assailed me. All I knew then was that not for anything in the world would I have approached one step nearer to that stiff, propped figure, flecked by the slanting shafts of the evening sun.

An undefined dread of my own half-formed, threatening thoughts seized me. Horror hovered—but no, no, no, I shut it out. My one imperative instinct was that on no account must Mademoiselle see what I had seen.

I wanted to get back to the hotel as quickly as possible. Yes, that was the thing to do—get back. Probably at the hotel I should find some quite simple explanation. Things would turn out to be all right, wouldn't they? Surely, surely! Anyhow, I wanted to move as quickly as possible and to be walking away and away from that sickeningly still figure. Somehow I couldn't bear to let Mademoiselle see my face. Muttering that I was fearfully thirsty, I passed her just as she had rebuttoned her boots. Feebly expostulating at my headlong pace, she followed.

Silently I plunged on, and, in spite of her corns, the devoted woman managed for some time to keep close behind. My thoughts were whirring, and for the last quarter of a mile I ran, reaching the hotel quite five minutes before Mademoiselle.

Just as I entered the courtyard, I heard the clop, clop of horse's hoofs, and a fly, driven by a fat man with a patch across one eye, rattled over the cobblestones.

Except for some luggage on the back seat, the fly was empty. Flinging the reins on to his horse's back, the driver jumped down from the box and clattered into the hotel. I followed him to the office, where, in his illiterate French and with much shrugging and gesticulating, he delivered himself of his strange story.

"The dark lady from here" with the luggage had told him to drive to a certain crossways in the forest. There she had got out, saying she went to fetch a friend whom she had left not far from the carriage drive, that she would return in at most ten minutes, and then they would proceed to the station.

He told how he had waited and waited, at first with and then without patience. For five hours he had been without food or drink, but the lady had never returned. He had not dared leave his horse and go and search the footpaths. He had shouted and shouted, but no answer had come.

What was he to do now? he asked himself, and how about his fare and his wasted day? He did not care for such customers! "No, thank you!"

The hotel staff volubly expressed their astonishment, but I did not stay to hear anything further. I rushed upstairs, and, to gain time, locked myself in the bathroom.

I could not face Mademoiselle, and yet I could not bear to be with my own thoughts. Could the lady with the lovely voice have failed to find the way to her friend? It was possible. But then surely she could have managed to get back to her carriage. It was scarcely conceivable that anyone could miss the broad carriage drive. Perhaps she was ill, as well as her friend, ill or : . .

Perhaps they had both been poisoned! I pleaded a headache and went early to bed. Mademoiselle ordered her evening meal on a tray, and did not go down again, so she heard no hotel gossip. The maid who brought up the dinner might have said something, but seeing me lying with closed eyelids she did not speak. By keeping my eyes tightly shut, I avoided all conversation with Mademoiselle, merely giving an inaudible grunt when she said: "Thank goodness that at least we have peace to-night, now those two ladies with their ceaseless chatter are happily gone."

Peace to-night? My ears could still hear their "chatter", just as clearly as last night. Their chatter? Yes, their chatter and their kisses. . . .

It is impossible to describe the following days and how my crumbling confidence was gradually soaked through by an infiltering flood of horror. It is difficult to distinguish what

I thought at the time from what I now think that I must have thought. A genuine headache and a subconscious shrinking from further news kept me long in bed the next morning. When at last I was stealing apprehensively down the stairs, I saw two gendarmes in the hall. They were surrounded by the entire staff of the hotel. Many voices were talking in shrill excitement, and there was a general impression of flustered emotion. When I had nearly reached the bottom stair, Mademoiselle, her face white and strained, detached herself from the gesticulating group and rushed towards me. Saying that I looked dreadfully ill, she scuffled me back to my bedroom and kept me there all day.

Early the next morning we left the hotel. I was given no explanation of our hurried departure, and was consistently treated like a very young child. To what extent this conspiracy of silence augmented my sufferings it is impossible to convey. If anyone had frankly talked to me of the mystery which obsessed me, I am sure my nightmare sufferings would have been less agonizing and less enduring.

But all my questions of Mademoiselle—in fact, any mention of the two Parisian ladies—were only answered by : "*Tais-toi.*"

I began to feel as though I had committed a crime, so haunted was I both when awake and when dreaming. In my dreams everyone had red hair and a kiss was death. And always before my eyes was that stiff propped-up figure—so gaily dressed—so shockingly still.

By bribing housemaids to procure me newspapers and cross-questioning everyone I saw as often as I managed to evade Mademoiselle's vigilance, I gradually pieced together the melodrama that for some time caused the hotel to be the most talked of in Europe. I will repeat the story, not in the sequence in which it filtered through to my own knowledge, but as the events succeeded one another.

On the evening of the angry coachman's return to our hotel, a woodcutter walking home from his work in the forest noticed a smartly dressed but hatless lady leaning against a tree. It was after sunset, and he thought it a little odd that she should be holding up a parasol. The next morning, as he set out to work by the same path, he was amazed to see the same figure in precisely the same position. His suspicions aroused, he approached, and discovered that the woman was dead. He immediately informed the police. The coachman's story of his missing fare told them which hotel to apply to, and before noon the sensation had spread like wildfire, and every servant in the hotel was basking in the glare of publicity.

The inquest revealed that the murdered woman had been drugged by means of an orange—half of which lay uneaten on her lap—and then pierced through the temple, probably by a hatpin.

The initials on the dead lady's handkerchief and underclothes did not correspond with either of the names under which the two Parisians were registered in the hotel book. It was remembered that the other lady had entered both their names.

The luggage left behind bore no name, and was merely labelled to one of the chief Paris stations, and its contents held no clue as to identity. No trace could be found at the station of this large provincial town of a dark-haired lady in a beige cloak and blue hat.

Months afterwards, by the merest chance, a black wig, a small blue hat, and a beige cloak were found flung away in a very thick, pathless part of the forest. Even though seven hundred people had taken travelling tickets on the day of the murder, the man who issued them might have remembered a surprisingly beautiful red-haired woman, probably attired in plain black, with a small winged hat, but for such a woman no enquiries were ever made. Under cross-examination he claimed to recall about twenty beautiful ladies with black hair and eyebrows. Neither had the porters noticed any dark woman travelling without luggage.

Whatever my dreams, no mention of "red hair" escaped my lips. For years afterward I could scarcely hear those two words without a start. It became a real "complex".

When she left the carriage, no doubt the lovely lady walked straight to the crowded station and left by the first train. No, not straight. She must first have taken the hat from her dead friend's head. She could not travel in that in which she had been seen leaving the hotel.

A photograph of the dead woman was circulated. This and her initials shortly led to her identification.

To me this identification was a second shock, the effects of which I can scarcely describe.

At that *"schwärmerish"* age my imagination had been
entirely captured by a young poet of remarkable personal
beauty, whose precocious and peculiar genius had newly taken
the reading world by storm.   I will give him the pseudonym
of Léon le Roi.   His moonlit muse was not destined to sur-
vive the daylight of posterity.   He is now long forgotten.
But at that time he had subjugated both critic and schoolgirl,
and his romantic features were as familiar to an adoring
public as are now those of the most popular of film stars.   I
myself cherished no less than three photographs of him, and
my memory was packed with his sonnets, laboriously committed to memory.   It had never occurred to me to speculate
as to his personal life.   To me he was a radiant emanation
rather than a fellow-creature—a "pard-like spirit, beautiful
and swift", not a Frenchman who ate luncheon, wore hats, and
must be either a married man or a bachelor.   Imagine my
feelings when it was established beyond doubt that the poor
murdered woman in the forest had been his wife !   That sallow
commonplace creature the chosen of Léon le Roi !   And he,
my imagination's idol, now in the blinding limelight of this
hideous melodrama !

No sort of an explanation was ever advanced, no shadow
of a motive discovered.   The poet was away from his house
in Paris on a distant visit to his mother.   When he returned,
his servants told him that his wife had gone away for a day or
two, leaving a letter for him.   In giving his evidence, he said
this letter informed him that she had gone away for a change
of air and would be back at latest on the day of his return.
She gave the name of her destination, but not the hotel, on
which she said she would decide on arrival.   He denied any
knowledge as to whom her companion might have been, and
insisted that she had made no mention of going *with* anyone.

When asked to produce this letter, telling of his wife's
plans, he expressed his great regret at having destroyed it
before he heard the terrible news.   He professed himself quite
unable to recall any friend of his wife answering to the description given by the witnesses from the hotel.   None of her very
few intimate associates happened to be dark.   She had left
her home and driven to the station alone.

Needless to say, *l'Affaire de la Forêt*, as it was called, became
one of the most sensational of undetected crimes.

Detectives were perhaps less redoubtable than they have

since become. In any case, the mystery remained unsolved. No arrest was ever made. Another murderer went unpunished by man.

Gradually the feverish interest subsided, and *l'Affaire de la Forêt* became a thing of the past.

Needless to say, every aspect of the tragedy remained vividly impressed on my mind. I was still haunted by the recollection of the vanished lady. I could hear her radiant voice, see her shimmering beauty, remember her brilliant, sweet gaiety. I could also see that sickeningly still figure stiffly propped against the tree. Gradually perhaps my impressions might have faded, but this was not to be.

My haunting experience had a sequel. The effect on me of that sequel I leave to the reader's imagination.

One summer's day, about two years after these events, I was strolling through the Bois de Boulogne. Passing a bench on which a woman was seated reading aloud, I was violently struck by the quality of her voice. Could there possibly be two such voices? My heart wildly beating, I turned and stared at the reader. I saw a lovely young woman of extreme and dazzling fairness of complexion. Her discarded hat lay on her lap, and the sun, stealing through the network of leaves, lit up the red-gold glory of her hair. Of her radiant loveliness there could be no question. If she had a fault, her eyebrows and lashes were perhaps too pale, but even this added something to the ethereal quality of her fairy-tale looks.

At her feet, his hands clasped round his knees, sat a young man, his dark head thrown back as he gazed up at her.

His beautiful face was as familiar to me as my own.

It was the famous poet Léon le Roi.

Almost startled out of my reason, I could scarcely suppress a cry, but I hurried past. In my first confusion I was only conscious of one impulse : to get out of sight, in case she should cease reading and look up and see me and the expression on my face.

She might recognize me.

I do not know what other girls might have done. I only know that to take any steps in this bewildering matter never for one second crossed my mind. God knows I was sufficiently troubled, but not by any questioning as to my own responsibility. That never occurred to me.

o

As one gets older, one often asks : "Is it all worth while ? Is life and its *potential* happiness worth such suffering as is inevitable ? Does Humanity ever get in bliss a tithe of what it pays in pain ? Apart from a man's opportunity, is his capacity for joy equal to his capacity for suffering ?" One or two recollections make me answer : "Yes, it is worth while." Amongst these evidences of human bliss, the most eloquent is the expression I can still see in that poet's eyes as he gazed on the face of that woman.

Come what might, to him life must be accounted worth while. For him the game *was* worth the candle. Never shall I forget that look on his face. Rapture and peace so seldom meet.

There is only one more thing to tell. Shortly after I saw these two in the Bois de Boulogne, my mother and I were visiting some friends in Paris.

The blood rushed to my face as I heard the lady who was pouring out my tea say to my mother, "Fancy, yesterday I met poor Léon le Roi's new wife. She's the most lovely creature."

"Yes," said my hostess's sister. "I remember seeing her once before. She made a great sensation at Madame de B——'s fancy-dress ball, where she appeared as Medea. I remember people said it was incorrect for Medea to have red hair, but I thought her so right not to sacrifice her own lovely colouring."

The next day in my doctor's waiting-room I came across some very far back numbers of a Society paper.

One of them contained an account of Madame de B——'s fancy-dress ball two years before. I looked at the date. The ball had taken place on August 31st, the evening of the day after that on which Léon le Roi's first wife had been murdered.

THE PLAYFELLOW

LAURA HALYARD wondered whether she would ever grow more accustomed to the loveliness of her new home. Each time she looked at the beautiful Tudor house she still wanted to rub her eyes.

After the din and glare of New York, the mellow beauty and green silence of Lichen Hall and its perfect surroundings lay like a spell on its new mistress. It was just six months since her husband Claud Halyard had succeeded to the property at the death of his elder brother, who had died childless. Since his marriage to Laura business had kept Claud in America, so he had never met her unfortunate brother-in-law. Yet she often thought of him, so strongly had his sad story impressed her imagination; the early loss of his adored wife, the accident which left him a hopeless cripple, and the ghastly tragedy of his only child, a girl of ten, who had perished in the fire which twelve years ago had destroyed a small wing of Lichen Hall.

The building had been so skilfully restored that it was difficult to believe in that fatal fire. Laura felt herself lapped in an atmosphere of peace, and found it impossible to associate anything so hideous as the death of that poor child with this place. Could such a thing have happened here, and only twelve years ago? In these serene surroundings it seemed so unimaginable.

Laura Halyard had the extraordinary adaptability of her race, and as she sat in the great hall one December evening, her slim, delicate beauty glowing in the flicker of the firelight, she looked wonderfully in tone with her setting. She was giving tea to the old parson, whose faded eyes blinked appreciatively at the grace and beauty of his hostess. He wished he didn't feel it was time to end his visit.

"If I may be permitted to say so," he said, reluctantly dragging his stiff limbs from the depths of the easy-chair, "if I may say so, Lady Halyard, it is very pleasant to have a châtelaine here again. Lichen Hall has been a sad place these last twelve years."

"Yes," responded Laura sympathetically. "I don't suppose my poor brother-in-law ever recovered from the terrible tragedy of that poor, poor child."

"A broken man is a phrase one often hears," said the parson, "but I am thankful to say that in the course of a long life it has only been my lot to know one man to whom I felt the phrase could be justly applied. That man was your brother-in-law. He did his duty by this place. No one could have done it better. But after Daphne's death, duty was all the world ever held for him. Nothing else remained. To see such grey ashes and have no power to kindle one spark has been a great pain to me. Such loneliness ! Scarcely anyone ever came here during these last years. Just a few old friends, but I always felt he only suffered them out of consideration for *their* feelings.

"I often wondered why your husband never came. In spite of the twenty years between them, they had always appeared to be such devoted brothers. It seems strange he should never once have returned to his own home until he succeeded to it."

"I know," said Laura. "Of course he was very tied by business, but still he could have managed it in his summer holiday. I often urged it, but he always said he thought next year would be better. I don't know why it was. Of course, Mr. Cloud, he's very sensitive. He shrinks from things. Perhaps—I sometimes think—he felt he simply couldn't face his brother's misery."

"Possibly," said the parson. "But I wish he had come. It might have made a big difference."

Laura detected a hint of reproach in the kind old voice.

"It isn't that he doesn't love this place," she eagerly assured him. "I can't tell you how much it means to him."

"I know, Lady Halyard, I know. You see, I remember him as a boy. Why, his love for his home was quite a household joke. Once he gave a visiting schoolfellow a black eye because he dared to say his home was more beautiful than this ! Bright days those were, when he and all his sisters were young." The parson's pale eyes widened as he stared wistfully back into the past. "I always think this garden clamours for children. It's wasted when there's none about. I assure you, it's a real joy to see your little girl tearing up and down the grass slopes."

"I can't tell you how happy Hyacinth is here," exclaimed Laura. "Her day is one long rapture."

"Bless her!" said the parson. "How lovely she is and how extraordinarily like——"

"Like? Like whom?"

"Like her poor cousin—like poor little Daphne. Why, surely the resemblance must have struck your husband?"

"No. At least he hasn't said anything, but then perhaps he wouldn't. Even after all these years he can't bear to speak of his niece. He never mentions Daphne's name."

"I know it was a great shock to him," agreed the parson. "He was so fond of her. I remember he was always playing with her. But then we all loved her. Yes, there was a real fascination about little Daphne."

"And was she really like our Hyacinth?"

"Like?" exclaimed the parson. "Why, it's the most astounding resemblance! I assure you it gave me quite a start the first time I saw your girl peering at me through the bushes. Yes, it took me back twelve years. She's ten, isn't she—your Hyacinth?"

Laura nodded.

"Well, you see, poor Daphne was just the same age the last time I saw her—the day before. Yes, yes, I can see her now. Just the same mop of red-gold hair framing the pale, pointed face—the wide eyes and the same eager look—something so extraordinary *vivid*."

"Really," said Laura. Her voice trembled and the hall swam in a blur of tears.

"Yes, a most extraordinary resemblance," continued the old man. "Voices a good deal alike, too. And your Hyacinth seems to have a similar passion for play. I never saw any being like Daphne for filling the day. She always seemed to want to cram as much fun into each hour as it could possibly hold. It was almost as though she knew she had no time to lose. Do you remember that passage in Maeterlinck about those he calls 'Les Avertis'?"

"Yes, I do." Laura's voice was heavy.

"Well, well, I must be going now," said the old man. "Thanks, dear lady, for a very pleasant afternoon. Give

my love to Daph—Hyacinth. She must come to tea with
me."

"Good night, Mr. Cloud. Come again soon," said
Laura rather mechanically. Turning to the fire she kicked
one of the large logs with her foot, and then stirred amongst
the embers with a poker until they blazed into flames. She
felt cold and tired. She started when the clergyman re-
entered the room. He apologized for having forgotten his
gloves.

"Oh, what colour are they?" asked Laura absently,
as though a variegated assortment of gloves were likely
to be lying about the hall.

"Grey. Here they are. I'm so sorry to have troubled
you."

"Stop one moment, Mr. Cloud. There was something
I meant to ask you. How do you think my husband is
looking?"

"I think he looks well, Lady Halyard, quite well. He always
was a magnificent fellow. Yes, I think he looks quite well. But,
since you ask me, the only thing I notice about him is a sort
of strained expression on his face—in his eyes, and on his
forehead. It's as though he were making some kind of mental
effort—as if he were trying to remember something."

"Trying to remember something?"

"Yes, he looks as I feel I must look when I'm struggling
with my daily crossword. No doubt it's the result of all his
work in that office. I'm so glad to see him out of it. Somehow I can't picture any Halyard in an office. Oh yes, Claud
was always made for country life. Good night, Lady Halyard,
good night."

Left to herself, Laura crouched over the blazing fire.
"Claud made for country life?" Yes, so she had always
thought. In America he had seemed an exile pining for
his native land. And yet, now that they were at his beloved
home, and it had proved more beautiful than even his rhap-
sodies had led her to expect, what was the matter? To her
growing disappointment she could not help admitting that
her husband's spirits—never steady—were on the whole
much lower than they used to be. A sultry gloom seemed
settling on him. Then that look of strain the parson had
noticed. Others had commented on this. What could
cause it, now that the present and the future seemed so

fair ? Business worries ? Laura wondered almost hope-
fully. No, what business worries could he have ? He told
her everything. Told her everything, did he ? Laura
almost laughed aloud. That very afternoon she had re-
encountered that threadbare phrase. The heroine of the bad
novel she had been reading, a woman in total darkness concerning her husband, had confidently asserted, "He tells me
everything !" How could any human being ever tell anyone
*every*thing ?

No doubt Claud had got something on his mind. Since
their home-coming, she had been conscious of a barrier
between them. In old days, if challenged, he would
often admit to a fit of depression. Now he seemed
rather to resent any inquiry as to his health or spirits. If
she said, "Is anything the matter ?" he would answer almost
irritably, "The matter ? No, nothing's the matter. Don't
suggest things."

Laura was not left to her reflections for long. Her
husband, a tall, handsome man, came into the room with
their daughter Hyacinth riding on his shoulders, her mop
of red-gold hair shining above his dark head.

The three of them settled round the fire. Hyacinth, with
her knees drawn up to her pointed chin, and her wide eyes
staring into the flames, made but a poor pretence of listening
to her father reading *Ivanhoe* for her benefit. The moment
the chapter was finished she sprang on to the tips of her toes
and stood quivering, like a flame released.

"May I go now   her whole eager being seemed to
express.

Struck afresh by the gleaming quality of her beauty, her
father gazed at her lovingly. So breathlessly full of life !
Ought she perhaps to have playfellows of her own age ?

"Are you lonely, Sprite ?" he asked her tenderly.

"Lonely ! Oh no ! I'm never, never lonely here !"
There was a note of exultation in the child's happy laugh.

"I must go now !" she said excitedly, and, slipping
out of her father's arms, she darted up the dark oak stairs
and, with a wave of her hand, disappeared from her parents'
gaze. Long after she had turned the corner that took her
out of sight, they heard her running footsteps and her voice
trilling out "Come, Lasses and Lads, Take Leave of your
Dads".

"Hyacinth's voice matches her face so marvellously, doesn't it, Claud?" said Laura. "Not many people's do. Hers has that piercing quality of crystal youth. It's like cold, cold water or biting into an apple."

Claud rose to throw another log on to the blazing fire.

"Laura, what does Hyacinth mean by saying she's never lonely *here*?"

"I don't know, Claud. But, now you ask, haven't you noticed how different she is since we came here? Do you remember how listless she sometimes used to seem? I often got quite worried, and thought that perhaps I ought to borrow some bright child to keep her company. But now she's always as happy as the day is long. In fact—to tell the honest truth—I can't help rather missing her moods—or at least her dependence on me. You see, she used so to want me. Don't you remember how she was always imploring me to read to her or tell her stories?"

"Doesn't she now?" asked Claud.

"No; nowadays I can scarcely ever persuade her to stay with me. She's always rushing away, as though she had something better to do. It's little I see of her beyond her heels and the back of her head! She's so strangely self-sufficient. Between you and me, Claud, I think she's almost disquietingly happy."

"Disquietingly happy? What do you mean, Laura?"

"Well—I mean—it's almost uncanny. Really, I don't know how to put it into words, but it's—it's as though she had some resource we don't know about. She seems so *occupied*. Yes, that's it—occupied. It sounds too silly, but it's as though being by herself were not being alone. She's grown a queer new sort of smile lately, too, a stealthy, sidelong smile, and the comings and goings of that smile don't have any connection with what any of us say or do. Haven't you noticed it? Claud, do you remember what that spooky friend of mine said about Hyacinth?"

"No, I don't," Claud answered shortly. "Some absurdity, I'm sure, from what I remember of her."

"She said, 'Now there's a child that should *see* things. Her "muddy vesture of decay" is too transparent to "close her in".' She said she had what she called 'listening eyes', and the thinnest lids she had ever seen. Nonsense I thought

it at the time, but now, Claud, I sometimes wonder . . .
This old place——"

"Oh, Lord! For Heaven's sake don't start any of that
psychical rot here."

Surprised at the annoyance in her husband's voice, Laura
laughed.

"I know, dear, you think no American can come near
a stately home of England without peopling it with ghosts,
but I assure you I haven't—to relapse into my native tongue
—'sensed' anything unpleasant here. I've had neither sight
nor sound of abbots carrying their heads, nor of ladies in
blood-speckled shrouds. No, indeed! On the contrary,
I am conscious of a something that's happy—gay—blithe—
I don't know what to call it, but there seems a sort of *liveliness*
about the atmosphere of this house—especially upstairs, and
most especially in that room Hyacinth insisted on having as
her playroom, the old day-nursery."

"I didn't want her to use that room," said Claud gruffly.

"I know, dear, I know," his wife responded sympathetically. "But she *insisted*."

Poor fellow, she thought, how sensitive he is! Of course
it had been his little niece Daphne's playroom. Probably
she had romped in it just before her life ended so tragically.
Laura reproached herself. She should never have allowed
Hyacinth to appropriate that particular room. For Claud,
its associations with Daphne were too strong. She should
have remembered how he winced at any reminder of that
poor dead child. Laura shuddered at the thought of the
horror of her death. Ten years old! Just the same age as
Hyacinth!

"I promise you there's nothing unpleasant in that room,"
Laura went on. "But—please don't think me silly—I do
feel an atmosphere in it—a happy, youthful one. When I
sit in that room, as I often do, memories of my own childhood
break out of the past and come thronging round me. I feel
the years simply slipping off me." She laughed. "Why,
I get funny impulses to play, to dance, to jump about. My
toes begin to twiddle. It's as though there were some *invitation* in the room. You'll think me too absurd, but once I
actually found myself hiding in the cupboard, just as though
I expected someone to come and search for me. And yet all
the time I knew Hyacinth must be in bed and asleep. Some-

times I long to mount the old rocking-horse and have a gallop. I would, too, only I'm so afraid of being caught by one of those terribly grown-up housemaids.

"Once I thought I heard light, scuffling steps and a sort of soft tittering. Imagination, of course ! . . . And yet, I suppose generations and generations of children have played in that room ?"

"Yes," said Claud. His voice was very gruff, and as he spoke he raised *The Times* and held it, like a wall, between him and any further confidences. Conscious of having annoyed him, Laura went away to tell Hyacinth it was bed-time. It was half an hour before she found her in the hayloft, and then she had great difficulty in coaxing her indoors. At last she handed her over to her maid, Bessy. The moment she returned to the hall her husband rose, saying he would go and say good night to Hyacinth.

"You won't find that little flibberty-gibbet in bed. I had such a tussle to get her in. It's the same thing every night. However late I leave her, she always says, 'I haven't had nearly time enough to play !' "

"Not nearly time enough to play ?" echoed Claud. "*She* doesn't say that ; not Hyacinth ?"

"Yes, why shouldn't she ?" exclaimed Laura, puzzled by the violence of his manner.

But, giving no answer, Claud hastened from the room. That night at dinner, when Laura asked him why he had been so struck by those very ordinary words of Hyacinth's that she had repeated, he said he had no idea to what she was alluding, couldn't remember her quoting Hyacinth, and that it must be one of her "silly fancies".

Puzzled and hurt, Laura dropped the subject. Claud did not look well, and to-night that expression of strain was very noticeable. How had the old parson described it ? "As though he were trying to remember something" ? No, she didn't think that was what the expression in Claud's cavernous grey eyes suggested. But when she tried to define it to herself, she felt completely baffled.

A few days later, the Halyards were walking in the garden. A strong wind blew, the trees were bare, and crisp leaves, the colour of Hyacinth's hair, rustled around their feet. As usual their thoughts turned on their adored child.

"I thought Hyacinth looked very pale at luncheon," said Claud.

"Yes," answered his wife. "Naughty child, she went out of doors last night!"

"Out of doors?"

"Yes. Bessy found her shoes and stockings drenched this morning, and when I asked, the little wretch owned she had gone out long after we were in bed. Just think how cold it must have been! She wouldn't tell me why she had done it, and when I said she must promise not to do it again, she burst into tears."

"Little sprite!" laughed Claud. "She still thinks of sleep as waste of time! I hope it may be—heavens! Just look at her now! What is she doing? I never saw a child run so fast, all alone."

Hyacinth, her face wildly tense, flashed past them on long, spindly legs. Her speed, surprising for her age, never slackened until, with arms outstretched to touch it, she reached an acacia tree, at the foot of which, panting and laughing, she flung herself to the ground.

Her parents approached.

"Well done, Hyacinth! You *were* going fast!"

"I nearly won that time!" exclaimed the excited child, her green eyes blazing. "Oh, so, so nearly!"

"You nearly *won*? What do you mean, by you 'nearly won'? Were you racing one leg against the other?"

Hyacinth flushed, smiled nervously, sprang to her feet and in an instant had run out of sight behind the great yew hedge.

"Funny child!" said her mother, with an uneasy laugh. "She's always running off, just as though she had an appointment elsewhere. She never seems to need me now. Do you remember how she used to think it such a treat to sleep with me? Now she never wants to. You know, Claud, it sounds ridiculous, but nowadays, when I go into that child's room, I feel as if I were—interrupting." As she spoke, Laura gave a slight shiver. Her own words seemed to crystallize vague misgivings of which she had scarcely been aware.

"In errupting?" echoed Claud. "Interrupting what?"

"I don't know," she answered hopelessly, and turned towards the house.

Claud whistled for his dogs and set off for a long walk.

That evening Laura went to see Hyacinth in bed.

"Darling," she said wheedlingly, "wouldn't you like to come and sleep with Mummie to-night? We'll have early morning tea together and play ludo on my big pillow."

An anxious look flitted across the child's sweet but rather set face.

"Thank you, Mummie darling," she answered shyly but decidedly, "only I'm so happy in my own lovely room. I love it, and I don't think it would like to be left."

Intense relief shone in her bright eyes when, in silent acquiescence, her mother kissed her good night.

"Good Mummie," she cooed, and, with a little ecstatic wriggle, she turned her radiant face towards the window.

That night it was very late before Laura rejoined her husband after dinner. The great bow window in the hall was uncurtained and the moonlight streamed in, its slanting green shafts mingling with the flickering red from the blazing fire by which Claud sat, an unopened book on his knee.

"Where have you been all this time, Laura?" he asked, glancing up at her face. "What have you been doing? I hope Hyacinth hasn't been up to any more of her pranks."

"No," Laura answered quickly. "But I have."

"What do you mean?"

"I mean, I've been what you'd call silly. You remember what I told you about those funny feelings I get in the playroom? Well, directly after I left you over your coffee, I felt I wanted to go to the playroom. Don't frown, Claud, I couldn't help it. I simply *had* to go. My feet just took me there. Well, as I went along the passage, I heard a faint noise—a queer sort of a rushing noise. I opened the door. What do you think I saw? Claud, the rocking-horse was plunging to and fro—going furiously—*without a rider!*"

"Well," said Claud, "no doubt Hyacinth heard you coming, and, knowing she should be in bed, jumped off and ran out of the other door."

"So I thought—so I hoped! But I rushed straight to her room, and found her fast asleep."

"Well, then it must have been one of the maids."

"No, there was no one about. They were all down at their supper. When I got back to the playroom, the rocking-horse was gradually subsiding. I watched it; and soon it was quite motionless."

"No. You *do* surprise me!" jeered Claud.

"The queer thing," said Laura solemnly, "was that even while the rocking-horse was galloping so fast, the stirrups were not swaying as they naturally would. No, they were quite taut—stretched out forwards—just as if——"

"Look here!" exclaimed Claud angrily. "What are you driving at? What have you been reading? What have you been eating? Rocking-horse, indeed! It sounds more like a nightmare! I never knew Hyacinth had a rocking-horse. Who gave it to her?"

"No one. We found it here. It was Daphne's. You must have seen it. Vermilion nostrils and minus a tail. But, do you mean to say—haven't you ever been in the playroom since you came home?"

"No."

"How extraordinary!"

"Why should I?" Claud's voice was fierce and he glared at his wife.

"Quite, quite!" said Laura nervously. She was surprised and shocked at the tone of his voice and the expression on his face. Why, for a second he had looked at her as though he hated her. Was it possible? Claud, her gentle, courteous husband, whose devotion to her was almost a joke to their friends. "Oh, I've forgotten my spectacles," she said confusedly, "I'll run up and fetch them. I shan't be two minutes."

With this excuse she ran upstairs, leaving her husband moodily staring at her spectacles, which lay, conspicuous, on the table where she had just placed them.

Five minutes later she returned. Glancing at her, Claud knew that if she had not been flushed she would have been very pale.

"What is it now?"

With her back to him, Laura stood facing the fire. She spoke quickly, in a very low voice, as though she feared to hear her own words.

"As I got near the playroom, I heard the gramophone playing. I thought I heard dancing feet, but when I opened the door there was no one in the room. You won't believe me, Claud, but there was no one in the room. No one! And yet a *record had just been set going.* It was 'Boys and Girls come out to Play'. Before I found the electric switch, I thought I felt something very light brush past me. Almost before I was aware of it, it had gone. Oh, so quickly—just like a puff of wind ! To make sure, I went to all the maids' bedrooms. One of them might have started the gramophone, but they were all in bed. Then I went to Hyacinth's room. I crept in, so as not to wake her, if she was asleep, and she was—yes, sound asleep. But as I looked at her, I heard a tap-tap at the window. It *might* have been a branch. Anyhow, it woke her. She sprang up in a second, wide, wide awake, with such a joyful welcoming expression on her excited little face. . . . Then she saw me, and she looked sort of scared and sorry—yes, *very* sorry to see me. Oh, Claud ! I couldn't bear the look on her face when she saw me !"

Laura's last words came from her like a cry, and she turned to Claud with outstretched arms, as though appealing against she knew not what.

"Damnation !" he cried, springing to his feet. "I can't stand any more of this ! Look here, Laura darling, we'll all three go away to-morrow. It's obvious you need a change. We've been here too long. After all, you aren't used to staying like a tree in one place. Besides, it will be great fun to take Hyacinth to London, won't it ? Laura, my sweet, darling Laura, say you like this plan !"

"Of course I should love it," murmured Laura, clasped in his arms.

It was such joy to feel herself carried on this wave of tenderness back into the haven of love, in which, until recently, she had felt so secure, that any proposal would have seemed welcome.

If only he would go on looking at her as now, with love in his eyes, what matter where they went ? And yet, even in the intensity of her relief, Laura was conscious of the irony of his wishing to leave the home he had always described as the Earthly Paradise. It was decided that they should leave the very next day, but, alas, when to-morrow came, their plan could not be carried out. Hyacinth had sprained her ankle very badly and was unable to put her foot to the ground. When told the news, Laura hurried to her daughter's room. She found her sitting up in bed. Her face was flushed and she looked shy.

"Poor darling! This is too sad. However did it happen?"

"I'm so sorry, Mummie." Hyacinth spoke hurriedly and nervously. "But I'm afraid I've been naughty again. Don't be very angry with me, but I went out again last night and——"

"You went out? Oh, Hyacinth darling, you promised you wouldn't!"

"I'm so sorry, Mummie, but it was such a lovely night —such bright, bright moonlight. It made me forget I mustn't, and I simply *couldn't* say no."

"The sooner you learn to say no to yourself the better. I shan't be able to trust you any more. You've hurt yourself, so I won't scold you, but you must never, never do such a thing again. Anyhow, what happened? How did you hurt your silly self?"

"I had a fall."

"What, running?"

"No," answered Hyacinth reluctantly. "I was climbing a tree."

"Climbing a tree? Good heavens! You might have broken your leg and lain out all night. Which tree?"

"The big elm. The one Daddie made a house in when he was little. A branch broke——"

"Well, you've had what Nannie used to call a 'natural punishment'. So I won't say any more. Lie still now until the doctor comes."

After the doctor had bound up Hyacinth's ankle, her mother went to look at the elm tree. She was appalled at the height of the broken branch. It seemed almost a miracle that the child was not more seriously hurt.

She returned to question her.

"You don't mean to tell me you fell from where a branch is broken off right up near the top of the tree?"

"Yes, but you see, there were so many branches that I paused on all the way down. I only really fell just the last bit."

"But I had no idea you could climb so high. Surely you can't have got all that way up without any help?"

"Oh yes, I did!" cried Hyacinth triumphantly. "And she climbed even higher, but then, of course, her legs are a little longer."

"She ?   Who is She ?"

Hyacinth flushed scarlet, and in confusion flung her arms
round her mother's neck.   Glancing quickly all round the
room, she put her finger in front of her mouth.

"Don't tell Daddie.   Oh, Mummie, *please, please* don't
tell !" she said in a scared, panting voice.   Not one word
more would she say.   After that one unguarded moment,
her whole being was clenched in silence.   At first her mother
tried to coax her into an explanation, but, alarmed by her
flushed excited face, she took her temperature.   Finding
her a little feverish, she did not like to press her any further.
She seemed so troubled.

Laura did not tell her husband of Hyacinth's strange
slip.

"*She* climbed even higher" ?   How could she tell him of
that ?   She dreaded to hear him speak in that new, sharp
way, so utterly unlike his old self.

After all, Hyacinth's fall must have been a considerable
shock.   Perhaps she had not known what she was saying.
The next day the child seemed better, and Laura made another
attempt to cross-question her about her accident, but, at the
first word of inquiry, the child's flower-like mouth set in a
thin, hard line, and an expression came into her eyes that was
like a shutter between her and her mother.

During the following days she was affectionate but somehow guarded, and Laura felt strangely out of touch with her.
On everyone's account she longed for a change and chafed
at the enforced postponement of their plans.   Claud, though
now uniformly gentle in his manner, seemed increasingly
depressed.   Laura was determined to leave the first possible
day, but unfortunately Hyacinth's injury proved more serious
than had been supposed, and her ankle took a long time to recover.   No bedridden child had ever been so little trouble.   In
fact she seemed almost unnaturally contented.   Whenever
her mother read aloud to her, she was politely acquiescent,
but her manner was that of one who makes a necessary
concession and waits with as good a grace as can be commanded.

Her gladness when the book was closed was evident,
and when her mother turned to leave the room she would
wave her hand over-gratefully, and raise herself a little on
her pillows, with a look of relief and a hovering smile of

happy expectancy. Though Laura tried to shut her mind
to the impression made by Hyacinth's manner, she could
not succeed. Stung out of her usual self-control, she once
cried out, "What is it, Hyacinth? Why are you always
waiting now—waiting for me to go?"

A look of fear quivered across the child's sensitive face.
"Waiting? What do you mean, Mummie? Why do
you think I want you to go?" And with unskilled evasiveness
she began to talk of irrelevancies—the cat's kittens, the
new gardener, the pony that had kicked the groom—anything
that came into her head.

With a heavy heart and a sense of absurdity, Laura
acquiesced in making conversation with the child whose
confidence she had once so completely possessed.

Though Hyacinth was full of strange whims, the one
her mother thought the queerest was her insistence on having
the rocking-horse brought into her bedroom.

"But, darling, it will take up so much room. And whatever is the use of having a rocking-horse you can't ride?"

But Hyacinth's pale, peaked face set in obstinacy.
"I want it. I need it," was all she would say.

So the shabby old rocking-horse was dragged along
the passage and stood in arrested prance at the foot of the
child's bed.

That evening, as Laura came into the room, Hyacinth
gave an obvious start, and, turning to her mother in flushed
uneasiness, said querulously :

"Aren't I old enough yet, Mother, for people to knock
at my door before they come into my room? You always
tell me I must knock at your door."

Amazed and hurt, Laura looked at the usually so gentle
child, whose worried gaze she noticed was now fixed on the
rocking-horse. Glancing at it herself, her glance became
a stare. Was it her fancy, or was it slightly, almost imperceptibly moving?"

"Have you been out of bed, Hyacinth?" she asked
suspiciously.

"Oh no, Mummie, why?"

"Only I thought perhaps you had been very naughty
and got on the rocking-horse. When I came in I thought
it was just moving, as if it had been in motion and wasn't
yet quite still. But of course it must have been my fancy."

With unwonted eagerness, Hyacinth said :
"Will you read to me now, Mummie?"

Laura readily consented.

"Before I begin, though," she said, "I must tell you some good news. The doctor says you may get up in a week, and the very day after you get up we are going to take you to London."

"You're going to take me to London?" Hyacinth's voice was sharp with dismay.

"Yes, darling. Won't it be fun?"

To her distress, Hyacinth burst into tears.

"Oh no, Mummie! No, no, no ! Please don't take me away from here. I can't go ! I won't go ! It wouldn't be fair !"

"What do you mean, you absurd child ? You'll have a lovely time in London. We'll take you to the Zoo and Madame Tussaud's and have pink ices at Gunther's. We'll do all the treats I used to tell you about in New York."

Hyacinth's eyes welled with tears.

"Oh, please, Mummie," she implored, "don't take me away from lovely here."

"But, my darling, I love you to love this place, but you can't always be here. It will be all the more fun to come back to it." She tried to laugh the child out of her distress. "After all, you goose, it won't run away because we leave it. Everything will be exactly the same when we return."

"I don't know, Mother," sobbed Hyacinth. "You can't tell. I'm afraid to go—besides, it wouldn't be fair."

"Not fair, what do you mean?" questioned Laura, now completely bewildered.

"Oh! I don't know, Mummie! But I'm so happy here. Mayn't I stay ? *Please*, please, *please* !"

Seeing Hyacinth so hysterically excited, Laura said firmly : "We won't talk about it any more now," and began to read aloud to unlistening ears.

The next day Hyacinth seemed much more sensible. Laura told her their departure was quite settled, and she made an obvious effort to accept the inevitable with as good a grace as possible, but she looked pale and strained and her manner was even more than usually preoccupied.

"She looks as though she were trying to propitiate herself," Laura explained to her husband.

"Trying to propitiate herself? What an absurd phrase!"
he laughed. "The ideas you have about that child!"

"I haven't any ideas about her." Laura was astonished
at the vehemence of her own voice.

Laura spent most of Christmas Eve decorating a small
tree for Hyacinth. When she brought it upstairs, gay with
glittering tinsel, gilded walnuts and shiny ornaments, the
child clapped her hands with delight. Saying she would
return in about an hour to light the candles, Laura placed
the tree on a table in front of the fire.

When she came back she was surprised to find the room
illuminated by the glimmer of little wax candles. Hyacinth
seemed asleep, but sat up as the door opened. Assuming the
child had prevailed on Bessy the maid to light the candles,
Laura merely said:

"Well, I must say, after all my trouble, I do think you
might have waited for me. Never mind. Now let's pull
the crackers together."

Shamefacedly Hyacinth pointed to the coloured tatters
of two dozen exploded crackers. Her bed was strewn with
paper caps, mottoes, and little tin musical instruments.

"Sorry, Mummie, I just couldn't wait," she mumbled.
"I *love* candles. Flames are such fun, aren't they? May
I have some toy fireworks? Please, Mummie!"

"I don't know. I think they're rather dangerous."

"Oh no, Mummie. They aren't! Please say I may
have some. I know! I'll ask Daddie to give me some. He
told me to tell him what I wanted."

Laura went to find Bessy.

"You should have asked me before lighting the candles
on the Christmas tree," she said severely. "It wasn't at
all safe to leave Miss Hyacinth alone in the room with all
those candles alight. They often set fire to a bit of the tree.
There should always be someone at hand with a wet sponge.
I'm surprised at you, Bessy."

"I didn't never light no tree, my lady," said the astonished
maid. "I haven't been into Miss Hyacinth's room, not for
two hours."

Laura hurried back to Hyacinth.

"I don't want to scold you on Christmas Eve, but it was
very naughty of you to get out of bed to light the candles,

when you know perfectly well you're still forbidden to put your foot to the ground. And isn't it rather selfish to pull crackers by yourself?"

Hyacinth blushed, but the expression on her face was unmistakably one of relief.

"Sorry, Mummie," she said, "so sorry," and impetuously she flung her arms around her mother's neck and kissed her quickly—lovingly—just as she used to in the days when she was lonely.

At last Hyacinth's ankle was sufficiently recovered to allow the Halyards to make all their plans for leaving the next day. That evening Claud was to dine out with an old schoolfellow who lived about four miles away. Before starting he went up to say good night to Hyacinth. Her half-packed trunk was open, and she was practising getting about the room.

"Don't ruin my tie!" he cried, as, hopping towards him, she flung her thin arms around his neck.

"Bother your tie!" she laughed. "Oh, Daddie, darling Daddie. Thank you for the lovely, lovely box of fireworks. They came by the afternoon post. Aren't they gorgeous? Look at the lovely pictures on the lid. Whizz-bangs, catherine wheels and all!"

"Oh, they've come, have they? Well, mind, you aren't on any account to touch them. I'll let them off for you the first evening we come home. I'll carry them away now and lock them up somewhere safe."

"Oh, mayn't they stay here, Daddie? I like looking at the pictures."

"Certainly not. I can't trust you not to touch them."

Hyacinth stood flushed and pouting. Suddenly she turned towards the window.

"Oh, look, Daddie," she cried, pointing. "Look at that great white owl. Oh, what a lovely Mrs. Fly-by-Night!"

"Where, Hyacinth? I can't see it."

"No, Daddie. You aren't looking where I'm pointing, can't you see? She's just flown over the church tower."

But look where he might, Claud could see no owl. He was still trying to be guided by Hyacinth's erratically pointed finger, when the butler came in and announced his car.

"Well, then, I must give the owl up," he said. "My friend's a great stickler for punctuality," and kissing Hyacinth, who made no effort to detain him, he left the room, quite forgetting the box of fireworks he had left lying on the table.

As he was about to step into his car, he overheard a mocking "To-whit-a-whoo!" Remembering an accomplishment of Hyacinth's—she could imitate an owl by whistling through her hands—he looked up towards her window. There she was, leaning far out, her red head gleaming, her pale face strangely elfin in the moonlight. Claud was startled by her beauty.

"Go to bed, Sprite," he called.

Hyacinth waved her thin white arms.

"Good night, Daddie. See you in the morning!"

Though bitterly cold, the still, starlight night was so beautiful that Claud decided to walk home, and dismissed his car. He and his friend found much to say to one another, and it was past midnight before he started home. As he strode across the frozen fields, he began to regret his dismissal of the car. The cold, clear silence was only broken by his own footsteps, the occasional hoot of an owl, and the far, far away bark of a lonely dog. He felt too much alone in a white, unshared world.

The present—in which Claud always strove to enwrap himself—receded and faded. Quite powerless to protect him from the past, it became a mere dissolving mist.

A man maimed by one memory, he depended on contact with immediate external things to preoccupy him, to claim his attention so urgently that his senses might not be re-assailed by certain ineffaceable impressions.

Just now he felt abandoned to the past, unprotected by the passage of time. What were time and space but modes of thought? There could be no putting distance between yourself and any experience. What had all the intervening years availed to release him? Nothing.

Claud Halyard had paid dearly for his inheritance. That strained expression friends noticed on his face was due not to the effort to remember, but to the effort to forget—to expunge from his consciousness a haunting memory from which there was no release.

And if I seek oblivion of an hour,
So shorten I the stature of my soul.

In Claud's life there is one hour of which he ceaselessly
and desperately seeks oblivion. Struggle as he may, he
is now caught back in that hour, forced to relive each agonizing instant. It is superimposed on his present, and all the
impressions of twelve intervening years are powerless to
soften any of its intensity.

Twelve years ago ; it is a moonlight night and, as now,
he is walking towards Lichen Hall, the beautiful home of
his childhood, the home which so obsesses his imagination
that to him it seems the core of the entire world. Such
love, he feels, should surely establish ownership, but Lichen
Hall is not entailed on the male line, and, at the death of its
present owner, his widowed and crippled brother, it will
pass to that brother's only child, Daphne, who in time will
marry and transfer all that wonderful beauty to strangers.
He reaches the edge of the park. What is it that so startles
him ? What strange, terrifying sounds ? God ! the alarm
bell in the great tower is clanging furiously. "Fire ! Fire !"
he hears the word shouted.

Sick with dread, he rushes towards the house from which
his horror-struck eyes see wreaths of smoke curling. Terrible
crackling sounds are coming from one wing, and from the
little turret tower in that wing long ribands of flame flutter
towards the white moon.

Breathless, he reaches the lawn. The distracted servants
have just carried someone out of the house. It is his crippled
brother. Claud rushes to him. Struggling to raise his
paralysed body, the agonized man clutches at Claud and,
pointing towards the house, shrieks, "Daphne ! Daphne !"

Claud realizes the situation. The fire brigade has not
yet arrived, and Daphne, who sleeps in the turret tower of
the burning wing, has not been got out. The alarm has
only just been given, as it is merely a few minutes since the
servants were aroused, the fire having gained a strong hold
before any of them awoke. So far they have only just had
time to carry down their helpless master. The child, they
hoped, would have woken and escaped. They expected to
find her outside but, to their dismay, she is nowhere to be seen.

With a reassuring shout, Claud dashes into the house.

The staircase leading up to the burning wing is already dense with smoke. Claud smashes a window and, choking, fights his way up and into the suffocating room where he sees Daphne on the floor—lying close to the window. The smoke has been too much for her. She is unconscious—quite unconscious, but breathing. He is in time! Quite easy to fling that light burden over his shoulder, to dash down the stairs and carry her safely out into the blessed air. Vividly Claud sees himself doing this—sees the joy blaze in his brother's eyes.

Simultaneously, an alternative picture presents itself. The child left lying as she is—unconscious—quite unconscious, not suffering, not dreading, not knowing, just *not reawakening*. Unaware. His own future? Lichen Hall?

His body seems to act without any conscious volition. Something takes command of his limbs. "I never told myself to do it! I never told myself to do it!" How often thereafter was he to mutter these words!

Stooping, he lifts the light body. The burnished red hair brushes against his cheek. In a moment he has shoved her safely out of sight. Now for the stairs. They have become almost impassable. He emerges, choking. "I can't find her!" he gasps to the horrified crowd. "She's not in her room. She must have got out." A frantic scream from his brother. Two minutes later the fire brigade dashes up. Claud takes control, directs the firemen to search for Daphne in every room except her own.

Now he sees the glowing, writhing roof of the little turret tower fall in. Soon the flames are extinguished. All the pictures are saved. The body of a child is found.

"Unfortunately the poor girl had taken refuge beneath her bed, and therefore her gallant uncle was unable to find her." The coroner's verdict!

Daphne's father. Oh, God, his eyes!

Claud has lived through each moment just as intensely as twelve years ago. Shaking, dripping with perspiration, he drops back into the present.

He still sees his brother's eyes.

Had he loved his Daphne as I love my Hyacinth? At the thought Claud's heart contracts agonizingly. Suppose he had. Why not? Was she not as lovely, as piercingly sweet and young? Her eagerness! Had he not loved her himself—his dear little niece. The "perfect playfellow" he used to call her. That last evening he had gone to say good night to her in her little Carpaccio bed.

"Time to go to sleep," he had said.

"Oh, bother sleep!" she had exclaimed, imploring him to remain. "I haven't had nearly time enough to play!"

Once more he feels the light burden in his arms, the unconscious little body that would so easily have revived to entertain its eager spirit—to welcome it back to the life it loved.

"Not nearly time enough to play?" Claud's mind struggled from the past to the present, to the past again and back to the present. Not nearly time enough to play!

The galloping, riderless rocking-horse? Hyacinth running races alone? His wife's strange impulses? Hide and seek? Who is it that seeks? These and other things flit through his strained mind.

He is nearly home now—home to Laura and Hyacinth —and to-morrow night they will all three be far from here. Yes, but in the meantime he is still so much in the grip of that fatal hour twelve years ago that he seems actually to hear that awful clanging and the cries of "Fire! Fire!"

Heavens, how *real*, how outside himself these hideous sounds seem! But this is past bearing. Are his senses hopelessly haunted? This way lies madness. He must go away—let the house—return to America.

The sounds are insistent—grow louder. The illusion is complete.

God, can it really be *now*?

Turning the corner which brings the distant house into view, Claud stares. Yes, it is true! The present and the past have fused. The bell, the shouts are actual—immediate! It is twelve years later, but Lichen Hall is again on fire, and burning— burning furiously. How can a fire have taken so strong a hold? Every modern device for extinguishing an outbreak had been installed. Claud tears up the hill and reaches the lawn. This time it is the other wing that has caught fire, that in which he, Laura and Hyacinth sleep. Its top story is already blazing. A crowd stares upward—pale faces red in the reflected glow. That shrieking woman, struggling to escape from arms that hold her back, can that be Laura? Disjointedly, from various voices, Claud learns the situation. The water-supply is frozen—all the pipes useless. The telephone wires are broken down, but the car has gone for the fire brigade. Any moment now they should be here. In the meantime the child—his child—is upstairs, and the wooden staircase is impassable, was already so before anyone was aware of the outbreak. His wife had not yet gone up to bed, and, as only the family sleep in that wing, no one was there. The child is alone up there, trapped in that red horror, and the longest ladder cannot reach to the window of her room. A second ladder? Yes, they are tying two together with ropes, and several men have offered to climb up.

Claud shouts that he will go himself. Thank God the ladders are now securely fastened together! There is still time, but none to lose. The roof must soon fall in.

The ladder has been placed against the wall under Hyacinth's room. Claud's foot is already on its second rung, when something catches his eye. At a window there to the right of the one to which he is climbing he sees a child appear. The window is open. Her long, thin arms are outstretched, her red head gleams in the flaring light.

"Move the ladder, quick, quick!" Claud yells distractedly. "She isn't in her bedroom. She's gone into the other room—the playroom. There! There! Can't you see her? There, hanging out of that window!"

No one sees anything, but blindly they obey. There is a rush and eager arms carry out his orders. The ladder is dragged away to the other window, at which Claud is pointing. It's ready now. Cheers ring out. Claud climbs up, up, up. Near the top he raises his head and finds himself staring into the smiling face of the girl who had perished in the flames twelve years ago. As Claud stares transfixed, the lovely, smiling face blurs and fades away. No one is there.

With a cry no one below could ever forget, Claud hurls himself down the ladder.

"The other window!" he gasps. "Back to the other window!"

Wonderfully quickly the ladder is moved and replaced, but not quickly enough. The delay has been fatal. Just as the fire engines roar up the drive, the roof falls in.

Again every picture is saved, and a little body is recovered.

D. H. LAWRENCE

THE ROCKING-HORSE WINNER

THERE was a woman who was beautiful, who started with all the advantages, yet she had no luck. She married for love, and the love turned to dust. She had bonny children, yet she felt they had been thrust upon her, and she could not love them. They looked at her coldly, as if they were finding fault with her. And hurriedly she felt she must cover up some fault in herself. Yet what it was that she must cover up she never knew. Nevertheless, when her children were present, she always felt the centre of her heart go hard. This troubled her, and in her manner she was all the more gentle and anxious for her children, as if she loved them very much. Only she herself knew that at the centre of her heart was a hard little place that could not feel love, no, not for anybody. Everybody else said of her: "She is such a good mother. She adores her children." Only she herself, and her children themselves, knew it was not so. They read it in each other's eyes.

There were a boy and two little girls. They lived in a pleasant house, with a garden, and they had discreet servants and felt themselves superior to anyone in the neighbourhood.

Although they lived in style, they felt always an anxiety in the house. There was never enough money. The mother had a small income, and the father had a small income, but not nearly enough for the social position which they had to keep up. The father went in to town to some office. But though he had good prospects, these prospects never materialized. There was always the grinding sense of the shortage of money, though the style was always kept up.

At last the mother said, "I will see if *I* can't make something." But she did not know where to begin. She racked her brains, and tried this thing and the other, but could not find anything successful. The failure made deep lines come

R

into her face. Her children were growing up, they would have to go to school. There must be more money, there must be more money. The father, who was always very handsome and expensive in his tastes, seemed as if he never *would* be able to do anything worth doing. And the mother, who had a great belief in herself, did not succeed any better, and her tastes were just as expensive.

And so the house came to be haunted by the unspoken phrase : *There must be more money ! There must be more money !* The children could hear it all the time, though nobody said it aloud. They heard it at Christmas, when the expensive and splendid toys filled the nursery. Behind the shining modern rocking-horse, behind the smart doll's-house, a voice would start whispering : "There *must* be more money ! There *must* be more money !" And the children would stop playing, to listen for a moment. They would look into each other's eyes, to see if they had all heard. And each one saw in the eyes of the other two that they too had heard. "There *must* be more money ! There *must* be more money !"

It came whispering from the springs of the still-swaying rocking-horse, and even the horse, bending his wooden, champing head, heard it. The big doll, sitting so pink and smirking in her new pram, could hear it quite plainly, and seemed to be smirking all the more self-consciously because of it. The foolish puppy, too, that took the place of the teddy-bear, he was looking so extraordinarily foolish for no other reason but that he heard the secret whisper all over the house : "There *must* be more money."

Yet nobody ever said it aloud. The whisper was everywhere, and therefore no one spoke it. Just as no one ever says : "We are breathing !" in spite of the fact that breath is coming and going all the time.

"Mother !" said the boy Paul one day. "Why don't we keep a car of our own ? Why do we always use uncle's, or else a taxi ?"

"Because we're the poor members of the family," said the mother.

"But why *are* we, Mother ?"

"Well—I suppose," she said slowly and bitterly, "it's because your father has no luck."

The boy was silent for some time.

"Is luck money, Mother ?" he asked rather timidly.

"No, Paul! Not quite. It's what causes you to have money."

"Oh!" said Paul vaguely. "I thought when Uncle Oscar said *filthy lucker* it meant money."

"*Filthy lucre* does mean money," said the mother. "But it's lucre, not luck."

"Oh!" said the boy. "Then what *is* luck, Mother?"

"It's what causes you to have money. If you're lucky you have money. That's why it's better to be born lucky than rich. If you're rich, you may lose your money. But if you're lucky, you will always get more money."

"Oh! Will you? And is Father not lucky?"

"Very unlucky, I should say," she said bitterly.

The boy watched her with unsure eyes.

"Why?" he asked.

"I don't know. Nobody ever knows why one person is lucky and another unlucky."

"Don't they? Nobody at all? Does *nobody* know?"

"Perhaps God! But He never tells."

"He ought to, then. And aren't you lucky, either, Mother?"

"I can't be, if I married an unlucky husband."

"But by yourself, aren't you?"

"I used to think I was, before I married. Now I think I am very unlucky indeed."

"Why?"

"Well—never mind! Perhaps I'm not really," she said.

The child looked at her, to see if she meant it. But he saw, by the lines of her mouth, that she was only trying to hide something from him.

"Well, anyhow," he said stoutly, "I'm a lucky person."

"Why?" said his mother, with a sudden laugh.

He stared at her. He didn't even know why he had said it.

"God told me," he asserted, brazening it out.

"I hope He did, dear!" she said, again with a laugh, but rather bitter.

"He did, Mother!"

"Excellent!" said the mother, using one of her husband's exclamations.

The boy saw she did not believe him; or, rather, that she paid no attention to his assertion. This angered him somewhere, and made him want to compel her attention.

He went off by himself, vaguely, in a childish way, seeking for the clue to "luck". Absorbed, taking no heed of other people, he went about with a sort of stealth, seeking inwardly for luck. He wanted luck, he wanted it, he wanted it. When the two girls were playing dolls, in the nursery, he would sit on his big rocking-horse, charging madly into space, with a frenzy that made the little girls peer at him uneasily. Wildly the horse careered, the waving dark hair of the boy tossed, his eyes had a strange glare in them. The little girls dared not speak to him.

When he had ridden to the end of his mad little journey, he climbed down and stood in front of his rocking-horse, staring fixedly into its lowered face. Its red mouth was slightly open, its big eye was wide and glassy-bright.

"Now!" he would silently command the snorting steed. "Now take me to where there is luck! Now take me!"

And he would slash the horse on the neck with the little whip he had asked Uncle Oscar for. He *knew* the horse could take him to where there was luck, if only he forced it. So he would mount again, and start on his furious ride, hoping at last to get there. He knew he could get there.

"You'll break your horse, Paul!" said the nurse.

"He's always riding like that! I wish he'd leave off!" said his elder sister, Joan.

But he only glared down on them in silence. Nurse gave him up. She could make nothing of him. Anyhow, he was growing beyond her.

One day his mother and his Uncle Oscar came in when he was on one of his furious rides. He did not speak to them.

"Hallo, you young jockey! Riding a winner?" said his uncle.

"Aren't you growing too big for a rocking-horse? You're not a very little boy any longer, you know," said his mother.

But Paul only gave a blue glare from his big, rather close-set eyes. He would speak to nobody when he was in full tilt. His mother watched him with an anxious expression on her face.

At last he suddenly stopped forcing his horse into the mechanical gallop, and slid down.

"Well, I got there!" he announced fiercely, his blue eyes still flaring, and his sturdy long legs straddling apart.

"Where did you get to ?" asked his mother.

"Where I wanted to go to," he flared back at her.

"That's right, son !" said Uncle Oscar. "Don't you stop till you get there. What's the horse's name ?"

"He doesn't have a name," said the boy.

"Gets on without all right ?" asked the uncle.

"Well, he has different names. He was called Sansovino last week."

"Sansovino, eh ? Won the Ascot. How did you know his name ?"

"He always talks about horse-races with Bassett," said Joan.

The uncle was delighted to find that his small nephew was posted with all the racing news. Bassett, the young gardener who had been wounded in the left foot in the war, and had got his present job through Oscar Cresswell, whose batman he had been, was a perfect blade of the Turf. He lived in the racing events, and the small boy lived with him.

Oscar Cresswell got it all from Bassett.

"Master Paul comes and asks me, so I can't do more than tell him, sir," said Bassett, his face terribly serious, as if he were speaking of religious matters.

"And does he ever put anything on a horse he fancies ?"

"Well—I don't want to give him away—he's a young sport, a fine sport, sir. Would you mind asking him himself ? He sort of takes a pleasure in it, and perhaps he'd feel I was giving him away, sir, if you don't mind."

Bassett was serious as a church.

The uncle went back to his nephew and took him off for a ride in the car.

"Say, Paul, old man, do you ever put anything on a horse ?" the uncle asked.

The boy watched the handsome man closely.

"Why, do you think I oughtn't to ?" he parried.

"Not a bit of it ! I thought perhaps you might give me a tip for the Lincoln."

The car sped on into the country, going down to Uncle Oscar's place in Hampshire.

"Honour bright ?" said the nephew.

"Honour bright, son !" said the uncle.

"Well, then, Daffodil."

"Daffodil ! I doubt it, sonny. What about Mirza ?"

"I only know the winner," said the boy. "That's Daffodil!"

"Daffodil, eh?"

There was a pause. Daffodil was an obscure horse, comparatively.

"Uncle!"

"Yes, son?"

"You won't let it go any further, will you? I promised Bassett."

"Bassett be damned, old man! What's he got to do with it?"

"We're partners! We've been partners from the first! Uncle, he lent me my first five shillings, which I lost. I promised him, honour bright, it was only between me and him: only you gave me that ten-shilling note I started winning with, so I thought you were lucky. You won't let it go any further, will you?"

The boy gazed at his uncle from those big, hot blue eyes, set rather close together. The uncle stirred and laughed uneasily.

"Right you are, son! I'll keep your tip private. Daffodil, eh! How much are you putting on him?"

"All except twenty pounds," said the boy. "I keep that in reserve."

The uncle thought it a good joke.

"You keep twenty pounds in reserve, do you, you young romancer? What are you betting, then?"

"I'm betting three hundred," said the boy gravely. "But it's between you and me, Uncle Oscar! Honour bright?"

The uncle burst into a roar of laughter.

"It's between you and me all right, you young Nat Gould," he said, laughing. "But where's your three hundred?"

"Bassett keeps it for me. We're partners."

"You are, are you? And what is Bassett putting on Daffodil?"

"He won't go quite as high as I do, I expect. Perhaps he'll go a hundred and fifty."

"What, pennies?" laughed the uncle.

"Pounds," said the child, with a surprised look at his uncle. "Bassett keeps a bigger reserve than I do."

Between wonder and amusement, Uncle Oscar was

silent. He pursued the matter no further, but he determined to take his nephew with him to the Lincoln races.

"Now, son," he said, "I'm putting twenty on Mirza, and I'll put five for you on any horse you fancy. What's your pick ?"

"Daffodil, uncle !"

"No, not the fiver on Daffodil !"

"I should if it was my own fiver," said the child.

"Good ! Good ! Right you are ! A fiver for me and a fiver for you on Daffodil."

The child had never been to a race-meeting before, and his eyes were blue fire. He pursed his mouth tight and watched. A Frenchman just in front had put his money on Lancelot. Wild with excitement, he flayed his arms up and down, yelling "*Lancelot ! Lancelot !*" in his French accent.

Daffodil came in first, Lancelot second, Mirza third. The child, flushed and with eyes blazing, was curiously serene. His uncle brought him five five-pound notes : four to one.

"What am I to do with these ?" he cried, waving them before the boy's eyes.

"I suppose we'll talk to Bassett," said the boy. "I expect I have fifteen hundred now : and twenty in reserve : and this twenty."

His uncle studied him for some moments.

"Look here, son !" he said. "You're not serious about Bassett and that fifteen hundred, are you ?"

"Yes, I am. But it's between you and me, Uncle ! Honour bright ?"

"Honour bright, all right, son ; but I must talk to Bassett."

"If you'd like to be a partner, Uncle, with Bassett and me, we could all be partners. Only you'd have to promise, honour bright, Uncle, not to let it go beyond us three. Bassett and I are lucky, and you must be lucky, because it was your ten shillings I started winning with. . . ."

Uncle Oscar took both Bassett and Paul into Richmond Park for an afternoon, and there they talked.

"It's like this, you see, sir," Bassett said. "Master Paul would get me talking about racing events, spinning yarns, you know, sir. And he was always keen on knowing if I'd made or if I'd lost. It's about a year since, now, that I put five shillings on Blush of Dawn for him : and we lost. Then

the luck turned, with that ten shillings he had from you :
that we put on Singhalese. And since that time, it's been
pretty steady, all things considering. What do you say,
Master Paul ?"

"We're all right when we're *sure*," said Paul. "It's when
we're not quite sure that we go down."

"Oh, but we're careful then," said Bassett.

"But when are you *sure* ?" smiled Uncle Oscar.

"It's Master Paul, sir," said Bassett, in a secret, religious
voice. "It's as if he had it from heaven. Like Daffodil now,
for the Lincoln. That was as sure as eggs."

"Did you put anything on Daffodil ?" asked Oscar
Cresswell.

"Yes, sir. I made my bit."

"And my nephew ?"

Bassett was obstinately silent, looking at Paul.

"I made twelve hundred, didn't I, Bassett ?   I told Uncle
I was putting three hundred on Daffodil."

"That's right," said Bassett, nodding.

"But where's the money ?" asked the uncle.

"I keep it safe locked up, sir. Master Paul, he can have
it any minute he likes to ask for it."

"What, fifteen hundred pounds ?"

"And twenty !   And *forty*, that is, with the twenty he
made on the course."

"It's amazing !" said the uncle.

"If Master Paul offers you to be partners, sir, I would,
if I were you : if you'll excuse me," said Bassett.

Oscar Cresswell thought about it.

"I'll see the money," he said.

They drove home again, and sure enough Bassett came
round to the garden-house with fifteen hundred pounds in
notes. The twenty pounds reserve was left with Joe Glee,
in the Turf Commission deposit.

"You see, it's all right, Uncle, when I'm *sure* !   Then we
go strong, for all we're worth. Don't we, Bassett ?"

"We do that, Master Paul."

"And when are you sure ?" said the uncle, laughing.

"Oh, well, sometimes I'm *absolutely* sure, like about
Daffodil," said the boy ; "and sometimes I have an idea ;
and sometimes I haven't even an idea, have I, Bassett ?   Then
we're careful, because we mostly go down."

"You do, do you ?   And when you're sure, like about Daffodil, what makes you sure, sonny ?"

"Oh, well, I don't know," said the boy uneasily.   "I'm sure, you know, Uncle ; that's all."

"It's as if he had it from heaven, sir," Bassett reiterated.

"I should say so !" said the uncle.

But he became a partner.   And when the Leger was coming on, Paul was "sure" about Lively Spark, which was a quite inconsiderable horse.   The boy insisted on putting a thousand on the horse, Bassett went for five hundred, and Oscar Cresswell two hundred.   Lively Spark came in first, and the betting had been ten to one against him.   Paul had made ten thousand.

"You see," he said, "I was absolutely sure of him."

Even Oscar Cresswell had cleared two thousand.

"Look here, son," he said, "this sort of thing makes me nervous."

"It needn't, Uncle !   Perhaps I shan't be sure again for a long time."

"But what are you going to do with your money ?" asked the uncle.

"Of course," said the boy, "I started it for Mother.   She said she had no luck, because Father is unlucky, so I thought if *I* was lucky, it might stop whispering."

"What might stop whispering ?"

"Our house !   I *hate* our house for whispering."

"What does it whisper ?"

"Why—why," the boy fidgeted, "why, I don't know ! But it's always short of money, you know, Uncle."

"I know it, son, I know it."

"You know people send Mother writs, don't you, Uncle ?"

"I'm afraid I do," said the uncle.

"And then the house whispers like people laughing at you behind your back.   It's awful, that is !   I thought if I was lucky——"

"You might stop it," added the uncle.

The boy watched him with big blue eyes that had an uncanny cold fire in them, and he said never a word.

"Well, then," said the uncle, "what are we doing ?"

"I shouldn't like Mother to know I was lucky," said the boy.

"Why not, son ?"

R*

"She'd stop me."

"I don't think she would."

"Oh"—and the boy writhed in an odd way—"I *don't* want her to know, Uncle."

"All right, son !   We'll manage it without her knowing."

They managed it very easily.   Paul, at the other's suggestion, handed over five thousand pounds to his uncle, who deposited it with the family lawyer, who was then to inform Paul's mother that a relative had put five thousand pounds into his hands, which sum was to be paid out a thousand pounds at a time, on the mother's birthday for the next five years.

"So she'll have a birthday present of a thousand pounds for five successive years," said Uncle Oscar.   "I hope it won't make it all the harder for her later."

Paul's mother had her birthday in November.   The house had been "whispering" worse than ever lately, and, even in spite of his luck, Paul could not bear up against it.   He was very anxious to see the effect of the birthday letter, telling his mother about the thousand pounds.

When there were no visitors, Paul now took his meals with his parents, as he was beyond the nursery control.   His mother went into town nearly every day.   She had discovered that she had an odd knack of sketching furs and dress materials so she worked secretly in the studio of a friend who was the chief "artist" for the leading drapers.   She drew the figures of ladies in furs and ladies in silk and sequins for the newspaper advertisements.   This young woman artist earned several thousand pounds a year, but Paul's mother only made several hundreds, and she was again dissatisfied.   She so wanted to be first in something, and she did not succeed, even in making sketches for draper advertisements.

She was down to breakfast on the morning of her birthday. Paul watched her face as she read her letters.   He knew the lawyer's letter.   As his mother read it, her face hardened and became more expressionless.   Then a cold, determined look came on her mouth.   She hid the letter under the pile of others, and said not a word about it.

"Didn't you have anything nice in the post for your birthday, Mother ?" said Paul.

"Quite moderately nice," she said, her voice cold and absent.

She went away to town without saying more.

But in the afternoon Uncle Oscar appeared. He said Paul's mother had had a long interview with the lawyer, asking if the whole five thousand could not be advanced at once, as she was in debt.

"What do you think, Uncle ?" said the boy.

"I leave it to you, son."

"Oh, let her have it, then ! We can get some more with the other," said the boy.

"A bird in the hand is worth two in the bush, laddie !" said Uncle Oscar.

"But I'm sure to *know* for the Grand National ; or the Lincolnshire ; or else the Derby. I'm sure to know for *one* of them," said Paul.

So Uncle Oscar signed the agreement, and Paul's mother touched the whole five thousand. Then something very curious happened. The voices in the house suddenly went mad, like a chorus of frogs on a spring evening. There were certain new furnishings, and Paul had a tutor. He was *really* going to Eton, his father's school, in the following autumn. There were flowers in the winter, and a blossoming of the luxury Paul's mother had been used to. And yet the voices in the house, behind the sprays of mimosa and almond-blossom, and from under the piles of iridescent cushions, simply trilled and screamed in a sort of ecstasy : "There *must* be more money ! Oh-h-h ! There *must* be more money ! Oh, now, now-w, now-w-w—there *must* be more money ! More than ever ! More than ever !"

It frightened Paul terribly. He studied away at his Latin and Greek with his tutors. But his intense hours were spent with Bassett. The Grand National had gone by ; he had not "known", and had lost a hundred pounds. Summer was at hand. He was in agony for the Lincoln. But even for the Lincoln he didn't "know", and he lost fifty pounds. He became wild-eyed and strange, as if something were going to explode in him.

"Let it alone, son ! Don't you bother about it !" urged Uncle Oscar. But it was as if the boy couldn't really hear what his uncle was saying.

"I've got to know for the Derby ! I've *got* to know for the Derby !" the child reiterated, his big blue eyes blazing with a sort of madness.

His mother noticed how overwrought he was.

"You'd better go to the seaside.   Wouldn't you like to go now to the seaside, instead of waiting?   I think you'd better," she said, looking down at him anxiously, her heart curiously heavy because of him.

But the child lifted his uncanny blue eyes.

"I couldn't possibly go before the Derby, Mother!" he said.   "I couldn't possibly!"

"Why not?" she said, her voice becoming heavy when she was opposed.   "Why not?   You can still go from the seaside to see the Derby with your Uncle Oscar, if that's what you wish.   No need for you to wait here.   Besides, I think you care too much about these races.   It's a bad sign.   My family has been a gambling family, and you won't know till you grow up how much damage it has done.   But it has done damage.   I shall have to send Bassett away, and ask Uncle Oscar not to talk racing to you, unless you promise to be reasonable about it: go away to the seaside and forget it. You're all nerves!"

"I'll do what you like, Mother, so long as you don't send me away till after the Derby," the boy said.

"Send you away from where?   Just from this house?"

"Yes," he said, gazing at her.

"Why, you curious child, what makes you care about this house so much, suddenly?   I never knew you loved it!"

He gazed at her without speaking.   He had a secret within a secret, something he had not divulged, even to Bassett or to his Uncle Oscar.

But his mother, after standing undecided and a little bit sullen for some moments, said:

"Very well, then!   Don't go to the seaside till after the Derby, if you don't wish it.   But promise me you won't let your nerves go to pieces!   Promise you won't think so much about horse-racing and *events*, as you call them!"

"Oh no!" said the boy casually.   "I won't think much about them, Mother.   You needn't worry.   I wouldn't worry, Mother, if I were you."

"If you were me and I were you," said his mother, "I wonder what we *should* do!"

"But you know you needn't worry, Mother, don't you?" the boy repeated.

"I should be awfully glad to know it," she said wearily.

"Oh, well, you *can*, you know. I mean you *ought* to know you needn't worry!" he insisted.

"Ought I? Then I'll see about it," she said.

Paul's secret of secrets was his wooden horse, that which had no name. Since he was emancipated from a nurse and a nursery-governess, he had had his rocking-horse removed to his own bedroom at the top of the house.

"Surely you're too big for a rocking-horse!" his mother had remonstrated.

"Well, you see, Mother, till I can have a *real* horse, I like to have *some* sort of animal about," had been his quaint answer.

"Do you feel he keeps you company?" she laughed.

"Oh yes! He's very good, he always keeps me company, when I'm there," said Paul.

So the horse, rather shabby, stood in an arrested prance in the boy's bedroom.

The Derby was drawing near, and the boy grew more and more tense. He hardly heard what was spoken to him, he was very frail, and his eyes were really uncanny. His mother had sudden strange seizures of uneasiness about him. Sometimes, for half an hour, she would feel a sudden anxiety about him that was almost anguish. She wanted to rush to him at once and know he was safe.

Two nights before the Derby, she was at a big party in town, when one of her rushes of anxiety about her boy, her first-born, gripped her heart till she could hardly speak. She fought with the feeling, might and main, for she believed in common sense. But it was too strong. She had to leave the dance and go downstairs to telephone to the country. The children's nursery-governess was terribly surprised and startled at being rung up in the night.

"Are the children all right, Miss Wilmot?"

"Oh yes, they are quite all right."

"Master Paul? Is he all right?"

"He went to bed as right as a trivet. Shall I run up and look at him?"

"No!" said Paul's mother reluctantly. "No! Don't trouble. It's all right. Don't sit up. We shall be home fairly soon." She did not want her son's privacy intruded upon.

"Very good," said the governess.

It was about one o'clock when Paul's mother and father drove up to their house. All was still. Paul's mother went to her room and slipped off her white fur cloak. She had told her maid not to wait up for her. She heard her husband downstairs, mixing a whisky-and-soda.

And then, because of the strange anxiety at her heart, she stole upstairs to her son's room. Noiselessly she went along the upper corridor. Was there a faint noise? What was it?

She stood, with arrested muscles, outside his door, listening. There was a strange, heavy, and yet not loud noise. Her heart stood still. It was a soundless noise, yet rushing and powerful. Something huge, in violent, hushed motion. What was it? What in God's name was it? She ought to know. She felt that she *knew* the noise. She knew what it was.

Yet she could not place it. She couldn't say what it was. And on and on it went, like a madness.

Softly, frozen with anxiety and fear, she turned the door-handle.

The room was dark. Yet in the space near the window she heard and saw something plunging to and fro. She gazed in fear and amazement.

Then suddenly she switched on the light, and saw her son, in his green pyjamas, madly surging on his rocking-horse. The blaze of light suddenly lit him up, as he urged the wooden horse, and lit her up, as she stood, blonde, in her dress of pale green and crystal, in the doorway.

"Paul!" she cried. "Whatever are you doing?"

"It's Malabar!" he screamed in a powerful, strange voice. "It's Malabar!"

His eyes blazed at her for one strange and senseless second, as he ceased urging his wooden horse. Then he fell with a crash to the ground, and she, all her tormented motherhood flooding upon her, rushed to gather him up.

But he was unconscious, and unconscious he remained, with some brain-fever. He talked and tossed, and his mother sat stonily by his side.

"Malabar! It's Malabar! Bassett, Bassett, I *know*; it's Malabar!"

So the child cried, trying to get up and urge the rocking-horse that gave him his inspiration.

"What does he mean by Malabar ?" asked the heart-frozen mother.

"I don't know," said the father stonily.

"What does he mean by Malabar ?" she asked her brother Oscar.

"It's one of the horses running for the Derby," was the answer.

And, in spite of himself, Oscar Cresswell spoke to Bassett, and himself put a thousand on Malabar : at fourteen to one.

The third day of the illness was critical : they were watching for a change. The boy, with his rather long curly hair, was tossing ceaselessly on the pillow. He neither slept nor regained consciousness, and his eyes were like blue stones. His mother sat, feeling her heart had gone, turned actually into a stone.

In the evening, Oscar Cresswell did not come, but Bassett sent a message, saying could he come up for one moment, just one moment ? Paul's mother was very angry at the intrusion, but on second thoughts she agreed. The boy was the same. Perhaps Bassett might bring him to consciousness.

The gardener, a shortish fellow with a little brown moustache and sharp little brown eyes, tiptoed into the room, touched his imaginary cap to Paul's mother, and stole to the bedside, staring with glittering, smallish eyes at the tossing, dying child.

"Master Paul !" he whispered. "Master Paul ! Malabar came in first all right, a clean win. I did as you told me. You've made over seventy thousand pounds, you have ; you've got over eighty thousand. Malabar came in all right, Master Paul."

"Malabar ! Malabar ! Did I say Malabar, Mother ? Did I say Malabar ? Do you think I'm lucky, Mother ? I knew Malabar, didn't I ? Over eighty thousand pounds ! I call that lucky, don't you, Mother ? Over eighty thousand pounds ! I knew, didn't I know I knew ? Malabar came in all right. If I ride my horse till I'm sure, then I tell you, Bassett, you can go as high as you like. Did you go for all you were worth, Bassett ?"

"I went a thousand on it, Master Paul."

"I never told you, Mother, that if I can ride my horse, and get *there*, then I'm absolutely sure—oh, absolutely ! Mother, did I ever tell you ? I *am* lucky !"

"No, you never did," said the mother.

But the boy died in the night.

And even as he lay dead, his mother heard her brother's voice saying to her: "My God, Hester, you're eighty-odd thousand to the good, and a poor devil of a son to the bad. But, poor devil, poor devil, he's best gone out of a life where he rides his rocking-horse to find a winner."

THE LOVELY LADY

At seventy-two, Pauline Attenborough could still sometimes be mistaken, in the half-light for thirty. She really was a wonderfully preserved woman, of perfect *chic*. Of course it helps a great deal to have the right frame. She would be an exquisite skeleton, and her skull would be an exquisite skull, like that of some Etruscan woman with feminine charm still in the swerve of the bone and the pretty, naïve teeth.

Mrs. Attenborough's face was of the perfect oval and slightly flat type that wears best. There is no flesh to sag. Her nose rode serenely, in its finely bridged curve. Only the big grey eyes were a tiny bit prominent, on the surface of her face, and they gave her away most. The bluish lids were heavy, as if they ached sometimes with the strain of keeping the eyes beneath them arch and bright; and at the corners of the eyes were fine little wrinkles which would slacken into haggardness, then be pulled up tense again to that bright, gay look like a Leonardo woman who really could laugh outright.

Her niece Cecilia was perhaps the only person in the world who was aware of the invisible little wire which connected Pauline's eye-wrinkles with Pauline's will-power. Only Cecilia consciously watched the eyes go haggard and old and tired, and remain so, for hours; until Robert came home. Then—ping !—the mysterious little wire that worked between Pauline's will and her face went taut, the weary, haggard, prominent eyes suddenly began to gleam, the eyelids arched, the queer, curved eyebrows which floated in such frail arches on Pauline's forehead began to gather a mocking significance, and you had the *real* lovely lady, in all her charm.

She really had the secret of everlasting youth; that is to say, she could don her youth again like an eagle. But she was sparing of it. She was wise enough not to try being young for too many people. Her son Robert, in the evenings, and Sir Wilfrid Knipe sometimes in the afternoon to tea ; then occasional visitors on Sunday, when Robert was home— for these she was her lovely and changeless self, that age could not wither, nor custom stale ; so bright and kindly and yet subtly mocking, like Mona Lisa, who knew a thing or two. But Pauline knew more, so she needn't be smug at all. She could laugh that lovely, mocking Bacchante laugh of hers, which was at the same time never malicious, always good-naturedly tolerant, both of virtues and vices—the former, of course, taking much more tolerating. So she suggested, roguishly.

Only with her niece Cecilia she did not trouble to keep up the glamour. Ciss was not very observant, anyhow ; and, more than that, she was plain ; more still, she was in love with Robert ; and most of all, she was thirty, and dependent on her aunt Pauline. Oh, Cecilia—why make music for her ?

Cecilia, called by her aunt and by her cousin Robert just Ciss, like a cat spitting, was a big, dark-complexioned, pug-faced young woman who very rarely spoke, and when she did couldn't get it out. She was the daughter of a poor Congregational clergyman who had been, while he lived, brother to Ronald, Aunt Pauline's husband. Ronald and the Congregational minister were both well dead, and Aunt Pauline had had charge of Ciss for the last five years.

They lived all together in a quite exquisite though rather small Queen Anne house some twenty-five miles out of town, secluded in a little dale, and surrounded by small but very quaint and pleasant grounds. It was an ideal place and an ideal life for Aunt Pauline, at the age of seventy-two. When the kingfishers flashed up the little stream in her garden, going under the alders, something still flashed in her heart. She was that kind of woman.

Robert, who was two years older than Ciss, went every day to town, to his chambers in one of the Inns. He was a barrister, and, to his secret but very deep mortification, he earned about a hundred pounds a year. He simply *couldn't* get above that figure, though it was rather easy to get below it. Of course, it didn't matter. Pauline had money. But then, what was Pauline's was Pauline's, and though she could give almost lavishly, still, one was always aware of having a *lovely* and *undeserved* present made to one. Presents are so much nicer when they're undeserved, Aunt Pauline would say.

Robert, too, was plain, and almost speechless. He was medium-sized, rather broad and stout, though not fat. Only his creamy, clean-shaven face was rather fat, and sometimes suggestive of an Italian priest, in its silence and its secrecy. But he had grey eyes like his mother, but very shy and uneasy, not bold like hers. Perhaps Ciss was the only person who fathomed his awful shyness and *malaise*, his habitual feeling that he was in the wrong place : almost like a soul that has got into a wrong body. But he never did anything about it. He went up to Chambers, and read law. It was, however, all the weird old processes that interested him. He had, unknown to everybody but his mother, a quite extraordinary collection of old Mexican legal documents— reports of processes and trials, pleas, accusations : the weird and awful mixture of ecclesiastical law and common law in seventeenth-century Mexico. He had started a study in this direction through coming across the report of a trial of two English sailors, for murder, in Mexico, in 1620, and he had gone on, when the next document was an accusation against a Don Miguel Estrada for seducing one of the nuns of the Sacred Heart Convent in Qaxaca in 1680.

Pauline and her son Robert had wonderful evenings with these old papers. The lovely lady knew a little Spanish. She even looked a trifle Spanish herself, with a high comb and a marvellous dark-brown shawl embroidered in thick, silvery silk embroidery. So she would sit at the perfect old table, soft as velvet in its deep, brown surface, a high comb in her hair, ear-rings with dropping pendants in her ears, her arms bare and still beautiful, a few strings of pearls round her throat, a puce velvet dress on, and this or another beautiful shawl, and by candlelight she looked, yes, a Spanish high-bred beauty of thirty-two or -three. She set the candles to give her face just the chiaroscuro she knew suited her ; her high chair that rose behind her face was done in old green brocade, against which her face emerged like a Christmas rose.

They were always three at table, and they always drank a bottle of champagne : Pauline two glasses, Ciss two glasses, Robert the rest. The lovely lady sparkled and was radiant. Ciss, her black hair bobbed, her broad shoulders in a very nice and becoming dress that Aunt Pauline had helped her to make, stared from her aunt to her cousin and back again, with rather confused, mute, hazel eyes, and played the part of an audience suitably impressed. She *was* impressed, somewhere, all the time. And even rendered speechless by Pauline's brilliancy, even after five years. But at the bottom of her consciousness was the *data* of as weird a document as Robert ever studied : all the things she knew about her aunt and her cousin.

Robert was always a gentleman, with an old-fashioned, punctilious courtesy that covered his shyness quite completely. He was, and Ciss knew it, more confused than shy. He was worse than she was. Cecilia's own confusion dated from only five years back. Robert's must have started before he was born. In the lovely lady's womb he must have felt *very* confused.

He paid all his attention to his mother, drawn to her as a humble flower to the sun. And yet, priest-like, he was all the time aware, with the tail of his consciousness, that Ciss was there, and that she was a bit shut out of it, and that something wasn't right. He was aware of the third consciousness in the room. Whereas, to Pauline, her niece Cecilia was an appropriate part of her own setting, rather than a distinct consciousness.

Robert took coffee with his mother and Ciss in the warm drawing-room, where all the furniture was so lovely, all collectors' pieces—Mrs. Attenborough had made her own money, dealing privately in pictures and furniture and rare things from barbaric countries—and the three talked desultorily till about eight or half past. It was very pleasant, very cosy, very homely even ; Pauline made a real home cosiness out of so much elegant material. The chat was simple, and nearly always bright. Pauline was her *real* self, emanating a friendly mockery and an odd, ironic gaiety—till there came a little pause.

At which Ciss always rose and said good night, and carried out the coffee-tray, to prevent Burnett from intruding any more.

And then—ah, then, the lovely, glowing intimacy of the evening, between mother and son, when they deciphered manuscripts and discussed points, Pauline with that eagerness of a girl for which she was famous. And it was quite genuine. In some mysterious way she had *saved up* her power for being thrilled, in connection with a man. Robert, solid, rather quiet and subdued, seemed like the elder of the two—almost like a priest with a young girl pupil. And that was rather how he felt.

Ciss had a flat for herself just across the courtyard, over the old coach-house and stables. There were no horses. Robert kept his car in the coach-house. Ciss had three very nice rooms up there, stretching along in a row one after the other, and she had got used to the ticking of the stable clock.

But sometimes she did not go to her rooms. In the summer she would sit on the lawn, and from the open window of the drawing-room upstairs she would hear Pauline's wonderful, heart searching laugh. And in winter the young woman would put on a thick coat and walk slowly to the little balustraded bridge over the stream, and then look back at the three lighted windows of that drawing-room where mother, and son were so happy together.

Ciss loved Robert, and she believed that Pauline intended the two of them to marry—when she was dead. But poor Robert, he was so convulsed with shyness already, with man or woman. What would he be when his mother was dead—in a dozen more years? He would be just a shell, the shell of a man who had never lived.

The strange, unspoken sympathy of the young with one another, when they are overshadowed by the old, was one of the bonds between Robert and Ciss. But another bond, which Ciss did not know how to draw tight, was the bond of passion. Poor Robert was by nature a passionate man. His silence and his agonized, though hidden, shyness were both the result of a secret physical passionateness. And how Pauline could play on this! Ah, Ciss was not blind to the eyes which he fixed on his mother—eyes fascinated yet humiliated, full of shame. He was ashamed that he was not a man. And he did not love his mother. He was fascinated by her. Completely fascinated. And for the rest, paralysed in a lifelong confusion.

Ciss stayed in the garden till the lights leapt up in Pauline's bedroom—about ten o'clock. The lovely lady had retired. Robert would now stay another hour or so, alone. Then he, too, would retire. Ciss, in the dark outside, sometimes wished she could creep up to him and say: "Oh, Robert! It's all wrong!" But Aunt Pauline would hear. And, anyhow, Ciss couldn't do it. She went off to her own rooms, once more. once more, and so for ever.

In the morning coffee was brought up on a tray to each of the rooms of the three relatives. Ciss had to be at Sir Wilfrid Knipe's at nine o'clock, to give two hours' lessons to his little granddaughter. It was her sole serious occupation, except that she played the piano for the love of it. Robert set off to town about nine. And as a rule, Aunt Pauline appeared to lunch, though sometimes not till tea-time. When she appeared, she looked fresh and young. But she was inclined to fade rather rapidly, like a flower without water, in the daytime. Her hour was the candle hour.

So she always rested in the afternoon. When the sun shone, if possible she took a sun-bath. This was one of her secrets. Her lunch was very light ; she could take her sun-and-air-bath before noon or after, as it pleased her. Often it was in the afternoon, when the sun shone very warmly into a queer little yew-walled square just behind the stables. Here Ciss stretched out the lying-chair and rugs, and put the light parasol handy in the silent little enclosure of thick dark yew-hedges beyond the old red walls of the unused stables. And hither came the lovely lady with her book. Ciss then had to be on guard in one of her own rooms, should her aunt, who was very keen-eared, hear a footstep.

One afternoon it occurred to Cecilia that she herself might while away this rather long afternoon hour by taking a sun-bath. She was growing restive. The thought of the flat roof of the stable buildings, to which she could climb from a loft at the end, started her on a new adventure. She often went on to the roof ; she had to, to wind up the stable clock, which was a job she had assumed to herself. Now she took a rug, climbed out under the heavens, looked at the sky and the great elm-tops, looked at the sun, then took off her things and lay down perfectly securely, in a corner of the roof under the parapet, full in the sun.

It was rather lovely, to bask all one's length like this in warm sun and air. Yes, it was very lovely ! It even seemed to melt some of the hard bitterness of her heart, some of that core of unspoken resentment which never dissolved. Luxuriously, she spread herself, so that the sun should touch her limbs fully, fully. If she had no other lover, she should have the sun ! She rolled over voluptuously.

And suddenly her heart stood still in her body, and her hair almost rose on end as a voice said very softly, musingly, in her ear :

"No, Henry dear ! It was not my fault you died instead of marrying that Claudia. No, darling. I was quite, quite willing for you to marry her, unsuitable though she was."

Cecilia sank down on her rug, powerless and perspiring with dread. That awful voice, so soft, so musing, yet so unnatural. Not a human voice at all. Yet there must, there *must* be someone on the roof ! Oh, how unspeakably awful !

She lifted her weak head and peeped across the sloping leads. Nobody ! The chimneys were too narrow to shelter anybody. There was nobody on the roof. Then it must be someone in the trees, in the elms. Either that, or—terror unspeakable—a bodiless voice ! She reared her head a little higher.

And, as she did so, came the voice again :

"No, darling ! I told you you would tire of her in six months. And you see it was true, dear. It was true, true, true ! I wanted to spare you that. So it wasn't I who made you feel weak and disabled, wanting that very silly Claudia— poor thing, she looked so woebegone afterwards !—wanting her and not wanting her. You got yourself into that per-plexity, my dear. I only warned you. What else could I do ? And you lost your spirit and died without ever knowing me again. It was bitter, bitter. . . ."

The voice faded away. Cecilia subsided weakly on to her rug, after the anguished tension of listening. Oh, it was awful. The sun shone, the sky was blue, all seemed so lovely and afternoony and summery. And yet—oh, horror !—she was going to be forced to believe in the supernatural ! And she loathed the supernatural, ghosts and voices and rappings and all the rest.

But that awful, creepy, bodiless voice, with its rusty sort of whispers of an overtone ! It had something so fearfully familiar in it, too ! And yet was so utterly uncanny. Poor Cecilia could only lie there unclothed, and so all the more agonizingly helpless, inert, collapsed in sheer dread.

And then she heard the thing sigh—a deep sigh that seemed weirdly familiar, yet was not human. "Ah well, ah well, the heart must bleed. Better it should bleed than break. It is grief, grief! But it wasn't my fault, dear. And Robert could marry our poor, dull Ciss to-morrow, if he wanted her. But he doesn't care about it, so why force him into anything?" The sounds were very uneven, sometimes only a husky sort of whisper. Listen! Listen!

Cecilia was about to give vent to loud and piercing screams of hysteria, when the last two sentences arrested her. All her caution and her cunning sprang alert. It was Aunt Pauline! It *must* be Aunt Pauline, practising ventriloquism, or something like that. What a devil she was!

Where was she? She must be lying down there, right below where Cecilia herself was lying. And it was either some fiend's trick of ventriloquism, or else thought-transference. The sounds were very uneven; sometimes quite inaudible, sometimes only a brushing sort of noise. Ciss listened intently. No, it could not be ventriloquism. It was worse: some form of thought-transference that conveyed itself like sound. Some horror of that sort! Cecilia still lay weak and inert, too terrified to move; but she was growing calmer with suspicion. It was some diabolic trick of that unnatural woman.

But *what* a devil of a woman! She even knew that she, Cecilia, had mentally accused her of killing her son Henry. Poor Henry was Robert's elder brother, twelve years older than Robert. He had died suddenly when he was twenty-two, after an awful struggle with himself, because he was passionately in love with a young and very good-looking actress, and his mother had humorously despised him for the attachment. So he had caught some sudden ordinary disease, but the poison had gone to his brain and killed him before he ever regained consciousness. Ciss knew the few facts from her own father. And lately she had been thinking that Pauline was going to kill Robert as she had killed Henry. It was clear murder: a mother murdering her sensitive sons, who were fascinated by her: the Circe!

"I suppose I may as well get up," murmured the dim, unbreathing voice. "Too much sun is as bad as too little. Enough sun, enough love-thrill, enough proper food, and not too much of any of them, and a woman might live for ever. I verily believe, for ever. If she absorbs as much vitality as she expends. Or perhaps a trifle more!"

It was certainly Aunt Pauline! How—how terrible!

She, Ciss, was hearing Aunt Pauline's thoughts. Oh, how ghastly! Aunt Pauline was sending out her thoughts in a sort of radio, and she, Ciss, had to *hear* what her aunt was thinking. How ghastly! How insufferable! One of them would surely have to die.

She twisted and lay inert and crumpled, staring vacantly in front of her. Vacantly! Vacantly! And her eyes were staring almost into a hole. She was staring in it un-seeing, a hole going down in the corner, from the lead gutter. It meant nothing to her. Only it frightened her a little more.

When suddenly, out of the hole came a sigh and a last whisper: "Ah well, Pauline! Get up, it's enough for to-day." Good God! Out of the hole of the rain-pipe! The rain-pipe was acting as a speaking-tube! Impossible! No, quite possible. She had read of it even in some book. And Aunt Pauline, like the old and guilty woman she was, talked aloud to herself. That was it!

A sullen exultance sprang in Ciss's breast. *That* was why she would never have anybody, not even Robert, in her bedroom. That was why she never dozed in a chair, never sat absent-minded anywhere, but went to her room, and kept to her room, except when she roused herself to be alert. When she slackened off she talked to herself! She talked in a soft little crazy voice to herself. But she was not crazy. It was only her thoughts murmuring themselves aloud.

So she had qualms about poor Henry! Well she might have! Ciss believed that Aunt Pauline had loved her big, handsome, brilliant first-born much more than she loved Robert, and that his death had been a terrible blow and a chagrin to her. Poor Robert had been only ten years old when Henry died. Since then he had been the substitute.

Ah, how awful!

But Aunt Pauline was a strange woman. She had left her husband when Henry was a small child, some years even before Robert was born. There was no quarrel. Some-times she saw her husband again, quite amiably, but a little mockingly. And she even gave him money.

For Pauline earned all her own. Her father had been a Consul in the East and in Naples, and a devoted collector of beautiful exotic things. When he died, soon after his grandson Henry was born, he left his collection of treasures to his daughter. And Pauline, who had really a passion and a genius for loveliness, whether in texture or form or colour, had laid the basis of her fortune on her father's collection. She had gone on collecting, buying where she could, and selling to collectors or to museums. She was one of the first to sell old, weird African figures to the museums, and ivory carvings from New Guinea. She bought Rénoir as soon as she saw his pictures. But not Rousseau. And all by herself she made a fortune.

After her husband died she had not married again. She was not even *known* to have had lovers. If she did have lovers, it was not among the men who admired her most and paid her devout and open attendance. To these she was a "friend".

Cecilia slipped on her clothes and caught up her rug, hastening carefully down the ladder to the loft. As she descended she heard the ringing, musical call: "All right, Ciss"—which meant that the lovely lady was finished and returning to the house. Even her voice was wonderfully young and sonorous, beautifully balanced and self-possessed. So different from the little voice in which she talked to herself. *That* was much more the voice of an old woman.

Ciss hastened round to the yew enclosure, where lay the comfortable *chaise-longue* with the various delicate rugs. Everything Pauline had was choice, to the fine straw mat on the floor. The great yew walls were beginning to cast long shadows. Only in the corner where the rugs tumbled their delicate colours was there hot, still sunshine.

The rugs folded up, the chair lifted away, Cecilia stooped to look at the mouth of the rain-pipe. There it was, in the corner, under a little hood of masonry and just projecting from the thick leaves of the creeper on the wall. If Pauline, lying there, turned her face towards the wall, she would speak into the very mouth of the tube. Cecilia was reassured. She had heard her aunt's thoughts indeed, but by no uncanny agency.

That evening, as if aware of something, Pauline was a little quieter than usual, though she looked her own serene, rather mysterious self. And after coffee she said to Robert and Ciss:

"I'm so sleepy. The sun has made me so sleepy. I

feel full of sunshine like a bee. I shall go to bed, if you don't mind. You two sit and have a talk."

Cecilia looked quickly at her cousin.

"Perhaps you'd rather be alone ?" she said to him.

"No—no," he replied. "Do keep me company for a while, if it doesn't bore you."

The windows were open, the scent of honeysuckle wafted in, with the sound of an owl. Robert smoked in silence. There was a sort of despair in his motionless, rather squat body. He looked like a caryatid bearing a weight.

"Do you remember Cousin Henry ?" Cecilia asked him suddenly.

He looked up in surprise.

"Yes. Very well," he said.

"What did he look like ?" she said, glancing into her cousin's big, secret-troubled eyes, in which there was so much frustration.

"Oh, he was handsome : tall, and fresh-coloured, with Mother's soft brown hair." As a matter of fact, Pauline's hair was grey. "The ladies admired him very much ; he was at all the dances."

"And what kind of character had he ?"

"Oh, very good-natured and jolly. He liked to be amused. He was rather quick and clever, like Mother, and very good company."

"And did he love your mother ?"

"Very much. She loved him too—better than she does me, as a matter of fact. He was so much more nearly her idea of a man."

"Why was he more her idea of a man ?"

"Tall—handsome—attractive, and very good company —and would, I believe, have been very successful at law. I'm afraid I am merely negative in all those respects."

Ciss looked at him attentively, with her slow-thinking hazel eyes. Under his impassive mask she knew he suffered.

"Do you think you are so much more negative than he ?" she said.

He did not lift his face. But after a few moments he replied :

"My life, certainly, is a negative affair."

She hesitated before she dared ask him :

"And do you mind ?"

He did not answer her at all. Her heart sank.

"You see, I'm afraid my life is as negative as yours is," she said. "And I'm beginning to mind bitterly. I'm thirty."

She saw his creamy, well-bred hand tremble.

"I suppose," he said, without looking at her, "one will rebel when it is too late."

That was queer, from him.

"Robert!" she said. "Do you like me at all?"

She saw his dusky-creamy face, so changeless in its folds, go pale.

"I am very fond of you," he murmured.

"Won't you kiss me? Nobody ever kisses me," she said pathetically.

He looked at her, his eyes strange with fear and a certain haughtiness. Then he rose, and came softly over to her, and kissed her gently on the cheek.

"It's an awful shame, Ciss!" he said softly.

She caught his hand and pressed it to her breast.

"And sit with me sometimes in the garden," she said, murmuring with difficulty. "Won't you?"

He looked at her anxiously and searchingly.

"What about Mother?"

Ciss smiled a funny little smile, and looked into his eyes. He suddenly flushed crimson, turning aside his face. It was a painful sight.

"I know," he said. "I am no lover of women."

He spoke with sarcastic stoicism, against himself, but even she did not know the shame it was to him.

"You never try to be," she said.

Again his eyes changed uncannily.

"Does one have to try?" he said.

"Why, yes. One never does anything if one doesn't try."

He went pale again.

"Perhaps you are right," he said.

In a few minutes she left him and went to her rooms. At least she had tried to take off the everlasting lid from things.

The weather continued sunny, Pauline continued her sun-baths, and Ciss lay on the roof eavesdropping, in the literal sense of the world. But Pauline was not to be heard.

No sound came up the pipe. She must be lying with her face away into the open. Ciss listened with all her might. She could just detect the faintest, faintest murmur away below, but no audible syllable.

And at night, under the stars, Cecilia sat and waited in silence, on the seat which kept in view the drawing-room windows and the side door into the garden. She saw the light go up in her aunt's room. She saw the lights at last go out in the drawing-room. And she waited. But he did not come. She stayed on in the darkness half the night, while the owl hooted. But she stayed alone.

Two days she heard nothing ; her aunt's thoughts were not revealed ; and at evening nothing happened. Then, the second night, as she sat with heavy, helpless persistence in the garden, suddenly she started. He had come out. She rose and went softly over the grass to him.

"Don't speak !" he murmured.

And in silence, in the dark, they walked down the garden and over the little bridge to the paddock, where the hay, cut very late, was in cock. There they stood disconsolate under the stars.

"You see," he said, "how can I ask for love, if I don't feel any love in myself ? You know I have a real regard for you——"

"How *can* you feel any love, when you never feel anything ?" she said.

"That is true," he replied.

And she waited for what next.

"And how can I marry ?" he said. "I am a failure even at making money. I can't ask my mother for money."

She sighed deeply.

"Then don't bother yet about marrying," she said. "Only love me a little. Won't you ?"

He gave a short laugh.

"It sounds so atrocious to say it is hard to begin," he said.

She sighed again. He was so stiff to move.

"Shall we sit down a minute ?" she said. And then, as they sat on the hay, she added : "May I touch you ? Do you mind ?"

"Yes, I mind. But do as you wish," he replied, with that mixture of shyness and queer candour which made him a little ridiculous, as he knew quite well. But in his heart there was almost murder.

She touched his black, always tidy hair with her fingers.

"I suppose I shall rebel one day," he said again suddenly.

They sat some time, till it grew chilly. And he held her hand fast, but he never put his arms round her. At last she rose, and went indoors, saying good night.

The next day, as Cecilia lay stunned and angry on the roof, taking her sun-bath, and becoming hot and fierce with sunshine, suddenly she started. A terror seized her in spite of herself. It was the voice.

"Caro, caro, tu non l'hai visto!" it was murmuring away, in a language Cecilia did not understand. She lay and writhed her limbs in the sun, listening intently to words she could not follow. Softly, whisperingly, with infinite caressiveness and yet with that subtle, insidious arrogance under its velvet, came the voice, murmuring in Italian : "Bravo, si, molto bravo, poverino, ma uomo come te non sarà mai, mai, mai !" Oh, especially in Italian, Cecilia heard the poisonous charm of the voice, so caressive, so soft and flexible, yet so utterly egoistic. She hated it with intensity as it sighed and whispered out of nowhere. Why, why should it be so delicate, so subtle and flexible and beautifully controlled, when she herself was so clumsy ? Oh, poor Cecilia, she writhed in the afternoon sun, knowing her own clownish clumsiness and lack of suavity, in comparison.

"No, Robert dear, you will never be the man your father was, though you have some of his looks. He was a marvellous lover, soft as a flower yet piercing as a humming-bird. Cara, cara mia bellissima, ti hoaspettato come l'agonissante aspetta la morte, morte deliziosa, quasi quasi troppo deliziosa per una mera anima humana. He gave himself to a woman as he gave himself to God. Mauro ! Mauro ! How you loved me ! How you loved me !"

The voice ceased in reverie, and Cecilia knew what she had guessed before—that Robert was not the son of her Uncle Ronald, but of some Italian.

"I am disappointed in you, Robert. There is no poignancy in you. Your father was a Jesuit, but he was the most perfect and poignant lover in the world. You are a Jesuit like a fish in a tank. And that Ciss of yours is the cat fishing for you. It is less edifying even than poor Henry."

Cecilia suddenly bent her mouth down to the tube, and said in a deep voice :

"Leave Robert alone ! Don't kill him as well."

There was dead silence in the hot July afternoon that was lowering for thunder. Cecilia lay prostrate, her heart beating in great thumps. She was listening as if her whole soul were an ear. At last she caught the whisper

"Did someone speak ?"

She leaned again to the mouth of the tube :

"Don't kill Robert as you killed me," she said, with slow enunciation and a deep but small voice.

"Ah !" came the sharp little cry. "Who is that speaking ?"

"Henry," said the deep voice.

There was dead silence. Poor Cecilia lay with all the use gone out of her. And there was dead silence. Till at last came the whisper :

"I didn't kill Henry. No, no ! No, no ! Henry, surely you can't blame me ! I loved you, dearest ; I only wanted to help you."

"You killed me !" came the deep, artificial, accusing voice. "Now let Robert live. Let him go ! Let him marry !"

There was a pause.

"How very, very awful !" mused the whispering voice. "Is it possible, Henry, you are a spirit, and you condemn me ?"

"Yes, I condemn you !"

Cecilia felt all the pent-up rage going down that rain-pipe. At the same time, she almost laughed. It was awful.

She lay and listened and listened. No sound ! As if time had ceased, she lay inert in the weakening sun, till she heard a far-off rumble of thunder. She sat up. The sky was yellowing. Quickly she dressed herself, went down, and out to the corner of the stables.

"Aunt Pauline," she called discreetly, "did you hear thunder ?"

"Yes. I am going in. Don't wait," came a feeble voice.

Cecilia retired, and from the loft watched, spying, as the figure of the lovely lady, wrapped in a lovely wrap of old blue silk, went rather totteringly to the house.

The sky gradually darkened. Cecilia hastened in with

the rugs. Then the storm broke. Aunt Pauline did not appear to tea. She found the thunder trying. Robert also did not arrive till after tea, in the pouring rain. Cecilia went down the covered passage to her own house, and dressed carefully for dinner, putting some white columbines at her breast.

The drawing-room was lit with a softly shaded lamp. Robert, dressed, was waiting, listening to the rain. He too seemed strangely crackling and on edge. Cecilia came in, with the white flowers nodding at her dusky breast. Robert was watching her curiously, a new look on his face. Cecilia went to the bookshelves near the door, and was peering for something, listening acutely. She heard a rustle, then the door softly opening. And as it opened, Ciss suddenly switched on the strong electric light by the door.

Her aunt, in a dress of black lace over ivory colour, stood in the doorway. Her face was made up, but haggard with a look of unspeakable irritability, as if years of suppressed exasperation and dislike of her fellow-men had suddenly crumpled her into an old witch.

"Oh, aunt !" cried Cecilia.

"Why, Mother, you're a little old lady !" came the astounded voice of Robert—like an astonished boy, as if it were a joke.

"Have you only just found it out ?" snapped the old woman venomously.

"Yes ! Why, I thought . . ." his voice tailed out in misgiving.

The haggard old Pauline, in a frenzy of exasperation, said :

"Aren't we going down ?"

She had not even noticed the excess of light, a thing she shunned. And she went downstairs almost tottering.

At table she sat with her face like a crumpled mask of unspeakable irritability. She looked old, very old, and like a witch. Robert and Cecilia fetched furtive glances at her. And Ciss, watching Robert, saw that he was so astonished and repelled by his mother's looks that he was another man.

"What kind of a drive home did you have ?" snapped Pauline, with an almost gibbering irritability.

"It rained, of course," he said.

"How clever of you to have found that out !" said his

mother, with the grisly grin of malice that had succeeded her arch smile.

"I don't understand," he said, with quiet suavity.

"It's apparent," said his mother, rapidly and sloppily eating her food.

She rushed through the meal like a crazy dog, to the utter consternation of the servant. And the moment it was over she darted in a queer, crab-like way upstairs. Robert and Cecilia followed her, thunderstruck, like two conspirators.

"You pour the coffee. I loathe it! I'm going. Good night!" said the old woman, in a succession of sharp shots. And she scrambled out of the room.

There was a dead silence. At last he said:

"I'm afraid Mother isn't well. I must persuade her to see a doctor."

"Yes," said Cecilia.

The evening passed in silence. Robert and Ciss stayed on in the drawing-room, having lit a fire. Outside was cold rain. Each pretended to read. They did not want to separate. The evening passed with ominous mysteriousness, yet quickly.

At about ten o'clock the door suddenly opened, and Pauline appeared, in a blue wrap. She shut the door behind her, and came to the fire. Then she looked at the two young people in hate, real hate.

"You two had better get married quickly," she said, in an ugly voice. "It would look more decent; such a passionate pair of lovers!"

Robert looked up at her quietly.

"I thought you believed that cousins should not marry, Mother," he said.

"I do. But you're not cousins. Your father was an Italian priest." Pauline held her daintily slippered foot to the fire, in an old coquettish gesture. Her body tried to repeat all the old graceful gestures. But the nerve had snapped, so it was a rather dreadful caricature.

"Is that really true, Mother?" he asked.

"True! What do you think? He was a distinguished man, or he wouldn't have been my lover. He was far too distinguished a man to have had you for a son. But that joy fell to me."

S

"How unfortunate all round!" he said slowly.

"Unfortunate for you? *You* were lucky. It was *my* misfortune," she said acidly to him.

She was really a dreadful sight, like a piece of lovely Venetian glass that has been dropped and gathered up again in horrible, sharp-edged fragments.

Suddenly she left the room again.

For a week it went on. She did not recover. It was as if every nerve in her body had suddenly started screaming in an insanity of discordance. The doctor came, and gave her sedatives, for she never slept. Without drugs she never slept at all, only paced back and forth in her room, looking hideous and evil, reeking with malevolence. She could not bear to see either her son or her niece. Only when either of them came she asked, in pure malice:

"Well! When's the wedding? Have you celebrated the nuptials yet?"

At first Cecilia was stunned by what she had done. She realized vaguely that her aunt, once a definite thrust of condemnation had penetrated her beautiful armour, had just collapsed, squirming, inside her shell. It was too terrible. Ciss was almost terrified into repentance. Then she thought: "This is what she always was. Now let her live the rest of her days in her true colours."

But Pauline would not live long. She was literally shrivelling away. She kept her room, and saw no one. She had her mirrors taken away.

Robert and Cecilia sat a good deal together. The jeering of the mad Pauline had not driven them apart, as she had hoped. But Cecilia dared not confess to him what she had done.

"Do you think your mother ever loved anybody?" Ciss asked him tentatively, rather wistfully, one evening.

He looked at her fixedly.

"Herself!" he said at last.

"She didn't even *love* herself," said Ciss. "It was something else. What was it?" She lifted a troubled, utterly puzzled face to him.

"Power," he said curtly.

"But what power?" she asked. "I don't understand."

"Power to feed on other lives," he said bitterly. "She was beautiful, and she fed on life. She has fed on me as she fed on Henry.   She put a sucker into one's soul, and sucked up one's essential life."

"And don't you forgive her ?"

"No."

"Poor Aunt Pauline !"

But even Ciss did not mean it.   She was only aghast.

"I *know* I've got a heart," he said, passionately striking his breast.   "But it's almost sucked dry.   I *know* I've got a soul, somewhere.   But it's gnawed bare.   I *hate* people who want power over others."

Ciss was silent.   What was there to say ?

And two days later Pauline was found dead in her bed, having taken too much veronal, for her heart was weakened.

From the grave even she hit back at her son and her niece.   She left Robert the noble sum of one thousand pounds, and Ciss one hundred.   All the rest, with the nucleus of her valuable antiques, went to form the "Pauline Attenborough Museum".

W. B. MAXWELL

THE PRINCE

In the little suburban slum between the railway and the river they called him indifferently "The Prince", "Prince Charles", or "Long Charlie".

He was a lean, tall, limping blackguard ; and at fifty years of age, with a leg stiffened by rheumatism, with his hawk nose broadened and swollen, his fierce eyes clouded and sometimes red at their rims, he showed but little of the clear-cut beauty that in youth had started his triumphs over the fairer sex. Nevertheless, he still had an air. Some quality of princeliness was still perceived by his inferiors. The costers, rag-pickers, and other riff-raff that formed the population of the river lane all bowed down before him.

Ever since adolescence he had lived upon women. As soon as he wooed and conquered one of them, he made her cook for him, sweep for him, and if necessary beg or steal for him. If she was troublesome he hit her. He did not do it as you or I would hit a woman, doubtfully and hesitatingly. He let fly. In lighter moments it was the back of his hand across her mouth, so that she abruptly seated herself on the pavement, bleeding and sobbing ; but if really incensed he drove with his right fist, and then the pavement seemed all soft as it rose to meet her, and she lay huddled, face-downward, unconscious. He allowed her to lie there until he wanted to move on. Then he stirred her with his boot. She got up, tottered, and followed him. For these and other reasons women loved him.

But a man, even though he is a prince, must have some visible means of support. Pride demands that he shall appear to earn a livelihood. Prince Charlie hawked pot-plants, limping after old ladies, bullying them, too, if he caught them unprotected, and he also cadged round the offices of all the charitable organizations of the suburb. He was known to the police and in the past had been watched by them, but they now disregarded him as mere trash.

347

At present his companion was a fine, strong, black-haired young woman named Maggie. They said that she had been an organ-grinder's girl and that there was Italian blood in her. If you washed her and made her tidy, she looked diabolically handsome. One of Maggie's own methods of washing was to take a dip in the river at dawn, or just before it. She ran down the lane and plunged.

The dark stream was almost invisible; the shadows beneath the poplars on the island, the barges, the further shore were dark as death; but the white stone bridge seemed to be made of ivory and opals, and it glimmered faintly as the first arrows of light struck it. The tale up and down the lane was that she swam stark naked. She was a good swimmer.

With the prince she proved passionate and adoring. She worshipped him. It was the devil in her that had taken his fancy and made him woo her. But the first time he wanted to chastise her she wouldn't have any.

It was up in their bedroom, with the window open to a gentle summer night, just above the lean-to shed and the rabbit-hutches of their neighbour.

"None of that, my lad," said Maggie. Quick as lightning she had snatched up a bottle and she promised to bash him with it, to split the glass all over his face.

"Put away that bottle."

"Not much."

"Put away that bottle," repeated the prince.

"Then do you promise not to touch me?"

"Yes."

"On your honour, Charlie?"

"Yes."

The moment she relinquished the bottle he knocked her down, of course. They got on well after this. Except for occasional tantrums, a fit of ugly temper once in a way, she was a sweet and docile helpmate. No one had ever worked harder for him than she did.

A good blackmailing lay of theirs was getting her clean and neat and putting her out in service as housekeeper to some innocent old gentleman. Few old gentlemen could resist her personality, and as soon as they showed any interest in it she made a false accusation. Then the prince pulled a locked trunk from under his bed, put on a comparatively decent

suit of clothes, and went to the house as the injured husband.
They made the victim pay.   If he was the sort of genuinely
nice old gentleman of whom his friends say they would never
have believed it, he paid handsomely.

A good lay!   The prince, rolling in hush-money, for a
little while resumed his full princehood.   He bought a new
suit of clothes, frequented the tavern that was used by the
bookmakers, went to Kempton Park with a train-load of the
unspeakable scoundrels that our noble English sport attracts
and maintains.   Night after night the bedroom was afloat
with liquor—black-browed Maggie filling the glasses, the
prince and two pals playing cards on the bed, and a smutty-
faced girl from the barges making music with a concertina.
It was frightfully jolly up in the bedroom.   And if you felt
sick, there was always the window.

When the company left, Maggie was eager to embrace
him, hungry for caresses.

"Oh, it's lovely to be 'ome agin with you, Charlie."

She loved him more and more.

Yet so perverse is the human heart, so limitless the in-
gratitude of princes, that he could not be true to her.

The other woman was a sort of taproom assistant at a
public-house close to the gasworks and some orchards that
now lay derelict.   After making her acquaintance, he used to
hang about this bit of waste ground and the neighbouring
roads, forgetting dinner-time in his desire for her, much as
a dog will prowl insatiable along the garden walls that hide a
female of his race.

She was a big blonde.   She had pallid blue eyes, a wide
loose mouth with a gap in the teeth that made her lisp, and her
age was uncertain—even to herself.   Why was he caught by
her?   How could he possibly prefer her, a stupid lump, to
that creature of mingled fire and fidelity?   Contrast.   Because
of her lighter colour.   Another piece of flesh, "with a different
smell to it", as he might have said himself.

He soon suspected that Maggie had discovered the intrigue.
In order to obtain freedom with his charmer, he manœuvred
Maggie to the seaside on their lay ; and the evening after her
departure he took the other home with him.

They were seated upon the bed holding each other's hands
when Maggie turned up very unexpectedly.

He was furious as well as disconcerted, but tried to pass it off in princely fashion.

"It's all right, Mag. I asked her upstairs to have a drink."

"Then why has she brought her leather bag?" And Maggie, snatching it open, pulled out a nightdress. "It's all right, yes. . . . Charlie asked you to come up the stairs. And I ask you to go down 'em—bloody quick, too."

When Charlie returned after escorting the intruder and carrying the violated bag for her, he found Maggie lying on the bed and crying as if her heart would break.

"Oh, Charlie, Charlie," she wailed despairingly. "I can't bear it. . . . Not this. You might have knocked me about—you could have done what you liked with me, but not this. . . . Oh, Prince, say you'll give her up."

He said so. He promised to give her up; and in due course he broke his promise. Once more Maggie knew. Instinctively, mysteriously, she divined the fresh betrayal.

"You've bin with that woman agin. You can't deny it."

Then a dreadful noisy scene ensued, nearly all the noise being made by Maggie. She was terrible in her passion. She frightened him. She tore her black hair; she raved, calling upon the shades of her Italian ancestry and imploring Heaven to strike her dead there where she stood if she didn't send him to kingdom-come for it. Before she had done he was trembling and stammering and meekly begging forgiveness. For the first time in his long disgraceful career one of the worms had turned. A woman had scared him.

He went out and strolled along the tow-path, feeling thoroughly upset.

Some hours later, when Maggie was absent from their room, he pulled the battered old trunk from beneath the bed and groped under all the garments and indescribable odds and ends in it for something that he kept right at the bottom—a revolver and some cartridges wrapped in oily rags. They weren't there. They were gone. Strangely, mysteriously, someone had got at them and taken them. The perspiration broke out on the back of his neck. Maggie?

When he came home that night fear was with him; quivering, disconcerting fear, fear that had pangs deeper than rheumatism, and nauseous qualms as distressful as

alcoholic sickness. There were horrid places in that lane
for a threatened man to pass—corners of walls, dark entries,
alleyways as black as pitch. He ran by some of them,
limpingly but swiftly. At home he crept up the stairs on all
fours, waiting a few moments at each tread. When he opened
the bedroom door he flung it right back and stepped aside.

But the bedroom was empty. Maggie was not there.
She did not come back that night, nor next day. She did not
come back at all.

Yet the fear remained with him. Maggie's absence was
too mysterious, too sinister. It got on his nerves.

On an evening in the autumn he had the other woman
in his room once more. Old as he was, he wanted to go
to Canada. He wanted her to go with him, but she didn't
take kindly to the notion. As he stood by the window
pleading with her, it seemed to him suddenly that Maggie,
or her ghost, was in the room. He moved hastily from the
window, and it seemed to him then that Maggie was on the
stairs. Maggie was outside too, waiting for him. Maggie
was all round the house.

"Come on. Clear out of this," he said brutally. "D'ye
hear? Go down ahead of me—an' see that there's nobody
down there. Then give me the signal, an' I'll foller."

The woman went down, and standing below the window
called up to him softly.

He came down himself and made her precede him by
a dozen paces as they went up the lane. She did not see
the motionless figure in one of the entries, and, whatever
the sensations of that watcher, she was allowed to pass.

Then as the prince came abreast, an explosion shook
the walls. The revolver made as much noise in that narrow
space as if it had been a shell bursting. Three shots were
fired, and before the third of them twenty people had come
out of their houses.

"Stop her!" screamed his lady-love. "She's killed him!"

But already men were in chase. They had seen her
running down the lane. She ran right down the lane and
plunged into the river.

The men peered and shouted, but could not see a sign
of her. There were things like her in the black flood as
it rolled by, but not her. A bargee hung a lantern over

the side of his barge, and its reflection, from the bank, looked like a dead face.

No one ever saw her again. Had her clothes drowned her, or had she succeeded in swimming across to the Middlesex shore and getting clear away ? She was a good swimmer.

THE LAST MAN IN

THE usual evening visitors were assembled in the tap-room of the Stag Inn, and Mr. Judd, the landlord, serving unassisted, had full employment. The "Stag" was a humble tavern in a poor street of a country town, but no doubt it seemed to its frequenters on this cold winter's night a snug and agreeable little club—a place of brightness and ease after the long day's toil.

Behind the tap-room was the commonly furnished and rather bare living-room, and here Mrs. Judd, the landlady, sat with a certain air of state. For her, too, the day's work was done. She amused herself, but did not labour, with some repairs to a large pile of Mr. Judd's socks and undergarments ; and, as she stitched and darned, she paused often to glance reflectively at the coal fire, the shabby armchair by the hearth, the brass clock, and the oleograph pictures, or to listen to the voices in the other room. The small-paned window between the two rooms had a red curtain drawn across it, so that one could not see the company ; but the open door permitted one to enjoy much of their jovial chaff, laughter and argument.

"Good evenin', Mrs. Judd."

Mr. Billett, an old customer, had appeared in the doorway, smoking his pipe and carrying his pot of beer.

"Good evenin', Mr. Billett. You're very noisy in there to-night. What's all the fun about ?"

"It isn't exactly fun," said Mr. Billett pompously. "We've been arguing out this London murder."

"Oh, Lor' !"

" 'Orrible business, ain't it ? But there's something very fascinating to me in a murder." And Mr. Billett put his pot of beer on the ledge just inside the door and came forward into the room.

"Yes," said Mrs. Judd. "I like a good secret murder as

much as anything in the paper. But not this sort—to be butchered in the open street. It makes my flesh creep to think of." She folded a garment with a decisive manner and laid it in her work-basket. "If that's London ways, I say you can 'ave London. Give me Bratford."

"Oh, don't be down on London. I lived there once. There's life in London."

"Yes, and death too—seemingly."

"The attraction to me of a murder," said Mr. Billett sententiously, "is the problem it offers the int'lect. To pierce the mystery, and put your 'and on the culprit. I argue in this case they'll catch him—the one as done it—the London P'lice will. The detection of crim'nals has been brought to a fine art in London."

While he spoke, a hand and arm appeared round the door jamb, and Mr. Billett's pot of beer was cautiously and stealthily withdrawn into the tap-room. Mr. Billett did not observe this action, and he smiled superciliously when the loud and jovial voice of an unseen triend addressed him.

"You talk too much, old boy," said the voice, and there were sounds of general merriment in the tap-room.

"I don't mind them," said Mr. Billett. "I won the argument in there. I was about to tell you, ma'am, that a cousin of mine belonged to the London P'lice Force once— but he dropped out of it. In many respects my cousin resembled me, for he——"

The appearance of the landlord interrupted Mr. Billett's stream of reminiscences. Mr. Judd, a red-haired, dry old fellow, had a short clay pipe in his mouth, and he carried a tray with a whisky-bottle, glass, and water-jug. On his way to his wife's table, he stopped and asked Mr. Billett a question in a confidential whisper.

"Who's that man in the corner—him that came in last ?"

"I dunno 'im. A new customer."

"None of the chaps seems to know him. And I don't care for the look of him. . . . Here y'are, missus." And Mr. Judd placed the tray beside the work-basket, and mixed a glass of whisky and water for his wife.

"Doctor's orders," said Mrs. Judd, with an explanatory wave of her needle towards Mr. Billett. "Doctor Page tells me I want it."

"I don't require a doctor to tell me that," said Mr. Billett facetiously. "I *know* I want it."

Mrs. Judd assumed considerable dignity.

"I'm not as young as I was—I'm over sixty-two years of age—and I do all my own housework still."

"That's a fact, Mr. Billett."

"We don't keep no servant," continued Mrs. Judd, "and I'm tired by the end of the day."

Mr. Judd handed her the glass. "There's your night-cap."

"Nightcap!" cried Mr. Billett. "He hasn't *laced* it like a nightcap should be. *That* ain't my style."

Mrs. Judd took the glass with the utmost dignity; but as she raised it her manner relaxed. The wrinkles about her eyes deepened, and her lips twitched under the stress of a humorous idea. "The King : God bless 'im !" And she took a sip. "Gentlemen, you may smoke." She looked round and pretended to be greatly surprised. "But you *are* smoking. Without permission—in a lady's drawn'n room? Oh, what manners !" And she laughed merrily.

"Mother," said Mr. Judd, grinning at her, "your good news has gone to yer 'ead," and he hurried back to his noisy guests.

"Ah yes," said Mr. Billett, coming to the table. "My congratulations, ma'am—and fully sincere. And may all the tale be true."

"What's the tale, indeed ?"

"Why, your son coming home."

"That's true—so far."

"And you to buy this place for your own—yes, and keep what servants you please."

"Oh, that's all neighbours' gossip." Mrs. Judd picked up a tattered sock briskly and cheerfully. "They know we expect our son, so they make him out to come home with a fortune."

"Ah, but there's more at the back of it than mere chatter-boxing." And Mr. Billett's tone had a friendly knowingness in it. "He said himself he was returning with money in his pockets."

"Yes."

"That was the expression in his letter, wasn't it ? Well, such words may mean a lot. It's how a rich man might put it—modest. A rich man don't want to boast—least of all to his own parents."

"We'll know what he meant in another month." Mrs. Judd was threading her needle with slightly tremulous fingers. "Sober and kind, Mr. Billett, is as good to a mother's heart as rich and free."

"You'll get both. Mark my words. It's the wild 'uns that turn out best in the end."

"I 'ope so," said Mrs. Judd, rather sadly.

"From what Mr. Judd has let fall now and again, I take it he *was* a wild 'un, but never a *wrong* 'un."

Mrs. Judd ignored the implied question.

"Eleven years, Mr. Billett! That's what he's been away from us. It's a long time—a long time."

"I'll drink you luck—and don't forget sincere old friends when the luck comes."

Then Mr. Billett, going back to the ledge by the doorway, discovered that his pot of beer had been removed.

"Who's taken my beer?" he asked excitedly and angrily as he plunged into the tap-room. "Which of you done this?"

"You talk too long-winded," said a voice. "Makes us dry to listen to you."

"I ask who done it!"

"You know so much," said another voice, "about the detection of criminals you can find it for yourself."

A chorus of laughter greeted this sally; one heard many voices mingling, and in the midst of the noise Mr. Billett still angrily protesting. Presently, during a lull of the animated chatter, Mrs. Judd looked up from her work and poised the darning-needle in a listening attitude.

"'Ark! That's the paper-boy. He's behind his time." And she glanced at the clock. "More'n 'arf an 'our."

The shrill voice of the newspaper-boy could be heard approaching in the narrow street.

"Horrible murder. . . . Latest particulars. . . . The London mur-der. . . ."

Mrs. Judd called to the open doorway.

"One of you gentlemen be so kind as get my paper for me—will you kindly? Don't let the boy pass the house. Young imp'll do that if there's——"

"Here he is."

The boy's shrill voice sounded at the outer door.

"Mrs. Judd's paper."

"That's right, sonnie."

Mr. Billett brought the newspaper to the doorway and stood there unfolding the double sheet.

"Would you, ma'am, grant me a glance at it ? . . . Yes—here we are. 'London's atroshus murder'." And he began to read.

"Well," said a voice, "have they caught him ?"

"Not yet. . . . Would you, ma'am, allow me to read it out, for the benefit of all parties ?"

"Certainly."

" 'It seems,' read Mr. Billett, with careful elocution, " 'that while Scotland Yard has been completely baffled——' "

"What price the p'lice now ?" asked a derisive voice.

"Don't be in an 'urry," said Mr. Billett. "Give 'em time. They're watching and waitin'. It's like a mouse in a hole, and a cat watchin'. She doesn't make any mewing. But when he shows himself, then *pounce* !"

"Go on with the print," said one of the voices.

" 'An important clue has been provided by a private individual——' "

"Brayro, puss !"—and a mocking voice attempted to imitate a cat. "Meeaw. Meeaw."

" 'The victim'—Mr. Billett read on, loudly and pompously—" 'is now practically identified as a sailor from a Monte Video cargo ship which has just left for the port of Hamburg. The evidence at the adjourned inquest to-day was of a shockin' description' "—Mr. Billett paused, looked round, and repeated with evident relish—" 'shockin' description. . . . It would seem that the face was totally unrecognizable as a human visage——' "

" 'O Lor' !" said Mrs. Judd shudderingly.

" 'So that the whole ship's company, were they here, might be unable to swear to a late comrade. The unhappy creature was prob'ly struck down from the back, and then with unparalleled ferocity the head was lit'rally beaten to a pulp.' "

"Oh," said Mrs. Judd, "it's too dreadful !" And she hid her face in her hands, as if to shut out the ugly vision that had been created by the newspaper report.

" 'But the problem becomes the more difficult of solution' "

—Mr. Billett looked round with an air of proud satisfaction. "That's what I said. It's the problem—very word I used."

"Go on with the print," said a voice in subdued tones.

" 'The myst'ry deepens. Here is a person of almost colossal statue and presoom—presoom'ble stren'th, done to death in a public and by no means unfrequented street, within fifty yards of a main art'ry of traffic, *i.* and *e.*, the Commercial Road.' (Bin there meself a score o' times.)

" 'Was the deed perpetrated by one man or by a gang? Was the motive plunder or revenge? It is like a crime woven by the morbid fancy of a sensashnal nov'list. One would say a horde o' madmen had broke loose, or demons possessed of power to render themselves invisible, or——' "

"Is that the print?" asked a voice, subdued now to a whisper.

"Yes," said Mr. Billett. "But he ain't got no more news. He runs on—embroidering like."

"Then that's enough of it."

"Yes," echoed Mrs. Judd with conviction, "that's more'n enough. It's too horrible."

Mr. Billett refolded the paper, laid it on the table, and returned to the convivial company of the front room.

Somehow or other the gaiety and light-heartedness of the assembled drinkers were evaporating. Mrs. Judd, stitching and listening musingly, heard no more laughter; the conversation had taken a serious turn; the voices, as they mingled, seemed to be sinking lower and lower towards a hushed solemnity of tone.

"Did you ever see the Tower Bridge from underneath?"

"No, I seen it from the train."

"There was a woman fell off it without hurting herself."

"Oh, that's a good 'un."

"What took you there? The football match?"

"No, the guv'nor sent me to the warehouses."

Thus the talk proceeded, but it was no longer spontaneous and easy. A silence fell once or twice, and there was a perceptible effort in the voice of the speaker who started a fresh topic. It was very curious, but it seemed as if an oppression of mind had descended upon all in the front room; and then soon it seemed as if the oppressive discomfort was spreading to the back room too.

Mrs. Judd got up, crossed to the fireplace, and put some coals on the fire.

"You're very quiet all at once," she said, turning towards the doorway.

No one answered; a silence had fallen. Mrs. Judd put on some more coals, dropped the shovel noisily, and went back to the table. Giving herself a shake, she sat down again and resumed her task.

"Well," said a voice, "I'll be saying good night."

"Good night, Mr. Price. . . . Excuse me a moment, gen'lemen."

Mr. Judd had appeared in the doorway, and he came to his wife's side.

"You're very quiet," she said, "in there to-night."

"Yes—you notice too?"

"What's caused it? Mr. Billett's reading?"

"No," said Mr. Judd confidentially, "it's the man in the corner—him as came in last. We don't know him—and it's a damper."

"Is he unpleasant? I haven't heard any strange voice all evening."

"He hasn't spoken. Just a damper. I wish he'd go."

Somebody called to the landlord, and he withdrew to fulfil the order.

"If I may trouble you again, Mr. Judd."

"Coming, Mr. Yates."

Left to herself, Mrs. Judd made a few thoughtful stitches; then she put down her work abruptly, got up, and, moving to the doorway, glanced into the tap-room without showing herself to customers, old or new. Moving again, she softly drew a chair to the red-curtained window, stood upon the seat of the chair, and cautiously peered through the glass above the curtain. Then she returned to her table once more and picked up her work. But in a moment or two the work was again abandoned with a jerk, and she called to her husband sharply.

"Judd."

"That's the missus calling you."

"What is it?" asked Mr. Judd, in the doorway.

"Come here. . . . Speak low. I took a peep, but I couldn't see him."

"No, I tell you, he sits in the corner."

"D'you say he don't talk—at all ?"

"Not a word."

"What's he had ?"

"Three glasses."

"Has he paid ?"

"No. He don't offer to pay or to go. He just sits there like a toad. And I see the others feel it same as me. Can't talk jolly. I on'y wish he'd go."

Mrs. Judd whispered sharply and decisively.

"Tell him to go."

"Shall I ?"

"Yes, you tell him to pay his score and clear out of this."

"Suppose he turns nasty !"

"Then make the excuse that you want to shut up. It *is* nigh on time. Let the lot go—and shut the door."

"Well; they're going a'ready—one after another "

"Don't stand here gaping. Do it, quick ! Tell that man to go."

The landlord went to dismiss the unwelcome guest ; and Mrs. Judd stood by her table, watching the doorway and listening intently. Her lips twitched nervously, and her hand, as it rested on the table, trembled.

" 'Ow goes the hour, eh ?"

The little company was apparently breaking up ; a cold breath of air came creeping in when somebody opened the street door ; one heard a note of leave-taking in the low-pitched voices.

"They say"—that was Mr. Veal's voice, slow and grave—"they say there's bin more influenza of the sort there has bin this winter than what there *ever* has been."

"Great deal o' sickness"—that was Mr. Carter's voice, low and solemn—"and, mind you, distress too—real distress—throughout the land."

"Good night, old boy."

"I'm on the move myself," said Mr. Billett.

"Good night to you."

Mrs. Judd, straining her ears, caught no sound of the stranger's voice.

"Well ?" she whispered anxiously, when her husband re-appeared. "Has he gone ?"

Mr. Judd put his finger to his lips as he approached.

"Has he gone?"

"No."

"Did you tell him?"

"No. But I've been speaking to him. Listen. He asks this! May he sleep here? Any shake-down will do. And he'll pay handsome."

"No, no. Don't you let him stop." Mrs. Judd had shown sudden fear. She seized her husband's arm, dragging it to her; her face was white, and she trembled violently. "Get rid of him. Get rid of him quick before all the others go. I'm scared."

"You needn't be afeared."

"It's the thought that come into my mind. . . . Suppose it was him they read of—the *murderer*."

"Oh!" Mr. Judd was looking at his wife in blank surprise. He added very feebly : "That ain't likely—at all."

"You go back—quick. No time to lose."

"Gentlemen," said Mr. Judd, hurrying into the tap-room, "you'll excuse me, but it's time I shut up—if you please. . . . What—are you off a'ready?"

The voices sounded in the street now, outside the tap-room door. "Good night. . . . Good night. . . . And good luck to you." The voices were dying away; soon all was silence.

Mr. Judd returned, rubbing his hands and speaking with unfeigned cheerfulness.

"Don't be afeared. He's gone."

"Thank goodness! It scared me."

"Must have gone while I was talkin' to you."

"Thank goodness!" Mrs. Judd gave herself a shake. "That's what I say. Thank goodness!"

"But he's sneaked off without paying."

"Never mind," cried Mrs. Judd vehemently. "I don't want that man's money. . . . Now you shut up carefully." And she packed her work into the basket. "Draw them door-bolts full—and see the chain's fast."

From the tap-room there came the noise of bolts and bars as the fastenings were adjusted.

"And put the rod firm across the shutter."

"That's firm enough," said Mr. Judd.

"Did you latch the window first?"

"Of course I did."

Then Mr. Judd turned out the gas in the tap-room and came back to the sitting-room. He laid his pipe on the mantelpiece, warmed his legs at the fire, and laughed.

"You *are* a one to get hold of rum ideas——"

Mrs. Judd had picked up a bedroom candlestick and was about to light the candle when suddenly she raised her hand as if signalling to her husband to keep quiet.

" 'Ark," she whispered. "What was that? I swear I 'eard something in there."

Judd moved hastily to his wife's side, and they both stood staring at the darkness behind the tap-room window.

"God! What's that?"

It was a tinkling crash of broken glass somewhere in the darkness; a tumbler had fallen on the tap-room floor.

"Wha—wha—what is it?" stammered Mr. Judd quaveringly.

There came a vague noise of movement; then more plainly, unmistakably heard—someone moving in the darkness of the tap-room.

"Look. Look."

A man was standing in the doorway. A slouch hat concealed the upper part of his face, but his red beard, growing high to the cheek-bones, gave him a fierce and terrible aspect. He seemed clumsy, loutish, stupid; and he spoke deliberately and slowly, with a rather thick utterance, but not as if he was drunk.

"All right," said the man. "I 'adn't gone. I was 'id be'ind the bar."

"Then outside you go now," said Mr. Judd feebly.

"I 'adn't sneaked off without paying," the man continued slowly, and with a slight chuckle. "I pay my debts. . . . You must let me stop here."

"Lis'n to me," said Mr. Judd, frightened but blustering. "You go straight to that door and draw the bolts and step out precious quick. You ought to be ashamed o' yourself."

"You can't turn me out. See? Because I want rest. I'm a boner fidy trav'ler. . . ." The man took off his hat and came forward into the room. "And I'm your own son."

Mr. Judd and his wife had drawn away to the wall as the man advanced. They were staring at him fearfully.

"Tom? No! I don't reco'nize *you* as my son."

" 'Adn't grown me beard, 'ad I ? It's all right. You can prove me. I wrote and told you I was coming. Well, I'm back sooner than I expected."

Mrs. Judd moved a few steps nearer to the man, stared at his eyes, and spoke with a breathless falter.

"Where did you write from ?"

"Rio der lar Plarter."

"Yes !" Mrs. Judd took another step towards him. "Yes—but that's no proof."

"Prove me by the fam'ly hist'ry. . . . You buried two before I was born. My sister Loo, what followed me, died o' the scarlet fever. I left for foreign parts because I'd disgraced meself over the club money that was left in the till. . . . But what's use ? Mother, don't yer *know* I'm yer son ?"

There was a pause, and then Mrs. Judd turned to her husband.

"Yes. It's Tom."

"Then what are you playing at ?" Mr. Judd looked at the man half timidly, half angrily, and, bringing out a handkerchief, wiped the perspiration from his forehead. "Where's the fun of scaring people ? Why couldn't you announce yerself like a reas'nable being ?"

"Didn't want to be messing about with a pack of strangers. . . . I'm a bit queer. See ? . . . But I was all right when I wrote. I was all right till I left Montevideo."

Mrs. Judd started and drew back.

"Montyvidyer !"

Mr. Judd echoed the word meaninglessly.

"Montyvidyer."

"When you been to Montyvidyer ?" asked Mrs. Judd in a shaky voice. "That's not the place you said—Lar Plarter."

"Same thing. That's the river. Montevideo's the city." The man put his hand to his brow and spoke with a dreamy air. "It's a grand city—Mon-te-vid-yo. . . ." He dropped his head and turned to Mrs. Judd with surly anger. "What yer looking at me like that for ? What's the matter with you ?"

Mrs. Judd had drawn right away to the wall again ; there was horror as well as fear in her starting eyes ; her lips were twitching.

"Well ? . . . Is this yer welcome 'ome ? Mother ! Aren't yer goin' ter kiss me ?"

There was a brief silence. Then Mrs. Judd shook herself, as if making a final successful effort to shake off the dark fears that oppressed her.

"Yes, of course I'm goin' ter kiss yer." She came from the wall, embraced her son, and with her arms round his neck, began to cry. "My boy! My own boy!"

"That's all right." And the son offered his hand to Mr. Judd. "Father!"

"How are yer?" And Mr. Judd shook hands. "Will you have another drink?"

"No. I mustn't drink. I tell you I'm queer—queer about the 'ead. Felt so dazed I could scarce find me way 'ome 'ere."

"Is that so?" Mr. Judd looked at his wife, who made a sign and whispered a few words to him. "I say, I think I best fetch the doctor to *you*. Doctor Page! Just acrost the road." And he moved towards the door. "He won't be gone to bed. He's a late bird—Doctor Page."

The son moved clumsily and intercepted him.

"No. You mustn't do that. I've seen a doctor—and I told him how it was. Bin pretty near choked—and then the inj'ry to th' 'ead." He looked at his parents stupidly and dreamily; then roused himself, as if trying to continue, but forgetting what he intended to say. "Yes, that's it. The doctor tells me, 'You're very queer, my fren'.' See? 'Take care,' he says, 'or you'll go off in a fit—and no doctors won't pull you out of that'."

He went to the hearth, drew the armchair before the fire, and put another chair by it to form his couch.

"I've money in my pockets—but I'm in trouble. See? I'm goin' on first thing mornin'." He said this slowly and dreamily. "Let me sleep and let me go. What yer lookin' at me, Mother? Want to hear my story, eh?" With an exertion he roused himself again to continue speaking. "Montevideo's a grand city—so's the river. Wonderful place." He stood staring in front of him; then once again roused himself. "You'd like to hear my story. Well, it's a wonderful place. Paradise for a sailorman—with money in his pockets. There's the drinking-saloons by the water, and these tamb'reen gals—Spanish half-breeds—dancing while you lap down yer liquor. Diff'rent from this set-out." And he waved his arm in the direction of the tap-room. "'Andsome and bright as parakeets—them tamb'reen gals." And he snapped his fingers. "Chikeeta! Chikeeta!"

He shuffled his feet, moved his hands as if beating a tambourine, and sang an unmelodious snatch of song. Then he stared in front of him fixedly, and there was a long silence before he went on dreamily :

"I wish I was in Montevideo now. That's where I wish I was now—down by the water, but out o' the sunshine."

Mrs. Judd had gone back to her table. She stood motionless, listening fearfully. Mr. Judd was at her side, by the table, listening stolidly and stupidly.

"Roughest lot ever I shipped with—and one as bullied me. Brought his grudge aboard with 'im." The man dropped his voice in a low grumble. "Bullying devil from hell. Thinks he'll choke me—out me in my bunk. See?" He put his hands to his throat, and gasped and grunted as if he really felt suffocation. "But they pulls 'im off of me. . . . Next time, he goes for me with an iron bolt"—and he put his hands to his head—"something cruel." Then he added dreamily, "You didn't ought to hit a man with iron.

"So that's my story, Mother." And he sat down in the armchair, and stretched his legs upon the other chair. "I'm dead beat. You must let me sleep. And you must watch and wake me. Rouse me daylight. I must go on." And he was about to settle himself in the chair when he looked round quickly. "See though. Wake me if I dream. Don't let me dream. I've been dreaming ever since. . . . Promise you'll wake me if I dream."

"Yes," said Mrs. Judd, in a dry, husky whisper, "I promise."

The man lay back in the armchair and almost immediately fell asleep. For a little while Mrs. Judd stood by her table, watching him. Mr. Judd looked at her stupidly.

"Should I turn out the gas?"

"Yes," said Mrs. Judd. "No. Turn it down—not out. Do it soft—so's not to disturb him."

Mr. Judd obeyed her ; then he pulled a chair to the table and sat down, making a slight rattling noise as his hand blundered against the tray and jug.

"Shush!"

She took a shawl, slowly crossed to the sleeping man, and

softly put it over his chest.   In all her movements she showed
dread and fear of the man.   Watching him apprehensively, she
knelt on the hearth and replenished the fire, picking the lumps
of coal from the scuttle with her fingers, making no noise.
She remained kneeling till the fire began to burn brighter, to
light up the figure of the sleeper, to throw monstrous shadows
on the ceiling and the wall.   Then she rose from her knees,
went back to her chair, and, leaning her elbows on the table,
hid her face in her hands.

The minutes dragged slowly and heavily.   Not a sound
now broke the silence, except the crisp ticking of the clock
and the stertorous breathing of the man.

"'Ark !"

The man was faintly muttering in his sleep.

"Chikeeta. . . .   Chikeeta."

He muttered indistinctly, but one could catch a sentence
here and there among the confused series of words.

"Chikeeta. . . .   All tamb'reen gals the same.   She's
my gal. . . .   Yes—my gal."

"He's on the dream," said Mrs. Judd.   "Go and wake
'im."

"Wake 'im so soon ?"

"Yes—now."

Mr. Judd got up, went across to the fire, and stood by the
man's side.   The man muttered again.

"Do as I tell you.   Wake 'im."

Mr. Judd laid his hand on the man's shoulder.

"Look 'ere.   Yer mother says time to wake up."

Then the man spoke loudly and distinctly.

"Let me and my gal alone.   See ?   My gal—an' me—
my gal."

"'Ere.   Stop it."   Mr. Judd shook the man's shoulder.
"Wake up."

"Let me alone," said the man loudly and snarlingly,
"let me alone, I say," and he threw off the shawl that covered
his shoulders.

Judd drew back, alarmed, and his wife, springing from her
chair, came and seized the man's left hand.

"Wake !" she cried.   "It's I—yer own mother. . . .
God, there's something wrong with his sleeping like this.
Wake—can't you ?"   And she pulled at his hand violently.

The man slowly released his hand and pressed it against

his breast, leaned forward in the chair, and went on talking. His eyes were still shut.

"No more your gal than my gal."

He spoke these words with an appalling fierceness; and Mrs. Judd shrank away from him, terrified.

"Any man's gal, while there's money in yer pockets. . . . Son of a dog, am I?" He was speaking with increasing passion. "Monkey-face, am I? If I am, *she* don't mind. She's chosen her monkey. See?" And his voice subsided again to indistinct mutterings.

Mrs. Judd in her terror had got behind the table; she was leaning on the table for support, as though all strength had gone from her knees.

"For the love o' mercy, wake 'im."

"I—I can't. I—I daren't."

Mrs. Judd frantically swept the tray, the jug, and the glass off the table, and they fell with a clatter and a smash.

"Wake. Why don't you wake?"

"Look 'ere. I—I'll fetch the doctor."

"No, no, don't leave me alone with 'im." And the terrified woman clutched at her husband's arm. "I can't bear it. . . . Yes, yes, I can. . . . Fetch Doctor Page. . . . Bring Doctor Page to wake 'im."

Her husband rushed through the tap-room, noisily drew the bolts of the outer door, and ran into the street, leaving the door open behind him.

The cold air crept into the warm room and seemed to freeze one's blood; the flames flickered behind the bars of the grate, lighting up the sleeper's face and his closed eyes, making fantastic shadows dance behind him on the wall; in the silence the ticking of the clock sounded like heavy, bursting heart-beats. Then the silence was broken; the man had begun to speak again.

"I'm not afraid of you—ashore or afloat. You don't put fear into me—on land or sea. . . . Bullying devil from hell."

"Wake."

Mrs. Judd came from behind the table and took two steps towards the dreaming man, as if she intended to try once more to rouse him. But her fear was too great. She stopped, with her hand on the table, as if paralysed by terror.

"Take your hands from me throat." He had lifted his

hands to his neck, was struggling in the chair. He pulled at his scarf, gasped and spluttered, as though choking. "Let me go. Let go o' me." He sank back on the chair, panting. "Thank ye, mates. Thank you kindly. He near done me that time."

"Wake!"

He was slowly coming forward in the chair.

"See here—ye swab. This don't end it. I'll pay you when we get ashore. I pay my debts. . . . Ye'll call me son of a dog! All right—but I'll pay you back. I'll swing for it—but I'll pay you."

"Wake!" The word came in a shrill scream of terror. "Wake!"

"There he goes—there he goes! . . ." He was whispering now; and, as he whispered, he raised himself, leaning right forward and pointing with an outstretched hand.

"There—there he goes." And his eyes opened, and he stared in front of him. The eyes were glassy, glittering, most horrible to watch in the silence while one waited with shuddering awe for the voice.

"Take that. Take that."

The voice had sounded loud and strong, bestially ferocious, and the dreamer was stooping from the chair and looking down at the floor.

"Where's your answer now? Speak up now. . . . There's more!" And he made violent, frightful gestures with the right hand. "There's more for you," he gasped. "And more, and more. . . . That's how I pay my debts."

He was breathless, panting; and, as he looked down at the floor, the words came in a low snarling rage.

"Answer back now. Now who's Monkey-face? Why, your own mother wouldn't know you now."

He drew back into the chair suddenly, shivering and gasping.

"No, no—not the dead man. Dead men can't—can't—can't . . ."

He raised both hands to his head with a swift motion and dropped back in the chair. Then his arms fell, hanging loosely; his head sank upon his left shoulder; and he lay quite still.

" 'Ere. This way—this way. 'Ere's 'elp at last."

Mr. Judd came hurrying through the tap-room, followed by the doctor.

Mrs. Judd stood by her table, unable to move, scarcely able to speak, in a frenzy of horror. Mr. Judd had turned up the gas and brought a lighted candle for the doctor. The doctor was stooping over the man, lifting his head, scrutinizing his eyes, feeling his breast.

"Wake 'im. Oh, wake 'im."

The doctor, looking round, spoke gravely.

"No one can wake him now. He will never wake."

"Dead ?"

"Yes."

Mrs. Judd stepped forward, dropped upon her knees, and raised his arms.

"Thank God! Thank God for that." And, sobbing and shaking, she covered her face with her hands.

C. H. B. KITCHIN

DISPOSSESSION

I

July. Two hours after midnight. The small windows of the first-floor room of 15 Cherry Lane, Chelsea, were wide open, but the blue curtains, closely drawn behind them, were shaken by no breeze. The night was hot in the street, and even hotter in the dark bedroom. Flat on its back, on the middle of an old four-poster bed, lay the body of Harry Duke, still as a corpse, and almost as cold.

Suddenly a muscle twitched beneath the sheets. The body grew warmer. A leg stirred, then a hand. The spine and loins shuddered. Drops of sweat crept through the skin. The mouth opened and gasped. An eyelid fluttered. Then the whole body heaved, while two brown hands jerked upwards over the chest and with one strong movement flung the bedclothes aside. The head shot forward. The unseeing eyes opened widely. The breath came quickly and violently.

Meanwhile the buried mind had taken shape, and struggled painfully upwards like a seed lying deep down in the earth and putting out a frail shoot past strata of peculiar perils. Each moment new visions pressed upon it, while old fears, writhing in sudden coils from a limbo of the brain, would have encircled it and dragged it down, had not the steady impulse of a growing will urged it onwards.

Half an hour later, the man got out of bed and, tottering to the door, switched on the light. At the sight of himself in a long mirror he stood for some minutes in bewilderment, and then, stripping off the silk pyjamas still drenched in sweat, looked with hesitant pride at his naked body, felt one hand with another, caressed with a lover's fingers his lips, moustache and eyes, and turning himself this way and that, as if the glass had never before reflected such an image, stroked trunk and arms and legs. Yet even while he surveyed

himself and rejoiced so strangely in his strength, a dizziness
came over him, and scarce had he staggered on to the bed
before the whole room swam round him and his eyes shut as if
never to open.   In vain he grappled with his wandering mind,
summoning all his wits to consider where he was and the
plans which were still to be made.   His senses ebbed away
and left the body as it had been before, quiet and untormented
and almost dead.

II

Harry Duke woke at eleven.   By five minutes past, he had
realized that the electric light was burning, that his pyjamas
were lying on the floor and that he was hungry and
unaccountably tired.   He wondered, also, why the alarm-
clock had not roused him at eight.   He had not expected to
be called, as the couple who attended to him had gone for
their holiday and he had counted on being well able to look
after himself for one night.   But it was irritating to have
missed the boat-train, even though there were other services
which he could take and the hour of his arrival at Wimereux
was of no great importance.
    He went to the bathroom and lit the geyser.   While the
water was being heated, he felt so ravenous that he went
downstairs in search of food.   There were some biscuits in a
canister in the sitting-room, and he ate them greedily, deciding
to have a proper meal in a restaurant as soon as he had dressed.
On his way back through the hall, he noticed two newspapers
in the letter-box.   He expected one ; but why two ?   He
hoped the Dennisons had remembered to stop the papers while
he was away.   He couldn't bother to go himself to the
newsagent that morning.   After all, a penny a day for ten
days is only tenpence.   Still, tenpence wasted . . .   Whatever had possessed the boy to leave two papers ?   With a
jerk he pulled them through the slit in the door, and looked at
them on the way upstairs.   A glance showed him that they
were different issues of the same paper.   The headlines were
not the same.   July 25, and July 26.   He'd had yesterday's
paper—but July 26—what could it mean ?   There must be a
mistake.   July 26 was to-morrow—Friday, July 26.   To-day
was Thursday.   On Wednesday, the night before, the Dennisons had left.   This was Thursday, the day he was to go to

Wimereux. On Friday he'd arranged to play golf with Grimwade's party.

After a little time, it dawned on him that he had overslept, not by a few minutes, but by more than twenty-four hours.

He lay in the bath and groaned. This time there was no escaping it. He was not well. He was—a moment's horror seized him. What could he do ? How could he go on hiding it ? What would be the end ? He was unused to mental suffering, and longed suddenly for someone to give him sympathy, for contact with another person, for an almost bodily comfort. Only one person had seemed able to understand his trouble, even to guess that he had one—that spectacled girl Joan Averil, a damned, inquisitive little fool. So far, she had been the only one to take him at a disadvantage, to realize the crisis when it came. He used the word "crisis" to describe one of a series of events which lay outside the process of his normal life. It was only lately that he had classed them together as a series. Having no gift for introspection, he had been very slow to notice any progress or similarity in the accidents which for the past eight months had been pursuing him. But now he was forced to "look facts in the face", to try to understand himself, to learn what it was that had to be cured, if cure there was.

He dried himself and, as he dressed, looked at "to-morrow's" paper. "Still no sign," he read, "of missing architect. Thousand pounds reward offered by solicitors." In his bedroom, he unlocked a drawer and brought out a bundle of manuscript, the very writing of which seemed full of fear and shame. The composition dated from his most serious attempt to take stock of himself—after the last crisis. At best, writing did not come easily to him.

The first page was headed October 26th, and the record was as follows :

"Dined with Embley and his wife and Mrs. Pole. About 10.30 went to party given by man called Grover (?) in St. John's Wood. Dancing and charades. E. said it would show me what Bohemian society was, though I must be careful not to use the word. I soon got too drunk to be shocked—not that I should have been if I'd kept sober. At 1.30 a good many people left, and a man and a woman, whose names I never caught, proposed we should go round to a party in the Adelphi. Got separated from the E.'s and Mrs. P., and faintly remember driving in a taxi with three women and another man. My head was rather clearer on arriving and I jibbed at going in, but it seemed rude to back out of it. The people at the new place were a very odd crew. I didn't know any of them and shouldn't recognize them again. There was some gambling, in which I felt too drunk to join, and some of the people seemed to be dressing and undressing and acting charades on their own. More drink. I was completely knocked out, and the last thing I remember is falling flat on a kind of divan, and someone saying, 'Come on, old chap, I'll see you home.'

"I awoke in my own bed the next day—feeling like death. My latch-key was on the dressing-table. I was too ill to get up, and as I felt even worse at night, I told Dennison to fetch a doctor. God knows I'd been drunk often enough before, but never like this. I thought I must have been poisoned—or doped. The doctor—a breezy fool—said there was nothing the matter with me except the obvious, and gave me some medicine. That night I had awful nightmares, which I can't remember. The day afterwards I felt better and got up. For about a week I had appalling dreams every night, though there seemed nothing the matter with me by day. I called in the doctor again, and he still didn't take me seriously. 'Constitution of an ox,' he said, and then murmured something about burning the candle at both ends. I paid him off, and decided to get better by myself. For a time I did.

"*December* 2nd.

"I'd been living very soberly—nothing in the nature of a binge for weeks, no worries to speak of. Physically quite fit. Dennison called me as usual, he said, and couldn't awaken me. I slept till three, and woke up in a sweat, feeling that something had happened. All the energy seemed to have been sucked out of me, and there was a kind of whirling at the back of my head, as if I was a corkscrew being drawn backwards through putty. I didn't want to eat, or read, or see anyone, and yet was terrified of going to sleep. When I did fall asleep, nothing happened. Awoke the next day feeling weak but better. Day after, quite well.

"*December* 15*th.*

"Same as December 2nd, but worse. Went to specialist to be overhauled. Cheered up on hearing there was absolutely nothing wrong with me.

"*December* 23*rd.*

"Went to the Partingtons for Christmas. The usual crowd, except for a Miss Averil, whom I hadn't met before—somebody's odd relation. Spectacles, no S.A., and very intelligent. She seemed to find me interesting.

"*Christmas Eve.*

"After dinner we had some bridge and then all sat round the fire talking and drinking punch. A cheery scene, holly and all that. Somebody told a ghost story or two, rather poor ones, and then it was suggested that we should take turns in telling what we thought was the most thrilling event in our lives. Edgar P. began with his old yarn about the bomb at the Gare du Nord. Phœbe produced an affair with a burglar, Jimmy Hale another ghost, and so on. Then it came to my turn, and I was racking my brains to see if I couldn't improve on my story of the puff adder, when the room swam round in circles, and I had the corkscrew feeling again, but somehow reversed. I managed to get out a few words, and then everything became a blank.

"N.B. The punch was fairly strong, and the room pretty hot, but I'll guarantee I've as good a head as most people, and I've never before found myself sensitive to heat or cold.

"I was naturally rather upset next day, and apologized to P. after breakfast. He seemed surprised and said he hadn't noticed anything unusual. 'How did I get to bed, then?' I asked. 'Why, by walking upstairs, I suppose,' he said. I pressed him a little further, but he seemed so convinced, in his dull way, that I hadn't done anything out of the ordinary, that I let the matter rest. He suggested I'd been having a nightmare as a result of the punch, and I half agreed with him.

"On Christmas afternoon I found myself alone with Miss Averil in the library. She made me feel uncomfortable, and I tried to escape but couldn't.

"'What regiment were you with during the war?' she asked me suddenly. I told her, and she went on to ask if I'd ever been attached to the Third Middlesex Rangers.

said I hadn't, and more than that, that I'd never even come
across anyone who had. I was a little annoyed by her curiosity,
and was afraid she was going to bring out some appallingly
sentimental memory, or tell me that I was the image of her
dead fiancé. But she hadn't finished yet, and asked me several
other questions. Where was I during the war? Partly in
England and partly in France. Whereabouts in France?
All over the place : Loos, Vimy, Arras, Fauquissart, Ypres,
Cambrai, etc. Was I ever at Miraumont? No, never. It
was one of the few bits of the line I'd given a miss to. 'But
in your story,' she said, 'on which I congratulate you, you
specially mentioned a dug-out beyond the front line between
Miraumont and Grandcourt.' 'I was never nearer either than
Albert,' I said, and went on to ask her what kind of a story
I'd told. 'D'you mean to say you don't remember?' 'I don't.
I'm afraid the punch must have gone to my head. I suppose
it was absolute rot.' 'Not at all,' she replied. 'Well, then,
what was it?' She seemed unwilling to tell me just then,
and before I had time to get it out of her we were interrupted. She had to go to London that night, and all she
managed to say to me before she left the house was : 'Give
me your address and I'll write to you.' I gave her my card,
and said good-bye, hoping that I should neither see her nor
hear from her again.

"The rest of the visit was quite ordinary, and I tried to
put the business of Christmas Eve out of my mind."

Next in the bundle of manuscript came some sheets of
blue notepaper covered with a careful and feminine hand.

January 4th.

Dear Mr. Duke,
*In case you have really forgotten the amazing story you
told us on Christmas Eve, I send it you now. I have a good memory,
and have tried to use your own phrases. You told it well. Indeed—
forgive me—I think you will find the style hard to recognize.*
*I feel I understand something about you that you don't. If I
can help you at any time, I shall be very glad to do so. I live normally
with my parents in Flat 50, Clarence House, Park Lane.*
Yours sincerely,
Joan Averil.

Mr. Duke's Story

"In January 1917, I was a junior subaltern with the 3rd Middlesex Rangers. The battalion had charge of a vast and vague area of mud in the Somme district. The whereabouts of the enemy's lines was hardly known. All landmarks had been destroyed, and what with the mist that overhung the desolate region and the absence of all tracks, means of communication were hazardous and primitive.

"With a few men, I was in charge of an outpost, the position of which was at the time recorded on none of our maps, somewhere between two ruinous areas which had once been the villages of Miraumont and Grandcourt. Apart from visits to my chilled and sodden sentries, I had little to do—or, rather, I did little; for I dare say I could have found many duties had I sought them. The deep dug-out left to us by the retreating enemy, in which I spent my idle hours, was divided into two parts, separated by a hanging blanket. My men lived in the larger and I in the smaller, which was so small that, though they were eight or nine, and I was only one, I was almost as cramped for room as they.

"One morning, before daybreak, my sergeant was shot in a sudden burst of machine-gun fire while on patrol. The men with him brought the body to the dug-out and I told them to let it rest in my cell till night; for it was impossible to carry it back to our headquarters during daylight.

"The body lay on the floor, covered by a waterproof sheet, and I on a wire trestle beside it. I had no horror of corpses that had met with a clean death. Indeed, it seemed companionable to have it there, and before long I lifted the waterproof sheet and looked at what lay beneath with sad curiosity. The only sign of the wound was a little stain on the tunic near the heart. Except for the absence of all breathing, you would have taken the body for that of a man who was asleep.

"It was a fine sergeant we had lost—a little stupid, but brave and magnificently strong. I remembered having seen him stripped at the baths, and noticing his healthy skin and well-built, powerful limbs. And now, as I looked at his calm face, it was not without a sense of jealous inferiority that I thought of my own poor body, stunted and thin, never free from some ache or uneasiness. You laugh as I say this, *but perhaps I am not the man I seem.* How wretchedly unjust, I thought, that I should go through life burdened with this corpse of mine, this miserable mass of nerves and skin perpetually hampering the exercise of my will and brain, and destined one day to harry me to death. Why could I not fall asleep and find myself rid of it, wake up as a new creature with a body equal in vigour to my mind? Must it be that these legs and arms beside me—and as the thought came to me, I stroked them gently—that firm flesh, those splendid muscles, still fully fit for living, even though dead, should moulder into decay and no use be found for them? So great was my disgust with Nature's law, so intense my despair at falling so far short of a perfection which, strangely enough, seemed almost attainable, that a mood of reckless agony came over me, and, hardly knowing what I did, I stretched myself out over the sergeant's body, my mouth on his mouth, my legs along his legs, as Elisha stretched himself upon the Shunammite's son whom he raised from the dead. . . .

"When I opened my eyes, it was my own face, pale and horrible, that I saw above me, my own body that lay on the top of me; but when I thrust it away, it was the sergeant's hand that moved. Triumphant in my new form, I stood up, and, gazing with hatred at the prostrate body that had been mine, I kicked it heavily in the ribs and covered it with the waterproof sheet that had covered the sergeant's body. Then, being still somewhat unsteady on my new-found legs, I sat down on the floor, lay back and laughed with joy.

"An hour later, my servant found me, bruised and numb, under the waterproof sheet."

III

At this point Duke pushed the bundle of papers aside, and lit a cigarette with nervous fingers. The story, not being written by himself, still moved him. When he had first received it, he had almost been amused. Later, when chastened by the next "crisis", he had written a short note to the sender, begging her not to bewilder him any more. Her reply, from the South of France, assured him that the story was substantially as he had told it. Then why, he had wondered, if by any strange chance this was the truth, had none of the others spoken to him about it ? Of course, they were a dull and stupid crowd. Perhaps they had all, except for the one attentive listener, been half asleep, half drunk, and hadn't understood what he was saying—or, if they had, disliked it and did not wish to mention it again.

One thing reassured him. The story was objectively untrue. Apart from regimental records, there were many living people who could vouch for his never having been near Miraumont and Grandcourt. At the beginning of 1917, he had been a company commander in a battalion stationed near Merville. This was a crumb of comfort, but his telling of the story, and its reference to himself, if any, was still mysterious. Was it a dream ? Had he talked in his sleep ? Perhaps. But he had had too many strange dreams to feel easy about even them.

Forgetting the need of breakfast, he walked round his bedroom in agitation. The newspaper—"to-morrow's" newspaper—was lying on a chair, and caught his eye. He picked it up and read it as he walked.

"Still no sign of missing architect. Thousand pounds offered by solicitors. . . .

"The whereabouts of Mr. de Milas are still unknown. He was last seen at his residence, 22 Amboyne Road, Adelphi Terrace, by his housekeeper, Mrs. Garley, about half past two on Wednesday afternoon. He was then going upstairs to rest in his bedroom. Mrs. Garley first became uneasy at nine o'clock, when a manservant, sent to the bedroom, reported that it was empty.

"Mr. de Milas is a gentleman of considerable means and somewhat eccentric habits. He is described as an architect, but it is not known when or where he exercised that profession. He served with the infantry during the war, and his age is now about forty-five. For some time his health has given cause for anxiety."

Anxiety, anxiety, anxiety, thought Duke, throwing the paper down in disgust. Was there no escape from trouble, other people's and one's own ? Was he never to get back to ordinary life, cheerful society, cards, games, and horses ?

How had this blight come upon him, this train of odd symptoms that seemed to pursue him from within, drawing him inwards, making him think too much about himself? Yet it had to be faced. He was worse, not better. With a sigh, he sat down and turned again to the manuscript :

"*February* 16*th*.

"I was to ride Lady Foyle's Halsettia in the Lauderbrake Steeplechase. A year ago I came in third on Diamond Claw, and this year hoped to win. The evening of the day before the race I had a feeling that something was wrong. A bad night, but no dream that I can remember. Felt very low at breakfast. Took my temperature. Normal. Very angry with myself. Wondered if it was simply funk, though I'd never been taken that way before. Decided to force myself to carry on, even if I broke my neck. Anything's better than being out of things. 11 a.m. violent headache. Had to go to bed, in great pain. Wired unwell. Headache easier by 4 p.m. Fit as a fiddle by 6. Johnson, who rode instead of me, was thrown and killed at the second jump. Outcry in papers about course being too dangerous.

"*March* 25*th*.

"Awoke very late. Dazed. Felt like a sleep-walker. Early to bed.

"*March* 26*th*.

"Too feeble to get up. Dozed most of the day. Refused to have doctor sent for.

"*March* 27*th*.

"The same. At night an extraordinary dream. These are the only bits I can remember.

"I seemed to be in a kind of orderly-room—bare boards and tables, and army forms, etc. Through holes in the wall, I could see wild flowers bending in the wind. The sun was setting, and I got caught in a long red ray, which made me unable to turn round. Suddenly a voice—behind me or in the ceiling—said, 'Is it impossible for us to get on better?' 'Who are you?' I asked. 'Can't you see?' I made a great effort and turned round, but could see no one.

"I went out into the fields, and all at once the voice said

again, 'You must take me for granted without seeing me, then. You laugh, *but I am not the man I seem*. After all, what have I done to you ? I have caused you really so little pain. Of course, I apologize for the Christmas joke. But I saved your life, though you may not know it. Oh, don't think I'm a clairvoyant. You are a good rider and might perhaps not have been killed. But you were too valuable for me to take the risk.'

"The voice went on speaking for a long time, till I found myself alone with someone in the room in the Adelphi where the party of October 26th was given. 'If ever you want a refuge,' the voice said, 'you can have what I can provide. Even you might be ill, or in trouble. Look !' At this point I felt as if I was going to learn an amazing secret, but the room was suddenly draped in thick red curtains, which opened and closed, showing me little pieces of something and blotting it out again. I can't remember what it was that I was so eager to see, but each time I looked I had the sensation that I was escaping from my body. Then the curtains swooped down on me and smothered me till I died. After my death, which wasn't painful, I looked into the orderly-room, and saw myself lying on the table. I longed terribly to be alive again, and took my body in my arms, intending to carry it home, but wherever I went, I found red curtains in the way. Then the voice spoke again, but I have forgotten what it said.

"Woke up very late the next day, weak, but better.

"*April 2nd.*
"To Vinton, nerve-specialist. Talked a lot about dual personalities and psycho-analysis. Don't trust him.

"*April 6th.*
"Hear that Phillips—poor chap—had been to Vinton for two months before he committed suicide. Panicked, and decided not to go to V. again.

"*May 18th.*
"No crisis, but since I've decided to keep notes on my 'case', had better put this down. Met Miss Averil, at the Jordans' party—only for a few minutes. She asked me if I had been telling any more stories. I felt very awkward, and she saw it. Suddenly I blurted out, 'Do you think I have a

double personality ?' She said, 'No, not exactly, in the ordinary sense of the words. Won't you tell me more about your trouble ?' Then we were interrupted, and feeling a fool, I managed to slip away.

"*June 4th and 5th.*

"Very like March 4th, 5th, and 6th, but no dream. Worried, on 'recovering', whether I'm becoming different from what I was. In my body, I feel as well as I ever did, but I can't be so certain of my mind. Remembered Jekyll and Hyde, which frightened me. If I have a 'double personality', can anything be done about it ? But Miss A. seemed to think it wasn't that. What does she know about these things ?"

IV

For luncheon, he had gone to a quiet restaurant near his house. He had given up all intention of going to France, but had made no other plans. He could think of nothing but himself, his mind and his body, and something that seemed to be occurring in both of them. As he walked back home, he noticed the newspaper placards : "Missing architect still untraced."

When he reached his house, he had a strong impulse to go to bed, but was afraid to do so. He felt himself to be in a state receptive of extraordinary influences. There was a continual drag on his brain, paralysing his capacity for action and urging him to look inwards. More and more, he seemed to be dreaming, and wondered how it is that we ever know the difference between dreams and waking life. Some of his thoughts seemed to be his own, and others the product of an alien mind. These would come suddenly, in the midst of his own mental sentences, interrupting them as a heckler might interrupt an orator. "*Give in, give in. Cease to struggle,*" an inner voice kept saying, and again with an insidious sweetness, "*Come with me. Follow me. Find where I am.*"

At four o'clock, when for a few moments the tension relaxed, he looked out Miss Averil's number in the telephone book.

"Miss Averil ?"

"Yes."

"My name is Duke."

"I remember. What is it?"

"I'm in great trouble. I need someone to help me badly. I'm slipping away—slipping out of myself. Can you help me?"

"I'm in bed, recovering from measles—not ill, but infectious. Tell me everything from the beginning."

"Wait a minute, then. I've got some stuff written down, which I could read you."

He put down the receiver, and went upstairs.

"Come with me. Follow me. Find where I am."

He looked for his manuscript in the wrong drawer.

"Give in. Give in. Let yourself go. Sleep, while I wake."

At length he found the manuscript, and went downstairs: "Miss Averil?"

There was no answer. He looked hurriedly in the directory and rang up again.

"Can Mr. Duke speak to Miss Averil, please?"

"Speak to whom?" asked the voice of an old woman.

"Miss Averil."

"I'm afraid you've got the wrong number. This is Mr. de Milas's house."

"Is there any news of Mr. de Milas?"

"Who is that speaking, please?"

Horrified, he rang off.

A newspaper-boy was shouting in the street. Duke went to the door, bought a paper, and took it with him him to the telephone. "Three o'clock results." . . . *"Follow me. Find me. . . ."* "Missing Architect. . . . Mrs. Garley admitted that she had been surprised by her master's absence from the house on one or two previous occasions, and, on being pressed for the dates of these, identified one of them with February 16th, which she remembered because it was the day of the Lauderbrake Steeplechase. Her nephew had persuaded her to put five shillings on Halsettia, the ill-fated horse which was killed with its rider, Captain Johnson. But her master had walked into the dining-room at about nine o'clock that evening, and she had thought no more of the matter. . . ."

"Follow me. Follow me. Follow me home."

"Mr. de Milas also, it seems, disappeared towards the end of March. It is true he had told Mrs. Garley that he might find it necessary to be absent from the house for a time, but as he seemed far from well, and gave no instructions about his luggage, she was uneasy till she saw him sitting in the drawing-room at tea-time three days later. . . ."

"Sleep, while I wake."

"He was also away on the fourth and fifth of June, but as he had packed a small handbag she felt no anxiety. The strangest part of the mystery is that on none of these occasions did Mrs. Garley see her master leave his house or return to it. . . ."

"You laugh, but you are not the man you seem."

Very quietly, Duke picked up the telephone receiver and asked for a number.

"Can I speak to Miss Averil, please ?"

"This is twenty-two Amboyne Road, Mr. de Milas's house. Who is that speaking, please ?"

"I am the missing architect, Mr. de Milas."

"Oh, sir, is that you ? This is Mrs. Garley speaking, sir. Doctor Polder made me notify the police the day before yesterday that you were missing from home. We've all been very anxious about you, sir."

"I shall soon be home."

"I'm sure I'm very glad to hear that, sir. We've———"

He put down the receiver, went up to his bedroom, and lay on the bed. A force seemed to be entering him, in spiral fashion like a corkscrew, while at the same time his normal will drained away, leaving the body without resistance. And yet at that very moment he had a sense, that he had never had before, of the preciousness of his body, its vigour and the perfection of all its organs. "This is your treasure," a voice seemed to murmur, "this is what you can give me. Forget your foolish little mind with its racing debts, its games of golf, its dances. Be generous to me, and give all you can freely. I have great need of you."

Then, after a period of silence during which Duke opened his eyes and saw the familiar things in the room shrinking and dwindling away, a rhythmical whisper seemed to flow gently along his spine. At first the words, if they were words, were too indistinct for him to catch, and sounded like a mere pulsation in common time. But soon the beat quickened, and became more staccato and articulate. "Go and find me. Go and find me. Leave this body. Go to mine. Go to mine.

Leave this body free for me." The words were repeated
monotonously, and at the same time Duke seemed to assent
of his own volition and to be persuading himself to yield.
"After all," he thought, "why shouldn't I do as he asks,
poor devil? Why shouldn't I give him a chance? He may
make better use of me than I can. Come! I'm ready."

But as if even this generous submission were not enough,
the rhythm of the summons grew suddenly more imperious,
irregular and desperate. "Let me in. The time is so short.
Let me in. Your place is in the black box, in the cupboard.
Go and hide there, in what I'm leaving you. Five minutes!
Only five minutes! Give me yourself for five minutes! The
black box in the little room. You've been there before. Go
again now, just this once, and save me. Save me, and give
me peace. Help! Help! I'm choking . . ."

The last word went through Duke's body as if a claw
were tearing him apart. For an instant, he seemed poised on
the edge of an unfathomable void, while the smell and touch
of clammy flesh came over him and squeezed him together
in a small and narrow space. "The grave," he thought, "the
grave!" And with a convulsive movement, he threw out his
arms and legs.

All at once the rhythm ceased, and he was filled with a
sane and miraculous calm. A distant lorry rumbled towards
the river. The clock on the mantelpiece ticked gently. Duke
opened his eyes and looked at it. Five minutes past six. Then
urgently the telephone bell rang downstairs.

"Hello. Is that you at last, Mr. Duke? Joan Averil
speaking. I've tried eight times to get you."

They had a long conversation, in which, full of wisdom,
she told him what to do.

v

"Missing Architect Found.

"Mrs. Garley's Extraordinary Story.

"The mystery of the disappearance of Mr. de Milas was
solved yesterday evening in an amazing and tragic fashion.
Mrs. Garley states that she was disturbed several times during

the afternoon by telephone calls from persons who had, as they thought, recognized Mr. de Milas from his photograph in the Press, and were eager to give information as to when and where they had seen him. In each case, Mrs. Garley requested the speaker to communicate at once with Mr. de Milas's solicitors or the police. Two of the calls, however, were of an unusual nature. On both occasions a man's voice began by asking to speak to a lady, whose name Mrs. Garley did not catch. On Mrs. Garley's suggestion of a wrong number, the speaker did not ring off at once, but in his first call asked for news of Mr. de Milas, and in his second call announced that he was Mr. de Milas himself. It is now thought that the inquiry was a piece of facetiousness on the part of some irresponsible person who had accidentally been given Mr. de Milas's number instead of the number he required, and that on a repetition of the same accident, the unknown was so far exasperated as to be guilty of a joke in exceedingly bad taste, pardonable only on the assumption that he was ignorant of the circumstances into which he was intruding.

"No further incident occurred till shortly after seven, when Dr. Polder, who had attended Mr. de Milas during his illness, called at the house and asked Mrs. Garley if she knew of a black box belonging to her master. It seems that the doctor had been rung up about a quarter to seven by a man who purported to be speaking for Mr. de Milas. The speaker had requested him with great urgency to visit Mr. de Milas's residence and search it for a black box, which he was to open immediately. He was assured that the opening of the box would throw a light on Mr. de Milas's disappearance, and that circumstances might arise in which medical skill would be essential. Mrs. Garley replied that there was such a box in a big cupboard opening out of Mr. de Milas's bedroom. To her knowledge the box—an old-fashioned leather trunk—had not been used or opened for some years. She accompanied Dr. Polder to the cupboard in question and saw the box in its usual position. The doctor attempted to lift it into the light, but could not do so owing to its great weight. He then asked Mrs. Garley to bring him a candle or lamp, and when she had left the room, he raised the lid of the box, which was unlocked. *Inside, huddled up on some blankets, was the dead body of Mr. de Milas.* The body was fully clad, and covered in part by a waterproof sheet such as was used extensively by soldiers during the war. . . . It is the opinion of Dr. Polder that death occurred about six o'clock the same afternoon, though the body might have been in a trance or state of catalepsy for several hours beforehand.

STOP PRESS:

"Call to Dr. Polder traced to Piccadilly Subway."

So ran the account of the finding of the missing architect as given to the public. Two people alone could have added substantially to it—Harry Duke, who was playing golf at Wimereux, and that devotee of psychical research, Joan Averil, who was recovering from measles in Park Lane. But neither of them cared to do so.

BEAUTY AND THE BEAST

A FAIRY TALE

FOR two hundred and fifty years the Jewish family of the
Lentworths had intermarried with the best English blood.
Unlike their weaker brethren, they did not try in any way
to hide the origin proclaimed by the Oriental fullness of
their lips and noses and their fine dark hair. Though no
one could remember a time when they did not profess the
Christian religion, they paid open homage to their ancestry
in their children's baptismal names, taking them neither
from pagan mythology nor from Anglo-Saxon roots. Instead
of Hermiones and Alexanders, Henrys and Harolds, we find
their pedigree composed of Daniels, Abrahams, Ruths and
Rebeccas, while the history of the line shows the same
character, proud, masterful and splendid, bequeathed from
generation to generation, no less constantly than the names.

Of one trait, commonly ascribed to the Jews, they had
perhaps too little. Though in the reign of Queen Anne
they had possessed great riches, two centuries of glorious
prodigality had so reduced them that, by the time Sir Abraham
Lentworth (thirteenth baronet and fifth to bear that fore-
name) was head of the family, his lands were but a fraction
of the old estate and cumbered with heavy mortgages. He
himself was far from thriftless—indeed, his parsimony bore
hardly on his three children, Deborah, Miriam and Gabriel—
but he had no gift for increasing his resources, and ill-luck
added to the havoc wrought by mismanagement. By nature
he was a lover of solitude, something of a scholar and a
collector of such antique curiosities as were not beyond his
means. All commonplace festivities filled him with dis-
pleasure, and he deprived his children, whose mother had died
when Gabriel, the youngest, was only three years old, not
only of those gaieties to which their rank entitled them, but

even of the common cheerfulness of a well-conducted home.

The children, especially Miriam and Gabriel, had much of that mercurial disposition which had often been remarkable in their forebears. Had there been wealth to squander, they would have squandered it—chance of adventure, they would have seized it greedily. Indeed, Gabriel, after coming many times into collision with his father, ran away to London and lived on the charity of an artist whom he had met during a holiday in France. At the time of his flight he was nineteen years old, and had great charm both of mind and body.

A few months after Gabriel's rebellion, when the quiet of Lentworth Manor was no longer broken by Sir Abraham's outcries against the conduct of his son, Miriam received an invitation from Lady Pinnerlee, a newly enriched neighbour in the county, to go with her to Monte Carlo as companion. Lady Pinnerlee, a widow and a person of no consequence either in her late husband's right or her own, was, after her period of mourning, setting about the enjoyment of those pleasures which her means made available for her, and had resolved to spend a long time abroad, where there would be fewer to recall her origin and early years. A Lentworth could not fail to add a lustre to her party. Moreover, she reflected, she was doing the girl a great service by taking her away from the dullest and most uncongenial of homes to an earthly paradise where there would be no lack of eligible youths to grace the Pinnerlee dinners.

Miriam, though her shrewdness allowed her no doubts as to the quality of Lady Pinnerlee's kindness, accepted the invitation at once. In this she was obeying her father's wish; for the old man, little foreseeing the amazing consequences of the visit, had reasoned that the maintenance of one daughter at home should cost but half the maintenance of two. Nor did he regret that it was Miriam who was to leave him, since she showed none of her sister's assiduity in waiting upon him, and had displeased him more than once by speaking in favour of her brother.

On leaving Lentworth, Miriam went to London, where she spent a week with her hostess. She had been given the present of a hundred pounds with which to buy such outfit as she needed. All the expenses of her journey were to be paid, and in addition she was to receive a wage cf five

pounds a week. To Miriam, who had never enjoyed such
riches before, the visit to London seemed so delightful that
she could not imagine herself happier. But her choice of
clothes was so exquisite and reckless that she had to borrow
a further sum from Lady Pinnerlee's younger daughter,
Gwendolen, to be repaid at her convenience. She had a
strong hold on Gwendolen's affections at the time, and did
not scuple to promote it, judging it wise to provide herself
with at least one ally among her fellow-travellers.

After an easy journey, the party, which numbered five
persons—Lady Pinnerlee, her daughters Hope and Gwendolen, a cousin named Vera Saunders, and Miriam—established itself at one of the best hotels on the Riviera. The
season was at its height, and the concourse of rich and idle
people, despite the manifest inferiority of many among them,
produced in Miriam an elation which she could scarce conceal.
She was enchanted, too, by the novelty of the scene, the
profusion of flowers, the palm trees, the blueness of the sea,
the clearness of the air, and most of all, it may be, by the
knowledge that the whole stretch of that coast existed shame-
lessly for the pursuit of pleasure. She had left behind all
sickly talk of duty and abstinence in the fogs of her own
country. For the first time she could consort with those
who shared her feelings on these matters ; for she had no
misgivings as to the best use a man may make of this life, into
which he is plunged willy-nilly at the whim of his parents,
and out of which he is taken, often when it is least convenient
for himself to go.

Thus it was that, having a greater readiness for enjoyment—as perhaps also for wretchedness—than any of her
companions, she flung herself with zest into the round of
festivities, and by her own adroitness contributed much to
the diversion of her fellow-guests. It may be that Lady
Pinnerlee felt a pang of jealousy when she saw the paid
attendant thus outshining her own daughters ; for it was
on Miriam that strangers first fixed their roving eyes. It
was to Miriam that the handsome manager of the hotel
gave his most gallant smile as he strutted each evening among
his dinner-tables. And it was Miriam, without a doubt,
who made the most desirable friends. Frequently, indeed,
men and women of distinction came up to her on learning
her name, and claimed acquaintance with her father or an

z

uncle or a cousin, while they showed no eagerness to prove any such link with Lady Pinnerlee.

At that time the pleasure of gaming had the chief place among the amusements of Monte Carlo, and Miriam was not unnaturally disposed to make trial of her luck at the tables, where a fortune might be won without effort, while her small means would not suffice to lose one, however great her folly. The first day she had a fine success and made her capital of one hundred francs into two thousand. The second day her stakes were larger, and she came away with a loss of seven hundred. The third day she lost the remainder of her winnings and three hundred francs besides.

Lady Pinnerlee, like all those who have no need of money, risked only the smallest sums, and when she did so rarely failed to win. On hearing of Miriam's losses she cautioned her severely, and urged her either to save such money as she had, or, if she must spend it, to lay it out in gloves and stockings, which could be bought more cheaply than in England. But Miriam paid no heed to this wise rebuke, and, whenever she could, would visit the Casino by stealth, raking together some forty or sixty francs in the hope of setting her affairs to rights. But she was still unlucky, and the continued drain upon her pittance caused her many an unhappy moment. She would often find herself without the money to pay for her tea or an omnibus ticket, and it was not long before she began to borrow small sums from any who would lend. Such lamentable conduct could not long be kept from Lady Pinnerlee, who was, moreover, but lately informed of the loan made to Miriam by Gwendolen. With much heat she forbade Miriam to go any more to the tables under pain of dismissal. It was dishonourable, she said, when under a monetary obligation, not to save every penny to pay back the debt.

But Miriam, despite a show of contrition, could not desist from her new habit. Waiting till she had at her disposition three hundred francs, she went once more to the gaming-rooms and played with desperate boldness. She first lost a louis on the number twenty-four, then gained four louis on the red but, leaving stake and winnings for another spin of the wheel, lost both. Nor was a five-louis piece on the middle dozen more successful. A sudden confidence then came to her that the next number would be twenty-nine, but so great was the crush of bodies round the table that she

:ould not stake her money till it was too late. One of the
ittendants threw the counter back to her as the ball ran into
he groove of the number she had chosen. Filled with anger,
he strove to make her mind receptive of another impulse,
ind after a few seconds' straining, it seemed to her that an
inward voice suggested number three—and on this number,
vhich she could not remember ever to have won, she placed
ier last five louis. To her undoing, and that of many others,
t was the turn of zero.

Nothing remained for her now save to quit the table
with an air of indifference; for every time she had used her
ast counter she felt as if the croupier had proclaimed her
iankruptcy aloud. While, then, she walked slowly away,
like one who debates whether to return home or to play
:lsewhere, where higher stakes are allowed, she was addressed
iy a fat man with a broad face and a vigorous brown beard.
He might have been sixty, but for all that was hale and hearty.
Miriam had seen him before, and fancied that he took an
nterest in her.

"It goes badly to-night?" he asked, with a foreign accent
hat was not French.

"Oh," she answered untruthfully, "not too badly."

"Still," he said, "it is not the moment when one would
lespise a fortune?"

"Indeed, no."

"Then spare me one moment in the gardens," he said,
'and I will put a fortune in your grasp."

Miriam had little doubt but that the old man was about
o make an infamous proposal to her, but this did not greatly
ilarm her. When the time came, she could weigh the merits
)f his offer, and in the meanwhile she might well find speech
with the stranger more diverting than the solitude of her room
n the hotel. Accordingly, she gave him her cloakroom
icket—glad to have his assistance in this, since she had not
o much as two francs left with which to make the gratuity
—and after he had obtained her wrap they went outside
ogether.

"If you fear," he said after a pause, "that I have dis-
ionourable intentions towards you, set your mind at rest.
All I ask is that you will perform a simple mission for me,
which, I promise, will bring you more than a thousand Eng-
ish pounds. Here is a key, and here is a letter addressed

to such-and-such a branch of the Deutsche Bank in Hamburg
You will leave this place to-morrow by the afternoon train
and, when you reach Hamburg, you will deliver the letter a
the address which is written on it.   You will then receiv
from the bank a tin box, which you will carry back to you
lodging and open.   What is to follow I leave to your dis
cretion ; for I see that you are a woman of uncommon bold
ness and resource.   Here I have five thousand francs wit
which to pay the expenses of your journey.   What is you
answer ?"

To come to quick decisions was part of Miriam's nature
She foresaw how dreary Monte Carlo must be to one in he
penniless state, and how hard it would be to resist the com
mission of a monstrous imprudence, such as pledging the cred
of her hostess.   She thought, moreover, that the old man wa
speaking the truth, and that she really would become possesse
of a thousand pounds ; for it was not likely that he woul
have given her five thousand francs had there been nothin
in what he said.   Added to this, the prospect of adventur
attracted her for its own sake.   It is not surprising, therefore
that she soon resolved to go, upon which the old man, answer
ing none of her questions, gave her the money, the envelop
and the key, and bade her good night with a low bow.

The next morning Miriam told Lady Pinnerlee that a
telegram had called her to the bedside of her father, anc
that she must go that very afternoon.   As a precaution
she sent a telegram to her sister Deborah, enjoining her to
post no more letters to Monte Carlo and also to hide any
letters which Lady Pinnerlee might send to Lentworth
She could count upon her sister's discretion, if not upon
her approval.   If anything went amiss with her plan, the
worst that could befall her was to lose her father's and Lady
Pinnerlee's good opinion.   And of that there was no longer
much to lose.

.   .   .   .

Having arrived in Hamburg without mishap, she chose
a cheap hotel, and lost no time in presenting the envelope
to the bank.   As the old man had foretold, the clerk gave
her a tin box, and asked her to sign a receipt for it.   She
did so, using the name of Constance Green.   She then

hastened back to her lodging, bolted her bedroom door, laid the box on her bed, and opened it. Great, indeed, was her joy when she saw what it contained—gold coins and banknotes of all countries. Having some knowledge of the rates of foreign exchange, she made a quick estimate of their value, which was no less than eleven hundred pounds. In the midst of this wealth was a sheet of paper, on which was written a message in several languages—English, German, French, Italian, and others which were unknown to her The English rendering ran thus :

So far, well done. To-morrow, at noon, go to 97 Baumwollenstrasse. Open the door with the key which opened this box, then bolt the door from within. Be faithful to your mission and you will earn great riches. If you speak of it to others, you do so at your peril.

Brown Beard.

Well might a more timid soul have quailed at these words, so peremptory and so mysterious. "Why not," urged prudence, "leave the country hurriedly, with such spoils as you have ?" But Miriam was cast in a robust mould, and, as she took her tea in one of the pavilions by the waters of the Alster, she thought with joy of her strange destiny. The possession of the money—a larger sum than she had ever been likely to handle in her life—filled her with joy and prepared her for bold deeds.

Early next morning she bought a map and found where Baumwollenstrasse lay. With guarded questions, she learnt that that quarter of the town was mean and squalid. But it seemed there still remained, though in great disrepair, a few streets of fine old houses, and she surmised that number ninety-seven might be one of these. In this she was right. After taking a carriage to a square which, from the map, she judged to be about half a mile distant from the street she wished to find, she made the remainder of her journey on foot, having committed all that portion of the map to memory. The first streets through which she went were ruinous and dirty. Children with pinched faces played in the gutters while their mothers and fathers were at work. The beginning of Baumwollenstrasse was not dissimilar, but the last five houses on the western side were of ample proportions, and in former days might have belonged to prosperous citizens. The last house of all, flanked by a muddy canal, was number ninety-seven.

Unhesitatingly Miriam went up the steep flight of steps which led to the door. A distant clock struck noon. Without pausing to try the handle, she thrust her key into the lock and turned it. The door opened easily, and after shutting and bolting it she walked into a somewhat dark and narrow hall, in which she could see no stairs, but a number of doors. On one of them was a piece of cardboard which bore the English words :

Come in and shut the door.

This she did, and found herself in a plainly furnished room, well lit by two tall windows of frosted glass. In the middle was a massive wooden table, with a wicker chair in front of it. A notice in English affixed to the chair enjoined her to sit down. She obeyed, trusting that the weight of her person would not set in motion any piece of infernal machinery. But nothing of the kind happened, and after she had sat still, in the full glare of the window, for some ten minutes, she was on the point of rising and searching the house further. Hardly, however, had she made a movement when, with a sudden jerk, a panel in the table opened, revealing a cluster of diamonds, and a piece of paper on which was written in English, but in a foreign handwriting, the words :

These are for you. Take them and go. But if you would like something more, come again to-morrow at noon.

With many an inward exclamation of delight Miriam placed the jewels, which were of a rare quality, in her bag, passed into the hall, and out into the street, scarce able to believe that she had accomplished the mission with such profit and so little inconvenience. Nor was it long before she regained the familiar parts of the town.

The next day, as the clock struck twelve, having repeated all the actions of her first visit, she entered the room in which she had received the jewels, and was about to seat herself in the wicker chair, when, with much amazement, she saw a man standing behind the table. For some minutes she

security, and the good opinion of those who are for the most part more mindful of our conduct than our joy.

How unlike Rudolph was General Sleaford-Clark! A bachelor, near upon forty, he was precise in his ideas and commonplace in his sentiments. He had a clean-shaven, intellectual face, denoting brain rather than sinew, the student rather than the soldier. His family had for many generations owned a large and flourishing estate in Lincolnshire, and it had but recently passed into his hands. He was indeed a man to whom Miriam (in the war of sense and sensibility by nature a stout champion of the former) would turn after a fall. A sympathy sprang up between them, and she soon understood that, if she wished, she could become his wife. After deliberating with herself for a few weeks on the matter, she resolved to do so, and when, on the last day of June, she was betrothed to him, she went to her rest with the conviction that her affairs were now set in a very favourable direction.

Her dreams that night, however, were not as comfortable as her waking thoughts, and it was in the middle of a gruesome nightmare that she awoke, warned by some inner faculty to prepare for a danger without. For a few minutes she listened, still harried by the terrors of her sleep, until, her perceptions quickened, she heard the sound of movement in her room. Was it a dog, she wondered, which had somehow been hidden there while she undressed? Unmistakably there was the noise of treading which heavy paws would make on the carpet. Soon something brushed the sheet hanging down at the bedside. She must, she thought, at all costs give no sign of life, and desperately she kept her hand from groping for the light. Then came a shock at the bedclothes on her left. Her own breathing seemed all too loud, but she could hear also the sharp intake of breath of a beast which scents its prey.

Then suddenly she almost laughed at her being still deluded by dreams, which a single ray of light would dispel, and, turning sharply on her side, stretched out a hand for the switch. Yet at the very instant when the light first blinded her, there was a bound towards the open window and she seemed to see the body of an immense and tawny animal springing into the darkness. A moment later she stumbled to the window and peered out; but nothing could she see save a ledge giving approach to the roof. The bedroom, despite the freshness of the night, was tainted with the smell of a wild beast.

After a second sleep, she awoke early and was soon looking round the room for traces of the night's encounter. But there was none to be seen, and, despite a lively remembrance of her fears, she was inclined to ascribe them to an overstrained imagination, or some more bodily cause. While, however, she was wondering whether it would not be wise to change her lodging, the tray bearing her breakfast roll and coffee was brought up to her, and with it a telegram from her sister Deborah announcing the dangerous illness of her father, and imploring her to return without delay.

She had no wish to disobey the summons, and after dressing hurriedly she called up the General on the telephone and told him of her enforced departure. He expressed admirably both his solicitude for her father and the pain of losing her even for a few days, and declared that he would follow her to England as soon as he could get leave of absence. When she went to the train, he met her on the platform and begged her to spare some thought for him even in the midst of calamity at home. To this injunction Miriam promised full obedience, and with a dexterous movement caught his pince-nez which were tumbling to the ground as he saluted in farewell. Without them, his tired eyes had a look of unwarrantable nakedness. But as the long train left the station she waved her bouquet of red roses with a will.

.   .   .   .

Arrived at Lentworth once more, Miriam found her father too ill to know who she was. An undutiful letter from Gabriel, who in London was leading a life of the vilest dissipation, had brought about a spasm of fury from which the old man had almost died. Of his recovery the doctors had no hope, though they suggested that the period of his passing might be long. Thus followed for Miriam a time of weary waiting, during which she had little to do save reply to the General's frequent and amorous communications, and walk desolately up and down the neglected paths of the Manor grounds, nourished only by bold plans for the future and her memories of the past.

As for the present, it was a time of unbearable monotony, each wasted hour creeping by on feet of lead. How much of life, she reflected, do we not squander waiting for this or that? How few are the moments which in truth youth contrives to fill with daring exploits? How often do we not find, on examining ourselves, that we are accomplishing nothing, have not even any sure promise of pleasure before us, and are but expectant loiterers on the road that leads for ever away from joy? By the very frenzy of the embrace with which we strive to clasp the flying shadow, can we not divine the swiftness with which it disappears?

At length, however, the General's homecoming put an end to these sour reflections, and about the same time Sir Abraham rallied sufficiently to make the moment favourable for his daughter's wedding. This project he viewed with great satisfaction. The Sleaford-Clarks were, in his eyes, a most desirable connection, and the thought that before he died he would see his house united with so distinguished a family contributed not a little to his partial recovery.

The wedding was solemnized in the village church at Lentworth. As soon as the ceremony was over, the bridal pair returned to the Manor, to hold a small reception, before they took an evening train to London and the Continent. Terrible indeed, then, was their dismay when, on entering the hall, freshly decorated for the joyful event, they heard that one of the servants had found Sir Abraham prone on the stairs, clutching a letter. Though he still lived, there was now no doubt but that the end was at hand. With a few sad words the guests were turned away, and death, instead of marriage, became the care of the house.

Hasty preparations were made for Miriam and her husband to remain at the Manor for the night. Gloomy and full of foreboding, they took their evening meal from the bridal refreshments, while Deborah went to and fro wringing her hands and sobbing. A nurse reported that Sir Abraham was likely to live through the night, and urged all who could to take their rest as usual. Miriam was by no means loth to do so. The hideous outcome of the day had filled her with so great a lassitude (more perhaps because she must spend yet another night in the hated house, than because she grieved overmuch for her father) that she kissed her sister good night soon after nine, and went upstairs to her bedroom, which was also to be her nuptial chamber, and undressed slowly, keeping a wrap at hand in case she were suddenly called to her father's room. Then, having surveyed herself in the glass—not without pleasure—she clambered into bed and lay there, full of turbulent thoughts. In the far corner of the room she could see the outline of the little bed made ready for her husband.

At what hour, she wondered, would he come upstairs? No doubt he would have too much respect for her grief to demand any full tokens of affection from her that night. Yet he could hardly be so brutish as to fall asleep without seeking one embrace, even if he dared no more than kiss her hand. And at this point Miriam's thoughts, under the guidance of a strange emotion, turned back to her arrival in Hamburg, her first entry into the house in Baumwollenstrasse, her meeting with Rudolph, the ripening of her acquaintance with him, their drives through the country in the early summer, and the sudden end of that strong affection. Despite the wretchedness she had felt at his desertion, she almost wished that it could be he who should creep into her room instead of his supplanter. Had she perhaps misjudged him? Had his going been, after all, as painful to him as to herself, his silence a test of her devotion? If that were so, she had indeed ill-used him, and at the thought of this she felt a melancholy so strange to her hard nature as in itself to be almost a delight.

While she was musing thus, the clock struck ten, then the half-hour, then eleven. At length, however, when she was drifting into sleep, there was a soft knock at her door, and her husband came in carrying a small lamp, which he shaded with his hand. He first went into a dressing-room, barely larger than a cupboard, to which the only door led from the bedroom, put down the lamp there, and came back to the bedroom to make ready for the night. Miriam, feigning sleep, heard the slight sound made by his pince-nez as he fumbled with them upon the mantelpiece, and marvelled at the modesty of a man who preferred to bear the hateful discomfort of undressing in the dark, rather than honestly reveal that shape which Nature had been pleased to give him.

Next, as she surmised, having laid down his outer garments on the chair beside his bed, he withdrew to the inner room, whence she could hear the sound of his ablutions. A

thin streak of yellow light showed through the crack of the
door, then disappeared as the lamp was extinguished and the
door opened, revealing to Miriam, through her half-closed
lids, the faint outline of her husband returning to the bedroom.
For a while he paused irresolutely, then approached her bed
and paused again, listening to her breathing. Then, seeing
that she stirred, he took her hand, which was uncovered, and
kissed it many times, uttering such endearments as are used by
lovers. Miriam, for her part, had now so strongly recalled
the image of Rudolph that she pictured it was he who stood
before her. But when she was about to make a sweet
response to her husband's caresses, the growing embrace was
interrupted by a scratching at the dressing-room door. A rat,
supposed the General, and for a short while paid no heed to
the noise. But it grew in a few moments so loud, and seemingly so purposeful, that Miriam was afraid, sat upright and
urged him to look to it. He rose obediently and was half-
way across the room when an awful thought assailed her.
"Stop!" she cried. "Go to it armed!"

"Only a rat," he answered, and would have continued
as he was, but Miriam leapt out of bed and held him back,
begging him to take some weapon, and assuring him that it
was no rat which made such a din. And at that moment,
as if to prove her wisdom, there was a crash upon the door,
which, though it was of stout oak, was almost burst open.
Without further ado the General seized his revolver, which,
with a soldier's habit, he kept by him, and stood in readiness
for what might happen, while Miriam crouched by the further
wall. They had not long to wait. There was another and
even fiercer shock upon the door, which, rent from its hinges,
fell down flat with a loud clatter, while at the same instant a
monstrous animal with blazing eyes sprang through the opening. The General stood his ground bravely and discharged
his weapon at the beast while it was yet in mid-air. With a
great thud it fell dead upon him, half stunning him with its
weight. Thereupon Miriam fainted, and had not come to
herself when, a few moments afterwards, her sister brought
word that Sir Abraham was dead.

．　　　．　　　．　　　．

It was no little distress to the General to find the family
into which he had married come tumbling to earth like a

house of cards. The death of Sir Abraham was indeed in the natural order of events, but its immediate cause was anything but usual. The letter which the old man had been clutching at the time of his fall was from his son Gabriel— the last word in a long and bitter correspondence. In this letter the wretched youth not only admitted to the truth of all the rumours about his evil conduct, but confessed to such hideous actions that hardly the most malicious imagination could have conceived them. He was, he said, in danger of arrest on several counts. His health was ruined. Nothing was left for him but to die, nor did he care if the manner of his death disgraced for ever a father whose narrow parsimony had brought about his downfall. Nor was this an idle threat, for, on the very afternoon of Miriam's luckless wedding, Gabriel was found hanged in a bedroom overlooking Piccadilly, while at his feet was a large journal in which he revealed the shameful secrets of his late associates, in such fullness that, during the outcry which followed, more than one person of distinction found it expedient to leave England.

Miriam and her husband also went abroad as soon as it was possible. The General was especially eager to be gone, fearing that the hubbub in the popular Press might drive his wife to despair. She was, indeed, slow to recover her strength, and the lassitude into which she had fallen seemed even less accountable to her than to her husband. The death of her father had brought with it no grief. Even the death of Gabriel, and the cloud of scandal which had gathered round her maiden name, did not weigh much with her. Against these calamities she did not feel it necessary to strengthen herself, and she could barely understand her husband's judicious words of comfort. He might have been a doctor prescribing cures for a disease from which she did not suffer.

Yet none the less she was ailing, and, the cause being hidden from her, she could think of no remedy for herself. No longer had she any wish to outshine others, to capture hearts, to display at every turn surprising talents. Her appearance she neglected. Day after day she would wear the same costume, though now, like Queen Elizabeth, she might have a new robe for every day in the year. Her speech was languid. Sentences barely formed, she broke off in the middle and did not finish. Her gestures were laboured and unpleasing. Her chief desire seemed to be to sit alone indoors holding a book which she did not read, or a piece of embroidery which she never touched with the needle. It was as though she were in love—with a lover who had crossed the sea never to return—a lover who had died.

At length the General, who was by now not a little alarmed, spoke of his wife to a friend of his who had knowledge of medicine, telling him in full all the events which followed the marriage service. This friend suggested that Miriam's affliction arose, not from the deaths of her father and brother so much as from the appearance of the tiger at the moment of her first love-making, and he urged the General strongly to give his wife the full story in the light of his after-acquired knowledge. The General followed his advice within a few hours of receiving it.

When he was alone with his wife in the evening, he recalled to her mind all the circumstances of the bridal night, the first alarm, her subtle instinct of the danger, the bursting open of the dressing-room door and the shot which had saved them. She listened intently, nodding assent to each point in his recital. He then went on to assure her that what had seemed a piece of devilish magic was nothing but an event in the ordinary course of nature, unusual perhaps, but none the less subject to the laws of cause and effect like the myriads of events which make up our lives without our heeding them.

The tiger, he said, was the property of a circus performing at Nottingham. The animals' booths were on the outskirts of that town, and the beast had escaped into the open country some time during the night before the wedding. On the wedding-day it had lain hid, probably in a long strip of wood which circled nearly to the Manor grounds, and at nightfall had continued its journey till it reached the Manor House, where, doubtless owing to the consternation which prevailed there, one of the doors or lower windows had as likely as not been left open to its approach. However it was, the beast had by some means made its entry into the house, passed unseen through Miriam's room, and taken refuge in the dressing-room beyond.

Here a difficulty arose in the General's narrative; for he had to show why, though it must have been hidden in the dressing-room before he retired thither, he had observed no trace of it. There was, however, a cupboard in the dressing-room containing old boxes and lumber. The door to this cupboard, which opened inwards, had been held open by a heavy trunk placed alongside it by a careless servant, and it was doubtless in this inmost recess that the tiger had lain sleeping till the General had finished his washing and shut the dressing-room door behind him. The rest was easily told. On hearing of the tiger's death, which was much spoken of in the neighbourhood, the owner of the circus had come in person to claim the carcass, but the General, wishful to preserve a trophy of so perilous an adventure, had bought it from the man, and sent it to a well-known taxidermist, who was even then preparing the skin to be a fine addition to the collection of stags' heads and antlers adorning the Manor hall.

Miriam, on hearing the story, expressed a dull satisfaction at its probability, and then, with barely a pause, asked the General if he would consent to an immediate return to Lentworth. For a while he resisted her, but she was so set upon going back, and showed such an unwonted vigour in urging her request, that he judged it wise to yield. After the lapse of a few days, therefore, they journeyed home once more and established themselves at the Manor, where they were alone; for Deborah, co-heiress with Miriam, was absent on a visit to some friends.

.   .   .   .   .

The General had small hope that a betterment of Miriam's condition would follow the return to Lentworth. For the first few days he watched her anxiously, striving to see signs of progress or decline in her every action, and soon had to admit that she was weakening both in mind and body.

At length he set out his apprehensions in a letter to the friend whose advice he had previously sought.

If you had seen my wife [he wrote], *when I first met her in Hamburg, you would be so much amazed at the change in her that you would think her the victim of some hideous enchantment. At the time of our first acquaintance I had never met anyone, man or woman, possessed of so great a zest for life, so complete a freedom from petty scruples or unhealthy thoughts. Her whole being seemed to give out a boundless sanity and an almost formidable common* sense. I was even a little grieved by the thought that she was perhaps lacking in kindliness and natural affection, so little did anything seem able to dismay her.

Compare with this picture my wife as she was when I presented you to her. And the comparison would be still more startling if you could see her as she is now. At her own request we have come here, in order, it would seem, that she may spend long hours wandering through the garden, which the autumn has enriched with a grave beauty, or walking up and down the corridors of this old house, with folded hands, as one walking in her sleep. For the last three days she has addressed no word to me. Twice I have proposed, with some air of authority, that we should quit the place, but each time she has been so distraught that I dare not insist. The newest turn of her trouble, which I can see, is that the indifference which she had shown for my person ever since the bridal night has now changed into loathing. When I come into a room in which she is sitting, her whole body is convulsed with shuddering.

I now sleep at the end of the house remote from her bedroom, which, by a morbid choice of hers, is the room in which we encountered the tiger. As to this tiger, by the way, there is a new tangle in the mystery. I am told that a few days after we had left, the body of a second tiger was found in a lonely ditch not far from Nottingham. It was a thin and starved beast, very different from the splendid creature which attacked me. The showman, it seems, admitted to some friends at an inn that this second tiger was the one which escaped from the circus, and that he knew no more than I did whence the first one came. Our luckless neighbourhood, therefore, has been overrun by two such animals, of which one has not yet been properly accounted for. As you advised, I gave my wife these tidings, but she, poor soul, when she heard them, did nothing but shake her head and cry, "I knew it! I knew it!" No doubt her thoughts were far away, in some sad region of her own imagination.

If you can give me further counsel, I shall be more than grateful. I have tried in vain to persuade Miriam to see a doctor, and even brought one to the house, giving out that he was a friend of mine. But, either because she saw through my device, or, by reason of her new hatred for any intercourse with strangers, she withdrew, after one disdainful glance, to her room, and did not come down till the unwelcome guest had gone. I am almost afraid now to summon another, lest he should declare her to be out of her mind.

By the time Deborah returned to the Manor it was well-nigh winter. The distress of her family had given such a gloomy cast to her feelings that she showed little surprise at the General's tidings of her sister, and had not even the heart to rally her upon her melancholy. "It is of little moment, after all," she thought, "whether Miriam lives or dies. Even should she overcome this apathy and regain something of her old spirit, I see in her no power to be of service to others or to herself. It may be that the joys for which she pines are no longer in this world. If they are in another, let her seek them there."

When the two sisters met, they kissed and did not speak. Deborah almost at once set about arranging some flowers in a bowl, while Miriam, lying in a long chair, watched her with flushed cheeks, as if she feared to hear some question which she would not understand. The room was large and well proportioned, and furnished with a fine simplicity. To the General, who spied upon them through a glass door at the further end, it seemed as if he were watching one of those plays in which the effects are attained by silence rather than speech, and the beauty of the scene is more eloquent than deeds. He was not one, however, to derive much comfort from the contemplation of so pitiable a sight, and soon went upstairs to make ready for dinner, cursing the fate which had not only given him a wife who was no wife, but had marred the promise of his career.

Better, indeed, he mused while he unpinned the sleeves of his stiff shirt—for he was one who would wear evening clothes even in the solitude of the Pole—better, indeed, had it been to marry Deborah, who, though she had once seemed her sister's shadow, had none the less a distinguished appearance and many high qualities of soul which endure after beauty's passing. The more he compared the two sisters, the surer he was that he had chosen badly, and the more desirable became she whom he had not chosen. And he remembered with shameful satisfaction that the law no longer forbade the marriage of a man with the sister of his dead wife.

Somewhat bewildered by the novelty of these thoughts, he made his way across the landing to the broad staircase which led into the hall. When he reached the head of the stairs he heard a sound as of a large object falling heavily, and saw that the tiger-skin, which had been hanging on the wall above, had fallen in a heap on to the lowest step.

Fearful that his wife might be alarmed by the absence of the skin from its accustomed place, he fetched a stepladder and tried to fix the skin to the wall; but whether the wall was unsound or his skill insufficient, he fell from the ladder with the full weight of the skin on top of him.

After this, much bruised and heated, he laid the skin like a rug on the floor of the hall and went to the dining-room, where Deborah soon joined him. During the meal they talked together of the conditions prevailing in the county, and he was pleased to find that his companion was both an eager and an intelligent listener; for he had long been used to taking his dinner alone, and the change from solitude was highly agreeable to him.

He did not speak of Miriam till they had finished their dessert—the garden that year being rich in autumn fruits—and then only by way of suggesting that Deborah might care to pay a short visit to her sister's room. To this she agreed, but hardly had she gone upstairs when she came down to say that Miriam was nowhere to be seen. At this the General was much surprised, and said that his wife was wont to go to bed at seven o'clock, as often as not taking no food after that hour.

"It must be that she is walking outside," he said, when they had searched the house. "In this cold air it is an imprudence. We must find her, and you shall persuade her to come indoors." So saying, he fetched two lanterns and went out alone with Deborah into the garden; for he was ashamed that any of the household should learn of his wife's new folly. For a while they took the nearer paths in vain, but at length, when they had walked down a long avenue of chestnut trees which led to a retired lawn, they saw by the dim light of their lanterns a shape lying by the base of a marble column, erected many years before to commemorate the coming of age of the third baronet.

There they found Miriam, her head pillowed by the mossy plinth, her arms outspread, and her body covered with the skin of the tiger—lifeless, but smiling, while her cheeks were reddened with the glow of health, and her eyes, which were open, shone with joy. But when, in silence, they lifted her upon a hurdle, to carry her back to the house, they saw that beneath the tiger-skin her naked body bore all over it the marks of teeth and claws.

HILDA HUGHES

THOSE WHOM THE GODS LOVE . . .

DAVID WILLIAMS walked slowly and wearily up the path to the farmhouse. The sun cast shadows over the meadows, but the hills in the background were dark and ominous. It had been a very red sky that morning.

He was a tall man with a rather handsome and refined face, but time had already imprinted itself upon it. He walked with long steps like one whose business it is to walk across open spaces, across land in the midst of cultivation. But to the observant there was something more in his gait than the characteristic tread of the farmer. He was a little weary of life—not merely tired through work that was well done.

He looked across at the forbidding hills as his hand touched the garden-gate latch, and then he entered the farmhouse which was typical of so many Welsh homesteads.

There was a row of copper kettles upon the kitchen mantelpiece, which made it a thing of splendour, and an enormous fire roared up the chimney, although it was summer. The teapot was, as almost always, to be seen upon the hob. And there, stretched before the fire, was Nan, the black-and-tan collie, with her sensitive face and faithful eyes—an excellently trained sheep-dog—while Bob, the other dog, an equally good worker though a less beautiful creature, peered through the door, as if master and mistress would not care for him to enter.

The rosy-faced girl who did the housework and made herself generally useful put the finishing touches to the table, and Blodwyn, David's wife, seated herself opposite her husband.

She was a healthy, good-looking woman, some six years older than her husband. But her face expressed discontent.

She carved the joint, handed David his portion, speaking but little.

He made a brave attempt at conversation, telling her of Mrs. Jones of Penmaenmawr, who had a new baby, and Mrs. Williams, whose son had gone to South Wales, and the Vicar, who was going to organize a concert in aid of the Church School.

When he mentioned music her face clouded still further.

Deirdre, the girl he loved, had won the prize at the Eisteddfod at Pwllheli that year. Deirdre was a beautiful girl who worked at a neighbouring farm, a lovely, delicate creature; she helped Mrs. Thomas with her baby, and milked the cows, though she looked too fragile to carry a milking-pail.

David had lived with Blodwyn long enough to read her mind, to know what kind of thought was about to seek expression, even if he could not actually foresee the words.

Before the phrase rose to her lips, the colour tinged his face and neck.

"Have you seen her to-day?"

"Who?" he asked, pretending not to understand her reference.

"You should know better than I, David—Deirdre, of course."

His cheeks grew a deeper red.

"No," he said rather vexedly. "You didn't want me to, I suppose—though how I could help seeing her if she chanced to come along the hill, Heaven alone knows."

Blodwyn was not soothed. She loved this husband of hers whose eye had wandered to someone years younger and fairer than herself. And her jealousy burned into her very flesh. She would have given much to know if Deirdre ever thought of him so—Deirdre who, she had heard it said, had had the cheek to refuse him before he married her. Deirdre was now being courted by both the sons at the farm where she worked. Why did she not accept one of them? This girl with her beautiful body, sensitive face and fanciful name might have changed her mind maybe, since David's marriage five years ago.

At any rate, Blodwyn knew that in spite of the money she had brought him—enough to buy their farm—David repented of his bargain very often. And if Deirdre cared, it must make it all the more bitter to him. Blodwyn could

not bear to face facts as they were. He was very good to
her—he did all that she expected of him.

But the fever in her blood would not be quieted.

"It's not so strange that I should be babbling of her,"
she said, "after all I know."

"I've never been untrue to you," David said sharply.
"You know that. You've talked of that girl to me until I
can't stand it any longer. You'll go crazy if you keep on.
Besides, I thought we decided not to speak of it any more."

She was silenced then; silenced, but not soothed. She
handed him the potatoes, and her mind all the time rushed on
in the same channels.

He finished his dinner. He sat by the fire and put on his
gaiters. He was going to the market town. Usually he
went to market early in the morning. To-day he merely
wished to see one or two of the farmers before they left for
home. He would be able to discuss business with them
before they took out their horses and motors. It was unfortunate that he had been hindered from going into town as
usual that morning, but in any case he should not be too late.

"Give me a kiss, Blodwyn, before I go," he said, his huff
turning suddenly to tenderness.

And, even as his kiss was fresh upon her cheek, she cursed
Fate because she could not control his mind, his heart, his
innermost spirit. She could nag him and extract promises
and see his obedience to her every whim, but his heart, his
mind with all its dreams, were out of her reach.

Blodwyn could not rest at home that day. Her troubled
spirit urged her to be off. And since her thoughts were
dwelling on Deirdre, she found herself walking to Mrs.
Thomas's farm, where the girl worked, as if to see that she
were still there.

There was a keenness in the air, and storm clouds were
gathering. Yet the sun still shone, and the clouds, passing
quickly, cast shadows over the exquisite expanse of green
hills. Nature's temper changes in an instant in a mountainous
country. Blodwyn, gazing at the dark outline of the mountains before her, knew that rain would fall before night-time.

She walked on past babbling mountain streams. Welsh
sheep with graceful bodies, small pointed faces and long
tails skipped out of her way, or peered at her as she passed

from behind some boulder or furze bush. The way was violet and pink before her with heather and ling. Little ferns grew all around, and one or two seagulls wheeled overhead.

The solitude would have been terrible to any city-dweller.

Rain suddenly began to fall.

Mrs. Williams looked down at the lake between the mountains. It was black, like some evil thing—black and threatening. Where, before, the sun had danced upon a shimmering blue surface, all was now chill and black and foreboding. There was a scream of wild birds in the air. Blodwyn turned up her coat collar and began to run.

She reached the farm at last, opened a peculiar iron gate almost like the door of an oven—North Wales is full of these—and took a short cut across the fields.

Outside the house there were white pebbles. It is the fashion for some farmers and many peasants to accumulate pebbles for the sake of decoration, but they must be white.

A dog barked as she advanced towards the door, and a woman who was working in the scullery peered out to see who was coming. But Mrs. Thomas herself opened the front door. It creaked a little, as though it was not used very often. Indeed the side door was in greater demand. The room into which Blodwyn was ushered had sporting pictures upon the walls, a case of stuffed birds and a text over the piano : "God is love."

"I wondered if you'd have gone to market," Blodwyn said to Mrs. Thomas, "but I thought in any case I'd just look in to see how you were. Has the gout left you yet ?"

"My foot's a bit troublesome," returned Mrs. Thomas, "and Deirdre went in my place. She's a very good girl. I can depend upon her."

Mrs. Williams sat down. This surely was what she had wanted to know.

"Your son's walking out with her, isn't he ?" she asked, knowing that this was not the case, but finding it impossible to get the girl out of her mind.

"I wish he was. Both of the boys would give their eyes for her—but she's keeping her own counsel. She's driven into market with William to-day. She's more like one of the family. I hope she will be before she's done. Did you see her prizes? She's been very lucky at Eisteddfods this season."

And Mrs. Thomas proudly displayed the trophies.

"A very fortunate girl all round. A darling of the gods, you might say," replied Blodwyn, putting the trophies down before she had so much as looked at them. This talk was going to her head.

They chatted about market prices and the new organ, and had a good deal to say about the Vicar's lady. Time after time Blodwyn looked at the clock, and always she delayed her departure.

The hour was getting late and Deirdre had not come home. Mrs. Thomas could not think what had kept them.

At last Blodwyn stirred. She decided to go home over the cliffs, since the path there would be drier. But she had left it rather late, and to anyone who had not been so sure of the way the route must have been fatal.

The tide was in and water dashed and swirled against the cliffs. A light flashed and faded, flashed and faded, out at sea. The gorse bushes looked almost like human forms in the uncanny dusk. The moaning of the sea was in her ears, the salt upon her lips and in her nostrils. A seagull wheeled overhead and pierced the darkness with its screams. A sheep crept out from behind a boulder and made Blodwyn start. Thunder rumbled in the distance.

And all the time Blodwyn's thoughts tortured her. She could see a pale and lovely face in her imagination, a pair of laughing eyes, a beautiful young figure. If only she could possess her husband's mind—if she could lay the ghost for once and all!

The wind whistled shrilly about her. Heavy drops of rain fell. She stumbled, picked herself up, went on her way. It was an evil night. Her thoughts were evil, too. She hated this girl to whom the gods had been so kind. As long as she lived she could not be sure that her husband would lose his dream. How could she rid herself of this girl for ever— this thorn in the flesh?

Her hatred grew, fed by a tortured imagination.

To live and see this girl till old age came! She could not face the prospect. Rather would she herself drain the life-blood from her veins—crush the flower beneath her heel, strangle the laughter on her lips. If only she might smother her in bed !

"God," she cried, and it was a prayer from the heart, "hear me, I beseech you ! Let her die ! Let her die !"

The significance of the act did not strike her. She wanted death for Deirdre. It was natural to her to call to her God, for her race was religious by instinct and religious from tradition.

"God !" she screamed. "God ! Kill her ! Kill her ! Let her die !" She shrieked the words aloud in the wind. She felt herself stiffen with passion and anger.

"If she were here now," she told herself, "I'd push her over the cliff, let her beautiful body fall into the sea, hear her scream, see her white face when the coastguard found her body later. It would be an accident. I would be able to escape the law. I'd stumble against her when the path was narrow, hurl her below to sudden death."

Was murder committed by people like herself, she asked, ordinary people ? "Whoso hateth his brother, the same is a murderer." But she did not care.

And then it seemed as though there was a wailing in the wind, a heart-piercing cry.

Something—she was sure she was not dreaming—brushed against her as she walked, seemed to clutch her skirt, made her heart stand still. Her knees trembled. She could scarcely walk. Her breath came in gasps. The tears were streaming down her face. She heard a distant clock strike nine, but the fact that the church was so near, that humanity itself would soon be within reach, brought no comfort to her. She was possessed with evil spirits. And phantoms seemed to pass her in the darkness. She felt something touch her face—heard ominous noises. Could it have been only the wind ? She saw her husband's face distinctly in the darkness —ashen white—with repulsion upon it for her.

She was moaning as she walked. Prayers and curses came in a strange jumble from her lips. She must be going mad. Even the white faces of sheep brought the perspiration out upon her brow. She felt that any moment she might fall, wished that death might come to her and bring relief.

She turned and left the sea behind her, crossed the range and found herself wading in a mountain stream. She turned again, and picked her way carefully between some cows, caught her ankle against a gorse bush and then pressed on as before. As she neared home her passion gradually died down. She found herself strangly calm after such a fury. She was tired physically and mentally. Strong emotion had worn her out.

She dragged her aching limbs along. Her shoes were sodden. She believed there was a blister on her heel. Her hair, too, was wet through, and as her damp clothes clung to her she shivered with cold—with cold and fatigue.

She opened her own garden gate, passed up the path, opened the front door.

Someone stirred in the sitting-room.

She saw William Thomas's face, very white in the lamp-light.

Her servant girl hovered about her and was gone. "Mrs. Williams, Mr. Thomas has been waiting for you. He has something to tell you, dear."

Blodwyn caught the note of endearment and turned a beseeching face to William Thomas.

His lips were blue.

"I've bad news, Mrs. Williams. It's a rotten world. Poor Deirdre . . ."

"Go on!" said Blodwyn, her voice quiet, her body icy cold.

"She's dead. Crumpled up like a flower as she crossed the road. It was just before nine."

And then his words verged into a sob.

"Just before nine!" The phrase re-echoed in her brain. She remembered hearing the clock strike. She had been planning murder, praying to God, just before then. She was a murderess—a murderess. She ought to hang. What was it they said—"Hang by the neck until you are dead"? She wanted to scream and yet she was fighting for breath. Her tongue clove to her mouth and her knees were trembling.

At last she forced herself to speak. "Poor lad!" she said. "It's cruel! But don't take on so!"

No blood had been shed, she thought, some higher power had stepped in.

"Just like a flower," said William Thomas brokenly.

Deirdre dead. She had killed her. . . . It must have been her spirit that had swept past her on the cliff.

"I've killed David's dream. I shall have him for myself now—nothing to come between."

"You mustn't grieve too much," she said aloud; "it's hard, poor boy, I know."

She thought with a rush of relief, "God has answered my prayer." She must really calm herself. Later she would be able to rejoice. Never would she and her man be separated in thought again. She would be very good to him.

"There's something else I must say," continued William Thomas, trying to drain the anguish from his voice.

"David . . . he went to market, as you know. He was leaving the 'Swan' when he saw her fall. A car was dashing round the corner. He thought she had fainted and the car would get her. He decided to throw himself between her and the car. So he rushed out into the road—pushed her back—not knowing she was dead already—had died suddenly in the street—something wrong with her heart I suppose—and . . . the car got him . . . poor David!"

"Killed?" said Mrs. Williams dully, knowing how he must reply.

And then she screamed aloud—screamed until there seemed no quieting her.

THE BIRTHRIGHT

MARTIN DRAKE was considered to be clairvoyant from a little child. At the age of ten he had dreamed of a drowning fatality in the brook on his uncle's farm, and the very next morning they had found his grandfather lying face downwards in the ditch. His clothes were sodden with water, and he was dead, as Martin had seen him in his dream

Two years later Martin, in the cold grey dawn in his waking hours had seen, as clearly as if it had happened before him, the horse on which Lord Karney was riding stumble and fall, with its rider thrown under it. And when they picked him up Lord Karney's neck was found to be broken.

Martin's mother, susceptible to her boy's gifts, which were looked upon with disfavour by his father, who gave all his affection to his firstborn Michael, took the vision as an evil omen. She had not been through the tragedy of her father's suicide for nothing. She rushed down to the Manor, asked to see Lord Karney himself, and begged him not to ride to hounds that morning. He scoffed at the superstition of his steward's wife who listened to the precocious prattling of her younger boy, and rode to the meet in the market-place. Three hours later his horse fell clumsily and rolled over upon its master. They carried Lord Karney home upon a hurdle—Karney with his broken neck and his mouth gaping. And Martin had felt a strange thrill of pleasure when he had been told. It was as he had predicted.

He became a person of some importance in the village after that. The schoolmaster, who dabbled in Spiritualism, suggested that Martin was mediumistic. The vision was, in his opinion, not due to the boy's clairvoyance, but to some spirit control. The child should be watched. Eminent research students who were investigating psychic phenomena should have an opportunity of talking with him. Mr. Drake, however, was indignant, and refused to consider "such an

2A

infamous piece of humbug". His wife's pleading left him
adamant. The boy was a prig, and should be thrashed until
he dropped his posing. And, when old women from the
village tried to encourage Martin to have premonitions about
themselves and their own concerns, Mr. Drake let it be understood that there was to be no more nonsensical talk of the
kind. Perhaps his anger merely veiled his fear. Nothing
Martin ever did could please his father, but any suggestion
of the boy's supernatural powers merely infuriated him.

And so during the next few years Martin's clairvoyance
—call it what you will—was discouraged, although his
mother, convinced of her boy's uncanny powers, secretly
regaled the ladies' sewing meeting with talk that brought a
gleam to the eyes of the least susceptible and made the superstitious experience a curdling of the blood.

When he was twenty-four Martin's father died. Mrs.
Drake, a sensitive woman who had experienced a good deal
of sorrow, lived on in the old house, because Michael had
followed in his father's footsteps and been made steward of
the present Lord Karney's estate.

A will, made several years before his death, left the entire
estate to the elder son, since the widow had money of her
own. In due course the will was proved, and Mrs. Drake
grieved secretly because the bitterness of her husband for her
younger son had lived on in his heart throughout his life,
had outlived his body. It was as if the father's evil, bitter
spirit towards her boy—their boy—brooded about the house,
even stronger in death than it had been in life. Once she
spoke to Martin about it.

"I couldn't understand your father as he got older,"
she said. "When I married him I saw only the gentle side
of his nature. He was loving and kind. But he faced all
kinds of trouble, and he couldn't weather the storms. He
was a bitter man—a cruel man. He did you a grievous
wrong, my boy. He hated you in his lifetime, and his hate
lives on. If he has any consciousness in that place where
the dead go he may come to be sorry. Perhaps it will
trouble him. I can't rest at night in the room where we
used to sleep. Perhaps you wouldn't mind changing bedrooms with me, my boy. It's silly, I know."

"Your nerves are going to pieces, Mother," he said.
"I'll change rooms with you."

He did as she bade him, and he too had many sleepless nights.

He gave them the shock of their lives at breakfast-time on the anniversary of his father's death.

"I couldn't sleep last night," he told them. "I knew there was something strange about the place. I knew, too, what I should see. It was that old power working in me. I dreaded to see my father."

His mother shuddered, her lips trembling, a strange sound whistling through her teeth. It was what she, too, had feared. But she dreaded still more that anyone should ever learn her secret, should know that her love for her man had slowly turned to hate and dread. She had trembled before him in his lifetime. She feared him still in death. It was terrible that, having hated him so much, she had been forced to give him her body. The horror of it had seared her mind. But what was her boy saying now ?

She looked at him, drawing his hand through his long, straight brown hair. His face looked distorted, as she watched him through narrowing eyes.

"I dreaded seeing him," Martin said in strange, thick tones. "He hated me so. I could feel his hate wrapping round me. The air seemed to be full of it. I couldn't breathe. I thought I should choke where I lay."

"You must have had nightmare," his brother interjected, but his mother hung upon every word, and then she turned her face aside and put her hand over her eyes so that they should not look into her soul.

"It was awful," he went on. "It was like a poisoned gas in the air, physical as well as spiritual, if you see what I mean. I tried to sit up and then fell back exhausted. I was sick to the heart and horribly afraid. And I can remember those trivial things which do stand out on days like this. I heard the cuckoo-clock in the hall, just as I heard it a few minutes before he died. I can remember noticing the awful ticking of my own watch, which lay on the dressing-table beside me and ticked with a terrifying insistence, seeming to get louder and louder.

"I could hear the leaves tapping on the window, and the head of Abraham Lincoln on the table looked strange in the moonlight. Even the knobs on the bedstead, with my dressing-gown thrown over the rail, were unnerving. I shall never forget it—the insistence upon my consciousness of all these things ; and yet I knew that something terrifying was going to happen, that I was a prisoner, numb with cold, yet suffocating slowly."

"Go on !" his mother screamed, and they were both shocked by her voice, hollow and toneless. But Martin's voice was deep, and what he said seemed inevitable. People might cry, might batter themselves against Fate ; these things were true, unalterable.

"I noticed the Thing near the window at first. Then it moved sickeningly towards the cupboard as though it could not see, but must feel its way. And then it swung round and faced me. And I saw my father's face with hollows where the eyes used to be—like a skull."

"A skull ! Oh, my God !"

"The face was white as he never was even in death. I can't remember what clothes he had, or if he had any, but he wrung his hands, and a terrible dry sobbing came from his lips. I tried to scream out, but I couldn't make a sound. I sat up in bed and clutched the sheets. And slowly I could understand what he meant. It was a voice all right, but the words were strange—like someone trying to speak who has been dumb for years."

"Oh, God !"

"And he shot out one hand towards me, and although it didn't touch me I had the sensation of something icy-cold. I've done you a wrong, my boy,' he said. 'Look in my old coat . . . open the family Bible. You'll find it in Genesis.' And then he turned aside and wailed and wrung his hands.

"I watched him as he went ; he seemed to merge into the dusk. He was like light—thin, white, transparent—but he seemed to fade away into the darkness, or else became lost in the moonbeam. I got out of bed when I could. I wanted to say something, but I couldn't find him. I got back into bed, and cold sweat poured off me."

"I don't wonder," said Michael, shocked to the depths but trying to make a pretence of calm.

"What do you think he meant ?" cried the mother.

Martin's long fingers played nervously with his lips.

"How should I know ?"

"You say he mentioned his old coat ?"

He nodded.

"I wanted to give it to Johnson two days before he died," said the widow. "It was so shabby, but he would cling to it. There was a scene."

"Where is it now ?" asked Michael. "Couldn't you, with your powers, tell us that, Martin, old boy ?"

Mrs. Drake spoke quickly before her elder son could notice that his brother was not prepared to reply.

"In the cupboard with all his other old clothes. I left them untouched after he died."

"*He* went towards the *cupboard* first," said Martin.

They looked at each other significantly, as people do when they think they have found a clue.

"We must go up at once," said Mrs. Drake.

Michael took her arm. Martin followed them.

They entered the bedroom where she had known so many unhappy nights. She knocked against the dressing-table and bruised one hip in her hurry. Then she crossed to the built-in cupboard beside the fireplace and flung open the doors. Some old clothes of her own, three or four pairs of shoes, an old hat or two met her gaze. She took them out, threw them upon the floor, took down her husband's frock-coat which had done duty at funerals, and, though very old, was not to be despised even now. Then she produced a dressing-gown, and lastly, from among a number of old garments, the coat in question. The outside pockets gave no clue. Then as Michael, sitting on the floor, ran his fingers over it, he heard a crackling and felt something in a breast-pocket. He took out a thin sheet of notepaper.

Kneeling on the floor together among the debris of the wardrobe, they read it.

I was unjust. I want to make amends before I die, and I have a premonition of death. For my last will and testament look in the family Bible—Genesis.

"Just as he said," put in Martin.

"You didn't say anything about a will," said his brother.

"He didn't exactly mention the word. But I remember him saying look in Genesis."

"Where is it, Mother ?"

"It's such a heavy book," said Mrs. Drake   "We never

use it now. It's got all your ages written upon the flyleaf. I remember your father's Cousin Jane would do it."

"Silly old girl!" said Michael.

"What does it matter?" sighed Martin.

Mrs. Drake went carefully through a pile of books in the cupboard, but could find no trace of the family Bible. They found it at last in the bottom drawer of the chiffonier in the dining-room. And between the pages of Genesis they found the will. It had been drawn up three years before and witnessed by Cousin Jane and Henry Deane. The premonition of death had evidently come to the strong man not a few days before he actually died, as they had at first supposed, but during a severe attack of influenza three years earlier.

"I remember now he was very nervous about himself," said the widow.

"Strong men always are when they're ill," said Martin.

In the will the property was to be divided equally between the two brothers.

"I'm glad your father didn't forget you, after all," went on Mrs. Drake.

"But the will's already been proved," said Michael.

"The last will must stand," his mother interposed. "You'll share and share alike now. It's only just. Your father regretted his bitterness—and to think I never knew!"

Her eyes strayed to the printed page of the Bible.

"And Esau said unto his father, Hast thou but one blessing, my father? Bless me, even me also, O my father. And Esau lifted up his voice, and wept."

It was the poignant story of Jacob and Esau. Her husband must have read that when he was ill. It had brought him to a new state of mind.

    .   .   .   .   .

The finding of the second will brought calm to Mary Drake's troubled spirit. Her boy—her baby—had not been forgotten. Perhaps her husband's heart had changed before he died. Perhaps he had become more like the man she once had loved passionately—not the fiend she had known in later life.

The proving of the second will took time. The technicalities of the Law always do. But the inheritance of the two brothers was shared equally at last. It was only Martin, benefiting by several thousands, who took it so calmly. His mother sometimes wondered if his father's change of spirit meant much to him. It was nice, of course, to have the money, but surely the justice of the thing must appeal to him. He must be sensitive. Was he not clairvoyant—perhaps a medium ?

Martin and his brother talked for a long time about investments one night beside the fire in the old-fashioned dining-room with its horsehair furniture and its copper kettles on the mantelpiece, and its willow-pattern china upon the dresser, and its sporting prints to decorate the walls. They had taken advice upon the subject that very afternoon, and were viewing themselves and each other as men of property. With the money well invested there was no knowing what they might do in the future. Neither of them had any responsibilities, any ties. Each had himself to consider, and money meant much to both of them, not merely because of the things it would bring them, but because it spelt power.

When Martin went to bed that night in the old four-poster, which his mother and father had once used, he went to sleep as soon as his head touched the pillow.

It was a large room with low beams and only one door. Rain fell outside and leaves rattled against the window-pane, but they had no power to disturb Martin. He had his fortune. He had power. His dreams as the night passed were fantastic. He could see himself as Master of the Hunt, living in the fine old Manor ; he could see more money coming from his mother later, and a wife and children sitting beside him at a table spread with silver and crystal. Yet he had never really loved in his life. But the woman in the dream was beautiful, and she was looking across the table with a smile. He could see himself lifting his glass and draining it . . . it was a funny thing to experience the sensation of good old wine in a dream. He could feel it nice to his palate, soothing to his stomach. His legs were tingling. He saw himself stand up and propose a toast. Then the scene changed. They were all at the Hunt Ball, he and his friends, and they were drinking at the bar, and then later dancing madly in a gallop. There seemed to be a fever in his blood. He danced the gallop, which had returned to fashion in order to round off a Hunt Ball programme, as he had never danced it before. A girl was looking up into his eyes—he bent over her—wanted to snatch a kiss—then he awoke.

There was something in the room. He could not see it, but he could feel. It was not the blind either, which was flapping at the open window, nor the curtain which was blown about and then seemed to bulge into the room. And how the wind howled ! It was on him before he knew. He could feel something scorching him—was it this fiend's breath, or the heat from the wood fire, crackling in the grate ?

He tried to get up, to escape. But small greenish eyes looked into his. His father stood over him, brooding over him, with intense hate and loathing on his face and in his eyes. There were no hollows, as in a skull. It was the face of a madman who acted with disconcerting logicality.

The Thing was trying to speak now.

"What was that nonsense you told them . . . the face of a skull ?"

The voice made him cower in his bed.

"You lied ! You never saw me ! I did not come !"

Martin put his hand before his eyes to shut out the sight. The feeling of heat was terrible.

"You lied ! You lied !" The voice screamed out the truth in a crescendo.

Sweat poured off Martin's face, his tongue was cloven. He lay trembling, as if in an ague. Words failed. Screams would not come, yet every nerve in his body cried aloud in pain, in horror for the peril that was to come.

And the Thing was drawing nearer . . . leaning over the bed.

"You forged my name—and the witnesses' names—upon that false will. You wrote letters in my handwriting about my premonitions, and I never so much as thought of death in all my life. Would to God I had ! You were a forger !"

The voice died away and then rose again in a scream. His father's great red hands with sandy hairs upon them reached out towards his throat.

Martin made a last effort to cry out. And then the Thing was upon him. His blood-curdling scream was his swan song.

His brother and a fireman forced their way into the room. The smoke was thick, but the fire had not done much damage.

Martin, however, lay white and still upon the bed. They lifted him before they realized.

The doctor came.

"It was not the fire that killed him," he said; "it didn't even touch him. But these things are easily explained. Death was undoubtedly due to shock."

MAY SINCLAIR

THE VILLA DÉSIRÉE

I

HE had arranged it all for her. She was to stay a week in Cannes with her aunt and then to go on to Roque-brune by herself, and he was to follow her there. She, Mildred Eve, supposed he could follow her anywhere, since they were engaged now.

There had been difficulties, but Louis Carson had got over all of them by lending her the Villa Désirée. She would be all right there, he said. The caretakers, Narcisse and Armandine, would look after her ; Armandine was an excellent cook ; and she wouldn't be five hundred yards from her friends, the Derings. It was so like him to think of it, to plan it all out for her. And when he came down ? Oh, when he came down he would go to the Cap Martin Hotel, of course.

He understood everything without any tiresome explaining. She couldn't afford the hotels at Cap Martin and Monte Carlo ; and though the Derings had asked her to stay with them, she really couldn't dump herself down on them like that, almost in the middle of their honeymoon.

Their honeymoon—she could have bitten her tongue out for saying it, for not remembering. It was awful of her to go talking to Louis Carson about honeymoons, after the appalling tragedy of *his*.

There were things she hadn't been told, that she hadn't liked to ask : Where it had happened ? And how ? And how long ago ? She only knew it was on his wedding-night, that he had gone in to the poor little girl of a bride and found her dead there, in the bed.

They said she had died in a sort of fit.

You had only to look at him to see that something terrible had happened to him some time. You saw it when his face was doing nothing : a queer, agonised look that made him strange to her while it lasted. It was more than suffering ; it was almost as if he could be cruel, only he never was, he never

427

could be. *People* were cruel, if you liked ; they said his face put them off. Mildred could see what they meant. It might have put *her* off, perhaps, if she hadn't known what he had gone through. But the first time she had met him he had been pointed out to her as the man to whom just that appalling thing had happened. So far from putting her off, that was what had drawn her to him from the beginning, made her pity him first, then love him. Their engagement had come quick, in the third week of their acquaintance.

When she asked herself, " After all, what do I know about him," she had her answer, " I know *that*." She felt that already she had entered into a mystical union with him through compassion. She *liked* the strangeness that kept other people away and left him to her altogether. He was more her own that way.

There was (Mildred Eve didn't deny it) his personal magic, the fascination of his almost abnormal beauty. His black, white, and blue. The intensely blue eyes under the straight black bars of the eyebrows, the perfect, pure, white face suddenly masked by the black moustache and small, black, pointed beard. And the rich vivid smile he had for her, the lighting up of the blue, the flash of white teeth in the black mask.

He had smiled then at her embarrassment as the awful word leaped out at him. He had taken it from her and turned the sharp edge of it.

" It would never do," he had said, " to spoil the *honeymoon*. You'd much better have my villa. Some day, quite soon, it'll be yours, too. You know I like anticipating things."

That was always the excuse he made for his generosities. He had said it again when he engaged her seat in the *train de luxe* from Paris and wouldn't let her pay for it. (She had wanted to travel third class.) He was only anticipating, he said.

He was seeing her off now at the Gare de Lyons, standing on the platform with a great sheaf of blush roses in his arms. She, on the high step of the railway carriage, stood above him, swinging in the open doorway. His face was on a level with her feet ; they gleamed white through the fine black stockings. Suddenly he thrust his face forwards and kissed her feet. As the train moved he ran beside it and tossed the roses into her lap.

And then she sat in the hurrying train, holding the great

sheaf of blush roses in her lap, and smiling at them as she dreamed. She was in the Riviera Express; the Riviera Express. Next week she would be in Roquebrune, at the Villa Désirée. She read the three letters woven into the edges of the grey cloth cushions : P.L.M. : Paris—Lyons—Mediterranée, Paris—Lyons—Mediterranée, over and over again. They sang themselves to the rhythm of the wheels ; they wove their pattern into her dream. Every now and then, when the other passengers weren't looking, she lifted the roses to her face and kissed them.

She hardly knew how she dragged herself through the long dull week with her aunt at Cannes.

And now it was over and she was by herself at Roquebrune.

The steep narrow lane went past the Dering's house and up the face of the hill. It led up into a little olive wood, and above the wood she saw the garden terraces. The sunlight beat in and out of their golden yellow walls. Tier above tier, the blazing terraces rose, holding up their ranks of spindle-stemmed lemon and orange trees. On the topmost terrace the Villa Désirée stood white and hushed between two palms, two tall poles each topped by a head of dark-green, curving, sharp-pointed blades. A grey scrub of olive-trees straggled up the hill behind it and on each side.

Rolf and Martha Dering waited for her with Narcisse and Armandine on the steps of the verandah.

" Why on earth didn't you come to us ? " they said.

" I didn't want to spoil your honeymoon."

" Honeymoon, what rot ! We've got over *that* silliness. Anyhow, it's our third week of it."

They were detached and cool in their happiness.

She went in with them, led by Narcisse and Armandine. The caretakers, subservient to Mildred Eve and visibly inimical to the Derings, left them together in the *salon*. It was very bright and French and fragile and worn ; all faded grey and old greenish gilt ; the gilt chairs and settees carved like picture frames round the gilded cane. The hot light beat in through the long windows open to the terrace, drawing up a faint powdery smell from the old floor.

Rolf Dering stared at the room, sniffing, with fine nostrils in a sort of bleak disgust.

" You'd much better have come to us," he said.

" Oh, but—it's charming."

" Do you *think* so ? " Martha said. She was looking at her intently.

Mildred saw that they expected her to feel something, she wasn't sure what, something that they felt. They were subtle and fastidious.

" It does look a little queer and—unlived in," she said, straining for the precise impression.

" I should say," said Martha, " it had been too much lived in, if you ask me."

" Oh no. That's only dust you smell. I think, perhaps, the windows haven't been open very long."

She resented this criticism of Louis's villa.

Armandine appeared at the doorway. Her little, slant, Chinesy eyes were screwed up and smiling. She wanted to know if Madame wouldn't like to go up and look at her room.

" We'll all go up and look at it," said Rolf.

They followed Armandine up the steep, slender, curling staircase. A closed door faced them on the landing. Armandine opened it, and the hot golden light streamed out to them again.

The room was all golden white ; it was like a great white tank filled with blond water where things shimmered, submerged in the stream ; the white-painted chairs and dressing-table, the high white-painted bed, the pink-and-white striped ottoman at its foot ; all vivid and still, yet quivering in the stillness, with the hot throb, throb of the light.

" Violà, Madame," said Armandine.

They didn't answer. They stood, fixed in the room, held by the stillness, staring, all three of them, at the high white bed that rose up, enormous, with its piled mattresses and pillows, the long white counterpane hanging straight and steep, like a curtain, to the floor.

Rolf turned to Armandine.

" Why have you given Madame this room ? "

Armandine shrugged her fat shoulders. Her small, Chinesy eyes blinked at him, slanting, inimical.

" Monsieur's orders, Monsieur. It is the best room in the house. It was Madame's room."

" I know. That's *why*———"

" But no, Monsieur. Nobody would dislike to sleep in Madame's room. The poor little thing, she was so pretty, so sweet, so young, Monsieur. Surely Madame will not dislike the room."

" Who *was*—Madame ? "

" But, Monsieur's wife, Madame. Madame Carson. Poor Monsieur, it was so sad——"

" Rolf," said Mildred, " did he bring her here—on their honeymoon ? "

" Yes."

" Yes, Madame. She died here. It was so sad. Is there anything I can do for Madame ? "

" No, thank you, Armandine."

" Then I will get ready the tea."

She turned again in the doorway, crooning in her thick, Provençal voice. " *Madame* does not dislike her room ? "

" No, Armandine. No. It's a beautiful room."

The door closed on Armandine. Martha opened it again to see whether she were listening on the landing. Then she broke out :

" Mildred—you know you loathe it. It's beastly. The whole place is beastly."

" You can't stay in it," said Rolf.

" Why not ? Do you mean, because of Madame ? "

Martha and Rolf were looking at each other, as if they were both asking what they should say. They said nothing.

" Oh, her poor little ghost won't hurt me, if that's what you mean."

" Nonsense," Martha said. " Of course it isn't."

" What is it, then ? "

" It's so beastly lonely, Mildred," said Rolf.

" Not with Narcisse and Armandine."

" Well, I wouldn't sleep a night in the place," Martha said, " if there wasn't any other on the Riviera. I don't like the look of it."

Mildred went to the open lattice, turning her back on the high, rather frightening bed. Down there below the terraces she saw the grey flicker of the olive woods and, beyond them, the sea. Martha was wrong. The place was beautiful ; it was adorable. She wasn't going to be afraid of poor little Madame. Louis had loved her. He loved the place. That was why he had lent it her.

She turned. Rolf had gone down again. She was alone with Martha. Martha was saying something.

2D*

" Mildred—where's Mr. Carson ? "

" In Paris. Why ? "

" I thought he was coming here."

" So he is, later on."

" To the villa ? "

" No. Of course not. To Cap Martin." She laughed.
" So *that's* what you're thinking of, is it ? "

She could understand her friend's fears of haunted houses,
but not these previsions of impropriety.

Martha looked shy and ashamed.

" Yes," she said. " I suppose so."

" How horrid of you ! You might have trusted me."

" I do trust you." Martha held her a minute with her
clear loving eyes. " Are you sure you can trust *him* ? "

" Trust him ? Do *you* trust Rolf ? "

" Ah—if it was like that, Mildred——"

" It *is* like that."

" You're really not afraid ? "

" What is there to be afraid of ? Poor little Madame ? "

" I didn't mean Madame. I meant Monsieur."

" Oh—wait till you've seen him."

" Is he *very* beautiful ? "

" Yes. But it isn't *that*, Martha. I can't tell you what it is."

They went downstairs, hand in hand, in the streaming light.
Rolf waited for them on the verandah. They were taking
Mildred back to dine with them.

" Won't you let me tell Armandine you're stopping the
night ? " he said.

" No, I won't. I don't want Armandine to think I'm
frightened."

She meant she didn't want Louis to think she was frightened.
Besides, she was not frightened.

" Well, if you find you don't like it, you must come to us,"
he said.

And they showed her the little spare-room next to theirs,
with its camp-bed made up, the bedclothes turned back, all
ready for her, any time of the night, in case she changed her
mind. The front door was on the latch.

" You've only to open it, and creep in here and be safe,"
Rolf said.

II

Armandine—subservient and no longer inimical, now that the Derings were not there—Armandine had put the candle and matches on the night-table and the bell which, she said, would summon her if Madame wanted anything in the night. And she had left her.

As the door closed softly behind Armandine, Mildred drew in her breath with a slight gasp. Her face in the looking-glass, between the tall lighted candles, showed its mouth half-open, and she was aware that her heart shook slightly in its beating. She was angry with the face in the glass with its foolish mouth gaping. She said to herself. Is it possible I'm frightened? It was not possible. Rolf and Martha had made her walk too fast up the hill, that was all. Her heart always did that when she walked too fast uphill, and she supposed that her mouth always gaped when it did it.

She clenched her teeth and let her heart choke her till it stopped shaking.

She was quiet now. But the test would come when she had blown out the candles and had to cross the room in the dark to the bed.

The flame bent backwards before the light puff she gave, and righted itself. She blew harder, twice, with a sense of spinning out the time. The flame writhed and went out. She extinguished the other candle at one breath. The red point of the wick pricked the darkness for a second and died, too, with a small crackling sound. At the far end of the room the high bed glimmered. She thought: Martha was right. The bed *is* awful.

She could feel her mouth set in a hard grin of defiance as she went to it, slowly, too proud to be frightened. And then suddenly, half-way, she thought about Madame.

The awful thing was, climbing into that high funeral bed that Madame had died in. Your back felt so undefended. But once she was safe between the bed-clothes it would be all right. It would be all right so long as she didn't think about Madame. Very well, then, she wouldn't think about her. You could frighten yourself into anything by thinking.

Deliberately, by an intense effort of her will, she turned the sad image of Madame out of her mind and found herself thinking about Louis Carson.

This was Louis's house, the place he used to come to when he wanted to be happy. She made out that he had sent her there because he wanted to be happy in it again. She was there to drive away the unhappiness, the memory of poor little Madame. Or, perhaps, because the place was sacred to him ; because they were both so sacred, she and the young dead bride who hadn't been his wife. Perhaps he didn't think about her as dead at all ; he didn't want her to be driven away. The room she had died in was not awful to him. He had the faithfulness for which death doesn't exist. She wouldn't have loved him if he hadn't been faithful. You could be faithful and yet marry again.

She was convinced that whatever she was there for, it was for some beautiful reason. Anything that Louis did, anything he thought or felt or wanted, would be beautiful. She thought of Louis standing on the platform in the Paris station, his beautiful face looking up at her ; its sudden darting forward to kiss her feet. She drifted again into her happy hypnotising dream, and was fast asleep before midnight.

She woke with a sense of intolerable compulsion, as if she were being dragged violently up out of her sleep. The room was grey in the twilight of the unrisen moon.

And she was not alone.

She knew that there was something there. Something that gave up the secret of the room and made it frightful and obscene. The greyness was frightful and obscene. It gathered itself together ; it became the containing shell of the horror.

The thing that had waked her was there with her in the room.

For she knew she was awake. Apart from her supernatural certainty, one physical sense, detached from the horror, was alert. It heard the ticking of the clock on the chimney-piece, the hard sharp shirring of the palm-leaves outside, as the wind rubbed their knife-blades together. These sounds were witnesses to the fact that she was awake, and that therefore the thing that was going to happen would be real. At the first sight of the greyness she had shut her eyes again, afraid to look into the room, because she knew that what she would see there was real. But she had no more power over her eyelids than she had had over her sleep. They opened under the same intolerable compulsion. And the supernatural thing forced itself now on her sight.

It stood a little in front of her by the bedside. From the

breasts downwards its body was unfinished, rudimentary, not quite born. The grey shell was still pregnant with its loathsome shapelessness. But the face—the face was perfect in absolute horror. And it was Louis Carson's face.

Between the black bars of the eyebrows and the black pointed beard she saw it, drawn back, distorted in an obscene agony, corrupt and malignant. The face and the body, flesh and yet not flesh, they were the essence made manifest of untold, unearthly abominations.

It came on to her, bending over her, peering at her, so close that the piled mattresses now hid the lower half of its body. And the frightful thing about it was that it was blind, parted from all controlling and absolving clarity, flesh and yet not flesh. It looked for her without seeing her ; and she knew that, unless she could save herself that instant, it would find what it looked for. Even now, behind the barrier of the piled-up mattresses, the unfinished form defined and completed itself ; she could feel it shake with the agitation of its birth.

Her heart staggered and stopped in her breast, as if her breast had been clamped down on to her backbone. She struggled against wave after wave of faintness ; for the moment that she lost consciousness the appalling presence there would have its way with her. All her will rose up against it. She dragged herself upright in the bed, suddenly, and spoke to it :

" Louis ! What are you doing there ? "

At her cry it went, without moving ; sucked back into the greyness that had borne it.

She thought : " It'll come back. It'll come back. Even if I don't see it I shall know it's in the room."

She knew what she would do. She would get up and go to the Derings. She longed for the open air, for Rolf and Martha, for the strong earth under her feet.

She lit the candle on the night-table and got up. She still felt that It was there, and that standing upon the floor she was more vulnerable, more exposed to it. Her terror was too extreme for her to stay and dress herself. She thrust her bare feet into her shoes, slipped her travelling coat over her nightgown and went downstairs and out through the house door, sliding back the bolts without a sound. She remembered that Rolf had left a lantern for her in the verandah, in case she should want it—as if they had known.

She lit the lantern and made her way down the villa garden, stumbling from terrace to terrace, through the olive wood and the steep lane to the Derings' house. Far down the hill she could see a light in the window of the spare room. The house door was on the latch. She went through and on into the lamp-lit room that waited for her.

She knew again what she would do. She would go away before Louis Carson could come to her. She would go away to-morrow, and never come back again. Rolf and Martha would bring her things down from the villa ; he would take her into Italy in his car. She would get away from Louis Carson for ever. She would get away up through Italy.

III

Rolf had come back from the villa with her things and he had brought her a letter. It had been sent up that morning from Cap Martin.

It was from Louis Carson.

My darling Mildred,

You see I couldn't wait a fortnight without seeing you. I *had* to come. I'm here at the Cap Martin Hotel.

I'll be with you some time between half-past ten and eleven——

Below, at the bottom of the lane, Rolf's car waited. It was half-past ten. If they went now they would meet Carson coming up the lane. They must wait till he had passed the house and gone up through the olive wood.

Martha had brought hot coffee and rolls. They sat down at the other side of the table and looked at her with kind anxious eyes as she turned sideways, watching the lane.

" Rolf," she said suddenly, " do you know anything about Louis Carson ? "

She could see them looking now at each other.

" Nothing. Only the things the people here say."

" What sort of things ? "

" Don't tell her, Rolf."

" Yes. He *must* tell me. I've got to know."

She had no feeling left but horror, horror that nothing could intensify.

" There's not much. Except that he was always having women with him up there. Not particularly nice women. He seems," Rolf said, " to have been rather an appalling beast."

" Must have been," said Martha, " to have brought his poor little wife there, after————"

" Rolf, what did Mrs. Carson die of ? "

" Don't ask *me*," he said.

But Martha answered : " She died of fright. She saw something. I told you the place was beastly."

Rolf shrugged his shoulders.

" Why, you said you felt it yourself. We both felt it."

" Because we knew about the beastly things he did there."

" *She* didn't know. I tell you, she saw something."

Mildred turned her white face to them.

" I saw it too."

" You ? "

" What ? What did you see ? "

" Him. Louis Carson."

" He must be dead, then, if you saw his ghost."

" The ghosts of poor dead people don't kill you. It was what he *is*. All that beastliness in a face. A face."

She could hear them draw in their breath short and sharp.

" Where ? "

" There. In that room. Close by the bed. It was looking for me. I saw what *she* saw."

She could see them frown now, incredulous, forcing themselves to disbelieve. She could hear them talking, their voices beating off the horror.

" Oh, but she couldn't. He wasn't there."

" He heard her scream first."

" Yes. He was in the other room, you know."

" *It* wasn't. He can't keep it back."

" Keep it back ? "

" No. He was waiting to go to her."

Her voice was dull and heavy with realisation. She felt herself struggling, helpless, against their stolidity, their unbelief.

" Look at that," she said. She pushed Carson's letter across to them.

" He was waiting to go to her," she repeated. " And—last night—he was waiting to come to me."

They stared at her, stupefied.

" Oh, can't you *see* ? " she cried. " It didn't wait. It got there before him."

DANIEL DEFOE

THE APPARITION OF MRS. VEAL

THIS thing is so rare in all its circumstances, and on so good authority, that my reading and conversation has not given me anything like it. Mrs. Bargrave is the person to whom Mrs. Veal appeared after her death; she is my intimate friend, and I can avouch for her reputation for these last fifteen or sixteen years, on my own knowledge. Though, since this relation, she is calumniated by friends of Mrs. Veal's brother, who think the relation of this appearance a reflection, and do therefore what they can to blast Mrs. Bargrave's reputation and laugh the story out of countenance.

You must know that Mrs. Veal was a maiden gentlewoman of about thirty, and for years had been troubled with fits. She was maintained by an only brother, and kept his house at Dover. She was intimately acquainted with Mrs. Bargrave from her childhood. Mrs. Veal's circumstances were then mean; her father did not take care of his children and they were exposed to hardships. And Mrs. Bargrave had in those days as unkind a father, though she wanted for neither food nor clothing, whilst Mrs. Veal wanted for both. So that it was in the power of Mrs. Bargrave to be very much her friend in several instances, which mightily endeared Mrs. Veal, so that she would often say, "Mrs. Bargrave, you are not only the best, but the only friend I have in the world, and no circumstances of life shall ever dissolve my friendship."

They would often condole each other's adverse fortune and read together *Drelincourt upon Death*, and other good books. Some time after, Mr. Veal's friends got him a place in the custom house at Dover, which occasioned Mrs. Veal, little by little, to fall off from her intimacy with Mrs. Bargrave, though there was never any such thing as a quarrel; but an indifference came on by degrees, till at last Mrs. Bargrave, then living in Canterbury, had not seen her for two years and a half.

On the 8th of September last (1705) Mrs. Bargrave was sitting alone thinking over her unfortunate life and sewing, when she heard a knock at the door. She went to see who was there and it proved to be her old friend Mrs. Veal, who was in a riding-habit. At that moment the clock struck twelve at noon.

"I am surprised to see you," said Mrs. Bargrave, "for you have been so long a stranger." She added that she was glad to see her and offered to give her a kiss. Mrs. Veal bent forward until their lips almost touched, then drawing her hand across her eyes, she said, "I am not very well," and so waived it. She told Mrs. Bargrave then that she was going on a journey, but had wanted to see her first.

"But," says Mrs. Bargrave, "how come you to take a journey alone? I am amazed at it, because I know you have so fond a brother."

"Oh, I gave my brother the slip, and came away, because I had so great a mind to see you before I took my journey."

Mrs. Bargrave led the way into another room, that was within the first, and Mrs. Veal sat herself down in an elbow-chair.

"My dear friend," says Mrs. Veal, "I am come to renew our old friendship and to beg your pardon for my breach of it."

"Oh, don't mention it. I have not had an uneasy thought about it. I can easily forgive it."

"What did you think of me?" says Mrs. Veal.

Says Mrs. Bargrave, "I thought you were like the rest of the world, and that prosperity had made you forget me."

Mrs. Veal, however, reminded Mrs. Bargrave of old kindnesses she had done her in former days, and of their time together when they had read *Drelincourt upon Death*. "Mrs. Bargrave," says she, "don't you think I am mightily impaired by my fits?"

"No," says Mrs. Bargrave; "I think you look as well as ever I knew you."

This talk between them lasted an hour or more, and then Mrs. Veal asked her friend if she would write a letter for her—a letter to her brother. She was to tell him that she wanted her rings given to such and such, and that there was a purse of gold in her cabinet, and that she would have two broad pieces from it given to her cousin Watson.

As she was talking quickly and passing her hand frequently across her brow, Mrs. Bargrave fancied a fit was coming upon

er. She therefore placed herself in a chair just before her
knees, to keep her from falling to the ground, if her fit should
occasion it. And to divert Mrs. Veal's attention she took
hold of her gown-sleeve and commended it. Mrs. Veal told
her it was a scoured silk and newly made up ; but she was not
to be turned from her request that Mrs. Bargrave would
write to her brother.

" But," said the latter, " surely it would be better for you
to do it yourself."

" No ; though it seems impertinent to you now, you will
see more reason for it hereafter."

Then Mrs. Veal asked for Mrs. Bargrave's daughter. She
said she was not at home. " But if you have a mind to see
her, I'll send for her."

" Do," says Mrs. Veal.

On which she left her, and went to a neighbour's to send
for her ; and by the time Mrs. Bargrave was returning,
Mrs. Veal was got without the door in the street, and stood
ready to part as soon as Mrs. Bargrave came to her. She
asked why she was in such haste, and Mrs. Veal said she must
be going, though perhaps she might not go her journey till
Monday ; and told Mrs. Bargrave she hoped she should see
her again at her cousin Watson's before she went whither she
was agoing. Then she said she would not take her leave of
her, and walked from Mrs. Bargrave, in her view, till a turning
interrupted the sight of her, which was three-quarters after
one in the afternoon of the 8th of September.

Mrs. Veal had died the 7th of September, at twelve
o'clock at noon, of her fits. The day after her appearance
being Sunday, Mrs. Bargrave was mightily indisposed with
a cold and a sore throat ; but on Monday morning she sent
a person to Captain Watson's to know if Mrs. Veal were
there. They wondered at Mrs. Bargrave's enquiry and sent
her word she was not there. At this answer, though Mrs.
Bargrave was ill, she put on her hood and went herself to
Captain Watson's to see if Mrs. Veal were there or not. They
said they wondered at her asking, for they were sure that if
she had been in town she would have been there. Says Mrs.
Bargrave, " She was with me on Saturday almost two hours."

They said it was impossible and, while they were disputing,
in comes Captain Watson with the sad news that Mrs. Veal
was dead and that her escutcheons were being made.

Strangely surprised, Mrs. Bargrave went to the person who had the care of them and found it was true.

Returning she related the whole story to the Watson family. " She had on a striped gown and told me it was scoured."

" You have seen her indeed," cried Mrs. Watson, " for none knew but Mrs. Veal and myself that the gown was scoured. And you have described the gown exactly, for I helped her make it up."

Mrs. Watson blazed this about the town, avouching that Mrs. Bargrave had truly seen the apparition of Mrs. Veal.

I should have said before that Mrs. Veal told Mrs. Bargrave that her sister and brother-in-law were just come down from London to see her.

" How came you," Mrs. Bargrave had enquired, " to order matters so strangely ? "

" It could not be helped," Mrs. Veal had replied.

And her brother and sister did come to see her and entered the town of Dover as Mrs. Veal was expiring.

All the time I sat with Mrs. Bargrave, which was some hours, she recollected fresh sayings of Mrs. Veal. And one material thing more she told Mrs. Bargrave, which was that old Mr. Breton allowed Mrs. Veal ten pounds a year, which was a secret, and unknown to Mrs. Bargrave until Mrs. Veal told her.

Mrs. Bargrave never varies in her story, which puzzles those who doubt of the truth or are unwilling to believe it. But Mr. Veal does what he can to stifle the story, and some of his friends report her to be a great liar, and that she knew of Mr. Breton's ten pounds a year. But the person who pretends these things has the reputation of a notorious liar among persons which I know to be of undoubted repute.

Why Mr. Veal should think this relation a reflection—as it is plain he does by his endeavour to stifle it—I cannot imagine ; for her errand was to ask Mrs. Bargrave's forgiveness for her breach of friendship and with a pious discourse to encourage her.

To suppose that Mrs. Bargrave could hatch such an invention as this, she must be more fortunate, witty and wicked too, than any indifferent person will allow.

" I would not," says she, " give a farthing to make anyone

believe my story, and, had it not come to light by accident, it would never have been made public."

The thing has very much affected me, and I am as well satisfied as I am of the best grounded matters of fact. And why we should dispute matters of fact, because we cannot solve things of which we can have no certain or demonstrative notions, seems strange to me ; Mrs. Bargrave's authority and sincerity alone would have been undoubted in any other case.

DENIS MACKAIL

THE LOST TRAGEDY

M R. BUNSTABLE'S book-shop represents a type of establishment which has pretty well disappeared from our modern cities. Indeed, but for the fear of becoming involved in correspondence with strangers, I should be prepared to go considerably further, and to say that it is the only shop of its kind still in existence. In any case, it is most distinctly and unmistakably a survival from the past.

As all who have considered the subject must agree, the principal object of any bookseller is to obstruct, as far as possible, the sale of books. The method generally adopted to-day is to fill the premises with intelligent young men with knobby foreheads who chase intending customers from shelf to shelf, thrusting novels at antiquarians, theological works at novel-readers, and two-volume biographies at those who obviously cannot afford them, until finally they have chased their victims right out into the street. This is called scientific salesmanship, and is largely responsible for the profits shown by the circulating libraries.

The old-fashioned method was directed at the same end, but by a totally different route. The intending customer was left utterly and entirely to himself. If he knew what he wanted to read, he read it without let or hindrance and equally without payment. If he were just vaguely in search of an unidentified book—let us suppose for a wedding present—then he would wait for a period which varied according to his patience and temperament, and ultimately would take his departure and buy a silver sauce-boat elsewhere.

Mr. Bunstable was, and still is, a skilled exponent of this second and earlier form of book-selling. He does not go in for window-dressing, and the wares which are visible from the street seem to have been chosen principally for their power to exclude the daylight from the interior of his shop, and secondarily for a lack of interest which shall ensure their remaining undisturbed. If you persist in disregarding the warning of this window, your next difficulty is with the door. Owing to a slight settlement in the fabric of Mr. Bunstable's premises it is impossible to open this door without the exercise of both strength and skill, but if you do succeed in opening it, then beware of the step which lurks just inside. Inexperienced customers usually arrive in the shop with a crash and a cry of alarm, and perhaps it is because of this that Mr. Bunstable has never troubled to repair the bell which hangs over his lintel, and was originally intended to give notice of his clients' approach.

As your eyes become accustomed to the darkness within, you now detect one or more figures, standing more or less erect with their legs more or less twisted round each other, and profoundly absorbed in the books which they are reading. Here again, and before they have discovered that these figures are wearing hats, inexperienced customers have mistaken them for members of Mr. Bunstable's staff. But no contretemps has ever arisen from this misapprehension. The figures are so intent on their studies that they are deaf to any words which may be addressed to them, and the customer can retrieve his error without any spoken explanation. One imagines that towards closing-time Mr. Bunstable must go round his shop removing the volumes from these students' hands, and gently pushing them back into the outer world. But it is almost as easy to suppose that some of them remain there all night, for so far as my own observation goes Mr. Bunstable regards them as part of the fittings and fixtures. One day I must really go there at closing-time and see what happens.

Meanwhile your eyes are becoming more and more acclimatised. You see vistas and vistas of books. Books heaped up on the dusty floor; books rising in tiers to the mottled ceiling; books on tables; books piled precariously on a step-ladder; books bursting out of brown-paper parcels; books balanced on the seats of chairs. You long to sneeze—for the violence of your entrance has sent a quantity of dust flying up your nose—but you control yourself heroically. The atmosphere of the place would make such an action an outrage. It would be worse than sneezing in church.

It was at this stage, in my own case, and just as I was wondering how on earth one ever bought anything in this extraordinary shop, that another of my senses was unexpectedly assailed. Somewhere—for the moment I couldn't tell where—

a tune was being whistled. A short, monotonous air which
suggested, " Here we go round the mulberry bush," and other
works of that nature, and yet refused to be identified as anything that I had heard before. I looked at the two drugged
readers who were the only other visible occupants of the shop,
but the sound wasn't coming from them. Nor, on the other
hand, did they give any sign of interest or annoyance at the
constant repetition of that little tune.

You will sympathise, I hope, when I say that it had now
become my most pressing requirement to track the whistler
to his lair ; and with this object in view I penetrated still
farther into the darkness of the shop, stepping over the heaps
of books and the brown-paper parcels, and soon losing all
sense of direction in a labyrinth of shelves. All this while the
tune continued, but as I felt my way forward I noticed another
peculiarity about it. The whistler seemed to have some rooted
objection to giving us the last note of his melody. Each
time that he reached this point, and each time that I was
convinced the key-note must be coming, he suddenly broke
off, paused for a moment, and began again at the beginning.
It was all that I could do not to supply the missing note myself.
And yet if, as I was now coming to believe, the music were
proceeding from the proprietor of the shop, this was hardly
the conventional way of introducing myself to his notice.

Again I controlled myself, and then suddenly—as I turned
yet another corner—I beheld the explanation of my puzzle.
I was at the door of an inner sanctum or den, bursting with
books also, yet differing from the dusty profusion through
which I had come in that they were all neatly and carefully
arranged ; and between me and the window, which opened
on to a prospect of unrelieved brickwork, there hung a small
bird-cage.

" Oh," I exclaimed aloud. " A bullfinch."

At the same moment a second, and human, silhouette
appeared before the window. Afterwards I saw that it had
risen from a large desk, but at the time it had the startling effect
of emerging as from a trap-door, and what with this and my
embarrassment at having been overheard, I took a hasty step
backward.

" Don't go, sir," said the silhouette. " Was there anything
I could find for you ? "

It was in this way that I first met Mr. Edward Bunstable,

the sole proprietor of the shop which I have attempted to describe, and the individual to whom I owe the story that I am trying to relate. He was, and still is, a shortish gentleman of a genial but moderate rotundity, the possessor of a beard and a pair of steel-rimmed spectacles. He knows more about out-of-the-way books than anyone I have ever met, and how in the world he keeps his trade going and pays rent, rates and taxes out of it, it is impossible to guess. I have enjoyed the privilege of his acquaintanceship for a number of years now, but though he has frequently shown me volumes which he has bought, I have never yet been able to discover any volume which he has sold. Sometimes I think that he must be an eccentric million-aire—so utterly unbusinesslike are his ways of business—at other times I am fain to believe that he is some kind of fairy, or ghost, or magician, or that he has escaped from the pages of one of his mustiest volumes—but I think this is because secretly he rather enjoys mystifying me. There has been a hint of a twinkle from behind those steel-rimmed spectacles during some of our talks which seems to me to support this view.

I have no idea where he sleeps, when he eats, or what—within about forty years—his age may be. On the other hand I know all these particulars about his bullfinch, for within three minutes of our first meeting—and while I was still trying to give him the name of the book that I wanted—he had told me that the bullfinch never left his room, that it subsisted on millet seed, and that it was fifteen years old. " I bought him cheap," he said, " because he never could learn the last note of his song. I spent ten years trying to teach it him, but it was no use. That bird's got *character*, he has."

" Oh yes," I said. " But about this book, I was wondering if——"

" That bird," interrupted Mr. Bunstable, " is a regular Londoner. He's as sharp as they're made, that bird is."

He told me a great deal more about his bullfinch's alleged characteristics before I could succeed in giving him the particulars of the book that I was after. Then he nodded his head with an air of infinite wisdom.

" I've got it," he said. " I can't just lay my hands on it at the moment, but if you were to come back—say in two or three days' time . . ."

Knowing no better, I did as I was asked. Mr. Bunstable said that he was still searching for the book. He was more convinced than ever that it was somewhere on the premises, but his general attitude towards the affair was that it was no use hurrying things. The suggestion conveyed to me at the time was that if once the book became aware that he was looking for it, it might take fright and disappear for good. After telling me a number of anecdotes of a literary flavour and showing me several of his most recent purchases—which he was careful to explain were not to be included in his stock—he proposed that I should pay him another visit, say in about a week or ten days.

"I'll be certain to have it for you by then," he added. "I *know* I've got it put away somewhere."

To cut a long story short, the object of my original enquiry has eluded Mr. Bunstable's search to this day. He is still hopeful about it, though I have long since abandoned any expectation of its ever coming to light—just as I have long since outgrown the whim which made me ask for it. If he should ever find it, of course I would offer to buy it. This would at least be due to a man who, at a very moderate reckoning, has spent about a fortnight of working days in trying to oblige a customer. I shall not be surprised, however, if—in the event of its turning up—Mr. Bunstable refuses to part with it. For in the meantime there have been one or two near shaves when I have tried to purchase other volumes from his collection, and each time he has managed to prevent the sale taking place.

"Don't take it now, sir," he has said. "I'll find a better copy if you'll wait." Or, "I wouldn't have it, if I were you, sir. There'll be a new edition out in the spring." If I am still persistent, he enmeshes me in one of his long and hypnotic anecdotes, edging me quietly towards the door as he tells it. By this means I am caused to forget the quest which had drawn me to his shop, and his honour as an old-fashioned book-seller is preserved.

An inexplicable old gentleman. Even now, as I set this description on paper, I find myself wondering whether he and his shop can really exist. And perhaps this uncertainty is one of the reasons why I keep on going back there. I want to convince myself that I haven't made it all up.

So we arrive at the story which Mr. Bunstable told me one evening last autumn—beginning it in the recesses of his inner sanctum, with the bullfinch contributing its familiar *obbligato* and finishing it at the front door of his shop, as he bowed me out into the foggy street. A good title for it might be " The Lost Tragedy."

Personally (said Mr. Bunstable) I'm a great one for reading, and perhaps you'll say that's natural enough. But there've been some big men in my trade—men who are up to all the tricks of the auction-room—who'd buy and sell books by the thousand, and yet never read anything but a catalogue or a newspaper, or maybe a railway time-table. Not that they weren't fond of books. But it was the bindings they cared for, or the leaves being uncut, or the first edition with all the misprints and the suppressed preface—*you* know, sir ; the things that run up the value of a book without any reference to what that book's about. Of course, we've all got to watch out for these details, but to my mind—when all's said and done— a book's a thing to read. You can't get away from *that*, sir.

But the man I learnt the business from—old Mr. Trumpett —I was twenty years in his shop in Panton Street before I set up on my own—*he* wouldn't have agreed with me. Not he, sir. He'd got an eye for rarities which was worth a fortune ; he'd got a collection of old editions which was worth another fortune ; and he could run rings round anyone in the saleroom. But he didn't worry about what was inside a book. Not he. Many a time he's hauled me over the coals for sitting reading in his shop. " You stick to the title-pages, my boy," he's said. " That's all a book-seller needs to know about." And I'll say this for Mr. Trumpett, he certainly practised what he preached.

He used to travel about a good deal, attending sales outside London or helping in valuations for probate where there was a big library ; and sometimes—though not as often as I'd have liked—he'd take me along with him. It was a wonder to me the way he'd go into a room full of books in an old country house—all arranged anyhow and with no catalogue or anything to help him—and yet he'd pick out all the plums within five or ten minutes of getting there. It was almost as if he could *smell* 'em out, sir. Uncanny, you'd have called it, if you'd seen him on the job. Partly for practice and partly to amuse myself I'd try sometimes if I couldn't find something valuable that he'd missed ; but I can't say that I ever succeeded. The nearest I ever came to it was with this book that I'm telling you about.

We'd gone down to a big country house where the owner had died, to see if we could pick anything up. The young fellow who'd come into the property was all for selling everything that he could, but when it came to the library the whole place was in such a mess that no one could trouble to make a proper inventory. The auctioneer's instructions were to sell the old books off in bundles as they stood on the shelves; and seeing the quantity of litter there was, I can't say it was a bad idea. The bindings had been pretty good in their day, though that had been some time ago, but as for the stuff inside —well, it was just the typical sermons and county histories and so forth that you could buy up anywhere. A regular lot of rubbish.

We got down there the morning of the day when that part of the sale was coming on, and old Mr. Trumpett didn't take long to size it all up. He marked down a few bundles which might about cover our railway fares, if he got them at a proper price, and then he was just thinking about getting some lunch when I pointed out to him that there was a shelf over one of the doors that we hadn't looked at.

" Nonsense," he said, for he didn't like admitting he could have missed anything. " I saw them when I first came in."

Of course we both knew quite well that he'd done nothing of the sort, but it wasn't going to pay me to get into an argument with him, so I just made up my mind that I'd come back after he'd gone and have a glance at those books myself. " Perhaps I'll get a chance," I thought, " to show him I'm not so ignorant as he thinks."

So just as we were going out of the front door, I pretended I'd left my pencil-case in the library and I went back there alone. To my surprise—for I hadn't been gone more than a minute and we certainly hadn't met anyone on the way—there was a gentleman standing on a chair with his back to me, reaching up at that particular shelf over the inner door. He'd got a cloak on—rather like people used to wear in Scotland—and as I could see a pair of rough stockings underneath it, I made up my mind he was a golfer. He was running through the books very quick and anxious-like, but he must have heard my step, for he stopped suddenly and turned round on his chair. He was rather a short gentleman, and a bit pale;

rather thin on the top, if you know what I mean, and with a little pointed beard. It struck me that I'd seen him somewhere before, or else his photograph, but I couldn't put a name to him at the time, and of course—well, I'll come to that later.

He was looking at me so curiously that I felt I had to say something, so I thought I'd better explain what I'd come back for.

"When you've finished, sir," I said, " I wanted to have a look through that shelf for myself." And as he didn't answer, though I was certain he'd heard me quite clearly, I added : "I've come down from London for the sale."

He nodded very gravely and politely, and turned back to the book-shelf. He kept on taking out one volume after another and shoving them back again as soon as he'd looked inside. Then all of a sudden he gave a little gasp, and I saw him staring at an old quarto, bound in calf, that he'd just opened. The next moment he'd popped it under his cloak and jumped off the chair.

Well, I'd seen some pretty cool customers in the book trade before now, but this seemed to me to be a bit *too* cool.

" Here," I called out, backing between him and the doorway. " What are you doing with that book ? You can't take it away like that."

" Can't I ? " he said—and it seemed to me that he spoke like some kind of West-countryman. " It's mine."

" But you're not Mr. Hatteras, are you ? " I asked—naming the heir to the property. For, you see, this gentleman was about fifty, I should judge.

" No," he said. " But the book is mine. If I choose to take it with me, what is that to you ? It should never have been printed."

Well, sir, at that last remark of his I'll admit that I thought he was a little bit—well, *you* know what I mean. (Here Mr. Bunstable tapped his forehead expressively.) But that didn't seem to me any reason why he should make off with something that wasn't his.

" Look here, sir," I said, " I don't want to make any trouble, but I saw you putting a book from that shelf under your cloak, and unless you put it back where it came from I shall have to tell the auctioneer."

" The auctioneer ? " he repeated, looking a bit puzzled.

" Yes," I said. " If you want any book out of this room,

you can bid for it at the sale this afternoon." And as he still looked kind of silly, I pointed to the card that had been pinned over the shelf. "Lot 56," I said. "If you want that book, the proper way to get it is to bid for Lot 56."

For a moment I thought he was going to make a dash past me, but I wasn't surprised when he changed his mind, for he was a very nervous-looking gentleman, and he wouldn't have stood much chance if I'd wanted to stop him.

"So be it," he said, and he climbed on to the chair again and put the book back where he'd found it. Then with a funny sort of look at me, he went straight out of the room. "I wonder where I've seen that face before," I kept on thinking—but still I couldn't put a name to it.

Well, sir, by this time I saw that if I was going to get any lunch I should have to run for it, and as I was a young man in those days I decided to leave that last book-shelf and try to slip in again before the sale started. As I was going out through the hall, I ran into the auctioneer's clerk, and I thought it mightn't be a bad thing if I told him what I'd seen.

"All right," he said, when I'd finished. "I'll lock the library door, if there's anything of that sort going on. But did you say the gentleman had come out just now?"

"Yes," I said. "Just about a minute before I did."

"That's funny," he answered. "I was in the hall here the whole time, and I could have sworn nobody came by."

Well, it *was* funny, if you see what I mean, sir ; and we both laughed a good deal at the time.

"Though apart from the principle of the thing," I said, "there's precious few books in there that are worth more than sixpence."

"That's as it may be," said the clerk cautiously. And I left him, and hurried off to the inn.

When I told Mr. Trumpett, he said, "H'm. That sounds like Badger of Liverpool. He'll get shut up one of these days if he's not careful." And he pulled out his copy of the sale catalogue and made a pencil mark against Lot 56. "He's a cunning old bird," he added. "If there's anything I've missed, we'll give him a run for his money."

And we did. I had no opportunity of seeing that shelf again, for the library was still locked when I got back, and the sale was to take place in the dining-room. But there was Mr. Badger of Liverpool, in his cloak and his golf-stockings, watching each lot as it came up and was knocked down, and when we got to Lot 56 he started bidding like a good 'un.

Mr. Trumpett sat there nodding his head to the auctioneer —for everyone but these two had soon dropped out—but when the price for the odd dozen books had run up to a hundred and twenty-five pounds, I suppose he felt he'd gone far enough for a pig in a poke. He closed his eyes and shook his head, in the way he had when he'd finished bidding, and the auctioneer brought his hammer down with a thump.

Of course I thought we'd heard the last of Lot 56, but just as I was crossing it off my list I heard the auctioneer having some kind of an argument with the successful bidder.

" These are no good to me," he was saying, holding out a handful of coins. " I can't take foreign money for my deposit."

Mr. Badger was a very nervous-looking gentleman, as I think I've told you, and he didn't seem to know what to make of this. He kept on snapping his fingers and starting sentences that he couldn't finish, but it was no use. The auctioneer simply dropped the money on his desk for Mr. Badger to take or leave as he chose, and announced that he was putting the lot up again. The little mystery and excitement that there'd been sent it up to seven-pound-ten, but at that figure the competition stopped and Mr. Trumpett got what he'd wanted. I could see the auctioneer looking pretty sick, but he was quite right, of course. Whatever those coins were, they'd have been no good to his employers. Why, some of them were scarcely even round !

Well, sir, we stopped on and picked up one or two more lots, and when we'd arranged for having them sent up to London we took a fly back to the station and caught our train. In the carriage I suddenly remembered rather a curious thing, and I mentioned it to Mr. Trumpett.

" Did you see where Mr. Badger went to ? " I asked. " I never saw him leaving the room, but he wasn't there when we came away ; that I'll swear."

Mr. Trumpett looked at me quite queer-like.

" Badger ? " he repeated. " What do you mean ? "

" Why," I said, " the gentleman who bid against you, sir, for Lot 56."

" That wasn't Badger," he says.

" Then who was it ? " says I.

But Mr. Trumpett had no idea.

" I feel as if I'd seen his face somewhere," he said presently ; " or else he's very like someone I've met. But I'm bothered if I can place him."

" If you ask me," he said, a little later on, " he'd broken loose from somewhere. Did you see the way his eyes were rolling ? "

" Yes," I said. " Quite a fine frenzy, wasn't it ? "

But of course my little literary allusion was wasted on Mr. Trumpett. He only grunted, and we dropped the subject for good.

Well (resumed Mr. Bunstable, who had now got me out of his labyrinth into the main part of the shop), a few days after that the packing-case came along from the sale, and though Mr. Trumpett would likely enough have let it lie in his cellar for weeks—for he took his time over most things— I thought I'd go down and look through the stuff myself. You see, I'd still got it in the back of my head that our golfing friend might have known a bit more than we'd given him credit for ; that there really might be some sort of " find " in Lot 56. And if there was, then I meant to get to the bottom of it.

So late that afternoon I took a candle down to the cellar— we'd no gas except in the shop itself in those days—and I got a tack-lifter and a hammer, and started opening the case. Out it all came—most of it just about fit for a barrow in the street, though every now and then I'd find one of the books that Mr. Trumpett had spotted—and presently I'd got right down to the straw. And there—the last book to come out—was the calf-bound quarto that the gentleman in the cloak had tried to make away with. The label had come off the back and the leaves were still uncut, but when I turned to the title-page— well, I tell you, sir, I thought for a moment I must be dreaming.

What would *you* say, sir, I wonder, if you picked up an old book and found it was a play by Shakespeare that no one had ever imagined as existing ? Would you believe your eyes ? I tell you, I could hardly believe mine. Yet there it was— paper, type and binding all above suspicion, as I knew well enough—and on the title-page *The Tragedie of Alexander the Great, by Mr. William Shakespeare*. I felt like Christopher Columbus and Marconi rolled into one. The biggest discovery of the century, and I—down there by myself in Mr. Trumpett's cellar—had made it. I sat down on the edge of that packing-case and fairly gasped for breath. It was the most tremendous moment of my life.

Of course I knew it was my real duty to rush up the ladder into the shop and tell Mr. Trumpett what I'd found, and, of course, I meant to do this as soon as I'd collected my wits. But while I sat there staring at that title-page, I realised more and more clearly what Mr. Trumpett would do. The book would go straight into his safe—uncut as it was, so as to keep up the value ; when it left the safe it would be to go direct to the saleroom, and from there—unless an Act of Parliament stopped it—to an American collector. If I carried out my duty without a thought of the consequences, my first oppor-tunity of reading the *Tragedie of Alexander the Great* would be in a facsimile or reprint, just as if the original had never been in my hands at all. And I wanted to read it *now*. I was enough of a bookseller to recognise its enormous value, but—unlike Mr. Trumpett—I was too much of a book-lover to let that American collector read it first.

I wasn't going to cut the leaves, of course. I knew better than to do that. But there were pretty wide margins, and by twisting the pages carefully I could manage well enough ; and so—sitting down on the packing-case and by the light of my candle—I began right away. " *Act I, Scene I. A Room in King Philip's Palace.*" Yes, sir ; I remember that. But I'm thankful that I can't remember any more.

Did I say " thankful " ? Well, sir, I'm afraid I mean it. I don't pretend to be a poet myself and in the ordinary way I'll admit there may be better critics. But when it comes to a real piece of downright incompetent, careless writing, of bad scansion and worse grammar, of loud-sounding, pretentious and meaningless clap-trap—then I'll take leave to say that I'm as good a judge as most men. It was awful, sir ; it was terrible, It was like a parody of the worst kind of Elizabethan poetry, and yet, if you see what I mean, it *was* Elizabethan poetry. Not a word, not a phrase to give the show away—as there are in Chatterton's forgeries. It was like Shakespeare read through some kind of distorting lens, with all the faults and weaknesses—for he *had* faults and weaknesses, sir—magnified ten thousand times, and all the beauty cancelled right out.

" No wonder they kept this out of the First Folio," I kept on telling myself. And yet I couldn't put it down. However

bad it might be, it *was*—unless some contemporary had played
an expensive practical joke—the discovery that I had taken it
for. And I was the first of my own contemporaries to read it.
In spite of myself, though, my excitement had given way to an
almost overwhelming sense of depression. If you're really
fond of books, sir, that's always the way a piece of thoroughly
bad workmanship takes you.

I don't know how long I'd been down in that cellar (resumed
Mr. Bunstable, after a short and mournful pause), when all of
a sudden I heard a kind of thud overhead ; and looking up I
saw that someone had closed the trap at the top of the ladder.
" Good heavens," I thought, " there's Mr. Trumpett going off
for the night, and if I don't hurry after him I shall be locked
in." I jumped up, picked up my candle and was just moving
to the foot of the ladder, when to my astonishment I saw that
two men were standing in my way. It seemed to me that they
were in some kind of fancy dress, and what with this and my
bewilderment at the way they'd managed to get in, I very
nearly dropped the candle. Then, as I recovered it, I recognised
the shorter of them. It was the old gentleman that I'd seen
last week at the sale down in the country ; the gentleman that
I'd taken for Mr. Badger of Liverpool.

" What's the matter ? " I asked in a shaking kind of voice.
" What do you want, sir ? "

He didn't answer me, but turned to his companion—a big
burly sort of fellow, who struck me as knowing pretty well
what the bottom of a pint-pot looked like.

" Did you bolt the trap, Ben ? " he asked. " Are you sure
the old man's gone ? "

" What do you take me for ? " said the big fellow, speaking
with a kind of rough, Cockney accent. " Of course he's gone.
Now, then," he added, looking at me, " we've come for that
book. Where have you put it ? "

I had it under my arm, but before I could answer him he'd
spotted it.

" Aha ! " he called out. " There you are, Will. What did
I tell you ? Didn't I say we'd find it here ? "

They both seemed tremendously excited, and I was convinced that they'd been drinking ; but I wasn't going to stand
any nonsense.

" I don't know what you're doing here," I said, retreating

behind the packing-case, " or how you've forced your way in. But this book has been bought and paid for by my employer, Mr. Trumpett, and let me remind you that you've no right in the private part of the shop."

The big man only laughed at this, but the other started talking sixteen to the dozen.

" And let me tell *you*," he said, " that that book was published without any authority, that the script was stolen from the theatre and that anyone who keeps it is a receiver of stolen goods. Do you know what I spent in buying up that edition from the blackguard who printed it ? Two hundred angels. And do you know how long I've been hunting for the copy he kept back ? Nearly three hundred years ! But I've found it at last, and I'm going to see that it's destroyed. I've got my reputation to protect the same as anyone else, and if I did a bit of pot-boiling because I'd got into debt that's no reason why it should be brought up against me now. I've had enough trouble over *Pericles* and *Titus Andronicus*, without being saddled with a bit of balderdash like *Alexander the Great*. You got the better of me down in Gloucestershire last week, but it's my turn now. I've got good friends, I have, who'll see that justice is done. If I'm a bit scant of breath myself, here's my old colleague Jonson, who's killed his man more than once and will do it again for the honour of the profession. Now, then, young sir, are you going to hand that play over, or do you want a taste of Ben's dagger in your gullet ? "

That's the way he ran on, sir, though I may not have got all his words quite right, and all the time the other man was rocking and shaking with laughter. I was so scared I could hardly think, for it was no joke being shut up down there with two fellows like that. Mad, they might be, or drunk, or both together ; but whatever they were, I could see they would stick at nothing. And yet . . .

Well, sir, it's no use reproaching myself now. And, besides, after all these years I'm not at all sure that the actual upshot wasn't the best for everybody. The big fellow had jumped right over the packing-case and twisted my arms together behind my back, while the little one snatched the book from where it had fallen, tore out the sheets and burnt them one by one in the flame of my candle. Then he threw the empty binding down on the cellar floor.

" All's well that ends well," he said. " He's had his lesson, Ben. You can let him go."

And then he stooped down and blew out the candle.

.   .   .   .

As he reached this stage in his remarkable narrative, Mr Bunstable stretched past me with one hand and opened the door of his shop. A cold draught accompanied by wisps of London fog blew in through the aperture, causing me to shiver and Mr. Bunstable to utter his little, dry, grating cough. Far away I heard the indomitable bullfinch once more embarking on his incomplete melody. The rest was silence.

" You mean," I said presently, " that it was a dream ? "

" Eh ? " said Mr. Bunstable, starting from his thoughts. " Well, sir, as to that I should hardly like to say. I certainly spent the night in that cellar, as Mr. Trumpett could tell you if he were alive. And I'll have to admit that there were no traces of that book on the floor—no ashes, even—when I looked for them in the morning. And yet that doesn't seem to me to explain everything. Because, sir, there was no calf bound quarto there either. You've only got my word for it, of course, but . . ."

And here, gently but firmly, Mr. Bunstable shut me out into the fog.

CLEMENCE DANE

SPINSTER'S REST

" Every day the poor girl had to sit and spin till her fingers
bled . . . and in the sorrow of her heart she jumped into the
well. . . . When she came to herself she was in a lovely
meadow where many thousands of flowers grew. Along she
went till she came to an oven, and the bread cried : ' Take me
out ! I shall burn ! ' . . . and to a tree covered with apples
which called to her : ' Shake me ! Shake me ! ' . . . and at
last to a little house out of which an old woman peeped and
called out : ' Dear child, stay with me ! If you will do the
work of the house properly you shall be the better for it. I am
Mother Holle.'

" So the girl took courage and agreed to enter her service.
She stayed some time, and then she became sad. At first she
did not know what was the matter with her, but at last she
said to Mother Holle : ' I have a longing for home.' . . .
Thereupon Mother Holle led her to a great door and, opening
it, said : ' This is the reward of your service.' "

Grimm's Fairy Tales.

" Holda (Hulda, Holle, Frau Holl) . . . A being of the sky
. . . a motherly deity. She assumes the shape of an old woman
and has the oversight of spinners. When it snows she is said
to be making her bed. She carries off unchristened infants."

Grimm's Mythology.

I

THE old woman had looked so kind. She had been such
a friendly sight after London, beastly London, crazy
London, after the struggle at the railway station and the sordid
rhythm of the train, after the solitary walk through the rainy
village and the soaked January lanes. She had been such a
cheerful heart, she and her firelit room, to the huge stone
house with its unlighted endless casement rows and its prison
front. The chance of such an employer, such a place of
employment, seemed too good to be true ! She was all
a-strain to fit herself into the picture, as she sat on the edge of
the chair, hands in lap, answering questions. Her body was
still, her manner was still, her eyes were fixed respectfully

upon the old woman's face. Yet the effect she produced, even to herself, was not a peaceful one. She felt like a wire stretched to snapping-point, like her own mantelpiece statue of the praying boy, beseeching hands eternally arrested in mid-air. Her voice as she answered was flat :

" Mary—Mary Pawle. No, quite alone. Both dead. I have a little money of my own. Oh no, I don't mind telling you—ninety pounds a year. At the office I got three pounds a week."

" I can't offer a companion more than board and lodging."

" I don't care. I want a change. I was ten years at the office."

" Ten years in an office ! A girl shouldn't be at any one piece of work for more than a year, my dear. We need change, we women. That's why we're given children."

Children ! That was the word that had driven like a wedge between the dry preliminaries of the interview and its fantastic heart of dreams. Children ! What devil's dice had tossed up that number ? What senile whim induced the old woman to strike just that forbidden note ? These rich old ladies, she thought, were like pampered house-cats ; too full-fed to claw, but they must pat you for their amusement. Well, she was yet her own mistress—where were her gloves ? Yet she had hoped to be approved : she had hoped to be taken on : it would have been a change. But such dissertations were more than even her sullen patience proposed to endure. You do not talk to an employer of the secret flowers withering in your heart like pansies in a London window-box—not in the first five minutes—no, nor for bed and board. She repeated stonily, her sallow cheeks flushing :

" I want a change, that's all ! " and reached for her handbag.

" Ah ? " The knitting-needles were flashing in the knotted ivory hands. Such bright pointed lights flickered from them : she could not take her eyes away.

" I hate London," she added, and flushed anew. She had not meant to say it.

" Quarrelled with him ? " said the old lady, for the first time fixing her with eyes sharper and brigher than the needles.

Then had come panic. She had risen hurriedly, giddily, so that her chair tilted backwards and fell clattering. She picked it up with fumbling hands, crying :

" I can't talk. I can't ! " in a high, terrified voice.

" To me? Oh, my girl, if we're to be companions——"

There were the velvet paws again! And yet the voice was sweet, like a dream she had had once of sighing trees. All her happy times had been in dreams. She was enchanted by that kind voice, even while she said, trembling :

" I'd better go. I don't think I should do." And saying it, gazing into the bright eyes of the old lady, she sat down again, slowly, obediently, like an animal quieted. She even answered the unspeakable question, saying, " It wasn't a quarrel." And then, " I haven't even that."

The bright steels that had stopped for a moment began to click again.

" Not even that, eh? Well—go on! "

And she went on. She felt the terrors and pangs of a prisoner tortured into speech as she cried out in spite of herself, twisting her fingers :

" He never looked at me. He only cared to spoil things."

" Spoilt things, did he? "

" Oh," she said piteously, " it was only a dream—like playing with dolls to some girls—but—but I'd lived for it somehow. I'd trained myself—fairy-tales and sewing and things. I wasn't silly. I wasn't horrid. It wasn't to get married. It was the children, to have children one day. But he—he spoilt it all. Did I ask to fall in love? "

So she spoke, her eyes fixed on those two bright eyes as if they were the crystals in which she read aloud her own fate. She listened, as if they were a stranger's, to her own shameless avowals.

" I always thought I'd get married, you see. One does. Home—husband—children—one knows it'll come. One's brought up to it. Can I help that? And I'm good with children. I looked so to have my own. One does. I know their names. I know how they look. I can feel their hands sometimes, touching me. I can—oh, I wish you'd let me stop! I wish——"

Again the movement of the needles had been passes in the air quelling and compelling her.

" You wish——? Go on! " said the old woman.

Go on? Of course she must go on. She could no more stop—she would like to see anyone stop her! All the agonies of her dying youth rose under the compulsion of those strange eyes to the surface of her mind at last, like some heaven or hell's brew on the bubble, on the boil, ready to brim over, to scald anew, to complete the ruin of the seared and suffering spirit; and yet, when she tried to speak, she could express herself only in the pitifully inadequate phrases of her untrained and illiterate consciousness:

"Husbands—love—troublesome, I used to think: rather hateful; but to be put up with, you know, because of children. Children get on with me. I'd have been such a good mother. But now——"

"Now——?"

"I can't have any, ever." And then, twisting herself like a prisoner straining in bonds, "I won't talk any more. I don't want to. I'm tired."

"Now——?" The bright eyes were becoming two lamps into which she must stare. She yielded.

"He stopped it, for good and all."

"Did you——?"

"Love him? He was at my boarding-house. He sat opposite me at meals. He talked to me. He used to smile when I came in. I thought for a little while—oh, I was so happy. I was a fool. He didn't even guess. He was killed, you know, in the war. He married a girl I know. They asked me to the wedding." And then fiercely, "Did I ask for it to happen to me? I could have married before, just nicely. But now—other men—how can I? It would be adultery. Besides, oh, besides, it's a blow, a thing like that, a blow to your mind. It's like a tree falling on you in a storm, crushing. Oh, it's nothing: I don't feel much any more. I'm only tired. I wish you'd let me shut my eyes."

"Shut them!" said the old woman's voice, a blessed decisive voice, a voice that knew your business for you, that told you what to do. She obeyed.

"'Once upon a time——'" began the old woman softly, and the clickings of the needles were like the tripping heels of a tune—"'Once upon a time there was a poor girl——'"

How familiar was the voice, the voice of her nurse telling her fairy-tales—dreams, nightmare; for the interview, of course, was a dream, the latest stage of the dull nightmare of her life. Well, if it lightened to mere dream again, at least it was a change. How familiar was the voice! It was her own voice, surely her own voice, dreaming over Grimm's on the hearthrug, spelling out by firelight her favourite fairy-tale——

" And at last she came to a house out of which an old woman was looking, and the girl was so frightened that she wanted to run away——"

Familiar words, familiar as a forgotten dream !

" ' What are you afraid of, dear child ? Stay with me for a year, and you shall be the better for it ; but you must take care to shake my bed till the feathers fly, for then it snows in the world. I am——' "

She broke in triumphantly :

" Mother Holle ! You're Mother Holle—Grimm's fairy-tales—the blue-and-gold cover ! I know you ! You're Mother Holle ! " And she would have risen from her chair as people rise in dreams from a strange bed ; but the needle lights flashed round her head like swords, like lightnings, and the soft voice forced her back into the dream's velvet deeps like a strong hand ramming home a sword into its protectant scabbard. She lost even the desire to struggle. With closed eyes and rested heart she let herself wander, as she had not done for twenty years, into the half-light, the half-consciousness of that accessible Middle Land that a child enters so easily, and that some children grow never too old to enter. She was such a child, though she had forgotten it, and it was as easy as waking to drift over the cobwebbed border on the wings of that controlling voice, a voice, a windy voice that spoke to her from the apple-tree : " Shake me ! Shake me ! " —a comfortable croaking voice from the oven-door : " Burning ! Burning ! Take me out ! "—as she shook down the apples and pulled out the scorched cakes, and so wandered on through its flowery grass and sunny weather, happy, happy, happy, in the happy land.

A timeless land—all its hours and minutes, its days and seasons melted into one, as a thousand scents puff by in every breath of summer. She did her year's service, wandering dreamily to and fro, from the cows with their aching udders to the dropping autumn apple-trees, and back to the little house with its spring garden quick with furtive life : newborn butterflies clinging weakly to the grey cabbage-leaves : young thrushes busy with snails : till (how eagerly she stooped !) under a gooseberry-bush one evening, one frosted, moon-lit evening, she found——

" That shall be the reward of your service ! " said Mother Holle. " In the meantime board and lodging."

She heard her own voice :

" I don't care : I wan't a change " : and so jerked herself back into consciousness, consciousness of herself, guiltily warm and relaxed on the sofa like a kitten on forbidden coverlets, facing the bright windows once more and the bright fire that leaped towards her like an eager dog, and near the fire, brighter than the fire, the bright eyes of her employer. " Employer " was the right term ; for the bargain, she found, had been struck, and her hand given and held a moment in a firm hand-clasp, in a clasp stirring words to life in her mind :

" Good-bye ! Good luck ! Come back safe ! Good-bye ! "

She tried to disengage her hand and herself, she tried to say, " I won't come to you ! You're bad to me. You're making me cry." But the words turned themselves on her lips to—

" Thank you ! Yes !—yes ! Very well ! "

She was to live at the inn in the village and come to Spinsters' Rest daily, " to be with me, to read aloud, and sew and be silent, and look after my guests."

" Guests ? "

" Not arrived yet," said her employer, and with a gleaming smile had closed the extraordinary interview.

II

She settled down, as far as unpacking a thin suit-case went, and learning her duties, and going, on her free afternoons, for aimless walks. It was the easiest place in the world for a poor girl—gratefully she admitted it. She might not have existed for all the ripple she made in the pond-like life of the village. She felt sometimes as if she and her employer were the only waking creatures in a tapestry world : that the sunlight outside the window was glimmering on mere stitch-work walls : that it was only her own shadow falling on them as she passed to and fro from her lodging that stirred her neighbours to unreal and momentary life. Yet she liked the faded quiet, just as she liked the grey street with its pebbled pavements and slate roofs streaked with velvet. The village was like herself, she thought, in a rare moment of self-analysis, stagnant, neither alive nor dead. She was in touch with it, and liked it better than the surrounding emerald wheat-lands set off with startling hedgerows of white and yellow ; for the winter was more than over. She could not but stare in daily wonder at the washed perfection of the spring ; but it had not lost, she found, its old power to hurt her. It roused her, made her think and remember and long for her own past with a sick violence of regret that thinned her cheeks till the skin grew taut and polished over the bones, and her eyelids were swelled and darkened with the weight of tears restrained. Before the spring was a month old she was as restless and hopeless as ever she had been in London.

She might be restless ; but she was not the only one. That discovery she made, and in a moment of expansion imparted it to her employer.

" How queer the village people are ! They whisper and point. They follow me, d'you know—truly it's not my fancy. One woman came right up to the door."

" A beggar ? "

" Yes—no. Begging, but not a beggar. A dog with a hurt paw, that's the look. And if I turn suddenly they back away."

Said her employer thoughtfully, compassionately :

" I can't do anything. It's too early in the year. They know that." And then—" Aren't the primroses out yet in the hedges ? "

She answered :

" I haven't looked." And was then amused and in the end half frightened by the look she got—such blue eyes were the old woman's, with such flashes in them when she chose. But the answer was merely whimsical. How else should she take it ?

" Not looked for primroses ? My dear, how wicked ! "

She shrugged her shoulders.

" I hate the spring. It makes one restless."

" You'll stay on through the summer all the same," said her employer placidly. " There'll be plenty to do." She clicked thoughtfully a moment, murmuring to herself in the fashion with which the girl had become familiar :

" ' Some to kill cankers in the musk-rose buds ;
Some war with rear mice for their leathern wings.' "

And then, flicking the words at her not so much from mouth or eye as from those sharp needle-points, flicking them forth at the end of invisible threads like a fisherman flicking a fly delicately forth upon the too clear water : " I've some children

coming down next week," and for an instant paused in her
eternal knitting, the girl felt, watchfully.

But this once-caught fish, sullen beneath her root, would
not rise : though she knew all about the slum children and
their yearly pilgrimage to shriek and scatter orange-peel and
wreck the byways of the garden. Her landlady had told her
their story, among others :

"Oh, yes, miss, the children come regular. Squalling
brats ! I don't hold—but children always have come, somehow, to Spinsters' Rest. My grandmother, she said her mother
said it was the same in her time."

"But that must be—oh, a hundred years ago ! She couldn't
—I mean, who lived there then ? "

"I don't know, miss, now you ask. But I'd say there'd
always been a friendly person, as it were, at Spinsters' Rest.
And children and beasts, they know it—oh yes ! I tell you,
miss, I seen a sick fox once walk in at the gate like a Christian.
And swallows—— ! Miss, where *do* the swallows go in winter
—our swallows ? Miss, there's an old man here, and his
father's mother told him what she saw once. She'd gone up
to Spinsters' Rest, wanting a herb or such—for the oldest
trouble in the country, she told him—and as she went up the
lane (in the autumn it was) she saw the swallows swinging
round and round the house like flies round a paper ball, she
said ; and up went the sash of a window, and there was a
hand that beckoned, and in they swept very quick and quiet,
every last one of them, like a flight of fish in clear water, the
woman said, and the window shut down. She said the sky
seemed so big and empty all at once, with the swallows gone,
and the house stood up so black against it, that she just took
and ran. And never a swallow seen again till April. Never
see birds here in winter, you know, nor squirrels and such.
They say the house takes them. They say it takes folks, too.
There was a time, miss, they say, when the house took too
many : poor creatures, you know, that nobody missed :
tramps and trollops and now and then a come-by-chance. Not
people to be missed. Then one day a young lady ! That
startled them, and they searched and searched, but they never
found anyone. So they took the woman of the house to be
a witch and swam her and stretched her and burnt her at last
on her own doorstep. They say the brickwork's blackened still
over the front door."

The modern girl shuddered.

" Yes, miss, and not her fault, as it turned out. For the beggars were back when the New Year came, trailing into the village again by twos and threes, and the young lady with them. They had nothing to say for themselves, just went about mooning, smiling, a bit too friendly. So it was put about that it was kidnapping, and they hanged the lot, all but the young lady. That was before they built the high wall round it."

" Who built it ? "

" I don't know, miss—one of the ladies. There's always been a lady living there, at least since the Queen's time."

" Which queen ? "

" The one on the sign. The story got about, you know, and she came to see for herself. Stayed in this very room. It's her bed you're setting on."

" But to see *what* for herself ? " For the assumption that she must understand irritated her.

" Well, miss, she never had chick nor child, did she ? Yes, she spent a day at Spinsters' Rest, they say, and she left a paper behind her that the house should never be troubled. The Rector has it."

" Is that history ? " demanded the girl.

" Not board-school, miss, but—well, they say so, hereabouts. The Rector'd tell you."

But the Rector was not interested in anything so modern as Good Queen Bess ; though, a mild amateur of antiquities, he was only too glad to chat with anyone employed in a house where a Roman pavement had been unearthed. He had not, alas ! been privileged to examine it himself. The occupant of Spinsters' Rest took little interest in matters parochial, was not, in fact (he lowered his voice), a communicant ; but he understood that it was a singularly interesting specimen. According to his theory—mere theory, my dear young lady ! —the local legends all pointed to a grove or temple in Roman times, of—Minerva, possibly ?—the patroness of spinners, eh ?—doubtless, resanctified later as a Christian fane. But in the sixth century, of course, all records were obliterated— Teuton hordes—" fierce Pagans," as Roger hath it—" setting up strange gods " ; but it was certainly a nunnery in later years. Hilda, Abbess Hilda (the convert, you remember ?) is said to have been the founder. The good nuns were famous

for their linen in—er—1250, I fancy, and privileged in consequence. Hence the name—Spinsters' Rest! Dispossessed
under Henry VIII, of course. An iniquitous business!
From him passed to his daughter—the spinster queen!
Explains your landlady's—er—surmise. Oh, mere surmise—
I know nothing of any paper; except, of course, the deed
of gift to a waiting-maid—dependant—who was, curiously
enough, burnt under James I. The road to Endor, eh?
Strait is the gate—yes, indeed! And now, alas! in private
hands: oh, no doubt very respectable hands; but, as
I say,—*not* being a communicant . . . He sighed himself
away.

She would lie at night listening to the curiously musical
creak of the Queen's Head board as it swung and started
beneath her window in the spring wind, and ponder these
things, and others: and not least among others, the fact that
she was sleeping where she was, and not, as would have been
so natural, in her employer's house.

" The rooms are wanted," her employer had stated in her
brief, unarguing fashion that inclined Mary Pawle, at least, to
accept any statement without question, without even an inward
stir of surprise. But in the stillness of the shortening nights
surprise would lift a head nevertheless, belatedly, like a
memory of wrongdoing long passed, long forgotten, but once
roused never again to be quieted. Who and what was her
employer? And what did the charwoman *do* on Sundays?

" And get me my meals on Sundays, my dear! I like
my good woman to get her Sundays off!" That had been
the actual phrase of her instructions, the wording of her bond:
and yet once—twice—for three Sundays running she had
come upon the clod-hopping familiar figure, in unfamiliar
Sunday clothes, lurking in the bushes in the early morning as
she let herself in, scurrying into the darkness of the drive as
she left the house behind her in the evening. And once, as she
swept away the breakfast crumbs, she had seen her through
the half-open door, passing across the patterned floorwork
of the vestibule, and heard her too, heard the labouring feet
creaking the stairs as she climbed them.

She had spoken then in her surprise:

" I thought she had her Sundays off!"

" So she does," said her employer. " Shake the crumbs to
the birds, my dear!"

She had laughed a little as she obeyed that regular command. No need to scatter the crumbs : she was accustomed to pushing the robins out of the way with her crumb-brush, to have the mixed crew on the threshold of the window rise but a bare half-yard into the air at her scattering gesture, and settle again a little nearer, always a little nearer. She said :

" But I see her here almost every Sunday."

Said the old lady :

" What do _you_ do with your afternoons off ? "

She considered the question as she went to her next duty, standing on the chair to snip the dead leaves from the great trail of old-man's-beard that had grown into the room through a crack in the cornice and now swung its powdery length over a blackened portrait (the original, she guessed, of the inn signboard). At last she said slowly, flushing :

" You know what I do."

" Sit and think ? "

" Sit and think." And then : " What else can I do ? "

" What my good woman does."

" Come back here ? "

" Why not ? Prowl about the house, my dear ! Amuse you. Fine pictures. Beds to rest on. Beautiful views—upstairs."

She got up irresolutely and opened the door as she spoke over her shoulder :

" I've never been upstairs."

The wide staircase was lighted by a skylight so large that you guessed the hall had once been open to the sky and the staircase ended in a landing, long, low-ceilinged, with doors to right and left. It turned sharply at its farther end like a rabbit's bolt-hole.

" However many doors ! "

" Many, many," chuckled the old woman, and startled the girl, for she had thought, not spoken.

" You wouldn't say it was such a long passage," she commented, " from the outside."

" It could be bounded in a nutshell," said her employer complacently.

She frowned, puzzled, because the incomprehensible phrase was somehow familiar. Then she turned back to the staircase. The problem of the charwoman had roused her curiosity.

" What does she do up there ? "

" Rests, I dare say. She's welcome. She's had a sad life.

She's a spinner," said the old lady. " That's why her back'
bent double."

" A weaver, you mean ? I thought that hand-looms———

" Factory-work, I mean," said the old woman. " Isn't i
factories now ? It was looms once. But always the spinning
wheel, my dear, behind it. Call it what you like, it works ou
the same. Swaddleclothes are always wanted, and bride-veil
and shrouds—and who thanks the spinners ? Fourpence a
hour—sweating, don't you call it, in your London ? Swea
of the spinners, it waters the earth. Bend 'em and break 'em
the women who spin, plenty more where they come from. On
man to one woman, and the women over—let 'em spin ! "

The girl stood staring, her duties dropping from her hands

" Me—they're in me, those bitter thoughts. That's wha
I'm thinking day and night. How do you know what
think ? "

Said her employer :

" You don't rest properly. You talk in your sleep."

It was her duty to laugh at the joke, and she laughed
shakily, as she stooped for the dusters and scissors.

" ' Spinster—An unmarried woman—so called becaus
she was supposed to occupy herself with spinning.' I foun
that in the dictionary." And then : " Do you hear my dream
across the village ? "

Said the old woman seriously :

" I hear the noise they make."

She had got herself in hand.

" I don't dream about noises."

" Oh, my dear," said her employer, " children are boun
to be noisy." And then, as the girl sat shivering, for she wa
never sufficiently on guard against the crazy accidents of thei
intercourse that ever and again, like a nail in an old pane
ripped up her garment in passing and bared the naked skin
" By the way, they're coming next week."

Almost she said :

" My children ? " so utterly had the baring of her thought
shaken her. But somehow she held to her sanity as she ha
done before in the crazy place. She could do it by sheer fierc
repetition of the epithet. " Crazy—it's a crazy place ! An
she—she's crazy ! A crazy old woman ! That's all ! She'
crazy ! " She said it inwardly now, as she said it twenty time
a day, while her tongue said in best companion's manner :

" The London children ? "

" Fifty of 'em. You'll see to things, my dear. Tea on
he lawn."

" But if it rains ? "

" It won't rain," said her employer. And then : " Better
give 'em strawberries and cream."

" But "—she was tentative after the snub—" there aren't
many. It's been so wet."

" There'll be enough," said her employer.

And when, a few days later, the children were at last ranged
in a great circle between the oak-tree and the house, and she
overlooked the quick-passing pottles that she had been filling
all the morning, she saw that there was indeed enough. And
he sky was as blue as a forget-me-not.

She was kept busy. The old lady's chair was pushed to
he very threshold of the French window, though she did not
leave it, did not put down her knitting even to greet the
London curate and the London ladies that topped and tailed
he excited column that filed past. (" My dear, I daren't !
The sun would go in.") She had said it with the swift glance
and smile that always dazzled her companion, physically
dazzled her, as if her eyes were too weak to support it unblink-
ing. And indeed, at that moment it had seemed to her as if
he long thin needles were indeed busy, not with threads of
wool but, fantastic notion, threads of sunlight.

However, it was not her business, and the children and
heir games were. She went down to play with them.

It was while they were playing Nuts-and-May that she first
noticed the child. It stood by itself, watching : a forlorn
manling, ridiculous in a woman's coat with gigot sleeves. As
hey passed and repassed, she made with her hand a little
gesture of invitation to join the end of the line. It backed from
her hastily, unsmiling, and she heard a laugh from the girl
whose hand she held.

" He won't come, miss : he's dumb. We don't play
wiv 'im."

" Oh, poor—— But why shouldn't he play ? "

" He won't, miss. He'll hit out at yer."

" Will he ? " She detached herself from the sticky clasp,
and went quickly after the small figure that was so pitifully
easy to overtake, for it limped in its hurry, and she could see
he stocking-shaped support of iron it wore on a pipe-stem leg.

She caught up with it and held out once more the inviting hand, though some delicate instinct restrained her from any premature touch.

"I say—look here—don't you want to play?" She was panting a little from her run.

The child, overtaken, had stopped: and its eyelids were lifted in that cold little look of inquiry with which all children await advances. It had the dark eyes, the pure, lustrous black circles, that so inexplicably shrink and lighten in later life to the common brown—"like mine," she thought ruefully, and smiled. And at that suddenly behind the eyes' blank surface something stirred, something looked out at her, signalled—she could swear it, for she felt her own eyes signalling in answer, in yearning answer—and was still again. It was as if a blind had been drawn up and down, as if two strangers had snapshotted each other's souls. But she was a woman grown out of girlhood and this starved child was—what? Four? Five? She bent forward in her eagerness, and as quickly knew her error. For, as she caught at the small hand it was snatched from her, and the child backed away again and at two yards' distance turned and fled, fled towards the open window at which her employer sat. She did not follow: she was well trained in putting her duties before her wishes; but as she took her place once more, and added her sweet shrill note to the song of the children, she was saying within herself over and over again: "It looked at me! It looked at me! What a fool I am!—but it looked at me!"

Later, she saw it again, momentarily, out of the corner of her eye, as she hurried along the terrace at tea-time. It had got itself over the threshold much, she fancied, as the birds did at breakfast, and was now as close as it could push to the big chair in the bewildering green-and-gold-barred shadows of the venetian blinds. Its hands, planted each on one of the old woman's knees, supported the whole weight of the eager, forward-thrust body. She had an odd fancy that the fingers were spread like the rootlets of some small tenacious tree, digging its home into a crag of the hill. The old woman, too, was bent forward till the two faces almost touched; and she heard a delicious whisper in the room, that faint, familiar hush of sighing trees. But the phrase that caught her ears as she passed them was only the banal phrase of old-age not used to coping with the youngest generation:

" Run away and play now, there's a good boy ! Upstairs—anywhere you like ! "

She had passed by then, but at the chink of iron she turned her head and stopped in time to see the dumb child push itself upright again and limp out of the room. The sunlight of the big hall showed it in silhouette for a moment, with the dark doorway of the sitting-room for frame. Then, as the creature began to climb the stairs, the lintel cut off the sharp, pallid little face. Once more the tenacious small fingers caught her eye, clutching and lifting, clutching and lifting, on the brown balustrade, and then the hall was empty again save for the shaft of sunshine from the roof and the glittering motes that danced against the darkness. She shot a glance sideways over the threshold. Her employer was knitting, knitting. And yet, as the girl shifted her pile of dishes to the other arm and went on again, she thought she heard a laugh.

When the telegram arrived three days later, she heard it again. Somehow, somewhere, on the route, one of the children had been mislaid. Could Spinsters' Rest help them ? Spinsters' Rest could not. For—" Think back, my dear ! "—the wagonettes had brimmed over with waving handkerchiefs and flushed faces, and trails of dog-roses whose petals fluttered from their golden holds, as the school-treat drove away, after farewells and false starts, and she had come to rest at the feet of her employer with a " Pouf ! And that's that ! "—had sat cooling as the garden cooled, till the little sounds of evening fell into the silence like pebbles flung into a lake ; but their peace had not been broken by any sight of any child.

An odd business, her employer agreed, as she soothed superintendents and interviewed inspectors. But what was to be done, when the children had not been counted, coming or going ? Tickets issued, eh ? Tickets, not names ! Blank tickets get exchanged, lost, picked up. Could they even be sure that the child was missing ? Had it ever started ? What did the parents—— ? Ah, no parents ! A step-sister. Not too heart-broken, eh ? And its absence had really gone unnoticed three days ? Three days astray in London—poor child ! Poor children ! God pity poor children ! They must report progress—let her know. No, nothing seen of any child here, eh, Miss Pawle ? No limping child wandering in our garden, with an iron round its leg. No child's voice —ah, dumb was it ? Dumb, too ! Well, Miss Pawle ?

But Miss Pawle, fascinated, had seen nothing. And it wa
odd, as her employer said to her in the later days of brown
August, it was odd how soon inquiries died down.

Odd—the phrase stuck in her mind though the inciden
faded from it—odd how inquiry died down, how soon, how
dully one accustomed oneself to change and novelty and a new
address. She had hoped to detach, to re-attach herself, to fling
new tendrils, to strike new roots ; and here, after the strangest
summer she had ever spent, after six months, only six months in
a new world, in a very factory of oddness (what stories might
she not have woven, what mysteries unravelled, what ghost
not laid in this forgotten coign of England, were the spirit of
adventure yet alive in her !), she could do no more than turn
back wearily upon herself, sated and indifferent. London
counting-house or Spinsters' Rest, it was all the same to her.
What more did Spinsters' Rest give her than London gave ?
Flowers for the picking and summer days : moonlit nights
the song of birds, children that came and went : and queer
tales such as she used to love. But if the salt has lost its
savour ?

" I want to leave ! " she blurted out.

Her employer shook her head.

" Soon, not yet."

She said :

" I want a change."

" You haven't earned your bonus. You must stay out
your year."

Again she said, as she had said nearly a year ago :

" I don't care. I want a change."

" Restless, eh ? "

" Desperate." And indeed, with her miserable eyes and
twisting hands, she looked it. " Could I—talk to you ? "

" I waited for that," said the sweet voice.

" I—I'm ill, I think. Oh, you know what it is! I've
nothing to care for." Suddenly she flung herself down at the
old woman's feet, caught at the knees as if they were the knees
of a god. " Can't you help me ? can't you ? You're older
than I."

Her eyes were a daze of tears. She saw no face. Yet she
heard the voice swell out in answer like a stir of many winds
like the thrash of saving rain :

" Yes, yes, older than you, my daughter, older than you.

And then, as she lay there, her face buried in the folds of the dress, crying as she had not cried for many days, came the voice again, the chirpy, commonplace voice of everyday life :

" You want rest, my dear ! You go upstairs and lie down."

She did as she was told, as children do, worn out with passion and tears.

III

As she reached the head of the stairs the door of the first room opened and out came the charwoman, breathless and staring.

" I beg your pardon, miss,—but do *you* come upstairs ? "

" She said I might," she said shyly, apologetically, forgetting her caste.

Said the woman harshly :

" You're young enough. What's *your* trouble ? " And then, softening : " But you're welcome. Quiet, ain't it ? I've been coming these twenty years. What I'd 'ave done without it——" Then, as the girl, making way for her, laid a hand on the door-knob behind them, she cried : " What are you doing ? That's my door, my young madam ! You leave touching other folks' doors ! " and, pushing by her, re-entered in haste, loosing a January draught on that hot August day against the girl's thin frock. She shivered. What a cold room to choose ! Was it only its north aspect that made it so bleak, or were there actually snowflakes afloat on the cold air ? Snowflakes ? How silly she was ! It was only the charwoman shaking up the bed. That must be her employer's room. " When they shake up my pillows, it snows in the world." Where did the phrase come from ? Shaking her head over that puzzle, she tried a second door, and a third. They were locked. She opened a fourth and went in.

She found herself in a nursery.

The nursery was her own. She was sure of that ; but whether the nursery of her yesterday or to-morrow she could not tell. The high guard round the fire was ancient history : so was the cork carpet and the spread tea-table, and golden-syrup in the jam-pot hand-painted with pink chrysanthemums ; but the frieze on the wall, that was the frieze she had always meant to paint round the walls of her children's nursery : and the floor games to teach a child geography, the history soldiers, the bricks for building the cities of the world, these existed no-where, she could have sworn, but in her own mind. Nor were the windows the small stiff casements of her childhood, but generous glass doors reaching to the ground, even as she had planned, as she had planned. As she threw them open hurriedly because of what she saw without, she tripped and all but fell over some object that clanked as she touched it.

It was a child's iron stocking.

The sight of it, she was aware, should have brought a memory to her mind, a memory factual not fantastic, a memory—but no! Though she picked up the ugly little instrument, fingering it critically, she could not at the moment crystallise the memory it evoked. For the windows were open and the wide champaign that spread itself without was calling to her with the voice of apple-trees sighing in the wind—"Shake me! Shake me!" "I burn! I burn!" rose the scent of cakes from the oven: and Mother Holle, it seemed, had once more taken her in; yet not to service, but to wander where she would, swinging from her fingers, as it were a divining-rod pointing to hidden treasure, a child's discarded stocking.

"Rested?" said her employer, not so much as looking up at her when, a thousand years later, she returned demurely to spread the evening meal.

She stretched out her hands, tiptoeing in a delicious yawn that sent the good blood to her cheeks with a rush.

"Rested," she said, and her smile was honest and her eyes at peace. Then, shyly, not knowing how to word it: "Did you call? I came back when I heard you call."

"In your sleep?"

"*Was* I asleep?"

In answer she got only:

"I should get your rest while you can. You've only another three months."

She started, all her new-found well-being poised for flight

"I don't want to go, not now," she submitted humbly.

"Didn't I engage you for a year?"

"I thought, if I give satisfaction——"

"Board and lodging for the year, and a present when you go, wasn't it?"

She pleaded, clutching wildly at the first excuse—

" The char—the old woman—she's been with you, years and years."

Said her employer :

" Yes, she stays on. She's too old to get the good of her wages. But yours are due by Twelfth Night, my dear, so take your pleasure while you can ! "

She took it, desperately she took it, as a man who has once starved hoards crusts against to-morrow. She came with the dawn : she stayed till moonlight blanched the dying fields. It was : " Can you spare me for half an hour ? " till her employer laughed as she spared her. Indeed, had she been less absorbed in her own dreaming, she might have wondered that she was spared so easily, have been startled at the restless little phrases that escaped her employer as she told stories in the early winter twilight—tales of swan-girls from Norway tucking men's hearts under their wings—of a ship out of Egypt that sailed on dry land, scattering corn and blessing through all the Middle Kingdoms, through all the middle years—of the spider in the cornice who was once a spinster too—of a limping queen whose son still drowses under the roots of the mountains with Arthur and Red-Beard and Ogier the Dane, awaiting the call to arms. " And his beard has grown through the stone table, and still he sleeps—or did, a year ago ! " And the shorter the days grew, the longer the tales, of journeys " in my car," and of adventures with obstructive village-folk merry-making on Twelfth Night. " Ah, yes, they're sorry when I go ! But here : I come again, my dear ! They know I come again ! " It was not till, years later, as she searched her memory for half-heard tales to please a listener, that she realised what she had lost, what she had wasted, yes, like the carpenter in one of the stories who had mended the car's broken wheels. ' When I threw him the chips for his pains, the fool left them lying ! And they were gold, my dear, they were gold ! "

But why listen to fairy-tales when fairy-land itself lay across a Roman pavement and up a flight of stairs ; when " Can you spare me for half an hour " was open sesame to her own country and her own kind ? For the land was peopled. None spoke to her, none crossed her path ; yet she was aware of shapes that lay under the poplars and stirred among the apple-trees, and looked down at her from the rails of laden ships that sailed to and fro upon the purple rim of the sea which edged that country as ghost moths sail across the blue of the dusk.

Some of the faces were familiar. She thought that she recognised a village crone who had followed her on one of her rambles, and there was a younger woman who might have been her landlady but for her full skirts and mob-cap. Once she saw a pretty girl with a plait of fair hair and a spindle in her hand, singing to herself as she sat on the edge of a well; but the words were in a strange language and the girl did not seem to see her: and once she came face to face with a pinched, white countenance, high-nosed like a parrot, in a parrot's flare of finery, that outfaced her a searching instant before a turn of the stiff shoulders swung the immense ruff between them for a screen, and that shadow crept away into the shadows with a screech of laughter that brought to her mind the creaking signboard of the Queen's Head Inn. "Neither chick nor child miss, had she?" The words returned to her. Was it indeed the same need that had brought them both to Spinsters' Rest? Was she still searching, the grand, starved ghost, for a heart's love to take back with her into history? "And are you jealous of me, poor queen, because the child has looked at me not you?"

For it was the dumb child who filled her hours. Ever since, on the threshold of enchantment, she had stumbled on that discarded instrument of pain, she had known what face would turn to her, what eyes would speak to her eyes in good time, unbeckoned. For would it not be lonely, the one male creature in the Spinsters' Rest? Summer is sweet, and draws a child with daisy-chains, but summer is a poor playfellow, she can grow you a cowslip ball, but—can she throw it? Furtively she observed it, flitting from tree to tree, from flower to flower, always wary, yet always circling her, always at play in the human safety of her shadow, and bided her time: and the while tried not to reckon, yet daily reckoned, up the shortening days. She had come to Spinsters' Rest on—Twelfth Night, was it not? And out in the winter world Twelfth Night was once more drawing near, was a month, a fortnight, was a week away. And now it had dwindled into a matter of days, into the last Sunday of all, and she had not won the child!

Lying in the sweet grasses by the river's edge, she watched it, not a yard away, as it hung over the clover-tufted bank engrossed in the image that wondered up at it from the clear deep water. And as she watched she began very softly to sing the old rhyme :

" Monday's child is full of grace——"

It did not so much as start. " It's grown accustomed to me," she thought. She sang on :

" Tuesday's child is fair of face——"

Was it ? Its grave eyes travelled doubtfully over its own reflection.

" Wednesday's child is loving and giving——"

She stretched out a hand and slipped a finger into the small fist that made room and closed again fast and friendly.

" Thursday's child——"

She shook he head ruefully at their two intent faces,

" ——must work for its living——
" Friday's child is full of woe——"

And it was clambering into her. lap, kneeling upright to stare into her face with piteous intelligence.

" Saturday's child has far to go——"

It was so light a burden to hold. She thought she could carry it to the ends of the earth and back, and never tire.

" But the child that is born on the Sabbath day——"

Its arms were at her neck, it was laughing and loving her as a child should. She finished with a little squeeze that made it chuckle :

" Is blithe and bonny and good and gay ! "

And, cheek grazing cheek, waited.

But before that for which she waited could be bestowed, the silence of the land was riven by a cry, a cry half triumph, half call, as it were the voice of a wild swan circling for the south, as it were a horn blowing for the departure of hosts. And at that sound the whole painted landscape, the meandering river with its white scarves of ranunculus, the gilded meadows and trees heavy with heat, the vaporous hills, the clouds, the purple yard of ocean, all, all quivered as the air quivers over a gipsy fire, and, rising like a painted gauze curtain, melted and passed utterly away.

She put her hand to her dazed eyes. She was in the garden, the common back garden of Spinsters' Rest, with its orange gravel so carefully swept, with its oak tree and evergreens, and its snow-covered, untouched lawn. And then fear took her, coldly as the winter air was taking her by the throat and shaking hands ; for she was standing, empty-armed, in the centre of that pure surface, and there was not, neither before nor behind her, neither to right nor to left, any track of human feet. Only, as she stared terrified, she could everywhere discern the innumerable tracks of birds.

She remembered the landlady's words—" Never see birds in winter-time ! " But now the birds had come back.

Thereupon she ran panicking into the house, half knowing what she should find, and found it—a garment discarded, a shrine abandoned, the body of an old, old woman, serenely laid down and left. The wind of winter sleeted in through the garden window and stirred the withered trail of clematis till seeded gossamers floated downwards to mingle with the stray and wind-borne flakes of snow. A brown shadow flurried for a moment at the wainscot and was gone. From the floor a robin rose into the air, hung fluttering, and dropped again to its crumb. . . .

It was a full week later that she turned for the last time into Spinsters' Rest. The weary business of a burying lay behind her and the agent's bored inquisition. Not that he had asked her what her plans were. Why should he ? It was of the fate of the house—" a fine property—neglected, of course!" —that he had talked. And on that she had asked, with an effort, who had inherited ? He did not know. A distant cousin, he imagined.

A—a woman ? She hung, breathless, on his answer, not daring to define what she expected.

A lady, yes. A spinster lady, he believed. A great traveller. As a matter of fact, the firm was uncertain at the moment of her exact whereabouts.

Was Mary Pawle needed ? Should she wait ?

He raised his eyebrows. He had already told her that they had appointed a former charwoman as caretaker. Why, then, should she wait ?

Why, indeed ? The train, the night train for London goes

at seven. The luggage has gone already. Say good-bye to Spinsters' Rest, and go!

For the last time she mounted the stairs, carpetless now, and opened the door of her room. Her room? She did not know it any more. The livid evening pressed its cheek against a curtainless high window: through a broken pane a little wind whistled as it bellied out the dirtied cobweb long since spun from latch to sill. Empty stood the room, empty as her future, empty as her life. Her feet made marks on the grey velvet dust, as she crossed to the casement and looked out.

What had she expected? She did not know; but whatever she looked for, she saw only below, below, not level with her feet, the orange paths, the dull garden, the dreary laurels. Well—there it was! another year frittered away, and—nothing to show! She was sorry that her employer was gone; but it was not for her that she was crying, weakly, miserably, in spite of herself. One dreamed dreams and paid for them. She supposed that it was something to be able even to dream. Some poor women had not even dreams. It had been at least a heaven's own vision. If it had lasted only a moment longer, only a little moment, the child would have kissed her of its own accord. It was something to win a child to you, if only in a dream.

Well—no use waiting: no use wishing. It was getting dark. She would barely grope her way to the station through the unlighted war-time lanes. So good-bye, room! Good-bye, dreams! Good-bye, Mother Holle! . . .

What was that?

She nearly fell with the violence of her own start. What, in God's name, was that shapeless sound? A damned soul clanking its chain? The wail of a lost child? Send us light in our darkness, O Lord, O Lord of spirits and little children!

As if in answer, over the edge of the sill, broad and benignant rose the winter moon, and the shadows fled before it to the far corners of the room, fled, settled, thickened to a stirring blackness on the silvered floor, to a crouched bundle with white face and wide eyes. She dropped to her knees beside it, and for an instant the two forlorn creatures stared at each other. Then the dark eyes knew her, the pinched lips smiled, the small unmothered arms reached up to her, caught, closed and clung, tightened about her neck till she could hardly breathe. Wild with wonder and delight, she rose to her feet and, flinging loose her cloak, wrapped it anew about herself and the child, so that the little creature might lodge on her breast, in the crook of her arm, hidden and safe and warm. Then, stealing down the stairway, tiptoeing over the pavement, she fled from that house of rest, unheard, unseen.

But even as she hurried down the evening lanes the smiling moon observed her : and the trees sighed after her—" This is the reward of your service."

EDGAR WALLACE

CIRCUMSTANTIAL EVIDENCE

COLONEL CHARTRES DANE lingered irresolutely in the broad and pleasant lobby. Other patients had lingered awhile in that agreeable vestibule. In wintry days it was a cosy place, its polished panelled walls reflecting the gleam of logs that burnt in the open fireplace. There was a shining oak settle that invited gossip, and old prints, and blue china bowls frothing over with the flowers of a belated autumn or advanced springtide, to charm the eye.

In summer it was cool and dark and restful. The mellow tick of the ancient clock, the fragrance of roses, the soft breeze that came through an open casement stirring the lilac curtains uneasily, these corollaries of peace and order had soothed many an unquiet mind.

Colonel Chartres Dane fingered a button of his light dust-coat, and his thin patrician face was set in thought. He was a spare man of fifty-five ; a man of tired eyes and nervous gesture.

Dr. Merriget peered at him through his powerful spectacles and wondered.

It was an awkward moment, for the doctor had murmured his sincere, if conventional regrets and encouragements, and there was nothing left but to close the door on his patient.

"You have had a bad wound there, Mr. Jackson," he said, by way of changing a very gloomy subject and filling in the interval of silence. This intervention might call to mind in a soldier some deed of his ; some far field of battle where men met death with courage and fortitude. Such memories might be helpful to a man under sentence.

Colonel Dane fingered the long scar on his cheek.

"Yes," he said absently, "a child did that—my niece. Quite my own fault."

"A child ?" Dr. Merriget appeared to be shocked. He was, in reality, very curious.

483

"Yes . . . she was eleven . . . my own fault. I spoke disrespectfully of her father. It was unpardonable, for he was only recently dead. He was my brother-in-law. We were at breakfast, and she threw the knife . . . yes . . ."

He ruminated on the incident, and a smile quivered at the corner of his thin lips.

"She hated me. She hates me still . . . yes . . ."

He waited.

The doctor was embarrassed and came back to the object of the visit.

"I should be ever so much more comfortable in my mind if you saw a specialist, Mr.—er—Jackson. You see how difficult it is for me to give an opinion? I may be wrong. I know nothing of your history, your medical history, I mean. There are so many men in town who could give you a better and more valuable opinion than I. A country practitioner like myself is rather in a backwater. One has the usual cases that come to one in a small country town, maternity cases, commonplace ailments . . . it is difficult to keep abreast of the extraordinary developments in medical science. . . ."

"Do you know anything about Machonicies College?" asked the colonel unexpectedly.

"Yes, of course." The doctor was surprised. "It is one of the best of the technical schools. Many of our best doctors and chemists take a preparatory course there. Why?"

"I merely asked. As to your specialists . . . I hardly think I shall bother them."

Dr. Merriget watched the tall figure striding down the red-tiled path between the banked flowers, and was still standing on the doorstep when the whine of his visitor's machine had gone beyond the limits of his hearing.

"H'm," said Dr. Merriget, as he returned to his study. He sat awhile thinking.

"Mr. Jackson?" he said aloud. "I wonder why the colonel calls himself 'Mr. Jackson'!"

He had seen the colonel two years before at a garden-party, and had an excellent memory for faces.

He gave the matter no further thought, having certain packing to superintend; he was on the eve of his departure for Constantinople—a holiday trip he had promised himself for years.

On the following afternoon at Machonicies Technical School a lecture was in progress.

". . . By this combustion you have secured true KCy, which we will now test and compare with the laboratory quantities . . . a deliquescent and colourless crystal extremely soluble. . . ."

The master, whose monotonous voice droned like the hum of a distant big stationary blue-bottle, was a middle-aged man to whom life was no more than a chemical reaction, and love not properly a matter for his observation or know-ledge. He had an idea that it was dealt with effectively in another department of the college . . . Metaphysics . . . or was it Philosophy? Or maybe it came into the realms of the Biological master.

Ella Grant glared resentfully at the crystals which glittered on the blue paper before her, and snapped out the bunsen burner with a vicious twist of finger and thumb. Newman always overshot the hour. It was a quarter past five! The pallid clock above the dais where Professor Denman stood seemed to mock her impatience.

She sighed wearily, and fiddled with the apparatus on the bench at which she sat. Some twenty other white-coated girls were also fiddling with test-tubes and bottles and gradu-ated measures, and twenty pairs of eyes glowered at the bald and stooping man who, unconscious of the passing of time, was turning affectionately to the properties of potassium. . . .

"Here we have a metal whose strange affinity for oxygen . . . eh, Miss Benson? Five? Bless my soul, so it is! Class is dismissed. And ladies, *ladies*, *ladies*! Please, please let me make myself heard. The laboratory keeper will take from you all chemicals you have drawn for this experi-ment. . . ."

They were crowding toward the door to the change room. Smith, the laboratory man, stood in the entrance grabbing wildly at little green and blue bottles that were thrust at him, and vainly endeavouring by a private system of mnemonics to commit his receipts to memory.

"Miss Fairlie, phial fairly ; Miss Jones, bottle bones ; Miss Walter, bottle salter . . ."

If at the end of his collection he failed to recall a rhyme to any name, the owner had passed without cashing in.

"Miss Grant . . . ?"

The laboratory of the Analytical Class was empty. Nineteen bottles stood on a shelf, and he reviewed them.

"Miss Grant . . . ?"

No, he had said nothing about "aunt" or "can't" or "pant".

He went into the change room, opened a locker, and felt in the pockets of the white overall. They were empty. Returning to the laboratory, he wrote in his report book :

Miss Grant did not return experrimment bottle.

He spelt "experiment" with two r's and two m's.

Ella found the bottle in the pocket of her overall as she was hanging it up in the long cupboard of the change room. She hesitated a moment, frowning resentfully at the little blue phial in her hand and rapidly calculating the time it would take to return to the laboratory to find the keeper and restore the property. In the end, she pushed it into her bag and hurried from the building. It was not an unusual occurrence that a student overlooked the return of some apparatus, and it could be restored in the morning.

Had Jack succeeded ? That was the thought which occupied her. The miracle about which every junior dreams had happened. Engaged in the prosecution of the notorious Flackman, his leader had been taken ill, and the conduct of the case for the State had fallen to him. He was opposed by two brilliant advocates, and the judge was a notorious humanitarian.

She did not stop to buy a newspaper ; she was in a fret at the thought that Jack Freeder might not have waited for her, and she heaved a sigh of relief when she turned into the old-world garden of the court-house and saw him pacing up and down the flagged walk, his hands in his pockets.

"I am so sorry. . . ."

She had come up behind him, and he turned on his heel to meet her. His face spoke success. The elation in it told her everything she wanted to know, and she slipped her arm through his with a queer mingled sense of pride and uneasiness.

". . . The judge sent for me to his room afterwards, and told me that the attorney could not have conducted the case better than I."

"He is guilty ?" she asked, hesitating.

"Who ? Flackman ? . . . I suppose so," he said care-essly. "His pistol was found in Sinnit's apartment, and it was known that he quarrelled with Sinnit about money, and here was a girl in it, I think, although we have never been able to get sufficient proof of that to put her into the box. You seldom have direct evidence in cases of this character, Ella, and in many ways circumstantial evidence is infinitely more damning. If a witness went into the box and said : 'I saw Flackman shoot Sinnit and saw Sinnit die,' the whole case would stand or fall by the credibility of that evidence ; prove that witness an habitual liar, and there is no chance of a conviction. On the other hand, when there are six or seven witnesses, all of whom subscribe to some one act or appearance or location of a prisoner, and all agreeing . . . why, you have him."

She nodded.

Her acquaintance with Jack Freeder had begun on her summer vacation, and had begun romantically but unconventionally when a sailing-boat overturned with its occupant pinned beneath the bulging canvas. It was Ella, a magnificent swimmer who, bathing, had seen the accident and had dived into the sea to the assistance of the drowning man.

"This means a lot to me, Ella," he said earnestly, as they turned into the busy street. "It means the foundation of a new life."

His eyes met hers and lingered for a second, and she was thrilled.

"Did you see Stephanie last night ?" he asked suddenly.

She felt guilty.

"No," she admitted, "but I don't think you ought to worry about that, Jack. Stephanie is expecting the money almost by any mail."

"She has been expecting the money almost by any mail for a month past," he said dryly, "and in the meantime this infernal note is becoming due. What I can't understand——"

She interrupted him with a laugh.

"You can't understand why they accepted my signature as a guarantee for Stephanie's," she laughed, "and you are extremely uncomplimentary !"

Stephanie Boston, her sometime room-mate, and now her apartmental neighbour, was a source of considerable worry to

2G

Jack Freeder, although he had only met her once. A handsome, volatile girl, with a penchant for good clothes and a mode of living out of all harmony with the meagre income she drew from fashion-plate artistry, she had found herself in difficulties It was a condition which the wise had long predicted, and Ella not so wise, had dreaded. And then one day the young artist had come to her with an oblong slip of paper, and an incoherent story of somebody being willing to lend her money if Ella would sign her name, and Ella Grant, to whom finance was an esoteric mystery, had cheerfully complied.

"If you were a great heiress, or you were expecting a lot of money coming to you through the death of a relative," persisted Jack with a frown, "I could understand Isaacs being satisfied with your acceptance ; but you aren't !"

Ella laughed softly and shook her head.

"The only relative I have in the world is poor dear Uncle Chartres, who loathes me ! I used to loathe him, too, but I've got over that. After Daddy died I lived with him for a few months, but we quarrelled over—over—well, I won't tell you what it was about, because I am sure he was sorry. I had a fiendish temper as a child, and I threw a knife at him."

"Good Lord !" gasped Jack, staring at her.

She nodded solemnly.

"I did—so you see there is very little likelihood of Uncle Chartres, who is immensely rich, leaving me anything more substantial than the horrid weapon with which I attempted to slay him !"

Jack was silent. Isaacs was a professional money-lender . . . he was not a philanthropist.

When Ella got home that night she determined to perform an unpleasant duty. She had not forgotten Jack Freeder's urgent insistence upon her seeing Stephanie Boston—she had simply avoided the unpalatable.

Stephanie's flat was on the first floor ; her own was immediately above. She considered for a long time before she pressed the bell.

Grace, Stephanie's elderly maid, opened the door, and her eyes were red with recent weeping.

"What is the matter ?" asked Ella in alarm.

"Come in, miss," said the servant miserably. "Miss Boston left a letter for you."

"Left?" repeated Ella wonderingly. "Has she gone way?"

"She was gone when I came this morning. The bailiffs ave been here . . . ."

Ella's heart sank.

The letter was short but eminently lucid :

I am going away, Ella. I do hope that you will forgive me. That wretched bill has become due, and I simply cannot face you again. will work desperately hard to repay you, Ella . . .

The girl stared at the letter, not realizing what it all meant, tephanie had gone away !

"She took all her clothes, miss. She left this morning, and old the porter she was going into the country ; and she owes ne three weeks' wages !"

Ella went upstairs to her own flat, dazed and shaken. he herself had no maid ; a woman came every morning to lean the flat, and Ella had her meals at a neighbouring estaurant.

As she made the last turn of the stairs she was conscious hat there was a man waiting on the landing above, with his ack to her door. Though she did not know him, he vidently recognized her, for he raised his hat. She had a lim idea that she had seen him somewhere before, but for he moment she could not recollect the circumstances.

"Good evening, Miss Grant," he said amiably. "I think ve have met before. Miss Boston introduced me—name of liggins."

She shook her head.

"I am afraid I don't remember you," she said, and wonlered whether his business was in connection with Stephanie's lefault.

"I brought the paper up that you signed about three nonths ago."

Then she recalled him and went cold.

"Mr. Isaacs didn't want to make any kind of trouble," he aid. "The bill became due a week ago, and we have been rying to get Miss Boston to pay. As it is, it looks very much s though you will have to find the money."

"When ?" she asked in dismay.

"Mr. Isaacs will give you until to-morrow night," said the

man. "I have been waiting here since five o'clock to see you.
I suppose it is convenient, miss ?"

Nobody knew better than Mr. Isaacs' clerk that it would
be most inconvenient, not to say impossible, for Ella Grant
to produce four hundred pounds.

"I will write to Mr. Isaacs," she said, finding her voice
at last.

She sat down in the solitude and dusk of her flat to think
things out. She was overwhelmed, numbed by the tragedy.
To owe money that she could not pay was to Ella Grant an
unspeakable horror.

There was a letter in the letter-box. She had taken it
out mechanically when she came in, and as mechanically slipped
her fingers through the flap and extracted a folded paper. But
she put it down without so much as a glance at its contents.

What would Jack say ? What a fool she had been, what
a perfectly reckless fool ! She had met difficulties before, and
had overcome them. When she had left her uncle's house
as a child of fourteen and had subsisted on the slender income
which her father had left her, rejecting every attempt on the
part of Chartres Dane to leave the home of an invalid maiden
aunt where she had taken refuge, she had faced what she
believed was the supreme crisis of life.

But this was different.

Chartres Dane ! She rejected the thought instantly, only
to find it recurring. Perhaps he would help. She had long
since overcome any ill-feeling she had towards him, for whatever dislike she had had been replaced by a sense of shame and
repentance. She had often been on the point of writing him
to beg his forgiveness, but had stopped short at the thought
that he might imagine she had some ulterior motive in seeking
to return to his good graces. He was her relative. He had
some responsibility . . . again the thought inserted itself
and suddenly she made up her mind.

Chartres Dane's house lay twelve miles out of town, a
great rambling place set on the slopes of a wooded hill, a place
admirably suited to his peculiar love of solitude.

She had some difficulty in finding a taxi-driver who was
willing to make the journey, and it had grown dark, though
a pale light still lingered in the western skies, when she
descended from the cab at the gateway of Hevel House.
There was a lodge at the entrance of the gate, but this had long

since been untenanted. She found her way up the long drive
to the columned portico in front of the house. The place
was in darkness, and she experienced a pang of apprehension.
Suppose he was not there ! (Even if he were, he would not
help her, she told herself.) But the possibility of his being
absent, however, gave her courage.

Her hand was on the bell when there came to her a flash
of memory. At such an hour he would be sitting in the window recess overlooking the lawn at the side of the house.
She had often seen him there on warm summer nights, his
glass of port on the broad window-ledge, a cigar clenched
between his white teeth, brooding out into the darkness.

She came down the steps and, walking on the close-
cropped grass bordering the flower-beds, came slowly, almost
stealthily, to the library window. The big casement was wide
open ; a faint light showed within, and she stopped dead, her
heart beating a furious rataplan at the sight of a filled glass on
the window-ledge. His habits had not changed, she thought ;
he himself would be sitting just out of sight from where she
stood, in that little window recess which was nearset to her.
Summoning all her courage, she advanced still further. He
was not in his customary place, and she crept nearer to the
window.

Colonel Chartres Dane was sitting at a large writing-table
in the centre of the room ; his back was toward her, and he
was writing by the light of two tall candles that stood upon the
table.

At the sight of his back all her courage failed, and as he
rose from the table she shrank back into the shadow. She saw
his white hand take up the glass of wine, and after a moment,
peeping again, she saw him, still with his back to her, put it
on the table by him as he sat down again.

She could not do it, she dare not do it, she told herself,
and turned away sorrowfully. She would write to him.

She had stepped from the grass to the path when a man
came from an opening in the bushes and gripped her arm.

"Hullo," he said, "who are you, and what are you doing
here ?"

"Let me go," she cried, frightened, "I—I——"

"What are you doing by the colonel's window ?"

"I am his niece," she said, trying to recover some of her
dignity.

"I thought you might be his aunt," said the gamekeeper ironically. "Now, my girl, I am going to take you in to the colonel——"

With a violent thrust she pushed him from her; the man stumbled and fell. She heard a thud and a groan, and stood rooted to the spot with horror.

"Have I hurt you?" she whispered. There was no reply.

She felt, rather than saw, that he had struck his head against a tree in falling, and, turning, she flew down the drive, terrified, nearly fainting in her fright. The cabman saw her as she flung open the gate and rushed out.

"Anything wrong?" he asked.

"I—I think I have killed a man," she said incoherently, and then from the other end of the drive she heard a thick voice cry:

"Stop that girl."

It was the voice of the gamekeeper, and for a moment the blood came back to her heart.

"Take me away, quickly, quickly," she cried.

The cabman hesitated.

"What have you been doing?" he asked.

"Take—take me away," she pleaded.

Again he hesitated.

"Jump in," he said gruffly.

Three weeks later John Penderbury, one of the greatest advocates at the Bar, walked into Jack Freeder's chambers.

The young man sat at his table, his head on his arm and Penderbury put his hand lightly upon the shoulders of the stricken man.

"You've got to take a hold of yourself, Freeder," he said kindly. "You will neither help yourself nor her by going under."

Jack lifted a white, haggard face to the lawyer.

"It is horrible, horrible," he said huskily. "She's as innocent as a baby. What evidence have they?"

"My dear, good fellow," said Penderbury, "the only evidence worth while in a case like this is circumstantial evidence. If there were direct evidence we might test the credibility of the witness. But in circumstantial evidence every piece of testimony dovetails into the other; each witness creates one strand of the net."

"It is horrible, it is impossible, it is madness to think that Ella could . . ."

Penderbury shook his head. Pulling up a chair at the other side of the table, he sat down, his arms folded, his grave eyes fixed on the younger man.

"Look at it from a lawyer's point of view, Freeder," he said gently. "Ella Grant is badly in need of money. She has backed a bill for a girl friend, and the money is suddenly demanded. A few minutes after learning this from Isaacs' clerk she finds a letter in her flat, which she has obviously read—the envelope was opened and its contents extracted— a letter which is from Colonel Dane's lawyers, telling her that the colonel has made her his sole heiress. She knows, therefore, that the moment the colonel dies she will be a rich woman. She has in her handbag a bottle containing cyanide of potassium, and that night, under the cover of darkness, drives to the colonel's house and is seen outside the library window by Colonel Dane's gamekeeper. She admitted, when she was questioned by the detective, that she knew the colonel was in the habit of sitting by the window, and that he usually put his glass of port on the window-ledge. What was easier than to drop a fatal dose of cyanide into the wine? Remember, she admitted that she had hated him, and that once she threw a knife at him, wounding him, so that the scar remained to the day of his death. She admitted herself that it was his practice to put the wine where she could have reached it."

He drew a bundle of papers from his pocket, unfolded them, and turned the leaves rapidly.

"Here it is." And he read :

"Yes, I saw a glass of wine on the window-ledge. The colonel was in the habit of sitting in the window on summer evenings. I have often seen him there, and I knew when I saw the wine that he was near at hand."

He pushed the paper aside and looked keenly at the wretched man before him.

"She is seen by the gamekeeper, as I say," he went on, "and, this man attempting to intercept her, she struggles from his grasp and runs down the drive to the cab. The cabman says she was agitated, and when he asked her what was the matter, she replied that she had killed a man——"

"She meant the gamekeeper," interrupted Jack.

"She may or may not, but she made that statement. There are the facts, Jack ; you cannot get past them. The letter from the lawyers—which she says she never read—the envelope was found open and the letter taken out ; is it likely that she had not read it ? The bottle of cyanide of potassium was found in her possession, and"—he spoke deliberately—"the colonel was found dead at his desk, and death was due to cyanide of potassium. A candle which stood on his desk had been overturned by him in his convulsions, and the first intimation the servants had that anything was wrong was the sight of the blazing papers on the table which the gamekeeper saw, when he returned to report what had occurred in the grounds. There is no question what verdict the jury will return."

It was a great and a fashionable trial. The court-house was crowded, and the public had fought for a few places that were vacant in the gallery.

Sir Johnson Grey, the Attorney-General, was to lead for the prosecution, and Penderbury had Jack Freeder as his junior.

The opening trial was due for ten o'clock, but it was half-past ten when the Attorney-General and Penderbury came into the court, and there was a light in Penderbury's eyes and a smile on his lips which amazed his junior.

Jack had only glanced once at the pale, slight prisoner. He dared not look at her.

"What is the delay ?" he asked irritably. "This infernal judge is always late."

At that moment the court rose as the judge came on to the Bench, and almost immediately afterwards the Attorney-General was addressing the court.

"My lord," he said, "I do not purpose offering any evidence in this case on behalf of the Crown. Last night I received from Dr. Merriget, an eminent practitioner of Townville, a sworn statement on which I purpose examining him.

"Dr. Merriget," the Attorney-General went on, "has been travelling in the Near East, and a letter which was sent to him by the late Colonel Dane only reached him a week ago, coincident with the doctor learning that these proceedings had been taken against the prisoner at the Bar.

"Dr. Merriget immediately placed himself in communication with the Crown officers of the law, as a result of which I am in a position to tell your lordship that I do not intend offering evidence against Ella Grant.

"Apparently Colonel Dane had long suspected that he was suffering from an incurable disease, and to make sure he went to Dr. Merriget and submitted himself to an examination. The reason for his going to a strange doctor is that he did not want to have it known that he had been consulting specialists in town. The doctor confirmed his worst fears, and Colonel Dane returned to his home. Whilst on the Continent, the doctor received a letter from Colonel Dane, which I purpose reading."

He took a letter from the table, adjusted his spectacles, and read :

"*Dear Dr. Merriget,*
    "*It occurred to me after I had left you the day before yesterday that you must have identified me, for I have a dim recollection that we met at a garden-party. I am not, as you suggested, taking any other advice. I know too well that this fibrous growth is beyond cure, and I purpose to-night taking a fatal dose of cyanide of potassium. I feel that I must notify you in case by a mischance there is some question as to how I met my death.*
                    "*Very sincerely yours,*
                            "*Chartres Dane.*

"I feel that the ends of justice will be served," continued the Attorney-General, "if I call the doctor. . . ."

It was not very long before another Crown case came the way of Jack Freeder. A week after his return from his honeymoon he was sent for to the Public Prosecutor's office, and that gentleman interviewed him.

"You did so well in the Flackman case, Freeder, that I want you to undertake the prosecution of Wise. Undoubtedly you will gain kudos in a trial of this description, for the Wise case has attracted a great deal of attention."

"What is the evidence ?" asked Jack bluntly.

"Circumstantial, of course," said the Public Prosecutor, "but——"

Jack shook his head.

2G*

"I think not, sir," he said, firmly but respectfully. "I will not prosecute in another case of murder, unless the murder is committed in my presence."

The Public Prosecutor stared at him.

"That means you will never take another murder prosecution. Have you given up criminal work, Mr. Freeder?"

"Yes, sir," said Jack gravely, "my wife doesn't like it."

To-day Jack Freeder is referred to in legal circles as a glaring example of how a promising career can be ruined by marriage.

EDGAR ALLAN POE

A DESCENT INTO THE MAELSTRÖM

WE had now reached the summit of the loftiest crag. For some minutes the old man seemed too much exhausted to speak.

"Not long ago," he said at length, "and I could have guided you on this route as well as the youngest of my sons ; but, about three years past, there happened to me an event such as never happened before to mortal man—or at least such as no man ever survived to tell of—and the six hours of deadly terror which I then endured have broken me up body and soul. You suppose me a *very* old man—but I am not. It took less than a single day to change these hairs from a jetty black to white, to weaken my limbs, and to unstring my nerves, so that I tremble at the least exertion, and am frightened at a shadow. Do you know I can scarcely look over this little cliff without getting giddy ? "

The " little cliff," upon whose edge he had so carelessly thrown himself to rest that the weightier portion of his body hung over it, while he was only kept from falling by the tenure of his elbow on its extreme and slippery edge—this " little cliff " arose, a sheer unobstructed precipice of black shining rock, some fifteen or sixteen hundred feet from the world of crags beneath us. Nothing would have tempted me to within half a dozen yards of its brink. In truth, so deeply was I excited by the perilous position of my companion, that I fell at full length upon the ground, clung to the shrubs around me, and dared not even glance upwards at the sky— while I struggled in vain to divest myself of the idea that the very foundations of the mountain were in danger from the fury of the winds. It was long before I could reason myself into sufficient courage to sit up and look out into the distance.

" You must get over these fancies," said the guide, " for I have brought you here that you might have the best possible view of the scene of that event I mentioned—and to tell you the whole story with the spot just under your eye.

" We are now," he continued, in that particularizing manner

which distinguished him—" we are now close upon the Norwegian coast—in the sixty-eighth degree of latitude—in the great province of Nordland—and in the dreary district of Lofoden. The mountain upon whose top we sit is Helseggen, the Cloudy. Now raise yourself up a little higher—hold on to the grass if you feel giddy—so—and look out, beyond the belt of vapour beneath us, into the sea."

I looked dizzily, and beheld a wide expanse of ocean, whose waters wore so inky a hue as to bring at once to my mind the Nubian geographer's account of the *Mare Tenebrarum*. A panorama more deplorably desolate no human imagination can conceive. To the right and left, as far as the eye could reach, there lay outstretched, like ramparts of the world, lines of horridly black and beetling cliff, whose character of gloom was but the more forcibly illustrated by the surf which reared high up against its white and ghastly crest, howling and shrieking for ever. Just opposite the promontory upon whose apex we were placed, and at a distance of some five or six miles out at sea, there was visible a small, bleak-looking island ; or, more properly, its position was discernible through the wilderness of wild surge in which it was enveloped. About two miles nearer the land, arose another of smaller size, hideously craggy and barren, and encompassed at various intervals by a cluster of dark rocks.

The appearance of the ocean, in the space between the more distant island and the shore, had something very unusual about it. Although, at the time, so strong a gale was blowing landward that a brig in the remote offing lay to under a double-reefed trysail, and constantly plunged her whole hull out of sight, still there was here nothing like a regular swell, but only a short, quick, angry cross dashing of water in every direction —as well in the teeth of the wind as otherwise. Of foam there was little except in the immediate vicinity of the rocks.

" The island in the distance," resumed the old man, " is called by the Norwegians Vurrgh. The one midway is Moskoe. That a mile to the northward is Ambaaren. Yonder are Islesen, Hotholm, Keildhelm, Suarven and Buckholm. Farther off—between Moskoe and Vurrgh—are Otterholm, Flimen, Sandflesen and Stockholm. These are the true names of the places—but why it has been thought necessary to name them at all is more than either you or I can understand. Do you hear anything ? Do you see any change in the water ? "

We had now been about ten minutes upon the top of Helseggen, to which we had ascended from the interior of Lofoden, so that we had caught no glimpse of the sea until it had burst upon us from the summit. As the old man spoke, I became aware of a loud and gradually increasing sound, like the moaning of a vast herd of buffaloes upon an American prairie; and at the same moment I perceived that what seamen term the *chopping* character of the ocean beneath us was rapidly changing into a current which set to the eastward. Even while I gazed, this current acquired a monstrous velocity. Each moment added to its speed—to its headlong impetuosity. In five minutes the whole sea, as far as Vurrgh, was lashed into ungovernable fury; but it was between Moskoe and the coast that the main uproar held its sway. Here the vast bed of the waters, seamed and scarred into a thousand conflicting channels, burst suddenly into frenzied convulsion—heaving, boiling, hissing—gyrating in gigantic and innumerable vortices, and all whirling and plunging on to the eastward with a rapidity which water never elsewhere assumes, except in precipitous descents.

In a few minutes more, there came over the sea another radical alteration. The general surface grew somewhat more smooth, and the whirlpools, one by one, disappeared, while prodigious streaks of foam became apparent where none had been seen before. These streaks, at length, spreading out to a great distance, and entering into combination, took unto themselves the gyratory motion of the subsided vortices, and seemed to form the germ of another more vast. Suddenly—very suddenly—this assumed a distinct and definite existence, in a circle of more than a mile in diameter. The edge of the whirl was represented by a broad belt of gleaming spray; but no particle of this slipped into the mouth of the terrific funnel, whose interior, as far as the eye could fathom it, was a smooth, shining and jet-black wall of water, inclined to the horizon at an angle of some forty-five degrees, speeding dizzily round and round with a swaying and sweltering motion, and sending forth to the winds an appalling voice, half shriek, half roar, such as not even the mighty cataract of Niagara ever lifts up in its agony to heaven.

The mountain trembled to its very base, and the rock rocked. I threw myself upon my face, and clung to the scant herbage in an excess of nervous agitation.

"This," said I at length to the old man, "this *can* be
nothing else than the great whirlpool of the Maelström."

"So it is sometimes termed," said he. "We Norwegians
call it the Moskoe-ström, from the island of Moskoe in the
midway."

The ordinary accounts of this vortex had by no means
prepared me for what I saw. That of Jonas Ramus, which
is perhaps the most circumstantial of any, cannot impart the
faintest conception either of the magnificence, or of the horror
of the scene—or of the wild bewildering sense of *the novel*
which confounds the beholder. I am not sure from what
point of view the writer in question surveyed it, nor at what
time ; but it could neither have been from the summit of
Helseggen, nor during a storm. There are some passages
of his description, nevertheless, which may be quoted for
their details, although their effect is exceedingly feeble in
conveying an impression of the spectacle.

"Between Lofoden and Moskoe," he says, "the depth of
the water is between thirty-six and forty fathoms ; but on the
other side, towards Ver (Vurrgh), this depth decreases so as
not to afford a convenient passage for a vessel, without the
risk of splitting on the rocks, which happens even in the
calmest weather. When it is flood, the stream runs up
the country between Lofoden and Moskoe with a boisterous
rapidity ; but the roar of its impetuous ebb to the sea is
scarce equalled by the loudest and most dreadful cataracts ;
the noise being heard several leagues off, and the vortices or
pits are of such an extent and depth, that if a ship comes
within its attraction, it is inevitably absorbed and carried down
to the bottom, and there beat to pieces against the rocks ;
and when the water relaxes, the fragments thereof are thrown
up again. But these intervals of tranquillity are only at the
turn of the ebb and flood, and in calm weather, and last but
a quarter of an hour, its violence gradually returning. When
the stream is most boisterous, and its fury heightened by a
storm, it is dangerous to come within a Norway mile of it.
Boats, yachts, and ships have been carried away by not guard-
ing against it before they were within its reach. It likewise
happens frequently that whales come too near the stream, and
are overpowered by its violence ; and then it is impossible
to describe their howlings and bellowings in their fruitless
struggles to disengage themselves. A bear, once, attempting

to swim from Lofoden to Moskoe, was caught by the stream and borne down, while he roared terribly, so as to be heard on shore. Large stocks of firs and pine trees, after being absorbed by the current, rise again broken and torn to such a degree as if bristles grew upon them. This plainly shows the bottom to consist of craggy rocks, among which they are whirled to and fro. This stream is regulated by the flux and reflux of the sea—it being constantly high and low water every six hours. In the year 1645, early in the morning of Sexagesima Sunday, it raged with such noise and impetuosity that the very stones of the houses on the coast fell to the ground."

In regard to the depth of the water, I could not see how this could have been ascertained at all in the immediate vicinity of the vortex. The "forty fathoms" must have reference only to portions of the channel close upon the shore either of Moskoe or Lofoden. The depth in the centre of the Moskoe-ström must be immeasurably greater; and no better proof of this fact is necessary than can be obtained from even the sidelong glance into the abyss of the whirl which may be had from the highest crag of Helseggen. Looking down from this pinnacle upon the howling Phlegethon below, I could not help smiling at the simplicity with which the honest Jonas Ramus records, as a matter difficult of belief, the anecdotes of the whales and the bears; for it appeared to me, in fact, a self-evident thing, that the largest ships of the line in existence, coming within the influence of that deadly attraction, could resist it as little as a feather the hurricane, and must disappear bodily and at once.

The attempts to account for the phenomenon—some of which, I remember, seemed to me sufficiently plausible in perusal—now wore a very different and unsatisfactory aspect. The idea generally received is that this, as well as three smaller vortices among the Ferroe islands, "have no other cause than the collision of waves rising and falling, at flux and reflux, against a ridge of rocks and shelves, which confines the water so that it precipitates itself like a cataract, and thus the higher the flood rises, the deeper must the fall be; and the natural result of all is a whirlpool or vortex, the prodigious suction of which is sufficiently known by lesser experiments." These are the words of the *Encyclopædia Britannica*. Kircher and others imagine that in the centre of the channel of the Maelström is an abyss penetrating the globe, and issuing in some very remote part—the gulf of Bothnia being somewhat decidedly named in one instance. This opinion, idle in itself, was the one to which, as I gazed, my imagination most readily assented; and, mentioning it to the guide, I was rather surprised to hear him say that, although it was the view almost universally entertained of the subject by the Norwegians, it nevertheless was not his own. As to the former notion, he confessed his inability to comprehend it ; and here I agreed with him—for, however conclusive on paper, it becomes altogether unintelligible, and even absurd, amid the thunder of the abyss.

" You have had a good look at the whirl now," said the old man ; " and if you will creep round this crag, so as to get in its lee, and deaden the roar of the water, I will tell you a story that will convince you I ought to know something of the Moskoe-ström."

I placed myself as desired, and he proceeded :

" Myself and my two brothers once owned a schooner-rigged smack of about seventy tons burthen, with which we were in the habit of fishing among the islands beyond Moskoe, nearly to Vurrgh. In all violent eddies at sea there is good fishing, at proper opportunities, if one has only the courage to attempt it ; but among the whole of the Lofoden coastmen, we three were the only ones who made a regular business of going out to the islands, as I tell you. The usual grounds are a great way lower down to the southward. There fish can be got at all hours, without much risk, and therefore these places are preferred. The choice spots over here among the rocks, however, not only yield the finest variety, but in far greater abundance ; so that we often got in a single day what the more timid of the craft could not scrape together in a week. In fact, we made it a matter of desperate speculation —the risk of life standing instead of labour, and courage answering for capital.

" We kept the smack in a cove about five miles higher up the coast than this ; and it was our practice, in fine weather, to take advantage of the fifteen minutes' slack to push across the main channel of the Moskoe-ström, far above the pool, and then drop down upon anchorage somewhere near Otterholm, or Sandflesen, where the eddies are not so violent as elsewhere. Here we used to remain until nearly time for slack-water again, when we weighed and made for home. We never set out upon this expedition without a steady side wind for going and coming—one that we felt sure would not fail us before our return—and we seldom made a miscalculation upon this point. Twice, during six years, we were forced to stay all night at anchor, on account of a dead calm, which is a rare thing indeed just about here; and once we had to remain on the grounds nearly a week, starving to death, owing to a gale which blew up shortly after our arrival, and made the channel too boisterous to be thought of. Upon this occasion we should have been driven out to sea in spite of everything (for the whirlpools threw us round and round so violently that at length we fouled our anchor and dragged it) if it had not been that we drifted into one of the innumerable cross-currents—here to-day and gone to-morrow—which drove us under the lee of Flimen, where, by good luck, we brought up.

"I could not tell you the twentieth part of the difficulties we encountered 'on the ground'—it is a bad spot to be in, even in good weather—but we make shift always to run the gauntlet of the Moskoe-ström itself without accident; although at times my heart has been in my mouth when we happened to be a minute or so behind or before the slack. The wind sometimes was not as strong as we thought it at starting, and then we made rather less way than we could wish, while the current rendered the smack unmanageable. My eldest brother had a son eighteen years old, and I had two stout boys of my own. These would have been of great assistance at such times in using the sweeps, as well as afterward in fishing—but, somehow, although we ran the risk ourselves, we had not the heart to let the young ones get into the danger—for, after all said and done, it *was* a horrible danger, and that is the truth.

"It is now within a few days of three years since what I am going to tell you occurred. It was on the 10th of July, 18—, a day which the people of this part of the world will never forget—for it was one in which blew the most terrible hurricane that ever came out of the heavens. And yet all the morning, and indeed until late in afternoon, there was a gentle and steady breeze from the south-west, while the sun shone brightly, so that the oldest seaman amongst us could not have foreseen what was to follow.

"The three of us—my two brothers and myself—had

crossed over to the islands about two o'clock p.m., and soon nearly loaded the smack with fine fish, which, we all remarked, were more plentiful that day than we had ever known them. It was just seven *by my watch* when we weighed and started for home, so as to make the worst of the Ström at slack water, which we knew would be at eight.

"We set out with a fresh wind on our starboard quarter, and for some time spanked along at a great rate, never dreaming of danger, for indeed we saw not the slightest reason to apprehend it. All at once we were taken aback by a breeze from over Helseggen. This was most unusual—something that had never happened to us before—and I began to feel a little uneasy, without exactly knowing why. We put the boat on the wind, but could make no headway at all for the eddies, and I was upon the point of proposing to return to the anchorage when, looking astern, we saw the whole horizon covered with a singular copper-coloured cloud that rose with the most amazing velocity.

"In the meantime the breeze that had headed us off fell away, and we were dead becalmed, drifting about in every direction. This state of things, however, did not last long enough to give us time to think about it. In less than a minute the storm was upon us—in less than two the sky was entirely overcast—and what with this and the driving spray, it became suddenly so dark that we could not see each other in the smack.

"Such a hurricane as then blew it is folly to attempt describing. The oldest seaman in Norway never experienced anything like it. We had let our sails go by the run before it cleverly took us; but, at the first puff, both our masts went by the board as if they had been sawed off—the mainmast taking with it my youngest brother, who had lashed himself to it for safety.

"Our boat was the lightest feather of a thing that had ever sat upon water. It had a complete flush deck, with only a small hatch near the bow, and this hatch it had always been our custom to batten down when about to cross the Ström, by way of precaution against the chopping seas. But for this circumstance we should have foundered at once—for we lay entirely buried for some moments. How my elder brother escaped destruction I cannot say, for I never had an opportunity of ascertaining. For my part, as soon as I had let the

oresail run, I threw myself flat on deck, with my feet against
he narrow gunwale of the bow, and with my hands grasping
ring-bolt near the foot of the foremast. It was mere instinct
hat prompted me to do this—which was undoubtedly the
ery best thing I could have done—for I was too much flurried
o think.

"For some moments we were completely deluged, as I
ay, and all this time I held my breath and clung to the bolt.
When I could stand it no longer I raised myself upon my knees,
ill keeping hold with my hands, and thus got my head clear.
resently our little boat gave herself a shake, just as a dog
oes in coming out of the water, and thus rid herself, in some
easure, of the seas. I was now trying to get the better of
e stupor that had come over me, and to collect my senses
o as to see what was to be done, when I felt somebody grasp
y arm. It was my elder brother, and my heart leaped for
y, for I had made sure that he was overboard—but the next
oment all this joy was turned into horror—for he put his
outh close to my ear, and screamed out the word ' *Moskoe-*
röm ! '

"No one ever will know what my feelings were at that
oment. I shook from head to foot as if I had had the most
iolent fit of ague. I knew what he meant by that one word
ell enough—I knew what he wished to make me understand.
With the wind that now drove us on, we were bound for the
hirl of the Ström, and nothing could save us !

"You perceive that in crossing the Ström *channel* we
ways went a long way up above the whirl, even in the
lmest weather, and then had to wait and watch carefully for
e slack—but now we were driving right upon the pool itself,
d in such a hurricane as this ! 'To be sure,' I thought,
we shall get there just about the slack—there is some little
ope in that '—but in the next moment I cursed myself for
eing so great a fool as to dream of hope at all. I knew very
ell that we were doomed, had we been ten times a ninety-gun
ip.

"By this time the first fury of the tempest had spent itself,
r perhaps we did not feel it so much, as we scudded before
, but at all events the seas, which at first had been kept down
y the wind, and lay flat and frothing, now got up into absolute
ountains. A singular change, too, had come over the
eavens. Around in every direction it was still as black as

pitch, but nearly overhead there burst out, all at once, a circula
rift of clear sky—as clear as I ever saw—and of a deep brigh
blue—and through it there blazed forth the full moon with
lustre that I never before knew her to wear. She lit up every
thing about us with the greatest distinctness—but, oh God
what a scene it was to light up !

" I now made one or two attempts to speak to my brothe
—but in some manner which I could not understand, the di
had so increased that I could not make him hear a single word
although I screamed out at the top of my voice in his ear
Presently he shook his head, looking as pale as death, and hel
up one of his fingers, as if to say ' *listen.*'

" At first I could not make out what he meant—but soor
a hideous thought flashed upon me. I dragged my watcl
from its fob. It was not going. I glanced at its face by th
moonlight, and then burst into tears as I flung it far away int
the ocean. *It had run down at seven o'clock ? We were behind th
time of the slack, and the whirl of the Ström was in full fury ?*

" When a boat is well built, properly trimmed, and no
deep laden, the waves in a strong gale, when she is goin
large, seem always to slip from beneath her—which appear
very strange to a landsman—and this is called *riding*, in se
phrase.

" Well, so far we had ridden the swells very cleverly ! bu
presently a gigantic sea happened to take us right under th
counter, and bore us with it as it rose—up—up—as if int
the sky. I would not have believed that any wave could ris
so high. And then down we came with a sweep, a slide, an
a plunge, that made me feel sick and dizzy, as if I was fallin
from some lofty mountain-top in a dream. But while we wer
up I had thrown a quick glance around—and that one glanc
was sufficient. I saw our exact position in an instant. Th
Moskoe-ström whirlpool was about a quarter of a mile dea
ahead, but no more like the everyday Moskoe-ström than th
whirl as you now see it is like a mill-race. If I had not know
where we were, and what we had to expect, I should not hav
recognized the place at all. As it was, I involuntarily close
my eyes in horror. The lids clenched themselves together a
if in a spasm.

" It could not have been two minutes afterwards when w
suddenly felt the waves subside, and were suddenly envelope
in foam. The boat made a short half-turn to larboard, and the

shot off in its new direction like a thunderbolt. At the same moment the roaring noise of the waters was completely drowned in a shrill shriek—such a sound as you might imagine given out by the water-pipes of many thousand steam-vessels, letting off their steam all together. We were now in the belt of surf that always surrounds the whirl ; and I thought, of course, that another moment would plunge us into the abyss —down which we could only see indistinctly on account of the amazing velocity with which we were borne along. The boat did not seem to sink into the water at all, but to skim like an air-bubble on the surface of the surge. Her starboard side was next the whirl, and on the larboard arose the world of ocean we had left. It stood like a huge, writhing wall between us and the horizon.

" It may appear strange, but now, when we were in the very jaws of the gulf, I felt more composed than when we were only approaching it. Having made up my mind to hope no more, I got rid of a great deal of that terror which unmanned me at first. I supposed it was despair that strung my nerves.

" It may look like boasting—but what I tell you is truth— I began to reflect how magnificent a thing it was to die in such a manner, and how foolish it was in me to think of so paltry a consideration as my own individual life, in view of so wonderful a manifestation of God's power. I do believe that I blushed with shame when this idea crossed my mind. After a little while I became possessed with the keenest curiosity about the whirl itself. I positively felt a *wish* to explore its depths, even at the sacrifice I was going to make ! and my principal grief was that I should never be able to tell my old companions on shore about the mysteries I should see. These, no doubt, were singular fancies to occupy a man's mind in such extremity—and I have often thought since that the revolutions of the boat around the pool might have rendered me a little light-headed.

" There was another circumstance which tended to restore my self-possession ; and this was the cessation of the wind, which could not reach us in our present situation—for, as you saw yourself, the belt of surf is considerably lower than the general bed of the ocean, and this latter now towered above us, a high, black, mountainous ridge. If you have never been at sea in a heavy gale, you can form no idea of the

confusion of mind occasioned by the wind and spray together
They blind, deafen, and strangle you, and take away all powe
of action or reflection. But we were now, in a great measure
rid of these annoyances—just as death-condemned felons ir
prison are allowed petty indulgences, forbidden them while
their doom is yet uncertain.

" How often we made the circuit of the belt it is impossible
to say. We careered round and round for perhaps an hour
flying rather than floating, getting gradually more and more
into the middle of the surge, and then nearer and nearer to
its horrible inner edge. All this time I had never let go of the
ring-bolt. My brother was at the stern holding on to ar
empty water-cask, which had been securely lashed under the
coop of the counter, and was the only thing on deck that hac
not been swept overboard when the gale first took us. As
we approached the brink of the pit he let go his hold upor
this, and made for the ring, from which, in the agony of his
terror, he endeavoured to force my hands, as it was not large
enough to afford us both a secure grasp. I never felt deepe
grief than when I saw him attempt this act—although I knew
he was a madman when he did it—a raving maniac through
sheer fright. I did not care, however, to contest the point
with him. I knew it could make no difference whether eithe
of us held on at all ; so I let him have the bolt and went asterr
to the cask. This there was no great difficulty in doing ; fo
the smack went round steadily enough, and upon an even kee
—only swaying to and fro with the immense swelters of the
whirl. Scarcely had I secured myself in my new position
when we gave a wild lurch to starboard, and rushed headlong
into the abyss. I muttered a hurried prayer to God, anc
thought all was over.

" As I felt the sickening sweep of the descent, I hac
instinctively tightened my hold upon the barrel, and closec
my eyes. For some seconds I dared not open them—while
I expected instant destruction, and wondered that I was no
already in my death-struggles with the water. But moment
after moment elapsed. I still lived. The sense of the falling
had ceased ; and the motion of the vessel seemed much as
it had been before, while in the belt of the foam, with the
exception that she now lay more along. I took courage anc
looked once again upon the scene.

" Never shall I forget the sensation of awe, horror, anc

admiration with which I gazed about me. The boat appeared to be hanging, as if by magic, midway down, upon the interior surface of a funnel, vast in circumference, prodigious in depth, and whose perfectly smooth sides might have been mistaken for ebony, but for the bewildering rapidity with which they spun around, and for the gleaming and ghastly radiance they shot forth, as the rays of the full moon, from that circular rift amid the clouds which I have already described, streamed in a flood of golden glory along the black walls and far away down into the inmost recess of the abyss.

" At first I was too much confused to observe anything accurately. The general burst of terrific grandeur was all that I beheld. When I recovered myself a little, however, my gaze fell instinctively downward. In this direction I was able to obtain an unobstructed view, from the manner in which the smack hung on the inclined surface of the pool. She was quite upon an even keel—that is to say, her deck lay in a plain parallel with that of the water—but this latter sloped at an angle of more than forty-five degrees, so that we seemed to be lying upon our beam ends. I could not help observing, nevertheless, that I had scarcely more difficulty in maintaining my hold and footing in this situation than if we had been upon a dead level ; and this, I suppose, was owing to the speed at which we revolved.

" The rays of the moon seemed to search the very bottom of the profound gulf ; but still I could make out nothing distinctly, on account of a thick mist in which everything there was enveloped, and over which there hung a magnificent rainbow, like that narrow and tottering bridge which Mussulmen say is the only pathway between Time and Eternity. This mist, or spray, was no doubt occasioned by the clashing of the great walls of the funnel, as they all met together at the bottom—but the yell that went up to the heavens from out of that mist, I dare not attempt to describe.

" Our first slide into the abyss itself, from the belt of foam above, had carried us a great distance down the slope ; but our further descent was by no means proportionate. Round and round we swept—not in any uniform movement—but in dizzying swings and jerks that sent us sometimes only a few hundred yards—sometimes nearly the complete circuit of the whirl. Our progress downwards, at each revolution, was slow, but very perceptible.

"Looking about me upon the wide waste of liquid ebony on which we were thus borne, I perceived that our boat was not the only object in the embrace of the whirl. Both above and below us were visible fragments of vessels, large masses of building timber and trunks of trees, with many smaller articles, such as pieces of house furniture, broken boxes, barrels, and staves. I have already described the unnatural curiosity which had taken the place of my original terrors. It appeared to grow upon me as I drew nearer and nearer to my dreadful doom. I now began to watch, with a strange interest, the numerous things that floated in our company. I *must* have been delirious—for I even sought *amusement* in speculating upon the relative velocities of their several descents toward the foam below. 'This fir tree,' I found myself at one time saying, 'will certainly be the next thing that takes the awful plunge and disappears'—and then I was disappointed to find that the wreck of a Dutch merchant ship overtook it and went down before. At length, after making several guesses of this nature, and being deceived in all— this fact—the fact of my invariable miscalculation, set me upon a train of reflection that made my limbs again tremble, and my heart beat heavily once more.

"It was not a new terror that thus affected me, but the dawn of a more exciting *hope*. This hope arose partly from memory, and partly from present observation. I called to mind the great variety of buoyant matter that strewed the coast of Lofoden, having been absorbed and then thrown forth by the Moskoe-ström. By far the greater number of the articles were shattered in the most extraordinary way— so chafed and roughened as to have the appearance of having been stuck full of splinters—but then I distinctly recollected that there were *some* of them which were not disfigured at all. Now I could not account for this difference except by suppos- ing that the roughened fragments were the only ones that had been *completely absorbed*—that the others had entered the whirl at so late a period of the tide, or, from some reason, had descended so slowly after entering, that they did not reach the bottom before the turn of the flood came, or of the ebb, as the case might be. I conceived it possible in either instance that they might thus be whirled up again to the level of the ocean, without undergoing the fate of those which had been drawn in more early or absorbed more rapidly. I made, also, three important observations. The first was, that as a general rule, the larger the bodies were, the more rapid their descent —the second, that, between two masses of equal extent, the one spherical and the other *of any other shape*, the superiority in speed of descent was with the sphere—the third, that, between two masses of equal size, the one cyclindrical and the other of any other shape, the cylinder was absorbed the more slowly. Since my escape, I have had several conversations on this subject with an old schoolmaster of the district ; and it was from him that I learned the use of the word ' cylinder ' and ' sphere.' He explained to me, although I have forgotten the explanation—how what I observed was, in fact, the natural consequence of the forms of the floating fragments—and showed me how it happened that a cylinder, swimming in a vortex, offered more resistance to its suction, and was drawn in with greater difficulty than an equally bulky body, of any form whatever.[1]

" There was one startling circumstance which went a great way in enforcing these observations, and rendering me anxious to turn them to account, and this was that, at every revolution, we passed something like a barrel, or else the yard or the mast of a vessel, while many of these things, which had been on our level when I first opened my eyes upon the wonders of the whirlpool, were now high up above us, and seemed to have moved but little from their original station.

" I no longer hesitated what to do. I resolved to lash myself securely to the water-cask upon which I now held, to cut it loose from the counter, and to throw myself with it into the water. I attracted my brother's attention by signs, pointed to the floating barrels that came near us, and did everything in my power to make him understand what I was about to do. I thought at length that he comprehended my design, but, whether this was the case or not, he shook his head despairingly, and refused to move from his station by the ring-bolt. It was impossible to reach him ; the emergency admitted of no delay ; and so, with a bitter struggle, I resigned him to his fate, fastened myself to the cask by means of the lashings which secured it to the counter, and precipitated myself with it into the sea, without another moment's hesitation.

" The result was precisely what I had hoped it might be.

[1] See Archimedes *De Incidentibus in Fluido*, lib. 2.

As it is myself who now tells you this tale—as you see that I *did* escape—and as you are already in possession of the mode in which this escape was effected, and must therefore anticipate all that I have further to say—I will bring my story quickly to conclusion. It might have been an hour, or thereabout, after my quitting the smack, when, having descended to a vast distance beneath me, it made three or four wild gyrations in rapid succession, and, bearing my loved brother with it, plunged headlong, at once and for ever, into the chaos of foam below. The barrel to which I was attached sunk very little farther than half the distance between the bottom of the gulf and the spot at which I leaped overboard, before a great change took place in the character of the whirlpool. The slope of the sides of the vast funnel became momentarily less and less steep. The gyrations of the whirl grew, gradually, less and less violent. By degrees, the froth and the rainbow disappeared, and the bottom of the gulf seemed slowly to uprise. The sky was clear, the winds had gone down, and the full moon was setting radiantly in the west, when I found myself on the surface of the ocean, in full view of the shores of Lofoden, and above the spot where the pool of the Moskoe-ström *had been.* It was the hour of the slack—but the sea still heaved in mountainous waves from the effects of the hurricane. I was borne violently into the channel of the Ström, and, in a few minutes, was hurried down the coast into the ' grounds ' of the fishermen. A boat picked me up—exhausted from fatigue—and (now that the danger was removed) speechless from the memory of its horror. Those who drew me on board were my old mates and daily companions—but they knew me no more than they would have known a traveller from the spirit-land. My hair, which had been raven-black the day before, was as white as you see it now. They say, too, that the whole expression of my countenance had changed. I told them my story—they did not believe it. I now tell it to *you* —and I can scarcely expect you to put more faith in it than did the merry fishermen of Lofoden."

CHARLES WHIBLEY

TWELVE O'CLOCK

IN 1779, the year of his mysterious death, Thomas, Lord Lyttelton had climbed the pinnacle of fame. Though he was but six and thirty, he was already known as "the wicked Lord Lyttelton." In what his wickedness consisted is not clear. Such reputations are seldom deserved, and are commonly founded upon flattery and vainglory. He is said to have had a great love of gambling, and was so unlucky in his youth that more than once he was compelled to leave his companions "abruptly" in far-off countries. But he presently became more artful and turned his sad experience to good account. "The pigeon turned into a hawk," we are told, and at his death he had gained by play some £30,000. For the rest, he had practised with much success those vices in which Whiggish ministers in his day had full licence to excel. There is no evidence that he was a genuine rival in dissipation to Charles James Fox, for instance, of whom a partisan has confessed that when he returned to Eton from the Continent his "Parisian experiences . . . produced a visible and durable change for the worse in the morals and habits of the place." In brains there was not much to choose between the two men. Dr. Barnard, the Head Master of Eton, who had had them both under his care, thought that the abilities of Lyttelton were vastly superior.

Whatever shape his legendary wickedness took, there is no doubt that he was shaped for nobler purposes. Fatigue is for rakes a better cure than repentance, and the years as they passed fashioned Thomas Lyttelton into a gravely ambitious statesman. Though he owned himself that his amendment was slow and progressive, it might be said of him, as was said of the great Rochester, whom he somewhat resembled, that "he seem'd to study nothing more than which way to make that great understanding God had given him most useful to his country." Like Rochester, too, he spoke in the House of Peers with general approbation. Men of all parties are agreed in his praise. Even his enemies were generous in extolling his gifts of eloquence and statesmanship. Sandwich, for instance, was

no friend of Lyttelton.   Lyttelton had attacked Sandwich with
a bitter ferocity, and this is what Sandwich found to say about
Lyttelton in 1775 : " I think that so far from reprehension, the
noble lord deserves commendation and thanks for so ably
defending and asserting the rights of the British Parliament
and the supreme legislative authority of the Mother Country. I
think I never before heard such a speech delivered by anybody,
and I am proud to testify my perfect approbation by affirming
that it was the finest ever delivered within these walls."

The praise, if excessive, was disinterested, and that Sandwich
was not alone in approbation is proved by Lyttelton's early
promotion.   At the age of thirty-two he was sworn of His
Majesty's Privy Council, and made one of the Chief Justices in
Eyre.   As a politician he was energetically and consistently
opposed to the rebels in America.   His speeches breathe the
true spirit of patriotism, and had he been able to carry the
administration with him, England would not have been forced
to endure an unjust, unmerited disgrace.   And by a freakish
accident we remember less clearly how he lived than how he died.
His once famous dissipations are but a rumour ; the speeches,
which were heard with a reluctant enthusiasm in the House of
Peers, are a vague echo from the past ; the ghostly apparition,
which heralded his death, still holds the wonder of the world,
and is an incitement to controversy after a century and a half.

I have said so much about the man and his character,
because without some understanding of them the story of
his death might fail of its effect.   He would not seem to be of
those who stand in awe of the invisible world.   His hard,
practical sense, his determination to snatch from life whatever
of pleasure it held, are not the qualities which we expect in
those to whom beckonings come from beyond the boundaries
of the world.   Yet he had always been a dreamer of dreams and
a seer of visions.   Not long before his death " I dreamt," said
he, " that I was dead, and was hurried away to the infernal
regions, which appeared as a large dark room, at the end of
which was seated Mrs. Brownrigg,[1] who told me it was

---

[1] Mrs. Brownrigg is the woman made immortal in *The Anti-
Jacobin:*   " Dost thou ask her crime ?
          She whipped two female prentices to death
          And hid them in the coal-hole.
          . . . For this act
          Did Brownrigg swing.   Harsh laws ! "

appointed for her to pour red-hot bullets down my throat for
a thousand years. The resistance I endeavoured to make to her
awakened me, but the agitation of my mind when I awoke is
not to be described, nor can I get the better of it." So ugly a
visitation as that of Mrs. Brownrigg visited him but seldom.
It was but the shadow cast by a disordered fancy. Far more
benign and amiable in aspect was the apparition which foretold
his death. The legend, repeated by many and divers tongues,
may be shaped into this : On Wednesday, 24th November,
1779, Lyttelton, at his house in Hill Street, saw, or dreamed
that he saw, a bird fly into his bedroom. He tried to clutch it,
and found it, like Macbeth's dagger, " of the mind, a false
creation." Presently it turned into a woman, draped in white,
and recalling by her ghostly features one whom Lyttelton had
treated none too well. In a solemn voice, as from the grave,
the voice with which spirits are said to intensify their effect,
the disembodied woman told Lyttelton that he must die.
" I hope not soon," he murmured, " not in two months."
" In three days," said she. In vain he attempted to speak to
her. She vanished from his sight, echoing as she went, " Three
days, three days ! "

Lyttelton was profoundly affected by this message from
the other world. Like most men of a doubting temper, he was
superstitious. He told those who lodged in his house what he
had seen, and the vision lost nothing of terror and persuasive-
ness in the telling. His allotted span must come to an end, if
the ghost spoke true, at midnight on Saturday. But even
though he were credulous, Lyttelton would not allow meanwhile the fateful message to turn him from the paths of duty
and pleasure. He went about his business with zeal and
address. Before the House of Lords he delivered the best
speech that ever he made. It was his swan-song. For the first
time he seceded openly from the Government, whose cowardly
conduct in America and in Ireland he attacked with pitiless
contempt and unrelenting logic. And all the while the visions
of the dove and the white lady were before his eyes. When he
said, in the solemn language which befitted the time and place,
and which gained in solemnity after the event, " It is true I hold
a place, but perhaps I shall not hold it long," the ministers
laughed. From them the irony was concealed. " The noble
lords smile at what I say," he retorted ; " let them turn their
eyes on their own pusillanimity . . . and then let them declare

in their consciences which is most fitly the object of contempt, my thus openly and unreservedly speaking my sentiments in Parliament . . . or their consenting, in a moment of difficulty and danger like the present, to pocket the wages of prostitution." While they thought of the place which he would not hold long, he remembered that, of the three days given him by the ghost, one was all but at an end.

On Friday morning George Fortescue called upon him, and presently the two of them took the air together. Lyttelton was still reflecting upon an early death, when they crossed the churchyard of St. James's Church. "Now look at all the vulgar fellows," said he, pointing to the tombstones; "they die in their youth, at five and thirty. But you and I, who are gentlemen, shall live to a good old age." A few hours later he went down to his house at Epsom, where he entertained a party, not such a party as the gossip of Walpole invented "a caravan of nymphs," nor "four virgins, whom he had picked up in the Strand"—but a party of ladies and gentlemen, whom he counted among his intimate friends. There was upon them all a certain foreboding, and when Saturday evening came, they thought of nothing but the ghost. Meanwhile, his friends all did their best to avert the depression, which settled upon Lyttelton, who, amid the shouting and the laughter of the others, exclaimed, "We shall jockey the ghost after all." A musician, named Russell, who had been summoned to entertain the company, noticed that despite the efforts of his friends, Lyttelton's melancholy still clung about him. So midnight drew on, the hour at which Lyttelton had been doomed to die by the ghost, and in spite of himself he kept an anxious eye upon the time. His valet, by an artful foresight, had put on the clock a quarter of an hour, in the hope that his master should not know when the foreordained minute came, and should not aid his death by a just fear. Slowly the seconds moved, and when Lyttelton saw that the clock marked the approach of midnight, he got up abruptly and bade good night to his guests. He had bilked the ghost, as he thought, and went upstairs to his bedroom with the light foot of a man reprieved. His thoughts were all of the morrow. He spoke to his servant with a cheerful voice, and "particularly enquired of him what care had been taken to provide good rolls for breakfast the next morning." He then bade the man prepare him a dose of medicine, and when he began to stir the medicine with a toothpick (or, according to another account, with a key), Lyttelton told him he was a dirty fellow, and bade him go downstairs and fetch a spoon. When the servant returned he found his master speechless upon his pillow and in the last agony of death. The attempt to cheat the clock had failed, for Russell, the musician, records that the moment when the servant came down to do his master's bidding, the clock of the parish church, which had not been tampered with, began slowly to strike the midnight hour.

Thus died Thomas, the second Lord Lyttelton, eminent alike in vice and virtue, renowned for eloquence in his life, most highly renowned for the manner of his death, which provided gossip for the malicious, and thought for the philosopher. Horace Walpole cut a new pen that he might share his contempt for the dead man with his friends. Samuel Johnson, the Commentator-General of his age, who heard the story with his own ears from Lyttelton's uncle, Lord Westcote, expressed at once his interest in it, and his faith. " It is the most extraordinary thing," said he, " that has happened in my day. . . . I am so glad to have every evidence of the spiritual world, that I am willing to believe it."

WASHINGTON IRVING

THE SPECTRE BRIDEGROOM

" He that supper for is dight,
He lyes full cold, I trow, this night !
Yestreen to chamber I him led,
This night Gray-steel has made his bed ! "
Sir Eger, Sir Grahame and Sir Gray-steel.

ON the summit of one of the heights of the Odenwald, a
wild and romantic tract of Upper Germany that lies
not far from the confluence of the Main and the Rhine, there
stood, many, many years since, the Castle of the Baron Von
Landshort. It is now fallen to decay, and almost buried
among beech trees and dark firs ; above which, however, its
old watch-tower may still be seen struggling, like the former
possessor I have mentioned, to carry a high head, and look
down upon a neighbouring country.

The Baron was a dry branch of the great family of Katzenellenbogen, and inherited the relics of the property and
all the pride of his ancestors. Though the warlike disposition
of his predecessors had much impaired the family possessions,
yet the Baron still endeavoured to keep up some show of
former state. The times were peaceable, and the German
nobles, in general, had abandoned their inconvenient old
castles, perched like eagles' nests among the mountains, and
had built more convenient residences in the valleys ; still the
Baron remained proudly drawn up in his little fortress,
cherishing with hereditary inveteracy all the old family feuds ;
so that he was on ill terms with some of his nearest neighbours,
on account of disputes that had happened between their
great-great-grandfathers.

The Baron had but one child, a daughter ; but Nature,
when she grants but one child, always compensates by making
it a prodigy ; and so it was with the daughter of the Baron
All the nurses, gossips and country cousins assured her father
that she had not her equal for beauty in all Germany ; and
who should know better than they ? She had, moreover
been brought up with great care, under the superintendence

of two maiden aunts, who had spent some years of their early life at one of the little German courts, and were skilled in all the branches of knowledge necessary to the education of a fine lady. Under their instructions, she became a miracle of accomplishments. By the time she was eighteen she could embroider to admiration, and had worked whole histories of the Saints in tapestry with such strength of expression in their countenances that they looked like so many souls in purgatory. She could read without great difficulty, and had spelled her way through several church legends, and almost all the chivalric wonders of the Heldenbuch. She had even made considerable proficiency in writing, could sign her own name without missing a letter, and so legibly that her aunts could read it without spectacles. She excelled in making little good-for-nothing ladylike knick-knacks of all kinds; was versed in the most abstruse dancing of the day; played a number of airs on the harp and guitar; and knew all the tender ballads of the Minne-lieders by heart.

Her aunts, too, having been great flirts and coquettes in their younger days, were admirably calculated to be vigilant guardians and strict censors of the conduct of their niece; for there is no duenna so rigidly prudent, and inexorably decorous, as a superannuated coquette. She was rarely suffered out of their sight; never went beyond the domains of the castle, unless well attended, or, rather, well watched; had continual lectures read to her about strict decorum and implicit obedience; and, as to the men—pah! she was taught to hold them at such distance and distrust that, unless properly authorized, she would not have cast a glance upon the handsomest cavalier in the world—no, not if he were even dying at her feet.

The good effects of this system were wonderfully apparent. The young lady was a pattern of docility and correctness. While others were wasting their sweetness in the glare of the world, and liable to be plucked and thrown aside by every hand, she was coyly blooming into fresh and lovely womanhood under the protection of those immaculate spinsters, like a rosebud blushing forth among guardian thorns. Her aunts looked upon her with pride and exultation, and vaunted that though all the other young ladies in the world might go astray, yet, thank Heaven, nothing of the kind could happen to the heiress of Katzenellenbogen.

But however scantily the Baron Von Landshort might be provided with children, his household was by no means a small one, for Providence had enriched him with abundance of poor relations. They, one and all, possessed the affectionate disposition common to humble relatives ; were wonderfully attached to the Baron, and took every possible occasion to come in swarms and enliven the castle. All family festivals were commemorated by these good people at the Baron's expense ; and when they were filled with good cheer, they would declare that there was nothing on earth so delightful as these family meetings, these jubilees of the heart.

The Baron, though a small man, had a large soul, and it swelled with satisfaction at the consciousness of being the greatest man in the little world about him. He loved to tell long stories about the stark old warriors whose portraits looked grimly down from the walls around, and he found no listeners equal to those who fed at his expense. He was much given to the marvellous, and a firm believer in all those supernatural tales with which every mountain and valley in Germany abounds. The faith of his guests even exceeded his own, they listened to every tale of wonder with open eyes and mouth, and never failed to be astonished, even though repeated for the hundredth time. Thus lived the Baron Von Landshort, the oracle of his table, the absolute monarch of his little territory, and happy, above all things, in the persuasion that he was the wisest man of the age.

At the time of which my story treats there was a great family gathering at the castle, on an affair of the utmost importance : it was to receive the destined bridegroom of the Baron's daughter. A negotiation had been carried on between the father and an old nobleman of Bavaria, to unite the dignity of their houses by the marriage of their children. The preliminaries had been conducted with proper punctilio. The young people were betrothed without seeing each other, and the time was appointed for the marriage ceremony. The young Count Von Altenburg had been recalled from the army for the purpose, and was actually on his way to the Baron's to receive his bride. Missives had even been received from him, from Wurtzburg, where he was accidentally detained, mentioning the day and hour when he might be expected to arrive.

The castle was in a tumult of preparation to give him a

suitable welcome. The fair bride had been decked out with uncommon care. The two aunts had superintended her toilet, and quarrelled the whole morning about every article of her dress. The young lady had taken advantage of their contest to follow the bent of her own taste; and fortunately it was a good one. She looked as lovely as youthful bridegroom could desire; and the flutter of expectation heightened the lustre of her charms.

The suffusions that mantled her face and neck, the gentle heaving of the bosom, the eye now and then lost in reverie, all betrayed the soft tumult that was going on in her little heart. The aunts were continually hovering around her; for maiden aunts are apt to take great interest in affairs of this nature: they were giving her a world of staid counsel, how to deport herself, what to say, and in what manner to receive the expected lover.

The Baron was no less busied in preparations. He had, in truth, nothing exactly to do; but he was naturally a fuming, bustling little man, and could not remain passive when all the world was in a hurry. He worried from top to bottom of the castle, with an air of infinite anxiety; he continually called the servants from their work to exhort them to be diligent, and buzzed about every hall and chamber, as idle, restless and importunate as a bluebottle fly of a warm summer's day.

In the meantime, the fatted calf had been killed; the forests had rung with the clamour of the huntsmen; the kitchen was crowded with good cheer; the cellars had yielded up whole oceans of *Rhein-wein* and *Ferne-wein*, and even the great Heidelberg Tun had been laid under contribution. Everything was ready to receive the distinguished guest with *Saus und Braus* in the true spirit of German hospitality—but the guest delayed to make his appearance. Hour rolled after hour. The sun that had poured his downward rays upon the rich forests of the Odenwald now just gleamed along the summits of the mountains. The Baron mounted the highest tower, and strained his eyes in hopes of catching a distant sight of the Count and his attendants. Once he thought he beheld them; the sound of horns came floating from the valley, prolonged by the mountain echoes: a number of horsemen were seen far below, slowly advancing along the road; but when they had nearly reached the foot of the

mountain they suddenly struck off in a different direction.
The last ray of sunshine departed—the bats began to flit by
in the twilight—the road grew dimmer and dimmer to the
view ; and nothing appeared stirring in it but now and then
a peasant lagging homeward from his labour.

While the old castle of Landshort was in this state of
perplexity, a very interesting scene was transacting in a different
part of the Odenwald.

The young Count Von Altenburg was tranquilly pursuing
his route in that sober jog-trot way in which a man travels
toward matrimony when his friends have taken all the trouble
and uncertainty of courtship off his hands, and a bride is
waiting for him, as certainly as a dinner, at the end of his
journey.   He had encountered at Wurtzburg a youthful
companion in arms, with whom he had seen some service on
the frontiers : Herman Von Starkenfaust, one of the stoutest
hands and worthiest hearts of German chivalry, who was now
returning from the army.   His father's castle was not far
distant from the old fortress of Landshort, although a
hereditary feud rendered the families hostile and strangers to
each other.

In the warm-hearted moment of recognition, the young
friends related all their past adventures and fortunes, and the
Count gave the whole history of his intended nuptials with a
young lady whom he had never seen, but of whose charms he
had received the most enrapturing descriptions.

As the route of the friends lay in the same direction, they
agreed to perform the rest of their journey together ; and,
that they might do it more leisurely, set off from Wurtzburg
at an early hour, the Count having given directions for his
retinue to follow and overtake him.

They beguiled their wayfaring with recollections of their
military scenes and adventures ; but the Count was apt to be
a little tedious, now and then, about the reputed charms of
his bride, and the felicity that awaited him.

In this way they had entered among the mountains of the
Odenwald, and were traversing one of its most lonely and thickly
wooded passes.   It is well known that the forests of Germany
have always been as much infested with robbers as its castles
by spectres ; and, at this time, the former were particularly
numerous, from the hordes of disbanded soldiers wandering
about the country.   It will not appear extraordinary, therefore,

that the cavaliers were attacked by a gang of these stragglers in the midst of the forest. They defended themselves with bravery, but were nearly overpowered when the Count's retinue arrived to their assistance. At sight of them the robbers fled, but not until the Count had received a mortal wound. He was slowly and carefully conveyed back to the city of Wurtzburg, and a friar summoned from a neighbouring convent, who was famous for his skill in administering to both soul and body. But half of his skill was superfluous; the moments of the unfortunate Count were numbered.

With his dying breath he entreated his friend to repair instantly to the castle of Landshort, and explain the fatal cause of his not keeping his appointment with his bride. Though not the most ardent of lovers, he was one of the most punctilious of men, and appeared earnestly solicitous that this mission should be speedily and courteously executed. "Unless this is done," said he, "I shall not sleep quietly in my grave!" He repeated these last words with peculiar solemnity. A request, at a moment so impressive, admitted no hesitation. Starkenfaust endeavoured to soothe him to calmness; promised faithfully to execute his wish, and gave him his hand in solemn pledge. The dying man pressed it in acknowledgment, but soon lapsed into delirium—raved about his bride—his engagements—his plighted word; ordered his horse, that he might ride to the castle of Landshort, and expired in the fancied act of vaulting into the saddle.

Starkenfaust bestowed a sigh and a soldier's tear on the untimely fate of his comrade; and then pondered on the awkward mission he had undertaken. His heart was heavy, and his head perplexed; for he was to present himself an unbidden guest among hostile people, and to damp their festivity with tidings fatal to their hopes. Still there were certain whisperings of curiosity in his bosom to see this far-famed beauty of Katzenellenbogen so cautiously shut up from the world; for he was a passionate admirer of the sex, and there was a dash of eccentricity and enterprise in his character that made him fond of all singular adventure.

Previous to his departure, he made all due arrangements with the holy fraternity of the convent for the funeral solemnities of his friend, who was to be buried in the cathedral of Wurtzburg, near some of his illustrious relatives; and the mourning retinue of the Count took charge of his remains.

It is now high time that we should return to the ancient family of Katzenellenbogen, who were impatient for their guest, and still more for their dinner ; and to the worthy little Baron, whom we left airing himself on the watch-tower.

Night closed in, but still no guest arrived. The Baron descended from the tower in despair. The banquet, which had been delayed from hour to hour, could no longer be postponed. The meats were already overdone, the cook in an agony, and the whole household had the look of a garrison that had been reduced by famine. The Baron was obliged reluctantly to give orders for the feast without the presence of the guest. All were seated at table, and just on the point of commencing, when the sound of a horn from without the gate gave notice of the approach of a stranger. Another long blast filled the old courts of the castle with its echoes, and was answered by the warder from the walls. The Baron hastened to receive his future son-in-law.

The drawbridge had been let down, and the stranger was before the gate. He was a tall gallant cavalier, mounted on a black steed. His countenance was pale, but he had a beaming, romantic eye, and an air of stately melancholy. The Baron was a little mortified that he should have come in this simple, solitary style. His dignity for a moment was ruffled, and he felt disposed to consider it a want of proper respect for the important occasion, and the important family with which he was to be connected. He pacified himself, however, with the conclusion that it must have been youthful impatience which had induced him thus to spur on sooner than his attendants.

" I am sorry," said the stranger, " to break in upon you thus unseasonably——"

Here the Baron interrupted him with a world of compliments and greetings ; for, to tell the truth, he prided himself upon his courtesy and his eloquence. The stranger attempted, once or twice, to stem the torrent of words, but in vain ; so he bowed his head and suffered it to flow on. By the time the Baron had come to a pause they had reached the inner court of the castle ; and the stranger was again about to speak, when he was once more interrupted by the appearance of the female part of the family, leading forth the shrinking and blushing bride. He gazed on her for a moment as one entranced ; it seemed as if his whole soul beamed forth in the gaze, and rested upon that lovely form. One of the maiden aunts whispered something in her ear; she made an effort to speak; her moist blue eye was timidly raised, gave a shy glance of inquiry on the stranger, and was cast again to the ground. The words died away; but there was a sweet smile playing about her lips, and a soft dimpling of the cheek, that showed her glance had not been unsatisfactory. It was impossible for a girl of the fond age of eighteen, highly predisposed for love and matrimony, not to be pleased with so gallant a cavalier.

The late hour at which the guest had arrived left no time for parley. The Baron was peremptory, and deferred all particular conversation until the morning, and led the way to the untasted banquet.

It was served up in the great hall of the castle. Around the walls hung the hard-favoured portraits of the heroes of the house of Katzenellenbogen, and the trophies which they had gained in the field and in the chase. Hacked corselets, splintered jousting spears, and tattered banners were mingled with the spoils of sylvan warfare: the jaws of the wolf and the tusks of the boar grinned horribly among crossbows and battle-axes, and a huge pair of antlers branched immediately over the head of the youthful bridegroom.

The cavalier took but little notice of the company or the entertainment. He scarcely tasted the banquet, but seemed absorbed in admiration of his bride. He conversed in a low tone, that could not be overheard—for the language of love is never loud; but where is the female ear so dull that it cannot catch the softest whisper of the lover? There was a mingled tenderness and gravity in his manner that appeared to have a powerful effect upon the young lady. Her colour came and went, as she listened with deep attention. Now and then she made some blushing reply, and when his eye was turned away she would steal a sidelong glance at his romantic countenance, and heave a gentle sigh of tender happiness. It was evident that the young couple were completely enamoured. The aunts, who were deeply versed in the mysteries of the heart, declared that they had fallen in love with each other at first sight.

The feast went on merrily, or at least noisily, for the guests were all blessed with those keen appetites that attend upon light purses and mountain air. The Baron told his best and longest stories, and never had he told them so well, or with such great effect. If there was anything marvellous, his auditors were lost in astonishment ; and if anything facetious, they were sure to laugh exactly in the right place. The Baron, it is true, like most great men, was too dignified to utter any joke but a dull one : it was always enforced, however, by a bumper of excellent Hoch-heimer ; and even a dull joke, at one's own table, served up with jolly old wine, is irresistible. Many good things were said by poorer and keener wits that would not bear repeating, except on similar occasions ; many sly speeches whispered in ladies' ears that almost convulsed them with suppressed laughter ; and a song or two roared out by a poor but merry and broad-faced cousin of the Baron, that absolutely made the maiden aunts hold up their fans.

Amid all this revelry, the stranger-guest maintained a most singular and unseasonable gravity. His countenance assumed a deeper cast of dejection as the evening advanced, and, strange as it may appear, even the Baron's jokes seemed only to render him the more melancholy. At times he was lost in thought, and at times there was a perturbed and restless wandering of the eye that bespoke a mind but ill at ease. His conversation with the bride became more and more earnest and mysterious. Lowering clouds began to steal over the fair serenity of her brow, and tremors to run through her tender frame.

All this could not escape the notice of the company. Their gaiety was chilled by the unaccountable gloom of the bride-groom ; their spirits were infected ; whispers and glances were interchanged, accompanied by shrugs and dubious shakes of the head. The song and the laugh grew less and less frequent : there were dreary pauses in the conversation, which were at length succeeded by wild tales and supernatural legends. One dismal story produced another still more dismal, and the Baron nearly frightened some of the ladies into hysterics with the history of the goblin horseman that carried away the fair Leonora—a dreadful, but true story, which has since been put into excellent verse, and is read and believed by all the world.

The bridegroom listened to this tale with profound atten-tion. He kept his eyes steadily fixed on the Baron, and, as the story drew to a close, began gradually to rise from his seat, growing taller and taller, until, in the Baron's entranced eye, he seemed almost to tower into a giant. The moment the tale was finished, he heaved a deep sigh, and took a solemn farewell of the company. They were all amazement. The Baron was perfectly thunderstruck.

"What! going to leave the castle at midnight? Why, everything was prepared for his reception; a chamber was ready for him if he wished to retire."

The stranger shook his head mournfully and mysteriously : "I must lay my head in a different chamber to-night!"

There was something in this reply, and the tone in which it was uttered, that made the Baron's heart misgive him ; but he rallied his forces, and repeated his hospitable entreaties. The stranger shook his head silently, but positively, at every offer ; and, waving his farewell to the company, stalked slowly out of the hall. The maiden aunts were absolutely petrified—the bride hung her head, and a tear stole to her eye.

The Baron followed the stranger to the great court of the castle, where the black charger stood pawing the earth and snorting with impatience. When they had reached the portal, whose deep archway was dimly lighted by a cresset, the stranger paused, and addressed the Baron in a hollow tone of voice, which the vaulted roof rendered still more sepulchral. "Now that we are alone," said he, "I will impart to you the reason of my going. I have a solemn, an indispensable engagement——"

"Why," said the Baron, "cannot you send someone in your place?"

"It admits of no substitute—I must attend it in person— I must away to Wurtzburg cathedral——"

"Ay," said the Baron, plucking up spirit, "but not until to-morrow—to-morrow you shall take your bride there."

"No! no!" replied the stranger, with tenfold solemnity, "my engagement is with no bride—the worms! the worms expect me! I am a dead man—I have been slain by robbers —my body lies at Wurtzburg—at midnight I am to be buried —the grave is waiting for me—I must keep my appointment!"

He sprang on his black charger, dashed over the drawbridge, and the clattering of his horse's hoofs was lost in the whistling of the night-blast.

The Baron returned to the hall in the utmost consternation, and related what had passed. Two ladies fainted outright ; others sickened at the idea of having banqueted with a spectre. It was the opinion of some that this might be the wild hunts- man famous in German legend. Some talked of mountain sprites, of wood-demons, and of other supernatural beings, with which the good people of Germany have been so grievously harassed since time immemorial. One of the poor relations ventured to suggest that it might be some sportive evasion of the young cavalier, and that the very gloominess of the caprice seemed to accord with so melancholy a personage. This, however, drew on him the indignation of the whole company, and especially of the Baron, who looked upon him as little better than an infidel; so that he was fain to abjure his heresy as speedily as possible, and come into the faith of the true believers.

But, whatever may have been the doubts entertained, they were completely put to an end by the arrival, next day, of regular missives confirming the intelligence of the young Count's murder, and his interment in Wurtzburg cathedral.

The dismay at the castle may well be imagined. The Baron shut himself up in his chamber. The guests who had come to rejoice with him could not think of abandoning him in his distress. They wandered about the courts, or collected in groups in the hall, shaking their heads and shrugging their shoulders at the troubles of so good a man; and sat longer than ever at table, and ate and drank more stoutly than ever, by way of keeping up their spirits. But the situation of the widowed bride was the most pitiable. To have lost a husband before she had even embraced him—and such a husband! If the spectre could be so gracious and noble, what must have been the living man? She filled the house with lamentations.

On the night of the second day of her widowhood, she had retired to her chamber, accompanied by one of her aunts who insisted on sleeping with her. The aunt, who was one of the best tellers of ghost stories in all Germany, had just been recounting one of her longest, and had fallen asleep in the very midst of it. The chamber was remote, and overlooked a small garden. The niece lay pensively gazing at the beams of the rising moon, as they trembled on the leaves of an aspen tree before the lattice. The castle clock had just tolled midnight, when a soft strain of music stole up from the garden. She rose hastily from her bed and stepped lightly to the window. A tall figure stood among the shadows of the trees. As it raised its head, a beam of moonlight fell upon the countenance. Heaven and earth! She beheld the Spectre

Bridegroom! A loud shriek at that moment burst upon her ear, and her aunt, who had been awakened by the music, and had followed her silently to the window, fell into her arms. When she looked again, the spectre had disappeared.

Of the two females, the aunt now required the most soothing, for she was perfectly beside herself with terror. As to the young lady, there was something, even in the spectre of her lover, that seemed endearing. There was still the semblance of manly beauty; and though the shadow of a man is but little calculated to satisfy the affections of a lovesick girl, yet, where the substance is not to be had, even that is consoling. The aunt declared that she would never sleep in that chamber again; the niece, for once, was refractory, and declared as strongly that she would sleep in no other in the castle: the consequence was that she had to sleep in it alone; but she drew a promise from her aunt not to relate the story of the spectre, lest she should be denied the only melancholy pleasure left her on earth—that of inhabiting the chamber over which the guardian shade of her lover kept its nightly vigils.

How long the good old lady would have observed this promise is uncertain, for she dearly loved to talk of the marvellous, and there is a triumph in being the first to tell a frightful story; it is, however, still quoted in the neighbourhood, as a memorable instance of female secrecy, that she kept it to herself for a whole week; when she was suddenly absolved from all further restraint by intelligence brought to the breakfast-table one morning that the young lady was not to be found. Her room was empty—the bed had not been slept in—the window was open—and the bird had flown!

The astonishment and concern with which the intelligence was received can only be imagined by those who have witnessed the agitation which the mishaps of a great man cause among his friends. Even the poor relations paused for a moment from the indefatigable labours of the trencher; when the aunt, who had at first been struck speechless, wrung her hands and shrieked out, " The goblin! the goblin! She's carried away by the goblin! "

In a few words she related the fearful scene of the garden, and concluded that the spectre must have carried off his bride. Two of the domestics corroborated the opinion, for they had heard the clattering of a horse's hoofs down the mountain about midnight, and had no doubt that it was the spectre on his black charger, bearing her away to the tomb. All present were struck with the direful probability; for events of the kind are extremely common in Germany, as many well-authenticated histories bear witness.

What a lamentable situation was that of the poor Baron! What a heart-rending dilemma for a fond father, and a member of the great family of Katzenellenbogen! His only daughter had either been rapt away to the grave, or he was to have some wood-demon for a son-in-law, and, perchance, a troop of goblin grandchildren. As usual, he was completely bewildered, and all the castle in an uproar. The men were ordered to take horse and scour every road and path and glen of the Odenwald. The Baron himself had just drawn on his jack-boots, girded on his sword, and was about to mount his steed to sally forth on the doubtful quest, when he was brought to a pause by a new apparition. A lady was seen approaching the castle, mounted on a palfrey attended by a cavalier on horseback. She galloped up to the gate, sprang from her horse, and falling at the Baron's feet, embraced his knees. It was his lost daughter, and her companion—the Spectre Bridegroom! The Baron was astounded. He looked at his daughter, then at the spectre, and almost doubted the evidence of his senses. The latter, too, was wonderfully improved in his appearance, since his visit to the world of spirits. His dress was splendid, and set off a noble figure of manly symmetry. He was no longer pale and melancholy. His fine countenance was flushed with the glow of youth, and joy rioted in his large dark eye.

The mystery was soon cleared up. The cavalier (for, in truth, as you must have known all the while, he was no goblin) announced himself as Sir Herman Von Starkenfaust. He related his adventure with the young Count. He told how he had hastened to the castle to deliver the unwelcome tidings, but that the eloquence of the Baron had interrupted him in every attempt to tell his tale. How the sight of the bride had completely captivated him, and that to pass a few hours near her he had tacitly suffered the mistake to continue. How he had been sorely perplexed in what way to make a decent retreat, until the Baron's goblin stories had suggested his eccentric exit. How, fearing the feudal hostility of the family, he had repeated his visits by stealth—had haunted the garden

2L

beneath the young lady's window—had wooed—had won—
had borne away in triumph—and, in a word, had wedded the
fair.

Under any other circumstances the Baron would have
been inflexible, for he was tenacious of paternal authority and
devoutly obstinate in all family feuds; but he loved his
daughter; he had lamented her as lost; he rejoiced to find
her still alive; and, though her husband was of a hostile
house, yet, thank Heaven, he was not a goblin. There was
something, it must be acknowledged, that did not exactly
accord with his notions of strict veracity, in the joke the
knight had passed upon him of his being a dead man; but
several old friends present, who had served in the wars
assured him that every strategem was excusable in love, and
that the cavalier was entitled to especial privilege, having
lately served as a trooper.

Matters, therefore, were happily arranged. The Baron
pardoned the young couple on the spot. The revels at the
castle were resumed. The poor relations overwhelmed this
new member of the family with loving-kindness; he was so
gallant, so generous—and so rich. The aunts, it is true, were
somewhat scandalized that their system of strict seclusion
and passive obedience should be so badly exemplified, but
attributed all to their negligence in not having the windows
grated. One of them was particularly mortified at having
her marvellous story marred, and that the only spectre she
had ever seen should turn out a counterfeit; but the niece
seemed perfectly happy at having found him substantial flesh
and blood—and so the story ends.

MARY WEBB

MR. TALLENT'S GHOST

THE first time I ever met Mr. Tallent was in the late summer of 1906, in a small, lonely inn on the top of a mountain. For natives, rainy days in these places are not very different from other days, since work fills them all, wet or fine. But for the tourist, rainy days are boring. I had been bored for nearly a week, and was thinking of returning to London, when Mr. Tallent came. And because I could not "place" Mr. Tallent, nor elucidate him to my satisfaction, he intrigued me. For a barrister should be able to sum up men in a few minutes.

I did not see Mr. Tallent arrive, nor did I observe him entering the room. I looked up, and he was there, in the small firelit parlour with his Bible, wool mats and copper preserving pan. He was reading a manuscript, slightly moving his lips as he read. He was a gentle, moth-like man, very lean and about six foot three or more. He had neutral coloured hair and eyes, a nondescript suit, limp-looking hands and slightly turned-up toes. The most noticeable thing about him was an expression of passive and enduring obstinacy.

I wished him good evening, and asked if he had a paper, as he seemed to have come from civilisation.

"No," he said softly, "no. Only a little manuscript of my own."

Now, as a rule I am as wary of manuscripts as a hare is of greyhounds. Having once been a critic, I am always liable to receive parcels of these for advice. So I might have saved myself and a dozen or so of other people from what turned out to be a terrible, an appalling, incubus. But the day had been so dull, and having exhausted Old Moore and sampled the Imprecatory Psalms, I had nothing else to read. So I said, "Your own?"

"Even so," replied Mr. Tallent modestly.

"May I have the privilege?" I queried, knowing he intended me to have it.

"How kind!" he exclaimed. "A stranger, knowing

nothing of my hopes and aims, yet willing to undertake so onerous a task."

" Not at all ! " I replied, with a nervous chuckle.

" I think," he murmured, drawing near and, as it were, taking possession of me, looming above me with his great height, " it might be best for me to read it to you. I am considered to have rather a fine reading voice."

I said I should be delighted, reflecting that supper could not very well be later than nine. I knew I should not like the reading.

He stood before the cloth-draped mantelpiece.

" This," he said, " shall be my rostrum." Then he read.

I wish I could describe to you that slow, expressionless, unstoppable voice. It was a voice for which at the time I could find no comparison. Now I know that it was like the voice of the loud speaker in a dull subject. At first one listened, taking in even the sense of the words. I took in all the first six chapters, which were unbelievably dull. I got all the scenery, characters, undramatic events clearly marshalled. I imagined that something would, in time, happen. I thought the characters were going to develop, do fearful things or great and holy deeds. But they did nothing.

Nothing happened. The book was flat, formless, yet not vital enough to be inchoate. It was just a meandering expression of a negative personality, with a plethora of muted, borrowed, stale ideas. He always said what one expected him to say. One knew what all his people would do. One waited for the culminating platitude as for an expected twinge of toothache. I thought he would pause after a time, for even the most arrogant usually do that, apologising and at the same time obviously waiting for one to say, " Do go on, please."

This was not necessary in his case. In fact, it was impossible. The slow, monotonous voice went on without a pause, with the terrible tirelessness of a gramophone. I longed for him to whisper or shout—anything to relieve the tedium. I tried to think of other things, but he read too distinctly for that. I could neither listen to him nor ignore him. I have never spent such an evening. As luck would have it the little maidservant did not achieve our meal till nearly ten o'clock. The hours dragged on.

At last I said: " Could we have a pause, just for a few minutes ? "

" Why ? " he enquired.

" For . . . for discussion," I weakly murmured.

" Not," he replied, " at the most exciting moment. Don't you realise that now, at last, I have worked up my plot to the most dramatic moment ? All the characters are waiting, attent, for the culminating tragedy."

He went on reading. I went on awaiting the culminating tragedy. But there was no tragedy. My head ached abominably. The voice flowed on, over my senses, the room, the world. I felt as if it would wash me away into eternity. I found myself thinking, quite solemnly :

" If she doesn't bring supper soon, I shall kill him."

I thought it in the instinctive· way in which one thinks it of an earwig or a midge. I took refuge in the consideration how to do it ? This was absorbing. It enabled me to detach myself completely from the sense of what he read. I considered all the ways open to me. Strangling. The bread knife on the sideboard. Hanging. I gloated over them. I was beginning to be almost happy, when suddenly the reading stopped.

" She is bringing supper," he said. " Now we can have a little discussion. Afterwards I will finish the manuscript."

He did. And after that, he told me all about his will. He said he was leaving all his money for the posthumous publication of his manuscript. He also said that he would like me to draw up this for him, and to be trustee of the manuscripts.

I said I was too busy. He replied that I could draw up the will to-morrow.

" I'm going to-morrow," I interpolated passionately.

" You cannot go until the carrier goes in the afternoon," he triumphed. " Meanwhile, you can draw up the will. After that you need do no more. You can pay a critic to read the manuscripts. You can pay a publisher to publish them. And I in them shall be remembered."

He added that if I still had doubts as to their literary worth, he would read me another.

I gave in. Would anyone else have done differently ? I drew up the will, left an address where he could send his stuff, and left the inn.

" Thank God ! " I breathed devoutly, as the turn of the lane hid him from view. He was standing on the doorstep beginning to read what he called a pastoral to a big cattle-dealer who had called for a pint of bitter. I smiled to think how much more he would get than he had bargained for.

After that, I forgot Mr. Tallent. I heard nothing more of him for some years. Occasionally I glanced down the list of books to see if anybody else had relieved me of my task by publishing Mr. Tallent. But nobody had.

It was about ten years later, when I was in hospital with a " Blighty " wound, that I met Mr. Tallent again. I was convalescent, sitting in the sun with some other chaps, when the door opened softly, and Mr. Tallent stole in. He read to us for two hours. He remembered me, and had a good deal to say about coincidence. When he had gone, I said to the nurse, " If you let that fellow in again while I'm here, I'll kill him."

She laughed a good deal, but the other chaps all agreed with me, and as a matter of fact, he never did come again.

Not long after this I saw the notice of his death in the paper.

" Poor chap ! " I thought, " he's been reading too much. Somebody's patience has given out. Well, he won't ever be able to read to me again."

Then I remembered the manuscripts, realising that, if he had been as good as his word, my troubles had only just begun And it was so.

First came the usual kind of letter from a solicitor in the town where he had lived. Next I had a call from the said solicitor's clerk, who brought a large tin box.

" The relations," he said, " of the deceased are extremely angry. Nothing has been left to them. They say that the manuscripts are worthless, and that the living have rights."

I asked how they knew that the manuscripts were worthless.

" It appears, sir, that Mr. Tallent has, from time to time, read these aloud——"

I managed to conceal a grin.

" And they claim, sir, to share equally with the—er— manuscripts. They threaten to take proceedings, and have been getting legal opinions as to the advisability of demand-ing an investigation of the material you have."

I looked at the box. There was an air of Joanna Southcott about it.

I asked if it were full.

" Quite, sir. Typed MSS. Very neatly done."

He produced the key, a copy of the will, and a sealed letter. I took the box home with me that evening. Fortified by dinner, a cigar and a glass of port, I considered it. There is an extraordinary air of fatality about a box. For bane or for blessing, it has a perpetual fascination for mankind. A wizard's coffer, a casket of jewels, the alabaster box of precious nard, a chest of bridal linen, a stone sarcophagus—what strange mystery is about them all ! So when I opened Mr. Tallent's box I felt like somebody letting loose a genie. And indeed I was. I had already perused the will and the letter, and discovered that the fortune was moderately large. The letter merely repeated what Mr. Tallent had told me. I glanced at some of the manuscripts. Immediately the room seemed full of Mr. Tallent's presence and his voice. I looked towards the now dusky corners of the room as if he might be looming there. As I ran through more of the papers, I realised that what Mr. Tallent had chosen to read to me had been the best of them. I looked up Johnson's telephone number and asked him to come round. He is the kind of chap who never makes any money. He is a free lance journalist with a conscience. I knew he would be glad of the job.

He came round at once. He eyed the manuscripts with rapture. For at heart he is a critic, and has the eternal hope of unearthing a masterpiece.

" You had better take a dozen at a time, and keep a record," I said. " Verdict at the end."

" Will it depend on me whether they are published ? "

" *Which* are published," I said. " Some will have to be. The will says so."

" But if I found them all worthless, the poor beggars would get more of the cash ? Damnable to be without cash."

" I shall have to look into that. I am not sure if it is legally possible. What, for instance, is the standard ? "

" *I* shall create the standard," said Johnson rather haughtily. " Of course, if I find a masterpiece——"

" If you find a masterpiece, my dear chap," I said, " I'll give you a hundred pounds."

He asked if I had thought of a publisher. I said I had decided on Jukes, since no book, however bad, could make his reputation worse than it was, and the money might save his credit.

2L*

"Is that quite fair to poor Tallent?" he asked. Mr. Tallent had already got hold of him.

"If," I said as a parting benediction, "you wish you had never gone into it (as, when you have put your hand to the plough, you will), remember that at least they were never read aloud to you, and be thankful."

Nothing occurred for a week. Then letters began to come from Mr. Tallent's relations. They were a prolific family. They were all very poor, very angry and intensely uninterested in literature. They wrote from all kinds of view-points, in all kinds of styles. They were, however, all alike in two things—the complete absence of literary excellence and legal exactitude.

It took an increasing time daily to read and answer these. If I gave them any hope, I at once felt Mr. Tallent's hovering presence, mute, anxious, hurt. If I gave no hope, I got a solicitor's letter by return of post. Nobody but myself seemed to feel the pathos of Mr. Tallent's ambitions and dreams. I was notified that proceedings were going to be taken by firms all over England. Money was being recklessly spent to rob Mr. Tallent of his immortality, but it appeared, later that Mr. Tallent could take care of himself.

When Johnson came for more of the contents of the box, he said that there was no sign of a masterpiece yet, and that they were as bad as they well could be.

"A pathetic chap, Tallent," he said.

"Don't, for God's sake, my dear chap, let him get at you," implored him. "Don't give way. He'll haunt you, as he's haunting me, with that abominable pathos of his. I think of him and his box continually just as one does of a life and death plea. If I sit by my own fireside, I can hear him reading. When I am just going to sleep, I dream that he is looming over me like an immense, wan moth. If I forget him for a little while, a letter comes from one of his unutterable relations and recalls me. Be wary of Tallent."

Needless to tell you that he did not take my advice. By the time he had finished the box he was as much under Tallent's thumb as I was. Bitterly disappointed that there was no masterpiece, he was still loyal to the writer, yet he was emotionally harrowed by the pitiful letters that the relations were now sending to all the papers.

"I dreamed," he said to me one day (Johnson always says

" dreamed," because he is a critic and considers it the elegan
form of expression), " I dreamed that poor Tallent appeared
to me in the watches of the night and told me exactly how
each of his things came to him. He said they came like
' Kubla Khan.' "

I said it must have taken all night.

" It did," he replied. " And it has made me dislike a master
piece."

I asked him if he intended to be present at the genera
meeting.

" Meeting ? "

" Yes. Things have got to such a pitch that we have had
to call one. There will be about a hundred people. I shall
have to entertain them to a meal afterwards. I can't very well
charge it up to the account of the deceased."

" Gosh ! It'll cost a pretty penny."

" It will. But perhaps we shall settle something. I shall
be thankful."

" You're not looking well, old chap," he said. " Worn
you seem."

" I am," I said. " Tallent is ever with me. Will you
come ? "

" Rather. But I don't know what to say."

" The truth, the whole truth——"

" But it's so awful to think of that poor soul spending his
whole life on those damned . . . and then that they should
never see the light of day."

" Worse that they should. Much worse."

" My dear chap, what a confounded position ! "

" If I had foreseen *how* confounded," I said, " I'd have
strangled the fellow on the top of that mountain. I have had
to get two clerks to deal with the correspondence. I get
no rest. All night I dream of Tallent. And now I hear that
a consumptive relation of his has died of disappointment at
not getting any of the money, and his wife has written me a
wild letter threatening to accuse me of manslaughter. Of
course that's all stuff, but it shows what a hysterical state
everybody's in. I feel pretty well done for."

" You'd feel worse if you'd read the boxful."

I agreed.

We had a stormy meeting. It was obvious that the people
did need the money. They were the sort of struggling, under

vitalised folk who always do need it. Children were waiting
for a chance in life, old people were waiting to be saved from
death a little longer, middle-aged people were waiting to set
themselves up in business or buy snug little houses. And
there was Tallent, out of it all, in a spiritual existence, not
needing beef and bread any more, deliberately keeping it
from them.

As I thought this, I distinctly saw Tallent pass the window
of the room I had hired for the occasion. I stood up ; I
pointed ; I cried out to them to follow him. The very man
himself.

Johnson came to me.

" Steady, old man," he said. " You're overstrained."

" But I did see him," I said. " The very man. The cause
of all the mischief. If I could only get my hands on him ! "

A medical man who had married one of Tallent's sisters
said that these hallucinations were very common, and that
I was evidently not a fit person to have charge of the money.
This brought me a ray of hope, till that ass Johnson contradicted him, saying foolish things about my career. And
a diversion was caused by a tremulous old lady calling out,
" The Church ! The Church ! Consult the Church ! There's
something in the Bible about it, only I can't call it to mind at
the moment. Has anybody got a Bible ! "

A clerical nephew produced a pocket New Testament,
and it transpired that what she had meant was, " Take ten
talents."

" If I could take one, madam," I said, " it would be enough."

" It speaks of that too," she replied triumphantly.
' Listen ! ' If any man have one talent . . . ' Oh, there's
everything in the Bible ! "

" Let us," remarked one of the thirteen solicitors, " get to
business. Whether it's in the Bible or not, whether Mr.
Tallent went past the window or not, the legality or illegality
of what we propose is not affected. Facts are facts. The
deceased is dead. You've got the money. We want it."

" I devoutly wish you'd got it," I said, " and that Tallent
was haunting you instead of me."

The meeting lasted four hours. The wildest ideas were put
forward. One or two sporting cousins of the deceased suggested a decision by games—representatives of the would-be
beneficiaries and representatives of the manuscript. They

were unable to see that this could not affect the legal aspect. Johnson was asked for his opinion. He said that from a critic's point of view the MSS. were balderdash. Everybody looked kindly upon him. But just as he was sunning himself in this atmosphere, and trying to forget Tallent, an immense lady, like Boadicea, advanced upon him, towering over him in a hostile manner.

"I haven't read the books, and I'm not going to," she said, "but I take exception to that word balderdash, sir, and I consider it libellous. Let me tell you, I brought Mr. Tallent into the world!" I looked at her with awesome wonder. She had brought that portent into the world! But how . . . whom had she persuaded? . . . I pulled myself up. And as I turned away from the contemplation of Boadicea, I saw Tallent pass the window again.

I rushed forward and tried to push up the sash. But the place was built for meetings, not for humanity, and it would not open. I seized the poker, intending to smash the glass. I suppose I must have looked rather mad, and as everybody else had been too intent on business to look out of the window, nobody believed that I had seen anything.

"You might just go round to the nearest chemist's and get some bromide," said the doctor to Johnson. "He's over-wrought."

Johnson, who was thankful to escape Boadicea, went with alacrity.

The meeting was, however, over at last. A resolution was passed that we should try to arrange things out of court. We were to take the opinions of six eminent lawyers—judges preferably. We were also to submit what Johnson thought the best story to a distinguished critic. According to what they said we were to divide the money up or leave things as they were.

I felt very much discouraged as I walked home. All these opinions would entail much work and expense. There seemed no end to it.

"Damn the man!" I muttered, as I turned the corner into the square in which I live. And there, just the width of the square away from me, was the man himself. I could almost have wept. What had I done that the gods should play with me thus?

I hurried forward, but he was walking fast, and in a moment

he turned down a side-street. When I got to the corner, the street was empty. After this, hardly a day passed without my seeing Tallent. It made me horribly jumpy and nervous, and the fear of madness began to prey on my mind. Meanwhile, the business went on. It was finally decided that half the money should be divided among the relations. Now I thought there would be peace, and for a time there was—comparatively.

But it was only about a month from this date that I heard from one of the solicitors to say that a strange and disquieting thing had happened—two of the beneficiaries were haunted by Mr. Tallent to such an extent that their reason was in danger. I wrote to ask what form the haunting took. He said they continually heard Mr. Tallent reading aloud from his works. Wherever they were in the house, they still heard him. I wondered if he would begin reading to me soon. So far it had only been visions. If he began to read . . .

In a few months I heard that both the relations who were haunted had been taken to an asylum. While they were in the asylum they heard nothing. But, some time after, on being certified as cured and released, they heard the reading again, and had to go back. Gradually the same thing happened to others, but only to one or two at a time.

During the long winter, two years after his death, it began to happen to me.

I immediately went to a specialist, who said there was acute nervous prostration, and recommended a " home." But I refused. I would fight Tallent to the last. Six of the beneficiaries were now in " homes," and every penny of the money they had had was used up.

I considered things. " Bell, book and candle " seemed to be what was required. But how, when, where to find him ? I consulted a spiritualist, a priest and a woman who has more intuitive perception than anyone I know. From their advice I made my plans. But it was Lesbia who saved me.

" Get a man who can run to go about with you," she said. " The moment *He* appears, let your companion rush round by a side-street and cut him off."

" But how will that——? "

" Never mind. I know what I think."

She gave me a wise little smile.

I did what she advised, but it was not till my patience was

nearly exhausted that I saw Tallent again. The reading went on, but only in the evenings when I was alone, and at night. I asked people in evening after evening. But when I got into bed, it began.

Johnson suggested that I should get married.

" What ? " I said, " offer a woman a ruined nervous system, a threatened home, and a possible end in an asylum ? "

" There's one woman who would jump at at. I love my love with an L."

" Don't be an ass," I said. I felt in no mood for jokes. All I wanted was to get things cleared up.

About three years after Tallent's death, my companion and I, going out rather earlier than usual, saw him hastening down a long road which had no side-streets leading out of it. As luck would have it, an empty taxi passed us. I shouted. We got in. Just in front of Tallent's ghost we stopped, leapt out, and flung ourselves upon him.

" My God ! " I cried. " He's *solid* ! "

He was perfectly solid, and not a little alarmed.

We put him into the taxi and took him to my house.

" *Now*, Tallent ! " I said, " you will answer for what you have done."

He looked scared, but dreamy.

" Why aren't you dead ? " was my next question.

He seemed hurt.

" I never died," he replied softly.

" It was in the papers."

" I put it in. I was in America. It was quite easy."

" And that continual haunting of me, and the wicked driving of your unfortunate relations into asylums ? " I was working myself into a rage. " Do you know how many of them are there now ? "

" Yes. I know. Very interesting."

" Interesting ? "

" It was in a great cause," he said. " Possibly you didn't grasp that I was a progressive psycho-analyst, and that I did not take those novels of mine seriously. In fact, they were just part of the experiment."

" In heaven's name, *what* experiment ? "

" The plural would be better, really," he said, " for there were many experiments."

" But what for, you damned old blackguard ? " I shouted.

" For my *magnum opus*," he said modestly.

" And what is your abominable *magnum opus*, you wicked old man ? "

" It will be famous all over the world," he said complacently. " All this has given me exceptional opportunities. It was so easy to get into my relations' houses and experiment with them. It was regrettable, though, that I could not follow them to the asylum."

This evidently worried him far more than the trouble he had caused.

" So it was *you* reading, every time ? "

" Every time."

" And it was you who went past the window of that horrible room when we discussed your will ? "

" Yes. A most gratifying spectacle ! "

" And now, you old scoundrel, before I decide what to do with you," I said, " what is the *magnum opus* ? "

" It is a treatise," he said, with the pleased expression that made me so wild. " A treatise that will eclipse all former work in that field, and its title is—' An Exhaustive Enquiry, with numerous Experiments, into the Power of Human Endurance.' "

ANN BRIDGE

THE BUICK SALOON

TO Mrs. James St. George Bernard Bowlby it seemed
almost providential that she should recover from the
series of illnesses which had perforce kept her in England, at
the precise moment when Bowlby was promoted from being
No. 2 to being No. 1 in the Grand Oriental Bank in Peking.
Her improved health and his improved circumstances made it
obvious that now at last she should join him, and she wrote
to suggest it. Bowlby of course agreed, and out she came.
He went down to meet her in Shanghai, but business having
called him further still, to Hongkong, Mrs. Bowlby proceeded
to Peking alone, and took up her quarters in the big, ugly grey-
brick house over the Bank in Legation Street. She tried, as
many managers' wives had tried before her, to do her best with
the solid mahogany and green leather furniture provided by the
Bank, wondering the while how Bowlby, so dependent always
on the feminine touch on his life and surroundings, had
endured the lesser solidities of the sub-manager's house alone
for so long. She bought silks and black-wood and scroll
paintings. She also bought a car. " You'll need a car, and
you'd better have a saloon, because of the dust," Bowlby
had said.

People who come to Peking without motors of their own
seldom buy new ones. There are always second-hand cars
going, from many sources; the leavings of transferred
diplomatists, the jetsam of financial ventures, the sediment of
conferences. So one morning Mrs. Bowlby went down with
Thompson, the new No. 2 in the Bank, to Maxon's garage in
the Nan Shih Tzu to choose her car. After much conversation
with the Canadian manager they pitched on a Buick saloon.
It was a Buick of the type which is practically standard in the
Far East, and had been entirely repainted outside, a respectable
dark blue; the inside had been newly done up in a pleasant
soft grey which appealed to Mrs. Bowlby. The manager was
loud in its praises. The suspension was excellent. (" You
want that on these roads, Mrs. Bowlby.") The driver and his

colleague sat outside. (" Much better, Mr. Thompson. If
these fellows have been eating garlic—they shouldn't, but they
do——") Thompson knew they did, and agreed heartily. Mrs.
Bowlby, new to such transactions, wanted to know who the
car had belonged to. The manager was firmly vague. This
was not a commission sale—he had bought the car when the
owner left. Very good people—" from the Quarter." This
fully satisfied Thompson, who knew that only Europeans live
(above the rose, anyhow) in the Legation Quarter of Peking.

So the Buick saloon was bought. Thompson, having heard
at the Club that the late Grand Oriental chauffeur drank petrol,
did not re-engage him with the rest of the servants according
to custom, but secured instead for Mrs. Bowlby the chauffeur
of a departing manager of the Banque Franco-Belge. By the
time Bowlby returned from Hongkong the chauffeur and his
colleagues had been fitted out with khaki livery for winter,
with white for summer—in either case with trim gold cuff-and-
hat-bands—and Mrs. Bowlby, in her blue saloon, had settled
down to pay her calls.

In Peking the newcomer calls first; a curious and dis-
couraging system. It is an ordeal even to the hardened. Mrs.
Bowlby was not hardened; she was a small, shy, frail woman,
who wore grey by preference, and looked grey—eyes, hair and
skin. She had no idea of asserting herself; if she had things
in her—subtleties, delicacies—she did not wear them outside;
she did not impose herself. She hated the calls. But as she was
also extremely conscientious, day after day, trying to fortify
herself by the sight of the two khaki-and-gold figures in front
of her, exhaling their possible garlic to the outer air beyond the
glass partition, she called. She called on the diplomats' wives
in the Quarter; she called on " the Salt " (officials of the Salt
Gabelle); she called on the Customs—English, Italian,
American, and French; she called on the Posts—French,
Italian, American, and English. The annual displacement of
pasteboard in Peking must amount to many tons, and in this
useful work Mrs. Bowlby, alone in the grey interior of her car,
faithfully took her share. She carried with her a little list on
which, with the help of her Number One Boy (as much a
permanent fixture in the Bank house, almost, as the doors and
windows), she had written out the styles, titles, and addresses
of the ladies she wished to visit. The late chauffeur of the
Banque Franco-Belge spoke excellent French; so did Mrs.

Bowlby—it was one of her few accomplishments ; but as no Chinese can or will master European names, the Europeans needs must learn and use the peculiar versions current among them. " *Ta Ch'in ch'ai T'ai-t'ai, Turkwo-fu* " read out Mrs. Bowlby when she wished to call on the wife of the German Minister. " *Oui, Madame !* " said Shwang. " *Pé T'ai-t'ai, Kung Hsien Hut'ung* " read out Mrs. Bowlby when visiting Mrs. Bray, the doctor's wife ; but when she wished to call on Mrs. Bennett, the wife of the Commandant of the English Guard, and Mrs. Baines, the Chaplain's wife, she found that they were both *Pé T'ai-t'ai* too—which led to confusion.

It began towards the end of the first week. Possibly it was her absorption in the lists and the Chinese names that prevented her from noticing it sooner, but at the end of that week Mrs. Bowlby would have sworn that she heard French spoken beside her as she drove about. Once, a little later, as she was driving down the Rue Marco Polo to fetch her husband from the Club, a voice said : " *C'est lui !* " in an underbreath, eagerly—or so she thought. The windows were lowered, and Mrs. Bowlby put it down to the servants in front. But it persisted. More than once she thought she heard a soft sigh. " Nerves ! " thought Mrs. Bowlby—her nerves were always a menace, and Peking, she knew, was bad for them.

She went on saying " nerves " for two or three more days ; then, one afternoon, she changed her mind. She was driving along the Ta Chiang an Chieh, the great thoroughfare running east and west outside the Legation Quarter, where the trams ring and clang past the scarlet walls and golden roofs of the Forbidden City, and long lines of camels, coming in with coal from the country as they have come for centuries, cross the road between the Dodges and Daimlers of the new China. It was a soft, brilliant afternoon in April, and the cinder track along the Glacis of the Quarter was thronged with riders ; polo had begun, and as the car neared Hatamen Street she caught a glimpse of the white and scarlet figures through the drifting dust on her right. At the corner of the Hatamen the car stopped ; a string of camels was passing up to the great gateway, and she had to wait.

She sat back in the car, glad of the pause ; she was unusually moved by the loveliness of the day, by the beauty and strangeness of the scene, by the whole magic of spring in Peking. She was going later to watch the polo, a terrifying game ; she wished Jim didn't play. Suddenly, across her idle thoughts, a voice beside her spoke clearly. *"Au revoir ! "* it said, *"mon très-cher. Ne tombe pas, je t'en prie."* And as the car moved forward behind the last of the camels, soft and unmistakable there came a sigh, and the words *" Ce polo ! Quel sport affreux ! Dieu, que je le déteste ! "* in a passionate undertone.

" That *wasn't* the chauffeur ! " was what Mrs. Bowlby found herself saying. The front windows were up. And besides, that low, rather husky voice, the cultivated and clear accent, could not be confounded for a moment with Shwang's guttural French. And besides, what chauffeur would talk like that ? The thing was ridiculous. " And it *wasn't* nerves this time," said Mrs. Bowlby, her thoughts running this way and that round the phenomenon. " She did say it." " Then it was she who said : ' *C'est lui ! '* before——" she said almost triumphantly, a moment later.

Curiously, though she was puzzled and startled, she realized presently that she was not in the least frightened. That someone with a beautiful voice should speak French in her car was absurd and impossible, but it wasn't alarming. In her timid way Mrs. Bowlby rather prided herself on her common sense, and as she shopped and called she considered this extraordinary occurrence from all the commonsense points of view that she could think of, but it remained a baffling and obstinate fact. Before her drive was over she found herself wishing simply to hear the voice again. It was ridiculous, but she did. And she had her wish. As the car turned into Legation Street an hour later she saw that it was too late to go to the polo ; the last chukka was over, and the players were leaving the ground, over which dust still hung in the low brilliant light, in cars and rickshaws. As she passed the gate the voice spoke again—almost in front of her, this time, as though the speaker were leaning forward to the window. *" Le voilà ! "* it said—and then, quite loudly, *" Jacques ! "* Mrs. Bowlby almost leaned out of the window herself, to look for whoever was being summoned—as she sat back, conscious of her folly, she heard again beside her, quite low, *" Il ne m'a pas vue."*

There was no mistake about it. It was broad daylight ; there she was in her car, bowling along Legation Street—past the Belgian Bank, past the German Legation ; rickshas skimming in front of her, Madame de Réan bowing to her. And just as clear and certain as all these things had been this woman's voice, calling to " *Jacques*," whoever he was—terrified lest he should fall at polo, hating the game for his sake. What a lovely voice it was ! Who was she, Mrs. Bowlby wondered, and what and who was Jacques ? " *Mon très-cher !* " she had called him—a delicious expression. It belonged to the day and the place—it was near to her own mood as she had sat at the corner of the Hatamen and noticed the spring, and hated the polo too for Jim's sake. She would have liked to call Jim " *mon très-cher*," only he would have been so surprised.

The thought of Bowlby brought her up with a round turn. What would he say to this affair ? Instantly, though she prolonged the discussion with herself for form's sake, she knew that she was not going to tell him. Not yet, anyhow. Bowlby had not been very satisfied with her choice of a car as it was— he said it was too big and too expensive to run. Besides, there was the question of her nerves. If he failed to hear the voice too she would be in a terribly difficult position. But there was more to it than that. She had a faint sense that she had been eavesdropping, however involuntarily. She had no right to give away even a voice which said " *mon très-cher* " in that tone.

This feeling grew upon her in the days that followed. The voice that haunted the Buick became of almost daily occurrence, furnishing a curious secret background to her social routine of calls and " At Homes." It spoke always in French, always to or about " Jacques "—a person, whoever he was, greatly loved. Sometimes it was clear to Mrs. Bowlby that she was hearing only half of a conversation between the two, as one does at the telephone. The man's voice she never heard, but, as at the telephone, she could often guess at what he said. Much of the speech was trivial enough ; arrangements for meetings at lunches, at the Polo ; for week-end parties at Pao-ma-chang in the temple of this person or that. This was more eerie than anything else to Mrs. Bowlby—the hearing of plans concerned with people she knew. " *Alors, dimanche prochain, chez les Milne.*" Meeting " *les Milne* " soon after, she would stare at them uneasily, as though by looking long enough she might find about them some trace of the presence which was more familiar to her than their own. Her voice was making ghosts of the living. But whether plans, or snatches of talk about people or ponies, there came always, sooner or later, the under-note of tenderness, now hesitant, now frank—the close concern, the monopolizing happiness of a woman in love.

It puzzled Mrs. Bowlby that the car should only register, as it were, the woman's voice. But then the whole affair bristled with puzzles. Why did Bowlby hear nothing? For he did not —she would have realized her worst fears if she *had* told him. She remembered always the first time that the voice spoke when he was with her. They were going to a *Thé Dansant* at the Peking Hotel, a farewell party for some Minister. As the car swung out of the Jade Canal Road, past the policemen who stand with fixed bayonets at the edge of the Glacis, the voice began suddenly, as it so often did, in French—" Then I leave thee now—thou wilt send back the car? " And as they lurched across the tramlines towards the huge European building and pulled up, it went on " But to-night, one will dance, *n'est-ce pas* ? "

" Goodness, what a crowd ! " said Bowlby. " This is going to be simply awful. Don't let's stay long. Will half an hour be enough, do you think ? "

Mrs. Bowlby stared at him without answering. Was it possible? She nearly gave herself away in the shock of astonishment. " What's the matter ? " said Bowlby. " What are you looking at ? "

Bowlby had not heard a word !

She noticed other things. There were certain places where the voice " came through," so to speak, more clearly and regularly than elsewhere. Intermittent fragments, sometimes unintelligible, occurred anywhere. But she came to know where to expect to hear most. Near the polo ground, for instance, which she hardly ever passed without hearing some expression of anxiety or pride. She often went to the polo, for Jim was a keen and brilliant player ; but it was a horror while he played, and this feeling was a sort of link, it seemed to her, between her and her unseen companion. More and more, too, she heard it near the Hatamen and the *hu-t'ungs* or alleys to the east of it. Mrs. Bowlby liked the East City. It lies rather in a backwater, between the crowded noisy thoroughfare of Hatamen Street, with its trams, dust, cars and camels, and the silent angle of the Tartar Wall, rising above the low one-story houses. A good many Europeans live there, and she was always glad when a call took her that way, through the narrow *hu-t'ungs* where the car lurched over heaps of rubbish or skidded in the deep dust, and rickshas pulled aside into gateways to let her pass. Many of these lanes end vaguely in big open spaces, where pigs root among the refuse and little boys wander about, singing long monotonous songs with a curious jerky rhythm in their high nasal voices. Sometimes, as she waited before a scarlet door, a flute-player out of sight would begin to play, and the thin sweet melody filled the sunny air between the blank grey walls. Flowering trees showed here and there above them ; coppersmiths plied their trade on the steps of carved marble gateways ; dogs and beggars sunned themselves under the white and scarlet walls of temple courtyards. Here, more than anywhere else, the voice spoke clearly, freely, continuously, the rounded French syllables falling on the air from nowhere, now high, light, and merry, with teasing words and inflection, now sinking into low murmurs of rapturous happiness. At such times Mrs. Bowlby sat wholly absorbed in listening, drawn by the lovely voice into a world not her own and held fascinated by the spell of this passionate adventure. Happy as she was with Bowlby, her life with him had never known anything like this. He had never wanted, and she had never dared to use the endearments lavished by the late owner of the Buick saloon on her Jacques.

She heard enough to follow the course of the affair pretty closely. They met when they could in public, but somewhere in the Chinese City there was clearly a meeting-place of their own—" *notre petit asile.*" And gradually this haven began to take shape in Mrs. Bowlby's mind. Joyous references were made to various features of it. To-morrow they would drink tea on the stone table under " our great white pine." There was the fish-pond shaped like a shamrock where one of the goldfish died—" *pourtant en Irelande cela porte bonheur, le trèfle, n'est-ce pas ?* " The parapet of this pond broke away and had to be repaired and " Jacques " made some sort of inscription in the damp mortar, for the voice thrilled softly one day as it murmured : " *Maintenant il se lit là pour toujours, ton amour !* " And all through that enchanted spring, first the lilac bushes perfumed the hours spent beneath the pine, and then the acacias that stood in a square round the shamrock pond. Still more that life and hers seemed to Mrs. Bowlby strangely mingled ; her own lilacs bloomed and scented the courtyard behind the grey Bank building, and one day as they drove to lunch in the British Legation she drew Jim's attention to the scent of the acacias, which drowned the whole compound in perfume. But Bowlby said, with a sort of shiver, that he hated the smell ;

and he swore at the chauffeur in French, which he spoke even better than his wife.

The desire grew on Mrs. Bowlby to know more of her pair, who and what they were and how their story ended. But it seemed wholly impossible to find out. Her reticences made her quite unequal to setting anyone on to question the people at the garage again. And then one day, accidentally, the clue was given to her. She had been calling at one of the houses in the French Legation; the two house servants, in blue and silver gowns, stood respectfully on the steps; her footman held open the door of the car for her. As she seated herself the voice said in a clear tone of command, " *Deux cent trente, Por Hua Shan Hut'ung !* " Acting on an impulse which surprised her, Mrs. Bowlby repeated the order—" *Deux cent trente, Por Hua Shan Hut'ung,*" she said. Shwang's colleague bowed and shut the door. But she caught sight, as she spoke, of the faces of the two servants on the steps. Was it imagination? Surely not. She would have sworn that a flicker of some emotion—surprise, and recollection—had appeared for a moment on their sealed and impassive countenances. In Peking the servants in Legation houses are commonly handed on from employer to employer, like the furniture, and the fact struck on her with sudden conviction—they had heard those words before !

Her heart rose with excitement as the car swung out of the compound into Legation Street. Where was it going? She had no idea where the Por Hua Shan Hut'ung was. Was she about to get a stage nearer to the solution of the mystery at last? At the Hatamen the Buick turned south along the Glacis. So far so good. They left the Hatamen, bumped into the Suchow Hut'ung, followed on down the Tung Tsung Pu Hut'ung, right into the heart of the East City. Her breath came fast. It must be right. Now they were skirting the edge of one of the rubbish-strewn open spaces, and the East Wall rose close ahead of them. They turned left, parallel with it; turned right again towards it; stopped. Shwang beckoned to a pancake-seller who was rolling out his wares in a doorway, and a colloquy in Chinese ensued. They went on slowly then, down a lane between high walls which ended at the Wall's very foot, and pulled up some hundred yards short of it before a high scarlet door, whose rows of golden knobs in fives beckoned the former dwelling of some Chinese of rank.

It was only when Liu came to open the door and held out

his cotton-gloved hand for her cards that Mrs. Bowlby realized
that she had no idea what she was going to do. She could not
call on a voice! She summoned Shwang, Liu's French was
not his strong point. " Ask," she said to Shwang, " who lives
here—the T'ai-t'ai's name." Shwang rang the bell. There
was a long pause. Shwang rang again. There came a sound of
shuffling feet inside ; creaking on its hinges the door opened,
and the head of an old Chinaman, thinly bearded and topped
with a little black cap, appeared in the crack. A conversation
followed, and then Shwang returned to the car.

" The house is empty," he said. " Ask him who lived there
last," said Mrs. Bowlby. Another and longer conversation
followed, but at last Shwang came to the window with the
information that a foreign T'ai-t'ai, " *Fa-kwa T'ai-t'ai* " (French
lady) he thought, had lived there, but she had gone away.
With that Mrs. Bowlby had to be content. It was something.
It might be much. The car had moved on towards the Wall,
seeking a place to turn, when an idea struck her. Telling
Shwang to wait, she got out, and glanced along the foot of the
Wall in both directions. Yes ! Some two hundred yards from
where she stood one of those huge ramps, used in former times
to ride or drive up on to the summit of the Wall, descended
into the dusty strip of waste land at its foot. She hurried
towards it, nervously, picking her way between the rough
fallen lumps of stone and heaps of rubbish ; she was afraid that
the servants would regard her action as strange, and that when
she reached the foot of the ramp she might not be able to get
up it. Since Boxer times the top of the Tartar Wall is forbidden
as a promenade, save for a short strip just above the Legation
Quarter, and the ramps are stoutly closed at the foot, theoreti-
cally. But in China theory and practice do not always
correspond, Mrs. Bowlby knew ; and as she hurried, she
hoped.

Her hope was justified. Though a solid wooden barrier
closed the foot of the ramp, a few feet higher up a little bolt-
hole, large enough to admit a goat or a small man, had been
picked away in the masonry of the parapet. Mrs. Bowlby
scrambled through and found herself on the cobbled slope of
the ramp ; panting a little, she walked up it on to the Wall.
The great flagged top, broad enough for two motor-lorries to
drive abreast, stretched away to left and right ; a thick under
growth of thorny bushes had sprung up between the flags, and

through them wound a little path, manifestly used by goats and goat-herds. Below her Peking lay spread out—a city turned by the trees which grow in every courtyard into the semblance of a green wood, out of which rose the immense golden roofs of the Forbidden City ; beyond it, far away, the faint mauve line of the Western Hills hung on the sky.

But Mrs. Bowlby had no eyes for the unparalleled view. Peeping cautiously through the battlements she located the Buick saloon, shining incongruously neat and modern in its squalid and deserted surroundings ; by it she took her bearings, and moved with a beating heart along the little path between the thorns. Hoopoes flew out in front of her, calling their sweet note, and perched again, raising and lowering their crests ; she never heeded them, nor her torn silk stockings. Now she was above the car ; yes, there was the lane up which they had come, and the wall beyond it was the wall of that house ! She could see the door-keeper, doll-like below her, still standing in his scarlet doorway, watching the car curiously. The garden wall stretched up close to the foot of the City Wall itself, so that, as she came abreast of it, the whole compound—the house, with its manifold courtyards, and the formal garden—lay spread out at her feet with the minute perfection of a child's toy farm on the floor.

Mrs. Bowlby stood looking down at it. A dream-like sense of unreality came over her, greater than any yet caused even by her impossible voice. A magnificent white pine, trunk and branches gleaming as if white-washed among its dark needles, rose out of the garden, and below it stood a round stone table among groups of lilacs. Just as the voice had described it ! Close by, separated from the pine garden by a wall pierced with a fan-shaped doorway, was another with a goldfish pond like a shamrock, and round it stood a square pleached alley of acacias. Flowers in great tubs bloomed everywhere. Here was the very setting of her lovers' secret idyll ; silent, sunny, sweet, it lay under the brooding protection of the Tartar Wall. Here she was indeed near to the heart of her mystery, Mrs. Bowlby felt, as she leaned on the stone parapet, looking down at the deserted garden. A strange fancy came to her that she would have liked to bring Jim here, and people it once again. But she and Jim, she reflected with a little sigh, were staid married people, with no need of a sceret haven hidden away in the East City. And with the thought of Jim the claims of everyday life reasserted themselves. She must go—and with a last glance at the garden she hastened back to the car.

During the next day or so Mrs. Bowlby brooded over her new discovery and all that had led to it. Everything—the place where the address had been given by the voice, the flicker of recognition on the faces of the servants at the house in the French Legation, the fact of the doorkeeper in the East City having mentioned a *Fa-kwa t'ai-t'ai* as his late employer, pointed to one thing—that the former owner of the Buick saloon had lived in the house where she had first called on that momentous afternoon. More than ever, now, the thing took hold of her—having penetrated the secret of the voice so far, she felt that she must follow it further yet. Timid or not, she must brace herself to ask some questions.

At a dinner a few nights later she found herself seated next to Mr. van Adam. Mr. van Adam was an elderly American, the *doyen* of Peking society, who had seen everything and known everyone since before Boxer days—a walking memory and a mine of social information. Mrs. Bowlby determined to apply to him. She displayed unwonted craft. She spoke of Legation compounds in general, and of the French compound in particular ; she praised the garden of the house where she had called. And then, " Who lived there before the Vernets came ? " she asked, and waited eagerly for the answer. Mr. van Adam eyed her a little curiously, she thought, but replied that it was a certain Count d'Ardennes. " Was he married ? " Mrs. Bowlby next enquired. Oh yes, he was married right enough—but the usual reminiscent flow of anecdote seemed to fail Mr. van Adam in this case. Struggling against a vague sense of difficulty, of a hitch somewhere, Mrs. Bowlby pushed on nevertheless to an enquiry as to what the Comtess d'Ardennes was like. " A siren ! " Mr. van Adam replied briefly—adding " lovely creature, though, as ever stepped."

He edged away rather from the subject, or so it seemed to Mrs. Bowlby, but she nerved herself to another question— " Had they a car ? " Mr. van Adam fairly stared, at that ; then he broke into a laugh. " Car ? Why, yes—she went everywhere in a yellow Buick—we used to call it ' the canary.' " The talk drifted off on to cars in general, and Mrs. Bowlby let it drift ; she was revolving in her mind the form of her last question. Her curiosity must look odd, she reflected nervously ; it was all more difficult, somehow, than she had expected. Her craft was failing her—she could not think of a good excuse for further questions that would not run the risk of betraying her secret. There must have been a scandal—there *would* have been, of course ; but Mrs. Bowlby was not of the order of women who in Peking ask coolly at the dinner-table : " And what was *her* scandal ? " At dessert, in desperation, she put it hurriedly, badly—" When did the d'Ardennes leave ? "

Mr. van Adam paused before he answered : " Oh, going on for a year ago, now. She was ill, they said—looked it, anyway —and went back to France. He was transferred to Bangkok soon after, but I don't know if she's gone out to him again. The East didn't suit her." " Oh, poor thing ! " murmured Mrs. Bowlby, softly and sincerely, her heart full of pity for the woman with the lovely voice and the lovely name, whose failing health had severed her from her Jacques. Not even love such as hers could control this wretched feeble body, reflected Mrs. Bowlby, whom few places suited. The ladies rose, and too absorbed in her reflections to pay any further attention to Mr. van Adam, she rose and went with them.

At this stage Mrs. Bowlby went to Pei-t'ai-ho for the summer. Peking, with a temperature of over 100 degrees in the shade, is no place for delicate women in July and August. Cars are not allowed on the sandy roads of the pleasant straggling seaside resort, and missionaries and diplomatists alike are obliged to fall back on rickshas and donkeys as a means of locomotion. So the Buick saloon was left in Peking with Jim, who came down for long week-ends as often as he could. Thus separated from her car, and in changed surroundings, Mrs. Bowlby endeavoured to take stock of the whole affair dispassionately. Get away from it she could not. Bathing, idling on the hot sunny beach, walking through the green paths bordered with maize and kaoliang, sitting out in the blessedly cool dark after dinner, she found herself as much absorbed as ever in this personality whose secret life she so strangely shared. Curiously enough, she felt no wish to ask any more questions of anyone. With her knowledge of Madame d'Ardennes' name the sense of eavesdropping had returned in full force. One thing struck her as a little odd : that if there *had* been a scandal she should not have heard of it —in Peking, where scandals were innumerable, and treated with startling openness and frank disregard. Perhaps she had been mistaken, though, in Mr. van Adam's attitude, and there had not been one. Or—the illumination came to her belated and suddenly—hadn't Mr. van Adam's son in the Customs, who went home last year, been called Jack? He had! and Mrs. Bowlby shuddered at the thought of her clumsiness. She could not have chosen a worse person for her enquiries.

Another thing, at Pei-t'ai-ho, she realized with a certain astonishment—that she had not been perceptibly shocked by this intrigue. Mrs. Bowlby had always believed herself to hold thoroughly conventional British views on marriage ; the late owner of the Buick saloon clearly had not, yet Mrs. Bowlby had never thought of censuring her. She had even been a little resentful of Mr. van Adam's calling her a " siren." Sirens were cold-hearted creatures, who lured men frivolously to their doom ; her voice was not the voice of a siren. Mrs. Bowlby was all on the side of her voice. Didn't such love justify itself, argued Mrs. Bowlby, awake at last to her own moral failure to condemn another, or very nearly? Perhaps, she caught herself thinking, if people knew as much about all love-affairs as she knew about this one, they would be less censorious.

Mrs. Bowlby stayed late at Pei-t'ai-ho, well on into September, till the breezes blew chilly off the sea, the green paths had faded to a dusty yellow, and the maize and kaoliang were being cut. When she returned to Peking she was at once very busy—calling begins all over again after the seaside holiday, and she spent hours in the Buick saloon leaving cards. The voice was with her again, as before. But something had overshadowed the blissful happiness of the spring days ; there was an undertone of distress, of foreboding, often, in the conversations. What exactly caused it she could not make out. But it increased, and one day half-way through October, driving in the East City, the voice dropped away into a burst of passionate sobbing. This distressed Mrs. Bowlby extraordinarily. It was a strange and terrible thing to sit in the car with those low, heart-broken sounds at her side. She almost put out her arms to take and comfort the unhappy creature— but there was only empty air, and the empty seat, with her bag, her book, and her little calling list. Obeying one of those sudden impulses which the voice alone seemed to call out in her, she abandoned her calls and told Shwang to drive to the Por Hua Shan Hut'ung. As they neared it the sobs beside her ceased, and murmured apologies for being *un peu énervée* followed.

When she reached the house Mrs. Bowlby got out, and again climbed the ramp on to the Tartar Wall. The thorns and bushes between the battlements were brown and sere, and no hoopoes flew and fluted among them. She reached the spot where she could look down into the garden. The lilacs were bare now, as her own were ; the tubs of flowers were gone, and heaps of leaves had drifted round the feet of the acacias—only the white pine stood up, stately and untouched by the general decay. A deep melancholy took hold of Mrs. Bowlby ; already shaken by the sobs in the car, the desolation of this deserted autumn garden weighed with an intense oppression on her spirit. She turned away, slowly, and slowly descended to the Buick. The sense of impending misfortune had seized on her too ; something, she vaguely felt, had come to an end in that garden.

As she was about to get into the car another impulse moved her. She felt an overmastering desire to enter that garden and see its features from close at hand. The oppression still hung over her, and she felt that a visit to the garden might in some way resolve it. She looked in her purse and found a five-dollar note. Handing it to the startled Shwang—" Give that," said Mrs. Bowlby, " to the *k'ai-men-ti*, and tell him I wish to walk in the garden of that house." Shwang bowed ; rang the bell ; conversed ; Mrs. Bowlby waited, trembling with impatience, till the clinching argument of the note was at last produced, and the old man whom she had seen before beckoned to her to enter.

She followed him through several courtyards. It was a rambling Chinese house, little modernized ; the blind paper lattices of the windows looked blankly on to the miniature lakes and rocky landscapes in the open courts. Finally they passed through a round doorway into the garden below the Tartar Wall, and bowing, the old custodian stood aside to let her walk alone.

Before her rose the white pine, and she strolled towards it, and sitting down on a marble bench beside the round stone table, gazed about her. Beautiful even in its decay, melancholy, serene, the garden lay under the battlements which cut the pale autumn sky behind her. And here the owner of the voice had sat, hidden and secure, her lover beside her ! A sudden burst of tears surprised Mrs. Bowlby. Cruel Life, she thought, which parts dear lovers. Had *she* too sat here alone ? A sharp unexpected sense of her own solitude drove Mrs. Bowlby up from her seat. This visit was a mistake ; her oppression was not lightened ; to have sat in this place seemed somehow to have involved herself in the disaster and misery of that parted pair. She wandered on, through the fan-shaped doorway, and came to a halt beside the goldfish pond. Staring at it through her tears, she noticed the repair to the coping of which the voice had spoken, where " Jacques " had made an inscription in the damp mortar. She moved round to the place where it still showed white against the grey surface, murmuring, " *Maintenant il se lit là pour toujours, ton amour !* "—the phrase of the voice had stayed rooted in her mind. Stooping down, she read the inscription, scratched out neatly and carefully with a penknife in the fine plaster :

> " Douce sépulture, mon cœur dans ton cœur,
> Doux paradis, mon âme dans ton âme."

And below two sets of initials :

A. de A.

de

J. St. G. B. B.

The verse touched Mrs. Bowlby to fresh tears, and it was actually a moment or two before she focussed her attention on the initials. When she did, she started back as though a serpent had stung her, and shut her eyes, and stood still. Then with a curious blind movement she opened her bag and took out one of her own cards, and laid it on the coping beside the inscription, as if to compare them. *Mrs. J. St. G. B. Bowlby*— the fine black letters stared up at her, uncompromising and clear, from the white oblong, beside the capitals cut in the plaster. There could be no mistake. Her mystery was solved at last, but it seemed as if she could not take it in. " Jim ? " murmured Mrs. Bowlby to herself, as if puzzled—and then " Jacques ? " Slowly, while she stood there, all the connections and verifications unrolled themselves, backwards in her mind, with devastating certainty and force. Her sentiment, her intuition on the wall had been terribly right—something *had* come to an end in that garden that day. Standing by the shamrock pond, with the first waves of an engulfing desolation sweeping over her, hardly conscious of her words, she whispered : *Pourtant cela porte bonheur, le trèfle, n'est-ce pas ? "*

And with that second quotation from the voice she seemed at last to wake from the sort of stupor in which she had stood. Intolerable! She must hear no more. Passing back, almost running, into the pine garden, she beckoned to the old *k'ai-men-ti* to take her out. He led her again, bowing, through the courtyards to the great gateway. Through the open red and gold doors she saw the Buick saloon, dark and shiny, standing as she had so often, and with what pleasure, seen it stand before how many doors? She stopped and looked round her almost wildly—behind her the garden, before her the Buick! Liu caught sight of her, and flew to hold open the door. But Mrs. Bowlby did not get in. She made Shwang call a ricksha, and when it came ordered him to direct the coolie to take her to the Bank house. Shwang, exercising the respectful supervision which Chinese servants are wont to bestow on their employers, reminded her that she was to go to the polo to pick up the *lao-yé*, Bowlby. Before his astonished eyes his mistress shuddered visibly from head to foot. "The Bank! The Bank!" she repeated, with a sort of desperate impatience.

Standing before his scarlet door, lighting his little black and silver pipe, the old *k'ai-men-ti* watched them go. First the ricksha, with a small drooping grey figure in it, lurched down the dusty *hu-t'ung*, and after it, empty, bumped the Buick saloon.

W. S. MORRISON, M.P.

THE HORNS OF THE BULL

I

"THEY call that rocky island '*Eilean an Tarbh*,' the Isle of the Bull. Why?—to be sure, you can see the horns of the Bull himself if we tack a little to the west." So said Donald, the ancient, the sea-wary, in a little boat, far out on the western coast of the Hebrides. The evening's fishing, for which I had chartered his boat, had not yet begun. The long Hebridean summer light clung tenaciously to the sky as if unwilling to leave so fair a prospect. "We have plenty of time before it is dark enough for fishing and, anyhow, there is a good bank there."

The dun lug-sail swung round. The little boat, at home in the great waters, slid with many whispers towards the sun's lair, and I could see at the southern extremity of the island two mighty pinnacles of shining brown rock, slanting in menacing fashion out to sea. It was easy to see how the little island had come by its name. "Could we land there?" I asked. Donald's look was significant. "We could—but, with your leave, we will not," he answered. Questions were clearly contra-indicated, as the doctors say. A silence fell, during which Donald was busy with the tackle.

"It is a good name for the island," said I. "The horns of it are just like a bull's horns."

"They are that," said Donald, "just like—as you say yourself—and maybe there has been something on them like what might be on the horns of a bull, and him loose in a field among the sheep."

"Is there a story about the island, then?" said I. "The spinner will be the best bait, I think, Donald."

"The spinner will be the best bait, as you said yourself, and this is the story about *Eilean an Tarbh* yonder; but I think we'll move a little further west. The bank is better there, and besides, the silly old wives yonder say the Isle's not canny. Not that I believe them, but . . . well, the fish

will be more plentiful a bittie more out to sea. You have the
Gaelic and I will tell you the story in the Old Tongue. It
will sound more natural-like, and I have a stronger grip on
the Gaelic for the story-telling.

.   .   .   .

In the very old days, when the men of Lochlainn—the
sea-rovers—were here, there lived a powerful old man on
Eilean an Uaine—the Isle of the Lamb. Where is that island?
. . . Not far from here. The old man had many things to
content his soul. He had the two islands of the Bull and the
Lamb, and he had two sons—fine, upstanding young men
both of them as I have heard, though mighty different from
one another in body and mind. The elder was as dark as the
raven and the younger was as fair as the sun's face. The old
man was a man of power. He had sailed far in his youth,
and he kept one of the grey birds that talk as men do. He was
more than that though; for they say he had the big knowledge.
The winds he would speak to as you would speak to me, and
they would be obedient and civil to him. He had a strange
shell that he had brought from some foreign place and he
would sit with it at his ear, listening. Now he would laugh
at what the shell told him, again, they say, he would be at the
curses, so that the birds on the rocks fell lifeless into the sea
with the fear of hearing him.

His two sons were from different mothers, women whom
he had loved, but I think he loved the first one the best, for
she was a dark woman of the old people, and they say it was
she who gave him his knowledge. However it was about
that, he was good to both his sons, and it was the sorrow of
his life that, instead of the love of brothers, it was the hatred
of fire for water that they felt for each other. How that hatred
arose I could not tell you; but hatred is like love—a thing
past finding out. When I was in the Naval Reserve in the
Black Prince, there was a man from the mainland, and though
no words of anger passed between us—but I was telling you
about the two sons of the powerful old man. Well, what
Iain did was hateful to Orm, and Orm's words and deeds
were like the vinegar in the mouth of Iain. It was the fear
of the old man's curses that kept the one from the throat of
the other, and he was that full of wisdom, that old man, that
there was no escaping the watch he put on them. They say

that once the two brothers took each one his sword in his
hand and set out in a boat to an island where they had it in
mind to fight till the one slew the other. But a tempest arose
and a darkness fell, and the voice of thunder came on them,
and they sailed till they knew not where they were on the
breast of the wide sea. When at the last they came in sight of
land, the land was *Eilean an Uaine*, from which they had set
out, and the one that met their boat on the shore was the old
man, their father, his beard streaming and his eyes on fire.
He was an old man of power, that one.

Well, the years passed by with the three of them as they do
with ourselves, my sorrow ! The two lads grew to be men.
Orm, the younger, was the more stirring and active of the
two. He was a good one at the fishing and in a boat, and he
was a warrior of might. They say he was a good farmer too,
and it was from copying him that the people round about
here learned their skill in breeding cattle and sheep and horses.
Iain was the dark brooder, the silent ponderer. What he
lacked of his brother's strength he made up with his deeper
thought and his darker devices. I think they were then both
false and selfish young men, as those are apt to be who have
more knowledge than their neighbours. Certain it is that they
were neither of them beloved of the people. They were
feared for their craft and force. I am thinking also that Orm
was the falser of the two, for, while Iain was dark and
dangerous to the eye, Orm was all smiles and heartiness, a
cajoler of men and of women. He would be like the man
from the mainland that was on the *Black Prince* with me.
You felt angry with yourself for having doubts of him, but
the doubts were there.

Well, well, the time came when, for all his power, Death
came walking along the seashore to fetch the old man. I am
thinking that the old man would make a brave battle of it,
but Death would have the victory in his own time. It was,
they say, a calm day like this about Beltane when the old man
called his sons to him, where they stood one on each side of
the bed. Iain with the black brows of him in a straight line,
and Orm with the frank, open face and the hard, blue eyes
which made the whole face hard, despite the smile on it.

"Sons," says the old man, "I am away with it this day,
and glad I am to be done with this world of feebleness and
decay. But though I am done with you, you are not done

with me. You must attend to my burial and my curse of the seven trolls will be on you if you fail me in this matter. The manner of my burial is this. I will go as my fathers went, with the east wind. You will put me afloat in my boat and send me off with the turn of the full tide. By my hand you will put my sword with the runes on it, and by my ear you will place the Shell of Power. You will do this, sons?" The sons said "Ay," and the old man said, "My curse is on the one that fails me. Now there is another matter. The enmity which your mothers bore to one another is in the marrow of your bones. While I lived, I kept your hatred in bounds, and no doubt you dream that when I am away the chains which bound you will bind you no longer. Sons, my power will command you to peace even when I am dead. I trust the words of neither of you, and I have made a spell and an arrangement about you. The terms of the spell are these. You, Iain, will have *Eilean an Tarbh* for your own. You are a brooder and a ponderer, and that isle is a faithful nourisher of true dreams. You, Orm, will have *Eilean an Uaine*. It is a green and fertile place and you will grow rich here. But, sons, if either of you leaves his island for the blood of the other, my curse will strike him who crosses the sea for his brother's life, and *his brother will triumph over him*. It is so written and arranged by me, and I have strong bonds on the Dark Ones to make sure that it will so happen. It is a spell on you that assuredly will not fail." As the old man made an end of speaking he smiled grimly to himself, for he could read the hearts of his sons and saw within them a seething of baffled anger and hatred. The triumph of his brother was the greatest word of evil that could blow in the ear of each.

"Now, sons, I have done with commands and I see the solid world floating and drifting like seaweed in the sea, and I see deep down through the dark earth as you would see through the calm sea. Nothing is fixed, but even the rocks are in perpetual drift like smoke. My time is come and I am glad." So he died, and they say his sons did as he had commanded them. They placed him lying on the deck, his sword at his hand and the shell at his ear. As the tide turned from the full, a firm breeze from the east filled the vessel's sails and out to see she went, goose-winged, into the red eye of the setting sun.

Iain would not put by the night on *Eilean an Uaine*, but set sail away out to *Eilean an Tarbh*, where he sailed in between the horns of the Bull yonder and anchored there. Orm watched his brother go without a word, and, when he was out of sight, he pushed off in a small boat himself. They were thus all three on the breast of the old sea. The old man with no thought in his head at all; one young man full of hatred of his brother, fleeing from his sight, and the other young man with more than hatred in his heart—with cunning and triumph over the living and the dead—singing a dull song of two notes in his heart. Some say that he thought of this ploy in his own heart, others that an old, wrinkled body of a hen-wife he had, put it into his mind. However that may be, he was from of old covetous of the Shell of Power, and he had craftily devised a means of taking it. There was an anchor set in the sea-bottom some distance from the shore, and to this there was tied a thin piece of fishing-line. When they were setting the old man straight for his last voyage, Orm had put the hook that was at the end of the line into a hole in the shell. When the ship bearing the old man had gone about half a mile from shore, the line tautened, and dragged the shell overboard, where it sank in the cool, green waters with a sigh, as if at the wickedness of a son that could thus rob his dead father. It was little Orm cared for that as he dragged about till he found the line, and there was the shell on the end of it right enough.

II

Now there was a man on *Eilean an Uaine* who was a shepherd. He was but a lad of sixteen years or so when the powerful old man died. Angus Og—Young Angus—he was called even till he became an old, old man. It is a funny thing, the way a name sticks to a man, but I am thinking that if a man keeps the name of Angus Og till the day of his death it is because he is one of those merry old men who keep the gift of mirth till the time of their passing. At the time I am telling you of, Angus Og was a young man of twenty-five or thereabouts, and he was a shepherd to Orm, who had been lord of *Eilean an Uaine* for the last ten years, and a great lord he was, by all accounts. The world had prospered with Orm since his father died. His flocks and his herds had increased and, moreover, he had carried war deep into the heart of the Isles, and he was the overlord of all within a day and a night's sail

2M*

of his swift galley. Bold and cunning though he had always been, men said there was a more than mortal fierceness and craft in his raids. They would speak of the shell, and how Orm would sit long with it at his ear. Less often than his father would he smile at its whispering. More often it was the curses with him, and if his father's curses made the birds drop lifeless in terror, they say that those of Orm smote into the great deep, so that the fishes would be seen floating belly upwards in the wash of the tides.

You can be thinking to yourself that *Eilean an Uaine* was no pleasant isle in those days for men and women to dwell in. Terror was on them all, and gloom. All, that is, except Angus Og, who had in the cheerful innocence of his heart a well of joy that no oppression could dry up, and curses affected him no more than the sound of rain on the thatch of a house. I am thinking that this is how it is with cursing. Evil speaks to evil, and if a man has no evil in his heart there is nothing for the curse to grip on.

There was one island where the rule of Orm did not run, and that was *Eilean an Tarbh*, where his brother Iain still dwelt, though in poor state compared with the glory and might of Orm. They say that the sadness had fallen on Iain, so that the world meant but little to him. With some men there comes a time when they suddenly see behind the smooth face of the world, and what they see there wipes all laughter from their lips and all striving from their hearts. So it was with Iain. He had his father's eyes, and the secret places of the earth were open to him. He lived quite alone on his little isle. He would be at the reading and the thinking, and that was how it was with him.

People would come to Iain now and then for the wisdom that was his. He would give medicines and words which would cure man and beast, and he would tell where lost men and things were to be found. But so sad and forbidding was his face that it was only in the direst need that a man would push off in his little boat and sail to *Eilean an Tarbh*. There was something stifling about the presence of Iain, so that men were glad to get away with their remedies and slip back in fear lest Orm should hear of their visit to his brother. For evil were Orm's thoughts, and heavy was his hand to such people. They say that he would allow no food to go to his brother, but it was little the poor man ate at the best ; and what he needed more than the sea and the island could give him, the people who came for his wisdom would leave on the rocks for him. There on *Eilean an Tarbh* lived Iain, the great world of loves and wars no more to him than the mist which streams at dawn along the surface of the sea.

But now, at the time I am speaking of, it fell to Angus Og also to have his mirth troubled by Orm. Angus Og had a young sister. Brigid was her name, and she was as fair as is the moonlight on a calm sea. In peace they lived together until the eye of Orm fell on her, and thereafter it was sorrow and fear for them both. The lot of a woman in Orm's long house was an evil one. What with carousing and violence, the cursing and the blood, there was no peace or security for anyone. Then there was the evil tongue of the old hen-wife and the fear of the shell, and all the witchery and devilment of a bad man's house. The young people clung together, and with tears waited the time when the creatures of Orm would seize her and carry her off to their master. But Angus Og thought to himself like a wise man, and he said to Brigid : " It is the part of a wise man to wait for good ; but it is the part of a fool to wait for evil." So saying, he prepared a boat and, being in great extremity, he said, " We will go to *Eilean an Tarbh* and see Iain. It is the one place where Orm may not come."

Sad at heart was Brigid to leave their little house. She sorrowed in particular over a lamb which she had nursed since its mother died. She would have taken the lamb with her, and glad the wee thing would have been to go, I am sure, but Angus said, " We will take nothing of his with us at all." Being a good, brave lassie, as well as beautiful to look on, Brigid dried her tears, baked them a bannock, and together they entrusted themselves in the boat to the old sea, and to Him whose praise it is daily occupied in singing, without pause. It was well that they did so, for that very night certain rough men, the thralls of Orm, broke down the door of the little house ; but all they found there was the little lamb, which ran out into the night, crying piteously.

You may think it was with fear that Brigid and Angus Og saw the horns of *Eilean an Tarbh* getting nearer to them out of the water, and I have no doubt that it was so, but the greater fear behind them made the bare rocks look like a garden of safety to them. As they drew nearer they saw Iain standing on the shore looking at them. " Poor leaves, dropping from the tree of life, what gust blows you here ? " he said, looking at them and beyond them. Angus Og said never a word, but lifted Brigid from the boat and together they ran past Iain to where they saw his little house. Iain followed them, and as he reached the door he was in time to see Angus Og bend down and touch with his hand the little fire of peats. " Sanctuary ! " he cried, " O master of this house. The avenger is behind us." It was with gloomy pity that Iain looked at them. " The ways of men are but little to me," he said, " but you have touched my fire." He looked at the girl and said, " This is some evil of my brother's." He looked at her again, and " Sanctuary you shall have," he said.

You may be sure that the young people were not long in telling their sorrows, and it was with a gloomy brow that Iain heard of the wickedness of *Eilean an Uaine*. No word escaped him, however, and he showed them where they might sleep and left them, going up to a blow-hole in the rocks as was his wont. This blow-hole ran down into a cave which came in under the island from the sea, and you could hear the sound of the sea thundering far below you on stormy days, and whispering and laughing to itself in fine weather. Here it was Iain's custom to go and listen with his ear to the rocks, and they say that the sea would tell him the news of the Isles and speak to him of things which are no concern of us mortal creatures.

It was not long after this that the men who came to *Eilean an Tarbh* saw a change in Iain and in his surroundings. The house was neater and warmer and less uncanny-looking. This was the work of Brigid. The fields were better tilled and the sheep and cattle were more numerous and fatter. This was the work of Angus Og. Iain himself seemed a changed man. Better clad and with more flesh on him, he would listen with more of a kindly interest to their tales of sick bairns and lost sweethearts, and he would give his powerful wisdom without the bitter word that had formerly made many a man sorry to have asked his help. In the course of Nature, it was not long after this that Iain took Brigid to be his wife, and with that the world came back to his eyes and the thoughts of men to his heart. So it was that the visits of men to *Eilean an Tarbh* became more frequent, and men spoke to one another on the wide seashore, or when they were alone in boats out at sea, of the hope that one day Iain might take the place of Orm and the Isles might have an end of thraldom.

It was safer, too, to visit Iain ; for shortly after the flight of Brigid and Angus Og, news came to Orm where they were, and thereafter he shut himself up with the shell and the old hen-wife, and it was the spells and the wizardry that they would be at, so that the clouds would gather darkly over *Eilean an Uaine,* and the lightning and thunder would break over it, though the sky in other parts was clear. Once or twice, too, men felt the island shake to its foundations as if it quaked at the devil's work that was being done on it. So thick with evil things did the air of *Eilean an Uaine* become that the people left it, all except a few wicked men who had nowhere else where they could go without a dirk in them for the feud of blood. Withdrawn to the one purpose, Orm heeded not their going. Innocence and beauty had fled from *Eilean an Uaine* and they were now on *Eilean an Tarbh* with Iain.

Innocence and beauty—I am thinking they are powerful words, these, and that they would have the victory over all the words in the deep.

III

But winter nights came and with them the closed houses and the empty, raging sea, where no boat would venture. The long nights passed one after another, and men waited for the sun's strength to return and cure the world's misery. Far off seemed the time of release, but its word had been whispered, men knew not when nor by whom. There was a movement in men's minds that had no shape. The men of the Isles felt as men feel who are foraying in one of the deep glens of the mainland, and know that soon the enemy will break down upon them and there will be dirk and sword and a decision of the matter, the one way or the other.

It was one dark night of storm that Iain was sitting with his wife Brigid in his little house. Heavy a little, and anxious had he been of late. His blow-hole had told him of dreadful preparations, forcing trolls and demons to labour in the roots of the earth. He had, this night, set Angus Og on watching from the cliffs, and the dark gaze of that one was turned to where *Eilean an Uaine* lay with its burden of terror and punishment. *Na Fir Chlish,* the Fighting Men—what they call in

English the " Northern Lights "—danced and glimmered and trod across the sky like champions in mortal combat. Bright they were that night, brighter than we have seen them, for the light of their flashing blades and shimmering spears showed Angus something at which his heart sank to the bottom of fear and there rested as if at home. Back he ran to the little house, and in he broke with " Master, *Eilean an Uaine* is adrift and bears down upon us ! "

It was up and out with Iain, sword in hand, with never a word, and Angus and Brigid after him, until they came to the hillock between the horns of the Bull yonder. The sky was on fire that night, and there stood Iain singing to himself in a high voice. It was a song about himself and Orm, telling of their boyhood and youth together, of the hate that was between them and of the old man, their father. The brother and sister, crouched under the crest of the hillock, could see the dim bulk of *Eilean an Uaine* closer than was canny and coming nearer and nearer. The air was full of voices and, now that they could see plain, there was Orm on a spur of his island with the shell in one hand and in the other—the drawn sword. The islands came close together, and " I have thee in spite of our father's spells ! " shouts Orm across the lessening waters.

" Fool ! " shouts Iain, " see who watches from his boat yonder ! " and there, when he turned, Orm could see, in a greenish glow of troubled sea, the burial boat of his father, and the corpse erect on its feet with its hands upraised with each starting grey hair.

" Now ! " says Iain, " help me the spirit of this Isle which I have not troubled ! " " Brave Isle of the Bull," said Brigid, " show us thy strength ! "

There was lightning and the voice of thunder between the worlds. There was a hot wind, and a powerful, with a smell of burning seaweed in it as if the rocks were melting. Twice and three times did the Isle of the Lamb strike the Isle of the Bull, but each time the valiant Bull shook his head clear. Ever nearer and nearer came the dread boat with the dead man in it. Sword in hand the brothers stood, burning to get at each other when the Isles should be joined, but shock after shock saw the Lamb recoil—and the dead man in his boat draw nearer.

Orm beat upon the shell with the flat of his sword so that

it gave out a whining, clangorous note like a creature in rage and pain. Then says he, " Thou hast come for thy shell, old one !—Have it then ! " and he flung the shell from him towards the glimmering boat.

There was a sound of wings and a piping of shrill voices. The Lamb rushed on the Bull and those on that Isle felt its recoil as the haunches tightened. In one roar and flash the isles united, but it was with the horns of the Bull in the flank of the Lamb. There was a heave which made the sky stoop to them, a roar of triumph from the old sea, and then darkness and no sound at all but the idle voice of the wind and the senseless chatter of the waves on the beach. . . . Ay, ay ! . . . It was all a long time ago.

And that is why, though we speak of *Eilean an Uaine*, we mean a bank under the sea where we are fishing just now. In the daytime you can see the dark bulk of it through the green sea. The seaweed clustering round it makes it show up dark against the white bottom. It was all a long time ago. Iain ? . . . Oh, he became a great and good Lord of the Isles. I am descended from him myself . . . but it was all long, long ago."

PHILIP MACDONALD

OUR FEATHERED FRIENDS

THE hot, hard August sunshine poured its pale and
blazing gold over the countryside. At the crest of the
hill, which overlooked a county and a half, the tiny motor-
car drawn up to the side of the dusty road which wound up
the hill like a white riband looked not so much mechanical
as insectile. It looked like a Brobdingnagian bee which,
wings folded, has settled for a moment's sleepy basking
in the fierce sunshine.

Beside the car, seeming almost ludicrously out of proportion with it, stood a man and a woman. The sum of their
ages could not have exceeded forty-five. The dress of the
girl, which was silken and slight, would not, at all events
upon her charming body, have done aught save grace a car
as large and costly as this one was minute and cheap. But
the clothes of the boy, despite his youth and erect comeliness,
were somehow eloquent of Norwood, a careful and not
unintelligent clerkliness pursued in the City of London, and
a pseudo-charitable arrangement whereby the bee-like motor-
car should be purchased, for many pounds more than its
actual worth, in small but almost eternal slices.

The girl was hatless, and her clipped golden poll glittered
in the sun-rays. She looked, and was, cool, despite the great
heat of the afternoon. The boy, in his tweed jacket, thick
flannel trousers, and over-tight collar, at whose front blazed
a tie which hoped to look like that of some famous school or
college, was hot, and very hot. He pulled his hat from his
dark head and mopped at his brow with a vivid handkerchief.

" Coo ! " he said. " Hot enough for you, Vi ? "

She wriggled slim, half-covered shoulders. " It's a treat ! "
she said. She gazed about her with wide, blue eyes ; she
looked down and round at the county-and-a-half. " Where's
this, Jack ? "

The boy continued to puff and mop. He said :

" Blessed if *I* know ! . . . I lost me bearings after that
big village place—what was it ? . . . . "

"Greyne, or some such," said the girl absently. Her gaze was now directed down the hillside to her right, where the emerald roof of a dense wood shone through the sun's gold. There was no breath of wind, even right up upon this hill, and the green of the leaves showed smooth and unbroken.

The boy put on his hat again. "Better be getting on, I s'pose. You've had that leg-stretch you were wanting."

"Ooh! Not _yet_, Jack. Don't let's yet!" She put the fingers of her left hand upon his sleeve. On the third of these fingers there sparkled a ring of doubtful brilliance. "Don't let's go on yet, Jack!" she said. She looked up into his face, her lips pouted in a way which was not the least of reasons for the flashing ring.

He slid an arm about the slim shoulders; he bent his head and kissed thoroughly the red mouth. "Just's _you_ like, Vi. . . . But what you want to do?" He looked about him with curling lip. "Sit around up here on this dusty grass and frizzle?"

"Silly!" she said, pulling herself away from him. She pointed down to the green roof. "I want to go down there. . . . Into that wood. Jest to see what its like. Haven't been in a reel wood since the summer holidays before last, when Effie an' me went to Hastings. . . . Cummon! Bet it's lovely and cool down there. . . ."

This last sentence floated up to him, for already she was off the narrow road and beginning a slipping descent of the short rough grass of the hillside's first twenty feet.

He went sliding and stumbling after her. But he could not catch up with the light, fragile little figure in its absurdly enchanting wisp of blue silk. The soles of his thick shoes were of leather, and, growing polished by the brushing of the close, arid grass, were treacherous. Forty feet down, on the suddenly jutting and only gently sloping plateau where the wood began, he did come up with her: he ended a stumbling, sliding rush with an imperfect and involuntary somersault which landed him asprawl at her feet.

He sat up, shouting with laughter. With a shock of surprise greater than any of his short life, he felt a little foot kick sharply—nearly savagely—at his arm, and heard a tensely whispered "ssh!"

He scrambled to his feet, to see that she was standing

facing the trees, her shining golden head thrust forward, her whole body tense as that of a sprinter waiting for the pistol's crack. As, wonderingly, he shuffled to take his stand at her shoulder, she said :

" *Listen !* . . . Birds ! . . . . Jever hear the like ? . . ." Her tone was a hushed yet clear whisper—like none he had ever heard her use before.

He said nothing. He stood scowling sulkily down at the grass beneath his feet and rubbing at the spot where her shoe had met his arm.

It seemed to him an hour before she turned. But turn at last she did. He still had his hand at the kicked arm, for all the world as if it really were causing him pain. From beneath his brows he watched her, covertly. He saw the odd rapt look leave the small face once more its pertly, pretty self ; saw the blue eyes suddenly widen with memory of what she had done. ; . .

And then soft warm arms came about his neck and by their pressure pulled down his head so that, close pressed against him and standing upon tiptoe, she might smother his face with the kisses of contrition.

He said, in answer to the pleas for forgiveness with which the caresses were interspersed :

" Never known you do a thing like that before, Vi ! "

" No," she said. " And you never won't again ! Reely, Jack darling ! . . . It . . . it . . ."—a cloud came over the blue eyes—" it . . . I don't rightly know what came over me. . . . I was listening to the birds. . . . I never heard the like . . . and . . . and I never heard you till you laughed . . . and I dunno *what* it was, but it seemed 's if I jest *had* to go on hearing what the birds were . . . 's if it was . . . was *wrong* to listen to anything else. . . . Oh, *I* dunno ! "

The small face was troubled and the eyes desperate with the realization of explanation's impossibility. But the mouth pouted. The boy kissed it. He laughed and said :

" Funny kid, you ! " He drew her arm through the crook of his and began to walk towards the first ranks of the trees. He put up his free hand and felt tenderly at the back of his neck. He said :

" Shan't be sorry for some shade. Neck's gettin' all sore." They walked on, finding that the trees were strangely further away than they had seemed. They did not speak, but every now and then the slim, naked arm would squeeze the thick, clothed arm and have its pressure returned.

They had only some ten paces to go to reach the fringe of the wood when the girl halted. He turned his head to look down at her and found that once more she was tense in every muscle and thrusting the golden head forward as if the better to hear. He frowned; then smiled; then again bent his brows. He sensed that there was somewhere an oddness which he knew he would never understand—a feeling abhorrent to him, as, indeed, to most men. He found that he, too, was straining to listen.

He supposed it must be birds that he was listening for. And quite suddenly he laughed. For he had realized that he was listening for something which had been for the last few moments so incessantly in his ears that he had forgotten he was hearing it. He explained this to the girl. She seemed to listen to him with only half an ear, and for a moment he came near to losing his temper. But only for a moment. He was a good-natured boy, with sensitive instincts serving him well in place of realized tact.

He felt a little tugging at his arm and fell into step with her as she began to go forward again. He went on with his theme, ignoring her patently half-hearted attention.

"Like at a dance," he said. "You know, Vi—you never hear the noise of the people's feet on the floor unless you happen to listen for it, an' when you do listen for it an' hear that sort of *shishing*—then you know you've been hearing it all the time, see? That's what we were doing about the birds. . . . " He became suddenly conscious that, in order to make himself clearly heard above the chattering, twittering flood of bird-song, he was speaking in a tone at least twice as loud as the normal. He said:

"Coo! . . . You're right, Vi. *I* never heard anything like it!"

They were passing now through the ranks of the outer line of trees. To the boy, a little worried by the strangeness of his adored, and more than a little discomfited by the truly abnormal heat of the sun, it seemed that he passed from an inferno to a paradise at one step. No more did the sun beat implacably down upon the world. In here, under the roof of green which no ray pierced but only a gentle, pervading, filtered softness of light, there was a cool peacefulness which seemed to bathe him, instantly, in a placid bath of contentment.

But the girl shivered a little. She said :

" Oh ! It's almost cold in here ! "

He did not catch the words. The chirping and carolling which was going on all about and above them seemed to catch up and absorb the sound of her voice.

" Drat the birds ! " he said. " What you say ? "

He saw her lips move, but though he bent his head, did not catch a sound. There had come, from immediately above their heads, the furious squeaks and flutterings of a bird-quarrel.

" Drat the birds ! " he said again.

They were quite deep in the wood now. Looking round, he could not see at all the sun-drenched grass plateau from which they had come. He felt a tugging at his arm. The girl was pointing to a gently sloping bed of thick moss which was like a carpet spread at the foot of an old and twisted tree.

They sauntered to this carpet and sat down upon it, the boy sprawling at his ease, the girl very straight of back, with her hands clasped tightly about her raised knees. Had he been looking at her, rather than at the pipe he was filling, he would have seen again that craning forward of her head.

He did not finish the filling of his pipe. The singing of the birds went on. It seemed to gather volume until the whole world was filled with its chaotic whistling. The boy found, now that he had once consciously listened for and to it, that he could not again make his ears unconscious of the sound ; the sound which, with its seemingly momentarily increased volume, was now so plucking at the nerves within his head—indeed over his whole body—that he felt he could not much longer endure it. He thrust pipe and pouch savagely back into his pocket and turned to say to the girl that the quicker they got away from this blinking twittering the better he'd be pleased.

But the words died upon his lips. For even as he turned he became aware of a diminution of the reedy babel. He saw, too, calmer now with the decrease of irritation, that the girl was still in rapt attention.

So he held his tongue. The singing of the birds grew less and lesser with each moment. He began to feel drowsy, and once caught himself with a startled jerk from the edge of actual slumber. He peered sideways at his companion and saw that still she sat rigid ; not by the breadth of a hair had she altered her first attentive pose. He felt again for pipe and pouch.

His fingers idle in the jacket-pocket, he found himself listening again. Only this time he listened because he wanted to listen. There was now but one bird who sang. And the boy was curiously conscious, hearing these liquid notes alone and in the fullness of their uninterrupted and almost unbearable beauty, that the reason for his hatred of that full and somehow discordant chorus which a few moments ago had nearly driven him from the trees and their lovely shelter had been his inability to hear more than an isolated note or two of this song whose existence then he had realized only subconsciously.

The full, deep notes ceased their rapid and incredible trilling, cutting their sound off sharply, almost in the manner of an operatic singer. There was, then, only silence in the wood. It lasted, for the town-bred boy and girl caught suddenly in this placid whirlpool of natural beauty, for moments which seemed strained and incalculable ages. And then into this pool of pregnant no-sound were dropped, one by one, six exquisite jewels of sound, each pause between these isolated loveliness being of twice the duration of its predecessor.

After the last of these notes—deep and varying and crystal-pure, yet misty with unimaginable beauties—the silence fell again ; a silence not pregnant, as the last, with the vibrant foreshadowings of the magic to come, but a silence which had in it the utter and miserable quietness of endings and nothingness.

The boy's arm went up and wrapped itself gently about slim, barely covered shoulders. Two heads turned, and dark eyes looked into blue. The blue were abrim with unshed tears. She whispered :

" It was *him* I was listening to all the while. I could hear *that* all . . . all through the others. . . ."

A tear brimmed over and rolled down the pale cheek. The arm about her shoulders tightened, and at last she relaxed. The little body grew limp and lay against his strength.

" You lay quiet, darling," he said. His voice trembled a

little. And he spoke in the hushed voice of a man who knows himself in a holy or enchanted place.

Then silence. Silence which weighed and. pressed upon a man's soul. Silence which seemed a living deadness about them. From the boy's shoulder came a hushed, small voice which endeavoured to conceal its shaking. It said :

"I . . . I . . . felt all along . . . we shouldn't . . . shouldn't be here. . . . We didn't ought to 've come. . . . "

Despite its quietness there was something like panic in the voice.

He spoke reassuring words. To shake her from this queer, repressed hysteria, he said these words in a loud and virile tone. But this had only the effect of conveying to himself something of the odd disquiet which had possessed the girl.

" It's cold in here," she whispered suddenly. Her body pressed itself against him.

He laughed ; an odd sound. He said hastily :

" Cold ! You're talking out of the back of your neck, Vi."

" It is," she said. But her voice was more natural now. " We better be getting along, hadn't we ? "

He nodded. " Think we had," he said. He stirred as if to get to his feet. But a small hand suddenly gripped his arm, and her voice whispered :

" Look ! *Look !* " It was her own voice again, so that, even while he started a little at her sudden clutch and the urgency of her tone, he felt a wave of relief and a sudden quietening of his own vague but discomfortable uneasiness.

His gaze followed the line of her pointing finger. He saw, upon the carpeting of rotten twigs and brown mouldering leaves, just at the point where this brown and the dark cool green of their moss-bank met, a small bird. It stood upon its slender sticks of legs and gazed up at them, over the plump bright-hued breast, with shining little eyes. Its head was cocked to one side.

" D'you know," said the girl's whisper, " that's the first one we've *seen* ? "

The boy pondered for a moment. " Gosh ! " he said at last. " So it is and all ! "

They watched in silence. The bird hopped nearer.

" Isn't he *sweet*, Jack ? " Her whisper was a delighted chuckle.

"Talk about tame!" said the boy softly. "Cunning little beggar!"

Her elbow nudged his ribs. She said, her lips barely moving :

"Keep still. If we don't move, I believe he'll come right up to us."

Almost on her words, the bird hopped nearer. Now he was actually upon the moss, and thus less than an inch from the toe of the girl's left shoe. His little pert head, which was of a shining green with a rather comically long beak of yellow, was still cocked to one side. His bright, small eyes still surveyed them with the unwinking stare of his kind.

The girl's fascinated eyes were upon the small creature. She saw nothing else. Not so the boy. There was a nudge, this time from his elbow.

"Look there!" he whispered, pointing. "And there!"

She took, reluctantly enough, her eyes from the small intruder by her foot. She gazed in the directions he had indicated. She gasped in wonder. She whispered :

"Why, they're *all* coming to see us!"

Everywhere between the boles of the close-growing trees were birds. Some stood singly, some in pairs, some in little clumps of four and more. Some seemed, even to urban eyes, patently of the same family as their first visitor, who still stood by the white shoe, staring up at the face of its owner. But there were many more families. There were very small birds, and birds of sparrow size but unsparrowlike plumage, and birds which were a little bigger than this, and birds which were twice and three times the size. But one and all faced the carpet of moss and stared with their shining eyes at the two humans who lay upon it.

"This," said the boy, "is the rummest start *I* ever . . ."

The girl's elbow nudged him to silence. He followed the nod of her head and, looking down, saw that the first visitor was now perched actually upon her instep. He seemed very much at his ease there. But he was no longer looking up at them with those bright little eyes. And his head was no longer cocked to one side : it was level, so that he appeared to be in contemplation of a silk-clad shin.

Something—perhaps it was a little whispering, pattering rustle among the rotting leaves of the wood's carpet—took the boy's fascinated eyes from this strange sight. He lifted them to see a stranger; a sight perhaps more fascinating, but with by no means the same fascination.

The birds were nearer. Much, much nearer. And their line was solid now; an unbroken semicircle with bounding-line so wide-flung that he felt rather than saw its extent. One little corner of his brain for an instant busied itself with wild essays at numerical computation, but reeled back defeated by the impossibility of the task. Even as he stared, his face pale now, and his eyes wide with something like terror, that semicircle drew yet nearer, each unit of it taking four hops and four hops only. Now, its line unmarred, it was close upon the edge of the moss.

But was it only a semicircle? A dread doubt of this flashed into his mind.

One horrified glance across his shoulder told him that semicircle it was not. Full circle it was.

Birds, birds, birds! Was it possible that the world itself should hold such numbers of birds?

Eyes! Small, shining, myriad button-points of glittering eyes. All fixed upon him . . . and—God!—upon *her*. . . .

In one wild glance he saw that as yet she had not seen. Still she was in rapt, silent ecstasy over her one bird. And this now sat upon the outspread palm of her hand. Close to her face she was holding this hand. . . .

Through the pall of silence he could feel those countless eyes upon him. Little eyes; bright, glittering eyes. . . .

His breath came in shuddering gasps. He tried to get himself in hand; tried, until the sweat ran off him with the intensity of his effort, to master his fear. To some extent he succeeded. He would no longer sit idle while the circle . . . while the circle . . .

The silence was again ruffled upon its surface by a rustling patter. . . . It was one hop this time. It brought the semicircle fronting him so near that there were birds within an inch of his feet.

He leapt up. He waved his arms and kicked out and uttered one shout which somehow cracked and was half-strangled in his throat.

Nothing happened. At the edge of the moss a small bird, crushed by his kick, lay in a soft, small heap.

Not one of the birds moved. Still their eyes were upon him. The girl sat like a statue in living stone. She had seen, and terror held her. Her palm, the one bird still motionless upon it, still was outspread near her face.

From high above them there dropped slowly into the black depths of the silence one note of a sweetness ineffable. It lingered upon the breathless air, dying slowly until it fused with the silence.

And then the girl screamed. Suddenly and dreadfully. The small green poll had darted forward. The yellow beak had struck and sunk. A scarlet runnel coursed down the tender cheek.

Above the lingering echo of that scream there came another of those single notes from on high.

The silence died then. There was a whirring which filled the air. That circle was no more.

There were two feathered mounds which screamed and ran and leapt, and at last lay and were silent.

AMBROSE BIERCE

THE STRANGER

A MAN stepped out of the darkness into the little illuminated circle about our failing camp-fire and seated himself
upon a rock.

"You are not the first to explore this region," he said
gravely.

Nobody controverted his statement; he was himself proof
of its truth, for he was not of our party and must have been
somewhere near when we camped. Moreover, he must have
companions not far away; it was not a place where one
would be living or travelling alone. For more than a week
we had seen, besides ourselves and our animals, only such
living things as rattlesnakes and horned toads. In an Arizona
desert one does not long coexist with only such creatures as
these; one must have pack animals, supplies, arms—"an
outfit." And all these imply comrades. It was, perhaps, a
doubt as to what manner of men this unceremonious stranger's
comrades might be, together with something in his words
interpretable as a challenge, that caused every man of our
half-dozen "gentlemen adventurers" to rise to a sitting
posture and lay his hand upon a weapon—an act signifying,
in that time and place, a policy of expectation. The stranger
gave the matter no attention, and began again to speak in
the same deliberate, uninflected monotone in which he had
delivered his first sentence :

"Thirty years ago Ramon Gallegos, William Shaw, George
W. Kent and Berry Davis, all of Tucson, crossed the Santa
Catalina Mountains and travelled due west, as nearly as the
configuration of the country permitted. We were prospecting
and it was our intention, if we found nothing, to push through
to the Gila river at some point near Big Bend, where we
understood there was a settlement. We had a good outfit
but no guide—just Ramon Gallegos, William Shaw, George
W. Kent and Berry Davis."

The man repeated the names slowly and distinctly, as if to
fix them in the memories of his audience, every member of

which was now attentively observing him, but with a slackened apprehension regarding his possible companions somewhere in the darkness which seemed to enclose us like a black wall, for in the manner of this volunteer historian was no suggestion of an unfriendly purpose. His act was rather that of a harmless lunatic than an enemy. We were not so new to the country as not to know that the solitary life of many a plainsman had a tendency to develop eccentricities of conduct and character not always easily distinguishable from mental aberration. A man is like a tree : in a forest of his fellows he will grow as straight as his generic and individual nature permits ; alone, in the open, he yields to the deforming stresses and tortions that environ him. Some such thoughts were in my mind as I watched the man from the shadow of my hat, pulled low to shut out the fire-light. A witless fellow, no doubt, but what could he be doing there in the heart of a desert ?

Nobody having broken the silence, the visitor went on to say :

" This country was not then what it is now. There was not a ranch between the Gila and the Gulf. There was a little game here and there in the mountains, and near the infrequent water-holes grass enough to keep our animals from starvation. If we should be so fortunate as to encounter no Indians we might get through. But within a week the purpose of the expedition had altered from discovery of wealth to preservation of life. We had gone too far to go back, for what was ahead could be no worse than what was behind ; so we pushed on, riding by night to avoid Indians and the intolerable heat, and concealing ourselves by day as best we could. Sometimes, having exhausted our supply of wild meat and emptied our casks, we were days without food and drink ; then a water-hole or a shallow pool in the bottom of an arroyo so restored our strength and sanity that we were able to shoot some of the wild animals that sought it also. Sometimes it was a bear, sometimes an antelope, a coyote, a cougar—that was as God pleased ; all were food.

" One morning as we skirted a mountain range, seeking a practicable pass, we were attacked by a band of Apaches who had followed our trail up a gulch—it is not far from here. Knowing that they outnumbered us ten to one, they took none of their usual cowardly precautions, but dashed upon us at a gallop, firing and yelling. Fighting was out of the question. We urged our feeble animals up the gulch as far as there was footing for a hoof, then threw ourselves out of our saddles and took to the chaparral on one of the slopes, abandoning our entire outfit to the enemy. But we retained our rifles, every man—Ramon Gallegos, William Shaw, George W. Kent and Berry Davis."

"Same old crowd," said the humorist of the party. A gesture of disapproval from our leader silenced him, and the stranger proceeded with his tale :

"The savages dismounted also, and some of them ran up the gulch beyond the point at which we had left it, cutting off further retreat in that direction and forcing us on up the side. Unfortunately the chaparral extended only a short distance up the slope, and as we came into the open ground above we took the fire of a dozen rifles ; but Apaches shoot badly when in a hurry, and God so willed it that none of us fell. Twenty yards up the slope, beyond the edge of the brush, were vertical cliffs, in which, directly in front of us, was a narrow opening. Into that we ran, finding ourselves in a cavern about as large as an ordinary room. Here for a time we were safe. A single man with a repeating rifle could defend the entrance against all the Apaches in the land. But against hunger and thirst we had no defence. Courage we still had, but hope was a memory.

"Not one of those Indians did we afterwards see, but by the smoke and glare of their fires in the gulch we knew that by day and by night they watched with ready rifles in the edge of the bush—knew that if we made a sortie not a man of us would live to take three steps into the open. For three days, watching in turn, we held out, before our suffering became insupportable. Then—it was the morning of the fourth day—Ramon Gallegos said :

" ' Señores, I know not well of the good God and what please him. I have lived without religion, and I am not acquaint with that of you. Pardon, señores, if I shock you, but for me the time is come to beat the game of the Apache.'

"He knelt upon the rock floor of the cave and pressed his pistol against his temple. ' Madre de Dios,' he said, ' comes now the soul of Ramon Gallegos.'

"And so he left us—William Shaw, George W. Kent and Berry Davis.

"I was the leader. It was for me to speak.

" ' He was a brave man,' I said. ' He knew when to die, and how. It is foolish to go mad from thirst and fall by Apache bullets, or be skinned alive—it is in bad taste. Let us join Ramon Gallegos.'

" ' That is right,' said William Shaw.

" ' That is right,' said George W. Kent.

" I straightened the limbs of Ramon Gallegos and put a handkerchief over his face. Then William Shaw said: ' I should like to look like that a little while.'

" And George W. Kent said that he felt that way too.

" ' It shall be so,' I said. ' The red devils will wait a week. William Shaw and George W. Kent, draw and kneel.'

" They did so and I stood before them.

" ' Almighty God, our Father,' said I.

" ' Almighty God, our Father,' said William Shaw.

" ' Almighty God, our Father,' said George W. Kent.

" ' Forgive us our sins,' said I.

" ' Forgive us our sins,' said they.

" ' And receive our souls.'

" ' And receive our souls.'

" ' Amen ! '

" ' Amen ! '

" I laid them beside Ramon Gallegos and covered their faces."

There was a quick commotion on the opposite side of the camp-fire. One of our party had sprung to his feet, pistol in hand.

" And you ! " he shouted, " you dared to escape ?—you dare to be alive ? You cowardly hound, I'll send you to join them if I hang for it ! "

But with the leap of a panther the captain was upon him, grasping his wrist. " Hold it in, Sam Yountsey, hold it in ! "

We were now all upon our feet—except the stranger, who sat motionless and apparently inattentive. Someone seized Yountsey's other arm.

" Captain," I said, " there is something wrong here. This fellow is either a lunatic or merely a liar—just a plain, everyday liar that Yountsey has no call to kill. If this man was of that party it had five members, one of whom—probably himself— he has not named."

" Yes," said the captain, releasing the insurgent, who sat down, " there is something—unusual. Years ago four dead bodies of white men, scalped and shamefully mutilated, were found about the mouth of that cave. They are buried there ; I have seen the graves—we shall all see them to-morrow."

The stranger rose, standing tall in the light of the expiring fire, which in our breathless attention to his story we had neglected to keep going.

" There were four," he said. " Ramon Gallegos, William Shaw, George W. Kent and Berry Davis."

With this reiterated roll-call of the dead he walked into the darkness and we saw him no more.

At that moment one of our party, who had been on guard, strode in among us, rifle in hand and somewhat excited.

" Captain," he said, " for the last half-hour three men have been standing out there on the *mesa*." He pointed in the direction taken by the stranger. " I could see them distinctly, for the moon is up, but as they had no guns and I had them covered with mine, I thought it was their move. They have made none, but, damn it ! they have got on my nerves."

" Go back to your post, and stay till you see them again," said the captain. " The rest of you lie down again, or I'll kick you all into the fire."

The sentinel obediently withdrew, swearing, and did not return. As we were arranging our blankets, the fiery Yountsey said : " I beg your pardon, Captain, but who the devil do you take them to be ? "

" Ramon Gallegos, William Shaw and George W. Kent."

" But how about Berry Davis ? I ought to have shot him."

" Quite needless ; you couldn't have made him any deader. Go to sleep."

A. J. ALAN

MY ADVENTURE IN NORFOLK

I DON'T know how it is with you, but during February *my* wife generally says to me : " Have you thought at all about what we are going to do for August ? " And, of course, I say " No," and then she begins looking through the advertisements of bungalows to let.

Well, this happened last year, as usual, and she eventually produced one that looked possible. It said : " Norfolk— Hickling Broad—Furnished Bungalow—Garden—Garage, Boathouse," and all the rest of it—— Oh—*and* plate and linen. It also mentioned an exorbitant rent. I pointed out the bit about the rent, but my wife said : " Yes, you'll have to go down and see the landlord, and get him to come down. They always do." As a matter of fact, they always don't, but that's a detail.

Anyway, I wrote off to the landlord and asked if he could arrange for me to stay the night in the place to see what it was really like. He wrote back and said : " Certainly," and that he was engaging Mrs. So-and-so to come in and " oblige me," and make up the beds and so forth.

I tell you, we do things thoroughly in our family—I have to sleep in all the beds, and when I come home my wife counts the bruises and decides whether they will do or not.

At any rate, I arrived, in a blinding snowstorm, at about *the* most desolate spot on God's earth. I'd come to Potter Heigham by train, and been driven on—(it was a good five miles from the station). Fortunately, Mrs. Selston, the old lady who was going to " do " for me, was there, and she'd lighted a fire, and cooked me a steak, for which I was truly thankful.

I somehow think the cow, or whatever they get steaks off, had only died that morning. It was very—er—obstinate. While I dined, she talked to me. She *would* tell me all about an operation her husband had just had. *All* about it. It was almost a lecture on surgery. The steak was rather underdone, and it sort of made me feel I was illustrating her lecture. Anyway, she put me clean off my dinner, and then departed for the night.

I explored the bungalow and just had a look outside. It was, of course, very dark, but not snowing quite so hard. The garage stood about fifteen yards from the back door. I walked round it but didn't go in. I also went down to the edge of the broad, and verified the boathouse. The whole place looked as though it might be all right in the summer-time, but just then it made one wonder why people ever wanted to go to the North Pole.

Anyhow, I went indoors, and settled down by the fire. You've no idea how quiet it was ; even the water-fowl had taken a night off—at least, they weren't working.

At a few minutes to eleven I heard the first noise there'd been since Mrs. What's-her-name—Selston—had cleared out. It was the sound of a car. If it had gone straight by I probably shouldn't have noticed it at all, only it didn't go straight by ; it seemed to stop farther up the road, before it got to the house. Even that didn't make much impression. After all, cars *do* stop.

It must have been five or ten minutes before it was borne in on me that it hadn't gone on again. So I got up and looked out of the window. It had left off snowing, and there was a glare through the gate that showed that there were head-lamps somewhere just out of sight. I thought I might as well stroll out and investigate.

I found a fair-sized limousine pulled up in the middle of the road about twenty yards short of my gate. The light was rather blinding, but when I got close to it I found a girl with the bonnet open, tinkering with the engine. Quite an attractive young female, from what one could see, but she was so muffled up in furs that it was rather hard to tell.

I said :

" Er—good evening—anything I can do ? "

She said she didn't know what was the matter. The engine had just stopped, and wouldn't start again. And it *had !* It wouldn't even turn, either with the self-starter or the handle. The whole thing was awfully hot, and I asked her whether there was any water in the radiator. She didn't see why there shouldn't be, there always had been. This didn't strike me as entirely conclusive. I said, we'd better put some in, and see what happened. She said, why not use snow ? But

I thought not. There was an idea at the back of my mind that there was some reason why it was unwise to use melted snow, and it wasn't until I arrived back with a bucketful that I remembered what it was. Of course—goitre.

When I got back to her she'd got the radiator cap off, and inserted what a Danish friend of mine calls a " funeral." We poured a little water in. . . . Luckily I'd warned her to stand clear. The first tablespoonful that went in came straight out again, red-hot, and blew the " funeral " sky-high. We waited a few minutes until things had cooled down a bit, but it was no go. As fast as we poured water in it simply ran out again into the road underneath. It was quite evident that she'd been driving with the radiator bone dry, and that her engine had seized right up.

I told her so. She said :

" Does that mean I've got to stop here all night ? "

I explained that it wasn't as bad as all that ; that is, if she cared to accept the hospitality of my poor roof (and it *was* a poor roof—it let the wet in). But she wouldn't hear of it. By the by, she didn't know the—er—circumstances, so it wasn't that. No, she wanted to leave the car where it was and go on on foot.

I said :

" Don't be silly, it's miles to anywhere."

However, at that moment we heard a car coming along the road, the same way as she'd come. We could see its lights, too, although it was a very long way off. You know how flat Norfolk is—you can see a terrific distance.

I said :

" There's the way out of all your troubles. This thing, whatever it is, will give you a tow to the nearest garage, or at any rate a lift to some hotel."

One would have expected her to show some relief, but she didn't. I began to wonder what she jolly well *did* want. She wouldn't let me help her to stop where she was, and she didn't seem anxious for anyone to help her to go anywhere else.

She was quite peculiar about it. She gripped hold of my arm, and said :

" What do you think this is that's coming ? "

I said :

" I'm sure I don't know, being a stranger in these parts, but it sounds like a lorry full of milk cans."

I offered to lay her sixpence about it (this was before the betting-tax came in). She'd have had to pay, too, because it *was* a lorry full of milk cans. The driver had to pull up because there wasn't room to get by.

He got down and asked if there was anything he could do to help. We explained the situation. He said he was going to Norwich, and was quite ready to give her a tow if she wanted it. However, she wouldn't do that, and it was finally decided to shove her car into my garage for the night, to be sent for next day, and the lorry was to take her along to Norwich.

Well, I managed to find the key of the garage, and the lorry-driver—Williams, his name was—and I ran the car in and locked the door. This having been done—(ablative absolute)—I suggested that it was a very cold night. Williams agreed, and said he didn't mind if he did. So I took them both indoors and mixed them a stiff whisky and water each. There wasn't any soda. And, naturally, the whole thing had left *me* very cold, too. I hadn't an overcoat on.

Up to now I hadn't seriously considered the young woman. For one thing it had been dark, *and* there had been a seized engine to look at. Er—I'm afraid that's not a very gallant remark. What I mean is that to anyone with a mechanical mind a motor-car in that condition is much more interesting than—er—well, it *is* very interesting—but why labour the point? However, in the sitting-room, in the lamplight, it was possible to get more of an idea. She was a little older than I'd thought, and her eyes were too close together.

Of course, she wasn't a—how shall I put it? Her manners weren't quite easy and she was careful with her English. *You* know. But that wasn't it. She treated us with a lack of friendliness which was—well, we'd done nothing to deserve it. There was a sort of vague hostility and suspicion, which seemed rather hard lines, considering. Also, she was so anxious to keep in the shadow that if I hadn't moved the lamp away she'd never have got near the fire at all.

And the way she hurried the wretched Williams over his drink was quite distressing ; and foolish, too, as *he* was going to drive, but that was her—funnel. When he'd gone out to start up his engine I asked her if she was all right for money, and she apparently was. Then they started off, and I shut up the place and went upstairs.

There happened to be a local guide-book in my bedroom, with maps in it. I looked at these and couldn't help wondering where the girl in the car had come from; I mean my road seemed so very unimportant. The sort of road one might use if one wanted to avoid people. If one were driving a stolen car, for instance. This was quite a thrilling idea. I thought it might be worth while having another look at the car. So I once more unhooked the key from the kitchen dresser and sallied forth into the snow. It was as black as pitch, and so still that my candle hardly flickered. It wasn't a large garage, and the car nearly filled it. By the by, we'd backed it in so as to make it easier to tow it out again.

The engine I'd already seen, so I squeezed past along the wall and opened the door in the body part of the car. At least, I only turned the handle, and the door was pushed open from the inside and—something—fell out on me. It pushed me quite hard, and wedged me against the wall. It also knocked the candle out of my hand and left me in the dark—which was a bit of a nuisance. I wondered what on earth the thing was—barging into me like that—so I felt it, rather gingerly, and found it was a man—a dead man—with a moustache. He'd evidently been sitting propped up against the door. I managed to put him back, as decorously as possible, and shut the door again.

After a lot of grovelling about under the car I found the candle and lighted it, and opened the opposite door and switched on the little lamp in the roof—and then—oo-er !

Of course, I had to make some sort of examination. He was an extremely tall and thin individual. He must have been well over six feet three. He was dark and very cadaverous looking. In fact, I don't suppose he'd ever looked so cadaverous in his life. He was wearing a trench coat.

It wasn't difficult to tell what he'd died of. He'd been shot through the back. I found the hole just under the right scrofula, or scalpel—what is shoulder-blade, anyway ? Oh, clavicle—stupid of me—well, that's where it was, and the bullet had evidently gone through into the lung. I say " evidently," and leave it at that.

There were no papers in his pockets, and no tailor's name on his clothes, but there was a note-case, with nine pounds in it. Altogether a most unpleasant business. Of course, it doesn't do to question the workings of Providence, but one couldn't help wishing it hadn't happened. It was just a little mysterious, too—er—who had killed him? It wasn't likely that the girl had or she wouldn't have been joy-riding about the country with him; and if someone else had murdered him why hadn't she mentioned it? Anyway, she hadn't and she'd gone, so one couldn't do anything for the time being. No telephone, of course. I just locked up the garage and went to bed. That was two o'clock.

Next morning I woke early, for some reason or other, and it occurred to me as a good idea to go and have a look at things—by daylight, and before Mrs. Selston turned up. So I did. The first thing that struck me was that it had snowed heavily during the night, because there were no wheel tracks or footprints, and the second was that I'd left the key in the garage door. I opened it and went in. The place was completely empty. No car, no body, no nothing. There was a patch of grease on the floor where I'd dropped the candle, otherwise there was nothing to show I'd been there before. One of two things must have happened : either some people had come along during the night and taken the car away, or else I'd fallen asleep in front of the fire and dreamt the whole thing.

Then I remembered the whisky glasses.

They should still be in the sitting-room. I went back to look, and they were, all three of them. So it *hadn't* been a dream and the car *had* been fetched away, but they must have been jolly quiet over it.

The girl had left her glass on the mantelpiece, and it showed several very clearly defined finger-marks. Some were mine, naturally, because I'd fetched the glass from the kitchen and poured out the drink for her, but hers, her finger-marks, were clean, and mine were oily, so it was quite easy to tell them apart. It isn't necessary to point out that this glass was very important. There'd evidently been a murder, or something of that kind, and the girl must have known all about it, even if she hadn't actually done it herself, so anything she had left in the way of evidence ought to be handed over to the police ; and this was all she *had* left. So I packed it up with meticulous care in an old biscuit-box out of the larder.

When Mrs. Selston came, I settled up with her and came back to Town. Oh, I called on the landlord on the way and told him I'd " let him know " about the bungalow. Then

I caught my train, and in due course drove straight to Scotland Yard. I went up and saw my friend there. I produced the glass and asked him if his people could identify the marks. He said, " Probably not," but he sent it down to the finger-print department and asked me where it came from. I said : " Never you mind ; let's have the identification first." He said : " All right."

They're awfully quick, these people—the clerk was back in three minutes with a file of papers. They knew the girl all right. They told me her name and showed me her photo-graph ; not flattering. Quite an adventurous lady, from all accounts. In the early part of her career she'd done time twice for shoplifting, chiefly in the book department. Then she'd what they call " taken up with " a member of one of those race-gangs one sometimes hears about.

My pal went on to say that there's been a fight between two of these gangs, in the course of which her friend had got shot. She'd managed to get him away in a car, but it had broken down somewhere in Norfolk. So she'd left it and the dead man in someone's garage, and had started off for Norwich in a lorry. Only she never got there. On the way the lorry had skidded, and both she and the driver—a fellow called Williams—had been thrown out, and they'd rammed their heads against a brick wall, which everyone knows is a fatal thing to do. At least, it was in their case.

I said : " Look here, it's all very well, but you simply can't know all this ; there hasn't been time—it only happened last night."

He said : " Last night be blowed ! It all happened in February, nineteen nineteen. The people you've described have been dead for years."

I said : " Oh ! "

And to think that I might have stuck to that nine pounds !

HONORÉ DE BALZAC

THE MYSTERIOUS MANSION

ABOUT a hundred yards from the town of Vendôme, on the borders of the Loire, there is an old grey house, surmounted by very high gables, and so completely isolated that neither tanyard nor shabby hostelry, such as you may find at the entrance to all small towns, exists in its immediate neighbourhood.

In front of this building, overlooking the river, is a garden, where the once well-trimmed box borders that used to define the walks now grow wild as they list. Several willows that spring from the Loire have grown as rapidly as the hedge that encloses it, and half conceal the house. The rich vegetation of those weeds that we call foul adorns the sloping shore. Fruit trees, neglected for the last ten years, no longer yield their harvest, and their shoots form coppices. The wall-fruit grows like hedges against the walls. Paths once gravelled are overgrown with moss, but, to tell the truth, there is no trace of a path. From the height of the hill, to which cling the ruins of the old castle of the Dukes of Vendôme, the only spot whence the eye can plunge into this enclosure, it strikes you that, at a time not easy to determine, this plot of land was the delight of a country gentleman, who cultivated roses and tulips and horticulture in general, and who was besides a lover of fine fruit. An arbour is still visible, or rather the debris of an arbour, where there is a table that time has not quite destroyed. The aspect of this garden of bygone days suggests the negative joys of peaceful, provincial life, as one might reconstruct the life of a worthy tradesman by reading the epitaph on his tombstone. As if to complete the sweetness and sadness of the ideas that possess one's soul, one of the walls displays a sun-dial decorated with the following commonplace Christian inscription : " Ultimam cogita ! " The roof of this house is horribly dilapidated, the shutters are always closed, the balconies are covered with swallows' nests, the doors are perpetually shut, weeds have drawn green lines in the cracks of the flights of steps, the locks and bolts are rusty. Sun, moon, winter, summer, and snow have worn the panelling, warped the boards, gnawed the paint. The lugubrious silence which reigns there is only broken by birds, cats, martins, rats and mice, free to course to and fro, to fight and to eat each other. Everywhere an invisible hand has graven the word *mystery*.

Should your curiosity lead you to glance at this house from the side that points to the road, you would perceive a great door which the children of the place have riddled with holes. I afterward heard that this door had been closed for the last ten years. Through the holes broken by the boys you would have observed the perfect harmony that existed between the façades of both garden and courtyard. In both the same disorder prevails. Tufts of weed encircle the paving-stones. Enormous cracks furrow the walls, round whose blackened crests twine the thousand garlands of the pellitory. The steps are out of joint, the wire of the bell is rusted, the spouts are cracked. What fire from heaven has fallen here? What tribunal has decreed that salt should be strewn on this dwelling? Has God been blasphemed, has France been here betrayed? These are the questions we ask ourselves, but get no answer from the crawling things that haunt the place. The empty and deserted house is a gigantic enigma, of which the key is lost. In bygone times it was a small fief, and bears the name of the Grande Bretêche.

I inferred that I was not the only person to whom my good landlady had communicated the secret of which I was to be the sole recipient, and I prepared to listen.

"Sir," she said, "when the Emperor sent the Spanish prisoners of war and others here, the Government quartered on me a young Spaniard who had been sent to Vendôme on parole. Parole notwithstanding he went out every day to show himself to the sous-préfet. He was a Spanish grandee! Nothing less! His name ended in os and dia, something like Burgos de Férédia. I have his name on my books; you can read it if you like. Oh! but he was a handsome young man for a Spaniard; they are all said to be ugly. He was only five feet and a few inches high, but he was well grown; he had small hands that he took such care of; ah! you should have seen! He had as many brushes for his hands as a woman for her whole dressing apparatus! He had thick black hair, a fiery eye, his skin was rather bronzed, but I liked the look of it. He wore the finest linen I have ever seen on anyone, although I have had princesses staying here, and, among others, General Bertrand, the Duke and Duchess d'Abrantès, Monsieur Decazes, and the King of Spain. He didn't eat much; but his manners were so polite, so amiable, that one could not owe him a grudge. Oh! I was very fond of him, although he didn't open his lips four times in the day, and it was impossible to keep up a conversation with him. For if you spoke to him, he did not answer. It was a fad, a mania with them all, I heard say. He read his breviary like a priest, he went to Mass and to all the services regularly. Where did he sit? Two steps from the chapel of Madame de Merret. As he took his place there the first time he went to church, nobody suspected him of any intention in so doing. Besides, he never raised his eyes from his prayer-book, poor young man! After that, sir, in the evening he would walk on the mountains, among the castle ruins. It was the poor man's only amusement, it reminded him of his country. They say that Spain is all mountains! From the commencement of his imprisonment he stayed out late. I was anxious when I found that he did not come home before midnight; but we got accustomed to this fancy of his. He took the key of the door, and we left off sitting up for him. He lodged in a house of ours in the Rue des Casernes. After that, one of our stable-men told us that in the evening when he led the horses to the water, he thought he had seen the Spanish grandee swimming far down the river like a live fish. When he returned, I told him to take care of the rushes; he appeared vexed to have been seen in the water. At last, one day, or rather one morning, we did not find him in his room; he had not returned. After searching everywhere, I found some writing in the drawer of a table, where there were fifty gold pieces of Spain that are called doubloons and were worth about five thousand francs; and ten thousand francs' worth of diamonds in a small sealed box. The writing said, that in case he did not return, he left us the money and the diamonds, on condition of paying for Masses to thank God for his escape, and for his salvation. In those days my husband had not been taken from me; he hastened to seek him everywhere.

"And now for the strange part of the story. He brought home the Spaniard's clothes, that he had discovered under a big stone, in a sort of pilework by the river-side near the castle, nearly opposite to the Grande Bretêche. My husband had gone there so early that no one had seen him. After reading the letter, he burned the clothes, and according to Count Férédia's desire we declared that he had escaped. The sous-préfet sent all the gendarmerie in pursuit of him; but brust! they never caught him. Lepas believed that the Spaniard had drowned himself. I, sir, don't think so; I am more inclined to believe that he had something to do with the affair of Madame de Merret, seeing that Rosalie told me that the crucifix that her mistress thought so much of, that she had it buried with her, was of ebony and silver. Now in the beginning of his stay here, Monsieur de Férédia had one in ebony and silver, that I never saw him with later. Now, sir, don't you consider that I need have no scruples about the Spaniard's fifteen thousand francs, and that I have a right to them?"

" Certainly; but you haven't tried to question Rosalie?" I said.

" Oh, yes, indeed, sir; but to no purpose! the girl's like a wall. She knows something, but it is impossible to get her to talk."

After exchanging a few more words with me, my landlady left me a prey to vague and gloomy thoughts, to a romantic curiosity, and a religious terror not unlike the profound impression produced on us when by night, on entering a dark church, we perceive a faint light under high arches; a vague figure glides by—the rustle of a robe or cassock is heard, and we shudder.

Suddenly the Grande Bretêche and its tall weeds, its barred windows, its rusty ironwork, its closed doors, its deserted apartments, appeared like a fantastic apparition before me. I essayed to penetrate the mysterious dwelling, and to find the knot of its dark story—the drama that had killed three persons. In my eyes Rosalie became the most interesting person in Vendôme. As I studied her, I discovered the traces of secret care, despite the radiant health that shone in her plump countenance. There was in her the germ of remorse or hope; her attitude revealed a secret, like the attitude of a bigot who prays to excess, or of the infanticide who ever hears the last cry of her child. Yet her manners were rough and ingenuous—her silly smile was not that of a criminal, and could you but have seen the great kerchief that encompassed her portly bust, framed and laced in by a lilac and blue cotton gown, you would have dubbed her innocent. No, I thought, I will not leave Vendôme without learning the history of the Grande Bretêche. To gain my ends I will strike up a friendship with Rosalie, if needs be.

" Rosalie," said I, one evening.

" Sir ? "

" You are not married ? "

She started slightly.

" Oh, I can find plenty of men, when the fancy takes me to be made miserable," she said, laughing.

She soon recovered from the effects of her emotion, for all women, from the great lady to the maid of the inn, possess a composure that is peculiar to them.

" You are too good-looking and well favoured to be short of lovers. But tell me, Rosalie, why did you take service in an inn after leaving Madame de Merret ? Did she leave you nothing to live on ? "

" Oh, yes ! But, sir, my place is the best in all Vendôme."

The reply was one of those that judges and lawyers would call evasive. Rosalie appeared to me to be situated in this romantic history like the square in the midst of a chessboard. She was at the heart of the truth and chief interest ; she seemed to me to be bound in the very knot of it. The conquest of Rosalie was no longer to be an ordinary siege—in this girl was centred the last chapter of a novel, therefore from this moment Rosalie became the object of my preference.

One morning I said to Rosalie : " Tell me all you know about Madame de Merret."

" Oh ! " she replied in terror, " do not ask that of me, Monsieur Horace."

Her pretty face fell—her clear, bright colour faded—and her eyes lost their innocent brightness.

" Well, then," she said, " if you must have it so, I will tell you about it ; but promise to keep my secret ! "

" Done ! my dear girl, I must keep your secret with the honour of a thief, which is the most loyal in the world."

Were I to transcribe Rosalie's diffuse eloquence faithfully, an entire volume would scarcely contain it ; so I shall abridge.

The room occupied by Madame de Merret at the Bretêche was on the ground-floor. A little closet about four feet deep, built in the thickness of the wall, served as her wardrobe.

Three months before the eventful evening of which I am about
to speak, Madame de Merret had been so seriously indisposed
that her husband had left her to herself in her own apartment,
while he occupied another on the first floor. By one of those
chances that it is impossible to foresee, he returned home from
the club (where he was accustomed to read the papers and
discuss politics with the inhabitants of the place) two hours
later than usual. His wife supposed him to be at home, in bed
and asleep. But the invasion of France had been the subject
of a most animated discussion ; the billiard-match had been
exciting, he had lost forty francs, an enormous sum for
Vendôme, where every one hoards, and where manners are
restricted within the limits of a praiseworthy modesty, which
perhaps is the source of the true happiness that no Parisian
covets. For some time past Monsieur de Merret had been
satisfied to ask Rosalie if his wife had gone to bed ; and on her
reply, which was always in the affirmative, had immediately
gained his own room with the good temper engendered by
habit and confidence. On entering his house, he took it into
his head to go and tell his wife of his misadventure, perhaps by
way of consolation. At dinner he found Madame de Merret
most coquettishly attired. On his way to the club it had
occurred to him that his wife was restored to health, and that
her convalescence had added to her beauty. He was, as husbands are wont to be, somewhat slow in making this discovery.
Instead of calling Rosalie, who was occupied just then in
watching the cook and coachman play a difficult hand at
brisque, Monsieur de Merret went to his wife's room by the
light of a lantern that he deposited on the first step of the
staircase. His unmistakable step resounded under the vaulted
corridor. At the moment that the Count turned the handle of
his wife's door, he fancied he could hear the door of the
closet I spoke of close ; but when he entered Madame de
Merret was alone before the fire-place. The husband thought
ingenuously that Rosalie was in the closet, yet a suspicion
that jangled in his ear put him on his guard. He looked at his
wife and saw in her eyes I know not what wild and hunted
expression.

" You are very late," she said. Her habitually pure, sweet
voice seemed changed to him.

Monsieur de Merret did not reply, for at that moment Rosalie
entered. It was a thunderbolt for him. He strode about the

room, passing from one window to the other, with mechanical motion and folded arms.

" Have you heard bad news, or are you unwell ? " inquired his wife timidly, while Rosalie undressed her.

He kept silent.

" You can leave me." said Madame de Merret to her maid ; " I will put my hair in curl papers myself."

From the expression of her husband's face she foresaw trouble, and wished to be alone with him. When Rosalie had gone, or was supposed to have gone (for she stayed in the corridor for a few minutes), Monsieur de Merret came and stood in front of his wife, and said coldly to her :

" Madame, there is someone in your closet ! " She looked calmly at her husband, and replied simply :

" No, sir."

This answer was heartrending to Monsieur de Merret ; he did not believe in it. Yet his wife had never appeared to him purer or more saintly than at that moment. He rose to open the closet door ; Madame de Merret took his hand, looked at him with an expression of melancholy, and said in a voice that betrayed singular emotion :

" If you find no one there, remember this, all will be over between us ! " The extraordinary dignity of his wife's manner restored the Count's profound esteem for her, and inspired him with one of those resolutions that only lack a vaster stage to become immortal.

" No," said he, " Josephine, I will not go there. In either case it would separate us for ever. Hear me, I know how pure you are at heart, and that your life is a holy one. You would not commit a mortal sin to save your life."

At these words Madame de Merret turned a haggard gaze upon her husband.

" Here, take your crucifix," he added. " Swear to me before God that there is no one in there ; I will believe you, I will never open that door."

Madame de Merret took the crucifix and said :

" I swear."

" Louder," said the husband, " and repeat ' I swear before God that there is no one in that closet.' "

She repeated the sentence calmly.

" That will do," said Monsieur de Merret, coldly.

After a moment of silence :

" I never saw this pretty toy before," he said, examining the ebony crucifix inlaid with silver, and most artistically chiselled.

" I found it at Duvivier's, who broughtit of a Spanish monk when the prisoners passed through Vendôme last year."

" Ah ! " said Monsieur de Merret, as he replaced the crucifix on the nail, and he rang. Rosalie did not keep him waiting. Monsieur de Merret went quickly to meet her, led her to the bay window that opened on to the garden and whispered to her :

" Listen ! I know that Gorenflot wishes to marry you, poverty is the only drawback, and you told him that you would be his wife if he found the means to establish himself as a master mason. Well ! go and fetch him, tell him to come here with his trowel and tools. Manage not to awaken anyone in his house but himself ; his fortune will be more than your desires. Above all, leave this room without babbling, other-wise——" He frowned. Rosalie went away, he recalled her.

" Here, take my latchkey," he said. " Jean ! " then cried Monsieur de Merret, in tones of thunder in the corridor. Jean, who was at the same time his coachman and his con-fidential servant, left his game of cards and came.

" Go to bed, all of you," said his master, signing to him to approach ; and the Count added, under his breath : " When they are all asleep—*asleep*, d'ye hear ?—you will come down and tell me." Monsieur de Merret, who had not lost sight of his wife all the time he was giving his orders, returned quietly to her at the fireside and began to tell her of the game of billiards and the talk of the club. When Rosalie returned she found Monsieur and Madame de Merret conversing very amicably.

The Count had lately had all the ceilings of his reception rooms on the ground floor repaired. Plaster of Paris is difficult to obtain in Vendôme ; the carriage raises its price. The Count had therefore bought a good deal, being well aware that he could find plenty of purchasers for whatever might remain over. This circumstance inspired him with the design he was about to execute.

" Sir, Gorenflot has arrived," said Rosalie in low tones.

" Show him in," replied the Count in loud tones.

Madame de Merret turned rather pale when she saw the mason.

" Gorenflot," said her husband, " go and fetch bricks from the coach-house, and bring sufficient to wall up the door of this closet; you will use the plaster I have over to coat the wall with." Then calling Rosalie and the workman aside :

" Listen, Gorenflot," he said in an undertone, " you will sleep here to-night. But to-morrow you will have a passport to a foreign country, to a town to which I will direct you. I shall give you six thousand francs for your journey. You will stay ten years in that town ; if you do not like it, you may establish yourself in another, provided it be in the same country. You will pass through Paris, where you will await me. There I will insure you an additional six thousand francs by contract, which will be paid to you on your return, provided you have fulfilled the conditions of our bargain. This is the price for your absolute silence as to what you are about to do to-night. As to you, Rosalie, I will give you ten thousand francs on the day of your wedding, on condition of your marrying Gorenflot ; but if you wish to marry, you must hold your tongues ; or—no dowry."

" Rosalie," said Madame de Merret, " do my hair."

The husband walked calmly up and down, watching the door, the mason, and his wife, but without betraying any insulting doubts. Madame de Merret chose a moment when the workman was unloading bricks and her husband was at the other end of the room to say to Rosalie : " A thousand francs a year for you, my child, if you can tell Gorenflot to leave a chink at the bottom." Then out loud, she added coolly :

" Go and help him ! "

Monsieur and Madame de Merret were silent all the time that Gorenflot took to brick up the door. This silence, on the part of the husband, who did not choose to furnish his wife with a pretext for saying things of a double meaning, had its purpose ; on the part of Madame de Merret it was either pride or prudence. When the wall was about half-way up, the sly workman took advantage of a moment when the Count's back was turned, to strike a blow with his trowel in one of the glass panes of the closet-door. This act informed Madame de Merret that Rosalie had spoken to Gorenflot.

All three then saw a man's face ; it was dark and gloomy with black hair and eyes of flame. Before her husband turned, the poor woman had time to make a sign to the stranger that signified : Hope !

At four o'clock, toward dawn, for it was the month of September, the construction was finished. The mason was handed over to the care of Jean, and Monsieur de Merret went to bed in his wife's room.

On rising the following morning, he said carelessly :

" The deuce ! I must go to the Mairie for the passport." He put his hat on his head, advanced three steps toward the door, altered his mind and took the crucifix.

His wife trembled for joy. " He is going to Duvivier," she thought. As soon as the Count had left, Madame de Merret rang for Rosalie ; then in a terrible voice :

" The trowel, the trowel ! " she cried, " and quick to work ! I saw how Gorenflot did it ; we shall have time to make a hole and to mend it again."

In the twinkling of an eye, Rosalie brought a sort of mattock to her mistress, who with unparalleled ardour set about demolishing the wall. She had already knocked out several bricks and was preparing to strike a more decisive blow when she perceived Monsieur de Merret behind her. She fainted.

" Lay Madame on her bed," said the Count coldly. He had foreseen what would happen in his absence and had set a trap for his wife ; he had simply written to the mayor, and had sent for Duvivier. The jeweller arrived just as the room had been put in order.

" Duvivier," inquired the Count, " did you buy crucifixes of the Spaniards who passed through here ? "

" No, sir."

" That will do, thank you," he said, looking at his wife like a tiger. " Jean," he added, " you will see that my meals are served in the Countess's room ; she is ill, and I shall not leave her until she has recovered."

The cruel gentleman stayed with his wife for twenty days. In the beginning, when there were sounds in the walled closet, and Josephine attempted to implore his pity for the dying stranger, he replied, without permitting her to say a word :

" You have sworn on the cross that there is no one there."

ALGERNON BLACKWOOD

THE STRANGER

THE flat lay deadly quiet, voices were hushed, and all moved to and fro on tiptoe. In the room where she lay —the woman who refused to die—this quiet was, of course, most marked, for there her breathing, so faint it was scarcely perceptible, alone broke the pall of silence. The last clearly audible sound had been the lowered voice of the family physician: " I won't wait now. There is little I can do. I will come back within an hour," and his heels tapping softly across the tiled floor of the narrow hall towards the lift.

Yes, she might last an hour or two, possibly even till to-morrow, this woman who so hated death that she always refused even to acknowledge it; but she would not wake from unconsciousness. She was sinking fast, the doctor said the intense vitality at length was unavailing ; there was nothing he could do.

And so now it was that the lowered voice, the tap of boots on the tiled floor of the landing, the rumble of the lift, still echoed on in the mind where all else lay muted and repressed.

Apart from two members of the family and these but nominally, dutifully, affectionate, Colonel Moreland alone was present in that room of silence. Elderly, grizzled, with features set in bronze, he sat motionless beside the bed. Looking like a Roman sentinel, he watched the grim, silent figure, whose arena was a few square feet of human frailty, and his was the mind in which the recent sounds seemed still to echo. The other, a stepbrother and an uncle, stood with their backs to him by the window, watching the dusk fall slowly over the dismal London street, not otherwise moved, probably, than by those practical considerations the approaching death of a tolerated relative involved. Priority of place, at any rate, they gave readily to the stern man who sat thus motionless beside the bed, almost a stranger to them, yet whose right, it seemed, they admitted gladly.

With the lessening traffic and the dropping of the winter's

night, the silence deepened. A slow wind mourned about the building. The stillness grew. If the faithful serving-woman in the kitchen wept, she wept inaudibly. That she did weep, however, is certain, for some half an hour later, when the Colonel looked into her face, the tears lay still upon her ashen cheeks. . . .

To her indeed, as to himself, this stealthy approach of death seemed an incredible occurrence, painfully dramatic for all its quiet method of arrival. To the old Scottish woman, a mere lassie from the Highlands when first she entered the family service years before, it seemed impossible that a mistress with such fierce love of living should ever cease to breathe. It was unnatural, almost wicked. A loathing of death, so intense that it amounted to a fixed refusal to die, must surely —somehow—keep her alive for ever ! Death, in her mistress's presence, no one ever dared to mention. Had she not proved it again and again : she—*would* not die !

To both soldier and servant, at any rate, death now seemed an outrage, something almost against the normal order. Yet to Colonel Moreland, though he shared with the humble serving-woman that rare worship of true love which had held faithful over a quarter of a century, the silent battle was painful, and dramatic for other, and very different, reasons. From time to time, as the minutes crawled, his eyes would open, gaze for a moment on the face he so passionately loved, then quickly close again, lest the intensity of his inner realisation be even by so much dimmed. His thoughts—pictures, rather than actual thoughts—were of long ago, of more recent years, to be exact, of two weeks before, when news of the dangerous seizure had brought him instantly to her side. No trivial, foolish convention had prevented then, as it had prevented years ago. No trumpery considerations of social rank, of thine and mine, differences that in youth appear so great, in later years so petty, had interfered with the overmastering power that impelled, even commanded, him to see her, before, in the final sense, it was too late, and—to make his long-concealed confession face to face. . . .

Twenty-five years ago, ignorance and timidity had sealed his lips. The V.C., gained on the North-West Frontier, proved a quality in him which yet had not availed a young man, finely self-forgetful, fighting for a loveliness that seemed wholly beyond his reach ; she, all unknowing, had given herself to another—and he had seen her go. Now, on his return from long sojourn in the East, he had heard in one and the same day both of her illness and of her present liberty. He had not hesitated. The late confession had been made that ought to have been made so many years before. She told him her own long secret, too. And in that very breath, which the doctor whispered might be wellnigh her last, she told him likewise—her whole being defiant with aggressive will :

" I shall get well again. I shall live for you. It is never too late for that . . . I *will* get well . . . ! "

The pathetic ignominy of it struck even the unimaginative soldier—the defiant little human will now helpless and inoperative as the last cold Shadow stole towards the bed. Death recked not of human desire and intention, however fierce, and the desolate battle, it seemed to him, was a foregone conclusion. Any moment now, the remorseless Figure must stand at the door, approach the bed, and steal her from his world. Colonel Moreland, overwrought perhaps a little, pictured in his mind a relentless and unbending Outline. . . .

The step-brother turned from the window, lighted a softly shaded lamp, then moved back without a sound to the post he held somewhat awkwardly with his companion. But the bronze outline beside the bed was too intent upon his poignant inner pictures to take much notice of what they did. Only the doctor's lowered voice, the tap of his boots upon the tiled floor outside, the rumble of the descending lift, still echoed on across the background of his mind. . . . These, indeed, and the frail outline beneath the sheets, seemed his sole relations with the outer world. When a step, therefore, became audible in the passage, it was natural he hardly stirred at first, and that the opening and closing of the front door, the murmur of confused voices, too, should have merged in that continuous memory of a mental sound.

There was a cold air that sent a faint shiver over him, but it was the whispering by the window that really disturbed his profound reverie :

" The doctor probably . . . sooner than he meant . . ."

he heard one say, and so was on his feet, startled rather, and out in the passage before either of them. But the woman from the kitchen was in front of him. He ran into her in his eagerness, noticed the tears upon her ashen cheeks, and saw at the same time the tall, thin outline of the stranger, who most certainly was *not* the doctor.

A very upright and unbending Outline it was, the stiffness, no doubt, adding to the appearance of the stature, beside which the woman seemed diminutive, almost dwarflike. The dreadful whiteness of her face he found unwelcome—more, it troubled him profoundly, though he recalled this only later. There was talk, confused and hurried, yet the voice of the stranger, he believed, was not once actually audible at all. It was the woman's voice and words he caught so distinctly, words whose incongruity must, at any other time, have brought a smile to his stern lips. This appearance, however, of rapid exchange between two persons was as clear to him as the certainty that there was a mistake as well, a mistake that seemed grossly stupid at this moment : the wrong name, the wrong door, the wrong building, of course.

Sharply, then, out of this muttering, the woman's words emerged, both fear and courage in the tone, as she repeated with insistent emphasis that her mistress was not at home : " She's *not* at home . . . to anybody. She's *dying*. . . . / "

Colonel Moreland, as he heard, found himself abruptly stopped. He stood stock-still, arrested in his tracks. The incongruity of the language gave him a sense of intolerant impatience, of anger, even. The stupid disturbance, at such a moment, was more than he could bear, while yet he took no immediate steps to relieve the fierce vexation that consumed him. His deep annoyance found no outlet. His mind, as well as his muscles, were arrested. There was about the tall, unbending outline of the stranger something indefinable, that produced a sudden shock, paralysing him unaccountably on the instant, and with it a flash that struck cold as winter's ice against his heart. The power of it caught him full : he remained motionless where he stood. . . . Thus, his first impulse to send the caller peremptorily about his business, to push him out of the still open door, was not obeyed ; and on turning an instant to see whether the others followed from the bedroom, he was aware of the woman close against him as though for protection, tears upon a face blanched like linen, terror in the staring eyes, and her body shaking like a leaf.

" I couldna' stop him," came her thick whisper. " He said he would—come back."

It was while she spoke he realised for the first time that

she was no longer accompanied. She stood now at his side —alone.

The soldier found his voice, though not yet his entire self-possession. " Come back ! " he managed to ejaculate. " Come back ! " he repeated. " At a time like this. . . . ! "

Words failed him then. He glared at the trembling woman, who now pointed, with helpless, unintelligent gesture, to the drawing-room door behind her. Her body, he noticed, was still quivering all over.

" In there," she muttered. " He went in there ! "

Something turned over in the soldier's heart. He did not argue ; he made at first no comment. The one weapon he really understood, a blow, was useless, for he knew not where to aim. His sense of outrage, his anger, moreover, were of a sudden curiously stilled. The ice pressed closer, but if the hair upon his scalp rose, he denied it violently.

" You are mistaken," he said presently, in his curtest tone. " You made a mistake," he repeated firmly, the anger now oddly gone from his voice as well. " He—he went out by the front door. He will not come back. It was all a mistake, I tell you."

The woman, beneath his compelling eyes, mumbled submissively, yet keeping close against him :

" If ye say so, sir," he heard her whisper. Flustered beyond belief she was, but she was unconvinced, her gaze still fixed in terror on the drawing-room door.

The other found his sternest voice, the one the Army knew, the voice of action.

" Get back to your kitchen," he commanded. " Kneel down ! Kneel down, I say, and pray to your God at once ! "

She crept away, shuffling, looking back over her shoulder before she disappeared. Her lips were moving, though no words came forth.

Colonel Moreland strode over and closed the front door, peering first along the bare stone floor, across the narrow landing where the gas jet flared, then down the darkened passage. There was no one visible. No sound broke the silence. He paused an instant, then abruptly did a curious thing. He said something without knowing why he said it:

" Your mistress," his sudden whisper followed the trembling woman, though probably inaudible to her, " will not die. She will recover."

As he spoke the words, wondering whence came his marvellously sure conviction, he pushed into the drawing-room. He felt his courage ebbing. A second's hesitation, and it must have failed him. He went in boldly.

Again, if the hair upon his scalp rose up, he denied it violently ; if that touch of ice pressed nearer on his heart, he faced it ; his muscles, if they trembled, were in a grip of iron.

Inside the threshold he felt for the light and switched it on. One glance at the chintz-covered furniture sufficed. There was no figure, there was no living presence. The room was empty.

Their marriage, late in life, proved beyond words a happy one, for passion's turbulence left no dread of a reaction, and the deeper ties were free to utter their fine call unhampered. If regret for unrealised glories tinged its glamour, it held at least no sordid pity for a gross remorse. To them it seemed unclouded, the gardened house in Kent, surrounded by gracious friends, its perfect setting.

The faithful serving-woman had gone her way, her curious problem with her—so far, at least, as Colonel Moreland had ever questioned. The soldier, indeed, kept his own counsel about a matter he had not cared to probe by cross-examination ; his wife, on this point, was never in his confidence. The puzzle remained, for him, unsolved. The woman had seen ; he, too, had seen. Yet, since both observers were in a condition of high nervous tension at the time—overwrought, he termed it —neither possibly, for that matter, had seen anything at all. This was the explanation laborious self-deception used ; temperament selected it, and stiff self-restraint maintained it, with an effort.

In his own inmost mind, none the less, there lurked a doubt no deliberate effort wholly could stifle. A note of interrogation, like a hidden flame, glowed and would not fade. As soldier, as Englishman, he had that abhorrence of the unordinary which was his due ; " supernatural " was a word not found in his vocabulary ; hostility, scepticism rose automatically when anything of the kind was mentioned. He had seen, more than most perhaps, what mysterious India had to show, and had enjoyed it ; for trickery might baffle the mind pleasurably without stretching it into uncomfortable postures. Through thick and thin he had always maintained this comfortable attitude ; he was not going to change it now for anybody in the world. The doubt, the note of inter-rogation, none the less, persisted ; there was a question, though a question never asked.

He was glad the serving-woman had gone to a world where questions were impossible, for the fear had been in him that one day he must ask her, worse still—that she might speak to him. He was now relieved of that anxiety. Yet there was another question, independent of an answerer. This was a faint, disturbing memory, though a memory he could never feel quite sure about, since he himself, the only person who might explain it, found no positive answer in him. Had he, indeed, caught that other voice, or had he not ?

A fitful wind, he remembered, moaned in gusts about the building at the time ; up the shaft it sighed, and through the opened door as well. A moaning wind could be responsible for sounds a strained mind might well twist into syllables, into the semblance of a voice with words, even into a definite sentence. It had made strange, restless noises, that fitful wind. He was a careful man : he would never positively swear to it. Yet to this sentence had been due his amazing conviction that recovery suddenly was certain, though only afterwards did he realise why he used the words he actually had used to the woman. . . .

There remained this disquieting, persistent memory of another voice, almost a whisper, little more, perhaps, than a breath of wind : " *I will come back* . . ." and so gently uttered it seemed to have been sighed into his understanding, rather than spoken audibly : " *I will come back.*"

Yet the doctor, he remembered, had used a similar phrase when he left half an hour earlier. Was not this second voice, perhaps, its reproduction in a mind troubled and overwrought, a mind still echoing the footsteps on the tiled floor, the rumble of the lift ? He would not positively swear ; as already said, he was a careful man. He realised only his sudden, positive assurance that recovery from that moment had become a definite certainty.

The note of interrogation thus remained. It haunted and troubled him for years, till with the passage of time it grew less present, less discomforting, at any rate. But it did not die. He could never entirely forget it.

Their happiness, meanwhile, if calm, was of the radiant kind that nothing, least of all differences of opinion, could disturb. Firmly based upon fundamentals, it was securely anchored in a deep need each had of the other. They supplied, indeed, respectively, one another's deficiencies, finding life's harvest rich and wonderful; and tolerance seemed their native gift. Yet a single dread they shared in common: lest one should be taken and the other left. That the final harvesting might come for both together was their intense desire.

The house, as a rule, had voices ringing through it, young voices, for they were the kind young people love. Friends of earlier years came with their children, a married niece, a holiday group, so that corridors and garden paths were alive with footsteps, calling, laughter; everywhere among the lawns and shrubberies moving figures darted, little people climbed the stairs, the children's quarters echoed, and young life had its happy way.

On this particular Sunday in late September, for the first time, indeed, during the entire summer, they found themselves alone. The Colonel's niece, with her brood of boys and girls, had left the day before, preparatory to Black Monday when schools reopen. It seemed as if a school treat, rather than four children with their mother, now left the house and grounds so still, so strangely quiet. The servants, as a reward for recent special services, had been given afternoon leave. . . . There was a touch of melancholy about both house and grounds, of emptiness, almost of desertion, and in their own hearts, too, there lay a certain emptiness, a silence that held half-ghostly whispers of unspoken questions. Though neither gave it utterance, the same thought echoed in that inner chamber, where, but for the trick the years had played them, might now have sounded the pattering of little feet, the cries and laughter, the presences, indeed, of children of their own.

To this thought, tinged with inevitable regret, neither ever permitted utterance; but now, as they sat after tea upon the lawn, each knew full well that the other's inmost chamber *was* thus tenanted. There was a happy telepathy between them they did not question. Inexplicable it might be, but frequent custom had established it beyond argument, so that even to Colonel Moreland's strict habit of mind it had become a commonplace. Some incalculable sympathy of love had taught them the code, the soldier himself acknowledging the results without demur. . . .

He made his suggestion quietly, glancing at her through the cigar smoke the air hardly stirred : " Aloud, dear—won't you ? " Then, seeing that she hesitated, he added : " You say them so beautifully always."

He touched her hand, yet turned his head away to listen, for poetry made him shy. He closed his eyes, as she began, his face in mask-like repose. It was the voice, perhaps, as much as the exquisite words that he enjoyed, floating to him over the still lawn and flower beds, where the sunset lay in slanting gold. Its music called up pictures of so many years ago . . . of bright, wondrous hours . . . of " hours that might have been, yet had not been . . ." and yet, it seems, of one Hour in particular :

> " The hour which might have been yet might not be,
>   Which man's and woman's heart conceived and bore
>   Yet whereof life was barren—on what shore
> Bides it the breaking of Time's weary sea ? "

She paused a moment. He was aware of her eyes upon his own, a question in them, so that he shyly turned to meet her gaze. Thrilled to a deeper understanding than he had ever known before, he divined that question instantly ; but he spoke no word, because no word came to him to speak . . . while the stillness deepened about them, and the shadows lengthened on the lawn. There was a new, sudden stirring in the depths within him. His whole being listened ; it was almost as though he waited, expecting something ; and the breeze that just moved the rose leaves behind her hair seemed to mingle with the voice, as she continued :

> " Bondchild of all consummate joys set free,
>   It somewhere sighs and serves, and mute before
>   The House of Love, hears through the echoing door
> His hours elect in choral consonancy . . ."

Again she paused a moment ; and again she raised her eyes to his ; listening, as it were, to the Hours Elect that had known realisation, yet for themselves had never struck. He, too, listened ; and, as he listened, understanding in him marvellously and sharply opened, so that his whole life rushed suddenly past, presenting with that lightning meaning due, they say, to drowning men, each separate item of failure or success, yet emphasised with its ultimate truth as wisdom or defeat. This lightning experience was abruptly his, lasting at most a second. The flash seemed timeless. . . . It passed . . . and he sat listening for her voice, and waiting with a sigh.

He remembered the lines to follow. That " Little Outcast Hour " lay in his inmost thought, perhaps, as he felt sure it lay in hers. There was a look in her eyes, he noticed, that gave him happiness and terror suddenly, the terror of some mighty happiness hitherto unknown, a happiness, he felt, that must be more than he could bear, unless she shared it with him.

The world, he realised at this moment, was, in any case, an inner world. Of this he was vividly aware. It held no shyness. In it, for him, only the mightier movements passed. . . .

A flooding wave broke over him. He took her hand.

" Beatuiful," he stammered, " beautiful and true. How— how could he know—— ? "

His words halted, as the wave momentarily withdrew. An inner breathlessness caught him, a groping almost physical, lest his feet be swept from under him, lest he be borne away from his known foundations. He held tightly to the fingers in his own.

" Your hand, dear," he heard himself saying. " It's cold." He waited a moment. It seemed to him he had been speaking for a long, long time; for days; for years; for centuries.

A new coolness, he noticed, had stolen into the air. It had been coming closer, ever closer; it had now invaded both of them.

Something was happening to her as well as to himself. The happiness, the terror, the returning wave. . . . His feet lost touch, his mind went groping. . . .

He made a prodigious effort, and it caused him an agony never before experienced.

" Shall we go in now," he managed to say, his breath difficult to control. " The damp—is rising."

The familiar words, the commonplace effort, made him realise abruptly that a few seconds only—a scarcely perceptible interval—had passed since her voice ceased on the spoken lines and she had looked into his eyes. But she was still looking into his eyes. Her lips, he saw, were moving. . . . Only a second had passed, he struggled to remember ; only a fleeting second, after all. . . .

It was, perhaps, a revelation that came upon them across that quiet English lawn, stealing past the roses, using the last sunset light to clothe itself, and taking the notes of a thrush that now burst suddenly into rapturous song in the cedar by the house. The low human tones surely came floating down the evening air rather than from her own lips.

> " But, lo ! what wedded souls now hand in hand
> Together tread at last the immortal strand,
> *With eyes where burning memory lights love home ?* "

The voice, the singing of the bird, hushed simultaneously, as a tide of happiness too great for human consciousness burst flooding over him, drowning all utterance in its wave. He saw her eyes—the way they now shifted from his own, searching the space behind him. She had stopped dead. His blood ebbed, then flushed again.

" Look ! " He caught her low voice. " What is it ? So upright, so unbending ; and—by the hand—a little child ? "

" Dear," he faltered, following the direction of her gaze, " but—I see no one—no one."

The lawn was empty.

The next lines—did she say them, or did he hear them singing within him as his feet lost their final touch with earth ?

> " Lo ! how the little outcast hour has turned
> And leaped to them and in their faces yearned."

He saw her try to rise. Her hands were stretched out beyond him. Her face was radiant with a burning glory. The last line yet hung upon her lips.

He made once again a prodigious effort. " No, no ! " he wanted to cry aloud. " Don't say it, dear—don't say it——"

It was too late. He struggled to his feet in vain. No muscle, either of tongue or limb, obeyed. A flood of light drove down the evening air, awful yet lovely, and from the heart of it a voice——

> " I am your child : O parents, ye have come ! "

It was the servant, returning in the dusk, who found them, not sitting in their chairs, but side by side upon the lawn, fallen, her right hand holding his, her other stretched out towards the house, as though . . . " as though," the old butler put in, " they had gone to meet someone. That's how they looked to me . . . and the faces both young and smiling." Between the roses they lay thus, close together.